*As the tracks crossed the plains,
desire thundered in two fierce hearts
and exploded across the
frontier. . . .*

Sunny: Heir to her father's empire, she shared his passionate obsession, but the price of her dream might be turning her back on the love of her life.

Colt: Bound to the land by blood and history, he knew the coming of the railroad would forever change the Plains, yet he knew he could not stop the future—nor silence his desire for a woman he believed he could never possess.

Vince: Consumed by anger and greed, Bo Landers's oldest son knew a secret that could destroy his sister—and he'd use it to force her into a loveless marriage and steal her birthright.

White Buffalo: Fated to side with his Cheyenne brothers, he pledged his friendship to the half-breed scout Colt Travis—never suspecting they would one day face each other on the field of battle.

Blaine: Wealthy and ambitious, he wanted Sunny as his bride and a share of the Landers millions—but his cruelty would break her heart.

THUNDER
on the
PLAINS

Rosanne Bittner

BANTAM BOOKS
NEW YORK · TORONTO · LONDON · SYDNEY · AUCKLAND

THUNDER ON THE PLAINS
A Bantam Fanfare Book

PUBLISHING HISTORY
Doubleday edition published January 1992
Bantam edition / August 1992

ISBN: 0-553-29015-0

Published simultaneously in the United States and Canada

PRINTED IN THE UNITED STATES OF AMERICA

RAD   0 9 8 7 6 5 4 3 2 1

To my husband, Larry, who helped me with the idea for this story. It takes a unique kind of man to be married to a writer, one with a lot of patience; a man who is not selfish about how his wife's time is spent, who understands the times when a writer needs to be left alone, and who understands that writing is as necessary for me as breathing.

Thank you, Larry, for believing in me through the years, for your love and support.

from the

Author

Just as the great Rocky Mountains are majestic in their reach toward the heavens, so is there a majesty to the Great Plains of the American West. They stretch for hundreds of miles of aloneness, sometimes flat, sometimes rising and falling like frozen ocean waves. There has always been a thunder on the plains . . . from violent spring storms that hit without warning . . . or in another time the pounding of buffalo hooves, or the rumbling locomotive that once snaked its way across vast stretches of grassland and wildflowers, its great steam engine dwarfed by the immensity of the land.

This story is about yet another kind of thunder, the kind that comes from two hearts beating, from a love as great and enduring as the land itself. Although the historical background for this novel is the building of the Union Pacific from Omaha, Nebraska, to Promontory

Point, Utah, it is more than the story of steel rails and eight-wheeled "iron horses." It is a love story that begins well before the railroad becomes a reality, a love story that endures through the Civil War and the assassination of a president.

Thunder on the Plains introduces the men who planned and schemed to build a railroad to reap great financial rewards; and the men who did the actual building, risking their lives against Indians, an unforgiving landscape, and the elements. It is equally the story of a woman of unusual courage and determination; a woman of great passion whose devotion to her father and her vow to finish his dream surpassed all other wants and needs; a woman of self-sacrifice whose strength and power was matched only by the great steam locomotives and the railroad empire itself.

The main characters in this novel and their personal stories are fictitious, and any resemblance to people who actually existed is purely coincidental. However, Dr. Thomas Durant and General John Casement are true characters so important to the building of the Union Pacific that I could not leave them out of this story. I like to imagine that all my other characters really lived. Certainly there were many like them during this exciting era.

I hope in reading this book you will share the human triumph as well as human tragedy, that you will feel the excitement and pride that came with the building of a railroad and with the growth of a nation. Most of all, I hope you will remember the love story that follows the rails west. . . .

Prologue

August 1869

Sunny opened the journal she had kept since her first trip west in 1857. It was a long time since she had the courage or the desire to continue the diary; but now, finally, there was an ending to her story . . . or was this just a beginning?

She picked up her fountain pen and made another entry. *Our love was born on the Great Plains, as wild and untamed as the land itself. Through these many years it has endured, like the land—solid, unchanging, always beckoning. . . .*

Part

One

Chapter 1

Annie Webster frowned when she opened the door. "I don't take nobody but gentlemen in my boardinghouse," she warned defensively, "and only them that bathes."

The young man standing on her porch removed a wide-brimmed leather hat, revealing a cascade of thick, nearly-black hair that fell in tumbled layers. "I don't know much about gentlemen, ma'am, except that I'm no troublemaker; and I *do* take baths, often as I can."

The woman studied him closely, noticing he was clean-shaven. Although he wore buckskins, they were not worn and dirty like those she had seen on so many other men in Omaha who dressed like this one. The young man smiled warmly, his teeth straight and white, too white, she thought. Maybe they looked that way because his skin was so dark. Whatever the reason, it was a very handsome, unnerving smile, and it destroyed her remaining defenses.

She stepped aside, allowing him inside. His lanky six-foot-plus frame towered over her as she closed the door and folded her arms, a look of authority moving into her eyes. "Well, what will it be? Money's got to be paid up front. I've had my share of men comin' in here and messin' up a room for a couple of nights, then takin' off without payin'."

"I'm not here for a room, ma'am. Name's Colt Travis, and I came here to see a Mister uh—" He stopped and took a folded piece of paper from where it was tucked into his wide leather belt. Mrs. Webster watched warily, for attached to the belt was a beaded sheath that held a huge knife. Around his hips hung a gun belt and revolver. The hands that unfolded the paper looked strong, and were tanned even darker than his face from exposure to the prairie sun, darker than any white man she had ever seen. "A Mr. Stuart Landers," he finished. He looked at her with soft hazel eyes, a gentle gaze that didn't seem to match the rest of his rugged frame. "This poster says I can find him here. He's looking for an experienced scout."

"Experienced? You don't look old enough to have much experience, but then I guess that's for Mr. Landers to decide."

"Is he here then?"

The woman nodded, squinting and eyeing him even more closely. "You an Indian?"

Colt felt the heat coming to his cheeks. It was a question he was sick of hearing every time he met someone new. "I'm just a man looking for a job."

Mrs. Webster straightened. "That's not what I asked."

Colt sighed. "Ma'am, will you please just get Mr. Landers?"

The woman sniffed. "Follow me." She turned and walked over a polished hardwood floor to a small but neat room with a brick fireplace. Vases and knickknacks lined the mantel. "Can't blame me for askin'," she muttered. "Them high cheekbones and that dark hair and skin, wearin' buckskins and all, what do you expect? I got a right to know who I'm lettin' in my door."

Colt said nothing. He glanced around the room, wondering if the woman scrubbed every item every day. It was hard to believe that anything in this dusty town could be kept so clean. The room was decorated with plants, and little tables, stuffed chairs, and a sofa with flower-patterned upholstery. "I'm Annie Webster," she said, turning to meet his eyes. "You can wait here in the parlor, Mr. Travis. I'll get Mr. Landers."

"Thank you, ma'am."

The woman started out, then stopped and glanced back at him as though trying to tell him with her eyes he had better not break or soil anything. Colt just nodded to her, and she finally left. Colt remained standing, deciding the furniture looked too fine to sit on. He wondered if Mrs. Webster was a Mormon. Several Mormons had chosen to stay in Omaha since they first settled there for one winter a good ten years before.

The Mormons had a way of making something out of nothing, and this house was an example. There were few fine frame buildings in Omaha, more log and tent structures than anything else; but the place considered itself a city nonetheless. Even in its young stage, it was all the city Colt cared to encounter. He felt closed in in the small parlor, as out of place as a buffalo might feel inside a house. He looked down at his boots, hoping he had stamped off enough dust so as not to dirty Mrs. Webster's immaculately polished floor and colorful braided rugs.

"Mr. Travis." Colt turned to see a man of perhaps thirty approaching. He guessed the man's suit was silk, as was the paisley-print vest he wore beneath the perfectly fitting jacket. A gold watch chain hung from the vest pocket. The man looked Colt over appreciatively. "Stuart Landers," he said, putting out his hand. "I am very glad to meet you. Mrs. Webster says you've come in answer to my poster."

Colt took his hand, thinking what a weak grip the

man had. Landers's dark hair was already beginning to thin dramatically, his temple area and the area just back from his forehead already bald. In spite of the man's obvious wealth, evident by his dress and manner, there was an honesty to his dark eyes that Colt liked right away. "Well, sir, the words *excellent pay* kind of struck my eye."

Landers laughed and motioned for Colt to be seated across from him. Colt reluctantly lowered himself into a stuffed chair, deciding not to lean back. "I am afraid I might have made a mistake putting those words in the ad," Landers told him. "Oh, the pay *will* be excellent, but the ad attracted every sort of man imaginable. Most of those who answered it so far have turned out either not to have near enough experience, or have been so dirty and dangerous-looking that I just felt I couldn't trust them." The man studied Colt intently as he spoke. "Mrs. Webster said you, on the other hand, gave a very good appearance and didn't, uh . . . well, to put it bluntly, she said that 'this one doesn't smell bad.' "

Colt frowned, trying to decide whether or not the remark was a compliment. He rested his elbows on his knees, fingering his hat. "Mr. Landers, I don't know what this is all about or why it matters, but before my folks died, I was raised to be clean and respectful. My father was a missionary, came west with the Cherokee back in the thirties. Fact is, my mother was a Cherokee herself, but she and my pa lived in nice houses and brought me up a Christian. I have to say, though, that whether or not a man is clean and educated doesn't have much to do with how good a scout he is."

"Oh, I am sure of that; but this is a situation that calls for both—an experienced scout who can ensure our safety, but a man presentable and mannerly enough to be around my younger sister. She's never been exposed to this rough frontier life. My father won't allow any nonsense around her—foul language, uncleanliness, that sort of thing. You're half Indian, you say?"

Colt felt the defenses rising again, but he did not detect an insulting ring to the words. "Cherokee. Lived most of my early years down in Texas. My folks were both dead by the time I was fourteen, and I've been kind of a wandering man ever since."

"Well, whether or not you're a half—I mean, being part Indian isn't really so important as long as you were raised by a white, Christian father. You speak well and give a good appearance. I must say, you look young, though, Mr. Travis. May I ask your age?"

"I'm twenty, but I've been on my own and lived a man's life for a lot of years. I've been to Oregon and back four times, and to California twice. I've fought Indians and killed my share, led wagon trains, hunted buffalo, you name it. I even know a little bit about surveying. After my mother died, my father moved to Austin and worked for a surveyor for a few years down in Texas, and I worked right alongside him."

Landers's eyes lit up. "Surveying! Why, that's wonderful! That kind of experience is just what we need! I *knew* if I took my time I'd find the right man."

Colt watched him warily. "I ought to tell you I have a partner, name of Slim Jessup," he said, speaking in a soft Texas drawl. "He's a little less prone to bathing, but I'd make sure he cleaned up. He's quite a bit older, taught me everything I know. He'd be here with me now, but he's over seeing a horse doctor about getting a tooth pulled."

"A *horse* doctor!" Landers grimaced. "For a tooth?"

"Out here you take help wherever you can find it," Colt said. "Slim's in a lot of pain."

Stuart Landers shook his head. "Well, will this Mr. Jessup be willing to come along?"

Colt rose, beginning to feel restless within the four walls. "I can't answer that until you tell me what this is all about, Mr. Landers. I haven't even said I'd do it myself for sure, but even without Slim, I can assure you I can do as good a job as anybody. I have a couple of letters of recommendation from people whose wagon trains I've helped guide west. I hang on to them to help me get new jobs. You want to see them?"

Landers rose. "Well, yes, I suppose I should." He studied Colt more closely as the young man took the letters from a small leather bag that was tied to his belt.

He took note of the weapons Colt wore, intuition telling him this young man did indeed know what he was about. Colt handed him the letters, which he had obviously been carrying around for a while. They were worn from being folded and unfolded often, but the writing was still legible.

Colt walked to a window while Landers read the letters. He looked out at the dusty, rutted street in front of the house, again wondering how Mrs. Webster kept the place so clean. It felt strange to be inside a normal home now, even though he had been brought up this way. It had been many years since he had lived in a real house. Since losing his parents, the whole West had become his home, the sky his ceiling, the earth his floor. He had grown to like it that way. Slim said it was the Indian in him.

"Well, these people praise you highly, Mr. Travis," Landers said. He walked over and handed the letters to Colt. "I am impressed and delighted. Time is getting short, and I wasn't sure I would find the right man. You're pretty young, but better qualified than anyone else I've interviewed. It would be good if your partner would accompany you. An extra man never hurts, but as far as protection goes, my father will be bringing along his own little army. What we need is someone who knows the way, at least as far as Fort Laramie; someone who can communicate with the Indians and keep us out of trouble; and a man who knows a little about surveying, well, that's all the better. We want the best, Mr. Travis, since my little sister is coming along." Landers reached into a vest pocket, taking out a little gold case and opening it. "Would you like a smoke, Mr. Travis?"

Colt eyed the five thin cigars inside the case. He nodded, taking one. "Never saw cigars this small before," he commented.

"Oh, they're quite pleasant and very expensive."

Landers closed the case and walked back to sit down. Colt put the thin smoke to his lips and wet the end of it. "I don't understand why your sister has to come along at all," he said then. "The land west of here is no fitting place for a young, pampered girl who's used to a fine

house and all the comforts." He moved to the fireplace
and took a large flint match from a pewter cup, striking
it and lighting the cigar. He puffed on it until the end
glowed good and red.

"You don't know Sunny, or my father," Landers answered, smiling almost sadly. "Sunny's got spirit. She'll
try anything. And she's the apple of my father's eye. He
named her Sunny because he says she brought a new ray
of sunshine into his life when she was born. He doesn't
go anyplace without her, and she wouldn't let him if he
tried." Colt sensed a tiny hint of jealousy in the words,
but it vanished in the next sentence. "Sunny's name
truly fits her," Landers added, looking away from Colt
and out a nearby window. "She has hair as yellow as the
sun, eyes as blue as the sky; and a smile that makes it
very hard not to love her, at least for me anyway. My
older brother, well, I suppose he loves her like any other
brother loves a sister, at least a half sister; but he's
afraid my father will give her a little too much of the
family fortune. Still—"

The man shifted in his chair and looked suddenly embarrassed. "Excuse me, Mr. Travis. I didn't mean to go
on like that about personal family matters that are of no
interest to you. I never answered your original question
—what this job involves." He leaned back, putting his
right foot up on the opposite knee. "It's about a railroad, Mr. Travis, a transcontinental railroad—one that
will link Chicago with California."

Colt's eyebrows arched, and he could not help grinning. He took another puff on the cigar then, thinking
what good tobacco it was. "A railroad clear across the
country?" He could not suppress a snicker at the ridiculous idea.

"Go ahead and laugh, Mr. Travis," Landers told him.
"You wouldn't be the first man to scoff at the idea. Even
I am no exception."

Colt shook his head and took the cigar from his
mouth. "To each man his own dream, I guess." He
walked back over to the chair but remained standing.
"Your *father* intends to build this railroad?"

"He and several other enterprising men who don't

know what else to do with their millions. I am perfectly aware there are plenty who think he's crazy, my older brother included. He won't have anything to do with any of this. Fact is, he thinks my father's foolish dreams are going to bankrupt us." The man rubbed at his neck. "Much as I tend to agree he's a little crazy, I personally don't believe my father would let the family business go under because of his dreams. He and his own father and grandfather worked too hard to build what they have, Mr. Travis. They come from rugged stock. My father and grandfather helped settle Chicago when it was just a trading post—Fort Dearborn. They survived the Pottawatomie massacre of 1812, built a trading and shipping empire that's worth millions today. Started out in the fur trade. We own ships that travel the Great Lakes, and we own a good share of stock in the railroads that come into Chicago. More railroads lead into Chicago now than any other city. I'll bet you didn't know that."

"I don't know a whole lot about anyplace east of here," Colt answered, sitting down again and taking another puff on the cigar. "And call me Colt. *Mr. Travis* is too formal for me." He met Stuart's eyes. "Actually, I don't even know much about railroads. Only saw a train once in my life myself, when I went through Iowa and met some people who'd taken a train out of Chicago as far west as it went, then went on with wagons. I have to say, I was pretty impressed with that big locomotive, but I'll tell you, laying rails clear across the plains and over two mountain ranges sounds impossible to me. Hell, it's hard enough to get mules and wagons over those mountains; but then I guess that's not my problem. All I want to know is what my role is in all of this."

Landers pulled at a dark, neatly trimmed mustache. "My father is on his way to Omaha. He'll be here in a few days. He wants an experienced scout who can give him a rough idea of what would be the best route to take in building a railroad west. He just wants to get a feel of the land, to see if it really could be done. He'll need to get a lot of financial backing for this, and before he can get others involved and talk them into investing, he wants to be sure he knows exactly what he's talking about." The man rose and began pacing. "Oh, there has been talk around Washington about such a railroad for a long time now, Mr.—I mean, Colt. There have even been one or two surveys done." He ran a hand through his thinning hair. "My father is convinced that Congress will eventually pass a bill supporting such a railroad. He wants to get in on the ground floor—sees the possibilities. If it is a success, he'll be an even richer man. Of course, if it fails, he'll be a much poorer one. At any rate, he asked me to come out here and set things up, find a good scout." He glanced at Colt and smiled nervously, a hint of fear in his eyes. "I would have hated to face him and tell him that after all this time I hadn't come up with anyone. When my father barks, people jump, except for my older brother, Vince. They never have gotten along very well. But my father really is a good man, Colt. He's just a man who worked hard all his life and is used to ordering people around, except for Sunny. She's got him wrapped right around her little finger, but she doesn't seem to take advantage of it."

Colt felt a little awkward hearing the added personal comments the man offered, wondering why he was telling him these things about their private family life. It mattered little to him, except that this sister the man kept mentioning did not sound like the type who should be trekking through dangerous country.

Landers walked closer to Colt, putting his hands in his vest pockets. "Will you take the job? There will be a few rules because of Sunny's presence, but I don't think they will be things you can't live with. I have a feeling you know how to behave around proper ladies. My father will pay five hundred dollars, and if something happens to your horse, he'll replace it. Whatever supplies you say are needed, he'll provide them."

Colt let out a light whistle. "Five hundred dollars?"

"To each of you, if your partner comes along."

Colt set the cigar in an ashtray and rose, standing a good four inches taller than Landers. "That's a lot of money. A man would be a fool to turn it down, but in a case like this, once we're out there, what I say goes. I can't be spending half my time arguing with your father.

I don't care how many millions he's worth, he's got to listen to me once we're out there on the trail."

"My father has great respect for your kind, Colt. Our business was built on traders and trappers. My father did a little wilderness trapping of his own when he was younger. He understands these things. He'll listen to you, especially if it means Sunny's safety."

Colt nodded. "I'll go talk to my friend and come back this evening with an answer."

"Fine." Landers put out his hand again, and Colt took it, trying to envision the "little sister" called Sunny. How little was little? And just how spoiled was she? He had a feeling it was the daughter who could end up being the real headache on this trip, but for five hundred dollars, he could put up with her smart-aleck talk and snooty ways. The girl would probably spend most of her time complaining about the discomforts of life on the trail and whining to go back home, but that was her problem. Besides, he'd spend most of his time scouting well ahead of the actual wagon train. He wouldn't have to listen to most of it.

Colt said his good-byes and donned his leather hat, walking on long legs to the front door, eyeing the lace curtains at the window and vaguely remembering his mother. He had been only five when she died, but he still remembered how lost and lonely he had felt. Every once in a while some little thing would remind him of her. He stepped out into the sunshine then, breathing deeply of the fresh spring air, glad to be out of the stuffy parlor.

"Here it comes." Slim Jessup craned his neck to see, then winced with pain, touching his swollen jaw. He had already decided that if he ever had tooth trouble again, he would just shoot himself before he would go through having one pulled. He took a flask of whiskey from inside his buckskin shirt and uncorked it, taking another swallow as he watched the approaching coach and the wagon train behind it.

"Watch that stuff," Colt warned. "We aren't supposed to drink, remember?"

Slim, a nickname applied because his physique was quite the opposite, wiped his lips. "I'm not so sure I'm going to like this job," he told Colt. "This is what I get for lettin' you do the choosin'."

"You find me another wagon train that will pay us five hundred dollars each, and we'll forget about this one."

Both men stood waiting on the porch of Mrs. Webster's boardinghouse. Stuart Landers had ridden out to greet his father in the distance, and the whole train stopped momentarily while a tall, husky man got out of a grand but very dusty coach. Colt and Slim watched the men talk. "That must be the old man," Slim grumbled. "A bastard to work for, I'll bet. And look at all them men with him, all them wagons. Hell, you'd think it was the President of the United States in that coach."

"Or the Queen of England," Colt commented. He glanced at Slim, wanting to laugh at the sight of the man in new buckskin pants and shirt, wearing a new hat, his face clean-shaven and his hair cut and combed. Slim Jessup was not a man prone to spruce up for anyone, and that was part of what Colt loved about him—he had done all this for him, respecting his decision to take this job. Slim had been like a father to Colt for years, ever since Colt saved his life.

Colt was only fourteen at the time. Having set out on his own after his father's death, Colt had come upon Slim's camp in the foothills of the Rockies. Slim invited Colt to share his coffee, and before their first conversation was ended, Colt had shot a rattler that had slithered up behind Slim and looked ready to strike. From then on the friendship deepened, and Colt began traveling with the seasoned scout, learning how to track, how to handle Indians, how to find food where it seemed none could be found. Colt had come to be as skilled as his mentor. The two men shared a mutual respect for each other and had traveled together now for six years.

"Somethin' tells me we'll dearly earn the five hundred, and wish we had asked for more," Slim commented.

"Relax. Lord knows we'll probably eat good. Stuart Landers has arranged for one hell of a supply of bacon and dried beef, potatoes, you name it. And he says two men are coming along who will cook for everybody. At least you won't have to eat cold beans out of a can, and we won't have to drink that rot-gut brew you call coffee."

"I make the best damn coffee this side of the Mississippi, and you know it."

"If that's true, I'd hate to taste the rest." Colt moved off the porch as the wagon train began moving again. "Jesus," he muttered. "Would you look at that coach? I've never seen anything like it."

"Special made for Her Royal Highness, I expect," Slim answered. He straightened, trying to pull in his big belly. He removed his hat and smoothed back his graying hair, then scratched at his chest. "All this pretty-smellin' junk you made me put on over at the bathhouse has got me itchin'," he complained. "I need a little dirt and sweat under this shirt."

Colt did not seem to be listening. Slim watched him push his own hat back, exposing a few dark waves that framed his finely chiseled face. Colt had his mother's dark skin and hair, his father's height, and hazel eyes. The young man's handsome looks had cost him run-ins a time or two over young white girls on wagon trains, girls who were quite taken with Colt in spite of his efforts to avoid them. Colt was fully aware that the girls' fathers considered a half-breed not good enough for their "chaste" young daughters.

Colt had learned the pleasures of being a man at the tender age of fifteen, in the arms of a whore in Portland whom Slim had paid to entertain Colt as a birthday present. Slim grinned at the memory. He supposed he loved Colt; felt almost like a father to him. Colt was as close to family as Slim figured he would ever get. It pained him to know that most of his life Colt had wrestled with not knowing to which world he belonged, white or Indian. Slim had tried to teach the young man that he was simply a man, his own man, worthy of being accepted with respect by both races.

The coach drew up beside them then, interrupting Slim's thoughts. Colt stepped back a little. Men shouted at the mules that pulled the following three wagons, and dust rose skyward. Besides the eight men who drove and rode shotgun on the coach and wagons, six more rode on individual horses, all sporting rifles and pistols. Some of them rode behind the wagons, driving a small remuda of horses and mules, apparently extras to be used to switch teams on the coach and wagons so that the animals would not be worked too hard.

The man has thought of everything, Colt thought. He glanced back at Slim, who shook his head in wonder.

Stuart Landers trotted his horse up to Colt and dismounted as the coach door opened and a well-dressed graying man stepped out. He looked even bigger now that he was closer, standing as tall as Colt but much heftier, a man who obviously ate well. "Hello!" he bellowed. "So, this is Omaha. Sure isn't much compared to Chicago." He took a quick look around, then reached inside the coach. "Come on out and have a look, honey."

A small, gloved hand took hold of Landers's hand, and in the next moment there appeared a young woman, certainly not the child Colt had expected. She wore a pink cotton dress that fit her slender waist and developing body enticingly. Although the dress had become wrinkled and dusty from the ride, its poor condition did little to detract from the beauty of the young lady who wore it. She stepped down, looking too warm in the long-sleeved dress. A feathered hat topped her golden hair, and when she looked at Colt, he wondered if anyone possessed eyes quite so blue. He could not help staring, especially when the young lady broke into a brilliant and genuinely sweet smile. "Hello," she said, little hint of shyness in her demeanor. "Are you the scout Stuart told us about?" Before he could answer she turned to her father. "Daddy, he doesn't look like those Indians we saw a few miles back."

"Those were full blood. Mr. Travis here is only *half* Indian." The man let go of his daughter and offered his hand to Colt. "You *are* Colt Travis, I take it. You certainly fit my son's description."

"Yes, Father, this is the one," Stuart put in.

Colt quickly looked away from the daughter, whose age and beauty surprised and intrigued him, but whose remark had left him wondering if it was meant as curiosity or an insult. He took Landers's hand. "I'm Colt Travis," he said. "The man up on the porch there is my partner, Slim Jessup."

Landers nodded to Slim. "I'm Bo Landers," he said loudly, "but then, I guess that's obvious by now." The man let go of Colt's hand and stepped back a little, eyeing him more closely. "Awful young, aren't you?"

"Old enough," Colt answered, feeling the daughter staring at him. It was the first time in his life a young lady had made him feel strangely uncomfortable, made him wonder if he looked presentable. "I've done a lot of scouting and can match anyone else you might pick."

"Stuart has already told me all of that. He says you even know a little bit about surveying."

"Well, I never learned it all, sir, but as far as the land to the west, I can tell you where the solid ground is, where it usually floods, where the ground is always too soft—that kind of thing."

"That's all I need. Pardon my daughter's remark about your Indian looks. It's just curiosity. Makes no difference to me. I've called many an Indian friend in my day. If a man is honest and hardworking and good at what he does, makes no difference to me what runs in his blood."

Slim eyed the conversation closely, grinning to himself. *Yeah,* he thought, *unless that hardworking half Indian man takes an interest in your daughter. What kind of a difference would it make then, Mr. Bo Landers?*

Landers thundered every word, unlike his quieter son. The skin of his face was a ruddy red, and when he removed his silk hat to apply a handkerchief to his sweating brow, the remaining hairs on his balding head were pure white. He replaced his hat and turned to his daughter, putting an arm around her. "This is Sunny, Mr. Travis. She's fifteen. Whatever else we do on this trip, the one thing to remember is that she is to be protected at all costs."

Colt glanced at Sunny, removing his hat. "Miss Landers," he said, nodding his head slightly. She smiled again, a bright, winning smile. Colt thought how her brother's description truly did fit her.

"We're glad to have you guiding us, Mr. Travis," she told him. "I'm so excited about the trip. It's going to be such fun."

Colt suppressed an urge to roll his eyes in exasperation. *Fun?* He looked back at her father. "I have to say, it might be better for your daughter if you left her here in Omaha or sent her back to Chicago, Mr. Landers."

"Oh, no." Sunny spoke up, taking her father's arm. "Wherever Daddy goes, I go. It's always been that way. I'll be just fine, Mr. Travis."

Landers patted her hand. "My daughter goes everywhere with me, Mr. Travis. We have plenty of well-armed men and plenty of supplies. Sunny's personal tutor is also with us, Miss Gloria Putnam. She's still in the coach, not feeling too well, I'm afraid, but she's getting used to the travel. Miss Putnam will help Sunny bathe and dress and do her hair, as well as continue her lessons. I keep my daughter well schooled, Mr. Travis. Sunny will be taking over a good share of my business someday, and by the time she does, she'll be as adept at doing accounting and figures as any man." The man beamed with pride. "Don't you worry about my Sunny. She's looking forward to the adventure. She's got more strength and spunk than you think, and she comes from rugged stock, brave and uncomplaining, loyal to the death." The man scowled then. "Which is more than I can say for my oldest son."

"Oh, Daddy, Vince will come around one day." Sunny tried to soothe him. "He'll see how right you are in this."

Colt allowed himself to look her over once more. *Rugged stock,* he questioned silently. *And she comes out here with her nanny, dressed like she's going to a dance.*

"I do hope the Indians farther west have tamed down some," Stuart Landers put in.

"We shouldn't have too much trouble if we stick to the main trail," Colt answered. "It would be wise to take along plenty of things to trade, like ribbons and tobacco and such."

"Right," Bo Landers agreed. "See to it, Stuart."

"Yes, sir. We'll have all the supplies we need. I already have a lot of things waiting in storage."

Colt took a quick inventory of the wagons and coach, deliberately not allowing himself to look at Sunny again. He had been prepared for a whining little child, but Sunny Landers was certainly no child, nor did she seem prone to complaining. More than that, she was beautiful.

He immediately chastised himself for the thought. Someone like Sunny Landers was as dangerous and wrong for him as a rattlesnake. Besides that, once they got going and she showed her feathers, she would probably prove herself to be spoiled to the point of unbearable. That sweet smile didn't fool him any. She was a "Daddy's girl," and her beauty would likely fade as her personality showed itself. "Your wife isn't coming?" he asked her father.

The light momentarily left Bo Landers's eyes. "Sunny's mother died shortly after Sunny was born," the man answered.

Colt chastised himself inwardly for asking the question, thinking that he should have realized why the man took his daughter everywhere with him, why she had a nanny along. He saw the pain in Landers's eyes, the same pain that had been in his father's eyes when his mother died. "I'm sorry, Mr. Landers. I didn't know."

Landers cast a scowl at his son. "Stuart should have explained," he grumbled. He looked back at Colt, his eyes brightening more. "Well, that was fifteen years ago, and I have learned to live with it. And my beautiful Lucille left me with an equally beautiful daughter, the light of my life. The older she gets, the more she reminds me of her mother." He patted Sunny's shoulder, and turned then, opening his arms to draw attention to his entourage. "So, are we well enough equipped, Mr. Travis?"

Colt stole one more glance at Sunny, feeling a little sorry that she had never known her mother. He thought he detected a distant loneliness in those blue eyes, even though she was smiling. He walked past her to the coach, glancing at the frail-looking Miss Putnam, who remained inside the carriage. He nodded to her, but she only held a handkerchief to her mouth and looked away. Colt guessed her to be perhaps in her mid-thirties, and he supposed she was coming along only for the money, or perhaps under the threat of losing her job if she refused. Then again, maybe she was along out of loyalty and love for her young charge.

He scanned the wagons and men, then nodded to Landers. "Looks like you've prepared yourself well." He crouched down to take a closer look at the coach. "That's a hell of an undercarriage," he commented. "Looks strong. I've never seen one quite like it."

"That's a swing suspension," Landers answered. He proceeded to explain that the coach was specially built for him by an Englishman. Sunny took the opportunity to stare at Colt while he and her father were involved in their conversation. Sometimes men came to Chicago dressed like Colt, mysterious beings from an unreal world. She had always thought of them as wild things, like a bear or a wolf. She had never spoken to such a man, nor had she ever seen one quite as clean and handsome as Colt Travis. She watched how he walked as he took a look at the rest of the wagons. He had an ambling gait that spoke of a young man who was relaxed and sure of himself. She wondered how people like him survived, living off the land and sleeping under the stars. Did Colt Travis have a place to call his own? Stuart had said the man's parents were dead. Did he just wander all the time, never staying in one place? It didn't seem like he could only be twenty. He had the sureness and build of an older man.

Another wagon clattered past them, and dust rolled. Sunny squinted and turned away, wondering at the primitiveness of this place called Omaha. Were all towns west of Chicago like this? Would such places turn into big cities once the railroad was built, as her father kept saying would happen? Oh, how she hoped that railroad would become a reality. It meant everything to Bo Landers, and what her father dreamed, she dreamed too. She knew others laughed at him, and it hurt terribly to see anyone scoff at her father, who was her whole world. He was more than a father. He was her best friend, and he needed her. She was sure she was the only one who truly loved him, who understood his dreams. A transcontinental railroad was a great challenge to him, and Bo Landers loved challenges. It took men like her father to make such ideas become a reality. *Your brothers have grown up taking everything they have for granted,* he had told her more than once. *They're satisfied to leave things as they are, but a man has to take chances in life, Sunny. We have to step out into unknown territory, take the bull by the tail and see where it kicks. That's how my grandfather and my father built all that we have.*

"Once you pick up the supplies your son and I arranged for, we can be on our way, by tomorrow morning if you like," Colt was saying. He and Bo Landers were walking back toward Sunny.

"We'll be ready," Landers answered. "Let me ask you, Mr. Travis, what do *you* think of the idea of a transcontinental railroad?"

Colt decided to weigh his words. "I suppose a man can do whatever he sets his mind to," he answered. *Especially if he has enough money behind him,* he wanted to add. He decided not to tell the man he thought the idea was crazy. If Bo Landers wanted to dump his millions into an impossible dream, that was his business.

"That's the kind of talk I like to hear," Landers answered. He began shouting some orders, and Colt allowed himself one more look at Sunny. He caught her staring right back at him. "I hope we can become friends on this trip, Mr. Travis," she told him. "I'd like to find out more about you. I'm keeping a journal about our trip and the interesting people we've met along the way. Tell me, what is that fascinating accent you have?"

Colt watched her stunning blue eyes, still trying to determine if this spoiled little rich girl was as genuinely nice as she appeared, or just trying to trick something out of him. "People down in Texas would say *you're* the one with the accent," he answered. He shifted his hat. "I, uh, I don't think you'd find much about me that's interesting enough to write about," he told her. He turned and walked away, mounting his horse then to join Slim and Stuart. Sunny took note of how he sat his horse, almost as if he were part of the animal. She wondered if she had offended him by commenting about his accent, and earlier about his Indian looks, hoping she had not gotten off on a bad footing with him.

Sunny began to compose her journal entry in her mind. *We have reached Omaha, and tomorrow we will head into the wilderness. Our guide is Mr. Colt Travis, and he seems quite skilled and knowledgeable. I am sure he will get us through safely, and that we will become good friends before this trip is over.*

Chapter 2

Slim rubbed his stinging jaw, where he had cut it shaving with cold river water that morning. "I ain't never seen the like," he grumbled, "a man bein' told he's got to shave just to suit some fancy gal he don't hardly know. It ain't right, Colt. I ain't never shaved on a trip like this in my life. Here we are out here huntin' game and Indians, and we've got to worry about keepin' our mugs smooth."

Colt laughed lightly. "You'll survive."

"Easy for you to say. You ain't old enough to have a beard that grows back on you before the sun sets." The man looked back at the elegant coach and the procession of wagons that followed it. "You gonna take supper with them?"

Colt sobered. "Do I have a choice? Her father practically demanded that I be there."

"He made it sound like he was askin' you to a ball or somethin'. I can't get over them settin' out a fancy table every night, spreadin' that white tablecloth over them boards, settin' out china. That Bo Landers sure keeps his help busy, them cooks stirrin' up a full meal every night under these conditions, that sour-pussed Miss Putnam fussin' after that little gal like she'd die if that there Sunny got dirty or got a hair out of place. I wonder why all of a sudden they invited you to sit at their fancy little table instead of sharin' grub with the rest of the men like always."

Colt scanned the wide horizon for trouble. "Who knows? I'd just as soon *not* join them, but Landers seemed pretty insistent."

Slim shrugged. "After two weeks on the trail and that little gal sittin' at your fire every night askin' you all them questions, I guess they figure you've earned the right."

"Earned? You make me sound like some servant who gets to come in the front door." Colt wrapped the reins of his horse around the pommel of his saddle, freeing his hands so that he could roll himself a cigarette. "All that money doesn't impress me any, and men like Landers bore me. Sometimes I find myself hoping his idea never gets off the ground. Do you realize what the railroad would do to this country? It would finish off the Indian and the buffalo, bring towns and noise and all sorts of no-goods out here, ruin the peace and quiet." He took a paper from a pocket of his buckskin shirt and lifted a pouch tied to his belt, pulling it open and managing to pour some tobacco onto the paper without spilling any. "We've been on the trail for only two weeks and already I'm wishing this trip was over with."

Slim adjusted his hat, casting Colt a sly glance. "I think you've got other reasons for wishin' this trip was over."

"Yeah?" Colt licked the paper and sealed the cigarette. "What the hell are you thinking?"

Slim sat a little straighter, forcing back a chuckle. "I think you'd like this trip just fine if you didn't have to always be lookin' at that pretty Miss Sunny, answerin' her questions, hearin' her voice, watchin' her move. I ain't exactly missed myself the way she sits a horse, wearin' them split skirts and straddlin' that horse like a man. I didn't believe her when she first said she could ride, but she does just fine."

Colt put the cigarette between his lips. "I never thought of you as a dirty old man, Slim Jessup. And as far as what you think *I'm* thinking, mind your own business. I'm not a damn fool. Besides, she's just a kid."

Slim chuckled. "And you ain't?"

Colt took the unlit cigarette from his mouth and cast the man a look of chagrin. "I stopped being a kid the day I saved your scraggly scalp from those Crow Indians when I was only seventeen. And don't forget that rattler. Anybody who's done what I've done the past few years isn't any kid."

Slim waved him off. "Just gettin' in my digs," he said with a wink. "You know how I like to get a rise out of you." They rode quietly for a moment while Colt slipped his hand into one of his saddlebags and took out a match. He flicked it with a fingernail to make it flame and he lit his cigarette.

"She *is* a looker, though," Slim teased. "You be careful, Colt. You've been down that road before."

Colt snickered and shook his head. "Lay off, will you? She's way above my head. I'm not ignorant enough to have any fantasies about someone who wears real gold and diamond brooches."

"Colt!" Colt turned at his shouted name to see Sunny riding hard toward them. "Jesus," he muttered, noticing how her riding skirt hugged her belly and hips.

"Speakin' of gold and diamonds, here they come," Slim joked.

"What's she doing riding up here by us again?" Colt grumbled.

Slim smiled. "You don't know? Better watch out, son, or ol' Bo Landers will hang you by your, uh, toes."

Sunny trotted her horse between the two men. She was all smiles and eagerness, her hair plaited into a thick blond braid down her back. "Father said I could come up and ride with you today," she said excitedly.

She looked at Colt. "I hope you don't mind. I wanted to watch you work. What do you look for? I mean, what does a scout actually do?"

Slim tipped his hat to Colt. "I'll let you answer that," he said with a wink. "I'm goin' on up ahead and find us a good spot to cross the river." He kicked his horse into a faster trot, and the animal lumbered away, carrying its heavy cargo.

Colt watched the wide shoulders of his companion, trying to decide how he could get back at the man for abandoning him at this awkward moment. He kept the cigarette in his mouth and his eyes forward when he answered Sunny. "Scouting is just—just scouting," he half grumbled. "You watch for tracks that show there's a buffalo herd up ahead, or Indians. You smell the air for a storm coming, shoot game when it's needed for food, dicker with pesky Indians—things like that." He finally looked at her. "Maybe your pa said you could come up here, but *I* didn't. You shouldn't just go riding out in the open like this unless I say it's okay."

"But we're only a couple of weeks out of Omaha! There certainly can't be any dangerous Indians here," she objected, tossing her head.

Colt allowed his gaze to linger. Did this woman-child understand what it did to a young man to see a blouse fit the way hers fit her, or to see such soft, fair skin? He was suddenly angry with her for being so beautiful, let alone for her assumption that she could ride up and join him anytime she felt like it. She and her father both were people accustomed to doing what they pleased without having to ask permission, and he decided to put a stop to it before she began thinking she could come up and join him whenever she got the yen. That was the last thing he needed.

"How the hell would *you* know where the Indians are?" he barked, deliberately using a swear word. "*I'm* the scout, remember? I told your father that once we got under way, things had to be like I say. You act like this is going to be one big picnic. You'll find out different after a few more weeks, and when I say you should stay hidden in that coach, you'd better do it! And I can't do my scouting with you tagging along asking questions. That's not what I'm getting paid for!" He looked away then and waited for her reply, hoping she would just turn around and ride back; but she trotted her horse right beside his, and he hated himself more with each passing silent moment.

"You're just like all the others," she finally said, so quietly he barely understood her. There was such a ring of sorrow to the words that he felt an odd sick feeling. Why had he let himself be short with her? She was as innocent as a sunrise. It wasn't her fault she was so damn beautiful, and dealing with it was *his* problem, not hers.

"What others?" he asked.

She let out a long sigh, then sniffed. Colt was not about to look and see if she was crying. "The people who don't know me," she answered. "They think that just because I'm rich and because my father dotes on me, I must be spoiled and arrogant. Most of the people I associate with back in Chicago who are my age *are* spoiled and arrogant. I don't like them at all, and people of a lower class think I'm too good for them; or maybe they think they're too good for me. Maybe they *are*. All I know is that it's awfully hard to make friends. Miss Putnam is older and domineering. I can't tell her anything."

She rode her horse forward, then turned it in front of him, halting and facing him. Colt rode closer, feeling like an ass at the sight of tears in her eyes.

"I wasn't being condescending when I asked about your work, Colt. Truly I wasn't," she told him. "I really am interested. You must know that from the times we've talked over campfires at night. And just because we're different doesn't mean we can't be friends. After all, you aren't that much older than I."

Colt took the cigarette from his mouth and grinned. "To begin with, I'm afraid I don't even know what *condescending* means," he told her.

Sunny thought for a moment, then smiled, realizing he was teasing her. She quickly wiped a tear. "It just means I wasn't trying to act superior or make fun of what you do. I respect your work very much, and I want to get things into words so that I don't forget. After this trip I'll probably never see you again."

Their gazes remained fixed for a moment, each realizing the other didn't dare say what was really felt. There was no future in such thoughts. In the past two weeks Colt had come to see her as an amazingly genuine, honest person, albeit a little spoiled. He couldn't help wishing she were a little older, and much less wealthy.

"I guess that's true," he answered. "I have to say, I never thought of somebody as wealthy as you as being lonely for friends. I'm sorry I lost my temper, but you really do have to be careful. You ought to stay back by the wagons."

"I'll ask first after this. Just tell me you aren't terribly angry, and that we can be friends. I might even write a story about you someday."

Colt shook his head in embarrassment and touched his horse's sides, goading the roan gelding into a gentle walk. "I don't think it would be a very exciting story," he told her.

"Oh, of course it would. A little boy of five, whose mother dies of cholera, goes on to the city of Austin with his missionary father and works for surveyors, then is orphaned at fourteen and strikes out on his own. And then that wonderful story Slim told me, of how you saved his life when you shot that rattler; and how you rode right into an angry band of Cheyenne warriors to rescue a white woman they had stolen from a wagon train; and what a good marksman you are, and—and the time you fought off Crow Indians who were attacking Slim, and—"

"Slim likes to exaggerate."

"I'll bet he's not exaggerating at all. I know you could tell me more if you weren't so bashful about yourself." She took a deep breath, watching Slim, now several yards ahead of them. "How do you even know where you are?"

Colt shrugged. "It's easy this first part of the way. You just follow the river. When you can't do that, you watch the sun by day and the stars at night. After you've done enough of this kind of traveling, you watch for certain landmarks. In our particular case you look for Chimney Rock, Independence Rock, things like that. Farther west the land gets hillier. You'll see bluffs and low mountains, more trees. You might even see one or two herd of buffalo before we're through. That's something you'll for sure want to write about."

"I've never seen such country. Except for along the river, there are no trees." She looked over at him. "Do you still think my father is crazy to think he can build a railroad out here?"

"I never said I thought he was crazy."

"No, but I could tell you were thinking it."

Colt laughed lightly, and Sunny thought she had never met a more handsome or more mysterious man. She was surprised at the feelings he stirred in her. Until she had made this trip with her father, she had not given fond thoughts to any young man. All the ones she knew back in Chicago were so empty, and so obviously interested in the wealth she would one day inherit. Somehow she suspected this young man didn't care about those things. Colt was the first young man who had actually drawn her attention from her father.

"It's really best if you go back," he told her.

How could she tell him she loved riding beside him? How could she ever explain to him or anyone how her heart pounded so that it hurt when he was near? Was she too young to feel this way? Would he laugh at her if he knew? Worse, was she being disloyal to her father and her responsibilities? Someday she would be one of the richest women in the country. What would someone like Colt Travis think of that? She had learned enough about him to know that he would hate the kind of life she led back in Chicago, and she carried too many obligations to ever leave that life. She was being silly and irresponsible to think of being anything but passing friends with this man; but even that much was exciting.

Colt turned to meet her gaze, and she reddened, wondering if he realized what she was thinking. Maybe he thought the same. "You *will* take supper with us tonight, won't you?" she asked. "We're having steak, boiled potatoes, biscuits, and peas. We'll even have a little wine."

Colt snickered and shook his head. "Your father sure knows how to travel." He took another drag on his cigarette. "I'll join you, but don't ask me too often. A man like me feels kind of out of place doing that sort of thing. I sure never thought I'd see the day when people ate off fancy plates out here. I can't even imagine the way you must live back in Chicago."

"Well, it's the only life I've ever known, so I suppose it isn't as grand to me as it might be to others. Our house is three stories high, and has twenty-five rooms. The third floor has a wonderful ballroom. Daddy loves to throw parties. We have ten servants and two cooks. You should come and visit us sometime when this trip is over. We could take you to the theater, and you could ride a train. Maybe you could come to my sixteenth birthday party. There will even be senators and congressmen there."

Colt kept the cigarette between his lips. "No, thanks. You can have your fancy life. Me and cities and wealth don't mix very well."

Her smile faded slightly. *Of course not,* she thought. How strange that she felt almost embarrassed about her wealth. "My father and his father before him worked very hard for what we have today, Colt." Suddenly she felt she had to explain. "You might think we live in the lap of luxury and lie around all day, but it isn't that way. I travel everywhere with Daddy. I've seen how hard he works. It isn't easy running several big companies, and when you have sons who don't help the way they should, well, it's even harder. My brothers have disappointed my father in a lot of ways. I'm the only one who understands him, the only one who knows how he hurts inside sometimes. I'm as excited about building this railroad as he is, and I pray every night that it will come to be."

Colt smoked the last of his cigarette, snuffing it out against the side of his canteen before throwing the stub into the tall spring grass. "That turned into quite a speech. I wasn't saying there's anything wrong with the way you live, Sunny. I was just saying some people aren't cut out to live that way. What the heck? It takes all kinds, right? If there weren't people like me, then people like you couldn't travel out here safely."

She smiled then, the warm smile that always made him want to see how her full lips might feel against his mouth. "Yes. Please do watch after Daddy. He thinks I'm the one to be looked after, but he is as important to me as I am to him. It frightens me sometimes to think of what it might be like to be without him. My brother Vince would—" She stopped, slowing her horse then. "I'd better go back now, like you said. I'll see you at supper tonight."

He tipped his hat, and she turned her horse and rode off. Colt watched after her, his smile fading. He was amazed at the loneliness she conveyed. He gathered from comments her brother had made and from her own that her family was very divided. There did not seem to be much love among them, except between Sunny and her father.

He turned his horse forward again and rode at a gentle lope, reminding himself that the Landers family problems, Sunny's in particular, were none of his affair.

Men hovered guardedly around the blanketed-off area where Sunny bathed in a tub of water that had been heated first over a campfire. Near one of the wagons the nightly ritual of setting up a table, by laying a wide, flat board on top of barrels, was completed. Colt never ceased to be astonished at the formality of the Landerses' nightly feast. The two cooks spread a tablecloth over the board and began setting out real china and silverware.

Over the past two weeks Colt had noticed Bo Landers's men jumped at his every command. Everyone worked with a kind of rhythm, no one questioning an order. Not one man gave an extra look to Sunny, and Colt figured they had learned it was better not to. Miss Sunny Landers was meant for something better than the likes of anyone who worked for her father. Even Sunny's brother Stuart marched to his father's tune. The man seemed decent enough, however. Stuart treated Sunny kindly, and he had written several letters to his wife, Violet, back in Chicago, although so far they had not passed by anyone who could carry the letters back for him. Stuart also talked often about his one-year-old daughter, Diana. It was obvious the man missed his family.

The scent of food drifted over from a second campfire, and a few items were hanging out to dry over a makeshift clothesline. The day had ended with a rough river crossing that had gotten people and belongings wet. It had been the first dangerous encounter of the trip. The Platte was high and deep this time of year, and it was always difficult to find a place to cross, but they had no choice if they wanted to avoid a lot of extra miles by having to circle around swampy ground.

For safety, Colt had taken Sunny across on his own horse, and he was still trying to forget the feel of her against him. He had changed into denim pants and a cotton shirt for supper, and at the moment he was wishing he had never agreed to sit and eat with these people. Slim camped farther ahead, preferring his own beans and coffee, and his own company.

"Come and have a seat," Bo called out. "I have some fine cigars here, Colt!"

Reluctantly, Colt walked over and sat down on a barrel, but he refused the cigar, preferring to roll his own smokes. "I might get too accustomed to that fine tobacco and not be able to smoke my own anymore," he told Bo.

Landers laughed. "Well, son, a man does get used to the finer things once he has them. I must say, this trip is a far cry from the trips I've taken to Washington by train. Someday, though, people will be able to travel in style and comfort all the way to California! I can see it already." He took a deep breath. "It's going to cost millions, but with the right backing I know we can convince the President and Congress to support us. Why, only two months ago I was talking with several senators who seem sold on the idea. It's not an easy thing to talk men who have no imagination into an idea they think is impossible. That's the trouble with most men, Colt. They don't think big enough. They give up too easily. I believe in a transcontinental railroad, and, by God, it's going to happen!" The man rose then, beaming. "Sunny! Come and sit. We'll eat soon."

Sunny approached them, her hair still wet but pulled into a thick tail at the back of her neck. She was fresh and clean and beautiful, and Colt wanted to leave so he wouldn't have to look at her. She walked up and kissed her father's cheek, then sat down across from Colt, journal and pen in hand.

Men began cleaning up Sunny's bathing area, and Miss Putnam hurried to Sunny's side, setting a bottle of ink in front of her. Colt thought the woman looked a little frazzled. Apparently, it was Sunny who got to clean up and relax first. Miss Putnam wore the same dress she had on earlier in the day, and the hemline was still damp. She looked pale and unhappy, and Colt could have felt sorry for her if it were not for the strange looks she had been giving him the last few days, as though he were something detestable. She nodded to him curtly. "Mr. Travis, how nice that you can join us." The words were spoken sarcastically, and her narrow gray eyes moved over him scathingly.

"Thank you," Colt answered guardedly. He wondered how the bony Miss Putnam kept from blowing away in the wind, and what it took to make the woman smile. The only thing he had found likable about her was her apparent loyalty to Sunny. It was obvious the woman had not wanted to come along on this trip, and she had been physically ill the first few days, but she seemed to be better now. Her hair, a mousy brown streaked with gray, was escaping from its normally neat bun, and she had apparently not had a chance to rest or change since the river crossing; yet she continued to fuss over Sunny.

Stuart and Bo talked business for a while, and Colt had never felt more uncomfortable or out of place. The few times he had eaten with families of other wagon trains, the people had been ordinary and down to earth, people with whom he could carry on a normal conversation and with whom he could feel welcome. To go to so much trouble to set a proper table out in the wilderness seemed to him absurd, let alone listening to talk of stocks and bonds and banking investments. He could not help staring when one of the cooks placed a candelabrum in the center of the table and lit the candles.

"Isn't this nice, Daddy," Sunny said. "Why didn't we use the candles before?"

"We would have if it weren't always so windy out here. This is the first evening that it's been still enough to light them."

Colt struggled not to laugh, realizing that Sunny actually thought this was absolutely wonderful. The food was served at the makeshift table first, after which the rest of Landers's men were fed. The others also ate from china plates, just like those at the table, but they and the cooks sat in their own little group. Only Bo and Stuart Landers, Sunny, Miss Putnam and Colt sat at the table, and Colt found himself hoping they did not expect him to sit here every night. Father and son were friendly enough, but between bites they continued to talk about politics and investments. Colt ate quietly while Bo talked about his friends who had already agreed to back his idea for the railroad, men who were willing to put up thousands of dollars, more money in a single contribution, Colt figured, than he would ever make in his whole life.

"We can't get Congress to vote on a railroad bill until we show we have backing of our own first," the man told Colt. "I'll say one thing, the more I see of this land, the more I am convinced this railroad can be built. A bridge here and there to keep us on the solid side of the river, or to avoid having to clear a lot of trees. Yes, yes, it can be done. And so far you have more than proved your worth, Colt, keeping us out of quagmires and such. Tell me, what in your estimation is the best way to get across the Rockies?"

Colt swallowed a piece of steak and gathered his thoughts while one of the cooks poured him some wine. "The only way I can see is through the South Pass, up in Wyoming country—same route the wagon trains take. If you want to take a more direct route, you'll have to do a lot of tunneling, and I don't see how any amount of men or equipment could tunnel straight through the Rockies."

Sunny was rapidly writing. When Colt stopped to sip his wine, she glanced at him with a look of admiration. "You know so much about the wilderness," she told him. "Some people in Congress call it the Great American Desert. They say it isn't worth anything, that there is no sense building a railroad because no one would want to go there."

Colt set down his wineglass, feeling Miss Putnam's eyes drilling into him again. He looked at Bo, who was also eyeing him strangely. In one tiny moment something had changed, and he wasn't quite sure if it was something he had said. "Oh, I think plenty of people will want to go," he answered. "After all, the Mormons certainly like it. Little towns are springing up all over, and look at the thousands of people who have gone to California. Now there are rumors of gold in the Rockies, around the Pikes Peak area. You know what that will mean. Personally, I'm not too crazy about the West being settled, and I can guarantee the Indians won't like it. But I can see already that things are bound to change."

"Like they changed for the Cherokee when they were sent to Indian Territory?" Miss Putnam put in. "That must have been very hard on your people."

Colt met her eyes, not sure why she had made the comment. Was she trying to drive home the point that he was part Indian? "I was pretty small. I don't remember most of it, but I was told enough stories to know how rough it was. A lot of my own relatives died."

"Oh, how sad," Sunny added. "I never thought to ask you about that part of your life. You must tell me about the Cherokee, Colt. What happened before they were sent to Indian Territory? Did they live like real wild Indians, in tipis and such?"

Colt told himself not to be angry with her natural curiosity and ignorance about Indians. "The Cherokee never lived in tipis. But that's beside the point. By the time they were kicked out of Georgia and Tennessee, they had become quite civilized, with brick homes and their own schools and—"

"Sunny! It's time for eating, not writing." Miss Putnam spoke the words softly but sternly, her interruption very obviously deliberate.

"Yes, yes, child, you'll need your strength," Bo put in. "Finish your food. Colt isn't here to talk about the tragic past of his ancestors. Besides, you've been through some rough times today and you got your clothes wet. I want you to eat and go straight to bed. God knows I can't have you getting sick on me."

Sunny looked a little disappointed. She set her journal aside and poked at some potatoes, and Colt finished his steak, feeling more awkward than ever, eager now for this meal to be over. This whole thing was making him even more aware of how different his world was from the Landerses'.

"Sunny tends to get a little carried away," Miss Putnam said then. "She *is* quite a good writer. Do you write, Mr. Travis?"

Colt wiped his mouth with a linen napkin, setting it aside then and meeting the woman's eyes boldly, understanding the intended insult. "Yes, ma'am, I know how to write. My father worked for a surveyor those last few years, but he was a missionary and a teacher at heart, and he taught me well." He glanced at Sunny and could see she was slightly hurt and embarrassed by Miss Putnam's remark. He gave her a light smile and turned to her father. "Stuart says you did some hunting and trapping in your own day," he said, deciding to change the subject and get the attention away from himself.

Bo brightened, a man who always enjoyed talking about himself. He bellowed about how his grandfather had settled at Fort Dearborn and started a trading business; and how he and his own father had survived the Pottawatomie massacre, but that his mother, a sister, and a brother had been murdered. He beamed about his shipping and railroad empire, about what a growing city Chicago was, and how, once the railroad was built across the country, there would be other cities as big or bigger. Colt glanced a time or two at Sunny, noticing how proudly she watched and listened to her father.

By the time the man finished talking, the meal was done and Landers was lighting another cigar. "You'd better get to sleep, Sunny," he said then. "We have a long day ahead of us tomorrow."

"But I want to sit here and listen," she objected.

"There will be many other opportunities," Miss Putnam put in. "Come, child."

A pouting Sunny picked up her journal, glancing at Colt. "I want to hear more about the Cherokee, Colt; and more about your other adventures, like how many Indians you have killed, people you have rescued. Have you ever been wounded yourself?"

"A couple of times."

"You have? Where? How badly?"

Colt gave her a patronizing smile, a little embarrassed. "You'd better go ahead and get your rest like your pa said." She held his eyes for a moment, and Colt sensed something shared in spite of how different their worlds were, something he could not quite name. "Good night, Sunny."

"Good night." She turned and gave her father a hug. "Good night, Daddy."

Both men watched her walk with Miss Putnam to the wagon, where she slept on double feather mattresses that were taken out each morning and evening and soundly shook and plumped. Mosquito netting had already been draped over the wagon openings to protect the girl from the pesky insects for the night.

The cooks began cleaning off the table, and several guards took positions to keep watch while others began bedding down for the night. Colt was about to rise and leave himself when Bo spoke. "My daughter is quite beautiful, isn't she?"

Colt glanced at Stuart, who gave him a limp smile. Colt looked at Sunny's father then, realizing he had better weigh his words. "Yes, sir, she's a very pretty young lady, and very nice. You've done well, raising her by yourself."

Bo held his gaze for a quiet moment. "Life hasn't

been easy for Sunny," he said. "Her oldest brother and his wife are not kind to her. Young ladies her own age are jealous of her because she's richer than any of them, let alone prettier. I suppose I've been a little too possessive of her and overprotective, but she means the world to me. When her mother died, I wanted to die too. Sunny is the only thing that kept me going."

The man puffed on his cigar, and Colt began rolling himself a cigarette, suspecting Bo Landers did not want him to leave just yet. "I think I understand," he answered. "My pa was pretty devastated when my mother died. It made us closer."

Bo sighed, glancing at Stuart. "My sons don't always understand."

"Father, you know the real reason—"

Bo flashed Stuart a warning look. "Don't say it," he almost snarled. "Don't ever say it! I have forgiven you, Stuart, but not Vince!" He looked at Colt again. "Sunny's mother was my second wife, very young when I married her. My sons resented the marriage for more reasons than loyalty to my first wife. I won't go into details. Suffice it to say their resentment grew when Sunny was born and I began giving her so much attention. I suppose it's partly my fault. The boys were pretty small when their own mother died. I was still terribly involved in a growing business empire as they were growing up, and they never got a lot of attention." He looked at Stuart. "There are other reasons for my sons' behavior, but as far as I am concerned, they are not valid. My oldest son is the most belligerent. He has no business treating Sunny so shabbily. At any rate, it makes things hard for my daughter."

Colt lit his cigarette and took a deep drag. "I, uh, I don't quite understand why you're telling me all this, sir."

Bo leaned closer, keeping his voice low. "I'm just trying to explain what life is like for Sunny. My oldest son makes things hard for her, and she leads a kind of sheltered personal life, but socially she's a hit wherever she goes. She's been to Washington with me several times, knows senators and congressmen by their first names.

Next year I'll be having a grand coming-out party for her sixteenth birthday. To the outside world Sunny is like a little queen, and she's *my* little princess. She's amazingly sweet and innocent and open, for all her pampering. By all rights she should be a wicked, demanding little witch, but she's a very giving and forgiving young lady. She understands my dreams, and if I died tomorrow, I think she'd go on to finish the railroad just because it was what I wanted. I'm training her to be a smart woman who will never let anyone use her for her money; but right now she's still learning, still a child in many ways, full of wonder, easily impressed. And in only a couple of weeks she has become very impressed with *you,* Colt."

The night air hung quiet as Colt took his cigarette from his lips. "Mr. Landers, if you think I'd—"

"Let's not put it into words, Colt. When Stuart and I hired you, we were thinking only of your skills and manners and neat appearance. Neither of us considered how you would look to someone like Sunny—handsome, exciting, mysterious. Girls her age can get silly crushes, and I think you're smart enough to understand how foolish and pointless it would be to let that happen. I have big plans for Sunny, Colt. I don't mean any insult. You're a fine young man, but no two people could be more different and mismatched. Someday, when Sunny is ready to marry, she'll need a man who understands her world, one who knows how to handle the kind of money she'll inherit. I've seen how you look at her. You're only twenty yourself, and young men can get fancy ideas. Just don't get them about Sunny. Not only could it never work, but she would get hurt, and that is the last thing I want. It's always better to nip these things in the bud, don't you agree?"

Colt just stared at him a moment, then rose, throwing down his cigarette and stepping it out. "Mr. Landers, I don't think you give your daughter enough credit for common sense. She's just a nice girl wanting to enjoy an exciting trip and wanting stories for her journal. I'm damn well aware of the circumstances here, and I've not done one thing to give your daughter any ideas. I've got no fancy thoughts about her, *or* her money. She's a nice girl who needs a friend, and I can be that much. If you want her to be a part of this railroad idea, then let her learn about the land. I can teach her. Just don't be worrying about anything more. Just sitting at this meal here tonight showed me how different—"

Colt hesitated, realizing then why he had been asked to share their table. He nodded. "I get it. Nip it in the bud, like you said." He snickered in disgust. "You didn't have anything to worry about to begin with, but you wanted to rub it in good, didn't you—show me how much I don't fit." He shook his head. "Sunny knows her place just like I know mine. You've taught her that—you and Miss Putnam. Give her some breathing room, Mr. Landers, and let her make some of her own decisions. You might be surprised at how much she's already learned."

Landers rose. "I just wanted to be sure we understood each other. I'd like you to be careful how you act toward her the rest of the trip." He put out his hand. "And I told you to call me Bo. You don't have to suddenly go back to calling me Mr. Landers."

Colt refused his hand. "You don't need to panic every time your daughter talks to me, *Mr.* Landers. I'm here to do a job, and I'll do it. When this trip is over, you'll go home and I don't expect any of us will ever see each other again. Now, you either trust me or you don't. If you don't, I turn back right now and you can get yourself somebody else."

Their eyes held in mutual challenge, and then Landers smiled and nodded. "I trust you," he said carefully. "And I damn well like you. I respect a man who isn't afraid to stand up to me. And like I said, call me Bo."

Colt breathed deeply, tempted to quit right then but too stubborn to do it. "Be ready to break camp and be on our way come sunrise," he told Landers. He turned and walked away, kicking at a rock as he headed for Slim's campfire.

Colt thought that it was going to be much easier now to avoid forbidden thoughts about Miss Sunny Landers. The more he saw the kind of world she lived in, the less attractive she was to him. Suddenly, rather than any kind of desire she might have stirred in him, he felt only pity for her, a lonely little girl trapped in a life of wealth that would probably bring her nothing but unhappiness. She all but worshipped her father, which meant she would never go against anything he wanted. Nice as she was, she was also one of "them," and the older she got, the more she would be like them. It was too bad, kind of a waste, he thought.

"You done with your socializin' already?" Slim sipped some of his own coffee as Colt loomed into the firelight.

"I'm done, period."

Slim watched him angrily unfold his bedroll, deciding this was not a time to tease. "What happened, son?"

"Let's just say Mr. Bo Landers and I know where each of us stands, and believe me, I wouldn't wear his shoes for all his millions. I'll tell you more when we ride out tomorrow. I don't want to talk about it right now." Colt removed his hat and weapons and boots, keeping his rifle beside him as he settled into his blankets. "Wake me up when it's time to take over for you." He put his head back and closed his eyes, but he knew sleep would not come easily. The night air rang with the singing of crickets, and in the distance came the faint sounds of the cooks cleaning up camp. "What a hell of a life," he grumbled then to Slim. "I should be envying them, but I feel sorry for them instead."

"Hmmm." Slim sipped some coffee. "Don't be feelin' sorry for the likes of Bo Landers. He's made his own bed and likes it just the way it is." He set his cup aside. "I expect it's the man's daughter you feel sorry for."

Colt looked across the fire at him, and one red coal popped, sending little sparks into the black night. "I'm not supposed to have *any* kind of feelings for her, if you get my meaning." He turned over then, his back to Slim.

Slim sighed and shook his head. "You're a good kid, Colt, good as the next man. Don't ever let anybody tell you any different," Slim said quietly.

Colt grinned a little in the darkness. "Thanks. And you're a good friend. Now let me sleep. We've got some long days ahead."

Chapter 3

Ten days ago a fierce thunderstorm and torrential rainfall put a halt to our travels, Sunny wrote. She sat next to a noon campfire while men prepared to leave out again. *The rain and wind were so violent that the cookwagon was blown over and our other two wagons got wet inside. Miss Putnam and I and two of my father's men suffered chills and colds, and I was too ill to make my daily journal entries. I am fully recovered now, but Miss Putnam still lies resting in our sleepwagon. I am very worried about her.*

We have moved past the Nebraska Sand Hills and are now in what Mr. Travis calls High Plains country. It is beautiful here, rolling hills and colorful rugged bluffs. I have never seen such country. The weather is finally sunny again, and I am going to ride horseback this afternoon. I am only allowed to ride two hours a day, and even then I must wear a wide-brimmed hat, for the western sun can age a person very quickly.

She put down her pen, deciding she would finish her writing later. It was almost time to leave. She thought about the terrible storm and their losses. With the muscle power of all the men, the overturned wagon had been righted. It had taken the rest of that rainy day just to sort through the mess—shattered china, spilled flour, dried peas scattered everywhere. Some food was useless and had to be thrown out, and over half the china was destroyed.

The cool, rainy weather had continued for six more days, making it difficult to dry out clothes and blankets, and bringing on the mosquitoes in a mighty force. Colt had continued to camp ahead of the wagon train, and Sunny wondered how a man could stand to spend day after day exposed to such weather and not get sick and die. She had wanted very much to ask him about survival in such weather, but for the past month he had almost completely avoided her.

Ever since the night he had eaten with them, Colt Travis had hardly spoken to her. Sunny could not help being confused over his sudden change, since he had seemed ready enough to talk to her those first couple of weeks of travel. Apparently, her enthusiasm for his exciting life had been interpreted as pesty nosiness, and now he avoided her. She felt like the silly child Colt probably thought she was, and sometimes it made her want to cry.

She finished her tea and stood up, shading her eyes. Colt had already gone over the next rise, and she could not see him. The land rose and fell here like great stationary waves, and a man could suddenly drop out of sight. A hawk circled overhead, and she looked up to watch it for a moment, thinking how lucky they were that their worst problem so far had been the storm and the loss of a little food and china. The farther west they got, the more graves they saw, some belonging to very young children. It gave her the shivers, especially when her father had mentioned they could be riding right over graves that had long lost their markings. "Those crude little markers can be so quickly destroyed by the elements," he had told her. She had written about the lonely graves in her journal, wanting to remember everything about this beautiful but dangerous country.

Her father rode up beside her then, bringing a saddled black mare that was her favorite. "You ready to ride, honey?"

Sunny smiled. "Yes!" She hurried over to put her journal into her wagon. She tied on her hat and mounted the mare, thinking how this trip had brought her and her father even closer. He was more determined than ever to build his railroad, now that he saw how much a better way of travel was needed. She watched him give orders to one of the cooks, proud of how hardy and determined he had remained through the hardships. Today, as every day, he wore a sturdy three-piece suit, but because of the inconveniences of the trip, his suits could not be properly cleaned and some were beginning to look wrinkled and soiled. Sunny could see the old ruggedness in him when she watched him carry on, dirty suits and all. She had discovered a new side to her father, one that was willing to sacrifice his own comforts for something he thought was much more important.

They trotted their horses up the gently sloped hill over which Colt had disappeared, hoping to spot him when they reached the top.

"It's such big country, Daddy. We've traveled hardly a third of it, and we've already been out here for six weeks. How long do you think it would take to build a railroad clear across it?"

Bo looked to the south, wondering how many miles it was possible to see with the naked eye. "Oh, I expect such a railroad will take years, and an awful lot of money, a whole lot more than what I might be able to raise through my connections. The important thing is to convince the President and Congress of the worthiness of such an idea. This trip has done wonders for my determination now to see this thing through."

They were nearly halfway up the hill, and already the horses were breathing harder. The animals grew tired more easily now, since the last few days the ground just seemed to swell higher and higher. Sometimes it was such a gradual ascent that they were hardly aware they were climbing, until the animals would begin to strain and sweat.

"Do you think we have enough food to reach Fort Laramie?"

"I expect so, if we go easy like Colt told us. Maybe he'll bring us some fresh meat. Trouble is, game is pretty scarce around here now, after so many coming through before us. Colt says that's what makes the Indians so angry. I can see already that once we bring a railroad out here, things are going to have to change for the Indians. Something is going to have to be done, more treaty-making, whatever. They can't just roam free wherever they please, and with a loss of game they're going to have to learn to live more like civilized people to survive."

Sunny thought about what Colt had said about the Cherokee being so civilized back in Georgia. If they were, then why had they been routed out and sent west? Just because they were Indians? Could the wilder Indians of the Plains learn to farm and live in brick homes? "Daddy, I do wish you would talk Colt into letting me ask him just a few more questions. There is so much I still want to know."

Bo stiffened, hoping the girl never discovered his deliberate attempt at keeping her and Colt Travis apart. He was glad Colt had been mature enough to see the foolishness in any kind of friendship with Sunny and had done his own part in helping stem his daughter's childish fantasies. "Well, maybe when we reach the fort. We'll have time to rest up, and maybe Colt can spend a couple of hours with you before he leaves us."

"Leaves us?"

"Yes. He agreed to go as far as Laramie, which is where we will probably turn around and come back. Maybe we'll go even a little farther west first, check out that South Pass Colt told us about. We'll be able to find new scouts at the fort, maybe even get permission to have a few soldiers accompany us. Colt and Slim will be going on from there, said they'd settle for two hundred and fifty dollars each for not returning with us. They're heading down to the Pikes Peak area, something about doing some scouting for the prospectors."

"But they agreed to stay with us on the whole trip." Sunny struggled not to show her terrible disappointment. Why did it hurt so to think of Colt's leaving them?

"Well, honey, maybe our little wagon train and our fancy ways have them a little bored. Men like Slim and Colt are always looking for new action and excitement. I suppose if we were part of a much bigger wagon train that was more of a challenge, they might stick it out. That's the way it is with such men. They're like the wind, blowing and drifting in different directions, not very dependable."

Sunny weighed her father's explanation, still finding it difficult to believe the reasons for Colt's actions. But then, what did she know about men like that? This was her first experience with this life and the kind of people who lived out in this wilderness, and it was true it would have to take a very different sort of man to want always to live this way. In some ways she could understand it, for she had grown to love this country and the peace she found here. But she knew deep down that she could not live this way the rest of her life. She sometimes missed the bustling streets of Chicago, the parties, the comforts of home, even the board meetings she attended with her father. She had grown to like the challenge of the business world, enjoyed watching her father bribe and cajole his cohorts and even congressmen to get what he wanted. He was a master at persuading others, and she had learned that bribing was just another tool a man had to use to accomplish his goals and dreams.

Her thoughts were interrupted then by Colt himself, who appeared at the top of the rise and rode toward them. In spite of what both Miss Putnam and her father had told her about how undependable and wild and worthless he surely was, she still could not help the rush of her heart whenever she saw him. How wonderful he looked, the way he sat a horse, his dark shoulder-length hair spilling from under his leather hat, the fringes of his buckskins dancing with his horse's gait. How intimidating he looked, sporting that big knife and that wide ammunition belt, a pistol at his side. This was his realm, as much a part of his life as mansions and boardrooms were to her and her father.

"You two have been wanting to see a herd of buffalo," he called to them, riding closer. "Now's your chance. Once you reach the top of the rise, hold up and just look. Don't move around too much and don't do any shouting. There's one of the biggest herds over that rise that I've seen in a while."

Bo nodded. "Ride back and tell the others."

Colt could not help glancing at Sunny, secretly relieved she was all right after taking the chills a few days earlier. He knew she must be wondering why he had suddenly begun ignoring her, and he wished sometimes that he could explain; but in spite of his fury with her father, he knew the man was right in insisting their friendship not be allowed to go any deeper.

He tipped his hat to her and left. He was glad, even relieved, that he had made the decision to leave their little excursion once they reached Fort Laramie. He wished Sunny had turned out to be more like he had first expected—spoiled, sassy, rude and complaining— but she had been nothing but sweet and cooperative, even strong and brave. The violent storm they had suffered through and her own illness afterward had not brought a complaint. He realized he had to stop thinking about her, and that was not going to happen unless he left her and her father behind once he got them to safety.

"Buffalo ahead," he told the rest of the men. "Leave the wagons here and go up on foot or horseback. When you reach the top of the ridge, don't do any shouting, and keep the horses still." He turned and rode back toward Sunny and Bo. Stuart and several others quickly mounted up and followed him, and the rest, including the cooks, ran up on foot.

Miss Putnam sat up and looked out the back of her wagon, deciding to stay inside. "Buffalo!" she muttered. She coughed and sneezed and settled back into her blankets. She had no interest in buffalo or Indians or anything else in this godforsaken land. Her only interest was in getting back to Chicago and the comforts of civilization.

Colt skirted around a washout in the side of the hill and headed higher. His horse snorted and shuddered as he forced the animal to climb back up the steep incline. When he reached the top, Sunny was pointing and exclaiming at the sight of a sea of buffalo almost as far as the eye could see. She spoke in whispers, as though they were in church, as did everyone else who gawked at the awesome sight.

"You could almost walk across their backs," Sunny said quietly.

"Soon as they get past us I'll ride down and try to kill one," Colt told Landers. "I want to wait until we're out of danger. They're heading northeast right now, away from us." His horse whinnied, and Colt patted its neck to quiet the animal. "Even a small one will keep us in meat for a long time. It will take me a couple of days to skin and clean it. I'll keep the hide for possible trade to Indians. At any rate, Slim will take over while I'm gone."

"Where is Slim now?" Sunny asked.

Colt scanned the wide plain before them, the hills beyond it. "He's around the west end there, checking out some tracks we've been keeping an eye on for a couple of days now. I think they're buffalo hunters. Scum of the earth, as far as I'm concerned."

Sunny studied his profile, the straight, proud nose, the full lips, the prominent brow. "Why do you say that?"

Colt leaned forward, crossing his arms and resting them on the pommel of his saddle. "Most of the ones I've met think they can make up their own laws, steal what they want from travelers and the like. There aren't many out here yet, but there will be more. Buffalo hides are becoming more popular back east. The biggest problem is the hunters kill the beasts for their hides alone and leave the rest of the animal to rot, wasting the meat, the bones, everything the Indians need to live on. That just makes the Indians angrier, and they take that anger out on travelers and settlers. As far as I'm concerned, there should be a law against such waste."

A shot suddenly rang out, startling everyone, including the buffalo herd. "What the—" Colt sat up straighter in his saddle. The buffalo grew restless, a few starting to run. There came another shot, two, three. The entire herd was suddenly in full stampede. The shots had come from the north side of the herd, making them turn south, toward the area of the Landers wagons.

"What's happening!" Bo asked, his horse rearing slightly.

Colt rode forward, spotting Slim. "It must be the buffalo hunters we've been following! The bastards have them in a run!" He rode along the top of the ridge, watching anxiously as Slim galloped his horse around the west end of the herd and charged right in front of them, trying to head the animals off more to the north and east again. Colt whistled and waved his hat, trying to help. It was to no avail. To his horror he saw Slim's horse stumble. He heard Sunny scream when they all watched Slim's bulky body quickly disappear along with his horse beneath the thundering buffalo hooves.

Colt felt as though his heart had just been crushed. There was no time to think about the loss, no time even to try to imagine the loneliness of being without the man who had been like a father to him for six years. It had all happened so quickly that he wondered if any of it was real.

The earth literally shook as he turned his horse back toward Bo and Sunny and the others. "Get down to that washout!" he yelled. "Those who don't fit, get under the wagons!"

Already it was difficult to hear him because of the hoofbeats. Some of the Landers men were confused. They turned their horses and rode hard. "Don't try to outride them!" Colt shouted. "You'll be killed! Get under the wagons! Under the wagons!"

His voice was lost in the terrific noise. Colt rode hard to catch up with Sunny and her father and brother, who charged down the hill and dismounted, dodging into the washout while the drivers and cooks made for the wagons. By now the noise was deafening. Colt reached the washout just in time to see Sunny bolt from its safety and run toward the wagons herself, screaming Miss Putnam's name.

"Sunny, come back!" her father screamed.

"Stay there or you're dead men!" Colt shouted to Bo and Stuart. "I'll take care of Sunny!" He galloped his horse toward Sunny, and already the buffalo were cresting the ridge. Colt reached down, grabbing Sunny up in one arm.

"Miss Putnam!" she screamed. "She's in the wagon!"

"You should have stayed in the washout!" Colt shouted as she fought him. "You can't help her now!" His horse reared and whirled, and Sunny slipped from his grasp. He quickly dismounted, and his horse ran off. Colt grabbed Sunny as the huge, shaggy beasts of the plains crashed into the wagons. One overturned, and the men crouched under it flattened themselves right next to it, the buffalo leaping over them and around them. Colt slammed Sunny to the ground between the overturned wagon and a barrel. He threw himself over her, putting his arms over her head. "Don't move!" he shouted in her ear.

He could hear her muffled scream as she cringed beneath him, while all around them the buffalo crashed and thundered past, the ground shaking as though hit by an earthquake. Dust billowed so densely that it was difficult to breathe. The fifteen minutes it took for the entire herd to stampede past them seemed more like an hour to those who huddled in terror. The other two wagons and the coach were also toppled. Finally the rumbling grew more distant, the ground more stable. The dust cloud began to settle, and Colt rose up slightly, touching Sunny's hair. "You all right?"

"I don't know," she answered, coughing. She looked up at him, her face dirty and streaked with tears. She was shaking, and Colt drew her close. She huddled against him, taking comfort in his protective arms. Finally, reluctantly, Colt let go of her. He rested on his elbows and looked into her eyes, struggling against an overwhelming urge to taste her mouth. She reached up and touched his face.

"Don't," he said softly, grasping her wrist. It was all he needed to say. A tear slipped down the side of her face into her ear, and he brushed it away, getting up and helping her to her feet.

"I think something cut me," she finally said. She felt a stinging pain at her left thigh, and she looked down to see her riding skirt was torn. She opened the tear to expose a bleeding cut, quickly turning away so that Colt could not see her bare skin.

"You'd better take care of that right away. Pour some whiskey on it if you can find some," Colt told her. "It will help prevent any infection."

"Sunny! Sunny!" Bo Landers was running in her direction, his forehead bleeding.

"Daddy!" Sunny scrambled away from Colt and ran to her father. "You're hurt!"

"I'm all right. I started to come to you and one of the beasts barely grazed me. I was forced to stay in the washout." The man hugged her tightly. "Thank God! I was sure you'd be killed!" He clung to her, looking over at Colt. "You saved her life."

Colt brushed himself off and picked up his hat. Sunny could see him struggling with his emotions. "I only wish I could have saved Slim too."

"I'm damn sorry, Colt." Landers scanned the damage, all three wagons overturned, teams trampled, the coach destroyed. "My God," he muttered. "What are we going to do?"

A few of his men began scrambling away from other wagons, one of them shouting that he had found Miss Putnam. "She's dead," he told the others.

Sunny burst into tears, and Colt could feel nothing but fury, wanting to kill the men who had caused this. "Your daughter's leg is cut," he told Landers. "You'd better tend to it, and to yourself." He turned to the others. "The rest of you see if you can find some of the horses. Some of your friends are probably lying dead out there. We'll have to bury them and salvage what we can. Maybe we can get at least one of these wagons into working order and save enough food and supplies to get us to Fort Laramie." He looked at Landers. "You can get more wagons and supplies there, and probably a few oxen. I'm going to go and bury Slim and then try to find my horse, if he's still alive. All of you make camp right here tonight. I'll be gone for a day or two."

"Gone! Gone where?" Stuart asked.

Sunny wiped her tears, looking up at Colt. His eyes had changed from the softness she had seen only a moment ago to a sudden look of fury that actually frightened her. Suddenly, he reminded her of how she had pictured wild Indians on the attack might look.

"I'm going to find the bastards who caused this," he nearly growled. "Somebody is going to *pay* for killing Slim!"

"But you can't leave us like this," Stuart protested. "You could get *yourself* killed!"

"And *they* tried to kill *us!*" Colt shot back. "They did this for a reason, Landers, and I'm not going to wait around for them to bushwhack us in the middle of the night. I prefer to be the *hunter* rather than the hunted. Just get your men to clean this mess up, I have a friend to bury."

Sunny was sure she saw tears in Colt's eyes before he turned away and kicked around some of the rubble until he found a shovel. He walked off toward the ridge, and Sunny watched after him until he was out of sight, aching to comfort him. She wondered what he was going to do about the buffalo hunters. Would he be killed, or would *he* do the killing?

She turned to look at the destruction the buffalo had left behind, reality sinking in then. Colt had not been the only one to lose someone close to him today. She limped over to Miss Putnam's body, which a couple of the men had removed from her wrecked wagon. The woman's face was blue and purple, but Sunny saw no blood. She ignored the pain in her leg and crumbled to the woman's side, weeping.

• • •

"Do you still think a railroad can be built out here?" Stuart asked his father. "It's a harsh land, Dad, big and unforgiving. We've sure learned that the hard way. Do you understand what you're proposing?"

Landers met his son's questioning gaze. They sat across from each other at a campfire, drinking coffee salvaged from the wreckage. This was the second night following the stampede, and both men were still struggling with the trauma of their loss. Sunny had cried herself sick over the loss of Slim and Miss Putnam. Her leg was bandaged but painful, and she lay exhausted near her father and the fire now, sleeping on a feather mattress that had been pulled from one of the wagons. The two cooks had survived the stampede, and they and the eight other men who had lived had buried Miss Putnam and the four men who had lost their lives. Colt had insisted on burying Slim alone. Now he was gone, and all they could do was wait and wonder if the man was going to make it back.

Everyone had saved what they could of food and belongings. A few horses and mules from the remuda had been rounded up, but a good deal of stock had been lost. The coach and two wagons were too damaged to be of any use, and wood from one of the destroyed wagons had been used to make the fire.

"I understand, all right," Bo answered his son. "I understand that this has all got to change, and the railroad will bring about that change. This land will by God be settled, and my railroad will lead the way! You don't give up because of things like this, Stuart. You just get mad and more determined!"

Stuart ran a hand through his hair, still badly shaken from his brush with death. "All right, Dad, build your railroad; but I think you ought to get the heck back to Chicago and take Sunny with you and let others come out here and do the footwork." He sighed deeply. "This has gone hard on Sunny. Miss Putnam has been right by her side for years."

"She's got me. She'll be all right."

Stuart frowned. *Yes, she's got you,* he thought. *You think that's all anybody needs, that you can run everyone's lives, don't you, Dad? You're Sunny's whole world. You've cut her off from everything and everyone else. What is she going to do when you're gone, especially if she finds out the truth about her mother?*

"Dad, look what's happened already, and we haven't even reached Fort Laramie. Do you realize there are two mountain ranges out there to be crossed, as well as a desert? You're talking about building a railroad through eighteen hundred miles of *wilderness!* I thought at first maybe it could be done, but now I don't know."

"I'll hear no more of that kind of talk. If I say it can be done, then it can! I hear enough protesting from Vince. I thought at least *one* of my sons was on my side."

Stuart closed his eyes in exasperation. "Dammit, Dad, you know I'm on your side."

"Then *act* like it! What has happened here just makes me more determined, and it should do the same for you. I'm building that railroad, Stuart, and if anything happens to me, I know Sunny will carry on the dream, because she loves me and she knows how important this is. With Vince giving her trouble every step of the way, she's got to at least have *your* support, and so do I!"

Stuart rubbed the back of his neck. "Fine. But as soon as we reach Laramie and get resupplied, I'm going back to my wife and baby. A man can die out here in the blink of an eye, and Vi is a little young to be left a widow. And don't tell me you aren't already thinking about going on to the South Pass. You've been thinking about it ever since you asked Colt about the best way through the Rockies. Do you intend to keep submitting Sunny to these dangers?"

Bo took a cigar from his pocket, sighing deeply. "She's got more guts than you and Vince put together. Sure I'll take her with me, if she'll go."

"You know she'll go. Has she ever said no to you? She worships the ground you walk on. She'd never—" Stuart hesitated when he thought he heard a grunt. He signaled his father to be quiet, and both men came alert. Since Colt had suggested the buffalo hunters might have deliberately stampeded the herd, they had all been on edge, the men taking turns keeping watch at night.

A shot startled them, and both men jumped to their feet just as the two cooks and six of Bo's remaining eight guards loomed into the firelight, herded forward by three filthy, bearded men whose body odor was noticeable even from several feet away.

"What is this!" Bo raged.

Sunny sat up, awakened by the gunfire. Her eyes widened in terror. "Daddy!"

"Stay right there, Sunny."

"I'm sorry, Mr. Landers," one of the guards spoke up. "I don't know how they snuck up on us like this. They shot Russell. I don't know what happened to Jimmy."

The huge figure of a fourth intruder loomed into the firelight, sporting the biggest rifle Stuart had ever seen. "Everybody rest easy," the man warned in a deep voice.

"What is going on?" Bo demanded. "Who the hell are you?" He stood as tall as the stranger but looked smaller because the other man was even heavier and wore a buffalo robe. Sunny wrinkled her nose at the smell of old blood.

"Names don't matter," the apparent leader replied. He held the well-chewed stub of a cigar in his yellowing teeth. "Me and my men figured if we waited till just the right time, we'd catch you and yours off guard. Been watchin' you for quite a few days, you and the pretty little gal there." The man rested his rifle barrel against Bo's neck. "You look like a rich old bugger. She's your daughter then, huh, Daddy?"

Bo's face reddened deeply with fury. "What the hell do you want? Money? I can pay you plenty. Just get out of here and leave us alone!"

Stuart seethed inwardly, wondering if he had survived the stampede only to be shot down in cold blood. "You're the ones who caused the stampede, aren't you?"

The man who held the rifle on Bo grinned. "Worked, didn't it? We figured you'd either all be killed, and we'd come here and loot your fancy wagons; or you'd lose enough men and be shook up enough that we'd catch you off guard, which is exactly what happened." He glanced down at Sunny. "You might as well stay on that nice soft mattress, honey. We'll all get some good use out of it. Maybe your pa would like to watch." He looked back at Landers. "Glad to see the little gal survived."

Sunny jumped to her feet. She tried to run to her father, but one of the hunters grabbed her from behind. She screamed and fought him, overwhelmed with horror when he grasped at her breasts.

"Shut up," the man growled, jerking her so tightly that she gasped for breath. "You want us to kill your pa right here and now?"

Their leader took his eyes from Bo long enough to give Sunny a good, long look. "Goddamn, you sure as hell don't look like somebody who ought to be callin' her pa Daddy. That's for little girls, and you ain't no little girl."

"Please! Leave her alone," Bo warned.

"Or what?"

Sunny remembered what Colt had said about these men, called them thieves and murderers. She felt so sick she thought she might vomit. She didn't know much about what men did with women, but she knew enough to realize she was in horrible danger. She struggled again, but the man's grip on her was so strong that her efforts were fruitless.

"Here's how it is," their leader said, fixing his eyes on Bo again. "From what we've been watchin', you're a man with a lot of money, and now you've admitted it. Now, first we'll loot what we can right here—watches, money, anything you got. Then me and my men here, we'll take the little gal with us when we leave. How much you figure she's worth, *Daddy?* A thousand? Ten thousand? A million? You tell me how much *you're* worth, and that's how much it's gonna cost you to get your daughter back. You try anything, you're dead, and she's ours to keep. You got any idea what a gun like this would do to you at this range? Your head will be lyin' on the other side of this ridge, your brains scattered all along the way."

"Bastards!" Stuart spat out at them.

One of the others fired a gun at his feet, making him jump, and they all laughed. Bo's men stood helpless.

"Colt!" Sunny cried out. "Where is he? What did you do to him?"

The leader moved his eyes to her again. "Who's Colt?"

She just stared at him, realizing then that the man was not aware someone else might be out there. Would Colt come, or had he deserted them?

"He's our guide," Stuart answered. "You killed his best friend in that stampede, and if you take off with Sunny, he'll by God kill you! All of you!"

The man grinned. "One man?"

Sunny squirmed and whimpered, tears of terror forming in her eyes.

"Let her go *now*," Bo pleaded. "I'll pay you anything you want if you don't harm her. But if you touch her wrongly, you won't get a cent!"

The man shook his head. "You'll pay anything, no matter *what* we do to her."

"You'd better listen to Mr. Landers," came a voice from the darkness. "Let her go!"

Everyone stood stiffly silent for a moment.

"Colt," Sunny whispered.

"Let go of the girl," the voice repeated, "or you'll be the first to die. You there, the big fat stinking bastard holding the rifle on the girl's father. I've got a bead on your gut, Mister. Nothing's worse than getting gut-shot. I guarantee, no matter what else happens, your belly will explode with lead before it's over if you and your men don't put down your arms right now. Tell your man to hand the girl over to her pa."

Several long, silent seconds passed. "Who the hell are you?" the leader asked.

"Like you already said, names don't matter," came Colt's voice. "Just do like I say."

Bo could hear the breathing of his abductor grow heavier. He watched a mixture of fear and stubbornness pass through the man's eyes, and he swallowed, wondering if he would pull the trigger and blow his head off.

Suddenly, the man whirled and shot into the darkness, apparently hoping to hit Colt. Sunny saw a flame from the shadows as Colt's revolver fired. The buffalo hunter's body flew backward and landed in the fire. He let out a short scream, then went silent.

Everything happened in a matter of seconds. The man holding Sunny gave her a push, and she heard another shot. Someone behind her cried out, then fell against her. Sunny gasped and ran for her father. "Let's get out of here!" someone else yelled. Sunny heard another shot, then the sound of a horse riding away.

Sunny stood clinging to her father, everyone frozen in place for a moment, not sure yet if they were safe. Finally Colt stepped into the firelight. Sunny whimpered his name, wanting very much to run to him, but there was still a viciousness in his eyes that frightened her. He walked up to the first man who had fallen into the fire. The man was so big that his body had actually put out most of the flames, but part of his buffalo skin jacket burned brightly so that there was still light. The rest of him smoldered in a stench, and the front of the man's clothing was covered with blood. Sunny put a hand to her stomach at the awful sight.

Colt kicked at the body as though it were no more than a dead animal. "Three are dead," he said matter-of-factly. "The fourth got away." He looked at Bo. "This makes up at least a little for what happened to Slim." He glanced at Sunny. "You okay?" he asked.

She nodded. "Thank you," she said softly.

He looked at her father. "Just doing my job." He turned to one of Bo's men. "Get rid of these bodies. Two more of your own men are dead. We'll bury them and get the hell on our way in the morning."

It took three men to lift the big man off the fire, and the flames flared up brighter again. Colt walked closer to Bo, and Sunny thought he looked suddenly older. With vengeance still lighting his eyes, and having just killed three men without an ounce of hesitation, he was an intimidating sight. Sunny clung to her father.

"I'll take one of those cigars you're always offering," Colt told the man.

Bo nodded, taking one of the smokes from an inside pocket of his jacket. "I don't know what to say, Colt. You saved my daughter from that stampede, and now this. I'll pay you Slim's share of the money when we reach Fort Laramie, plus an extra two hundred fifty."

Their eyes held for a moment, and Colt took the cigar. "I don't want your damn money. Slim told me not to take this job, but I didn't listen. Now he's dead. It's my fault, not yours. And saving your daughter's life and virtue isn't something a man can put a price on, now, is it?" He turned away, stooping over the fire to light the cigar. "I found my horse," he explained when he straightened. "Followed the hunters' tracks and realized they were heading right back here. I just figured I'd wait till dark and surprise them." He puffed the cigar a moment, then took it from between his teeth. "I'll make my own camp." He held up the cigar. "Thanks." He turned, then hesitated, looking at Bo again. "This dream of yours has cost a lot of lives already. After all this, you'd better build that damn railroad."

He disappeared into the darkness, leaving the rest of them stunned. What had just happened so quickly seemed unreal, until Sunny looked again at the bloody, smoldering body of the big man who had threatened her and her father. She told herself that what Colt did was simply a necessary evil in a violent land, where survival went to the strongest and the fittest, sometimes to the cleverest. She understood that out here there was no room for hesitation or remorse. Off in the distant hills coyotes began to yip and howl, and it hit her with much more clarity just how drastically different Colt Travis's world was from her own. She felt like a foolish child for giving him even the slightest romantic thought.

Chapter 4

Sunny struggled to write without scribbling as the wagon in which she sat bounced and jolted over the rough terrain. Her leg hurt so badly now that walking or riding a horse was too painful.

Five days have passed since the buffalo stampede. We are down to one wagon that carries a mixture of salvaged necessities, mostly food and cooking utensils and extra ammunition, along with the feather mattress on which I sleep inside the wagon. Father and Stuart are forced to sleep under the stars with the other men. Other than my father and brother and the two cooks, there are only six men left, plus, of course, our guide.

The comforts she had been afforded at the beginning of their journey were gone. She had managed only one bath over the past five days, amazed that the battered tin tub she used did not leak. Her father had set it up

behind some thick, blooming bushes along the river-
bank.

*Thank goodness I found my journal among the wreck-
age,* she wrote. *We are following the North Platte now,
and I am anxious to reach Fort Laramie, where we will
buy extra wagons and supplies. It is strange not to have
Miss Putnam helping me bathe and do my hair and such,
and I miss her very much. I pray she is someplace happy
now. The rest of us carry on like real pioneers. I never
thought I could survive such a life. It is a real test of our
stamina.*

She dipped her pen into the ink bottle again. *Thanks
to Colt Travis, we at least do not have to go hungry. Colt
managed to shoot an antelope three days ago, and just
yesterday he shot two rabbits. To watch him clean and skin
an animal is like watching an artist, for he is quick and
very skilled, leaving the skins in quite beautiful shape. They
now hang drying on the wagon, in case they are needed for
trade with Indians.*

She leaned back, moving to try to get her sore leg in a
more comfortable position. Now that they had lost Slim
and four other men, Colt stayed closer to the wagons as
their little group limped toward Fort Laramie. Enough
horses had been salvaged so that the men all had something to ride, with four extras. Only seven of the original
eighteen mules had survived and been found, and six of
them pulled the wagon, the two cooks taking turns driving.

Sunny looked back down at her journal. *Mr. Travis has
been very quiet since Mr. Jessup died, and I think he is in
deep mourning. I feel bad for him, especially since he has
saved my life twice so far on this awful trip.*

"Now what?" One of the two cooks sitting in the
wagon seat had spoken the words. "Whoa!" the driver
yelled. The wagon came quickly to a stop.

Sunny set aside her journal. "Keep the girl inside,"
she heard Colt shout.

"Stay out of sight, Miss Landers," the driver called to
her.

Sunny wondered what new catastrophe they had encountered. She winced with pain as she turned to peek

out from the side of the wagon, lifting the canvas just enough to see at least twenty painted warriors sitting on their ponies on a rise south of the wagon. "Indians!" she gasped. Surprisingly, this was the first time they had encountered any of the wilder Plains tribes.

"No women along," one of the cooks commented. "Didn't Colt tell us once that when women weren't along it was probably a war party?"

Sunny's heart pounded with dreadful imaginings of what the painted warriors might do to her if they decided to attack. Her father's men lined up alongside the wagon, weapons ready.

"Don't anybody make a move unless I say so," Colt warned. "They probably just want to trade." Sunny watched him ride out to the Indians, wondering how it felt to him to have to deal with people so similar to his own heritage. Surely he knew that what had happened to the Cherokee could also happen to these Plains Indians. If the West was settled, like her father believed would happen, where would these nomadic people go? Up until now it was a matter of pushing eastern tribes westward into Indian Territory; but once whites filled the West, what would be left for the Indian? Still, this was such a big country. Surely there was room for everybody. The Indians could find a place to call their own.

Colt seemed to be arguing with the apparent leader of the warriors, and Sunny felt goose bumps rising on her skin. She expected at any moment to see one of the Indians sink a tomahawk into poor Colt. Finally Colt rode back to Sunny's father, whose horse was close to the wagon.

"There's been trouble, but I think we can get through this without losing our scalps," Colt told the man. "Believe me, all of us together are no match for those men up there. Those are Cheyenne warriors, some of the best fighters on the Plains. There are at least twenty-five of them, and one angry warrior is equal to three ordinary men. I told them we're just a small party of government men headed for Fort Laramie and that we mean them no harm. Thinking you're representatives of the Great White Father in Washington will make them think twice about giving us trouble, especially if we co-operate. Just don't let them see Sunny."

"What do they want?"

"Practically everything we've got, and we'd better give it to them."

"But we're down to almost nothing ourselves!"

Colt's horse whinnied and pranced in a circle, as though sensing the danger. "There's no arguing about it, Landers. Their people have been harassed by soldiers, whole villages with food and weapon supplies destroyed, women and children killed. Now the army has confiscated the government issue down at Bent's Fort and won't give them promised supplies, including guns and flint and powder. Those men up there are in a real ugly mood. They're looking for weapons they can use to hunt, as well as tobacco and whatever food we can spare. I want at least six of your men to give up their rifles and ammunition to them."

"So they can turn around and use them against us?" Stuart's face was red with fear and anger.

"They've given me their word they'll ride off and leave us alone."

"And you *believe* them? They're *Indians!*" Stuart retorted.

Sunny could see Colt stiffen. For a moment his own face reminded her of the very warriors they were dealing with. "You trust *my* word, don't you? *I'm* Indian!"

Stuart rolled his eyes. "You know what I mean, Colt. You're different!"

"I'm *no* different! An Indian's word is good as long as we don't betray them in some way. Now get the rifles together, and be glad they were willing to settle for only six instead of taking every damn gun we have!" Colt looked up at the cooks. "Get that extra meat and put it in a flour sack or something; and get out that last can of tobacco. We'll have a little left for ourselves, and I can always do more hunting. We aren't that far from Laramie."

The cooks scrambled to retrieve the necessary items. Bo ordered six of his men to hand over their rifles and to take extra ammunition from their saddlebags. The men dismounted and walked forward, laying the rifles in a pile; the cooks added the food and tobacco.

They all backed away, and Colt shouted something in the strange, clipped Cheyenne tongue. Several of the warriors rode cautiously closer then, while their leader hung back. Sunny lowered the canvas to a tiny crack, petrified of being spotted. Her eyes widened at the nearly naked bodies of the warriors, who dismounted and picked up the supplies. Their faces were painted, their skin even darker than Colt's. She had heard many stories about these fierce warriors, the awful things they did to white prisoners. It was difficult to imagine that they could have human feelings, yet a couple of them glanced up at Colt with no animosity. They spoke to him, and although Sunny could not understand what was said, she sensed it was a form of thank-you.

Her stomach felt as though it had climbed up into her heart as she watched. The warriors took the supplies and rode back up the ridge. Their leader raised a hand to Colt, and Colt returned the apparent farewell gesture. "Stay put," he said quietly to her father and his men. The Indians finally rode off, disappearing over the ridge.

Colt turned to face Bo and his men. "Don't be surprised if we see them watching us for a while. They're going to make sure we keep going." He gestured to Bo. "Come with me." Colt trotted his horse around to the back of the wagon, and Bo followed. Colt looked inside at Sunny. "For the next couple of days, you stay in there as long as it's light. Try to hold your personal needs until dark. It's very important that they don't see you."

She nodded, still wide-eyed from a mixture of wonder and terror.

"It hurts her leg too much to walk anyway," Bo told him.

Colt frowned with concern. "Is it really that bad, Sunny?"

She didn't want to sound like a baby in front of him, but the leg had gotten too sore to hide it any longer. "It hurts worse every day. But I'm sure it will be all right."

Colt turned to her father. "You'd better let me have a

look. That cut should be getting better by now, not worse."

Worry moved into Bo's eyes. "I just figured it would be all right. She hasn't even let *me* look at it." The man turned his gaze to Sunny. "Is that wound worse than you're letting on? You'd better let me see it, Sunny."

Sunny reddened with embarrassment. "Daddy, it's clear up on my thigh!"

The man sighed and dismounted, climbing into the wagon, grunting from the effort. "Sunny, I wish Miss Putnam was here, but she isn't," he said, crouching close to her. "If that cut is infected, we need to know. Now, let me have a look. For heaven's sake, I'm your father."

Sunny knew she could no longer object. The ugly cut was beginning to worry her, too, but she hadn't wanted to seem whiny about it. Reluctantly, she pulled up her skirt and pushed up one leg of her bloomers, exposing her outer left thigh. Her father began unwrapping the bandage she had put on herself, and before he even finished he detected the smell of infection.

"Keep a lookout," Colt was shouting outside.

"I don't see anybody," one of the men answered.

"Colt, you'd better look at this," Bo called out to him.

"Daddy! He *can't* look at it."

"This is no time for modesty, Sunny. My God, child, you should have *told* me!"

Colt dismounted and climbed over the wagon gate with ease. Bo moved out of the way so that a shaft of sunlight made it easier to see. Sunny closed her eyes and looked away, one tear spilling down her cheek.

"Damn," Colt muttered. She heard him sigh deeply, and he spoke her name. Sunny looked at him, some of her humiliation leaving her when she saw the true concern in his eyes. She thought how strange it was that he could look so much like the fierce warriors who had just left them, and a moment later those hazel eyes could hold such gentleness. "Sunny, something has to be done about this. You could lose your leg."

"My God!" Bo gasped. "What have I done, bringing her out here?" He touched her hair lovingly.

"What can you do?" Sunny asked Colt, stifling an urge to cry openly.

Colt looked at her father. "The only thing that might kill off the infection is to burn it out of there."

Sunny gasped in a whimper, and Bo's eyes widened. *"Burn* it! But that would be so painful, and it will leave a worse scar than the cut!"

"A little pain now and a scar are a hell of a lot better than losing the whole leg, wouldn't you say? Besides, it's not exactly in a spot anybody will ever see, except maybe her husband, who shouldn't give a damn."

Sunny felt the embarrassment returning, and she covered her face. "Let him do it, Daddy," she whimpered.

"I've seen these things before, Landers," Colt told the man. Ever since the man had told him to stay away from Sunny, Colt had been unable to call Bo by his first name. "There's no other way to do it."

"Good God," Bo muttered, suddenly looking like the aging man that he was.

"We'll do it tonight after we make camp. We don't dare sit here too long right now. Those Cheyenne might return and wonder what we're still doing here." Colt gently pulled Sunny's skirt back over her leg, leaning closer. "Sunny, it's not as bad as you think. I promise that the infection in that wound hurts a lot more than the burn that will be left after we get rid of it, but you have to be braver than you've ever been so far."

She shook, wiping at her eyes and meeting Colt's gaze. She felt better when he smiled softly. "You're one strong, brave woman, Sunny. You've got the Landers spunk, just like your pa said. I want you to know that you fooled me good on this trip. I figured you'd cause one hell of a problem and whine all the way out here, but you've been as brave as any woman on any wagon train I've ever worked for. Your pa can be proud of you." He looked at Bo. "Stay with her awhile."

"Of course."

Colt left them, and Sunny rested her head against her father's chest as he held her, but it was not Bo Landers's arms that comforted her. It was the thought of Colt's last words. It was not just that he had called her strong and brave. He had called her a woman.

Sunny's father embraced her firmly from behind, and Sunny kept her arms wrapped around a pillow, which she would use to cover her face when the awful moment came. Her screams had to be muffled so that no Indians would hear. She was too frightened now to cry, or to care about the embarrassment of having to bring in Stuart to hold her legs. Just outside, a piece of flatiron that had been saved from one of the destroyed wagons was being heated in the hot coals of the campfire. One of the cooks wrapped a towel around one end of it, lifting it out to see that the other end glowed red. He carried it over to where Colt waited inside the wagon. "This good enough?" he asked.

"That's fine." Colt took the hot iron from him, turning to Sunny, who lay on her right side. His heart ached at the look in her eyes when she saw the glowing piece of metal. "I'm sorry, Sunny. There's no time to wait. I don't want this to cool down." He looked at her father, whose eyes betrayed his devastation. "Hang on to her."

Sunny buried her face in the pillow, and Stuart grasped her ankles more firmly. By the light of a lantern that hung overhead, Colt pressed the red-hot iron to the wound.

Sunny had never known such pain, and she prayed she never would again. She could not help the screams as she pushed her face into the pillow. Her father's grip tightened, and her body lurched in a natural instinct to get away; but there was no escaping what must be. In her mind it seemed that Colt held the iron to the wound for a very long time, and she wondered if she would pass out.

Finally, she heard Colt telling someone to take the flatiron away. The burning sensation continued until Sunny felt an unexpected gentle touch. Colt was applying something very soothing to the burn. "What is that?" she heard her father asking.

"An old Cherokee remedy," Colt answered. "My

mother taught it to my father when I burned my hands once, and he taught it to me. It's a mixture of cornmeal and slippery-elm bark—good for burns. It will help take away the pain and make this heal faster."

"Where did you get the bark?" Stuart asked. "There's no elm trees out here."

"When your life depends on your own doctoring, you make sure you always have the right supplies along," Colt answered. "Places like Bent's Fort always carry such things to sell to traders and scouts. They know men like us use the old Indian remedies. There is another poultice made from buffalo fat that the Plains Indians use, but I don't have any buffalo fat with me. Lift her leg a little and we'll get it wrapped up." Someone touched her hair. "Sunny?"

Still shivering with sobs, Sunny finally took her face from the pillow. She curled her nose at the smell of her own burned flesh.

"You did good," Colt told her. "How does it feel now?"

"I don't know," she sniffed. Her father stroked the hair back from her face. "Kind of numb."

"That's because of the poultice," Colt told her. "We'll get it wrapped up, and I guarantee by tomorrow morning it will feel one hell of a lot better."

She watched his eyes, loving him for all he had done for her. "Thank you," she whimpered.

Colt grinned. "That's a hell of a thing to have to thank a man for." He turned to take some gauze from Stuart and began wrapping her leg. Sunny watched him, wanting to remember his every feature, wondering how she was going to forget Colt Travis once this trip was over.

"I'm so damn sorry, Sunny," her father said, his voice choked. He rocked her in his arms. "I could have lost you. I'll get you back to Chicago as fast as we can go, and by God we'll get a railroad bill passed so others don't have to suffer like this. I've seen all I need to see to know that we have to bring civilization to this land, towns with doctors and supply stores, a better way to travel out here." He leaned down and kissed her forehead. "I wouldn't want to go on living if something happened to my Sunny."

Colt finished wrapping her leg, wondering how he was going to forget the sight of her slender thigh, or how smooth her skin was. Forbidden thoughts raced through his mind, how he would like to hold her himself, see the rest of that satiny skin, make a full woman of her. He pulled her skirt back over her leg. "Get some rest," he told her, picking up the tin cup in which he had mixed the poultice. "We'll check the wound tomorrow night."

"Thank you again," she told him, shivering.

He nodded, a new look in his eyes she could not quite read. "I'm glad you're all right," he answered. He seemed to want to say more, but he glanced at her father and his eyes changed again. "Let's all get some sleep." He climbed out of the wagon.

"Stuart and I will be right outside, honey," her father told her, kissing her cheek. "You just yell if you need anything." He drew a blanket over her, and Sunny relaxed into the feather mattress, thinking about how Colt had looked at her, as though it had hurt him deeply to have to bring her pain. There was something in that look that told her what she needed to know, that he cared about her after all, much more than she had thought. She wished he wouldn't leave them when they reached the fort, wished she were older and knew more about men. If Stuart's wife were here, she could tell the woman about her feelings. Vi would understand. Since she had married Stuart, Vi and Sunny had become close. Vi was nothing like Vince's wife, who could be cruel.

For now, she could not even talk to Vi. She could only pour out her feelings in her journal. She wondered how she would feel years from now when she got out that journal and read it . . . and remembered Colt Travis.

"Well, it's too bad about all your misfortunes, Mr. Landers. I'll find you a good scout and authorize a few of my men to accompany you back through Nebraska, at least to Fort Kearny."

The words came from the fort commander, a Lieutenant Amber, who had invited Sunny and her father and brother, as well as Colt, to supper. His cook had prepared a special meal for them of venison, potatoes, and carrots, followed by apple pie. After rationing their meager food supplies for weeks, the food tasted wonderful to everyone; but Sunny was unable to eat. Knowing that Colt would be gone tomorrow brought an ache to her stomach.

"Thank you for your offer," Bo told Amber. "I'll never quite forgive myself for bringing Sunny out here. If I had known all that would happen, well, let's just say I'm more determined than ever now to build that railroad."

"That will be a sight to see, a great boon to the army, I'll say that."

Sunny was hardly aware of the conversation. All she could think about was how she could speak alone to Colt before he left them. Somehow she had to have a last good-bye. She wondered if he thought she looked pretty tonight. Here at the fort they had gotten new supplies and wagons, and Sunny was given the luxury of a room where she could take a real bath again. From her salvaged belongings she had retrieved a yellow cotton day dress that was one of her favorites. One of her father's cooks had ironed it for her, and she wore it tonight. It fit her blossoming form perfectly, and she had pulled back the sides of her hair with yellow bows. She was becoming more aware of her femininity, thinking of herself as a woman now, not a child. Colt Travis himself had called her a woman, and she was proud that he thought of her that way.

"I'm sorry about your tutor, Miss Landers," the lieutenant said. "And your own accident. It must have been quite an ordeal for you. You're lucky you had someone along who knew what to do about that infection."

Sunny had been staring at Colt, wishing he would look at her, but he seemed to be deliberately averting his eyes. She turned her attention to the lieutenant. "Yes," she answered. "Colt saved my life more than once. I'll be forever grateful to him. My leg is healing beautifully, and I don't even limp now."

Colt finally glanced at her while a private walked around the wooden table pouring everyone a glass of wine. A rush of something wonderful and unexplainable pulsated through Sunny when Colt's eyes met hers, making her feel too warm.

Colt directed his gaze at Lieutenant Amber then. "All part of the job," he told the man. He felt almost guilty enjoying the fine meal the commander had served them while the rest of Bo's men camped outside, eating their own cooking around a campfire. He knew Amber would never have done this for the ordinary traveler, but the soldier had discovered that Bo Landers was one of the richest men in the country, and the man had catered to Landers ever since, following him around, ordering his men to see to their every need, ogling Sunny.

Colt could not imagine having people lick after a man just because of his money. He couldn't stand such fakes, and he decided it was probably a good thing he would never be rich. He would probably be landing a fist into people every day for their stupid groveling. He was getting a headache watching the lieutenant kowtow to Landers's every wish, but Landers was eating it up. He was used to such treatment and enjoying every minute of it. Colt was getting a good idea of what life was like for the man back in Chicago, everyone jumping at his every command, people impressed by his money and power.

"Well, if you ever want to do some scouting for the army," the lieutenant was telling Colt, "just let me know. You're pretty young, Travis, but apparently very skilled. I'm sorry about your friend getting killed." The man took a sip of wine. "By the way, which way do you think those Cheyenne went?" he asked casually. "They can't be too far from here if you had your run-in with them only a couple of days ago."

Colt downed his own wine in two gulps, setting his glass down and giving the lieutenant a look of disdain. "You offered me a job as a scout, but I didn't take it, Lieutenant Amber, which means I don't have to tell you which way they went. Besides, I wouldn't have any idea where they were headed. I think all they want right now is to be left alone." He looked around the table and rose. "If you'll all excuse me, I intend to turn in early tonight. I'll be leaving for Colorado at sunup."

"Already?" Bo asked him. "We haven't even settled up yet."

"I've got some things to get in order, some repacking to do. I'll be camped over near the livery. You can come there when you're finished. Go ahead and visit awhile." He turned his eyes to Sunny, and he saw her own eyes were starting to tear. "I—I'm glad you're all right, Sunny. It was real nice knowing you." Sunny felt on fire when his gaze moved to her bosom for a moment before moving to Bo and Stuart. "All of you," he added.

Sunny thought he seemed a little defensive when he shook her father's hand, then Stuart's. "It was a hell of a trip, wasn't it? Thanks for hiring me, Stuart. I'm sorry things didn't turn out quite like we had planned. Good luck on your return trip. I'm sure things will work out for you." He looked at Bo again. "And for your railroad. It sounds like one hell of an impossibility, but I have a feeling if anybody can get the thing built, it's you." He glanced at Sunny again. "You and your daughter."

Sunny could not take her eyes from his. Finally, it was Colt who looked away first, turning to the lieutenant. "Thanks again for the fine meal." He left, and Lieutenant Amber turned to Sunny's father.

"You say he killed three men?"

"In the blink of an eye. I must say they deserved it, but you don't often see a man kill another with no hesitation and no regrets. He's killed others before this. Hard to believe, him only twenty."

"Well, he's part Indian," the commander answered. "It's in their blood. It's no wonder he won't help me track down those Cheyenne."

"I like him, but he's a strange one," Stuart put in. "One minute he's blowing a man away and the next he's all worried about a cut on my sister's leg."

"Daddy, I'm not very hungry tonight," Sunny said

then. "May I go back to the wagons? I want to write some things in my journal."

"Well, it's dark out there, Sunny. Why don't you stay with me until I leave?"

"There are lanterns at most of the buildings, and soldiers everywhere. Our men are camped around the wagons. I'll be all right."

Bo frowned, setting down his wineglass. "I suppose it's all right."

"She's quite safe, Mr. Landers." The lieutenant rose. "Miss Landers, never has my table been graced with such elegance and beauty." The man looked her over in a way Sunny was not accustomed to being looked at. Had men been eyeing her this way for a long time, and she just never noticed before? She didn't mind when Colt looked at her that way, but she didn't like it when others did.

"Thank you, Lieutenant," she answered. She pulled her shawl around her shoulders and excused herself. As soon as she was out the door she hurried off into the darkness, trying to remember where the livery was. Crickets sang as she scurried across the parade grounds to a building that was lit across the way. When she reached it she saw through the window a man sitting at a desk. She quickly entered, realizing she didn't have a lot of time before her father would look for Colt to pay him what he had coming. The soldier at the desk seemed surprised at seeing her, and he jumped up from his chair. Sunny noticed he looked her over the same way as the lieutenant and other soldiers had eyed her. She had even become aware that her father's own men watched her that way sometimes. It gave her a strange feeling of power.

"Miss Landers!" the soldier exclaimed. "What are you doing here? Where's your father?"

"I'd like to know where the livery is. I—my father sent me to give a message to a couple of his men who are over there right now." She hadn't dared to ask in front of her father where the livery was, or he would know why she wanted to go there. Surely he wouldn't mind that she wanted to say a last good-bye to Colt

Travis, but for some reason she didn't want him to know.

The soldier wondered why Bo Landers would send his pretty daughter out into the night to find a couple of his men, but the young lady who stood before him represented several million dollars, or so he'd been told. He was not about to question her. "The livery is only four buildings down from here." He pointed. "That way."

"Thank you!" Sunny hurried out, running along the buildings, counting. She stopped when she saw a campfire behind the fourth building. A man was bent over it, adding a little wood to get the fire going better. She recognized the tall frame, the fringes of his buckskins that danced in little shadows in the firelight. Her heart pounded as she cautiously walked closer, wondering if he would be angry that she came. "Colt?"

He turned, looking surprised. "Sunny!" He looked around. "You alone?"

"Yes. I—I made an excuse to go back to the wagons, but I really wanted to come and see you by myself. I just, well, it didn't seem right, you leaving without us being able to talk a little. I mean, you did so much for me." She stepped a little closer, thinking how handsome and dangerous he looked in the firelight. She wasn't sure what had driven her here. Her heart raced, and her blood surged with all kinds of new feelings. "I had to thank you once more, for everything. I know you don't much like people like us, and you blame us for Slim's death, but—"

"*Blame* you?" He walked closer. "Sunny, that could have happened anytime, some other way. Men like me and Slim, we see death staring at us every day. You didn't have anything to do with that stampede, and I took care of the men who did."

She shivered, wondering if it was because of the cool night, or if it was the realization that she was standing there alone with a young man who was half Indian and who killed men with the ease of shooting a rabbit. Part of her wanted to run, but the woman in her wanted to stay. He was so close.

"There were so many things I wanted to ask you," she told him. "I guess I made a pest out of myself. I'm sorry —about Slim, about everything. But I had to tell you . . . I'll miss you terribly, Colt. For some reason, I can hardly stand the thought of never seeing you again." Her voice choked. "I never felt this way before about anybody."

Colt felt as though someone had stabbed his heart. He wondered if she had any idea of the feelings she stirred in him. Still, what good would it do to let her know? It would only make her feel worse, and somehow, not voicing them made it easier for him too. He reached out and grasped her arms. "Hey, don't cry, Sunny. You're not a cryer, remember?"

"But I don't want you to go," she sniffed. "Please tell me we're at least friends. You said once, that day I was riding with you, that you were my friend."

"Jesus, Sunny, you know that I am." He wanted so much to take her in his arms. "I never thought of you as a pest. You're the nicest person I've ever met. You really showed your stuff on this trip." He couldn't stand her tears. "Dammit, Sunny, I liked you, maybe too much. I was afraid if we got too close, maybe . . . I don't know how to explain it. You're awfully young, and we couldn't be more different. Sometimes people have to make certain decisions that are for the good of everybody involved. You understand what I'm saying?"

She looked up at him, trembling at his touch. "I think I know what you mean," she answered. "You really liked me that much?"

He gave her a smile that melted her heart. "Come on, Sunny. We both felt it. Let's just say I liked the woman you're *going* to be someday, except that that woman belongs in a world of mansions and servants, a world of senators and businessmen, carriages and theaters and fancy clothes. You're the very breath your father breathes, and someday you'll inherit a fortune and help run a financial empire. It wouldn't make much sense for somebody like me to get too interested in a woman like that, now, would it? You know the kind of world I live in, and I like it just fine this way. In this life some things are just the right thing to do, and some are wrong."

She studied his eyes in the flickering firelight. "I'll never forget this trip or you for the rest of my life, Colt. No matter what else happens in my life, I'll always think of you as the most wonderful, special person I ever met." She couldn't help more tears then, and Colt gently wiped them with his fingers.

"I'll think of you the same way. I'll bet someday I'll read about you in the newspapers, Miss Sunny Landers, part owner of a transcontinental railroad. You'll go home and next year your pa will have that coming-out party for you, and every eligible young man in Chicago who is anybody important will be wanting to court you. You'll be flirting with congressmen and going to operas and signing million-dollar deals. Your pa has a big dream, and I don't think he can finish it without you at his side; and I don't think you'd let him. You're his whole world, and right now he's yours, and that's probably the way it should be."

She took a deep breath and forced a smile. "And you'll be out here leading wagon trains and chasing buffalo, and that's how it should be for you."

He smiled more. "Now you've got it right."

He held her gaze, and for a moment she thought he might kiss her. "Thanks for coming to see me, Sunny. Your brother told me once that your name fits you perfectly, and he was right. Don't ever change. You're going to have to deal with a lot of power, make big decisions, handle an empire. Don't let it make you into a different person."

She held back tears. "I owe you so much. I owe you my life, Colt."

"You don't owe me anything, except maybe some good words in that journal of yours. You'd better get going now before your pa finds you out here alone with me. It wouldn't look good."

She could not help the sudden urge to hug him. Colt felt his arms going around her, and he wondered if she realized what the feel of her did to him. He breathed deeply of her sweet scent, telling himself his feelings might have been the same for any pretty girl in the same situation. A man got lonely out here.

"Good-bye, Colt," she said, pulling away from him. "I'll never forget you, never."

"Bye, Sunny."

She studied him a moment longer, then turned and ran off into the darkness, feeling on fire, her heart torn with mixed emotions. Was this how love felt? She found the wagons and climbed inside her own, quickly searching for her journal and pen. She sat down on the feather mattress and began to write.

Colt Travis is leaving us. Tomorrow will be the saddest day of my life, for from then on I will never see Colt again. It seems strange to say it, but in spite of how different he is from anyone I have ever known, we were good friends, and I feel special having known him. I went tonight to tell him good-bye, and he held me. I think I love—" She heard footsteps outside the wagon then, and her father looked inside. Sunny quickly closed the journal, hoping it wasn't too obvious that she had been crying. "Father," she said, not even aware that she had called him Father for the first time rather than Daddy. "Did you already pay Colt?"

"No. I'm on my way over there now." He looked at her strangely, and she wondered if he knew where she had been.

"Do we *have* to go right back to Chicago, Father?" she asked.

"What do you mean?"

"You wanted to go on, at least to the South Pass. I'm well now, and we have new supplies and a new scout and even soldiers to go along. I want to go on. I love it out here, Father, and it's important for you to see what might be the best route. It will help you understand what will be needed in the way of money and all."

"Sunny, I hate to expose you to any more danger. I almost lost you more than once. Nothing is more important to me than you."

"Father, I'm a Landers. I'll be fine. I want to go on."

He frowned. "What happened? I thought you were eager to go back."

"I never said I was. You just *thought* it. Let's keep going."

"You're not afraid?"

She leaned back, feeling alive and beautiful. She was a woman, a strong and brave woman at that, according to Colt. If someone like Colt thought it, then it must be so. She felt so sad, yet so proud. She had found a new confidence, a new power. And not leaving this country just yet would help her feel close to Colt a little longer. "I'm not afraid of anything anymore," she answered.

Bo smiled, shaking his head. "All right, by God, we'll go," the man told her. "Stuart can go back if he wants, but you and I will go on. I'm damn proud of you, Sunny! *Damn* proud! You *are* a Landers, all right! You get some sleep and I'll go back and talk to the lieutenant about the possibility of going on west instead of going back." His eyes sparkled with excitement. "Thank you, Sunny."

He left her then, and Sunny pressed the journal against her breast, leaning back and remembering the feel of Colt's strong arms around her, his gentle touch when he put the poultice on her burn. She could not help the new tears that wanted to come, and she wondered if she could ever again feel about any man the way she felt about Colt Travis.

She did not know just when her tears subsided into sleep. She knew only that when she awoke the next morning she was surprised that she had slept at all. She quickly rose and washed, changing her dress and preparing to go to breakfast with her father and Stuart and the lieutenant. She told her father to go ahead without her. She would be along. As soon as he and Stuart left, she climbed out of the wagon and hurried over to the livery. One more good-bye, she promised herself. Just one more!

She reached Colt's campsite and her smile faded. The campfire was cold. Colt Travis was gone.

Part

Two

Chapter 5

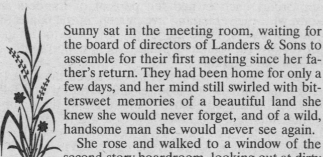 Sunny sat in the meeting room, waiting for the board of directors of Landers & Sons to assemble for their first meeting since her father's return. They had been home for only a few days, and her mind still swirled with bittersweet memories of a beautiful land she knew she would never forget, and of a wild, handsome man she would never see again.

She rose and walked to a window of the second-story boardroom, looking out at dirty snow and a gray day. It was November. The rain had turned to snow and then back to rain again. She imagined what the weather might be like out on the Great Plains and in the mountains—wicked blizzards, bitter cold. Colt was out there somewhere, perhaps huddled alone against a snowstorm. How sad that he could not have Slim's company. It was hard to imagine what it must be like to wander alone and homeless.

Below her a train rumbled by. B&L R.R. was painted on the boxcars. The letters stood for Beauregard Landers Rail Road, a line owned one hundred percent by her father. It ran from Chicago to Columbus, Ohio; Memphis, Tennessee; St. Joseph, Missouri; St. Paul, Minnesota, and Louisville, Kentucky. Her father also owned considerable stock in the Illinois Central and the Chicago & Rock Island. He had already told her that someday it would all belong to her, as well his forty percent stock in Landers Great Lakes Shipping and Landers Warehousing, in which Vince had already been awarded a forty-nine percent control, the remaining eleven percent in the hands of outside investors. Her father also owned forty percent stock in Landers Overland Freighting and Landers Supply, in which companies it was Stuart who owned forty-nine percent. Besides his full control of all railroad holdings and his thirty percent in all subsidiary companies, Bo Landers held seventy-five percent of the stock in Landers & Sons, the company that owned and controlled the subsidiaries. Vince and Stuart each owned ten percent of Landers & Sons, with the remaining five percent in the hands of other investors, close associates who had to be approved by Bo Landers himself before becoming a part of the company.

The thought of her father's power, and the knowledge that someday that power and wealth would fall into her hands, only drove home to Sunny the reality of her situation, and how right Colt was to recognize that their feelings for each other could never have come to anything. Much as she had fallen in love with the beautiful but dangerous land west of the Missouri River, and in spite of her special feelings for a young man who was as untamed as that land, this was where she belonged. This was the life she was born to, and her father trusted her to safeguard all that he owned.

Ever since she could remember, she had traveled and attended meetings with her father. When she was little he would perch her on his knee, and her presence would help soften board members and investors and aid in Bo's efforts to get what he wanted. Now she was becoming more aware that she could charm men in a different way. She had returned from the West a woman, the memories of her trip preserved forever in her precious journal. For now it still hurt to think of Colt, to think of the peace and wonder of the Great Plains and the magnificent Rockies; but she knew that as time passed, those memories would gradually fade. The important thing now was to help her father in his even more determined quest to build a railroad that would connect Chicago with the Pacific, a railroad that would bring Oriental trade to the heartland of America and would at the same time give people a safer way to travel through the wilderness.

Stuart had left them at Fort Laramie and had returned to Chicago to be with the wife and child he had so dearly missed; but Sunny and her father had gone on into the Rockies. Sunny would never forget the rugged, overwhelming beauty of the mountains. She believed the railroad could be built, but now that she knew how big the West was, she was sure such a railroad would take years. Her father was already sixty-three years old, and the trip west had aged him more. She hoped and prayed that Bo Landers would live to see his dream come to be.

She turned away from the window, smiling and greeting her father when he came into the room, his arms full of papers. "Come and sit at the table, Sunny," he told her excitedly. "Everyone will be here soon." He looked toward the doorway. "Bring in that coffee, and some fresh cigars," he boomed to a young errand boy in the outer offices.

Sunny's several slips rustled as she moved back to the table. She wore brown taffeta today, a perfectly fitted dress that showed off her tiny waist, then billowed to the floor in gentle puffs. Hand-crocheted ivory lace graced the high neck, and a row of thirty buttons with tiny diamonds in their centers decorated the front closure of the dress. The cuffs of the long sleeves were trimmed in the same ivory lace, and she wore a short mink cape around her shoulders to guard against the cold, damp November air that seemed to find its way into the building in spite of the coal heating system.

"Do you think we'll win their support, Father?" Sunny asked, aware that today her father meant to garner financial support for a Pacific railroad from his own board of directors.

"Of course we will," he answered. "The board has never gone against me on anything I've asked for. After all, I hold seventy-five percent of the stock."

"Vince was awfully quiet at supper the other night, and he hasn't come to visit since. I thought he would want to hear more about our trip and about the railroad."

"You know Vincent. He was against the trip in the first place. Your stubborn brother is not about to let himself show any interest, but he'll by God be interested once I announce what I want to do."

Men began filtering into the room, and the errand boy hurried in with a tray that held several china cups and a silver pot filled with coffee. He placed the tray in the center of the table, then took from it a small gold box that held some of Bo's cherished expensive cigars. He set the cigars near Bo's chair and hurried out again.

Several of those who entered the room nodded and smiled at Sunny. Again she felt an awareness that men did not look upon her as a little girl anymore. Some had probably already heard about how she had survived the stampede, and about her hideous infection. Absently, she moved her hand to her skirt, touching her left leg, remembering that awful night; she also remembered Colt's gentle touch when he put the poultice on her burn. She still carried an ugly scar, yet oddly, she didn't care, for it was her permanent reminder of the most thrilling time of her life, in spite of losing poor Miss Putnam; and it reminded her of a man who would always hold a special place in her heart.

More men arrived, all greeting her father with loud

welcomes and handshakes. Some seemed almost too enthusiastic, and Sunny detected a distinct tension in the air in spite of the hellos and the laughter and questions about their adventurous journey. Something was not quite right, but Sunny could not determine just what it was. When Vince entered the room, the tension only increased. Sunny was sure her father must feel it too, although everyone was friendly and seemed happy to see that she and her father had returned safely. Stuart finally joined them, bringing the board of Landers & Sons to full attendance.

Chairs scraped and all the men seemed to be talking at once as everyone took their seats. The coffeepot was passed around, and Bo lit a cigar. To Sunny, who sat down at her father's right hand, everyone's chatter seemed almost nervous. The men laughed a little too much, some glancing at Vince and exchanging some kind of knowing look. Her oldest half brother moved his eyes to meet Sunny's gaze, and he gave her his usual condescending look, making sure, as he always did, that she was aware that he didn't think she had any right attending these important meetings. Vince was as big as his father, with thick, sandy hair and the same intense blue eyes. At thirty-three, he was solid and strong, a formidable-looking man who tried to be as commanding as his father but usually took the wrong approach.

Stuart more closely resembled his and Vince's long-dead mother, with his darker coloring and smaller build. He was two years younger than Vince, and the brothers were as different in personality as they were in looks and build. Both often disagreed with their father on business decisions and policy, but Stuart usually crumbled to his father's wishes, sometimes seeming almost afraid of the man. Vincent, on the other hand, argued with his father to the point of screaming matches, and more than once Sunny had worried that her father was so angry he might have a heart attack. Both boys were spoiled, and Bo never failed to accuse them of being too cautious when it came to expansion and taking risks. They did not have their father's desire to keep building and investing, or his talent as an entrepreneur.

Neither brother had been very loving toward Sunny, although Stuart had changed considerably since marrying Vi and becoming a father. Vi, a sweet-natured woman whose warm personality made up for her plain dark looks, had brought out a softer side to Stuart, and had been genuinely loving toward Sunny. Besides her father, Vi was the only one in the family who made Sunny feel loved.

Vince's wife, Eve, was another story. She and Vince had a seven-year-old son and a four-year-old daughter, as well as another baby on the way, but Eve's motherly affection stopped at her own doorstep. She could be a cold, cruel woman to others, and she had had no affect on Vince's personality. When Sunny and her father first returned home, it was Stuart and Vi who had come right over to see them. Vince had waited for two days, until Bo had invited him to supper. Vince had asked few questions about the trip, and he and Eve had not even brought the children, which had hurt Bo deeply.

Sunny had only painful memories of her youth, a deep hurt at how her brothers had treated her. Although neither Vince nor Stuart had ever put it into words, she knew as she grew older that both men resented her being born, resented the love her father had had for her mother, which they considered a betrayal to their own dead mother's memory. Bo had always told her only good and wonderful things about her mother, and Sunny couldn't understand why her brothers had hated the woman so. Once, Eve had cornered her and had warned her that she had better not think she could wrap everyone around her little finger as she had done with Bo, and as her "scheming" mother had.

You think that if you play your hand right, you can control all of your father's holdings, the woman had said. *Vince and I have you all figured out, Sunny, all your sweetness, the way you dote on Bo, just like your mother did! If not for you, Vincent and Stuart would inherit every penny and every business your father owns, and when Bo Landers dies, if you get more than your fair share, you can expect a court battle over it! You're just a daughter, a half sister at that! Vincent won't begrudge you a small share, but if Bo Landers thinks he's going to put his business holdings in your hands and deny Vincent and Stuart what is rightfully theirs, he can just think again!*

Sunny had never forgotten the cruel words. Why Eve had attacked her with such venom, she would never understand, unless the woman was simply jealous of how Bo pampered her. She had never been anything but friendly toward Eve, and loving toward her niece and nephew. Eve's whole countenance was as sharp as her words. She was tall and bony, her dark hair always in a bun, sharp lines to her face, a prominent brow and nose. Bo had commented once that he thought Vincent had married her because she had a good mind for business and because he stood to be even richer when her own father, who owned a bank in Chicago, died.

You can bet your brother didn't marry for love, her father had told her once. *He doesn't know the meaning of the word. Now, Stuart, he married for love. Lord knows Vi doesn't have a head for business, but she's a good woman. Still, neither Vi nor Eve can hold a candle to you. You not only have a good heart, but you're beautiful and damn smart.*

Sunny had never told her father about her confrontation with Eve, afraid of upsetting him too much. She had no idea what he intended to will to her, and she didn't really care. Whatever fell into her hands, she would respect Bo Landers's wishes and carry on in his memory, fully accepting any responsibility he gave her, for no daughter could be more loved. She only prayed that such responsibilities were many years down the road.

"Gentlemen, let's come to order," Bo announced. He puffed the cigar, and the room quieted as he rose from his chair. "It's good to be home," he continued.

"I'm sure Stuart filled you in on some of our adventures and mishaps out in the Wild West."

There came a round of nervous laughter, and Sunny looked at each man, studying his eyes, developing the same protective feelings for her father that he had for her. She could not get over this new awareness, not only of how men looked at her, but a kind of defensiveness of her womanhood. The knowledge that Vince apparently did not think her capable of carrying on in her father's footsteps used to only hurt her. Now, with the new maturity she had found through her harrowing adventures, she had a feeling of pride, a sureness, and to think that just because she was female she was incapable of understanding the workings of a business as big as Landers & Sons made her angry.

Everyone listened as Bo recounted his experiences, and Sunny reddened slightly when the man bragged about her own bravery. When he mentioned how their scout, Colt Travis, had saved her life more than once, pain again visited her heart at the realization Colt had been but a tiny part of her life that she would never know again.

"There is no doubt left in my mind, gentlemen, of the need for a transcontinental railroad," Bo went on, beginning to pace around the table. "Now, I intend to get to a normal business meeting shortly, but I am simply too excited about the railroad to put off telling all of you what I've learned. The land out west is big and wild, but, by God, it can be tamed! A fast, safe connection to California will mean being able to get in on trade with the Orient right here in Chicago. There is vast, untapped wealth in the West, no matter how much others tell you it's a useless desert. Already gold has been discovered around Pikes Peak. Who knows how much more in the way of precious metals lies out in those hills? It's a land just itching to be settled. It needs towns and doctors, a safe way for people to travel through it. The profits on transportation alone are worth the effort of laying the tracks."

The man came back around to his chair at the head

of the long, freshly polished oak table, his eyes dancing with excitement. "Next week I'm meeting with former congressman Abe Lincoln. His popularity is growing again, and there is a good chance he could become president—a man from our own state! I'm told Lincoln is very receptive to the idea of a transcontinental railroad. He even owns land out near Omaha, so he is also aware of the potential value of the country. I will also be meeting with Dr. Thomas Durant in New York City. Durant is a strong supporter of the railroad, and has already been lobbying in Washington to promote the idea and has founded the Pacific Railroad Company."

Bo leaned forward, the cigar between his teeth, his hands resting on the table. "I want and need all of your support," he said. "I'll tell you right now that I'll be investing a good deal of the profits of Landers & Sons into Durant's company. I intend to get in on the ground floor. Those who act now are going to profit the most in the long run, and I want all of you to have a share in this. I'm asking for, in fact I'm counting on, your support, your personal investments. I am also counting on investments from the profits of the shipping and warehousing companies, and the freighting and supply businesses." He looked at Stuart. "Son, you were out there. You know it can be done. Besides that, we have to invest heavily from the freighting business. After all, once the railroad is built, Landers Overland Freighting will cease to exist. We will simply meld it into the railroad, and by so doing, we technically won't be losing business at all! We'll just become part of the Pacific Railroad!"

Bo puffed the cigar, removing it from his mouth then and setting it in an ashtray. "Well? Let's hear your offers. You all stand to make a fortune. I want to be able to go to Durant and tell him Landers & Sons is willing to sink a good share of its profits into investing in a Pacific railroad."

He looked around the table at men he had called friends for years, men who owned banks and factories, hotels and theaters, and who were heavily invested in Landers & Sons. He did not see the eagerness in their eyes that he had expected, and he was beginning to understand the reason for the tense smiles and nervous talk he had noticed when they first greeted him. He straightened, glancing at Stuart, who kept his eyes averted. He looked then at Vince, who met his gaze boldly.

"We have all already decided this whole idea is ridiculous, Dad," Vince told him. "I said it before you left, and I still believe it."

Sunny watched her father's face begin to redden, and she saw another storm coming in the Landers family. "You started that sentence with *we,*" he said, obviously struggling to stay calm. "You said *we* already decided. Would you mind explaining that?"

Vince sighed, looking around the table, then back at his father. He rose, standing just as tall and commanding as Bo Landers. "We talked about the whole ridiculous idea while you were gone, and we took a vote," Vince said. "First I held a meeting with the board of directors for my company, and we decided—"

"*Your* company? You hold forty-nine percent of the shares of Landers Shipping and Warehousing. Other investors and I hold the other fifty-one percent." Bo seethed. "It isn't *your* company."

"I'm president and major stockholder," Vince retorted, "just like Stuart is for the freighting and supply businesses. You can't order him to give up the overland freighting to the railroad just like that! And you can't order me to risk the profits of my company in something as harebrained and impossible as a transcontinental railroad!"

Bo moved his eyes to Stuart. "Did *your* board of directors also take a vote?"

Stuart shifted in his chair. "They all had a right to know what was going on," he answered. "I just wanted to get an idea how they felt about it."

"After what you saw and learned on that trip?" Bo fumed.

Stuart finally met his eyes. "I saw a land so rugged

and untamed that to think of settling it is to think crazy!" he answered. "I saw people die! I saw a vast, open land that's worth *nothing,* and I saw that if anyone tried to build a railroad out there, a lot of men would lose their lives doing it—to Indians, the elements, buffalo, outlaws, you name it! Such a project would take years, and millions of dollars! It can't be done, Dad!"

Sunny felt like crying at the crestfallen look on her father's face. The rest of the fourteen men in the room sat quietly, some embarrassed at the emotional confrontation between father and sons, although they had seen such arguments before, some looking ashamed of their betrayal of a good friend. There was a long, agonizing moment of silence in the room. The laughter and greetings of moments before had turned to bitterness and anger. "Tell them, Sunny." Bo finally spoke up, almost startling her. "Tell them what *you* think."

"We don't need to hear what a fifteen-year-old girl thinks," Vince raged. "My God, Dad, she's just a kid, and everybody in this room knows that if you told her jumping into Lake Michigan was a good idea, she'd go and *do* it! What the hell does *she* know, except what *you* tell her! She wants the railroad because *you* want it!"

"I want it because I don't want innocent people like Miss Putnam to *die* out there," Sunny answered, too angry at the moment to realize she had spoken up on her own at one of these meetings for the first time, let alone talked back to Vince. She rose and looked around the table. "All any of you can think about is money! Even if you were in favor of this, it would be because you think you might get richer because of it! Our scout lost his best friend out there, and I lost my friend and tutor. Six other good men died, and all along the way we passed grave after grave, old people, little children. No matter how useless any of you might think that land is out there, thousands of people think otherwise. They keep going west, most of them heading for California and the coast, many stopping in the Rockies to look for gold. People will keep going out there and they'll keep *dying!* If they can go by train, they can be safer, get there faster, be sheltered from the elements and the Indians! And the thing for all of *you* to remember is that they'll *pay* to go by rail! At the same time, we can bring silks and spices and other expensive items from China back to places like Chicago and New York. People will be able to get them cheaper because they can be sent straight across the country instead of having to go around Cape Horn or across the Isthmus of Panama."

She turned her blue eyes to Vince, surprising him with the determination he saw there, and with her knowledge of the subject she had suddenly so passionately defended. "I am not such a stupid little kid as you might think, Vince," she added. "I might be only fifteen, but I've grown up learning everything about this business, and I know this company can afford to make this investment. I've done my homework. I have also been out west. *You* haven't! I've not only seen, but have experienced for myself the suffering. That railroad *can* be built, but it will take men who can dream big, men who are willing to take risks, men who love a challenge!" She looked at the others again. "I thought those were the kind of men who called themselves my father's friends."

She struggled against tears, angry with herself for suddenly feeling like crying. That would be a childish thing to do, and she did not want to appear childish at this crucial moment. She glanced at her father, who was almost as surprised as the others. She saw the intense pride in his eyes, and she was glad she had spoken up.

"Well," he said, taking a deep breath. "I couldn't have said it better myself." He looked at Stuart, then at Vince. "While my daughter was out risking her life to support me, going on to the mountains when all she had to do was tell me she wanted to come home, my sons were here plotting against me."

"Dad, it wasn't like that," Stuart put in.

"Maybe you didn't think so in your heart, Stuart, but Vince certainly did!" He faced his elder son, who was reddening with anger. "You call the shipping and warehousing *your* company. It's yours only because you're my son and I decided to *give* you the bigger share after you got married. You never *earned* it, Vincent. You never had to struggle to build it. It was handed to you on a silver platter, just like I handed Stuart the freighting and supply businesses! At heart they're still *my* companies, and *I* own seventy-five percent of this *controlling* company!" Bo took another deep breath, glaring at the rest of the men with a cold, accusing look before looking back at his son. "So, let's hear what it is you and *your* board voted on."

Vince closed his eyes for a moment, gritting his teeth. He faced his father squarely, keeping his chin high. "We voted not to allow you to use any profits from Great Lakes Shipping or from Landers Warehousing to invest in your transcontinental railroad idea. Our votes represent sixty percent of the companies, so you can't override them."

Bo held his eyes, nodding his head with a look of disgust. He turned to Stuart. "Is it the same with the freighting and supply board?"

Stuart looked almost ashamed. He forced himself to rise and meet his father's stare. "We, uh, we just took a mock vote. No one wanted to allow profits to be invested in the railroad, but it's not an official vote yet."

"Why not?" Vince barked. "You said you'd hold a legal vote and get it on record! Why do you chicken out every time it means standing up against Dad!"

Stuart stiffened. "I didn't chicken out," he said quietly. "I simply thought it wasn't right to take a final vote until Dad returned. He founded those companies, Vince. He has a right to get in his say!"

Bo's eyebrows arched in surprise. "Well, I got *that* much out of *one* of my sons, at least."

Stuart shook his head. "The fact remains, Dad, that no one on the board wants to invest in your idea, not individually, and not with company profits. We've talked to these men here, and it's the same. The board of directors of Landers & Sons is not willing to take the risk. There's been no official vote among this board, but we've discussed it."

Bo picked up his cigar. "Sit down, both of you," he ordered his sons. Stuart sat down right away, but Vince took his time. Bo puffed on his cigar for a moment, and everyone waited quietly, tension filling the air. "Well, well," Bo said. "I have certainly found out who my friends are."

"It's got nothing to do with friendship, Bo," one man said. It was Harold Regis, owner of one of the biggest banks in Chicago. "It's simply a matter of logistics. I think the whole idea is ridiculous and impossible, but that doesn't mean I don't value our friendship."

Bo glared at him. "You have as much as called me a fool. I don't call that any kind of friendship."

"Give us some solid figures, Bo," another man said, "something that will ensure we won't be risking bankruptcy by putting our money into this thing. After all, it's nothing more right now than the dream of a couple of men. You have no solid support from Congress, no solid support from other investors, no—"

"I'll get the support!" Bo interrupted. "I told you I'll be talking with Abe Lincoln and Thomas Durant. I'll be going to Washington and lobbying for a railroad act. I'm telling all of you, right now, that I *am* going to make this happen! I'll get land grants from Congress, government money to back us. I'll *buy* votes if I have to! I've done it before and I'll do it again!"

He paced around the table again, and as he passed each man, Sunny could see that man cringe slightly, as though he thought her father might hit him. "I have learned a lot here today," Bo went on. "I have learned that I can't count on my friends, or even on my own sons! All of you have been scheming behind my back, preparing to defeat me before I even had the chance to explain my position. The only person in this room who supports me is my daughter." He walked back to his chair but remained standing. "So be it." He looked at Vince. "You will always remember this day, Vincent, long after I'm gone."

Vince's eyes widened with indignation and near fear. "What the hell does that mean?"

"You figure it out, son." He looked at the others. "I still own seventy-five percent of Landers & Sons, and therefore I control what happens to the profits of this parent company. I'll invest them as I see fit, as well as the profits from the railroad companies, which, I am glad now to say, I own fully! When the transcontinental railroad is completed, the B&L will connect with the Pacific Railroad, and I'll be richer than any of you can ever hope to be! I'll get this thing done—or I should say, *Sunny* and I will get it done! You can all go to hell!" He picked up his papers. "I'm not staying for the rest of the meeting. Since you all think you can conduct business so well without me, go ahead and do it. Sunny and I have to plan a trip to New York and Washington."

Whispers went around the table as Sunny rose, and she decided that if looks could kill, Vince's glare would surely leave her dead. She walked with her father toward the door, where Bo stopped and turned. "By the way, you can add to your official records today that Bo Landers, the major shareholder of Landers & Sons, has decided to change the name of this company to Landers Enterprises. I want the 'Sons' removed from the company name."

"You can't do that!" Vince yelled, rising again, his face purple with rage.

"I can and I have," Bo answered. "You've shown your true colors, Vincent. You can pay the price. And I might add that you can also make it a matter of record that as of today, Sunny is an official board member, with full voting rights."

They left, and Sunny could hear shouting and a buzz of talking. She felt a little sorry for Stuart, but not for Vince. It hurt to see such hard feelings be-

tween father and sons, and although she had done
nothing wrong, she knew Vincent would find a way to
make all of this look like her fault. In spite of her
young age, she could see that deep family turmoil lay
ahead for her, and she wondered if she could handle
it.

A board member with full voting rights! She had
not expected that. More and more she felt the weight
of the responsibilities she would one day inherit, including having to stand up to Vincent. What had her
father meant when he told Vince he would remember
this day long after Bo was gone? She wanted to ask
her father not to place such a burden on her, but she
knew how hurt he was, and she could not bring herself to hurt him even more.

"It will be all right, Father," she told him.

"You bet it will! You pack your things, Sunny.
We're going to Springfield to talk with Lincoln, then
on to New York and Washington."

They climbed into her father's carriage and Bo ordered his driver to take them back to the house. Outside, the wind blew hard and cold, and Sunny's heart
felt suddenly heavy at the thought of going even farther east, so far from the land from which she had so
recently returned, so far from the rolling plains and
the beautiful mountains, so far from Colt Travis. She
told herself she had to get over her childish fantasies
and face these new responsibilities. Her father had a
railroad to build, and she was going to do all she
could to help him build it.

Chapter 6

1858

The gunshot cracked in the cool autumn air, and Colt jumped up from his noon campfire, a tin cup filled with coffee still in his hand. He listened carefully, sure the shot had come from somewhere to the east. All was silence again, except for the soft moan of the wind in the pines. He decided perhaps it was only a hunter. Since gold was discovered in this area a year ago, thousands of people had poured into the mountains in search of the usually elusive metal, and many had already given up and gone back, discovering the gold was not so easy to find, some convinced it was all a hoax. For most of them life in the Rockies had been a lot harder than they had bargained for, but a few brave souls had stayed, settling along Cherry Creek farther to the north, where more gold had supposedly been found.

An eagle circled overhead, calling to its mate somewhere in the higher mountains. Colt thought he heard another sound at the same time. He waited for the majestic bird to wing its way toward the mountains, then listened intently. He frowned when he heard the strange wail again, unlike the eagle, unlike any animal with which he was familiar. It was more like a cry of pain, perhaps a woman weeping.

He set down his cup and picked up his rifle, going to his still-saddled horse and shoving the rifle into its boot. "Let's go take a look, boy." He took hold of the buckskin-colored gelding he had purchased not long before at Bent's Fort, after the roan horse he had ridden for years had stumbled on a steep mountain trail and broken its leg. It still hurt to think about losing the animal. He had loved that horse, as he had loved Slim. Now both were gone. He was growing more attached to his new mount, which he called simply Buck; but his loneliness had deepened since Slim died, and a horse certainly was not the answer. He had not been this lonely since his father died.

He mounted up and headed Buck through a thick grove of pine and golden aspen. He knew now that he couldn't lead this life of wandering forever. A man had to have some kind of direction, something to cling to, sons to carry on his name. A man had to have a woman, not the loose kind that provided quick sexual relief, but a woman who truly loved him, who gave herself only to him and gifted him with children. He figured if Slim were still alive, maybe he wouldn't be thinking this way yet. Or maybe if he had never met Sunny Landers and started thinking how nice it might be to have a pretty, devoted woman sharing his bed at night, he wouldn't have this new yen for female company.

He figured he would never really forget Sunny, and he often wondered what life must be like for her back in Chicago. Did she ever think of him? Were wealthy young men fighting each other over the privilege of wooing her, now that she was sixteen and had probably had her grand "coming-out" party? She was back where she belonged, now only a sweet memory to him; but she had made him hungry for a woman, hungry for a different kind of companionship than he'd had with Slim.

He trotted his horse up and down two swelling hills, weaving through more pines, his keen ears still picking up the sound. He could hear it better now, knew it was a woman who was either hurt or in great mourning. He reached a clearing and saw a wagon farther out in a shallow valley of yellowing grass. A woman was bent over a body, weeping. He looked around, seeing no other wagons, no Indians, wondering who had shot a gun, and why. "Get up there, Buck." He urged the horse into a gentle lope.

The woman looked up then and noticed him. Colt saw her reach for something, and in the next moment she raised a rifle and aimed it at him. He quickly drew his horse to a halt, Buck's hooves pushing up the sod. The horse turned in a circle and whinnied, shaking his mane. "I'm here to help," Colt called out to her. "I heard a gunshot, heard you crying."

"Don't you come any closer!" she screamed. "I'm alone here!"

The voice and slender figure told him she was young.

"Ma'am, I don't mean you any harm! My name is Colt Travis, and I'm a scout. I know this country. Please, put the rifle down and let me help you. What's happened?"

She stood rigid for several long seconds, her shoulders jerking with each sob. She finally lowered the rifle slightly. "You can . . . come closer," she said, the words choked.

Colt cautiously approached, seeing the terror and sorrow in her pretty brown eyes. He guessed she was perhaps seventeen or eighteen years old, and her thick dark hair hung past her shoulders. He could see the body on the ground now, an older man. Part of his head was missing, and the grass around his shoulders was soaked with blood. Colt drew up his horse, still hanging back, noticing then that there was blood on the girl's hands and arms and dress. "That your pa?" he asked.

She nodded, her face wet with tears, her nose running. "My mother . . . is in the wagon. She died last night . . . had a bad cough for weeks. Pa wouldn't bring her out of the wagon and bury her . . . couldn't face her death. He blamed himself . . . for bringing her out here. And then today I . . . I tried to tell him again he had to bury her. He said he would. I went . . . inside the wagon to dress her and fix her hair . . . and then I heard the gunshot." She shook with more sobs, lowering the rifle a little more and staring at it a moment. "He must have just . . . turned the rifle around and . . . put it to his head. I guess he just couldn't . . . live with the guilt."

Colt's heart went out to her, a young girl orphaned in a strange land. He knew the feeling of being suddenly alone, and this was a horrible way to lose one's parents. He slowly dismounted. "Why don't you put down that rifle? I'll bury your folks for you and I'll get you to some help."

She looked at him helplessly, and suddenly her eyes rolled back and she slumped to the ground. Colt hurried to her side, kneeling down and pulling her partially into his arms. He smoothed the hair back from her face, studying her pretty features, wiping her tears. "I don't even know your name," he muttered. She groaned and he gently laid her back into the grass, then went to his horse to retrieve a canteen. He rushed back to her, kneeling down and dripping a little of the cool water over her face. She gasped and opened her eyes again, staring at him a moment, looking confused. She reached up for him, and he pulled her into his arms.

"Everything will be all right," he told her gently. "I'll take care of you."

November 12, 1858

Mr. Lincoln has lost the senatorial race, but I do not believe he is through politically. His loss was only because of the way our districts are divided. Although Mr. Lincoln and his antislavery Republican Party actually received the greater share of votes, Mr. Douglas won the majority of seats by district and thus is again senator. However, the speeches Mr. Lincoln gave during his many debates with Mr. Douglas over the past months have made him very popular in Illinois and, in fact, throughout the North.

Sunny put down her pen, wondering if her father was right in fearing the country could end up going to war over the slavery issue. She could not imagine that anyone could think slavery was right, but the South was standing firmly in favor of keeping the long-used, barbaric practice. She and her father had followed Abraham Lincoln's political career, and Bo was convinced Lincoln's eloquent, impassioned debates with Douglas would eventually take him to the presidency. He had contributed heavily to the antislavery Republican Party during the current senatorial race, and soon they would travel to Springfield to speak with Lincoln and urge him to run for president. Bo was ready to contribute even more to such a campaign; but although he was firmly against slavery himself, his intentions for getting Lincoln elected were not to end slavery, but rather to have a man in the White House who was in favor of a transcontinental railroad.

Mr. Lincoln has time and again shown a great interest in a railroad that would span the continent. The only thing that could hold up a vote for such a railroad is the awful possibility of a war between northern and southern states. I dread the thought of such a war, and I also dread knowing that it could be several more years yet before we can even begin thinking about building the railroad. I am so afraid Father will not live to see his dream. He has had a little trouble with his heart, and it frightens me, for I am not sure I could go on living if something happened to him.

She again put down the pen, wishing they had made more progress toward the railroad so that her father could see that the project was at least under way. So far they had still not even been able to convince close friends to contribute a dime toward the dream. Her father had been forced to pay certain congressmen to introduce a railroad bill, but that bill lay dying, overlooked now because of the growing political problems over slavery. They kept in contact with Thomas Durant, who was also campaigning heavily for the railroad, and Bo had invested in Durant's Pacific Railroad Company, the bare beginnings of what they hoped would one day be the parent company of a lucrative transcontinental railroad.

Through her father, Sunny was personally acquainted with both Lincoln and Durant, and with several congressmen and senators. She was only sixteen and a half, but she felt much older and wiser for all she had learned over the past months since returning from the West. Her sixteenth birthday party had been one of the more spectacular parties in Chicago. She had made her grand entrance, coming down the spiral staircase of the Landers mansion on her father's arm, presented to a crowd of over one hundred fifty dignitaries and their wives, Chicago's wealthiest, as well as several political figures, including Abraham Lincoln.

She had worn baby-blue silk, the full bustle skirt of the dress cascading in a tumble of lace and diamond-trimmed tufts. The skirt trailed out in a train at the back, and the scooped neckline of the bodice revealed her bosom in a more enticing cut than she had ever dared to wear before. A brilliant diamond necklace glittered at her throat, a gift from her father, and she had worn elbow-length white silk gloves, silk stockings, and white slippers. She had Vi to thank for helping her dress and giving her encouragement that nervous day. Although her father had hired a new tutor, a widow named Hannah Seymour, and had also hired a personal maid for her, the only woman she could really talk to now was Vi, with whom she had grown even closer. Still, she had not even told Vi of her secret wish that day, that Colt Travis would be in the crowd of spectators, seeing her as beautiful as she could possibly be. She wondered what she might have seen in his eyes.

The thought made her turn back in her journal to the notes from her trip west. *We have moved past the Nebraska Sand Hills and are now in what Mr. Travis calls High Plains country,* she read softly to herself. She scanned further ahead. *I never thought I could survive*

*such a life. . . . Mr. Travis has been very quiet since Mr.
Jessup died, and I think he is in deep mourning. I feel sorry
for him. . . .* She turned a few more pages. *Colt Travis
is leaving us. Tomorrow will be the saddest day of my life,
for from then on I will never see Colt again. . . . I went
tonight to tell him good-bye, and he held me.*

She put her head back and sighed. Colt had become
just a pleasant memory now. Young men had begun calling on her, with particular attention coming from
twenty-four-year-old Ted Regis, the son of board member and bank owner Harold Regis. Her father had had
time to cool down since the big blow-up with the board
of directors, and they were on speaking terms again. He
had not objected when Regis's son had asked to call on
Sunny, and Sunny had decided it was time to begin seeing young men. In fact, Ted would be there soon to take
her to the theater. Mrs. Seymour, who accompanied
Sunny wherever she went, would act as a chaperone.
Ted was a mannerly but somewhat cocky young man
who seemed totally taken with her, but Sunny had no
special feelings for him, nothing like the wonderful feelings she used to get around Colt.

She rose and walked to her dresser, taking another
look at herself in the mirror. She recognized her own
beauty, but she recalled Miss Putnam telling her, "Don't
let your looks go to your head." What mattered was a
person's heart and strength. Still, she had become very
aware that her looks could sway a congressman's vote.
Sometimes her father swore it was more her beauty
than his money that got them into the offices of men
who at first refused to see him and listen to him talk
about his "damned railroad."

Someone knocked on the door to her room then, and
Mae Bitters, her personal maid, came into the room.
"Your Mr. Regis has arrived for you," the young woman
told her.

"*My* Mr. Regis? He's just a friend, Mae."

Mae giggled, looking Sunny over. "Sure he is. I
wouldn't want to be 'just friends' with the likes of him.
Those gray eyes and that handsome smile would melt
me right away!"

"Mae Bitters, I swear *all* men make you melt."

"All men with *money* are good-looking to me, Miss Sunny, and that's the only kind of man who ever comes around here!" She laughed again, and Sunny could not help a giggle of her own. Mae was from a poorer section of town and had been delighted to get a job in the Landers mansion. She was close enough to Sunny's age that there were things they could share; but Mae was too flighty to share truly deep feelings with her, and too uneducated for Sunny to talk to her about political events or some of the bigger financial decisions Sunny knew her father was plagued with making. Still, in many ways Mae was already a better, more loyal friend than the young women of her own class.

Mae helped Sunny pin on her hat, a deep red velvet with pink feathers in it. It matched her red velvet dress that had been perfectly tailored to her voluptuous figure. Forty tiny velvet buttons fastened the dress down the middle of her back, and the puffed shoulders were tapered into tight-fitting long sleeves. Mae draped a fur cape around her shoulders and tied it at her throat, then stood back.

"How do I look?"

Mae shook her head. "Do you know how women envy you? I would hate you myself if I didn't know how nice you are, Miss Landers. When I was first hired, I thought you would be bossy and rude to me, but you've made my job so pleasant." Mae smiled, a gentle smile in a plain face. She was slight of build, her coloring pale, her hair a light brown.

"Thank you, Mae," Sunny answered. "That was a very nice thing to say. Did my father get home yet?"

"No, ma'am. He's still at his office, I think."

Sunny wished her father would not put in so many long hours. She did as much for him as she could, and would be with him now if he had not insisted she accept this date with Ted Regis. The man seemed concerned that his workload was interfering with Sunny's social life, and she could not convince him that she would rather be with him, going over books and helping plan his railroad investments.

She went to the door to leave, hearing a commotion downstairs as she stepped into the hall. She recognized Eve's voice, and her heart fell. What did the woman want now? Vince and Eve hardly ever came to visit, and Vince was often conspicuously absent from board meetings where his father was in attendance. The two men had hardly spoken since the argument over Bo's railroad investments. Stuart, on the other hand, had apologized and helped his father convince at least two men on the board of directors for the freighting and supply companies to make a contribution toward his father's project.

"Her date can wait," Eve was saying loudly to Mrs. Seymour downstairs.

Sunny looked over the balcony rail to see an embarrassed-looking Ted Regis running his fingers nervously between his collar and his neck. Eve was already heading up the stairs, skirts rustling, her steps deliberate and stomping. Eve had given birth to a third child the past summer, another daughter. The birth had been difficult, leaving her weak and sick for several weeks. But she was fully recovered and as ornery as ever, motherhood having done nothing to soften the woman.

Mae watched in wide-eyed fear as the woman came to the top of the stairs. She had never liked Eve Landers, who was rude and demanding. "Leave us!" the woman barked. Mae scurried past them to the backstairs that led up to her own room, but Sunny held Eve's eyes boldly.

"I was just leaving for the theater, Eve," she told the woman. "It's very rude and unmannerly of you to barge in on us this way. What on earth do you want?"

"We'll talk alone." Eve stormed into Sunny's bedroom, and Sunny reluctantly followed, closing the door. "*I* think it's very rude and unmannerly of *you* to keep us in the dark on some of the things your father is up to." The woman looked her over scathingly, her jealousy of Sunny's beauty obvious.

"What on earth are you talking about?"

"I'm talking about your father investing a good sum of money from Landers Enterprises into some fly-by-night company called the Pennsylvania Fiscal Agency. It's already done now. Vince came home and told me about it, but don't tell me you didn't know he was going to do it!"

Sunny pulled on her silk gloves. "Of course I knew, but as owner and founder of Landers Enterprises, it's my *father's* business who he confides in when he makes investments."

"Things like this have to be brought up before the board! You know that!"

"The board is there only to help run the business and make certain policy decisions, Eve. My father might not be able to control all the funds of the subsidiaries anymore because he gave them over to Vince and Stuart, something, I might add, that he now regrets doing. But he *does* have control over the parent company, *and* over the railroads, thank goodness. As a seventy-five percent stockholder, he can make certain investments of his own choosing without consulting *anyone*. When it comes to investments that have to do with the railroad, he doesn't bother taking it to the board because Vince and most of the others have made it very clear how they feel about the idea! They don't want any part of it, so my father is making sure they *have* no part in it!"

Eve glowered at her, her face darkening with rage. "That man is going to bankrupt us!"

"The Pennsylvania Fiscal Agency is a very solvent company founded by Thomas Durant. Do you really think anything Mr. Durant creates and supports is going to be a fly-by-night company, as you put it?"

"Mr. Durant is as crazy as your father when it comes to this ridiculous transcontinental railroad! I swear, both men would sell their *teeth* for it!"

"Mr. Durant is a very wealthy man. He and Father have some excellent connections in Washington, and are on very good terms with Abraham Lincoln, who just might be our next president! They know what they're doing, Eve. They have vision. They see far beyond the small world you and Vincent live in!"

"Oh, yes, *you* would know! It's *you* he takes to New

York and Washington with him, *you* he confides in, instead of his *sons!*"

"Vince made it very plain what he thought of his father's dreams, Eve. This is the way he wanted it, so don't come crying when Father goes ahead with certain investments without consulting people who don't *give* a damn!"

It was the first time Sunny had used a swear word. Eve's eyes widened, and she straightened, surprised not just by the word, but by Sunny's firm retort. Always before it had been easy to make the girl shiver in her shoes, but in the last few months Sunny had changed dramatically. It worried Eve, who had been sure that once Bo Landers died, it would be easy to browbeat Sunny into giving up control of what she received in Bo's will.

"I suppose you think that just because Father has been seeing a doctor about his heart, it's time to stop him from spending too much money before he dies," Sunny said coolly. "That way there will be more left for you when he's gone."

"It's something that must be considered," Eve answered. "The man is getting senile, Sunny. Can't you see that?"

Sunny struggled against tears at the thought of her father's somewhat failing health. She forced herself not to show her panic in front of this woman who would love to see her crumble. "I'm only sixteen, Eve. Would you say I'm senile? *I* think the same way *he* does. I see nothing wrong in his investments, so that makes him no different from me. Father is as bright and creative as he ever was! And I won't have someone in my house who is waiting with baited breath for him to die! Now, get out!"

Eve's face turned even darker. "I see he's training you well. He's making a real *man* out of you, isn't he? When are you going to be a woman, Sunny? When are you going to learn to leave the business world to men, take a husband, have children, and let the *men* make the decisions?"

"Is that what *you're* doing by being here trying to talk me into changing my father's mind?"

"This is the only way I have of doing my part. I'm not privy to the board meetings and the books like *you* are! And God knows you're the only one who might be able to talk some sense into Bo Landers!"

"I don't need to. He's doing some very sensible things, as far as I'm concerned. I told you once to leave. Shall I get the butler to show you out forcefully?"

Eve sucked in her breath and shook her head. "You poor thing," she scowled. "You might be beautiful and feminine on the outside, but you're becoming ugly and domineering on the inside." The woman turned and stormed out, failing to notice Mae Bitters scurry away from the door where she had been listening. Sunny struggled against an urge to scream and weep. She knew Eve's words were meant to deliberately undermine her self-confidence and create self-doubt, and she would not let that happen. If she folded now and wept as she wanted to, Eve would win.

She took a deep breath, holding her chin high, and marched out of the room and down the stairs just as Eve slammed the door on her way out of the house. Sunny walked up to Ted, who still looked embarrassed. Mrs. Seymour stood quietly by, accustomed to the rancor in the Landers family.

"I'm very sorry for the interruption, Ted," Sunny told him. "It's a family matter and it has been settled. We can go now." She took his arm. "Tell me, do you think of me as ugly and domineering?"

The handsome, blond-haired young man looked at her in surprise. "Why on earth would you ask a thing like that, Sunny? You're the most beautiful, nicest girl I know."

Sunny smiled victoriously. "Thank you," she answered. "Shall we go?"

LeeAnn Harding answered a knock at the door of the boardinghouse where she worked, which was in the tiny town of Denver City. It was 1859, and in just the one year since she had come here, the little settlement had grown rapidly. Gold had a way of creating towns out of the earth like mushrooms.

She gasped and smiled with joy when she saw Colt Travis standing on the porch, holding a fistful of wild-flowers. "Colt!"

"Hi, LeeAnn." Colt smiled the melting smile that made the eighteen-year-old girl's heart rush. He held out the flowers and she took them, her eyes misting.

"Oh, Colt, where have you been?"

In an instant he swept her into his arms. Colt breathed deeply of the smell of her dark hair, enjoyed the feel of her against him. "I'm sorry I was away so long. I just had to think about some things before I came back here and asked you to marry me."

She leaned back, his arms still around her. *"Marry* you? Oh, Colt, do you mean it?"

"Sure I do." He studied her dark eyes, aching for her. Ever since rescuing LeeAnn from her predicament in the foothills a year before, he had been unable to stay away from her. The pitiful way she had been orphaned had tugged at his heart, and they both shared a loneliness each could understand in the other.

LeeAnn had no family to return to back in Ohio, from where her father had brought his wife and daughter to Colorado in hopes of finding riches. Colt had brought her to this crude settlement along Cherry Creek, where a woman whose own husband had just died took her in. Joanna Scott's husband had left her enough money to have a real frame house built, and she had begun renting out rooms. LeeAnn worked for the woman to help earn her keep.

"I missed you, LeeAnn. I wasn't sure I was ready to marry and settle, but now I know it's time. I can't think of anybody I'd rather settle with than you, if you'll have me."

Her eyes teared. "Did you think that I wouldn't?"

He studied her eyes, wanting her, needing her. He leaned closer, meeting her mouth in a kiss that quickly became hotter, more searching. Someone else flashed into Colt's memory for just a moment, a girl with white-blond hair and amazingly blue eyes, but he quickly dismissed the thought. Sunny Landers was just a fond memory, a pretty young woman he would never see again and who could never have shared his world anyway.

He kissed LeeAnn's mouth once more, then moved his lips to taste her sweet neck. LeeAnn fit him perfectly. She came from a simple background, a family that had little money. There was nothing about her life that would draw her attention from her husband or would interfere with living a normal, quiet life on a little farm out on the Plains. He still had the full $750 that Bo Landers had paid him, plenty of money to start a homestead. He wanted nothing to do with searching for gold. He would get richer than most of the prospectors by growing food to sell to them.

"I've found a nice piece of land where we can settle," he told her. "I've even started building a cabin. You don't mind, do you?"

LeeAnn studied his handsome face, her heart racing at the thought of being Colt Travis's wife. She didn't care about the fact that he was half Indian. She had never known anyone as handsome or as kind, as brave and skilled. When she was in his arms she was not afraid of anything.

"Why would I mind? It sounds wonderful!" She finally pulled away, sniffing the flowers, and Colt moved into the narrow hallway, closing the curtained door. "I can't wait until Joanna returns," LeeAnn was saying. "She'll be so happy for me." She turned and looked at Colt again. "She's been so good to me, Colt." She sighed, looking him over. "I was so afraid you wouldn't come back."

His eyes moved over her in a way that made her shiver with desire. "We got to know each other pretty well, LeeAnn. How could you think I wouldn't come back, after telling you I loved you?"

She looked down, reddening. "I don't know. You're so . . . so wild and free and all. I thought maybe you felt I was trying to pin you down, taking away your freedom or something."

"I'm twenty-two years old, LeeAnn. I've been wandering with no aim in life since I was fourteen. There comes a time when a man has to own up to his manhood, his needs. I went off to be alone in the mountains for a while, wanting to make sure I was doing the right thing—not because of me, but because of you. I didn't want to do something that would hurt you any more than you've already been hurt. I thought I'd see if I could stay away, but I couldn't. I know what I want now. I want a wife, kids. I want to settle."

She looked up at him, her eyes misting with love and joy. "When?"

"Whenever you want. Today isn't too soon as far as I'm concerned. Is there a preacher in this pitiful place?"

"Yes." Their eyes held, their hearts racing, their desire intense. "Just let me bathe and change first, and I'd like to find Joanna. She should be there. She's been like a mother to me."

He nodded. "Whatever you want. Actually, I was hoping you'd agree to today. I set up camp just outside of town. It's just a tent, but I thought we ought to be alone." He grinned suggestively. "You know what I mean?"

She felt her cheeks quickly grow hot. "I know."

"It's not very fancy, but then, there isn't anything fancy any place around here. It would be nice to stay here, but I thought it might be a little awkward for you, with Mrs. Scott and boarders here and all."

She nodded. "You're right." She searched his eyes, and he read the mixture of anticipation and fear in her own.

"It'll be all right, LeeAnn," he promised her. "I haven't been mean to you or broken any promises yet, have I?"

She shook her head. "I love you so, Colt. I'm so glad you're back." Tears spilled over in her eyes. He pulled her into his arms once more.

"Thank you," he whispered. "I'll be a good husband, LeeAnn."

"I know you will."

He held her so tightly she could hardly catch her

breath. Again she brushed his mouth, their lips meeting in a hot, passionate kiss that made both of them feel they must do this or die. Today she would become Mrs. Colt Travis, and no woman could ask for a more handsome, gentler, braver man to call her husband.

Chapter 7

Sunny clung to her father's arm amid a crowd of hundreds of cheering men. Brass bands played while banners and signs supporting Abraham Lincoln and the Republican Party waved above people's heads. Bo Landers had been instrumental in urging the Party to hold their national convention of 1860 in Chicago. He had taken a suite in one of Chicago's finest downtown hotels so that he and Sunny could be close enough to attend nearly every hour of what would become a historic event. Each time more votes came in for Abraham Lincoln, the Party favorite, the huge hall would resound with a barrage of cheers and more band-playing.

Sunny laughed and held up her own banner while the party chairman pounded his gavel and tried to bring the gathering back to order. "Father, he's going to win!" Sunny said excitedly.

"It looks that way." Landers held up a fist, cheering the important victory. To have a president who backed a continental railroad was one big boost in the right direction. The crowd finally quieted enough so more states could cast their votes, and Lincoln continued to gain strength through the third balloting. When Ohio finally went against Salmon P. Chase, a candidate from their own state, taking four votes from him and giving them to Lincoln, the nomination was sealed in Lincoln's favor.

Again the crowd broke into mighty celebrating. Sunny wondered if some of the southern states would really secede if Lincoln was elected. Many had threatened to do so. Still, he was not president yet. That was the next big step.

Speeches and celebrating continued until the wee hours of the morning, and Sunny and her father were among the last to leave the convention hall. Bo talked excitedly all the way out to their waiting carriage.

"This is the best thing that could have happened, Sunny! The only problem will be if those damn southern states make trouble. Why can't they behave like civilized men and give up their hideous practice of owning slaves?"

"I agree that it's immoral, Father. Some of the things we've heard—I can't imagine they really happen; but you know why the South won't give it up. Farming is their wealth, just like industry and railroading is ours. I wonder sometimes if we had built all that we have on slavery, if we would want to give it up."

"Those plantation owners can just start paying their labor, just like we have to do. It's one thing for a man to make his fortune while treating other men like human beings, quite another for him to make it by breaking other men's backs. I might be demanding of the men who work for me, but by God I respect them, and they respect themselves for earning their way."

They climbed into the carriage, and Bo closed the door. Sunny leaned back into the plush velvet seat. "What would happen to those poor slaves if they were freed, Father? I mean, where would they go? Apparently, they're completely cared for by their owners, poor as some of that care might be. If they're freed, they'll have no money, no homes, nothing."

Landers leaned out the window and waved to someone before answering. "I don't know what they would do, but there's no sense worrying about it right now. Ending slavery isn't something that is going to happen overnight, but I do think this thing is going to come to a head very soon, and I don't like to think of what could happen. Already the fighting in Kansas over the slavery issue has been terribly bloody, and there are those awful border wars between Kansas and Missouri." He reached over and patted her hand. "That is one area we'll avoid when we do our campaigning. Some of the western territories are in a real turmoil over this because they have to choose to be free or slave."

As always, when someone reminded her of the land to the west, sweet memories stirred Sunny's soul. Did Colt know or care about the problems over slavery?

"The first step to keeping this country united and getting our railroad built is to get our Mr. Lincoln into the White House," her father was saying, "and we'll by God do it. We'll hit every major industrialist in the North and New England, every man who is anyone important, get them to contribute to the campaign and to do their own talking to their employees and such. I'll make speeches myself. Then at the same time we can talk to people about the railroad."

Sunny squeezed his hand. "Father, are you sure you're well enough to go stomping all over the country campaigning? I'm worried about you."

Landers forced a laugh. He was secretly glad that the last couple of days he had been able to hide the fact that he had not felt well at all. What bothered him most was shortness of breath and a constant feeling of a weight on his chest. For a year his doctor had been preaching at him to slow down, telling him his heart was no longer strong. Such talk only angered him. "Bo Landers slow down? Never! I'm fine, honey. Don't you worry about your ol' dad. You just worry about helping me get Lincoln elected."

Sunny sighed, putting her head on his shoulder. Sometimes she wanted to tell him how it frightened her to think of being without him, of bearing the responsibilities that would be hers when he was gone, let alone the trouble she knew Vince would make for her. At least now, because of Vi, she had Stuart on her side; but Stuart was not someone who could stand up to Vince. She kept her thoughts to herself, hating to burden her father with them, always afraid of upsetting him and maybe making him get sick. He was so proud of her strength and spunk. How could she tell him how afraid she was sometimes?

She told herself she was being foolish to worry anyway. Bo Landers was a hefty, energetic man who would probably live to be a hundred. The carriage clattered over the bricked streets, now and then splashing through fresh puddles left by a summer rain. Weariness claimed Sunny as she began to drift off to sleep. The splashing sounds combined with riding in the carriage recalled another time . . . a wagon, crossing a river . . . a horse splashing through water . . . her skirt getting wet . . . someone holding her so she wouldn't slip into a cold river. In her mind's eye she saw a picture of vast, endless grasslands. She glided across them on a horse, floating, feeling nothing except the strong, protective arms of the man who rode with her, a dark man who wore buckskins. She was happy and free, and no one could hurt her in the sweet dream, not while those arms were wrapped around her.

Colt galloped Buck across the open grassland, a fresh-killed antelope and two jackrabbits tied to the horse's rump. He smiled at the thought of how glad LeeAnn would be to see him coming with a fresh supply of meat, and he wondered why God had seen fit to give him such happiness. Ten months after their marriage LeeAnn had given birth to a son. Little four-month-old Ethan was named after LeeAnn's father. Colt had helped deliver the baby himself, since there was no one close by to help. Never would he forget the joy and miracle of that moment. As far as he was concerned, a man's life could not be fuller or more satisfying than his was. For years he had never dreamed things could be like this for him, or that he would even want to be a settled man. Life with LeeAnn and Ethan had changed all of that.

The sky was a brilliant blue, with just a hint of coming winter in the cool air. He thought about how nice it was going to be to get inside the warm little cabin and eat some of LeeAnn's cooking. He didn't like leaving her and Ethan alone, but he had not gone far and had been gone only since morning. This was the time of year a man had to think about getting in a supply of meat for the winter. The corn and beans were already in, and he never ceased to be amazed to discover that he actually didn't mind farming. He intended to expand each year, maybe even hire some help, begin taking produce to the fast-growing city of Denver, one of the few gold towns that looked as though it might last.

He crested one of the rolling foothills that stood between him and home, only to see smoke beyond the next rise, which was where his own little cabin lay. He stared for a moment, telling himself not to panic, then kicked Buck into an even faster run, galloping down one slope, charging up the next, his horse making little sound in the soft sod. When he crested the next rise, his eyes widened in horror. The cabin was on fire! To his right Indians were herding away his four plow horses, and six more wild horses he had managed to capture and corral. A small barn and another horse shed were also on fire.

"My God!" he groaned. He ripped his rifle from its boot and screamed a war whoop, charging down the steep slope toward everything that had ever meant anything to him since he was a little boy. He raised the rifle while still in the saddle at a hard ride, aiming and firing. One Indian fell. More began to flee from the front side of the cabin, which he could not see yet. He told himself it was not possible that anything could have happened to LeeAnn and Ethan. God simply wouldn't let them come to harm. He wouldn't take away such a beautiful, loving woman and a tiny baby boy. It couldn't happen!

His hope dwindled in the seconds it took to get closer, for he saw by their paint and hair that they were Pawnee, bitter enemy of the Sioux and Cheyenne, Indians who sometimes seemed to kill simply for the pleasure of it.

"Bastards!" he screamed. Dread boiled in his belly like hot tar. He fired the rifle again, over and over, not even sure how many men he hit, not caring that he was outnumbered. He had to get them away from LeeAnn and Ethan! Why had he left this morning? Why had he let himself become so happy and complacent as to think he could leave a woman and baby alone?

He rounded the cabin, and it was then he felt the horrible hot sting to his right ribs. He cried out, trying desperately to hang on to his rifle but unable to do so, unable even to stay on Buck. He felt himself crashing to the ground, and through a haze he saw Buck gallop off. An Indian grasped the horse's bridle and took Buck away with him, fresh meat and all.

Acrid smoke from the burning cabin stung Colt's nostrils. He lay on his back, realizing somewhere deep in his confused mind that he had taken an arrow. Knowing the Pawnee, they had probably dipped it in horse dung first to make sure that if the wound itself did not kill him, infection would. He stared up at the sky, thinking that if LeeAnn and Ethan were dead, he didn't want to live anyway. He could never bear the guilt of leaving them, or the horrible loneliness of having to live without them.

"LeeAnn!" In his mind he had screamed the name, but it was only a mumble. He scooted on his back, forcing himself then to roll to his left side. His right arm bumped against the arrow that still protruded from his ribs, and he cried out with the ugly pain. For a moment he blacked out, then came around again, opening his eyes, forcing them to focus. The only sound was the crackling of the burning buildings. The Pawnee had gone.

He crawled across the ground on his left side, most things still blurry. He tried to get over what he thought was a rock, until he felt how soft it was. He looked down to push it out of the way, only to realize then that it was his son's dead body, his head brutally crushed.

Colt gasped, rising up slightly. He screamed Ethan's name, screamed God's name, retched until he thought his insides would explode. How could this be? Ethan, his son, his baby! He had watched him be born, remembered how happy he had been to see that he was healthy and perfect.

His vomiting was followed by bitter sobbing, and in spite of his own grave wound, he dragged himself over and pulled the baby to him, touching him, begging him to come back to life. He looked around again, calling LeeAnn's name through tears. Surely by some miracle at least LeeAnn had lived. To lose them both was more than a man could be expected to bear. He realized then that if she *was* alive, he had to find her, help her.

He carefully laid the child aside, finding the baby's blanket nearby and covering him with it. With the greatest effort he managed to get to his feet and stumbled toward the cabin, vaguely aware that the roof had just fallen in. Finally, his vision cleared enough so he could see things in more detail. He saw LeeAnn then, lying on the ground at a far corner of the cabin. Her body was naked, several arrows protruding from it. He could see she had been sexually abused by the men, and part of her hair was gone.

Colt just stared in disbelief. He turned away, looking over at his dead son. Grief consumed him in one great convulsion, bringing him to his knees. He raised his arms, needing to scream out his horror, for he was again alone, more alone than he had ever been, but his voice would not come. He had no idea how much blood had already poured from his own wound. All consciousness left him then. He collapsed, sprawled between his wife and son.

The sweet smell of sage filled Colt's nostrils. He could hear a strange chanting, and when he opened his eyes he saw a lovely dark woman bending over him. At first he thought it was LeeAnn. He groaned her name, but as his vision focused he saw that it was an Indian woman. He tried to sit up, and a sickening pain tore at his side, making him gasp and fall back again. The woman said something to someone, and Colt recognized the Cheyenne word for "awake." Someone grasped his shoulders firmly.

"Go and get White Horse," came a man's voice, again in the Cheyenne tongue. "You must not move," the same man told him, leaning closer then. "You are very, very sick."

Colt opened his eyes to see a white-haired Indian with a wrinkled face. The old man smiled. "You will live, if you rest for many more days. It might be another full moon before you can rise."

It felt to Colt as though his whole body were on fire, and he felt sweat trickle from his forehead. "Where . . . am I?" he asked, struggling to remember how to say it in Cheyenne.

"It is the village of Many Beaver, whose son is White Buffalo. Three winters ago you gave us rifles and food. Many Beaver remembered you. When he found you wounded eight sunrises ago, and saw that you were still alive, Many Beaver said we must help you because once you helped him." Colt struggled to remember. Wounded? Still alive? "Many Beaver says you are a man who has good medicine. Not many men survive the wound of a Pawnee arrow," the old man added.

Pawnee arrow? The horror returned then as Colt began to remember. Pawnee! They had attacked his home, raped and tortured and scalped LeeAnn, killed his baby son! The memory moved over him like a herd of buffalo, beating, pounding, torturing. He gasped in a sob. "Let me die," he groaned.

The old man applied something cool to his forehead. "We are a people who know grief," he said soothingly. "Time heals many things. For now your sorrow makes you say foolish things, but you are young. You will live, and there will be other loved ones in your life."

"Never." Colt could not stop the tears that ran from his eyes across his cheeks, some trickling into his ears. LeeAnn. Ethan. It was true. This was not some awful nightmare, but reality. Why had he let himself think that the happiness he had found could last? A man had to be a fool to take such things for granted. The worst part was that it was his fault. He should never have left them. They died alone. Alone! LeeAnn had probably screamed his name, hoping he would come and help her. But he had been off enjoying a good hunt. He put a hand to his face, his body shuddering in sobs.

The woman returned, two other men with her. *"Saaa,"* the woman said softly, "what is this?" She wet a rag and applied it to his forehead. "You will heal, friend, in body and in spirit."

"Will he live?" The question came from one of the men.

"I think so," the old medicine man answered. "But his grief is very strong."

"I know a way to make him *want* to live," came another man's voice, this one a little younger.

Colt sensed a change of positions. Someone different had crouched beside him. "Open your eyes," the man told him.

Colt swallowed back an urge to vomit. The woman had moved around to his other side, the old medicine man moving away slightly. The woman continued to bathe his face, washing away his tears. Colt opened his eyes to see a handsome young Indian he guessed was about his same age.

"Who are you?" the young man asked. "We can see you have Indian blood. What kind of Indian are you?"

Colt swallowed again. "Cherokee," he answered. "My father . . . was white."

The young Indian sniffed. "Just as we thought. A half-blood." He looked back at a more middle-aged man who was crouched on his knees near Colt's feet. Colt thought he recognized him, but couldn't remember from where. "Three winters ago, in the time when summer is coming, did you not give rifles and food to the Cheyenne?" the younger Indian asked.

Colt strained to remember. It was so hard to think when he was so sick with grief. Three years ago. The only time he had handed rifles over to Indians was when a small party of Cheyenne had stopped what was left of the Landers party after the buffalo stampede. Why did that seem more like twenty years ago? It was the first time he had thought about Sunny Landers since marrying LeeAnn, and somehow the thought comforted him. "I . . . remember," he answered. "Yes, I was scouting . . . for a man heading . . . for Fort Laramie."

The young man looked over at the Indian sitting at Colt's feet. "So, it *is* the same man!" He looked back at Colt. "I am called White Buffalo. My father, Many Beaver, and I were with the warriors you helped that day." He pointed to the middle-aged man. "That is Many Beaver. He is the one you spoke with. Do you remember?"

So, Colt thought, that was why the man looked familiar. "Yes," he answered.

"Because you helped us, we are helping you," White Buffalo told him. "The woman who cares for you is my wife, Sits Tall. The medicine man is Dancing Otter. For many sunrises he has cared for you. He cut the Pawnee arrow out of your side and has put the magic herbs and medicines on your wound to bring out the infection. Many times we thought you would die, but you are a strong man. What are you called?"

Colt shivered, struggling against a new surge of tears that threatened to overwhelm and consume him. "Colt . . . Travis," he answered.

"You are a brave man, Colt Travis. We found six dead Pawnee when we found you. We buried your woman and child the white man's way, but we did not bury the Pawnee. Let the buzzards take care of them!" White Buffalo turned and spit in a sign of his hatred and disrespect for his longtime Cheyenne enemy.

Colt closed his eyes. "LeeAnn," he groaned. "It's . . . true? My wife . . . my baby boy . . ."

"*Ai.* We grieve with you, Colt Travis, but there is one way a man can help the pain in his heart."

Colt opened his eyes again, looking first at Many Beaver, who nodded. "You know what you must do," the man told Colt. "The Pawnee also attacked our village.

We, too, have lost loved ones. Soon we will be joined by many more of our People. We will make sacrifices and fast and pray. We will make much magic so that we are very strong. Then we will go after the Pawnee when the snows are deep. That is when they will least expect us. Their blood will stain the snow! Many will die!"

Colt looked at White Buffalo, who grinned. *"You* will *not* die, Colt Travis, because if you live, you can ride with us against the Pawnee. Is that not a much more pleasant thought than dying?"

The image of killing Pawnee brought a surge of new life into Colt's veins. "Yes," he answered. Was it his Indian blood that made him understand the glory and satisfaction of vengeance? Part of him wanted to die, to be with LeeAnn and Ethan. But a stronger part of him wanted to live, not just to taste Pawnee blood, but also because his death would only mean another Pawnee victory. "You would . . . let me ride with you?"

"If you are strong enough," White Buffalo answered. "Every extra man who hates the Pawnee means another Pawnee death!"

Colt looked at Sits Tall, in his agony and sorrow seeing only LeeAnn's face smiling down at him. "I will be strong enough," he answered. He looked over at Dancing Otter. "Help me," he told the old man. "I'll do whatever you tell me to do. I want to live long enough to ride with your warriors against the Pawnee."

The old man nodded, and Many Beaver raised a fist. "So, the half-blood will become a full-blood for a while, yes?" He looked over at his son, and both men laughed.

Colt looked at White Buffalo, wondering what kind of a man his little Ethan might have become. He would never know now. *"Ai,"* he answered. "I will be an Indian, long enough to drink Pawnee blood."

White Buffalo gave out a shrill cry, throwing back his head.

"For now you must rest," Sits Tall told Colt, pressing the cloth to his head again.

He closed his eyes. Yes, he would rest so that he would heal. He could think of no better way to deal with his grief than to kill, and kill, and kill, until he was so weary that he could no longer raise his arm. If he was lucky, after he had felt enough warm Pawnee blood on his hands, some warrior's arrow would end his own life so he could find peace with LeeAnn and Ethan.

Sunny took the message from the courier, opening the note that a fellow campaign worker had sent to her from Republican headquarters. "Lincoln won," it read. Her heart raced with a mixture of joy and sorrow. This was what her father had worked so hard for, but now he might not even live to see Lincoln's inauguration. Several southern states were close to secession, and the close of 1860 brought with it dark clouds over a divided country, and closer to home, the very real possibility of Bo Landers's death.

She thanked the messenger, turning and lifting her skirt to go up the stairs to her father's room. She prayed that this news would revive him, that by some miracle he would heal and be whole again, the big, strapping man he had always been, not the shell of a man who lay in his bed in his second-story room.

She was only eighteen, but today she felt old and weary from the strain of having to watch her father slowly die. She could hardly believe that a man could fail so quickly, especially someone as hardy as Bo Landers had always been. She kept waiting for him to get better, but she knew now that that was not going to happen. She had not wanted him to do so much traveling to campaign for Lincoln, but he had insisted, and two weeks before, it had caught up with him. He had collapsed while giving a talk in Indiana, and he had been brought back home on his own train. The doctor said that his heart was slowly failing him, and that there was nothing he could do. It seemed strange to have so much money, to have the best doctors at one's beck and call, and still not be able to stop the ugly hand of death.

Sunny suspected that the only reason her father had lived this long was to know for certain whether Lincoln had won the election. It had become an obsession with him, just like his dream of a transcontinental railroad.

He expected her to finish that dream for him. He had told her so more than once, had trained her well, taught her everything he knew. She was acquainted with all the important people who could help her make the dream a reality; but the thought of going on without him, of taking on such a tremendous responsibility without her father's strength and know-how, weighed heavily on her.

She never dreamed it would happen this way. Men like Bo Landers didn't die. He was supposed to wait until she was much older, wait until she was married so that she had a husband and family to fall back on. If only she had not been born so late in his life. Now he sometimes mumbled about going to be with her mother. "The love of his life" he had called her so many times. Sunny wished with all her heart she could have known her, wished her mother were here with her now; but the woman would forever be no more to her than a painting that hung over the fireplace in the parlor, a painting that Vince had grumbled several times didn't belong there, even though Bo kept a painting of Vince and Stuart's mother in the dining room.

Sunny wondered how her brothers had treated her mother when Bo married her. She was sure they were as mean to the poor young woman as they had been to her. She thought how her mother had been only her age when she married Bo Landers, but at the moment Sunny could not picture herself married. If her father died, marriage would be an even greater impossibility. She would have far too many responsibilities to think of taking on a husband and having a family.

She dreaded the smell of death when she walked into the room, but it was always there. A nurse sat beside Bo, and Vi turned from a stand where she had been pouring a glass of water. She set the glass down and rushed over to Sunny, taking her arm.

"I told you to take the day shopping or something," the woman told her. "I'll watch him today."

Sunny was grateful for the genuine concern in her sister-in-law's dark eyes. Vince and Eve seldom had a kind word about Vi, both insisting Stuart had made a grave mistake marrying the plain, plump young woman whose family was not part of the Landers circle of friends. Eve was sure Vi had married Stuart for his money, but Sunny didn't believe it. She was simply a good-hearted woman who loved Stuart in spite of all his shortcomings.

"I was thinking of going out, but I got this message," she told Vi. "I have to tell Father. Lincoln has won."

Vi saw the mixture of triumph and sorrow in Sunny's eyes. "Yes, you should tell him right away." She walked with Sunny to the bed. As always, Bo's eyes lit up when he saw his daughter.

"Sunny! Is there any news yet?"

She smiled for him. "Yes." She sat down on the edge of the bed. "Lincoln won."

He broke into a smile, and Sunny thought how thin his face looked. "I knew it," he said. He closed his eyes for a moment, his breathing labored. "Thank God." He reached for her hand, enfolding it in his own. "You know what to do, Sunny. You're my only hope. You know that, don't you?"

She tried not to let her tears and terror show. "Yes, Father, I know what to do."

"You're by God a Landers from the inside out." His eyes teared slightly. "Don't let them take it away from you, Sunny. You're a fighter, and you know what needs to be done. You can't do it if Vince takes away some of your inheritance. That money and what you will own means power, Sunny, power to get done whatever you want to get done! Build my railroad, Sunny. Promise me you'll do it."

She could hardly bear to look at him this way, her own father, thin, failing, giving up. "I need *you,* Father. You've got to get well and help me."

"I want to, Sunny. I want that more than anything." How weak his voice was, compared to the old, booming Bo Landers. "But there are some things money and power can't buy, and health's one of them. I'm just sorry I was already getting old when you were born." He squeezed her hand lightly. "Sunny, my precious, beautiful Sunny. Oh, how I hate leaving you. I'm so sorry I've placed such a burden on you, but I wouldn't do it if I didn't think you were capable."

A tear slipped down her cheek. "Don't leave me, Daddy," she said, feeling at that moment like a little girl again.

"Oh, no, girl, I'll never leave you. I might not be here in body, but I'll by God be with you in spirit. When you need strength, when you need to give somebody what-for and make yourself heard, you just think of me. I'll be standing right behind you. And when you get that railroad built, I'll be right there at the celebrations, watching them drive that last spike. You can do it, Sunny. There is no doubt whatsoever in my heart."

She leaned down, resting her head against his shoulder, and he touched her face, stroking her hair back from her forehead. "My little ray of sunshine," he mumbled. "Don't let them take it away from you. You fight for what's yours."

She could not stop the tears. How was she going to go on without her pillar of strength, the only person in her life who loved her totally and unconditionally? She would gladly give up Lincoln's victory, her wealth, everything . . . if it meant Bo Landers would live.

Chapter 8

Colt could hear the cries again, smell the blood, feel it on his hands. The dream became a mixture of memories and horror. He was lying flat on the ground, and hundreds of Pawnee warriors were riding down on him. The hooves of their horses made his body tumble, and after rolling over several times he thought he heard LeeAnn screaming his name. He got to his feet, searching through the hundreds of Pawnee, who kept shooting arrows at him, but he kept walking, searching. He stumbled over something, looking down to see a baby, bloody but smiling at him. He reached down to pick it up, holding it close in his arms.

LeeAnn called his name again, and he looked to see her approaching. The Pawnee were gone. LeeAnn's image kept flashing back and forth from a bloody, naked woman he could not recognize, to his beautiful wife, smiling and reaching out for him. When she came close he could smell the lilac in her hair.

"We're home, Colt," she told him, reaching for the baby. He handed it over to her, and the child was no longer bloody. "See? We're all right," LeeAnn said. "And so are you. Go back to the living, Colt."

She turned away with the baby, and Colt reached out for her; but suddenly a painted Pawnee warrior jumped up in his face and screamed, slashing at him with a huge knife. Colt started to cry out, in reality letting out a groan and jerking awake. He sat up quickly, his body bathed in sweat. His breathing came in near gasps for a moment as he struggled to get his bearings. He looked around the tipi, which was dimly lit by the fading coals of an earlier fire.

He was alive. He touched his face, wiping sweat from himself, throwing off his heavy covers of buffalo robes, not even realizing at first how cold it was inside the tipi, for outside the January winds howled across the northern Kansas plains so fiercely that the tipi skins billowed in and out. He had seen enough of these well-constructed dwellings to know it would not blow apart, but it was getting a mighty test tonight.

"You have had a bad dream."

Colt looked over at White Buffalo, who had risen up on one elbow, looking across the glowing coals at him. Sits Tall stirred slightly, snuggling closer against her husband. The sight made Colt's insides ache for LeeAnn. He nodded in reply to White Buffalo's statement.

"It is common to have such dreams after losing loved ones or after making war," White Buffalo told him. "Do you want to talk?"

Finally the cold air made Colt shiver, and he pulled a robe back over himself. Because of the severe cold, he was fully dressed under the covers. He lay back down. "I saw her this time . . . my wife," he said quietly. "She took our son from me and told me that they were home now, that they were all right. She told me to go back to the living."

White Buffalo moved out from under his robes, making sure his wife was well covered. He reached over to a backrest, where another robe lay, and put it around his shoulders, coming to sit cross-legged near the dwindling fire. He reached to his right, where some buffalo chips were stacked, and added some to the fire. A few flames flickered upward.

"You drew much Pawnee blood, and you needed that," he told Colt. "Now it is done. You carry the scar of a Pawnee knife across your forehead, a sign that you sought vengeance for what was done to your family. You even took three Pawnee scalps. It was good that you could do these things, but, my friend, at heart you are a white man. It is the white man's world in which you were raised, and it is the white man's world to which you must return. I think maybe that is what your woman was telling you—to go back to where you belong."

Colt sat up straighter, listening to the moaning wind outside and thinking how it resembled the way he felt. "I have nothing there anymore."

White Buffalo poked at the fire with a stick. "As my father would say, you are still very young. You have much life ahead of you. You will find a reason to live again."

Colt looked across the fire at him, thinking how White Buffalo and Many Beaver had become the best friends he had had since Slim was killed. "I don't know if I ever want to leave."

"When you think about it more, you will know it is the right thing to do. I will not like saying good-bye to you, Colt Travis; but you do not really belong here, not forever. You must go back to the world that is familiar to you, and I must go on struggling to save what land is left to us. I am not such a fool as to think I can keep this life until I am old man. Already your white brothers are filling up the land, killing our game, bringing their diseases. Your white man's government makes promises and breaks them again, sends its soldiers to hunt us down when we have done nothing wrong. You should leave us while I still think of you as my good friend, and before soldiers or others come who will force you to choose. It is then I might come to hate you, and I do not want to hate you."

His eyes held Colt's gaze, and Colt felt the painful loneliness again squeezing at his heart. Where would he go? Who was there left in his life that mattered? Still, he knew White Buffalo was right. This was not a world in which he could forever remain. He turned and grasped his parfleche, pulling it to his lap and opening it. He reached inside, taking out a gold-plated chain watch that had been his father's. White Buffalo had seen it before, and had admired it greatly. Colt handed it across the fire. "Here."

White Buffalo frowned, reaching out to take the watch. "I can listen to the little sound it makes again?"

"You can keep it. Do you remember what I showed you, how to wind it?"

White Buffalo nodded, surprise in his eyes. "You wish to give it to me? A gift?"

Colt nodded. "A gift." White Buffalo looked at the watch almost reverently. "It's a thank-you gift, White Buffalo. You and your people saved my life, helped me find a reason to want to live again. Thank you for letting me join you on the Pawnee raids, for letting me taste my share of Pawnee blood."

White Buffalo closed the watch into his fist. "This is a fine gift, Colt. It was your father's. It is not an easy thing for you to give away."

"You've been good to me, fed me, gave me shelter, friendship."

White Buffalo rose, walking to a looped string of rawhide that hung from a tipi pole and to which his painted prayer pipe was attached. He untied the pipe, turning then and walking back to the fire, handing it to Colt. "We do not accept a gift without giving one in return. This is my gift to you."

Colt took the pipe, holding it carefully, recognizing the friendship such a gift represented. "I accept your gift with great honor. I will always treasure it."

"You will leave us, then?"

Their eyes held in mutual friendship and feelings of sorrow. "I think I must," Colt answered. "But I will wait until the spring."

White Buffalo nodded. "It is the right thing to do. I will not forget you, Colt Travis."

Colt's throat suddenly ached. "And I will not forget you, White Buffalo." He thought he detected tears in White Buffalo's eyes. "Life is just a series of good-byes, isn't it? People move in and out of our lives, they go on to new places, sometimes they die." He sighed. "Seems like somebody wants me always to be alone."

White Buffalo shook his head. "It will not always be so. We have the company of our memories, and someday another will come into your life to help you forget your woman."

Colt shook his head. "Maybe to love in a different way. But I will never forget. Nor will I forget that it was partly my fault."

"It is easy to blame oneself. But you should not. My father says all things happen for a purpose, that some people are just gifts that are with us for a while until we grow in a new way and are ready for new things. There is another purpose for your life, Colt."

Colt smiled sadly, watching the small fire for a moment. "I can't imagine right now what it would be, my friend, but I hope you're right. I hope you're right."

In spite of the heavy fur coat and hat and muff Sunny wore, the cold January wind bit at her mercilessly, only emphasizing the loneliness and horror of the moment. She stared at the deep hole into which her father would soon be lowered, almost oblivious to the hundreds of people, including congressmen and businessmen from Washington and New York, who had come to pay their last respects to Bo Landers.

Sunny was not even sure how she had gotten to the burial site. The entire funeral service was just a blurred memory. She remembered only grabbing hold of her father and pleading with him to come back to life.

"Ashes to ashes, dust to dust," the Methodist minister said.

Not Bo Landers, she thought. *Men like that don't die. They don't turn to dust. It isn't possible!*

She heard nothing of the final eulogy. She heard only a booming voice, a little girl's laughter. She felt herself being bounced on her father's knee, smelled his cigar smoke. She saw ledgers, saw her father's hefty finger pointing out figures and explaining to her everything about Landers Enterprises, explaining that someday it would all be hers. That was to be seen, for the will was still to be read. Oh, how she dreaded it, dreaded what Vince would say and do.

She looked across the grave at Vince, saw the tears in his eyes and the resolute tenseness of his tightly clenched jaw. He was not about to cry over a father he felt had somehow cheated him. Sometimes she felt sorry for Vince, who somehow had come to think his father didn't love him and who had struck back in vicious ways, done things he must have regretted. Was he wishing his father were alive again so he could apologize and tell him he loved him? Was he wishing he had visited his father more often before he died?

Eve stood beside him, not a tear in her eyes. She was a cold woman from a cold family that fed on money and attention. Eve was an only child who had had anything she wanted all her life. Now she would want Vince's fair share of Landers Enterprises, and she would most certainly force Vince to do what was necessary to get it.

She felt Vi's arm wrap around her then, giving her a tender hug. How could she have gotten through this without Vi's companionship, her help in caring for her father? Stuart stood next to Vi, weeping openly. In spite of his own differences with his father, Stuart seemed genuinely grief-stricken. Sunny was glad that he and Bo had become a little closer before Bo's death.

For the moment none of that mattered. The fact remained that Bo Landers *was* dead, and it all seemed like a bad dream. Sunny wondered if her near collapse during the funeral had sapped all her energy and bled her of all her tears, for now there were none to shed. There was only a kind of numbness.

"These things always hit harder after a few days or weeks have gone by," she remembered someone saying.

Was it the doctor, or Vi? "You've got to share your feelings, Sunny, turn to others, let us help you."

Sunny wondered if anyone truly understood her grief and need. All her life the center of her world, the person in whom she confided, the person she spent most of her time with, was her father. She had a few girlfriends, and they were spoiled and giddy. None of them would ever have to shoulder the responsibilities that were soon to be given to her. How could she share that with them? Mae was good to her, sympathetic, but she came from a world that didn't understand the kind of life she would lead now.

Vi kept an arm around her. At least Vi understood a little of what she was feeling. Vi had married into this world of wealth and power and responsibility. "It's time to go, Sunny," Vi was telling her.

Sunny blinked and looked at her. "But I . . . I didn't hear what the preacher said," she objected. "It can't be over yet. Make him say it again! It's too soon! And too cold! They can't put Daddy in the ground when it's this cold! He'll get the chills!"

She felt more people gathering around her, grasping her arms, making her leave. She began screaming at them that she had a right to stay, that they should put plenty of blankets over her father to keep him warm. Finally, she called to her "Daddy" to make them stop pulling at her. She screamed for him, felt herself being dragged into a coach.

Moments earlier she had thought she had cried as much as anyone could, but now the tears came again, in sobs so bitter and deep that they made everything hurt. Vi's arms came around her again, trying to soothe and comfort. She heard Stuart telling her everything would be all right. "I'll help you, Sunny. No matter what happens with the will, you aren't in this alone. I'll cooperate however I can."

He didn't even realize her devastation was over the personal loss of part of herself. She couldn't care less if she was left with one penny. Her father was gone, and nothing mattered anymore.

"Think of something that makes you feel at peace,"

Vi was telling her. "Of Christ, or wildflowers, the mountains. You've talked so much about the mountains, Sunny. Think of the land out west, how quiet it was, how much you loved it."

Sunny struggled through her sobs to remember the serenity of another time, another place, saw herself riding over the rolling hills. But that was another Sunny, one who supposed her father would live forever and who had given no thought to what she would do when he was gone. It wasn't fair that people had to die, not fair to the deceased, and not fair to the loved ones left behind to struggle on alone. She clung to Vi, wondering how long it would be before the ache of it left her. Maybe it never would.

Activity at Fort Kearny was high, soldiers everywhere, one regiment riding out just as Colt was riding in. Several emigrants were camped about the fort, but Colt knew it was too early in the spring for many to have made it this far yet on their journey west.

Colt trotted his prize Appaloosa gelding, called Dancer, toward a small log structure that carried a sign reading PONY EXPRESS. The horse was a gift from White Buffalo, and the sight of the soldiers leaving brought memories of his good friend, as well as worry. He called out to a soldier passing nearby, slowing Dancer. "Where are those soldiers going?" he asked. "There isn't some new campaign being waged against the Indians, is there?"

"Hell, no," the soldier answered. "Haven't you heard? The country's at war, North against South. Those soldiers are headed back east."

"War!" Colt drew the reins tight on Dancer. "I knew there was a problem over the slavery issue, but I never thought it would lead to war. Is it that bad?"

The soldier frowned as though he thought Colt was a little crazy. "Where in hell have you been, Mister? We've got a new President, Abraham Lincoln. Ever since he was sworn in, southern states have been seceding right and left. Lincoln is against slavery. Now some forces from South Carolina have attacked Fort Sumter. Hell, the damn Union commander there surrendered. Now the South thinks it can win other battles. They want to form their own country, elect their own president. Can you believe that one?"

Colt shook his head, realizing that since wandering off alone after Slim died, then marrying LeeAnn and living out on the Plains with no neighbors, he had not kept up much on national events, nor had he cared, especially after losing LeeAnn and Ethan. For months he had lived the even more remote life of a nomadic Indian, giving little thought to what might be going on in the white man's world.

"Thanks for the information," he told the soldier. *War*, he thought. *What the hell kind of a mess is this country getting itself into?* He had never even heard of Abraham Lincoln. He shook his head in wonder as he trotted his horse to the Pony Express building, dismounting and looping the reins of Dancer's bridle around a hitching post. He walked on long legs into the building, where another sign hung over a desk reading RUSSELL, MAJORS, AND WADDELL. "Morning," he said to a bearded man who sat at the desk.

"Morning," the man answered. "What can I do for you?"

"I'm looking for work. I rode partway here with a man driving a freight wagon, and he told me about the Pony Express. Sounded like something I'd like to do."

The man behind the desk looked him over warily, and Colt didn't think he had ever seen anyone with quite so red a beard. "And why do you think that?" the man asked.

Colt shrugged. "Sounds exciting. I know the country, and I'm a good rider; and right now I need something that will keep me real busy, keep my mind off personal things."

"Like what?"

Colt shifted his hat, revealing part of a fresh scar that began above his right eyebrow and ran down his right temple to his ear. "That's my business. Do you need a rider?"

The bearded man scowled, deciding that from the looks of the tall, strong-looking young man before him, it was best not to pry. "Have a seat," he told Colt, indicating a wooden chair, the varnish worn from its seat. Colt obliged, removing his hat. "My name is John Stanley," the man told him. He rolled up a newspaper and swatted a fly.

"Colt Travis," Colt answered, studying the man's thick reddish eyebrows and the mass of freckles on his aging face and on his arms and hands.

"How old are you, Travis?"

"What's the date?"

Stanley grinned a little, glancing at his calendar. "May 27, 1861."

"Then I was twenty-four seven days ago."

"We generally hire only young boys, some only fifteen, up to about twenty. The less weight, the faster the horse." Stanley pulled open a drawer and took out a wad of tobacco. "And they have to be orphans."

"I was orphaned at fourteen," Colt answered, watching the man put the tobacco in his cheek. "I can assure you there isn't one person in this country who gives a damn whether I live or die. And like you say, it's true less weight makes a faster horse," he added. "But there's also something to be said about experience. I've led wagon trains since I was orphaned—been to Oregon four times, California twice. I've fought Indians and I've lived with them—can communicate with Sioux, Cheyenne, Crow, Blackfoot, Shoshone—" He hesitated, the bitter hatred still burning in his gut. "Pawnee," he finished. "I can shoot straight, even from a galloping horse. I know what to do for wounds, and I know this country like the back of my hand."

Stanley just stared at him a moment, chewing on the tobacco, then turning to spit into a can beside his desk. "You've made your point," he said. "We've lost two riders recently, quit because of being shot at by outlaws looking to steal the mail—probably think there's money in it. At any rate, some have the courage for the job, and some don't. I expect there ain't much that scares off the likes of you. Pay's a hundred and twenty-five a month, but there's no guarantee the job will last long. The government is already building a telegraph line clear across the country. A lot of the more important news will be carried that way after that, so there won't be so much need for us riding hard to carry it. The Butterfield Overland stage line carries mail too, so we figure the job is good for as long as it takes for the telegraph to get finished. After that I expect we'll be out of business."

Colt grinned, slightly embarrassed. "What the hell is a telegraph?"

Stanley smiled in return, turning and spitting again. "Where in hell have you been boy?"

"Someone else already asked me that. Let's just say I've kind of been off alone for quite a while."

"Mmmm-hmmm. Where'd you get that scar?"

"Pawnee. His scalp is tied to my gear."

Stanley chuckled. "Well, ain't you somethin'? No doubt you've got Indian blood. What kind?"

"Cherokee."

"You've got a drawl. I don't want any Confederates working for Russell, Majors, and Waddell."

"I don't even know what a Confederate is, Mr. Stanley. All I can say is I was raised in Oklahoma and Texas."

The man laughed more, shaking his head. "Boy, you really *have* been off alone, haven't you? You know about the war?"

"I just found out about it. The men driving the freight wagon didn't know anything about it either, but then, they were heading west to east. I guess the news hadn't reached them yet."

"Well, a Confederate is somebody who's on the side of the South."

Colt sighed, leaning forward to rest his elbows on his knees. "I don't take *any* side. I don't give a damn about the war, Mr. Stanley. I just want a job that will keep me busy and will let me be alone and travel the country I love."

"Fine." Stanley picked up the newspaper he had used to swat the fly. "Sounds to me like you need to brush up on what's goin' on. Can you read?"

"Yes, sir."

"Well, take that paper there and study on it. It's a few days old, out of Omaha, but you can get an idea of what's been happening. And by the way, a telegraph is a way they've invented to send coded messages clear across the country. You ride a little bit north of here and you'll see the poles, with wire strung across their tops. There will be stations set up all across the country, places where men sit and use an instrument to send messages by something called Morse code. The messages go through the wire by way of what they call electricity. It travels through the wires on the poles on over to another station—takes only seconds, mind you—and that station sends it on to the next and so forth."

Colt ran a hand through his thick hair, his mind swirling with all this new information. "I'll be damned. Electricity, they call it?"

Stanley nodded. "Newspapers say it's the thing of the future, figure someday this electricity will be used all kinds of ways to speed things up and such. Next thing you know, there will be a damn railroad out here. There's talk of it. Can you imagine? A *railroad* that goes clear across the country? I say it can't be done, but now that they're building this telegraph thing, who knows? I'd sure like to see how they think they'll get a railroad over the mountains."

A railroad! The comment brought back memories. It was the first time Colt had thought of Sunny Landers in a very long time. Did her father still plan to build a transcontinental railroad? It had been nearly four years since he had guided them to Fort Laramie.

"Who knows?" he said. "People seem intent on getting themselves to California or Oregon, and going by wagon is still an awfully risky way to go, especially with a family." He remembered how he had first found Lee-Ann, and the sick grief swept over him again. He wondered if it was going to be like this for the rest of his life, these bouts of horrible grief suddenly slamming into him, making all his muscles ache.

"Well, not all of them go on to the coast," Stanley was

saying. "A lot of them are starting to settle right out here. I bet you'd be surprised at how Omaha is growing, and now there's Denver and Cheyenne and Salt Lake City." He shook his head. "Never thought I'd see the day this godforsaken country actually started to fill up with settlers. At any rate, you come back here tomorrow morning and we'll talk about what you need to do, get you started. That all right with you?"

"Fine." Colt rose, picking up the paper. "Thank you."

"Have a good day, Travis."

Colt nodded, turning to take his hat from where he had hung it on the arm of the chair. "Thanks for the paper," he said as he put on his hat. He walked outside to Dancer. "Let's go find a spot of shade, maybe a place where it's a little more quiet, boy."

A wagon clattered past, and in the distance the sound of someone giving an order mingled with the cry of a baby that came from a settler's wagon. It gave Colt a strange feeling to be around the bustling activity of so many people again, after spending months in quiet Indian camps. He wasn't sure he was ready for all of this yet, but he supposed a man had to get back to living sometime, even if it didn't seem there was anything to live for. He took hold of Dancer's reins and led the animal away, heading for a grove of cottonwood trees north of the fort, where he retied the horse to a small tree. Dancer snorted and shook his mane, bending his head down to nibble at some grass.

Colt stepped away from the trees, deciding he'd ride out later to find the telegraph poles Stanley had told him about. He wanted to see the strange invention for himself. He couldn't picture how anything could move through wires, taking only seconds to travel over several miles. He shook his head, wondering what White Buffalo would think of such a thing. He sure wouldn't like to hear what Stanley had just told Colt, about more people coming here to settle.

He sat down with his back against a tree, reading by sunlight. *More States Secede from Union,* one headline read. "Virginia and Arkansas have become the eighth and ninth states to secede from the Union," Colt read aloud. "President Lincoln has called for more volunteers to help end the insurrection that has torn the United States and has now caused casualties. A secessionist mob stoned Union troops in Baltimore, Maryland, killing four men."

Colt shook his head, hardly able to believe what was happening. "Jesus," he muttered. He scanned the paper again, reading article after article about possible all-out, bloody fighting between North and South. He found one article about the progress of the telegraph, another about how the West was growing and how there was talk of a transcontinental railroad. *Congress continues to argue the value and necessity of such a railroad,* the article read, *and the best route, should such a railroad come to be. Now that the South has chosen to withdraw from the Union, it is unlikely that the southern route they have wanted will be used. Mr. Thomas Durant is urging the consideration of Omaha as a starting point for the railroad, but some congressmen claim it should be St. Louis. However, with the clouds of civil war hanging gray and heavy over Congress, it is unlikely there will be a vote on the railroad anytime soon.*

Colt set the paper aside, and began to roll a cigarette. He lit it and leaned his head back, unable to help wondering what LeeAnn would have thought of all these new happenings. Again, her memory brought a very real pain to his stomach. He closed his eyes. Little Ethan would have been a year old now, maybe walking. He had never been able to bring himself to go and see their graves, hadn't even bothered to look for the four hundred dollars he had hidden under a floorboard of the cabin. Retrieving it was not worth having to view the scene of his horrible loss, having to see the burned-out cabin that LeeAnn was once so proud of, where they had made love and shared meals, where Ethan was born.

He had never found Buck or gone back to see if there was anything salvageable. If someone else wanted to settle there, they could have the tools and the plow he

had left behind. He supposed he should go and see Mrs.
Scott someday and tell her what had happened, but he
still couldn't bear talking about it. Maybe he would just
write her a letter. That would be easier than facing her,
for he still had not gotten over his own shame and anger
at feeling LeeAnn's and Ethan's deaths were partly his
fault.

He smoked in silence, wondering how long it was going to take to get over the pain of it, or if maybe that
would never happen. A gentle wind rustled the newspaper, disturbing his thoughts. One page blew over, and as
he grasped the paper to keep it from blowing away, he
caught the name—*Landers*. He frowned, keeping the
cigarette in his mouth as he picked up the paper for a
closer look.

*Miss Sunny Landers, daughter of the late Beauregard
Landers, shipping and railroad magnate of Chicago, Illinois, has been awarded the full inheritance willed to her
upon her father's death January second of this year,* he
read. Colt quickly put out his cigarette. Bo Landers,
dead! What a terrible loss for Sunny. Suddenly, the
memories came flooding back as though that last good-
bye had been only yesterday. *The decision, handed down
by Circuit Court Judge Howard Seymour, ends a bitter
family feud, instigated by Vincent Landers, firstborn son of
Beauregard and half brother to Miss Sunny Landers.*
"Poor Sunny," Colt muttered. *The contested will has
been settled, leaving Miss Landers full ownership of the
B&L Rail Road, a major stockholder of the Illinois Central and the Chicago and Rock Island Railroads, and 75
percent stockholder of Landers Enterprises, the parent
company for the family's several subsidiaries as well as
another 40 percent stock in all subsidiary companies. Also
in the award is the family home, a mansion on Lake
Michigan valued at one hundred thousand dollars, ownership of all property on which Landers Enterprises and its
subsidiaries are located, vacant land that borders two
miles of Lake Michigan shoreline, and stock in the Pacific
Railroad Company, plus an undisclosed but reportedly
substantial sum of money held in trust. Landers's sons,*

Vincent and Stuart, will retain their major stock in Landers Great Lakes Shipping, Landers Warehousing, Landers Overland Freighting, and Landers Supply. A picture of the first Mrs. Landers and some of her jewelry was awarded to Vincent Landers and was not argued by Miss Sunny Landers.

The court's decision ends a four-month struggle by Miss Landers to have the will administered according to her father's wishes, and it leaves her one of the richest women in the country, and one with extraordinary power for a female only nineteen years of age. Miss Landers has gone into seclusion at the family home and was unavailable for comment, but it is rumored that when she reenters society, she will carry on her father's campaign for a transcontinental railroad, in which Landers had invested heavily. It is well known that Miss Landers and her father were close to President Lincoln, who has made it known publicly that he favors such a railroad, but no bill for such a project is expected to be passed anytime soon.

Colt let out a soft whistle. Sunny Landers was a very, very rich lady, and only nineteen. What a burden her father had placed on her! And what a horror it must have been, having to go up against her brother and fight to keep what had been given to her. He remembered when she and Bo and Stuart had talked about the older brother, Vincent. Sunny had seemed almost afraid of him. What kind of hell had he put her through, and all the while she must have been grieving so deeply over her father. He was all she had ever known, her protector, apparently the only one in the family who had loved her the way she deserved to be loved.

How well he understood grief and loneliness. He wondered if she ever thought about him anymore, if she still kept that journal. His heart went out to her for her loss. It was difficult enough to lose one's father under any circumstances, but to be left with such tremendous responsibilities could only be an added strain, especially on a woman so young.

He reread the article, noticing that apparently only Vincent had contested the will. At least she didn't have both brothers against her, a small consolation in the midst of such responsibilities. He wished there were something he could do to help console her. He wondered if he should write her, express his concern over her loss. Maybe she would like hearing from him. Then again, maybe she had practically forgotten him.

Chapter 9

"Are you sure you're ready to go out and face the world, Miss Sunny?" Mae finished pinning a straw hat to Sunny's hair.

"I don't have much choice." Sunny turned to look into the mirror, hardly able to believe the image she saw reflected there. She had lost weight, too much weight, and the circles under her eyes could not be hidden by powders. Losing her father had been cause for enough grief, but Vince's contesting of the will had not only dragged her through public attention and court appearances that put a temporary stop to any control she had over her railroad holdings and Landers Enterprises. The turmoil Vince had caused had left her no time to truly grieve. She had spent the month since the court's decision in seclusion, taking the time she needed to weep, to think, to pray. She wondered if she would have survived at all if not for Vi's kind support and their long talks.

She had visited her father's grave many times, praying that somehow he would visit her in spirit and help her know what to do. She had a big job ahead of her, and she still struggled with depression. Her doctor had given her a special tonic to take twice a day, and Stuart had promised to help as much as he could, but he also had the responsibility of running his own companies, and he had a family who needed him. He could not go running off with her to Washington whenever it was necessary, and she knew he probably wouldn't be much help there anyway. A person had to be aggressive and he had to know what he was talking about. Stuart still knew little about the railroad. He had not bothered to try to learn.

"Well, today I begin playing the part of Bo Landers," she told Mae. She rose and turned. "A slight difference in size, wouldn't you say?"

Mae smiled sadly. "Only physically. I've seen you stand up to the worst of them, Miss Sunny, and I'll bet facing congressmen and fellow businessmen won't be half as hard as having to face that cruel brother of yours and his witch of a wife." She gasped, her eyes widening. "Pardon me! I shouldn't have said that about your family."

Sunny smiled. "What you said isn't half as bad as what I'm thinking about them, so don't worry." She took a deep breath. "Leave me alone for a few minutes, will you, Mae?"

The young woman nodded. "Good luck, Miss Sunny."

"Thank you."

Mae left and Sunny walked across an Oriental rug to the library table she kept at the front window of her bedroom. She took out her journal, opening it to a new page. She sat down in the ornate cabriole chair kept at the desk, she picked up her pen, and dipped it into an inkwell.

Today I go out to face the world, she wrote. *Actually, this is my first day of official business since Father died five months ago. I think I am strong enough now. In a few days I will travel to New York and Washington to get back to lobbying for the railroad. I hope those who were working*

*on a railroad bill have not given up. With the country in
full civil war, I fear the task ahead is great.*

*My grief will always be with me, but each day it gets a
little easier. Writing these entries helps me cope.*

She set aside the pen, deciding to wait and write more
after her first board meeting as chairman of Landers
Enterprises. She thumbed back through some of her
first entries, seldom able to open the journal without
going back to the passages about her trip west. How she
longed at the moment for the peace and beauty she had
known there! It seemed strange, with all she had suffered and lost on that journey, that she should remember it so fondly. In her grief she had discovered that
thoughts of the beautiful land and the mountains were a
great comfort.

She closed the journal, deciding this was not a time
for daydreaming or longing for what could not be. She
walked back to the mirror and checked herself once
more. Her hat was trimmed with dark brown velvet ribbon and no flowers. Her dress was relatively plain, white
poplin with a carter's frock draped apronlike over a
dark brown and white striped sateen underskirt. White
lace trim decorated the cuffs and high neckline of the
dark brown bodice of the dress. She would rather have
worn something with shorter sleeves and a lower neckline because of the July heat, but today she wanted to
look as businesslike and proper as possible, no frills,
nothing to make her look too feminine. It was going to
be difficult enough to garner the respect of the other
board members, who now must look to her for final
decisions.

She picked up her handbag, turning and looking at
the canopied four-poster, wanting to run back to it and
hide out for another day; but there was work to be done.
She thought of how strong and energetic her father had
always been, what he would expect of her now. It was
time to carry on.

She marched out the door and down the stairs, saying
good-bye to Mae. There was no room for tears or
doubt. She had a job to do. She just prayed she would
have the strength to do it. She walked to the waiting

open carriage, smiling at the driver, an old black man called Page.

"Mornin', Miss Landers." Page opened the carriage door.

"Good morning, Page." Sunny climbed inside, situating the skirt of her dress as she settled into the freshly cleaned leather seat.

"Glad to see you're finally up and about. You're too young to keep yourself cooped up in that big ol' house all alone."

Page closed the door and climbed up into the driver's seat. Sunny liked the graying man, whose eyes always showed respect, even now. It seemed most of her help was kinder to her than her own family. "Take me to the office, Page," she said.

"Yes, ma'am." He snapped the reins, getting the shiny black mare that pulled the carriage into motion. "Fine day, isn't it?"

Sunny studied the manicured lawns and gardens of neighboring mansions. "Yes, it is." She studied the man a moment from behind, realizing she didn't know much about him in spite of all the years he had worked for her father. She knew he had four grown children and he and his family lived in a little brick house near the stables on the Landers estate. "Page, tell me, what do you think of this war? Were you ever a slave?"

"No, ma'am," he answered, watching the road ahead. "My father was, though, before I was born. He worked for a good man who gave him his freedom papers, and he came up here right off because he was afraid some other slaver would catch him and destroy his papers. He met my mama down by St. Louis and they came up here —had his own little farm north of Chicago. Me, I came to the city to find work, only had a couple other jobs before I started working for your father thirty years ago. Far as the war, fighting is always a bad thing, especially when it's among a country's own people. I expect those in the South think they have a right to defend their way of life, but from the things my father used to tell me about how slaves got treated on other farms that he knew of, if it takes a war to end it, then I guess we've got to have one. I just thank the Lord that most all the fighting will be in the South and not up here."

"Yes, I suppose we can be grateful for that much. I just hope it's over with soon. It's frightening to think of people in the same country fighting each other."

"Some folks say it's going to get mighty ugly before it's over."

Sunny shivered, deciding to change the subject. She was not ready to think about this war. "Thirty years is a long time," she told Page. "Didn't you ever want to do anything else besides drive for my father?"

"No, ma'am. Your father was always good to me. I like this job just fine, and I've got a nice house to go along with it."

Sunny realized as she watched him that while her father was alive, she had never questioned how or why others had come into the Landers employ. Even his business associates were simply people that had always been in Bo Landers's life. Now she would find out who had been kind to her out of sincerity, and who had only been kowtowing to Bo Landers because of his wealth and power. She did not look forward to this day, but seeing to her father's wishes had to start sometime, and no day was going to be a good day for it.

The carriage clattered over the brick streets, and Sunny caught the smell of the lake in the air. She had spent many long days sitting on the bluff looking out at Lake Michigan, sometimes imagining that the rolling waves were the rolling grasslands of Nebraska, or speculating what it might be like to sail across that lake and never come back.

She nodded to a few people who recognized her, thinking about what the general public might be saying about her—that she was a spoiled brat, that she was the one who had created problems over the will, that she had talked her father into giving her practically everything, made sure the rest of the family got cheated out of their fair share.

She decided to let them think what they wanted. She had never asked to be given so much, and she had worked hard at her father's side to learn all that she knew. She was the only one who had believed in his dreams, the only one who would make sure those dreams got finished.

"Page, I never thought to ask you, but you must have known my mother, didn't you?"

The man was silent for a moment. "Yes, ma'am," he finally answered.

"What was she like? Was she as beautiful as in the painting in our house?"

"No painting could do her justice," he answered. "And she was right kind to everybody."

To Sunny's dismay, she realized how little she knew about her mother's heritage or past. While her father was alive, she had never asked anyone else about the woman, since her father was always right there to answer all her questions. Who better to ask than Bo Landers? It never seemed necessary to ask anyone else, and she always felt that her jealous brothers would not have told her the truth anyway.

Still, she realized now that her father had never told her much, except that he had all but worshipped the woman, who had brought him new joy and vitality. She had no doubt whatsoever that they had loved each other very much. As far as personals about her mother, she knew only that Bo had met her in New York. He had told her that the woman's parents were dead and she had no brothers or sisters. Her maiden name was Madison, Lucille Madison, a beautiful woman in a lovely painting who had never held her, whose touch Sunny had never felt. She wished she could hear her voice just once.

She remained quietly lost in thought as Page headed the carriage into town. She could not help being nervous, wondering now if she was ready for this. The carriage pulled up in front of the seven-story Landers Enterprises building, the tallest building in Chicago. Page climbed down and opened the carriage door, helping her out. "You go get 'em, Miss Sunny," he told her with a grin.

Sunny smiled. "Thank you, Page. I needed to hear that. Be back here at four o'clock, will you?"

Page nodded, and Sunny faced the front door, holding her chin high and taking a deep breath before walking inside, where she greeted secretaries and managers. She sensed their smiles were false, felt a few accusing looks. She ignored them, deciding that in time she would win them all over. She thought how strange it was that when her father was alive and she was just "Bo's daughter," everyone was kind to her. Now that everything belonged to her, there came the jealousy and the gossip. Only one of the several young women she had once called friends had bothered to come and see her the last few weeks, and Sunny suspected even that visit was out of curiosity. *Some thought you had lost your mind and would never return to society,* Helen Graves had told her, looking her over as though she were something dangerous and insane.

Now they know I have returned, she thought, glad now she had not warned anyone she would be in today. Catching them by surprise helped her get an idea of how they truly felt. If they knew she was coming, they might be ready with flowers and falsely kind greetings.

She entered the elevator, never ceasing to be amazed at the new steam-powered invention her father had had installed just last year. After riding in such a contraption in New York City, he had promptly decided that the Landers Enterprises building must have one, and what Bo Landers wanted, Bo Landers got. She hoped she would be able to deal with people with the same authority.

She reached the top floor, pushing open the elevator gate and stepping into the hall. Her heart ached when she stared at the door to her father's spacious office. BO LANDERS was still painted on the glass of the outer door. She touched it lovingly, forcing back tears as she stepped inside the secretary's office. Thirty-two-year-old Tod Russell jumped to his feet in surprise. "Miss Landers! You're here!"

Sunny watched him closely, seeing the confusion and sudden defense in his eyes. Tod had worked for her father for twelve years, through a marriage and two children. He was good at what he did, a loyal employee who was paid well.

"In the flesh," she answered. "I sent a messenger out last night to all the board members that I'm calling a meeting today. I guess I should have told you too. I'm sorry, Tod. Would you prepare the boardroom, make sure there are ashtrays, coffee, and all? We aren't meeting until ten o'clock, so there's plenty of time. I'd like you to fill me in on what's been going on. Stuart says that you and he and Vince have been able to keep things going reasonably well, but there must be certain things that need attention right away." She headed for the door to her father's office. "If it weren't for all the legal problems Vincent gave me, I could have attended to these things much sooner. Heaven only knows what Vince has managed to deliberately ruin during all of this."

She hesitated at the door, realizing Tod had not spoken or made a move. She turned to look at him, and he stood staring at her strangely. He was a short, rather stocky man with looks as plain as a door. Tod was all business, usually prompt, efficient, scurrying; but he was making no moves at the moment. "Is something wrong, Tod?"

His eyes moved over her strangely, showing none of the pleasant welcome he had always given her when she came here with her father. "Well, I, uh, I've been handling a lot of things alone, Miss Landers, and I've had all this time to think; but I, well, you surprised me before I had a chance to decide."

"Decide what?"

"Well, I'm just not sure I can work for you. I mean, to work for a woman is bad enough, but your age. I mean, how would it look, a man my age taking orders from an unmarried nineteen-year-old woman?"

Sunny's blue eyes blazed with the affront. "I am the same Sunny Landers who has always been coming here, Tod, the same one you used to greet with a smile. You took orders from me when my father was alive, so what is the difference?"

He reddened slightly, touching a sideburn nervously.

"But everybody knew then that Bo was the real boss. You were just, I don't know, just Sunny."

"Well, I'm not *just* Sunny anymore! If it helps, you can think of me as my father." She faced him more fully, putting her hands to her waist. "I am not entirely happy with the tremendous burden all of this means for me, Tod, but if you had any respect for my father, then you should respect his choice as to who should be his successor. You know perfectly well that I am capable of carrying on in his place."

She took a deep breath to boost her courage, hooking the strings of her purse over her arm and removing her white gloves finger by finger. "I suppose the decision is yours, Tod, but I will remind you that this has always been a good-paying job. You have been able to provide for your family well because of it. If it helps your pride any, I will give you a ten dollar a week raise. I have far too much to do to have to worry about breaking in someone new. It would be a great help to me if you stayed on." She held his gaze, deciding to play up to his pride. "In all honesty, I need you. I don't think anyone else could handle the job nearly as well as you."

She saw his eyes soften a little. "Well, thank you," he said almost humbly. "I didn't mean any offense, Miss Landers. You have to admit it's a rather strange situation for me."

"I can see where it might be, but you will find me all business, Tod, just as eager to get to what needs doing as my father would be. In fact, I want you to make arrangements for me for a trip to New York in three days. It *is* still safe to travel by train to the east, isn't it? I'm afraid I haven't kept abreast of what is happening with the war."

"Not much has happened yet, except that eleven southern states have now seceded, and General Robert E. Lee resigned from the army and will join the rebels. That's, uh, that's what northerners are calling the southerners. Poor President Lincoln has walked into an awful political mess, I'm afraid. As far as travel goes, there is nothing dangerous in it so far."

"Good, then I will be going to New York."

"Yes, ma'am. By the way, there is some recent mail on your father's—I mean, your desk. There is one there from Thomas Durant. I just thought you should be aware of it."

"Fine." Sunny opened her purse and put her gloves inside.

"And thank you, Miss Landers, for the raise. I wasn't asking for one."

"I know that, but you probably deserve it." Sunny put her hand on the knob of the door that led into her father's office. "And you always called me Sunny before, Tod."

"I know. But now that you're my boss, I just feel better calling you Miss Landers."

Sunny closed her eyes in exasperation. "Whatever suits you." She opened the door to her father's office.

"Miss Landers—"

She turned, meeting Tod's eyes expectantly. "Yes?"

"I, uh, I'm awful sorry about your father. He was always real good to me. I wanted to talk to you at the funeral, but, well, you were pretty bad off. I've done some grieving of my own."

The pain returned to Sunny's stomach. She still remembered so little about the funeral. "Yes, thank you," she told Tod.

He shook his head. "In spite of feeling strange working for you, I do want to compliment your courage, Miss Landers. I can't help wondering what the business world will think, dealing with a young woman."

"They'll just have to get used to it, I guess."

Sunny turned and went into her father's office, closing the door and leaning against it. She reminded herself that this room was hers now, and it gave her the shivers. She gathered her courage and walked across the deep green plush carpeting, and immediately the memories came flooding over her, the lingering smell of cigar smoke making them even sharper and more painful. She could almost see Bo Landers sitting behind the huge mahogany desk. "Lord, help me," she whimpered. The room was cool, and dark as a tomb. It made her shiver, and she hurried over to jerk open the green velvet drapes that hung at three huge windows, letting in the morning light.

Since the room was on the seventh floor, it was sheltered from the noise of the streets below. The only sound was the quiet ticking of a grandfather clock that stood in one corner. Sunny felt surrounded by Bo Landers, wished she were little again and could sit on his lap and let him take care of everything. Tears stung her eyes at the hurt of it, and she decided she would redecorate the office in a more feminine way. She couldn't bear to come in here every day with so much of her father in everything she saw and touched. She looked up at the painting of her at ten years old that still hung behind his desk. That would have to come down. Maybe she would replace it with a painting of a locomotive. That would be more fitting.

Mustering her courage, she moved behind the desk and sat in the huge leather chair. The chair too, would have to be replaced. It simply did not fit her small frame. She felt lost in it. She blinked back tears and picked up the mail, thumbing through it, seeing the letter from Thomas Durant and setting it aside.

The door opened then, and she looked up to see Stuart standing there. She smiled softly. Over the past weeks, because of the close relationship she had developed with Vi, she had inadvertently grown closer to Stuart, who had been surprisingly kind since Bo's death. "Most people knock first," she said, teasingly as she stood up.

"I would have, except that I was so surprised to hear you had come in already. I didn't think you'd be here before nine." He walked closer. "You sure you're ready for this, Sunny?"

"Is there ever a right time for these things?"

He looked her over with a smile. "You've got to put on some weight. And your eyes—you look terrible."

"Thank you," she said with a mock smile.

"You know what I mean. Vince will hit you with everything he's got right off. He's out to break you, Sunny. He's been talking to everybody on the board about how they can get around you, telling them how you'll need all kinds of help, how a girl of nineteen can't handle this."

"I can handle it, and I can handle Vince. I've already proven that. If the others don't want to cooperate, I'll buy them all out if I have to. I wonder how Vince would like it if I bought up the eleven percent investor-owned portions of the shipping and warehousing? That would give me fifty-one percent ownership, and Vince only forty-nine percent. Maybe the threat of *that* would shut him up."

Stuart grinned. "I can see you've already thought about how to handle him."

"When it comes to Vince, it's necessary to try to stay one step ahead. If he does anything to block my railroad investments or anything else to do with Father's dreams of a transcontinental railroad, he will regret it."

Stuart smiled and shook his head. "By God, you *are* a chip off the old block."

Sunny sat down again, suddenly weary. She leaned back, the big chair dwarfing her. "Why does he hate me so, Stuart? Is it just the money? It seems like the hatred is directed right at me, like he'd hate me even if he *had* gotten what he wanted in the will."

Stuart shrugged, averting her eyes. How would she feel if she knew the truth about her mother? "Vince isn't really as bad as you think. And he doesn't hate you. I guess he just, I don't know, resents you, I guess. He knows nothing is really your fault, but it's just easiest to take it all out on you. He and Dad haven't gotten along for years. That's just the way it is. I don't know how to change it. You know I kind of resented you myself, but Vi has taught me a lot about tolerance and such. It's hard to live with her and remain a ruthless businessman."

Sunny smiled again. "I can understand, and I'm glad you married her. I don't know what I would have done without her help these past months. I know Vince makes things hard on you and Vi too, Stuart. Maybe we can help each other."

He leaned over her desk, and Sunny noticed he seemed to get a little balder every day. "Well, that's part of the reason I came in here—to tell you I'll help all I can. Are you keeping Tod as a secretary?"

"I have to. He knows too much, and he's too efficient; but he told me straight out he didn't like the thought of working for a woman. I'm afraid I had to bribe him with a raise to get him to stay."

Stuart laughed lightly and straightened again. "He'll get used to the idea. Besides, who wouldn't want to work for someone as sweet and beautiful as you?"

"A lot of people," she answered sarcastically, "all male."

He waved her off. "There might be a few stubborn ones, but you'll win them over. I have no doubt that in six months time they'll all be eating out of your hand. So will those men in Washington. You can charm them into giving you any vote you want." He headed for the door. "I'll give you some time to get ready. We'll get things set up in the boardroom."

"Thanks, Stuart."

He left, and Sunny put her head back for a moment, glad she had at least one brother on her side. She picked up the rest of her mail and quickly thumbed through it, deciding most of it could be read later, except for Durant's letter. She was about to set it all aside when she noticed an unusual return address. She studied it closer, her eyes widening with shock. "Travis, Pony Express, Fort Kearny, Nebraska."

"Travis," she whispered. Colt? It seemed impossible. A prickly chill moved over her as she quickly tore open the envelope, pulling out the folded letter. It was written on plain, cheap paper, and the penmanship was a little shaky. She smiled at the thought of how little opportunity such a man had to write at all, and she was impressed with the apparent effort at neatness. But why on earth had he written her after four years?

Hello, Sunny, she read. *Please excuse the handwriting. It's been a long, long time since I had to write anything. I guess you must remember me. I'm the man who scouted for you and your father when you came west back in '57.*

Immediately, the old girlish flutter returned, and she

smiled. "How could I forget you, Colt Travis?" she said softly. She read on.

I am writing because I only recently read in an Omaha newspaper about your father's death and something about trouble with your brother over the will. It's too bad he had to cause you trouble when you are in so much sorrow. I remember how much your father meant to you, and you still aren't all that old. I remember and understand the grief and have had more grief of my own. I will not burden you with the details. Just want you to know someone is thinking about you. I remember you as a very strong woman, so I expect you will get through your sorrow and do a good job handling your father's estate. I would never want the job myself, but if anybody is made for it, you are.

I am currently riding for the Pony Express, so if you would want to answer my letter, just write me in care of them at Fort Kearny. I don't have any kind of home right now. I ride between Fort Kearny and Fort Laramie and sleep at either place or at stations in between. I actually settled once, a real wife and a house and everything. Can you believe that? But I am alone again now, and I suppose that's the way it's supposed to be.

I just wanted to express my sorrow and remind you that somebody way out here in the Wild West thinks about you. You don't have to write back. You're a busy lady. Just want to tell you to stay strong and keep faith.

An old friend, Colt Travis.

She read the letter again, hardly able to believe he had written to her. He had apparently not lied about being taught well. Every word was spelled right. She wondered what he meant about having more grief of his own. He had settled once, but now he was alone again. What had happened to his wife? She sensed tragedy between the lines, and her heart ached for him. Suddenly, it seemed only yesterday that she had told him good-bye.

She set the letter aside, rising and walking to a west window, looking out at the horizon, wishing she had the time to go back out to the land she had never forgotten, wondering what Colt looked like now, wondering if he, too, needed a friend.

Someone knocked lightly on the door, bringing her back to reality. "Everything is ready in the boardroom, Miss Landers," came Tod's voice. She thought how much easier it might be to ride for the Pony Express and face Indians and outlaws and the elements than to have to face the board of Landers Enterprises.

"Tod."

"Yes?"

"Get me some stationery, would you? I want to write a letter right away."

"Yes, ma'am."

Tod left, and Sunny sat down again, glancing at the letter from Durant. She picked it up and opened it.

Dear Miss Landers, I again express my deepest sympathy for your loss, a loss felt by many, many people, including myself. I am sorry if I am speaking too soon, but it is vitally important for me to know if you intend to continue your father's work in support of the Pacific Railroad Company, now that the problems over your inheritance have been settled.

Mr. C. P. Huntington, part owner of the Central Pacific out of California, is making his own efforts at a transcontinental railroad, and we must stay on top of this or the Central Pacific will be awarded the rights all to itself. I have managed to get a bill introduced into Congress for our own railroad, to be called the Union Pacific; but with a war going on, there now is a problem with rising costs. I have discovered that the price of rails has soared from $55 a ton to $115! I am still having trouble convincing investors to buy stock in the Union Pacific, and Huntington is having the same problems, so he is not ahead of us yet. There is so much to discuss. Please contact me at your earliest opportunity and let me know if I can depend on your continued support.

Again, my deepest sympathies, and my apologies for interrupting you in a time of sorrow; however, time is of the essence, and your beautiful, charming presence could have a great effect on influencing certain congressmen who were close to your father. I feel a vote will be taken in the next few months, and we must work together to make sure a railroad bill is passed.

A sincere friend, Thomas Durant.

She set the letter aside and leaned back in the chair again, thinking what a contrast the two letters were, representative of the two places in her heart. One place was more like a fantasy, the other, naked reality. Tod came back inside and laid some stationery on her desk.

"Send a wire to Mr. Durant telling him I will be arriving in about four days," she told him. "I'm glad I had already decided to go and try to meet with him. His letter says it's urgent that I do so." She sighed. "I just hope I haven't been away from things so long that I have hurt the political work for the railroad."

"I'll send the wire," Tod told her, leaving her again.

Sunny picked up the blank envelope he had brought her. "First things first," she muttered. *Mr. Colt Travis,* she wrote, *c/o Pony Express, Fort Kearny, Nebraska.*

Chapter 10

Colt waited while the mail was sorted. At Fort Kearny it had to be checked to make sure which mail went on to Fort Laramie. At Laramie it was checked again for what would be ridden into Cheyenne and Denver and what would go on to Fort Bridger and beyond.

"I'll be damned," Stanley said to him, pulling at his red beard. "Here's one for you. Who the hell do you know in Chicago, boy?"

Colt took the letter. "Sunny," he said quietly. He looked at Stanley. "Just an old acquaintance, somebody I helped guide to Fort Laramie a few years back."

"Well, you'll have to finish your run before you read it. Time's wastin'." The man shoved the necessary mail into the rainproof Pony Express pouch, and Colt slid Sunny's letter inside his buckskin shirt. He grabbed the bags and hurried outside, slinging the bags over the front of his saddle. He mounted the horse in one swift, graceful movement, quickly tying a rawhide cord around the mail bags before riding off at a hard gallop on one of the many swift ponies owned by Russell, Majors, and Waddell.

The journey began, a job he had grown to love and wished would not end when the telegraph was finished. The constant riding of the past weeks, the danger, the responsibility, all had helped him keep his thoughts from painful memories. He charged across the Nebraska Plains, quickly leaving the fort behind, enjoying the feel of the wind in his face.

Sometimes he thought riding hard was just another outlet for his anger, as though he could run from the memories by riding as hard and fast as possible. There had even been times when he screamed, letting go of the reins and opening his arms, begging God to just strike him down and end his agony.

He galloped over soft sod, sometimes following the ever-lengthening telegraph lines. He touched his pocket, making sure Sunny's letter was still there, hardly able to believe she had written back to him. It made him ride even harder, eager to get to the end of his run so he could read it. It gave him a good feeling to know that somewhere there was one person who remembered him and cared enough to answer a letter. How strange that someone who lived in a city like Chicago, someone who could probably buy the whole city, should write to a lonely drifter with nothing more to his name than his horse and the hundred and twenty-five dollars he had made so far riding for the Pony Express.

It was the first of August, and terribly hot and humid. Already his horse was lathered, the constant run hard on an animal in such weather. The relay stations were set up every ten to fifteen miles so that it took only fifteen to twenty minutes to reach the next station, where he would get a fresh horse.

Man and horse rose and fell with the undulating hills, one small dot against the massive landscape of green and yellow. Colt leaned into the wind, smiling at the thought of Sunny writing to him. He tried to guess how long he had ridden—ten minutes? Fifteen? He couldn't be far from the next station.

Suddenly, he heard a gunshot. His horse whinnied and stumbled forward. Colt was catapulted out of the saddle, his body rolling head over heels for several yards until it landed against a small boulder. Colt cried out with the jolt. He lay stunned for a moment, trying to gather his thoughts. He thought he heard someone give out a yell, and he knew he was in grave danger, although he remained too confused to realize at first what was happening.

He managed to sit up and look around. Five men were riding hard down a far hill, obviously after the mail. He scooted around behind the boulder, wincing at a vicious pain in his ribs. His saw his horse lying in the distance, bleeding from the shoulder but snorting and kicking. The mail bags were still secured to the saddle.

Colt quickly drew one of his two revolvers, sweat pouring from him because of his pain, combined with the intense heat. These men were out to kill, he had no doubt, and his duty was to protect the mail. He hunched his shoulder and wiped perspiration from his forehead so that it would not sting his eyes; then he took careful aim, waiting until they drew close enough that he could not miss. Every shot had to count, since the boulder behind which he crouched was not nearly big enough to hide him completely.

He fired, and a man cried out, his body jerking back and tumbling from his horse. Colt fired again, and a second man came crashing down, horse and all. Colt flattened himself to the ground when the remaining men returned fire, their bullets making little zinging noises when they hit the rock. He rolled to his knees, again firing. A third man cussed and grabbed his arm.

"Let's get the hell out of here!" one of them yelled.

Colt shot the hat off another.

"Goddamn sonofabitch!" the man cried out. "You said they was just kids!"

"Drop your weapons before you're all dead!" Colt shouted.

A couple of the men raised their arms. "He ain't no kid," one of them grumbled.

"Let us pick up our friends' bodies," another called out.

"The murdering bastards can lie right where they are!" Colt quickly switched his second, fully-loaded pistol to his right hand, holstering the first pistol and getting to his feet. He held the revolver steady. "Drop your weapons like I said, and get down off your horses!" The three men looked at one another hesitantly. "Try firing at me again, and one of you will join your dead partners. Which one wants to take that chance?"

"Jesus Christ," one of them muttered, climbing down from his horse. He threw his gun aside, and the other two followed suit.

Colt continued to keep a steady aim on them, ordering them to walk a considerable distance from their weapons. He eased himself over to his horse. "Sorry, boy," he said, hating to see the animal suffer. He lowered the pistol and shot the horse in the head, and the three men jumped in fright. The horse gasped for a couple of seconds, then shuddered in death. Colt again aimed the pistol at the outlaws as he quickly untied the mail bags, then walked over to the other horse that had stumbled. He could tell without touching it that a leg was broken. He fired again, killing the second horse, and the men cussed and backed away more.

Colt slung the bags over the saddle of one of the other outlaws' horses, then mounted the animal, the pain in his ribs bringing even more perspiration. "Let's go," he told the three remaining men.

"Go where?"

"To the next station. You three get to walk."

"But it's another two or three miles! It must be a hundred degrees out here!"

"The heat didn't stop you from waiting out here and trying to kill me and rob the U. S. Mail. Now, start walking! Once we get to the next station I'll see about getting you back to Fort Kearny. The soldiers will take care of you from there. And walk fast, or I'll shoot to wound and leave you sitting in the heat! I've got mail to deliver, and I've got no sympathy for a man who tries to kill me!"

"What about the wound in my arm?" one of them asked. "I'm bleedin' bad."

"You break my heart," Colt told him.

"What about our friends?"

"They're resting in peace. Maybe soldiers from the fort will come out and bury them." Colt grasped the reins of two other horses. The fifth horse had run off. "Get moving," he told the three men. "I can't trust you not to ride off on me if I let you use your horses."

"Goddamn bastard!" one of them grumbled.

"Looks like a goddamn Indian to me," another muttered. "No wonder he ain't got no feelin's."

For the next hour and a half the men marched on aching feet to the next station.

"You're late!" the attendant called out. "What the hell you got there?"

"Thieving murderers!" Colt called back. "You got another man who can go on from here? I think I've got a couple of cracked ribs. They shot my horse, and I took one hell of a fall."

The man hurried inside, coming back out with a rifle and another man as well as a boy Colt recognized as Dave Hicks, only seventeen. Dave ran over and grabbed the mail bags. "Glad you're all right, Colt," the young man told him. He rushed over to a waiting fresh horse, throwing the bags over the saddle and riding off. The attendant herded the three outlaws inside the station, which was nothing more than a log-and-mud hut, and the second man, a Pony Express employee named Matt Willett, helped Colt dismount.

"Come on inside and I'll wrap your ribs."

"I have something else I want to do first," Colt answered. "Later on you can help me herd those three back to Fort Kearny and let the soldiers take care of them. I've also got to pick up my gear that's still out there."

"Sure, Colt, but you don't look too good. You'd better let me take care of those ribs."

"I'll be all right. I just won't be able to take a deep

breath for a while." He walked over to a wash bucket next to the station and splashed some of the cool water onto his face. "Just give me a minute. I've got a letter to read." He took a towel from a hook on the side of the building and wiped it over his face and through his hair, then draped it around his neck, walking to a stool on the shaded end of the building.

He sat down gingerly, taking a cigarette paper from his front pocket and some tobacco from the leather pouch on his belt, rolling a cigarette and lighting it. The pain hit him again when he tried to take a deep drag from the smoke. He grunted, keeping the cigarette between his lips as he pulled Sunny's letter from his pocket. He had sweated so much that the ink on the envelope had run into an illegible blur, and he worried that the letter would also be unreadable, but to his relief the letter was dry and the writing was clear.

Dear Colt, he read. *So, you're riding for the Pony Express. How exciting! Is it dangerous?* He could not suppress a laugh, in spite of the pain it brought him. It hit him then that it had been a very long time since he had laughed. It had taken only one opening line from Sunny Landers, and he remembered how he once thought she truly fit her name. He wondered what her personality was like now, since losing her father and taking on the responsibility of Landers Enterprises. Was she still the same young woman, full of so much life and determination? Did she smile anymore?

I have no trouble picturing you riding across the Plains with the mail, he read on. *I suppose it is fitting work for a man like you, but I am concerned about your remark that you have suffered your own grief. You said that you had married but that you are alone again. You must tell me what happened. You wrote to tell me that you share my sorrow, but you must also let others share yours.* His smile faded as the ugly memories returned. How could he tell her, knowing that it was partly his fault?

I thank you so much for remembering me and writing to express your sympathy. This has all been very hard for me, and I am just today getting back to the work of carrying on in my father's footsteps. I never thought this would all be left to me at such a young age. Father was always so big and strong. It is a terrible thing to watch your father, the pillar of your life, waste away into death. It seems so unfair for someone like Bo Landers to die that way, but then, my sister-in-law Vi has tried to help me understand that death is just a part of life.

Yes, I will continue Father's work toward a transcontinental railroad, even though the rest of my family and the board members of our various companies are against it. I promised Father I would carry on the dream, and already there is a bill being reviewed by Congress in support of just such a railroad. I will be traveling to Washington soon to do what I can to get the required votes.

Our biggest problem at the moment is the war and the rising costs of material. It will be difficult to get funding, as most industrialists are more concerned with the money they can earn from making supplies for the war than investing in a railroad they think can never be built. For such men money comes above all things, and we who want the railroad will have our work cut out for us in getting others to invest. After all these years of trying, we still have only a few hundred thousand dollars toward the railroad, and most of that has come from our own pockets.

Colt grinned again. "Only a few hundred thousand dollars, huh?" He shook his head. "Just a drop in the bucket." He thought how he risked his life daily for a hundred and twenty-five dollars a month.

So, here I am, preparing to go into my first board meeting as chairman of Landers Enterprises while you ride horses across the Plains, fighting Indians and such. Our lives are a fine contrast, aren't they?

Do write me again. You have no idea how welcome your letter was. It really brightened my day, and I need all the help I can get. Somehow, thinking of you doing brave things out there in that wild land gives me more courage to face my own daily life. Believe it or not, I face dangers too, but they are not the kind a man can see, or feel physically. When you are young and a woman, and you have just inherited a fortune, you have many enemies; but Father trained me well, and I know what to watch for and who to trust.

*Thank you so much for your letter, and for remembering
me. How could you think I would not remember you? I
still have my journal from our trip west, and I often open it
and read it. Somehow it comforts me to think of that beautiful land and the peace I felt there. I don't blame you for
loving it and wanting nothing more than to do exactly what
you are doing. Some of us have duties handed to us in life
that we might not really want, but we do them anyway,
because it's right and necessary. I am old enough now to
know the difference between fantasy and reality, and my
reality is right here in Chicago.*

*If you ever have reason to come this way, you must visit
me. You would always be welcome. Just look up Landers
Enterprises, and anyone there can tell you where my home
is. Just because four years have gone by, and we live in two
different worlds, doesn't mean we can't remain friends.
Right now I could use a pen pal who has nothing to do with
my daily life here. I will be very upset if you don't write
back.*

God bless you and keep you safe. Sincerely, Sunny.

Colt folded the letter, managing to take another deep
drag on the cigarette in spite of his pain. He tried to
picture himself visiting Sunny in her mansion of a home,
and the thought made him grin again.

He stomped out his cigarette and stood up, shoving
the letter into the pocket of his denim pants, afraid if he
put it back into his shirt it would get wet. He wondered
what others would think if he told them he was corresponding with Sunny Landers, one of the richest women
in the country. They would probably laugh and call him
a liar, and he wouldn't blame them one bit. He decided
it was best to keep this one to himself.

All ten men at the round table in Thomas Durant's elegant boardroom rose respectfully when Sunny walked
into the room. Some literally gawked. In spite of the
wealth they all represented, and the beautiful women
such men were accustomed to associating with, Sunny
was still a sight to behold. How many nineteen-year-old

women held so much power, as well as being so stunningly attractive?

Sunny's wide blue eyes scanned the circle of men, all in silk suits and vests, wearing gold watches and expensive rings. She was perfectly aware that some of them thought of her only in the way all men thought of beautiful women, that they were nice to have on their arms and to flaunt in public, but that they had no head for business. She would set these men straight.

She strolled into the room, wearing a soft lavender silk dress overlaid with white lace that cascaded in an apron down the front of the dress and trimmed its hem. The fitted bodice and bustle in the back accented her tiny waist. The neckline was scooped just enough to reveal a diamond and amethyst necklace. Her hair was drawn up to the crown in a cascade of curls and topped with a fancy silk bonnet that matched the dress, plumed feathers of white and lavender putting a finishing touch to the hat.

Mae, whom Sunny had brought along as an aide, had spent over an hour fussing with her hair, pinning the hat just so. Sunny wanted to look perfect for this first meeting alone with Durant and his men. Hannah Seymour and two bodyguards waited outside in her special coach. Because of her wealth and importance, Sunny had decided it would not be wise to travel alone, and the entourage with which she had arrived in New York had made the society column in *The New York Times*.

"Good afternoon, gentlemen," she said. They all replied in near unison, their eyes following her as she was escorted to her seat. She thanked the man who had shown her in and sat down. The men took their seats again, and Durant himself introduced them, some of them from his own newly formed Union Pacific Railroad Company, some from the Pennsylvania Fiscal Agency, the company that "the Doctor," as everyone called Durant, had set up to raise funds for the railroad. Sunny knew several of them from other meetings, but there were a few new faces at the table.

Durant himself was the most elegantly dressed of the men. He was rather handsome, of slender stature and impeccable taste, and, everyone knew, a man with splendid manners. His hair, mustache, and goatee were dark, his eyes a warm brown that did not always reveal the schemes behind them. Sunny knew what a clever businessman Durant could be. Her father had taught her well when it came to men of power. She had grown up with one of the best, and she knew how they thought.

Durant had given up a medical career as well as his family's grain business in New York to help build the Michigan Southern Railroad; and he had had a hand in the Chicago & Rock Island lines in which she now owned considerable shares. He was a railroad man at heart, and, Sunny knew, very important to her cause. He was the only other man of wealth and influence, besides her own father, who had a passion for seeing that a transcontinental railroad was built.

Durant ordered an office boy to bring a bottle of his finest wine from his own cellars in the basement of the office building. Another young man hurried in with crystal goblets, quietly setting a glass at each man's position, as well as in front of Sunny.

"We're all so glad you are finally getting out," Durant told Sunny as he took his own seat. "I told you in my letter how sorry I am about your father. He will be sorely missed by a lot of people."

"Thank you," Sunny answered. "It has been hard for me. I'm sure you have all read about my problems with my brother." She moved her eyes around the circle again, gauging the looks, picking out the ones she could tell doubted her abilities. "At any rate, I can assure you I am getting back to normal, and that I do own all the railroad stock that was my father's, including his investments in the U.P. I am here to carry on for him. As you all know, a transcontinental railroad was his last big dream. I will do what I can to help make that dream come true."

Most of them smiled and nodded, one man in particular, whom Sunny had never met before, staring at her so intently it made her a little uncomfortable, albeit flattered. He was exceedingly handsome, his hair dark and wavy, his eyes dark brown, every feature in his face seeming flawless. With one or two quick glances, Sunny guessed he was in his late twenties or early thirties. Durant introduced him as Blaine O'Brien, son of the late William O'Brien, a shipping magnate who had invested in railroading. "Blaine is interested in the potential of the logging industry of the Northwest," Durant had explained. "Obviously a transcontinental railroad would do such an industry a great service."

The young man who had been sent for the wine came back into the room and began pouring some into each glass. Sunny looked around the cheerful room, decorated, as all of Durant's offices were, with potted palms and rococo statues. There was even a canary in a hanging cage in one corner. Sunny liked the sound of its singing and decided something similar would be a nice change to her own office in Chicago, for which she had left redecorating orders before she left. She decided she would wire Tod and tell him to make sure a canary was included in the decor.

Durant held up his glass. "To the Union Pacific," he said.

Sunny and the others held up their glasses and replied the same, a couple of the men gulping their wine, Sunny and the rest just sipping theirs. Sunny had tasted wine only three times in her life. She had seen what too much drink did to some men, and she decided to be careful with such things herself, a hard thing to do when constantly being invited to parties and dinners; but the last thing she ever wanted to do was make a fool of herself, especially now that she was on her own.

Durant began mapping out the extensive work that lay ahead for them. "Each of you will have to press your business associates to rethink their refusal to invest in the U.P. Never has the future of our railroad been more promising," he told them. "A vote is very near, and if we can convince just a few more congressmen to vote in our favor, the bill will be passed and the groundwork will be set for government aid in this thing."

"What about Huntington and the Central Pacific?" Sunny asked.

Blaine O'Brien grinned. "We've been keeping an eye

on him," he answered for Durant. "With this war going on, the Central Pacific is having one hell of a time getting any kind of supplies. Prices are up to begin with, and after paying freight charges to get around Cape Horn or through Panama, there is simply no profit for the C.P., and other supplies are often impounded by the War Department for their own use. The C.P. line has barely made it out of Sacramento."

"We still can't underestimate Mr. Huntington's clever business mind," Sunny answered. "And don't forget that he has three wealthy associates, Charles Crocker, Mark Hopkins, and the governor of California."

O'Brien was stirred, not only by Sunny's beauty, but by her knowledge and assertiveness. He nodded. "Agreed that we can't be too careful. But they have even more problems—trouble from Wells Fargo and other shipping companies who don't want the competition, the danger of investing nearly all their personal profits from their grocery and hardware businesses, and the simple fact that they don't all get along that well."

Sunny looked around the table. "There is one thing my father said they have done and will keep doing, and that's buying elections in California, making sure the right men are elected who will go over the heads of companies like Wells Fargo and vote to help finance the C.P. with California money, and we all know California has plenty of that. If we don't want the Central Pacific to be the primary builders of the transcontinental railroad and get the greater share of government help, then we will have to do a little under-the-table bidding ourselves in Congress."

Sunny was finding it difficult to be cool and firm under O'Brien's stare. He kept watching her as she spoke, making her feel as though he could tell how she looked naked.

"The lady also has no scruples when it comes to getting votes," he said with a grin. "Your father *did* teach you well."

The others laughed lightly.

"Scruples or not, Miss Landers has a point," another spoke up. "I think we should all set up meetings with various congressmen. We're all pretty well aware of who can be bribed and who can't."

"And there is no room for scruples when it's for the U.P.," Sunny added. "There are a few men I know I can handle myself. I was always with my father when he met with them, and I've seen them take money from him before."

"And you have them wrapped around your pretty little finger, no doubt," O'Brien said. "Would that we all had the weapons you have."

There came another round of light laughter, and Sunny felt the heat in her cheeks. She rose, her eyes meeting O'Brien's boldly. "I don't care for the insinuation that I use myself like a harlot, Mr. O'Brien," she said firmly. "I happen to be in charge of one of the biggest business enterprises in Chicago. My father would not have handed over something he spent his life building to someone who knew nothing more about how to handle it than how to sway when she walks. I live in a man's world, and when it comes to business, there is nothing female about me. I will not sit here and be taken lightly just because I am a woman. I'll wager I can outtalk you on stocks and bonds and Wall Street activities any day of the week. Maybe you feel I should be questioned, to see if there are really any brains under this feathered hat."

The others lost their smiles, and O'Brien reddened slightly. "You take offense too easily, Miss Landers. I was envying you, not insulting you. I'm sorry I spoke out of line." *God, I like this woman,* he thought.

"I can assure all of you that keeping Miss Landers with us is very important," Durant said in defense of Sunny. "Don't any of you let her youth and beauty fool you. She is as on top of things as any of us, and she has invested a good deal of money both in the U.P. and in the Pennsylvania Fiscal Agency, which I will incorporate into the U.P. as soon as we get federal support." He looked at Sunny. "I also apologize, Miss Landers. I didn't ask you here for you to be offended."

Sunny tore her eyes from O'Brien, sitting down again. "Apology accepted." She looked at the others. "The fact remains that between the money we can raise through investors and money the government might vote to give us, it will likely take a good hundred million dollars to finance a transcontinental railroad. It is a mind-boggling figure, and that is part of the reason we're still having trouble getting private investors interested. They still simply don't believe it can be done."

"Then the key is to first be able to tell them that we do have federal support," Durant said. "Once we can say that the government is footing most of the bill, private investors will be much more willing to take a chance. All we have to do is get Congress to pass a bill that will set some guidelines so we know what we have to work with. One good thing about this war is that most southern states have dropped out, so we have fewer men we'll have to approach about this. Without the South present to argue about the route the line should follow, we have eliminated one big barrier. Most of those in the Senate and Congress now favor the northern route. I personally think Omaha would be the best starting point, but we can iron that out later."

The man went on, naming certain congressmen who were most likely to take bribes. His mention of Omaha took Sunny away for a moment, to another time, another place. She thought about Colt's letter and wondered if he had hers yet. Her trip to New York had been delayed by three weeks because of more problems Vince had caused at home. The letter had been sent off nearly a month before.

"We will decide here today which of us will visit which congressmen," Durant was saying, "and after today none of us will even mention the word *bribery*. We don't deal in such underhanded methods, do we, gentlemen?" He turned to Sunny. "Miss Landers?"

Sunny smiled. "Of course not."

There came another round of laughter, and Durant ordered that more wine be poured, but Sunny refused, some still left in her glass. Durant raised his glass again. "Gentlemen, Miss Landers, good luck to each of you. The first order of business, then, is to get a railroad bill passed so that we have something to work with when we go after the private investors."

"Hear, hear!" another cheered.

They all raised their glasses and drank again. The meeting went on for another two hours before it finally broke up. Durant pulled Sunny's chair out for her and thanked her for coming all the way from Chicago.

"I needed to get away anyway," she answered. She shook the man's hand. "Thank you for your condolences, and for showing me the same trust and respect you always showed my father."

Durant smiled. "He taught you well. You're quite a woman, Sunny."

She picked up the list of congressmen she was to visit. "I will study this tonight and decide what it will take to talk some of these men into helping us," she said. "I know a couple who will simply take money, others want to buy into Landers Enterprises, some may just want a promise that I will endorse them in the next election, or will want campaign money."

"Well, I trust you'll handle each one according to his need," Durant told her with a sly wink. He looked past her. "Ah, I see another apology coming." He turned then to talk to someone else, and Sunny turned around to see Blaine O'Brien standing behind her. She looked up into his dark eyes, thinking how there were things about him that resembled Colt Travis, his height, his dark hair; but his looks were too smooth, not ruggedly handsome like Colt's, nor was his skin as dark. She wondered then why she had made the comparison at all.

"My apology isn't enough, Miss Landers," the man was telling her. "Please, let me take you to dinner tonight. We'll go to the most expensive, elegant restaurant in New York. Where are you staying? I'll send a coach for you."

"It isn't necessary, Mr. O'Brien. Besides, I have a lot of thinking to do tonight over this list, some notes to take. I'll be leaving early tomorrow for Washington."

The man folded his arms, studying her with a scowl. "Okay, I was wrong about your abilities," he told her. "I can see you *are* all business, and I have to admit I am very impressed. But tell me, do you *ever* let yourself be a woman? Do you have a male interest back in Chicago?"

His eyes dropped to her breasts, and Sunny felt the odd flutter again. Ted Regis had never made her feel quite this way, but then, there had never been anything seriously romantic between her and Ted. After her father's death she had refused to see anyone for a long time except Vi and Stuart, putting a total halt to her social life. She had heard that Ted was now seeing someone else.

She wondered at the feelings Blaine O'Brien stirred in her. It was not that she was attracted to O'Brien in particular, she thought, but more the fact that she had begun realizing lately that womanly needs were beginning to stir in her. She had never forgotten Eve's remark to her about behaving like a man, and she realized she had never explored the feminine, sexual side of herself. Something about O'Brien's attentions had awakened her curiosity. Besides, she told herself, this man was important to the railroad. "All right, Mr. O'Brien," she answered. "One dinner. Pick me up at eight at the Waldorf. I will be bringing a companion, a Mrs. Seymour. I don't go out in public with a man I hardly know without a chaperone."

"Fine. Bring her along, then." He bowed slightly. "Thank you for accepting and giving me a chance to make up for my blundering remark. I really did mean it as a compliment."

"I'm sure you did," she answered, thinking what an attractive man he was at that. "You have to understand that things have been very difficult for me, Mr. O'Brien, since stepping in for my father. People don't always treat me with the respect I deserve, and they doubt my abilities. It makes me rather defensive."

"Of course. I don't blame you." He grinned. "I think you underestimate your own beauty, Miss Landers, and what it does to a man's thinking. The fact is, we find it hard to think at all when we see something as beautiful as you. If we get flustered and say the wrong things, it's because of our own shortcomings when we're near an attractive woman."

Sunny could not help a rather embarrassed smile. "Well, thank you, I guess. I will expect you this evening, then, at eight."

"My pleasure, I'm sure," he answered.

Sunny nodded and walked away, talking to a few more men before leaving the room. O'Brien watched after her, breathing deeply with the pleasure of knowing she had accepted his invitation. For years he had been looking for just the right woman to share his wealth. This one could even add to that wealth, and she was pretty enough to make a man want to beg. *By God,* he thought, *I believe I've just met the future Mrs. Blaine O'Brien. All I have to do is break down that brick wall she's built around herself.*

Chapter 11

I had to laugh when you said in your letter that you hoped I wasn't in too much danger, Sunny read. She smiled, turning her new velvet chair around so that its back was to her large oak desk, on which sat a vase of fresh flowers. *I had to take off on a routine run when I got your letter, so I couldn't read it right away. During my ride I was attacked by outlaws— killed two of them, took the other three in to be arrested. When they shot at me, they got my horse instead, and when he fell, I went down with him and cracked three ribs, but didn't take a bullet, so I'm okay. Got the mail through just fine.*

Sunny laughed then, shaking her head. "I'll bet you did," she said softly. Only Colt Travis would write about such a thing as though it were nothing. *So when I opened your letter, which was before I would even let them wrap my ribs, and read your first comment, I couldn't help laughing, which, I might add, didn't help the pain in my ribs.*

I'm so glad you wrote back, Sunny. Something about that letter made me feel kind of special, like somebody in this whole big world knows about Colt Travis and actually gives a damn. My best and only real friend up to this point, who is still alive I should say, is a Cheyenne Indian called White Buffalo, but I haven't seen him for quite some time. I lived with him for a few months last winter. I feel sorry for him and his people, with all the settlement going on out here now. The Indians' way of life is changing, and it's killing them. Because of that I probably shouldn't hope that your railroad gets built, but I can't help rooting for you anyway.

You should come back for a visit, at least to Omaha. I bet you'd be surprised how things have changed. They say the telegraph will be finished by this fall. I don't know what I'll do then. I need something to keep me busy, keep my mind off things that hurt too much to think about.

You asked about my wife, how she died. It was Pawnee Indians. I was off hunting, and I don't think I will ever forgive myself for leaving her and our baby son alone.

"Baby son!" she murmured aloud. He had not mentioned a child in the first letter.

It is still hard for me to talk about. Or to even write about it. Picture the most awful thing you can picture. I don't know how else to put it. My son's name was Ethan. He was only four months old. By the time I got there, it was too late. I took an arrow in my side and would have died if not for White Buffalo and his people finding me and nursing me back from death, although I really didn't want to live anyway.

"Oh, Colt," she muttered. "Dear God!"

Maybe if we ever get to visit in person again I can tell you more. For now, I would rather tell you how beautiful the weather is here today, except that it's very hot. My ribs are mending just fine, and I will get back to riding my route again soon. They get copies of the Omaha paper here about once a week, and I look through every page to see if there is any news about you. I saw an article that said you had traveled to New York and Washington to lobby for the railroad, and that you were even going to see the President. I can't get over the fact that you took the time to answer my letter in the middle of your busy schedule. It must not be easy for you.

I have to hurry and finish this. Another rider will be by anytime to take it on to Omaha. I just wanted to thank you for your letter. Please don't feel obligated to answer every time I write you.

An old friend, Colt.

Sunny refolded the letter, turning back around and putting it in the top right drawer of her desk, where she had placed the first letter. She liked keeping them where she could reread them once in a while. She would answer his letter, whether he expected it or not. To think of the tragedy he had suffered, the horror with which he had to live, brought pain to her own heart. To lose not only a young wife, but a baby son too . . . how dreadful! She could almost feel his anguish. It seemed everyone in his life who loved him and was close to him ended up dying. It had to be very lonely for him.

She took out a piece of paper and a pen and began writing, unable to put it off for one minute in spite of the mountains of other work that needed to be done. This was a quiet time of the day, late afternoon. The grandfather clock still ticked away in one corner of the huge room, but it was about all that was left of her father's original decor. All furniture was now oak and velvet instead of mahogany and leather. The carpeting and draperies were mauve instead of dark green. Paintings of mountains and flowers hung on the walls. Potted plants were placed strategically about, and a bird cage hung near a window in which a canary flitted about, lifting her heart and spirits with its singing.

The wallpaper had also been changed to a mauve and beige flower design, and the picture of herself behind the desk had been removed. Soon it would be replaced by the painting she had originally decided she wanted—of a locomotive. She had hired a professional artist to paint it for her, instructing him that she wanted a background of the Great Plains. Since the artist had never been west of Chicago, she had made an appointment with him so that she could describe the land she loved. She decided she would bring along her journal and read to him some of her fresh descriptions of the Plains. She couldn't wait until the picture was finished, and already planned to frame it in gold.

The refurbishing had been done while she was gone so that she would not have to come back and be hit again with the agony of her father's death. She could still smell the wallpaper glue, and she thought how much easier it was to breathe that smell than the lingering odor of her father's cigars. If she was ever going to get over this painful loss, she had to stop looking for things that reminded her of Bo Landers.

Someone knocked at the door, and she looked up, closing the desk drawer that held the letters. "Who is it?"

"Vince."

Oh, how she had grown to hate even his voice! What did he want now? "Come in," she said.

To her surprise, her brother entered carrying a huge bouquet of flowers. He stopped and looked around, and Sunny knew this was the first time he had seen the office since she made the changes. She waited for the expected blow-up, perhaps a speech about how she had no business changing his father's office this way; but whatever he wanted to say, he managed to force it back, putting on a pleasant face.

"I was on my way up to see you when these were delivered downstairs," he told her. "I said I'd bring them up. Are they from who I *think* they're from?"

Sunny took the flowers and laid them on her desk, all defenses alert, since Vince almost never came to see her casually. "And who *do* you think they're from?" She took the card from the flowers.

"Blaine O'Brien, one of the wealthiest men in the country."

Sunny looked at him in surprise, amazed to see a smile on his face. "How do you know about Blaine?"

"Hell, everybody knows, Sunny. It was in the society column of the *Tribune* before you got back from Washington."

Sunny frowned in exasperation, realizing now why Mae had been so mysteriously giggly that morning when she helped her dress. "I just got back yesterday. I hadn't heard," she said, staring at the card.

For the most beautiful woman in Chicago or New York or anyplace else, it read. *I am coming to Chicago soon. I must see you again. Always, Blaine.*

Sunny could feel the color coming to her cheeks. "Yes, they're from Blaine."

"So, are you going to tell me about it?"

She rolled her eyes. "There is nothing to tell. I don't know why or how it got into the newspaper. I had one chaperoned dinner date with the man, and that was because he owed me an apology. It meant nothing." She folded her arms authoritatively. "And why do you, of all people, care, Vince? What did you come up here for in the first place?"

He grinned almost nervously. "Well, for this." He indicated the flowers. "I wanted to find out about the rumors, and lo and behold, the man is sending you flowers. You must have made quite an impression on him. I've heard he's quite handsome and *very* eligible." His eyes moved over her appreciatively. "You aren't going to let somebody like that get away, are you?"

Sunny's eyes narrowed with suspicion. "Vince, you couldn't care less about my love life, except how it might affect you and Landers Enterprises. Don't be so eager to marry me off. Even if I *were* to marry, I would draw up some kind of legal papers that would leave me in control of what I have. I am not about to let some man who never even knew Father take over all my holdings. Is that what you're worried about? Or are you *wishing* I would marry, maybe settle and have babies and drop out of my job here?"

His smile faded, and the old familiar hostile look returned. "You *do* neglect your social life, Sunny. You *should* get married, behave like a woman is *supposed* to behave! And I do hope you will be careful to marry properly. There aren't many men who are worthy of becoming part of this family, you know. Blaine O'Brien, I am told, is a man of impeccable taste, with a good reputation and as much or more money than we have. He would be a *wonderful* match for you. I hope you won't fall for some worthless nobody and marry below yourself, like—" He reddened slightly.

Sunny put her hands to her waist. "Like who?"

Like our father, he wanted to tell her. Oh, how he longed to tell her the truth, to tell her the *real* reason he resented the thought of her inheriting so much! But he had promised his father, under the threat of losing what little he did still hold. Although Bo Landers was dead, he still couldn't bring himself to break that promise. What was the sense in torturing Sunny with it when he had already lost his bid to his share of the fortune? It had been his father's place to set things right, and he had not done so. The man had refused to admit that Lucille Madison was anything but sweet and wonderful and the love of his life, and Vince wondered if he would ever stop hating the man for it, or hating Sunny, even though she had had no control over events.

"Well, like . . . like Andrew Hipple's daughter. She married a no-good gambler, and look what happened. He gambled away everything she had inherited, then left her."

Sunny shook her head, picking up the flowers and carrying them over to a table and placing them into a Chinese vase. "I'm not going to marry any worthless gambler, Vince."

"Yes, but do you realize what it could mean for Landers Enterprises if you *did* marry badly? My God, we could lose everything! You need to marry a man who understands business and wealth. More important, you need to marry a man who has as much or more money than we do. You'll know then that he loves you for you and isn't after your money and the company."

She turned to face him, anger in her eyes. "Vince, stop pretending that you care about whether or not a man marries me for love. Why don't you just admit that you're worried only about losing the company to someone who doesn't know how to run it? I told you I intend to stay in control and keep what is mine, no matter what, even if I have children. If a man can keep up his business life after children, so can a woman. That's what nannies are for." She frowned, studying him closely. "What brought this on? Is it something more than the rumors about me and Blaine O'Brien? Why did you feel you had to warn me about marrying a man with no money?"

Vince ran a hand through his still-thick but graying hair, hesitating for a moment, then walking closer to her, using his old tactic of towering over her like a bully. "Stuart says Vi told him you've been corresponding with that scout you met when you went out west. Is that true?"

Sunny just stared at him for a moment, then burst out laughing. She turned away and walked back behind her desk. "I don't believe what I'm hearing," she said, laughing again.

"Well? *Is* it true?"

Her smile faded. "Yes. But I can assure you, Vince, the *last* thing Colt Travis cares about is my money."

"Money is the only thing most men *do* care about, especially when they don't have any of their own."

Anger began to move into Sunny's eyes, replacing the humor. "You don't know anything about Colt. He wrote me out of pure concern for my loss. He had read about it in an Omaha newspaper. He was sorry my *brother* had given me so many problems during my time of mourning!" She enjoyed the color that came into his face at the remark. "Who I write letters to is *my* business, Vince! Colt is nothing more than an old friend, who, I might add, saved my life more than once on that trip! He has suffered his own losses—a wife and baby son murdered by Indians! He has absolutely no one in this world who cares a whole lot what happens to him or if he's lonely or hurt. He takes comfort in my letters and I take comfort in his, and do you want to know why? Because he represents a kind of peace and serenity I found out there, a world apart from the gossip and stares and hatred and decision-making and fighting I have to put up with here, mostly thanks to *you!*"

She pulled open the drawer where the letters were kept and whipped them out. "Here! Do you want to censor my mail? You'll find the letters are perfectly respectable!" She slammed them down on the desk. "I have a right to my private life, Vince. And give me a little credit for common sense. Believe me, Colt Travis wouldn't come here and take over Landers Enterprises for all the money in the *world!* Believe it or not, there *are* men in this world who don't put money first! Besides that, the man has no romantic inclinations anyway. It's obvious by his letters that he is still haunted by the deaths of his wife and son. I highly doubt he's ready to fall in love again, especially with someone he hasn't seen in four years and who is as far a cry from what he would want in a woman as she could get!"

She turned away. "Get out, Vince. Every time you come around I get a headache. I might have known you didn't come to see me just to offer your help or to try to start being a real brother."

He stared at her a moment, tempted to explain. "Sunny, I am just looking out for your welfare. For Christ's sake, you're only nineteen. What do you know about men?"

She slowly turned proud eyes to meet his gaze. "I know when a man doesn't respect my intelligence. I know when my own brother hates me. I know that most men put money above all things. I grew up around the most scheming kind of men there can be, remember? Father taught me better than you think. I know I have to be careful." She looked away again. "Besides, I have far too much work ahead of me before I can devote my time to *any* kind of a relationship, whether it's with someone like Blaine O'Brien or anyone else. I have a railroad to build."

She heard him sigh deeply. "A railroad that is never going to come to be. What will happen then, Sunny, to all the money you're putting into it? It will be gone, lining the pockets of men like Thomas Durant."

"Mr. Durant has kept me totally informed every step of the way. If the railroad fails, he and a lot of others will have lost, not just me." She faced him again. "But we aren't *going* to lose, Vince."

"You'll never raise the money you need, not while there is a war going on."

"Let me worry about that. You worry about Great Lakes Shipping and Landers Warehousing."

His mouth moved into a sneer. "When it comes to that goddamn railroad, you're as much of a fool as Dad was! I hope you aren't as foolish about the men you take to your bed!"

Her eyes widened with indignation. "How dare you say such a thing! I've never given one thought to going to bed with *any* man!"

His gaze moved over her strangely. Was she still a virgin, or was she going to be like her mother, he wondered secretly. "Just remember my advice about Blaine O'Brien. Don't waste a good thing, Sunny, and don't be stupid enough to think that this Colt Travis, or whatever his name is, doesn't see dollar signs every time he gets another letter from you!" He walked to the door, stopping to gaze around the room once more. "I see you didn't waste any time getting rid of everything that speaks of our father."

"I changed this room because it hurt too *much* to leave it the way Father had it! Why in God's name do you continue to reopen old wounds, Vince, to make life hell for me!"

He stiffened and closed his eyes for a moment. How could he explain? "I'm sorry."

He turned and left, and Sunny stared after him, furious at how he always found a way to upset her. Why had he made the remark about taking men to her bed? She had never done anything more than let Ted Regis kiss her once, and that had been merely a kiss of friendship. She turned back to her desk, picking up Colt's letters, realizing he was the only man about whom she had ever had any truly romantic thoughts, and that was when she was a daydreaming child. She scanned one of the letters again, refusing to believe Colt would write her for any reason other than out of true concern.

She looked over at the magnificent spray of flowers Blaine had sent her. He was coming to Chicago soon to see her. She could not deny he was a charming man whom any woman would consider a perfect catch. She also could not deny that Vince was right in saying that she had to be careful who she allowed into her life, but the way he had said it left her somewhat stunned.

She sat down and again picked up her pen. She was determined to keep writing to Colt no matter what anyone thought of it. *I might not know much about men, Vince Landers, but I know of one man for certain who couldn't care less if I was worth no more than the clothes on my back.* She told herself she was not foolish enough to entertain romantic thoughts about Colt, for just as she had told Vince, it would be ridiculous, considering their different life-styles. But that didn't mean they couldn't continue to be friends, and it didn't mean she couldn't still daydream about a beautiful land and correspond with someone who was part of a lovely memory. She needed Colt's letters, and she was sure that he needed hers.

Dear Colt, she wrote. *I can't begin to tell you my sorrow at hearing about your wife and son. I can't think of one thing I could possibly say that would make the pain of your loss any more bearable, except that you should never blame yourself. God works in mysterious ways, and sometimes we just have to accept what happens.*

She set the pen aside again, a sudden shot of jealousy moving through her at the thought of Colt loving another woman, sleeping with her, having a child with her. She put his letters back in the drawer and stared at the beginnings of her reply. Was she asking for trouble by continuing the correspondence? Was she risking an awakening of that childish crush?

She let out a sigh of disgust with herself. Colt Travis was a lonely man who had loved and lost and was surely not about to love again for a long time. He knew back on that trip that they could never be anything but friends, and now that they both were older and more mature, what was wrong with corresponding? If her letters did some little bit to help him feel less lonely in his time of loss, then it was good that she kept writing him.

She took up her pen and continued. Neither Vince nor anyone else was going to stop her from helping a friend in need, especially one to whom she owed her life.

Colt headed Dancer up the gradual slope, his heart pounding with dread. For some reason he thought it was necessary to come here, that somehow seeing the graves would help him forget. He had stopped in Denver first to see Joanna Scott and tell her what had happened to LeeAnn, but he had discovered the woman had died, which only reawakened his grief. Mrs. Scott had been his last link to LeeAnn's memory. Now that she was dead, it was as though poor LeeAnn and her whole family had never existed.

A biting February wind stung his face, yet it felt as if a piece of hard, hot iron were lying in his stomach. Since leaving his employ with the Pony Express in November 1861, he had again wandered, moving from town to fort to town along the Oregon Trail. He'd written his fourth and last letter to Sunny in late November. He had told her their correspondence would have to end for a while, since he would have no permanent address.

He never realized how much he would miss her letters, and he couldn't help wondering if she missed hearing from him. He thought perhaps he should write her again, even though she couldn't write back. He wasn't sure what he would do with himself now. He was only sure that before he could go on, he had to visit Lee-Ann's and Ethan's graves and face the reality of their deaths once more. Maybe if he finalized things in his mind, it would be easier to go on.

He crested the rise, and pain ripped through him like fire. There lay the little homestead, still vacant and burned out, the plow still there, the broken-down fencing. Someone had either buried the Pawnee bodies, or come and taken them away, for as he came closer, he saw no bones or remnants of any kind. He grasped at his stomach, the awful memories from that ugly day coming back in sharp images.

He trotted Dancer to the burned-out cabin, every muscle tense, his heart pounding so that it hurt. He dismounted, tying Dancer and turning up the collar on his wolfskin jacket against the cruel wind. He walked through the cabin's ruins, remembering—a smile, a warm embrace, LeeAnn sitting by the fireplace breastfeeding little Ethan. That fireplace was all that remained now. The rocker in which LeeAnn used to sit still stood in front of it, but it was a charred skeleton of a chair, debris lying on top of it.

Colt shuddered, but it was not from the bitter cold. His whole body began to tremble, and he went to his knees beside the rocker, letting the tears come, telling himself it was better to let it out. Sobs racked at his body. He had no idea how long he knelt there before he managed to get control of himself. He struggled to his feet, throwing back his head and screaming, turning and kicking at the debris while sleet turned to snow and began to whiten the ugly black ruins.

After a rage of kicking and throwing things about, he stumbled upon the hinged door he had built into the floor of the cabin, under which LeeAnn stored potatoes and other vegetables. With a growl he shoved away more debris and lifted the door, kneeling down then to see a sack of potatoes still there but they were shriveled and dry, totally covered with long viney sprouts. He pushed the potatoes aside, and to his surprise, the four hundred dollars he had hidden behind them were still there. He grasped the money angrily and sat back and stared at it a moment, finding it ironic that out of all of this, only the damn money had survived.

He stood up and shoved the money into his pants pocket, staring around the cabin ruins, sometimes wondering if those few precious months he had had with LeeAnn had really happened. It seemed he had already done so many things in his life, yet he was going to be only twenty-five in three months. He felt like seventy.

He wished that for a little while he could have them all back, his mother and father, Slim, LeeAnn, Ethan. He had tried to find White Buffalo, but the ever-more-warlike Cheyenne were becoming very elusive, and bad weather had forced him into Denver for shelter. He had come here during a break in the weather, but it had again grown worse on his way out.

He walked away from the cabin, and the wind began to howl as he looked around for the graves. He tied his hat under his chin to keep it from blowing off his head, and he huddled his mouth and chin down into the front of his jacket as he walked around searching for some sign of where his wife and son were buried. The wind blew so hard that the snow swept across the ground, mixed with sand, leaving the earth bare in spite of the snow getting heavier by the minute.

Colt finally spotted a mound near what was once the horse shed. He hurried over, seeing that it had rocks laid over it in the shape of a cross. *I marked your woman and baby's grave with stones in the shape of the white man's sign of God,* White Buffalo had told him. *I learned of this sign from your missionaries. If you go to find it, look for the sign of the cross. The boy is buried with his mother.*

Colt stared at the grave. So, it *was* real. LeeAnn and Ethan really were dead! He had never quite gotten over little spells of disbelief, the thought that somehow, somewhere, he would find them alive.

He knelt beside the grave, grateful to see that no animals had dug at it. "My poor LeeAnn," he groaned, reaching out and touching the rocks. "I'm so sorry." More tears came, and he hung his head, hardly aware of the wind and snow. Finally, he lay down, stretching himself across the hard mound, pretending his wife and son were in his arms. Snow drifted up against him and began to cover him, and somewhere in the distant hills, wolves began a mournful wail.

Blaine draped Sunny's fur cape around her shoulders, nodding to several of Chicago's most elite as others began leaving the theater. "Quite a good symphony, wasn't it?"

"I enjoyed it very much, Blaine," Sunny answered. "Thank you for taking me."

He took her arm, aware that people were staring.

Blaine O'Brien and Sunny Landers were the hot topic of the society columns. Everyone in Chicago seemed to know who Sunny was, and any man who might be a love interest gained instant public attention. Blaine didn't mind one bit. He had big plans for the future, a career in politics. Public attention was just what he needed. He had deliberately taken time away from his business in New York to stay in Chicago for a while and court Sunny. As far as he was concerned, he had found the perfect woman, but sometimes he wondered just how long it was going to take to get her to marry him.

He was determined to keep trying. It wasn't just her beauty that fascinated him. He had dated many beautiful women in his thirty years. Nor was it just her intelligence and abilities, both of which she had proved in a grand way over the last few months. He decided that what frustrated him and made him want her most was the fact that she still had not put him on a pedestal the way other women had. He could not get the sexual response from her that he wanted and needed, nor could he get her to commit to him in any serious way. Her father's business and the railroad still came above all else.

They stopped and talked to a few people on their way out, people who looked admiringly at the couple, women getting flustered when Blaine kissed their hands, men ogling Sunny's exquisite beauty. Blaine himself had been unable to keep his eyes from the way Sunny's dress was cut, just enough to reveal a tempting portion of the crests of her untouched breasts, breasts he dearly wanted to touch and taste, wanted to own. He escorted her outside to his waiting carriage, both of them ducking against a bitter March wind. Blaine shouted to the driver to take them to Sunny's home, then helped her climb into the carriage and settled in beside her, commenting again about the symphony.

Sunny put her head back. "Oh, I needed a night away from things, Blaine. Thank you again."

He leaned closer. "There are a lot of things you need that you neglect to let yourself enjoy, Sunny."

"Oh? Like what?"

Before she could protest, he put a hand to the side of her face and covered her mouth with his own, giving her his most provocative kiss, one that usually made other women putty in his hands. He felt her soften, moved his hand over her neck, traced his fingers toward her breasts. The kiss deepened when he moved a hand over a breast, but Sunny quickly grasped the hand and pulled it away. She turned away from the kiss, and he continued to kiss her cheek and neck, trembling with the want of her.

"Don't do this to me, Sunny. I've wanted you since that first day I saw you at Durant's meeting last fall. We've done a lot of things together, and our dates aren't even chaperoned anymore. There must be a reason you wanted us to be alone."

She sighed, pulling away slightly, watching out the window for a moment as the coach clattered over brick streets lit with gaslights. "Blaine, part of me wants to be a woman. I'm twenty years old. Most women my age are already married and having babies."

"And *you* should be too." He pulled her closer, kissing her again. How she wished she could feel that special rush of desire she had felt only once in her life, with a man she could not have. Why couldn't she feel that around Blaine? She had to admit she was attracted to him, but always there was that fear of what men really wanted from her, a round in bed and a chance at her fortune. Vi had heard the rumors of Blaine's womanizing, but then, as far as she knew he had been true to her since he first started courting her. Nearly every day he sent flowers or other gifts. It was almost too much.

She put her hands to his chest and turned her face away again. "Blaine, I don't think we should see so much of each other. I have so many things to think about, so much to do. I . . . I sort of promised myself that I wouldn't get involved with anyone until my feet were solidly on the ground with Landers Enterprises, and until the railroad becomes a reality. I don't have time for anything serious, and I can't trust my own decisions right now."

He sighed deeply, taking her hand. "Sunny, you're a

beautiful woman with so much to give. You'd make a wonderful wife and mother. I'm not—well, I'm not actually proposing this minute, and I'll admit I've had my share of women; but dammit, I've never wanted one quite like I want you. I've never come this close to wanting to marry. You're everything a man could want. And how are we going to know how things might be between us—" He pulled her closer. "Sexually," he continued in a near whisper, "if we don't do a little exploring, experimenting. Jesus, Sunny, let go of the sexual woman inside the businesswoman and just be female for once. You just might like it."

His words and touch made the thought so tempting. He searched her mouth again, his lips trailing over her neck, down to her breasts. She felt only curiosity and a desire not to hurt his feelings, but she did not feel the passion she was sure she should feel. She touched his hair, and suddenly imagined that it was Colt Travis doing this to her. The thought startled her so that she gasped and pushed him away again. "Blaine, don't."

He scowled, moving into his own corner of the seat, saying nothing for several long seconds. Sunny blinked back tears, wondering if the pressures of her business life were ruining her own femininity, her ability to love and want and— She shivered when she realized what had made her push him away. Why on earth had she thought of Colt? She hadn't heard from him since that last letter in December, telling her not to write anymore because he didn't know where he would be. He was a man from another world whom she hadn't seen in five years and would very likely never see again. Was she throwing away the best years of her life?

"I'm sorry, Blaine. You deserve better. I'm just not ready." She felt the sudden ache to her throat. "You have to understand that other women . . . other women don't have the responsibilities I have. They have more time to socialize and go to parties and think about their personal lives."

"Is there someone else?"

"What?"

"You heard me."

She looked out the window again, thinking of Colt. "No, of course not. That's a silly question. You know yourself I hardly have time to see *you* as often as you would like."

"As *I* would like? What about you? Do you see me just because it's what *I* want? God, woman, don't patronize me."

Sunny blinked back tears. "It isn't that way. I do like being with you, Blaine. I guess I'm just not as mature a woman that way as you need." She thought then how he had said only that he wanted and needed her, not that he loved her. Perhaps that was the problem. Until she heard those words, she could not be sure.

The carriage rolled up in front of her home, and Blaine got out his side, slamming the door. He came around and opened her door, helping her down, his grip on her arm a little tighter than necessary as he walked her to the huge double oak doors of the mansion.

"I have to go back to New York for a few weeks," he told her. "Maybe we'll see each other in Washington. You *will* be there for the vote, won't you?"

"Of course I will." She put her hands to the satin lapels of his wool overcoat. "Blaine, don't be angry, please. Maybe it's good that you'll be gone for a while. I need time to think about things, and I just can't bring myself to get involved until the railroad bill is passed. Give me at least that much."

He shook his head. "*I* don't need any more time to know what I want." He let out a short sarcastic laugh. "You do know how to get back at a man, don't you?"

"Get back at him?"

"Is this your way of paying me back for insulting you that first day?"

She smiled. "I would love to be mean and say yes." She leaned up and kissed his cheek. "No, Blaine. I forgot about that after that first dinner." The brisk wind blew her cape wildly, and she stepped back to grab hold of it. Blaine stared at her a moment, as though he didn't believe her.

"You ever get any more letters from that half-breed scout you told me about?" he asked.

Sunny felt a flush to her cheeks at the unexpected question. "No. Not since December. I don't even know where he is."

A strange look came into his eyes as his gaze moved over her in that way he had of making her feel naked. "Do me a favor. If he writes you again, don't answer."

Her eyebrows arched in surprise, mixed with anger. "Why!"

"I just don't think it's a good idea, that's all. A woman shouldn't be corresponding like close friends with some man when she's serious about another. It doesn't look good and it isn't proper, especially a woman of your station writing to a worthless drifter. Leave it alone, Sunny." He turned and went down the steps, getting into the carriage. "I'll see you in Washington," he called out to her.

"Maybe," Sunny muttered, still angry. She stood on the portico and watched the carriage clatter away. She shivered, not sure if it was from the wind or from Blaine's warning. How dare he give her orders as to whom she could choose for friends! In spite of the cold she walked around the house to the backyard and to steps that led down the steep sandy bank to the lake below. The blustery wind tore at her, and she listened to the waves crashing to shore, wondering what Colt would think of Lake Michigan.

She closed her eyes then, realizing that again she had allowed Colt to come into her thoughts. As much as it angered her to be told what to do, she wondered if perhaps Blaine was right in telling her she shouldn't answer him if he wrote again.

She touched her breast where Blaine had caressed it with his lips. Part of her had wanted him to do that and more. It wasn't that she didn't have the same desires as any woman; it was just that she had never done such things before . . . and she wasn't sure she wanted Blaine to be the one to enjoy her favors.

She felt a mist of cold rain then and turned to hurry back to the house. She decided she was better off for the time being not getting involved with any man. If the railroad bill passed the House and Senate and was signed by Lincoln, then the *real* work would have just begun. She would be busier than ever. It wouldn't be long now before they would all know if the Union Pacific was going to become a reality, and at this time in her life, that was more important than worrying about hurting Blaine O'Brien's feelings, although there were times when she wondered if he had any feelings at all.

Chapter 12

Colt reached over and pulled the letter from the pocket of his buckskin shirt, lying back in the bed and opening it to reread it for the tenth time. He strained to see by the light of a nearby oil lamp that the prostitute lying next to him had turned down so she could sleep. He smoked quietly, wondering how much had changed since Sunny had written the letter seven months ago.

He missed hearing from her, missed the unusual friendship he had developed with her through their letters. He supposed it was best to end it after all, considering that their paths would never cross again. Even if they did, where would he fit into her life, or she into his? Still, he could not help wondering if she was still all right. Anything could happen on her many trips to New York and Washington, with the damn war escalating the way it was.

This is an exciting but also frightening time, he read again, always trying to picture how she might look, sitting at a desk, slender fingers creating the lovely handwriting. *As I begin this letter, I am sitting in a hotel room in Washington, D.C., where I have come to again discuss the railroad with senators and congressmen. It is not easy to get their attention. Everyone here is, of course, afraid of a Confederate attack. The train I rode on to come here was packed with volunteers for the Union Army, and when I arrived in Washington, the city was a rush of thousands more volunteers, men from New York, Vermont, Ohio, Michigan, Rhode Island, Pennsylvania, Illinois, nearly every northern state. Never have I seen such movement and chaos, even in my own big city of Chicago. The capital is in a state of near panic, main thoroughfares guarded, common citizens who live on the borders of Virginia and Maryland flooding in for protection. Troops guard the Potomac and the James rivers, and it is rumored there will be a Union campaign to capture the Confederate capital of Richmond, Virginia, which is very close to Washington.*

I have never seen such a mess—people tenting in the streets, a shortage of water and a lack of sanitary conditions. It is times like this that I like to daydream about being out there where you are, where it is quiet, and a person can go for miles without seeing another human being.

Colt smiled at the remark, sometimes feeling like she was sitting right next to him telling him these things. He remembered how she used to love to write in her daily journal, wondered if she still did that.

In spite of the mass of soldiers to guard our own capital and president, I wonder about our Union leadership. We have suffered two major defeats, at Manassas, Virginia, and at Leesburg, Virginia, where the ghastly number of nineteen hundred Union soldiers died. We do at last have a blockade set up around southern ports, and recently the Union fleet captured two Confederate forts on Port Royal Sound in South Carolina, so we are now able to attack from the coast.

It seems strange to talk about this awful war, our own people fighting against each other. This is the saddest,

*most hideous kind of war. My sister-in-law Vi has volun-
teered to work at a big hospital in Chicago, where some of
the more seriously injured Union soldiers have been
brought, as well as injured but captured Rebels whose
wounds are to be treated before they are sent to our Union
prison at Rock Island. I have helped out occasionally at
the hospital, but I am afraid I do not have the constitution
for it that Vi has.*

*In the meantime, I pray that none of the trains I take on
my own trips are attacked by Rebels, a constant danger.
Still, I feel compelled to continue my own work for the
railroad in spite of what is happening. I refuse to let the
issue be forgotten because of the war, and a bill has finally
been introduced that might be voted on next spring.*

Colt sighed, refolding the letter before finishing it. It
was dated late October 1861. Now here it was almost
June of '62, and the war was apparently in full explo-
sion. He had read in an Omaha newspaper about terrible casualties in a conflict called the Battle of Shiloh, in
Tennessee. Nearly twenty-five thousand men had been
killed and wounded. The numbers that were being
printed in the newspapers were staggering, and sometimes Colt wondered how there could be that many men
in the entire country, to lose so many in one battle and
still be able to carry on the war.

Brother against brother, the headlines had read. What
kind of hell was taking place back east? He was feeling
more and more uneasy about it, wondering if it was
right for him to be sitting in bed with a whore in Omaha
while men his age were fighting and dying to save the
Union. The more he thought about it, the more he realized there couldn't be a much better way for someone
like him to pass his time—excitement, danger, certainly
no time to think about the graves he had left back in
Colorado. War was the perfect answer for a man who
didn't give a damn if he lived or died.

He had hoped that the Homestead Act President Lincoln had recently signed would mean some kind of work
for him, but people were just beginning to trickle in. It
was predicted they would soon start arriving by the
thousands, but rather than whole wagon trains to lead

to Oregon and California, it was already obvious they would come in more individual groups, one to three wagons at a time, with no need for a guide because they didn't intend to go much farther. They were being aided by land speculators, sinfully cheated by some, Colt suspected. At any rate, the new Homestead Act had not provided the kind of work he was looking for.

Actually, he considered the act as nothing more than another thorn in the side of the Indian. A new flow of settlers would begin arriving, many of them deciding to homestead on lands the government had promised would forever belong to the Indians. So much for the white man's promises.

He figured Sunny was thrilled about the new settlement act. The more people who came out here to live, the more need there would be for a railroad. There were times when he wanted to hate her for being part of a system that was changing the West as he had once known it, but he knew that what was happening was inevitable. If not Sunny and her cohorts, then someone else. It was going to happen simply because progress and settlement were so much a part of the white culture, and he couldn't hold himself blameless. After all, he had led many a wagon train himself.

He laid the letter back on the night table next to him, then snuffed out the cigarette, turning to the young woman stretched out naked beside him. Her name was Billie White, short for Belinda, and she was about Lee-Ann's age, with LeeAnn's coloring and small build. Still, she was not LeeAnn, no matter how hard he tried to imagine that she was.

He was lonely and he had a need. It was as simple as that. He had met Billie in the tavern downstairs, and he had stayed with her every night for the past three nights, taking out his pent-up frustrations on her, even crying on her shoulder one night. Wild as she was, she had a heart and a good ear, and he thought how under other circumstances, a man could love her for his own. But this one belonged to any man with the right amount of money, although when a man was with her, she treated him as if he were the only one in her life.

"Wake up, Billie," he said softly, moving between her legs again.

"Oh, you're mean," she groaned. "I'm sleepy, Colt."

"And that's my money lying on your night table."

He wondered how someone so young and pretty had ended up selling herself to lonely men, but he had not asked questions. Most whores didn't want to talk about why they did what they did, the same as he didn't always want to talk about why he was there in the first place.

He pushed himself deep inside her, and she responded with the exotic precision of a woman who knew all the ways there were to please a man. Still, it was not as satisfying as lying with a woman who truly loved him, a woman who wanted to give him children, a woman he in turn loved more than his own life. What a difference there was between having sex and making love. There was a physical relief in this, but no emotional joy. He took her almost violently, angry that she was not LeeAnn.

He rose to his knees and stared down at her small breasts, their pink nipples taut from the sudden arousal. He deliberately took a long, hard look at her nakedness, wanting simply to get rid of the strong physical needs that months of being without a woman had left him with. He would get this out of his system, but it wouldn't make the loneliness go away. It wouldn't bring back LeeAnn or Ethan. It would simply tide him over for a while as far as his natural needs were concerned.

He grasped her slim hips, and she gasped his name and arched up to him in an exquisite gyrating motion. He rammed himself hard into her, wanting it to last as long as possible. He moved with such energy that he began to perspire, letting go of her hips then and bending down to taste each nipple. He grabbed her hair then, and buried his face against her neck, his broad shoulders hovering over her. He felt her fingers lightly caress his own nipple, and she wrapped her legs around his waist. With one final thrust his life spilled into her once more, life that would never come to fruition. The scar across her belly was proof she would never have children. He had not asked how or why she had come to have the operation, satisfied that it was simply an added convenience that left both her and her customers less to worry about.

Colt shuddered a last sigh and rolled away from her. Billie lay spent and panting, looking like a wilted flower. "You could have been a little more gentle," she complained, "especially after waking me up like that."

Colt rubbed his face and sat up. "Sorry." He got up and walked to a washstand, pouring water from a pitcher into a bowl. He soaped up a rag and began washing his privates. "You'd better be as clean as you say you are."

"That's part of the high price. I don't sleep with just any bum who comes in here, you know. I'm careful. Hurry up and wash so I can wash too."

Colt finished, turning to see her sitting with a towel between her legs but otherwise completely naked. She was smoking a thin cigar, her dark brown hair in a tangle. He studied her a moment, thinking how, if she didn't wear all that paint and would dress like a decent woman, she could be anybody's proper, churchgoing and quite pretty daughter.

Her sultry eyes fell to his privates as he walked back over to the bed. "You sure are hung," she commented. "You going to stay in Omaha? I wouldn't mind being your favorite—you know, reserving myself for you and not taking any other customers? I'd be willing." She licked at her lips. "Something as good-looking and built like you doesn't come along very often."

He smiled almost bashfully. "I guess that's supposed to be a compliment." He reached over and took his longjohns from where they hung on a post of the brass bed. "I don't know what the hell I'm going to do right now. I'm thinking I ought to be doing something about the war. I took a room in Denver for a couple of days when I was there. Somebody had left a book there called *Uncle Tom's Cabin.* I was bored as hell, so I read it. It was about slavery. Gave me the shivers. Between that and not feeling right about the country being all torn up like it is—" He shrugged. "Just seems like a man with no family and no responsibilities ought to do his part." He pulled on the longjohns and sat on the edge of the bed, taking a cigarette paper and his pouch of tobacco from the night table and rolling himself another cigarette.

"War has to be awful ugly, Colt, especially a civil war. I read the papers too, you know. I read about those thousands of men killed and wounded at Shiloh. I had a customer not long ago who said he was a volunteer medic for the Union. He was at Shiloh, and he deserted —said what he saw made him so sick he couldn't look at it anymore—men screaming, dying of awful infections, getting their legs or arms cut off. You ought to stay right here."

Colt rose, bending over the oil lamp and lighting his cigarette, then walking to a window, watching the activity in the dimly lit street below. He was still surprised how much Omaha had grown since he brought Sunny here five years ago. "Somebody has to do it, Billie. Might as well be men like me who won't be missed if they're killed."

She stuck out her lower lip. *"I'd* miss you."

He looked over at her and snickered. "Only until somebody hung bigger came along."

She smiled seductively. "They don't come any bigger."

He laughed lightly and shook his head, looking out the window again to see a gang of five men ride up to the front of the tavern just below, apparently in quite a hurry. They stormed inside, and Colt could hear a commotion downstairs. He frowned, hurrying over to open the door to Billie's room.

"What is it, Colt?"

He put up his hand for her to be quiet and walked farther out onto the balcony, still in his underwear. Billie listened intently to men shouting in the tavern below. Colt looked over the railing at the intruders, who were brandishing guns and yelling threateningly at the tavern patrons.

"We saw that black bugger run in this direction," one of them was bellowing. "There's laws against hiding fugitive slaves!"

"Why don't you go back south where you belong and fight with them that's dying so you can *keep* your damn slaves," someone grumbled. "We haven't seen any nigger in here, and we don't have no use for anybody that would use humans like damn mules."

"Mr. Tibbs is willing not to press any charges if you're hiding him," one of the other gang members told the customers. "Just turn him over." He gave a signal to one of his men, and Colt watched warily as the second man turned and headed upstairs.

"You all might say you're nigger lovers," the man talking below went on, "but do you love them more than money? Our boss will pay good money to the man that turns the nigger in. He's small built, eighteen years old, wearing a fancy suit. Tibbs treats his niggers good, especially his personal servants. Nothing's going to happen to him if you turn him in."

"Except a good whipping that will open up his back, right?" someone said with a sneer.

Colt boldly met the eyes of the man who had come upstairs. The man hesitated, his eyes moving over Colt, taking the several scars on his face and naked torso into account. After years of hard living and personal loss, Colt looked older. The scar above his right eye indicated a man who could be mean when necessary, let alone the fact that he stood over six feet tall, his arms and chest hard-muscled. He kept his cigarette between his lips, literally frightening the intruder with his eyes as he stared him down. "There's nobody in there but my own personal whore," he said firmly but quietly. "You've got no right coming up here and disturbing people. Get the hell out."

The man kept a gun on him, moving to peek around the doorway. Billie, still sitting stark naked on the bed, smiled and waved at him. The man took a moment to get a good look before turning back to Colt, clearing his throat nervously. "There's a reward, if you're interested. The nigger's name is Elam. He's the boss's favorite, if you know what I mean. Mr. Tibbs will pay plenty to get him back." The man turned and went downstairs, leav-

ing with the others then to continue their search. Colt
went back inside Billie's room and began dressing.

"Where are *you* going?" Billie asked him.

"Out for some fresh air. I just saw something that
made me feel a little sick. Besides, I'm wide awake
now."

"You're going to look for that Negro kid yourself,
aren't you?"

"No. I just have a sudden urge to get the hell out of
here, maybe go for a ride. I've got some things to think
about." He finished dressing and strapped on his gun.
He picked Sunny's letter up from the night table and
shoved it back into his saddlebag, then shoved in other
personal articles. He tied his tobacco pouch onto his
belt and picked up the saddlebags and his carbine.

"You won't be back, will you?" Billie asked.

He met her eyes, seeing a hint of sadness. "Probably
not. Thanks for the last three days. I needed it."

"I'm sorry about your wife and all. I just wish you
wouldn't go get yourself involved in that war, Colt.
You're a nice man, way down deep inside that mean-
looking exterior. If you get wounded, lose a leg or something, who's going to take care of you?"

He smiled sadly. "I've always found a way to get by.
Take care of yourself, Billie. Be careful who you invite
up here."

She grinned. "They'll all be a disappointment after
you."

He laughed lightly, showing the melting smile that
made her wonder if maybe she could love a man at that.
But then, what man would love her back? "Bye, Colt.
You're one hell of a man."

Colt just shook his head. "Bye, Billie." He headed out
and down the stairs, walking out into the cool night air
and taking a deep breath. He could hear the gang of
searchers pounding on doors and shouting farther up
the street. Suddenly, he wanted to get the hell away
from all of it. He walked in the opposite direction to the
livery where his horse was kept. He had already paid the
owner for Dancer's stall for tonight, so he decided it
wouldn't matter if he got his horse and left.

He reached the livery only to find that the front doors of the shed were padlocked. "Damn," he muttered. He paced in front of the building, frustrated. He started for the back then, remembering there were more double doors on the opposite end of the shed. If those were simply board-locked from the inside, then if he could get inside himself, he could open them and get the hell out of there. He had no idea where the owner lived, and he was not about to wait for the man to open up in the morning. When Colt Travis got an itch to ride, there was no waiting around.

He checked the back doors, secured from the inside, just as he had suspected. He looked up—no window. He walked back around the side of the building, remembering he had seen a window there. It was then that he noticed some crates stacked against the side wall of the shed, leading right up to the window, almost as though they had been put there deliberately. The window had been pushed open.

Frowning with curiosity, Colt slung the saddlebags over his shoulder and climbed up on the crates to the window, which was only eight feet off the ground. He peeked inside the darkened shed. A couple of horses whinnied, but he wasn't sure if it was from his appearance, or if someone else was inside.

He let his eyes adjust to the moonlight that came through another window at the front of the shed, and he saw a stack of hay below him. He swung his legs over the windowsill, throwing down his saddlebags first, then keeping hold of his rifle as he jumped into the hay. A few more horses whinnied and snorted. Colt picked up the saddlebags, talking softly to the horses to calm them, then making his way over to where he knew Dancer was kept. He found an oil lamp, then felt around in his saddlebags for a match, taking one out and lighting the lamp just enough so he could see to saddle Dancer.

He looked around the shed, seeing nothing, hearing nothing. He cautiously walked over to Dancer, hanging the lamp nearby and setting his rifle and saddlebags aside. He stroked the horse a moment to keep him calm, then turned and took his saddle blanket from a hook and slung it over the animal's back. He lifted his saddle from where it was perched on the stall gate and set it on Dancer, reaching under the horse's belly to grab the cinch.

It was then he saw movement under a small stack of hay in the opposite corner of Dancer's stall. Colt hesitated, slowly reaching for his revolver. Quietly, he moved around the other side of Dancer, then aimed the revolver at the stack of hay. "Who's there?" he demanded.

The only answer was a strange whimpering sound, certainly not what he would expect to hear from a horse thief, unless the thief were a child. He stepped a little closer, suddenly thinking about how the crates had been stacked by the window. Maybe whoever was under the hay had simply come in here to hide. He could still hear shouting farther up the street. "Damn," he whispered. "Elam? That you?"

There came another whimper. Colt had seen a few Negro slaves when he was younger, down in Texas, and he had always felt sorry for them. Since coming into the Plains country, he had seen almost no Negroes, slave or free. Kansas and Nebraska tried to keep them out to avoid trouble over the slavery issue. If there was a Negro under that hay, it had to be the one called Elam.

"I won't hurt you, and I won't turn you in," he tried to explain. "My name is Colt Travis, and right now I've got no particular plans but to get the hell out of Omaha. You want to come along?" He put his gun back in its holster. "Let me help you, Elam. I'm riding out of here tonight. I can take you into country where those boys up the street would never find you."

He finally saw movement again. Some of the hay tumbled away, and a slender boy who looked to Colt more like fourteen than eighteen scrambled from under the straw. He was quite handsome, with a face that could almost be called pretty. He stared at Colt wide-eyed and shivering, reminding Colt of a scared deer.

"You *are* Elam, aren't you?" Colt asked.

The boy swallowed and nodded. "Please, please don't turn me in, Mister! Mr. Tibbs, he'll hurt me good."

Colt looked him over. He wore a tight-fitting suit with a ruffled shirt, and his hair hung in curls to his shoulders. "How come your owner dresses you fancy like that? That suit looks like silk." He squinted. "You *really* a boy?"

"Yes, sir, I'm a boy. Mr. Tibbs, he makes me wear my hair long and makes me wear these clothes. He likes to dress his servants good, pretend he treats them just fine. But he don't. Not really. Don't make me go back to him, please!"

"Where is this Tibbs from, and what's he doing in Omaha?"

"He's from Kentuck, sir," Elam answered, his voice still that of a younger boy. "He come out here to maybe buy some land, have him a big ranch on account of that Homestead Act. He brung me with 'cause I'm his favorite." The boy sniffed and shivered. "I was waiting till we got far enough north that maybe I could get away. You know a place called Canada?"

"I've never been there, but I know how to find it."

"Take me there! Please, Mister! I be free there! You done said you could take me into country where those men wouldn't come looking for me. You said it. You said you was riding out of Omaha tonight!"

Colt scowled slightly. "You didn't do something wrong, did you, like steal something? Kill somebody?"

"No! No, sir! I just gotta get away from Mr. Tibbs, that's all. It ain't right, what he makes me do. I ain't no woman, you know? I gotta do what he say, you know? Or else he hurts me bad. I don't mind doing housework, working in fields, none of that. But I ain't no woman, and it makes me throw up sometimes. And when he gets tired of me, or when I start looking like the man I'm gonna be, he'll have his men shoot me. I've seen him do it to others. I'm just his newest, you know? Pretty soon he'll be done with me and he'll kill me! I gotta get away, get to Canada!"

Colt thought about the remark the man who had

come upstairs with the gun had made about this young man being the boss's "favorite."

"What do you mean, you're no woman?"

Elam looked down at the floor. "You know, don't you? I'm Mr. Tibbs's favorite. He don't like real women, jus' boys."

Colt stared at him, dumbfounded, feeling like a fool for not immediately grasping what the poor kid was trying to tell him. "Jesus Christ," he swore, finding it hard to believe there really were men like that. "Stay put." He walked back around and finished cinching his saddle. He tied on his bedroll and saddlebags, then shoved his rifle into its boot. "Come on over here," he told Elam.

The young man obeyed, still looking fearful. He swallowed when he looked up at Colt. "You an Indian? I ain't never seen one, but you look like how I'd picture one."

"Half Indian. Cherokee. You ever ride a horse?"

"No, sir."

"Come over here and put your foot in this stirrup and climb up."

The young man just gawked at him a moment. "You won't . . . you ain't like Mr. Tibbs, are you? I'd just as soon you shot me."

Colt let out a sigh of disgust. "No, I'm not like Mr. Tibbs. Look, I'm a wandering man with no job at the moment and no particular plans except a sudden urge to get the hell out of Omaha."

"You takin' me to Canada?"

"If that's where you want to go. Soon as we get a good ride away from here, I'll see about getting you into some clothes that aren't so damn conspicuous."

"How do you know them men won't come after us?"

"Because nobody in his right mind wants to ride into Sioux country."

"Sioux! Sioux *Indians?*"

"Don't worry. I've dealt with them before, and I know the country. Now, which would you rather do—have those men up the street find you, or take your chances with the Sioux?"

Elam took a deep breath and managed a limp smile. "Help me up," he answered. He put his left foot in the stirrup and Colt gave him a boost. As soon as Elam was in the saddle, his feet were no longer in the stirrups because his legs were so much shorter than Colt's.

Colt took Dancer's bridle from where it hung on a nail and he slipped it over the horse's head and ears. He took hold of the reins and blew out the lamp, leading the horse to doors at the back of the shed, which were locked from inside with a simple board shoved through iron bars. He pulled the board away and cautiously pushed open the doors, leading Dancer out into the dark alley behind the livery. "Move to the back of the saddle," he told Elam quietly.

The young Negro obeyed, and Colt mounted up. "Hang on to me," he told Elam. "We'll leave very quietly and stay to the shadows. Once we're beyond hearing, I'm going to be riding hard, so be ready."

"Yes, sir. I . . . I don't know what to say . . . how to thank you."

"Don't worry about it. Besides, if you end up on the wrong end of some Sioux arrow, you might not be so grateful."

"Don't matter, sir, long as I don't have to go back to Mr. Tibbs."

Colt gently touched Dancer's sides, trotting the horse through the back alley and keeping out of the light.

The Senate gallery was filled, mostly with reporters who were certain the Pacific Railway Act would be defeated. Sunny was certain it would not. She and Durant and others had spent far too much money bribing some of the men who sat below. For months the Pacific Railway Act had been tossed back and forth from House to Senate, studied by various committees, read, changed, reread. Congressmen and senators alike had given long speeches for and against the idea, and Thomas Durant, Sunny herself, and several other of their wealthy cohorts had presented their own arguments before Congress.

Now, finally, the act was down to the final Senate

vote, after being approved by the House. Sunny was beyond worrying about whether her own bribery techniques were moral or immoral. She had paid men directly, promised others she would contribute to future campaigns, awarded shares of railroad stock free, and had even invested in one senator's fledgling textile mill. Part of her considered it abhorrent that so many of the elected officials below would so easily take bribes. They were supposed to be law-abiding men, the pillars of their communities. *Just about any man can be bought, Sunny.* She could hear her father's words. *And when it comes to what's best for Landers Enterprises, and what's best for this transcontinental railroad, then we will pay the price, right or wrong.*

Pay she had. If she were not so sure that C. P. Huntington and other Central Pacific officials were doling out their own payoffs, she might have thought twice about what she had done; but in her world it was the rich against the richest. Bribes were as natural a part of daily business as sales and inventory. She was in this now for the long haul, and dangerous as it had been to come to Washington again, she was not about to stay away during this historic moment.

Blaine reached over and took her hand as they listened to each senator give his "yea" or "nay." Until the last two weeks, she and Blaine had not seen each other since he left Chicago in March. It was now the end of June. Blaine had met her at the train station when she arrived in Baltimore and had ridden the train the rest of the way with her to D.C. It was a trip Sunny hoped she would not have to make again for a while. Skirmishes between North and South were taking place in and around Virginia, the Confederates trying to protect Richmond from being taken by federal troops. Every trip she made now was dangerous.

The names of senators from each state were called, more votes recorded. No one doubted that if the act was passed now by the Senate, President Lincoln would give his approval. The final wording of the act gave the Central Pacific and the Union Pacific equal opportunity and the same requirements for obtaining money. The U.P.

would build westward from Omaha, the Central Pacific eastward from Sacramento, the two railroads uniting somewhere in the West. Already Sunny could feel the excitement of what was sure to be a construction race.

Blaine was making plans to go to northern California and southern Oregon to investigate the logging industry. He was sure there was an untapped source of great wealth there, and if the railroad bill was passed, it could open many new doors for lumbering.

Sunny was almost glad he was going. Since seeing him again, Blaine had inundated her with flowers and attention, and she knew that if they were together too much over the next few months, things would again come to the point where decisions would have to be made, decisions she didn't want to think about yet. Already Blaine talked of wanting her to marry him and go with him to the South of France, where his mother and sister lived, and to Africa, where he had himself done big-game hunting. He had all kinds of wonderful plans, but none of them excited her the way the thought of being a part of the transcontinental railroad made her heart rush, and now the railroad was becoming a reality.

She decided that once this new act was approved, she would immediately go to Omaha and hire builders to begin construction on new Landers Enterprises offices there, maybe even a new home. She would move the center of her U.P. interests to Omaha and make her home there while the railroad was being built so that she could be close to what was going on.

"That's it!" Blaine let go of her hand and jumped up, clapping his hands. Durant and the rest of his men were also standing and cheering now. Reporters began talking among themselves, some running out of the gallery, others coming over to talk to Durant. On the other side of the Senate gallery Central Pacific men were also cheering.

Sunny stayed in her seat, almost stunned. The bill had passed the Senate! She could hardly believe it, after years of fighting and talking and bribing and traveling and praying. She slowly rose, staring down at the circle of seats below, her eyes tearing. *We did it, Daddy,* she thought. *We did it.*

Now the real work began. There were two thousand miles of track to be laid across a dangerous country and impossible mountains, and she was going to be a part of it! No matter what Blaine or Vince or anyone else thought of it, she was going back out to the land she loved and see this thing through to the finish. If possible, she was going to be at the joining of the rails, wherever that ended up taking place, and no matter how many years it took to get there! Nothing, and no one, would stop her now.

Chapter 13

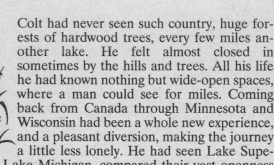

Colt had never seen such country, huge forests of hardwood trees, every few miles another lake. He felt almost closed in sometimes by the hills and trees. All his life he had known nothing but wide-open spaces, where a man could see for miles. Coming back from Canada through Minnesota and Wisconsin had been a whole new experience, and a pleasant diversion, making the journey a little less lonely. He had seen Lake Superior and Lake Michigan, compared their vast openness to the Great Plains.

He had managed to get poor Elam to Canada, something that had turned out to be a harrowing experience. Just before reaching the Canadian border, there had been a Sioux uprising in Minnesota. He had no idea what had set it off, but he didn't doubt it had something to do with some white man doing something insulting and stupid, or maybe over another broken promise.

Whatever the reason, he and Elam had seen the terrible results at two different settlements. They had encountered one group of fleeing settlers who had just vacated an entire small town and were heading for Wisconsin; and he and Elam had spent the rest of their journey doing their best to stay out of sight, hiding not only from the Sioux but from whomever Elam's master might have sent after them.

Elam was safe in Canada now, with a free Negro family who had kindly taken him in. He had learned a lot from the young Negro, and what he had heard he would not soon forget. It didn't seem right for a Christian-minded, freedom-loving country to allow slavery. He had vague memories of his father talking against the issue years earlier, as well as memories about how it felt to be treated like something worthless himself. The banishment of his people, which they now referred to as the Trail of Tears, was something he barely remembered, but sometimes a face would come to mind, an old woman crying, a child being buried. In spite of being so young at the time, he was aware that the experience had left him terribly defensive of his heritage and his person, as well as hurt at being treated as something less than human. He could understand how it must feel to be owned by another man. No man would own him, ever.

He headed Dancer up a sandy slope along Lake Michigan. The only other place he had seen sand like this was in southern Colorado, but there had certainly been no lake to go along with it. Dancer snorted in objection to the difficult climb. "Come on, boy," Colt prodded. "Just a little more. I saw smoke on the horizon. I expect we're getting close."

Horse and man finally reached the top of the sandhill, which had a much steeper descent on the other side. Colt had not realized he was already on some of the highest ground in the area. To the south, along the shoreline and west of it, the land dropped and spread out wide and flat. What it held made Colt stare in awe. He pulled Dancer's reins. "I'll be damned," he muttered.

So, this was Sunny's Chicago. He thought Omaha was

big, but there was no comparison. The city lay sprawled in the distance, smoke coming from tall brick stacks that Colt figured were some of the factories he had read about. Six- and seven-story buildings rose skyward. A river wound through the middle of the mass of tall buildings, and several bridges connected one side to the other, both riverbanks packed with what some men would call civilization. To Colt it was ugly. He would take his mountains any day.

"No wonder Sunny daydreams about the Plains," he said to Dancer. He remembered one article he had read in an Omaha newspaper that spoke of how Omaha would soon be connected by rail to Chicago, "the world's busiest rail center," it had read. Ten major railroad lines led into Chicago, one hundred trains a day coming into or leaving the city. He had taken special note of it because he knew Sunny owned one of those railroad lines outright, and a good share of stock in some of the others. Not only that, but there was Landers Great Lakes Shipping, Landers Warehousing, a freighting and supply company—he shivered. He had not imagined anything this big. Only now did it strike him full force just how rich and powerful Sunny Landers must be.

Was he a fool to come here and try to see her before going off to war? He had to come back south anyway, and someone in Wisconsin had told him that if he wanted to join the Union forces, he should go to Chicago. As long as he was here, it seemed only logical he should pay Sunny a visit. It hardly seemed fair to either of them to be so close and not try to see her. Now he was not so sure. He had not expected this. He thought he had a pretty good idea how big Chicago would be, but he had grossly underestimated what he would find, even though he had read that the city boasted a population of over one hundred thousand people.

He took a moment to gather his courage, deciding he would rather face Indians or stampeding buffalo than to ride into that noisy, smoky mess. He had to admit some of his nervousness had nothing to do with the city. He was worried about seeing Sunny. Maybe she never expected him to show up. Maybe she would be embarrassed or too busy.

Still, he could tell by her letters that she meant every word when she had told him to come. He could see her blue eyes as she wrote those letters, see her smile. It would be almost cruel to be right here on her turf and not go to see her. He squinted, scanning the horizon more, studying a scattering of homes that lay between him and the city proper. It was his understanding that Sunny's home was along the lake. Only about a quarter of a mile in the distance he could see one astounding mansion of a home. It made sense that was the area in which Sunny lived.

His heart raced as he headed Dancer down the steep sandy bank that was dotted with bunches of grass. He breathed in the smell of fish and water, new scents to which he had grown accustomed since arriving in this sometimes swampy country. He suspected that once he got into the city, the air would not smell so sweet. He scowled at the way smoke from the factories darkened the sky. White Buffalo and his people were right about one thing—the white man sure knew how to dirty up the land.

He wondered if it was possible cities could grow this big out west. Omaha was growing, as was Denver and Salt Lake City. None of them came close to Chicago, but neither did those cities have railroads feeding them. If Sunny's railroad got built, a lot of things would change. Still, the money it would take for such a project was enough to send a man's head spinning, certainly bigger numbers than he could imagine.

But Sunny can imagine that kind of money, he thought. He shook his head, his astonishment that she had answered his letters renewed. He slowed Dancer again as he reached the outlying homes. He decided he had better think about this. Perhaps he would just ride into the city first, get a damn good look at this place called Chicago, see what factories looked like, visit the rail yard, find out where to sign up for the army. He'd ask around, find out where Sunny lived for sure. That would give him time to decide if he should bother seeing her at all.

•   •   •

Tod looked up from his desk, a chill creeping down his spine at the sight of the tall, buckskin-clad, wild-looking young man who stood in front of him. He looked dangerous, obviously part Indian, a light scar running across his right eyebrow and down over his temple. Tod swallowed, glancing at the gun and knife the man wore on his wide beaded leather belt. "Can I—help you?"

The man removed his hat, revealing neat, clean, dark hair that hung in waves about his neckline. A surprisingly friendly look came into his hazel eyes, and when he smiled, Tod thought he was outright handsome, or at least he could be if he were not dressed so crudely.

"I'm Colt Travis. I, uh, I don't know if Miss Landers ever mentioned me, but I was her guide a few years ago when she and her father—"

"Travis! So, *you're* Colt Travis!" Tod rose, hardly coming to Colt's shoulders, glad there was a desk between them, since he still wasn't sure he could trust the man. He looked him over, hardly able to believe this was the man Sunny had corresponded with and of whom she talked so fondly. "Yes, I know who you are. I'm Tod Russell, Miss Landers's personal secretary."

Colt frowned. "You work *for* her?"

Tod reddened slightly. "Yes. I worked for her father, and stayed on after he died. Miss Landers took over everything, you know. She needed my expertise to help her through the transition, and she is very pleasant to work for."

Colt grinned. "I'll bet she is." He decided to keep his thoughts to himself. He supposed in this crazy city maybe nobody thought anything about a middle-aged man working for a young woman. He had already given up being surprised at much stranger things he had seen. "Is Sunny in?"

"No. She went home about three o'clock. She had some things to do to prepare for quite a large dinner party she is having tonight at the mansion. I, uh—" Tod hesitated. Was it safe to tell this man where Sunny lived? He could not see why he shouldn't. She seemed to be very fond of him and to trust him, and, after all, there were plenty of men who guarded the mansion and the grounds. "I can explain to you how to find her if you like."

Colt nodded. "Yes, I would." He glanced at another door that read SUNNY LANDERS. "Is that where she does her work when she's in?"

Tod nodded. "Would you like to see her office?"

"Sure, if it's all right."

Tod looked him over again. "I don't know why not." He walked around the desk and opened the door to Sunny's office, standing back and letting Colt inside.

Colt whistled softly as he looked around. "Damn," he muttered. He walked farther into the huge room, admiring the beautiful plants and statues. He heard a birdsong and glanced over at the cage, walking closer. Tod took the opportunity to shake his head and smile disdainfully at how easily impressed this Mr. Travis seemed to be.

Colt studied the canary for a moment, and for some reason it made him think of White Buffalo. "Doesn't seem right, keeping a bird in a cage like that." He thought how the bird seemed kind of a symbol of how the wealthy and powerful could stick people right where they wanted them to be, servants, slaves, cages for animals, reservations for Indians. It wasn't that he blamed someone like Sunny, but she was, after all, a part of the same system. Again it struck him that he must be an idiot for being here at all. He turned and gazed around the office, glancing then at the grandfather clock when it began to chime. He walked closer to it, studying the fine oak cabinet, enjoying the rich sound it made as it sounded out five o'clock.

What beautiful things Sunny had surrounding her. This room reeked of power and money. He turned to study the gilt-framed painting that hung on the wall behind her desk, stepping closer to admire it. "Well, well," he muttered, smiling at the background for the magnificent locomotive. The train was set against wide-open prairie land. It was a beautiful painting, so real that it made him homesick for the West.

He sighed, turning to face Tod. "Can you draw me a map or something, show me how to get to Sunny's home?"

Tod looked him over again. "Of course. The way Miss Landers talks about you, she would probably fire me if I didn't."

Colt followed him to the outer office. "She talks about me that much?"

"Oh, she did for a while there, when you wrote her those letters. But lately she hasn't said so much. She's been so involved with her plans for offices and such in Omaha, what with the railroad act being passed and all. She's a very, very busy lady now."

"They passed a bill for a transcontinental railroad?"

"Yes." Tod sat down and took out a piece of paper and a pen.

"Sunny is going to have offices in Omaha?"

"That's what she says. She might even build a home there. She's in the process right now of finding someone to take over for her here. She wants to take her brother Stuart with her, and of course she would never allow Vince to step into her shoes here. There is no love lost between those two. At any rate—" Tod hesitated, taking a moment to draw some lines and name some streets. "At any rate, between the railroad act and Omaha and a certain Mr. Blaine O'Brien, Miss Landers has her hands full."

"Who is Blaine O'Brien?"

Tod looked up at him. What was this man's interest in Sunny Landers? Was he really just a friend, or was he someone out to get Sunny's money, as Vince yelled at Sunny once? He decided that whatever this Colt Travis wanted, someone like Sunny would never even remotely consider such a primitive, unrefined man as a lover or a husband, discounting the fact that he was half Indian. It gave Tod the shivers to think of how vicious this man could be when necessary, from the stories he had heard. At any rate, he supposed Colt ought to know where things stand before he saw Sunny.

"Mr. O'Brien is Miss Landers's, uh, love interest, you might say." He watched Colt's eyes, caught the little flash of jealousy. So, there *was* a little more here than friendship. He decided that if there was, it was certainly one-sided. This Colt Travis nowhere near compared to Blaine O'Brien. "Mr. O'Brien is one of the richest men in the country," he added, deciding to do his part in discouraging any romantic thoughts this foolish young man might have about Sunny. "His father was owner of O'Brien Shipping, one of the biggest freighting and passenger lines between the United States and Europe. Mr. O'Brien inherited the business. He is also one of the primary investors in the Union Pacific Railroad—that's what the new railroad will be called. He is interested in investing in land in the Northwest. Once the railroad is completed, he believes there will be a huge new market for lumber, and he wants to get in on the ground floor."

Tod enjoyed the idea that he must be greatly impressing Colt with his description of Blaine O'Brien, whom he greatly respected. He looked down and finished his drawing. "Mr. O'Brien has been courting Miss Landers for about a year and half now," he added casually. "Everyone believes they'll end up getting married in the not-too-distant future, but right now Miss Landers says the railroad has to come first. She isn't quite ready for a full commitment, although no one doubts that she loves the man. I suppose her first loyalty is still to her father's memory and his dream of a railroad. Bo Landers was quite a man. I miss him very much." Tod sighed and stood up. "Here you are."

He met Colt's eyes again, but he did not see the disappointment there that he thought he would see. Instead, he saw only a look of contempt. Colt took the paper. "You didn't have to go to so much trouble to make your point, Mr. Russell," he told Tod. He smiled, but it was more of a sneer. "I assure you, I am here only to pay a respectful visit to an old friend, whose life I happened to save more than once, I might add. Believe it or not, people who run in different circles *can* be friends sometimes. Thanks for the map."

"Mr. Travis," Tod said as Colt turned to leave. Colt looked at him, impatience in his eyes. "I was just, well, I wanted you to be aware, that's all. As I told you earlier,

Miss Landers is having a dinner party tonight. You might like to know that Mr. O'Brien will be there, as well as several prominent people from Chicago and New York. It's a kind of celebration dinner for the passing of the railroad act. Miss Landers is leaving day after tomorrow for Omaha."

Colt stared at him a moment, furious at the fact that the man was suggesting he shouldn't go to see Sunny tonight. Was he afraid that he would embarrass her? He turned and left without another word, avoiding the elevator someone downstairs had tried to show to him. He didn't like contraptions that made him feel caged. He took the stairs, his mind racing with indecision. *Would* he embarrass Sunny? One thing was certain—going over there tonight was a damn good way to find out if she had changed. The old Sunny would not be embarrassed at all, and the old Sunny was the one who had come through in the letters.

He stepped into the street, where a few passersby gawked at him as though he were from another world. *Hell, I guess I am,* he thought. He looked at the map, seeing a square marked "office" and another marked "Sunny's home," several blocks to the northeast on the lake. He untied Dancer and mounted up, thinking how painfully ironic it was that he was headed farther east to join the war, while Sunny was heading for his home country. If he had stayed in Omaha a little longer, he might have seen her there, in *his* world, where he would have felt so much more relaxed meeting her again.

He looked up at the tall Landers Enterprises building and shook his head. He was tempted to find a room for the night and say the hell with it, but the fact remained that he was here, and after the letters they had exchanged, no amount of reasoning was going to keep him from seeing her. After all, it would probably be years before he would have this chance again, and he was going off to war while Sunny Landers had a railroad to build—and a man to marry. What was the harm in saying hello?

"Well, boy, let's see if we can find a bathhouse," he told Dancer, turning the horse away from the hitching post. "Apparently, I'd better spruce up a little before experiencing the honor of stepping into the grand household of Miss Sunny Landers."

"Well, what do you think?" Sunny stood back and opened her arms, turning in a circle. Both Mae and Vi smiled with envy but happiness for Sunny's victory.

"I don't believe a more beautiful young woman exists in the whole country," Vi said, shaking her head.

"I have to agree, ma'am," Mae added, thrilled that Sunny had already told her she wanted her to go to Omaha with her.

"I wasn't referring to whether or not I look beautiful," Sunny said with light laughter. "It's just that I have to look just right—I don't know, like a woman of authority. Everyone coming tonight is so important to the railroad."

"Sunny, if you haven't proven your abilities by now, then anyone who still doubts you is a fool," Vi told her. "Stop worrying about how you will be accepted just because you are female." She sighed, looking Sunny over admiringly again. "You have it all, you know—looks, brains, power, wealth—"

"And a man some women would die for," Mae added.

Sunny shrugged and turned to look in the full-length mirror again. "Blaine is the least of my concerns tonight," she told them. "Everyone is so eager to get us together, but I don't know if I love him enough; and right now the Union Pacific is all that matters." She laughed. "I'm in love with a railroad. How do you like that?"

"You're Bo Landers's daughter, all right," Vi told her.

Sunny adjusted the position of the bodice of the dress, moving it down just a little more off her shoulders. The dress had been specially made by her personal tailor, fashioned after the latest designs in England, with dropped sleeves that exposed her milky-white shoulders and a tempting portion of her breasts. A fall of exquisite hand-made lace graced the upper edge of the bodice, hanging down six inches to her elbows. The dress was a deep lavender-blue, with a tight-fitting pointed waist, below which billowed an upper skirt of white tulle and more delicate lace, draped diagonally over an underskirt of lavender-blue silk gathered in hundreds of puffings, each tied with white satin ribbon. She wore the glittering diamond necklace given to her by her father when she turned sixteen, and on her wrist she wore a bracelet of more diamonds, given to her by Blaine as a celebration gift before she left Washington. Tiny diamond earrings graced her earlobes, exposed by an upswept hairdo that came together at her crown in a tumble of waves and curls that fell down her back. Diamond-studded combs decorated her golden hair.

"I have to look just right, especially with Vince coming," she told Vi and Mae. "I can't believe he actually accepted the invitation. I hope he isn't going to do something to ruin the evening."

"I don't think he will," Vi assured her. "Let him eat crow tonight, Sunny."

Sunny turned to face her, smiling lovingly. "What would I have done these last few months without you to talk to?" She sighed deeply. "I hope I'm not the one eating crow a few months from now. All we've done is get government approval and a little help. Actually building the railroad will be another matter."

"You'll do it, ma'am," Mae told her. "I've got no doubt you can do anything you make up your mind to do."

"Thank you, Mae." Sunny walked up and hugged Vi. "I haven't even told you how lovely you look tonight. How rude of me to be fussing over myself like this. Here you are such a busy woman yourself." She stepped back, studying Vi's much plainer dark blue dress. It was elegant and obviously of the best material and design. After all, what Landers woman would wear anything less? But it was a simpler style, fitting for someone like Vi. Sunny thought how the woman's personality made her so beautiful from the inside that a person hardly noticed her plump build and plain features. "You have given me too much of your time, Vi," she told her. "With three children at home and now working at that hospital, I want you to quit worrying about me. I'm going to be fine now." She glanced at Mae. "Would you mind leaving us alone for a few minutes, Mae?"

"Oh, no, ma'am." Mae hurriedly picked up the clothes Sunny had discarded and left the room.

Sunny walked closer and took Vi's hand. "Are you sure you don't mind my taking Stuart to Omaha with me?"

"Of course not," Vi answered, squeezing her hand. "I'm just happy Stuart is willing to go. I hated the way he treated you when I first met him. Besides, he's kind of looking forward to going back out. Actually, it might be good for Stuart to get away from Vince. Vince is always after him about something, deliberately upsetting him. While he's gone I have my work at the hospital."

Sunny studied her kind eyes. "What's it like, Violet? The war seems so far away and unreal, until I see all those soldiers at the railroad station, see the ones coming in wounded and crying with pain."

Vi's eyes misted. "It's terrible. This war is the ugliest thing I've ever seen." She let go of Sunny's hand and turned away. "When I volunteered to help out at the hospital, I thought I was doing my good deed for the day. But it has become something more than that. There is nothing worse than telling a boy of only nineteen or twenty that his leg has to come off, or his arm, or that he'll never live long enough to go home again. I never thought I could bear up under so much pain and tears and blood, but something keeps me going, something helps me ignore the smell and the horror of it." She faced Sunny again. "I guess it's the terror I see in the eyes of those young men. I hold their hand, and I become their wife, their mother, their sweetheart, their comfort."

Sunny sighed, fingering the bracelet at her wrist. "I feel like I should be doing something, too, to help."

"Right now you're doing what *you* have to do, Sunny. We all have our duties in life. Someday soon, I hope, this ugly war will be over, and when it is, that railroad will be needed more than ever. In the meantime life has to go on, and you have a big job ahead of you. Tonight is your night, Sunny. It's the culmination of years of work on your part and your father's before you. Enjoy your victory, and don't let Vince or anyone else do anything to spoil it for you."

Sunny searched her eyes, thinking how Vi had become the closest thing to a mother she would ever have in spite of the fact that the woman was only eight years older than she. "What do you think of Blaine? Am I crazy not to marry him right now? Be a wife? Have children?"

Vi smiled, touching her arm. "I'll tell you something, Sunny. When the right man comes along, you won't wonder and doubt and put other things first. You'll know. Blaine seems wonderful, and no one would argue his looks. But I am not totally certain his personality and yours fit together. A man of so much wealth and power needs a woman who fits in a slightly lower place —a wife, but not a business partner. I worry that you having equal wealth and power might cause problems after a time. I don't think Blaine likes to share the spotlight, but then, you probably know him better than I. He certainly does dote on you. He seems totally smitten."

"I don't know." Sunny looked at the bracelet again. "Sometimes I feel like I'm just another conquest for him. And I always worry that a man is just trying to get his hands on my wealth, even Blaine. Lord knows he doesn't need it, but I don't want to risk losing all that Father worked for to someone who wouldn't love and respect it all the way I do. And sometimes, when Blaine kisses me, I don't know. It's like something is missing, yet he's so good to me, so generous. Sometimes I think there is something wrong with me not being able to respond to him the way I should. I see how other women look at him, and sometimes it makes me a little jealous; but I don't have the passion for him I feel I should have for a man I want to marry."

Vi put an arm around her shoulders. "Give it time, Sunny. Part of your problem is that you have all these other things on your mind. If you aren't ready to be serious, then accept that. Blaine will have to accept it too. Don't marry someone because you feel it's what others expect of you. Do what your *heart* tells you to do."

Mae knocked at the door and peeked into the room. "Excuse me, ma'am, but the butler says to tell you your guests are arriving and the table is ready."

Sunny lit up with excitement. "Thank you, Mae." She took a last look in the mirror, then turned to Vi. "Let's go down and find Stuart. I should be down there greeting my guests."

Vi laughed lightly. "Have fun, Sunny." She followed her out, and guests in the marble foyer looked up at her, a couple of women whispering to each other. Lights from hundreds of candles that flickered in a crystal chandelier hanging from the third story down to the foyer cast a lovely glow on Sunny as she greeted the new arrivals.

Blaine came in from the dining room, and he took Sunny's arm, his face lighting up with pleasure and desire at the sight of her. "My God, Sunny, I've never seen you look more beautiful," he told her, leaning down and kissing her cheek. "Come, come! Vince and Eve are here, and the whole Landers board and four representatives for Durant. They have brought a letter from the Doctor, expressing his regrets that he couldn't be here himself. Oh, and Senator Cunningham is here."

He turned from her a moment to greet more newcomers, the owner of a steel mill and the owner of a coal processing plant, and their wives. Sunny watched him, thinking what a fitting husband he truly would be. Blaine was the epitome of wealth and grace and manners, a man totally comfortable with the rich and powerful. Surely she was a fool not to see that he was the perfect match, yet there was that nagging doubt. Was Vi right in saying that perhaps they were each too wealthy in their own right to get along?

She decided this was not the time to worry about it. Blaine understood that for now the railroad came first, and this was her night to shine. She walked with him into the dining hall, where a forty-foot-long table displayed the finest of china and silver and crystal. Silver candelabra shed an elegant light on the setting, and servants were moving about the crowd, carrying silver trays of drinks. Sunny greeted guests, felt the stares of envy, knew the women were gossiping about her and Blaine.

Blaine left her for a moment and returned with two glasses of white wine. He put one into her hand and took her aside, kissing her cheek again. He held up his glass. "To the Union Pacific," he said softly, his eyes glittering with intense desire, "and to us." He touched her glass.

"To the railroad, and to us," she answered. They each took a sip of wine.

"You are absolutely gorgeous tonight, Sunny. Sometimes you drive me insane with your beauty."

Sunny smiled. "And you are too—" Her voice left her then, and she slowly lowered her glass.

The room had quieted, and Blaine turned to see what Sunny and the others were staring at. At the entrance to the dining hall stood a tall, dark, rugged-looking man wearing denim pants and a simple clean white shirt. He was handsome in his own right, and looked part Indian, certainly not a man of the social standing that belonged in a place like this; and there was a wild look about him, a scar over his right eye.

"My God," Sunny said in a near whisper. "It's Colt!"

Chapter 14

"What the hell?" Blaine's eyes widened with instant jealousy combined with embarrassment when Sunny suddenly handed him her wineglass and rushed over to the man standing at the entrance to the dining hall. He watched her eagerly take his hand, and everyone else in the room turned to stare in surprise.

"Colt!" Sunny exclaimed, her heart pounding with joy and excitement. "Is it really you? I can't believe my eyes! Where have you been? What brings you to Chicago?"

He squeezed her hand. "Hello, Sunny." Colt was surprised at how he felt at finally seeing her again—warm, even a little shaken. He had no doubt that she would be beautiful, but this was more than he had expected. He studied the eyes that he had forgotten were so intensely blue, and he saw no disappointment or embarrassment there, only a great joy at seeing him. "Why I'm here is a long story, but I should have warned you. I guess I came at a bad time."

Sunny looked him over, as surprised by how she felt as Colt was, both of them struggling to hide their true feelings. She in turn had not pictured him quite like this —even more handsome, the fullness of a man to him. In those gentle hazel eyes she could see beyond the momentary joy, could see the tragedy in his life. Where had he gotten the scar over his eye?

"There could never be a bad time for you to come and see me, Colt," she answered, feeling suddenly too warm. "I just—I'm so surprised! This is wonderful! Just wonderful!"

Colt glanced around the room, beginning to feel uncomfortable under the critical stares of Sunny's well-to-do guests. "I, uh, I really do think I should come back. I came only to let you know I was here and to arrange a time to come back when you're not so involved." Why was it so hard to let go of her hand?

"After all these years, and as elusive as you are? I'll not let you out of my sight for one minute!" Sunny declared. She gave him that smile he remembered, the one that made her look so delicious. She kept hold of his hand and walked closer to the huge table, tugging him along. Blaine and Vince both watched in horror as Sunny seemed to lose all composure. "Everyone! This is someone you *must* meet! This is—"

"Colt! Colt Travis!" Stuart had reentered the dining hall after giving some instructions to the cooks. "My God, man, is it really you?" He walked up to Colt, beaming. He put out his hand.

Colt finally let go of Sunny in order to shake hands with her brother. "Hello, Stuart."

"By God, it's good to see you! What on earth are you doing in a place like Chicago?"

Vince moved closer to Eve, his face deep red with anger. "I can just imagine what he's doing here," he muttered to his wife.

"Yes. So can I," Eve answered, raising her chin slightly to give Colt a haughty, defensive stare. "Look at him, how he's dressed. He's dangerous. He's probably never carried more than ten dollars on him his whole life."

Others whispered among themselves as Colt and Stuart talked, and Blaine struggled to keep calm and act as though the intrusion was really nothing. He headed over to Sunny.

"I've signed up for the Union Army," Colt was telling Stuart.

"The army!" Sunny could not hide her disappointment and fear. "Why!"

"A Texan fighting for the Union?" Stuart grinned. "Well, you never were one to do the expected."

Colt grinned a little. "I have my reasons."

"Well, Sunny, how about a more formal introduction for the rest of us?" Blaine put on his best smile and placed his hands on Sunny's bare shoulders, a possessive gesture Colt did not miss when he turned to greet the tall, handsome man who had spoken. Blaine reached across Sunny's shoulder and held out his hand. "Blaine O'Brien. Sunny and I are, well, close to being married, I guess you'd say."

Colt read the animosity in the man's eyes, wondering what "close to being married" meant. He had not actually said Sunny was his fiancée. "Colt Travis," he answered. "Sunny has no doubt told you about me." He did not miss the meaning of the way O'Brien squeezed his hand a little more firmly than necessary.

"And how soon will you be joining the army?" Blaine asked, putting his hand back on Sunny's shoulder.

Colt watched his dark eyes. *The sooner better as far as you're concerned, I'll bet,* he thought. "Tomorrow." He saw the relief in O'Brien's eyes.

"Oh, Colt, so soon?" Sunny took his hand again, and Colt noticed she wore no engagement ring. In spite of the fact that he had no romantic notions about her, he could not help feeling protective, and a surprising jealousy at the way Blaine O'Brien touched those bare, milky-white shoulders; nor could he help another glance at the full, firm breasts that were teasingly exposed by the cut of her dress. He had never seen such a beautiful gown, or such smooth, unblemished skin. And he had certainly never seen so many glittering diamonds.

"No sense putting it off," he told her. Was that really fear and concern he saw in her eyes? Sunny kept hold of his hand and led him away, leaving Blaine standing alone and again struggling with his anger.

Sunny walked closer to Vi then. "Vi—everyone—this is Colt Travis, as all of you know by now," she announced. "Colt was our scout when Father and I went out west five years ago. You should know that this man saved my life—more than once." Most everyone smiled and nodded their greetings, murmuring and staring. Colt could almost hear the unspoken remarks and began feeling more uncomfortable by the minute. "Colt, this is Violet, Stuart's wife, and a dear friend."

Colt shook Vi's hand, seeing in her eyes a true joy at meeting him.

"Sunny has told me so much about you," she said. "Apparently, without you Sunny wouldn't be with us at all." Vi glanced at Sunny, realizing she had never seen her look so totally happy and enraptured as at that moment. Sunny again took hold of Colt's hand, as though she were afraid he would bolt and run at any moment. She led Colt around the room, which was so big that the voices echoed against the high walls decorated with expensive paintings. "This is my tutor, Hannah Seymour," Sunny was saying. "I'm studying German and French. We expect to have a lot of foreign investment in the Union Pacific, and I think I should know some foreign languages. . . . This is Ted Regis, and his fiancée, Naomi West. Ted's father is Harold Regis, owner of the biggest bank in Chicago—oh, this is Harold right here."

In spite of its size, Colt felt the room closing in around him. He was introduced to bankers, lawyers, doctors, industrialists, and even a senator. He was meeting some of the wealthiest people in the country, some of whom, including Sunny, were even well acquainted with the President of the United States. He sensed a genuine welcome from only a few of them, knew exactly what the rest were thinking when they looked him over with those judgmental eyes. He hated their limp handshakes and condescending smiles, and he suspected that some of them could be as vicious as the worst outlaw or Indian, except that they did not deal their blows physically. They did their back-stabbing and scalping in other ways.

"And this is my brother Vince and his wife, Eve," Sunny was saying.

"Well, the famous Colt Travis," Vince said. He did not offer his hand. "We've heard a lot about you, most of it like something out of a dime novel, I must say. According to Sunny, you are nothing short of a hero, but then, that was a long time ago, wasn't it? And Sunny was such a young thing." He looked Colt over as though there were something reprehensible about him. "And now here you are, just an 'old friend,' right?"

Colt held his eyes, understanding now the kind of hell Sunny must have been through with this man as an enemy. Vince was big and arrogant, and apparently capable of being very rude. He knew exactly what the man was thinking. "Right," he answered. "Just an old friend. I guess I can thank you for instigating the letters between me and Sunny. Your lawsuit against Sunny made the Omaha newspaper. That's how I found out your father had died. I decided to write Sunny and tell her how sorry I was about her loss—and her troubles," he added with a menacing glare. In spite of having just met the rather infamous Vince Landers and realizing none of what had happened was any of his business, he could not help an instant dislike of the man for the way he had treated Sunny. He wondered at these ridiculous protective feelings as if he were suddenly again responsible for Sunny's safety.

Sunny anxiously watched the two men stare at each other, fearful of what Vince would say next, rejoicing inside at Colt's clever rebuff. Vince moved his gaze to her then. "You remember some of the things I told you." He glanced past her. "Blaine is waiting for you, and he doesn't look too happy. Don't shame yourself, Sunny." He took Eve's arm and walked off to greet someone else.

Sunny watched after him, and Colt saw her stiffen

and raise her chin. She looked up at him apologetically. "I'm sorry. I don't even know why I invited him tonight. I guess I just thought that because he's my brother it was the right thing to do. I'm sure he accepted the invitation only to make himself look good in front of all the other important people here tonight."

Colt glanced over to watch Vince laughing and shaking hands with the senator. "Now that I've met him, I can't help thinking you're some woman, Sunny. He must have put you through hell."

She stopped a servant carrying a tray of filled wineglasses and took two, handing one to Colt. "It's over now. I've handled all of it the best I can." She took his arm and put on a smile. "And I feel only pride at having you here. Don't listen to anything Vince says. Let's get back to the table. You are staying and eating with us, and I won't take no for an answer." She led him to the chair at her right hand and ordered a servant to set an extra place at the other end of the table and rearrange the seating.

Blaine managed to continue to check his own rage when he saw Sunny offer Colt the place that was supposed to be his. *Audacious sonofabitch!* he fumed inwardly. Men like Colt Travis didn't deserve to be at such an elegant gathering, let alone sit at the right hand of someone as important as Sunny. He forced himself to keep a friendly look on his face as he moved around to the first seating on Sunny's left. The waiter hurriedly readjusted the white and gold lace-trimmed seating cards, and guests began gathering at their proper places, but remained standing as Sunny raised her wineglass for a toast.

"I want to tell all of you that this is the most wonderful moment of my life," she said. "I only wish Daddy—my father—could be here." She blinked back tears and took a deep breath. "I planned this dinner party to celebrate the passing of the railroad act—the beginning of the realization of a grand dream, begun by men like Dr. Durant, and my father. All of you know I intend to carry on that dream and will be leaving for Omaha very soon." She glanced at Colt again, and both of them felt the irony of their situation, at the same time wondering at the painful nostalgia that had engulfed them the moment they set eyes on each other. "This celebration has taken a new twist," she continued, again scanning the fifty-four people who stood at their places, smiling and listening. Colt could not help wondering how many of them would disappear from Sunny's life if she suddenly lost all her money. "Now we can also welcome a man deserving of our friendship and praise," she was saying. "If any of you has ever wanted to meet a real hunter and scout from the Wild West, he is standing right next to me. Colt saved me from a buffalo stampede, from outlaws who threatened my person and my father's life; and it was his quick thinking that saved me from an infection that could have caused me to lose my leg, maybe even my life."

Colt felt a warmth in his cheeks at the praise, a little embarrassed. He grinned and shook his head as remarks of "good man" and "well done" moved around the table.

"Colt is an honest-to-goodness scout and Indian fighter," Sunny went on. "He has led wagon trains and hunted buffalo. When we first met him he was only twenty, and he had already been to Oregon and California several times. When we were corresponding, he was riding for the Pony Express; and more recently, he lived among the Cheyenne, who had saved his life." There came a few gasps and intense stares that made Colt want to disappear.

"Not so unusual, considering he's half Indian himself," Vince added. It was obvious to everyone that Vince was already feeling his wine, that he had been drinking before he arrived. "Tell the gentlefolks here, Mr. Travis—how many Indians and, uh, outlaws, have you killed? Do you prefer to knife them or shoot them, or what?"

The table quieted, and Sunny paled, her eyes widening with rage. "Vince!"

"Well, hell, if he's such a hero, we'd like to hear all the gory details. After all, none of us has ever been exposed to that barbaric kind of life. It's quite a thrill to hear about it. Imagine, having a near savage at our very table. Tell us, Mr. Travis, have you ever taken scalps?"

Colt's eyes bore into the man, all gentleness gone. The room hung so silent, people could hear one another breathing. Everyone stared at Colt, some feeling sorry for him, others feeling near fear at the wildness about him, and the look he was giving Vince that very moment.

"Yes, if you want the truth," Colt finally answered, his voice low and firm. "I've taken scalps—Pawnee. They raped and murdered my wife and smashed in the head of my four-month-old son. Things like that can make a man do a lot of things he wouldn't normally do."

Gasps and whispers moved around the table, and Sunny's eyes stung with tears of sorrow for Colt, and rage at Vince. Vince reddened with embarrassment but refused to show any remorse for his remark.

Colt's jaw flexed in anger. He fixed his gaze on Vince a moment longer, then glanced at Blaine O'Brien, still seeing the challenge and contempt in the man's eyes. He felt it was Blaine's place to step in for Sunny in some kind of word or deed that would help her through this awkward moment, but it was obvious Blaine was as eager for Colt to look bad in front of Sunny and the others as Vince was. What kind of people were these vultures that surrounded Sunny? No one said a word.

He directed his gaze to each person at the table, women wearing diamonds, their hair coiffed into curls, pinned with fancy combs; the men scrubbed clean, even to their fingernails, gold watches hanging from their vests. "I've killed men," he told them, "white and Indian alike, and all of them deserved to die. Out west the code of life is different from what it is here in what you call civilization. Out west it's survival of the fittest, and for people like me violence sometimes becomes a way of life. I've got the scars to prove it." He set down his wineglass. "There are a lot of graves along the Oregon Trail, and Sunny's railroad is going to save a lot of lives in the future—maybe bring some law and order to a violent land. I hope all of you with your millions will do what you can to help her." He looked at Sunny. "I'm sorry I broke in on your party. Like I said before, it's better that I leave." He turned to go, but Sunny grasped his arm.

"No," she said firmly. "You are the most honored guest at this table. I owe you my life." The words were spoken with fire, her voice suddenly lower and almost threatening. Colt looked at her in surprise, seeing the complete change in those blue eyes. The almost childish joy and excitement she had shown a moment earlier had been replaced by a firm determination. For the first time he saw the hard side of Sunny Landers, the strength and resolve one would expect from her father. She had turned her attention to Vince, and the look in her eyes was almost frightening.

"My brother has insulted a dear friend," she said, obviously talking to everyone present, but keeping her eyes on Vince. "As everyone knows, I didn't need to invite you here tonight, Vince. I did it because you are my brother, and because I thought now that the railroad act had been passed, you would see that Father's dream can become a reality. I thought you would want to celebrate with us, maybe even take an interest. But since you have seen fit only to be insulting, then I think you and Eve had better leave. Besides, you're already drunk."

"Sunny, don't do this because of me," Colt said quietly.

"This has nothing to do with you," she answered, her eyes still on Vince. "It's more than that."

Several guests cleared their throats, some looking down at their plates, everyone trying to hide their embarrassment for both Sunny and Vince, all well aware of the problems the two of them had had in the past.

"I agree with Sunny." Stuart spoke up, glaring at Vince.

Vince sneered at him. "Well, you always were one to go with the flow, weren't you, Stuart?" His eyes glittered with contempt as he turned them again to Colt. "Well, Mr. Travis, enjoy your meal. Where you are going, it could be your last one; but then, at least the Union

Army is getting a man who won't hesitate when it comes to shooting another man down, isn't that right?"

"At least the people I hurt are the enemy," Colt answered boldly. "Men who would kill me first if they could. I don't go around attacking the people I am *supposed* to *love,* people with my own blood running in their veins."

Vince stiffened at the intended slam, and others let out little gasps, some even grinning at the well-aimed remark. Sunny could not help a subtle smile of her own.

"This is an outrage!" Eve spat out.

Vince took her arm. "All we have done is try to keep Sunny from destroying Landers Enterprises," he said, looking around the table. "If the rest of you want to throw your money away on this railroad, be my guest."

"Get out, Vince," Sunny told him firmly.

Vince glared at Colt a moment longer, then looked at Sunny. "Someday you'll understand that everything I've done was to try to protect you."

"The only thing you think you're protecting is your source of income," Sunny answered. "Please leave before I have someone come and take you out bodily."

He glowered at her a moment longer, and Colt was astonished that the man could look that way at his own sister, especially one as sweet as Sunny could be; although at the moment all that sweetness had vanished. It was easy to see that Sunny Landers could be tough as nails when necessary. Vince turned and left without another word, Eve holding up her chin defiantly and following him out, skirts rustling, feet stomping.

"My apologies," Sunny told her guests. She closed her eyes a moment, breathing deeply to regain her composure. As soon as Vince was gone she again became the sociable, generous, smiling Sunny Landers. She raised her wineglass again. "Now, I want all of you to enjoy yourselves. The servants will be bringing food until you think you cannot eat another bite—oysters, ham, turkey, shrimp, beef. I want you to eat and drink to your heart's content. In a little while an orchestra will entertain you upstairs in the ballroom. This is meant to be a night of celebration, and I am personally proud and excited to have a man here who was a part of helping Bo Landers see for himself that a railroad certainly can be built across the western plains and mountains." She looked at Colt again. "To Colt Travis—and the Union Pacific!"

Colt studied her eyes as others repeated the toast and drank their wine. He saw a strength in the woman that amazed him, and he also saw the side of Sunny Landers that belonged to this world of wealth and power. She ordered the servant who had been pouring wine to "give the signal." Colt watched as the man pulled a cord that hung at the wall, and in moments more servants began streaming in, carrying silver trays stacked with food. Chairs made scraping sounds on the marble floor as everyone sat down. Blaine pulled out Sunny's chair for her and she took her place. "Are you all right?" the man asked, leaning down to kiss her shoulder from behind before taking his own seat.

Sunny blushed, turning to give him a disgruntled look. "You could have said something on my behalf."

Blaine frowned, taking his own chair. "Darling, you know I'm no fan of Vince's. But I don't feel I have a right to get involved in your family squabbles just yet. Once we're married I'll handle the bastard myself. You won't have to ever face him again." He put a hand over hers, but she drew hers away, looking at Colt.

"Thank you for what you said about the railroad—and for what you said to Vince. I suppose I never should have invited him."

Colt glanced at Blaine again, realizing the man must be furious that Colt had inadvertently stepped in where Blaine should have. Blaine looked ready to kill. "I was probably out of line, Sunny," Colt answered, "but I don't lie back for insults. And don't be upset with Mr. O'Brien," he added, trying to smooth things over so as to avoid more confrontations. "The insult was directed at me, and it was my place to answer it, not his." He looked at Blaine again and saw a hint of appreciation; but there was no doubt that the man considered Colt some kind of a challenge. Colt thought it absurd that he should think Colt had any intention of taking his place in Sunny's life. This world he had walked into was as far from anything he would want as it could be.

Still, he could not help the irritation he felt at the thought of Blaine O'Brien touching Sunny the way he had; could not help wondering just how deeply Sunny had fallen for the man's charms. Did she give him more than kisses? He looked away, staring at an assortment of silverware, wondering which fork or spoon he was supposed to use first. More than that, he wondered why in hell he cared what kind of sexual favors Sunny gave to her "almost" husband.

"I see you're wearing the bracelet I gave you," Blaine was saying. While Colt's thoughts had been reeling with confusion, Sunny had apologized to Blaine, and now he was rubbing her forearm affectionately. He glanced at Colt. "I gave Sunny this bracelet in Washington, after the railroad act was passed," he explained. "Diamonds do fit her, don't they?" He took Sunny's hand and kissed it. "Even diamonds don't seem good enough."

Sunny blushed, and Colt felt he was being given the same subtle hints that Bo Landers had given him that night he had asked him to eat with them out on the prairie. He scooted back his chair a little. "I—uh, I really am not hungry, Sunny," he said. "I ate a pretty big meal before I came. I'm very sorry about my timing. I'll just leave you to your guests and—"

"No! Don't go, please." She looked at him with the same pleading look he had seen the night before he left Fort Laramie. It was awfully hard to say no to those blue eyes.

"Sunny, I don't belong here."

"Don't eat if you don't want to. But please do stay until we get a chance to talk. And you belong here just as much as anyone in this room. As far as I am concerned, your timing couldn't be better, considering the reason we are celebrating here tonight."

"Not to worry, Mr. Travis," Blaine said. "If Sunny wants you here, you're welcome, I'm sure. I personally am glad to have the chance to meet you and talk with you. After all those letters you exchanged with Sunny, I have to admit my curiosity was getting the better of me.

Are you really only twenty-five? With all the things you've done in your life, I should think you would be older."

Colt drank down his wine. "I'm really only twenty-five." He pulled his chair back in a little, but he still was not sure he should stay.

"I wonder how hunting buffalo compares to hunting elephants in Africa," Blaine was saying. "I've done big-game hunting myself, you know. Now, there is something you would probably really enjoy. Of course Indians, that's another story. I have no experience in that area, but then, I just might soon. I'll be leaving in a few days for Oregon. I'm interested in the logging business —figure once the railroad goes through, there will be quite a market. A man has to always be looking for new investments, you know. That's how the money grows."

"Is that so?" A waiter started to set a bowl of oysters in front of Colt, but Colt waved him off. "The most investing I've ever done is to buy a damn good horse," Colt added, accepting more wine from another waiter. He looked at Sunny and caught the smile at the corner of her mouth.

Blaine stiffened slightly. "Yes, well, I suppose there is a comparison. Of course, when you own an ocean freighting and passenger service, you have a little more to think about than buying a horse, but then, it's a matter of perspective."

Colt did not miss any of the innuendos, nor did he miss the deliberate loving looks and touches O'Brien gave Sunny. "Sunny here is quite a woman, isn't she? She's done a hell of a job taking over Landers Enterprises and working to get the railroad act passed. That's how we met, you know. I'm part of Thomas Durant's investment group—president of his Pennsylvania Fiscal Agency. Sunny came to one of our meetings, and one look was all I needed. When she started talking and spouted all that business know-how and showed she was not only beautiful but intelligent, I knew what I wanted."

"A perfect match, I'd say," a lawyer sitting near Colt

said. "Put them together and they could buy all of Chicago and then some!"

A round of laughter and cheers made its way around the table, and Sunny glanced at Colt almost apologetically. Colt felt dizzy with a mixture of emotions, wishing their first meeting could have been alone instead of in the middle of all this distraction.

"Another toast," Stuart suggested. "To Sunny and Blaine."

"Hear! Hear!" someone added.

Sunny could not take her eyes from Colt, could not help the shiver she felt when his gaze fell to her breasts. For a brief flash she remembered how she had thought of him when Blaine was kissing her breasts that night in the carriage. She felt the color come to her cheeks, and she forced herself to look at Blaine and smile as everyone raised their glasses and drank to them.

Blaine's eyes also moved over her in that way he had of making her feel undressed. "Maybe it won't be long before we're holding an engagement party," he told her.

Vi watched Sunny, wondering about the remark she had made about having special feelings for the man she would marry. She had not missed the light in Sunny's eyes when she greeted Colt Travis. Where was the poor girl's heart leading her? She had nothing against the handsome and apparently very brave and skilled Colt Travis, but an attraction beyond friendship between the two of them could lead only to disaster. Two people could not be more different.

More food was served, as well as more wine. Sunny's guests began loosening up from the alcohol in their blood, and social conversation moved into a more frivolous mood. Several of those at the table began peppering Colt with questions about the West and Indians—could a railroad be built out there? Was it really just a big, worthless desert? Did every man who went west have to worry about his scalp? Were there really millions of buffalo? They wanted descriptions of the land, explanations as to why the Indians were so warlike. Why had he lived with the Cheyenne?

Blaine's insides burned with frustration at the way

Sunny's eyes lit up as she listened to Colt's answers. He wondered what the hell she saw in the man. He didn't have much use for Vince, but at the moment Blaine had to agree with what he suspected Vince felt about all of this—that Colt Travis saw in Sunny a tremendous opportunity to become a rich man the easy way; but if Colt Travis thought someone of Sunny's social status would ever consider linking up with a worthless drifter, a half-breed no less, the man was crazy! Still, Sunny had never looked at him the way she was looking at Colt tonight.

The bastard! Look at him, showing up out of nowhere, pretending just to be on his way to join the army. He hoped Mr. Colt Travis was destined to be shot and killed in the line of duty and would never return. He wanted dearly to challenge him, to show him up in front of Sunny for what he really was, but he knew he didn't dare insult him at this particular moment. The mood Sunny was in, she would never forgive him. He noticed Colt studying his silverware, apparently confused. Blaine realized it was the perfect opportunity to get in another subtle insult. "It's this one," he said aloud, putting on a friendly smile and holding up a tiny fork to show Colt. "That's shrimp they've put on your plate. Ever tasted it?"

Colt stared at the strange-looking food for a moment, thinking it looked horrible, but he was not about to admit it in front of Mr. Blaine O'Brien. "Of course I have," he lied. He picked up the ridiculously small fork and stabbed one of the shrimp. He bit off a piece, surprised at how good it was after all. It reminded him of rattlesnake.

"But you prefer a good, tender piece of buffalo, I'll bet," Blaine said with a patronizing grin.

Colt set down his fork, returning the fake smile. "Actually, I would," he answered. "And raw. It's always better raw. Tell me, Mr. O'Brien, have you ever held the heart of a buffalo in your hands while it's still warm and taken a bite out of it?" He watched Blaine pale, his smile fade. "Best thing in the world," he added. "That's what keeps Indians tough."

Blaine looked wide-eyed at Sunny when she laughed

at the comment rather than being appalled. "I'm afraid we don't have any raw buffalo heart tonight, Colt," she told him. "If I had known you were going to be here, I would have put it on the menu." Colt laughed with her, glancing at Blaine again and feeling the hatred behind the weak smile.

The rest of the guests were lost in their own chatter, a man here talking about how he had only ten thousand to invest, a woman there talking about the latest fashions, their empty laughter making Colt long for the quiet of the prairie. He tried to guess how long the table was, how much the china and silver settings must be worth. He looked around the room, noticing the chandelier above the table, the delicate scrollwork of the wooden beams that decorated the cathedral ceiling. He had no idea what kind of wood it was, but it was beautiful.

He wished now that he had followed his impulse when he first set eyes on the Landers mansion and had just kept riding. The ornate home was situated on the shores of Lake Michigan, surrounded by other imposing homes. The whole area, this house, these people, all reeked of money and power. In spite of her basic sweetness, Sunny herself eminated that same aura. He had seen her wield that power against her domineering brother, and he could just imagine how forceful and demanding she could be in business when necessary. She would never have survived to this point if she were not able to be as ruthless and clever as the people with whom she associated.

He sure as hell didn't fit into any of this. Again he felt stifled, felt as though the whole house were going to fall in on him at any moment. He scooted back his chair again, feeling a sudden need for fresh air. "I really don't belong here, Sunny," he said then, sobering. "And don't beg me to stay another minute. I'm leaving, and that's that. I'll come back in the morning, as God is my witness."

The joy left her eyes. "Oh, Colt, you shouldn't feel you don't belong here. You're always welcome in my home. You know that."

"I do know it. But not when your home is filled with people who look at me like a wild animal who's been let off his leash. We'll talk after all these people are gone and things are nice and quiet. I'll have a little time in the morning before I leave." He rose. "Thanks for inviting me in and introducing me to everyone; but this is your night. I'm really sorry I put a dent in things."

"Colt, you aren't leaving!" Stuart excused himself and rose.

"I think it's best," Colt answered.

A few people turned to stare, but most continued with their meal and chatter, forks clinking against plates, wineglasses being emptied as fast as they were filled. Two men playing violins came down the wide circular staircase that led to the upper balconies and the ballroom. They began walking around the table, playing soft music.

Sunny felt helpless and pressured, suddenly frantic that if Colt left, he wouldn't come back, yet realizing she couldn't run after him and beg him not to go. Colt gave her a nod. "Thanks, Sunny. I'll see you tomorrow."

Sunny started to rise, but Blaine touched her arm. "Stuart and I will see him to the door, dear. You really should tend to your guests."

"Oh, is he leaving?" one woman asked. "You ought to stay, Mr. Travis. We do want to hear more about your wild Indians and such. Is it true that a buffalo is nearly as big as an elephant?"

Colt ignored the question. "I have an appointment to keep," he lied. "Thank you for your hospitality." He glanced at Sunny once more, trying to assure her with his eyes that he would be back.

"What an intriguing young man," one woman mentioned as he turned and left.

"Sunny, did you really correspond with him?" The question came from Ted Regis's fiancée. "Does he actually know how to write?"

Sunny could hardly concentrate for wanting to run and give her apologies to Colt. "Of course he can write," she answered. "Colt was raised by a missionary father who was also a teacher. He isn't nearly as uncivi-

lized and uneducated as all of you think. He has just
grown up in a violent land and had a lot of bad luck. He
has no family, no one who cares."

Except for you, Vi thought. *Watch your heart, Sunny.*

"I hope we didn't scare him away, dear," another
woman put in.

Sunny hardly heard the remark. She turned to look at
the entrance to the room, but Colt and Stuart and
Blaine were gone.

At the front door Stuart shook Colt's hand. "It's just
too damn bad we don't have more time to talk, Colt,"
he told him. "What a shock it was to see you. I'm damn
sorry about your wife and son, and the best of luck to
you in the army. It's a hellish war, from what I read. My
wife works at a hospital here in Chicago, where
wounded men who need long rehabilitation are brought.
I hate to think of you getting wounded like that. You
watch yourself." He laughed. "Well, I guess I don't have
to tell you that, do I?"

"Thanks, Stuart. Maybe after the war I'll see all of
you again."

"Yes, you should do that. I imagine we just might be
living in Omaha by then."

"And Sunny and I will be set up in our own home,"
Blaine put in. "I don't know if it will be Chicago or
Omaha, maybe even New York. I'll let Sunny decide
that. Makes no difference to me, as long as she is Mrs.
Blaine O'Brien."

Colt tried to ignore the remark, saying another good-
bye to Stuart. "I hate to leave it like this, but I do have
to get back to the dinner," Stuart told him. "Do take
care of yourself, Colt." The man left, and Colt walked
outside, feeling Blaine close on his heels. He reached
Dancer and began untying the reins, turning to face
Blaine. "Nice meeting you," he said, trying to keep
things civil.

"I wish I could say the same," Blaine answered, the
bitterness coming through full force now. "Tell me,
Travis, what is the *real* reason you're here?"

Colt sighed. "Exactly what I said," he answered. "Just

visiting an old acquaintance who was nice enough to care when I lost my wife and child."

Blaine faced him squarely. "I'm sorry about your tragedy, Mr. Travis, but the point is you're alone again, so let's get something straight. Sunny Landers is going to be my wife someday. She needs a man of her own social status, one who understands money and power—one who has plenty of both all on his own. I have bought and sold men like you many times over. If you think you can come here and pick up on some old childish crush Sunny might have had on you, think again. You would be destroyed—by wealth and power that would overwhelm a man like you. And if you do anything to turn Sunny's eyes from me, *I* will destroy you! Fighting your Indians and buffalo hunters and whatever else you've done won't compare to what I can do to a man like you, with one snap of a *finger!* You remember that when you have your little talk with her in the morning. Make sure it's a final good-bye. And don't think I won't be joining the two of you for breakfast!"

Colt stared at him, a look coming into his eyes that made Blaine swallow and tremble, although he kept his eyes boldly locked on Colt. "If you're this unsure of Sunny's love for you because of a visit from an old friend, the two of you must not have much of a relationship," he told Blaine. "And from what I've seen, you aren't any better suited for her than *I* am!" He turned and mounted Dancer. "Don't worry, O'Brien. I came here as a friend, whether you want to believe that or not. When a man sees his wife's nude body filled with arrows and his son's head smashed, he doesn't have much stomach or desire for letting himself care about another woman, not for a long time." He leaned closer. "You actually think I'm after Sunny's money, don't you?" He shook his head. "Jesus," he muttered. He pulled back on Dancer's reins, making the horse turn in a circle. "I care about *Sunny,* nothing more. Her money means no more to me than cow shit. And I'm more impressed by a good horse than I am by you, O'Brien. Don't ever challenge me like that again. I don't take threats lightly, and if we were on *my* turf, you'd be begging for your *life* right about now!"

He kicked Dancer's sides and rode off, the horse's hooves clacking against the brick drive. He headed down the street, his head aching with a need to hit someone. He cut between two thick rows of neatly trimmed shrubs, guiding Dancer down a sandy bank toward the lake.

"Bastard," he muttered. "We'll outsmart him, boy," he told Dancer. "We'll just camp out on the beach below the bluff behind her house and wait for the party to end."

They reached the damp sand, and the sound of the waves was music to Colt's ears compared to the laughter and empty talk going on inside the Landers mansion. He dismounted and spread a blanket out on the sand. He stretched out on the blanket, lying on his back and looking up at the stars. "God, this feels good," he said aloud. "I couldn't breathe in there."

The night was warm, with just enough of a soft breeze to keep away the mosquitoes. He would wait until the party was over. He argued that he was probably a fool to do this at all. He should leave and forget the whole thing. But now that he had looked into Sunny's blue eyes again, remembered the kindness in her letters, he couldn't go yet. Besides, he had promised her they would get a chance to talk alone, and alone it would be. If Mr. Blaine O'Brien thought he was going to horn in on their morning meeting, then he would just have his talk with Sunny tonight, right down here on the beach.

Chapter 15

Sunny approached the campfire tentatively, remembering another night, when a young Sunny Landers had a painful crush on the tall, handsome Colt Travis. She told herself this was different. They were both older now, leading lives worlds apart from each other. She had learned a lot about life, was more mature, better able to be rational about matters of the heart. She realized Blaine would be furious if he knew she was coming to the beach alone, but Blaine O'Brien did not own her, and she had not decided yet if she ever wanted him to.

She wondered why Colt wanted to meet her at this ungodly hour. After Blaine and the guests had all left, a kitchen maid had come to tell her that a man calling himself Colt had come to the back door with a message that she should come down to the beach. It seemed a ridiculous time to be doing such a thing, but then she realized this was just like something Colt would do, never one to do the expected, just like Stuart had said earlier in the evening. And if the whole thing *was* ridiculous, then she was as crazy as Colt for being here at all.

Why had she felt so compelled to come? Why had she not even questioned whether it was right or wrong? Blaine had stirred enough womanly instincts in her to make her realize there was something inherently dangerous about this, the soft, warm night, a full moon casting a brilliant glitter on Lake Michigan, the mixed feelings she had had earlier tonight when she first set eyes on Colt after such a long time.

She breathed deeply, feeling fifteen again. She touched her hair, now brushed out from the fancy hairdo she had worn earlier. Mae had quickly braided it into one thick plait at her back. She had changed clothes, from her magnificent party dress into a simple blouse and skirt, and she had given Mae instructions that no matter how long she was gone, the girl was not to become alarmed and was not to tell a soul where she was. Mae had barraged her with a thousand questions until Sunny had simply left while the girl was still jabbering.

Waves rolled softly onto the beach, their rushing sound shrouding the scrunch of Sunny's high-top shoes stepping through the sand. She drew closer to the figure sitting cross-legged on a blanket near the fire. "Colt?" she called from the darkness.

Immediately, he jumped to his feet, looking in the direction of her voice. "I'm not used to the sounds in this place," he told her. "Out on the prairie you never would have snuck up on me like that."

She smiled, stepping into the light of the fire. "I was so surprised when the kitchen maid brought your message. I thought you were coming back later this morning."

"I was, but—" He contemplated telling her about Blaine's threat, then decided he had better not bring it up. Looking at her now, he could hardly blame the man for his feelings, and maybe Blaine thought he was looking out for Sunny's best interest after all. Besides, if he told her what had happened, it would make this whole visit look like some kind of romantic challenge, which it wasn't—at least that was what he told himself it shouldn't be. Still, those blue eyes in the soft firelight did something to him. "I thought this would be nicer for both of us. With all those servants you have, we wouldn't really be alone up at the house."

She laughed lightly. "Quite a change from where you come from, isn't it?"

He smiled almost bashfully, taking a deep sigh. "Quite." He glanced at the lights high up on the bluff. "I thought that music would never end. When you throw a party, you do it up right, don't you? I imagine a few of those people are going to wake up with magnificent headaches in the morning."

She laughed more. Colt thought how full and tempting her lips were, how much prettier she was when she dressed simply, as she was now.

"Of that I am sure," she said, sobering. "I just hope Vince is the sickest. I'm so terribly sorry about the things he said, Colt."

"It doesn't matter. I didn't come here to impress him or Blaine or anyone else. I just wanted to see you."

How she loved to hear him talk with that soft drawl. There was that wonderful melting smile she remembered. Again she thought about that last night she saw him at Fort Laramie. Was that five whole years ago? Or was it just yesterday? They watched each other a moment, hardly aware they were moving closer, neither of them quite sure how or why they were suddenly in each other's arms. She rested her head against his chest and he pressed her close, relishing the feel of her against him, remembering how nice it was to hold someone sweet and beautiful and pure.

"Oh, Colt, I'm so glad you decided to do this," she said, feeling safe and protected in his embrace. "I was so tired and was thinking of nothing but sleep; and then I got your message and suddenly I was wide awake. I still can't believe you came to Chicago, but I'm so glad you did." They held each other a moment, both of them confused by their emotions.

"I am too," he told her.

She leaned back slightly to look at him. "Why, Colt? Why do you want to join the army? It's so dangerous. Vi has been working part-time at the hospital, and the awful injuries—men losing legs and arms, even dying of infection from much simpler wounds. It's an ugly, ugly war, Colt, and you have already been through so much."

He watched her eyes, saw her own sudden embarrassment that they had so easily embraced. Colt felt a dangerous stirring deep inside and pulled away from her. "A man has to do *something* with his life. I can't think of a better way to be useful and still have something to do that will help me stop thinking about things that make me want to go crazy." He took her hand. "I put out a blanket here so we can sit." He sat down cross-legged, and Sunny, her cheeks still feeling hot from having let him hold her, tentatively took a place beside him, her legs curled under her. She wondered why, after all these years, she felt such a wonderful comfort in his arms.

"I know what you're thinking, Colt," she told him, her concern for his welfare overpowering a sudden shyness. "You think you're expendable because you're a man without responsibility or family—because you think no one cares. But *I* care, Colt. And I know Stuart thinks a lot of you and so do Vi and a few others, simply because I've told them so much about you." She hesitantly touched his arm. "Please don't go, Colt. You could stay here. I would find some kind of work for you. I'm leaving for Omaha soon. Maybe you could go back and work for the railroad. For heaven's sake, they'll need surveyors, scouts, guides—there are any number of things you could do."

Colt reached in front of him and took his tobacco pouch and a cigarette paper from his saddlebag. "It's something to think about, but not right now." He opened the bag and carefully shook some tobacco from it onto the paper, turning slightly to shelter the loose tobacco from the gentle breeze. "It's going to be a long time yet before your railroad gets under way, Sunny.

I've had enough experience with the government and the Indians to know how long it takes Washington to move on anything, even after they have decided to take action." He packed the tobacco tightly and licked and sealed the paper. "My guess is it will be at least a year before things get off the ground. You're more familiar with how our fine legislators operate. What's your guess?"

Sunny watched him strike a match and light the cigarette. She studied the handsome, hard lines of his face as he smoked. What was it about him that stirred her so? He was nothing like the kind of man to whom she should be attracted. Was it his heroic nature? The hint of danger about him? Or was it simply that he was so forbidden? She moved her eyes to watch the fire. "You understand politics better than I thought," she told him. "Yes, I figure a year, maybe even longer. But it *will* get done, Colt."

He blew smoke into the night air as he let out a sigh. "I have no doubt about that. In the meantime, I have to make myself busy or go insane. I know you care, and I appreciate that; but you're just one person, Sunny. And right now it wouldn't matter *how* many people cared. For the moment I don't give a damn what happens to me, and nothing can change that. There are moments when I would welcome death."

She closed her eyes against the pain of the words. "It was terrible, wasn't it?"

He hesitated a moment, staring at his cigarette. "Worse than anything your imagination could ever conjure up," he answered almost absently. "After that, revenge was all I had to live for. The thought of going after the Pawnee was my medicine. And I by God went after them." The last words were spoken low and mean. He drew deeply on the cigarette. "When I'm not in such civilized places, I still tie the three Pawnee scalps I took that day into Dancer's mane. Dancer is that fine Appaloosa you see hobbled nearby. He's a gift from White Buffalo."

Sunny could just make out the horse's silhouette beyond the fire. The reality of what Colt was telling her made her shiver. What was she doing here, sitting beside this half-breed man who had lived among the Cheyenne, had attacked the Pawnee like the wildest savage, had taken scalps? She remembered how calmly and coldly he had shot the buffalo hunters. It was hard to believe a man like that could turn around and be so thoughtful and caring, could settle with a wife and son, or could have written such wonderful letters.

He was a man of contrasts, and of all the wealthy, famous, and important people she knew, none was as interesting or exciting as Colt Travis. "Did you get that scar over your eye from the Pawnee?" she asked. He did not answer right away, but she could feel his hatred.

"I did," he finally said. "You know, Sunny, a man can kill and kill and kill, and still not be satisfied, because killing a thousand men isn't going to bring back the loved ones you've lost."

She drew up her knees and folded her arms around them. "I don't know what to say. I'm so sorry about all of it. Maybe you need to talk about her, Colt. I'd be willing to listen. What was she like? What was her name?"

He studied his cigarette thoughtfully. "Her name was LeeAnn," he finally said. "We didn't meet the way people normally meet. Actually, I *found* her. She had been traveling with her mother and father. Her mother got sick and died, and before she was buried her father shot himself in his grief—blamed himself, I guess, for bringing her west. I was camped nearby—heard the gunshot. When I went to investigate, I found LeeAnn in hysterics, covered with her father's blood."

"Dear God," Sunny whispered. "How awful!"

"Pretty pitiful. I buried her parents and took LeeAnn to Denver—found a woman who took her in. It took some time for her to recover. We did a lot of talking— kind of identified with each other, you know? Neither of us had one damn person left who knew or cared we existed. I guess it was the loneliness in both of us that—"

He stopped, the words catching in his throat. Sunny

again felt the unwanted jealousy gripping at her. "That made you fall in love," she finished for him.

Colt took another deep breath, and it was obvious he was having trouble finding the words. "I, uh, I used the money your father paid me to set up a little farm in eastern Colorado—built a cabin. We got married, and to my own surprise I actually enjoyed being settled. Then Ethan was born. I helped deliver him myself—my 'little colt' LeeAnn called him, seeing as how the only thing I had ever helped deliver before that was foals."

He smoked a moment longer, and Sunny waited quietly, letting him tell it at his own pace. "I can't even begin to describe how it feels to a man to have a son. I thought I had finally found what I needed in life. And then one day I—" He cleared his throat. "I went hunting. We needed the meat. I've had people tell me I shouldn't blame myself, that I did what any man would do in the same situation. But that doesn't help. I'll never stop blaming myself for being gone that day." His voice turned gruff with anger and bitterness. "Ever since then I've been able to understand why LeeAnn's father shot himself for feeling responsible for his wife's death."

His voice broke on the last few words, and Sunny's heart went out to him. She touched his back in a caring gesture. "My God, Colt, I hope you haven't thought of doing such a thing."

He cleared his throat again and took another drag on the cigarette. "I suppose I've hoped it would happen in a roundabout way. When I went after the Pawnee, I literally prayed I would get killed, but luck wasn't with me, I guess. I still wake up in cold sweats, sometimes screaming. I keep seeing it all in my dreams—the cabin on fire, my son's little face gone, LeeAnn's naked body full of arrows. If I told you the other things they did to her, you'd be sick . . . like I still sometimes get sick." His voice withered on the last words, and he rubbed at his eyes.

"Colt—"

He waved her off, putting the cigarette to his lips and rising. He walked off into the darkness for several minutes, and Sunny could not help her own tears. Finally, he reappeared, carrying a couple of pieces of dried wood he had found washed up on the beach. He put the wood on the fire, and Sunny could see his eyes were red from silent tears. He no longer had the cigarette.

"It's pretty here," he said. "The Great Lakes are beautiful, but I miss the mountains. Too bad there aren't nice big fresh-water lakes like this out west. I have a feeling that as things get more settled out there, people will be killing each other over water rights." He sat down next to her again, and neither of them spoke for several long seconds.

"Colt," Sunny finally said, "you aren't joining the army to preserve the Union or fight slavery, or because you have no family, are you? You're just joining up in the hope you'll be killed."

He rested his elbows on his knees, staring at the fire. "I'm not sure. I do think the slavery thing is completely wrong. Before I came here I helped a young Negro boy escape to Canada. That's what got me interested in joining up—hearing the things he told me, and reading a book called *Uncle Tom's Cabin.*"

"Yes, I've read it myself. This country should be ashamed it lets such things go on."

Colt picked up a small stick and poked at the fire. "I know this war is more political than anything else, but the fact remains that if the Union wins, there will be no more slavery in the South. And if my death comes in the process of doing some kind of good, then it hasn't all been for nothing."

She closed her eyes and sighed. "Colt, the others are right. You can't blame yourself for what happened to your wife and son. It isn't like you to just *let* yourself die, and I don't believe you want to. It's just something that sometimes sounds easier than facing the pain of your loss." She turned to face him better. "I know how it feels to want to die. I know there is no comparison, but there were moments when I didn't want to go on after Father died. I've suffered my own form of hell, Colt. I know my life looks fancy and easy, but believe me, my enemies are just as real and vicious as yours. The only difference is you can easily point yours out and physically face them. Mine are hidden behind smiles and handshakes and fancy clothes." A piece of her hair came loose and drifted across her face. She grasped it and pushed it behind her ear. "You and I are as different as night and day, but in some ways our worlds are a lot alike."

Colt thought about what he had seen earlier in the evening—the ostentatious mansion, the class of people he had met, the way Sunny had looked, the air of authority and smell of money about her. "Well, I suppose in a very abstract way our worlds are alike, but in reality I can hardly see a comparison."

Sunny smiled softly. "All right. I guess I have to agree with that one."

He turned and looked at her. "Enough of me." He leaned down on his side, resting on one elbow. "What about you? You said I needed to talk. Maybe you do too. Tell me about your father, and Vince. You must have gone through hell the last few months, from what I read in the papers."

Sunny drew a deep breath, allowing herself the liberty of spilling out her emotions, the trauma of losing her father, followed by the ugly court proceedings Vince had dragged her through. "I had a nervous collapse after everything was over," she said, swallowing back tears. "It wasn't just Father's death and all that hell with Vince. I think it was more from the realization that at the young age of eighteen everything would fall into my hands." She reached out and began sifting some sand through her fingers. "I wasn't ready emotionally. Father had taught me so much, but I thought I would be older when all this happened, maybe married, with a husband who could help me."

Colt could feel her pain, hear it in her voice. "Your brother should have wanted to help you, not make things worse for you. I've met him only once, and I can see what a bastard he is. You're a hell of a woman to have come through it all like this."

She shrugged. "I don't know. It took me five months to come out of my grief enough to take over my duties. A person simply does what she has to do, I guess. I thought about Father, what he expected of me. In everything I do I think of him, what he would say, how he would react, how strong he'd be. That's all that gets me through." She turned to face him. "And your letters. I got the first one the very day I started back to work. I can't tell you what it meant. Something about it just, I don't know, it made me stronger, gave me more courage." She leaned down beside him. "I don't know why you thought I might have forgotten you, Colt. You know how I felt."

Their eyes held in remembered emotions, and Sunny felt the flush coming to her cheeks again in sudden embarrassment. "I mean . . ." She looked down at the blanket. "I was young and full of fantasies then. I know that. I acted like a silly child, but my feelings about the kind of person you are, my respect for you, and my appreciation for the things you did for me—that never changed these past five years." She met his eyes again. "And neither have my memories of the West and how much I loved it. I can hardly wait to get back to Omaha. This whole thing is so exciting, Colt. I want to be a part of every aspect of building the railroad. I want to be right there, visit the construction sites. It's like—I don't know, like if I'm there, Father will be there too. He would have dearly loved to have been a part of all of it! I prayed so hard that he would stay well and that it would happen for him."

Colt grinned, cautiously touching her hand with his own. "Something tells me he knows exactly what is going on, and he's very proud of you. Finishing his dream, that means a lot to you, doesn't it?"

How was it that after five years this man could instantly give her such comfort? "I think you understand that better than anyone in my whole family. It means everything, especially with all the things Vince has done to try to stop me. He even tried to stop my father before he died, tried to keep people from investing in the Union Pacific. I'll never quite understand Vince. It's like he literally hates me, and I've never done anything against him. He has a strange contempt for me. Father used to say he was angry that my mother had taken

Vince's mother's place, and Vince thought that was wrong. Stuart did, too, for a long time, but he's changed a lot since marrying Vi. Vi and I have become very close. She's a good woman, very sincere and honest."

"I could tell by her eyes in that one introduction. I'm glad there's *somebody* in your family you can turn to." He squeezed her hand. "What about Blaine? Does he support you? Can you talk to him?" Colt caught the hint of nervousness in her quick little laugh.

"Blaine is the kind of man who can talk business all night. He's a wonderful support as far as discussing financial problems, investments, the railroad. Sometimes I almost feel in competition with him. But it's—it's hard for me to explain how I feel about other things. He's very eager to marry me, and he doesn't understand why I need to wait. I can't make a commitment like that until the railroad is at least well under construction. There's so much to do, and it's going to take a lot of my time. I think when a woman marries she should be ready to devote all her attention to her husband, ready to have children. I'm not ready for either." *Why am I telling you these things, Colt? Why do I already know you understand when no one else does?*

He rubbed a thumb across the back of her hand. "Do you love him?"

She looked down at the strong fingers that held her hand. "I honestly don't know. Sometimes I think I do, or at least that I should. As you could tell at the party, everyone thinks we're the perfect match." She looked into his eyes and smiled nervously again. "Vi thinks just the opposite. She thinks we're too much alike for it to work. He would want to take over everything that's mine, and I couldn't let him do that. I couldn't let *any-one* do that. Vi says that if I'm so full of doubt, I must not love Blaine. She says when the right man comes along—" *My God, Colt, she says I'll feel about him the way I have sometimes felt about you! No,* she argued inwardly. *This is ridiculous!* She pulled her hand away from his. "That I'll just know," she finished.

"She's probably right. Just don't go marrying a man because everybody else *thinks* you should, or because you think it's time to marry. You ought to really want him. It makes the things that come after easier." Colt immediately regretted the remark. *Jesus, why did I say that? What the hell am I doing talking to her about marriage and sex?* He watched Sunny turn away, and he knew he had embarrassed her. "I'm sorry, Sunny. I had no right saying that."

"It's all right. You care, and that's nice." She allowed her eyes to meet his own, feeling a desperation, realizing this might be their only chance to talk for a long time to come, maybe forever. "It does scare me sometimes, but if I really love a man, it shouldn't, should it?"

Colt searched the blue depths of her trusting eyes. "No," he answered in a near whisper.

Sunny swallowed, shivering with the need to say it. "I wouldn't be scared with you." Why did she say it? Why? She covered her face with her hand and started to sit up, but he grasped her arm, pulling her back down, gently taking her hand from her face. "I'm sorry," she whispered. "It's so easy to talk to you, so easy—"

Colt put a big hand to the side of her face. "Maybe Blaine doesn't know how to treat a woman so she's not afraid," he told her. "And maybe I can't stand the thought of him doing that to you."

Part of her wanted to run, but Sunny lay still as he came closer. Yes, they *were* older now, and both had suffered great loss and heartache. Such a good friend he had become through his letters. Why *shouldn't* they have the right to take comfort in each other? Neither of them had any real ties to another, and there was something they both needed to know, wasn't there?

In a moment his warm lips were pressing against her own, so gently, searching with a feathery touch, making her mouth open just slightly. No, there was no fear here, only a wonderful desire to taste his lips back, to let this wild, dangerous, forbidden man pull her tight against him as he was doing then, to let him move his weight on top of her, let his tongue search deep in a kiss that was becoming hotter, more demanding.

Sunny thought of the night Blaine had kissed her neck and breasts. There had been a kind of forcefulness about it that frightened her. Yet nothing Colt did made her afraid. The kiss became almost desperate, and Colt made a soft groaning sound as he finally left her mouth, his lips traveling to her eyes, back to lick her lips, down over her throat, and to the open neck of her shirt.

"My God, Sunny," he groaned, pressing a strong hand against her side, moving it to the fullness of her soft breast. "You looked so beautiful tonight. I've never in my life seen anything as pretty as you."

She grasped his hair, whispering his name, part of her screaming that she should stop him, that this was wrong, yet finding no strength or any desire to say no. What was this wild, foolish thing she was doing? She had not seen him for five years! But the letters . . . his terrible need. She whimpered when he moved his hand to the opening of her blouse and ran a thumb inside over the white of her breast. He moved it farther inside to feel her taut nipple, and both of them shivered from the thrill of the touch.

Colt whispered her name and gently pushed the blouse and her camisole away to expose one breast. He leaned closer and took her virgin nipple tenderly into his mouth, tasting it gently, his tongue rubbing over her hard ripe fruit. Sunny grasped his hair, her whole body on fire, painful urges surging deep inside that Blaine had never roused in her. She thought how right Colt was. A woman should never be afraid if it's the right man touching her.

She felt Colt begin to tremble as he sucked lovingly at the breast as though it was something delicious. Finally his lips moved back over her throat, met her mouth again in a near-savage kiss. Both of them groaned when he moved a hand down to her skirt and under it, over the scar left on her thigh from when he had burned out her infection years before. Their kiss grew deeper and hotter as she felt his strong hand move over her bottom, between her legs, pushing gently so that she whimpered his name. He moved the hand to the waistline of her bloomers and down inside them, and Sunny cried out with ecstasy at the feel of Colt Travis touching private places. It was so easy to let him touch her intimately, as though she already belonged to him. He began working wonderful magic with his fingers.

"It has to be you, Colt," she whispered. "Love me. Just love me. It doesn't matter what happens after tonight."

After tonight, Colt thought. *After tonight.* He stiffened. What the hell was he doing, using this sweet woman to soothe his own sore heart, taking advantage of this moment when he knew he was going off to war tomorrow, a war from which he might never return? Part of him wanted her to be LeeAnn, and that wasn't fair to Sunny. He relished the feel of her satiny juices on his fingers, would like nothing more at this moment than to plant himself in her virgin depths. But it was wrong, and he damn well knew it!

He took his hand away and pulled down her skirt, kissing her eyes as he did so. He gently moved her camisole and blouse back over her breast, kissing her ever so lightly then as he squeezed and caressed her breast once more. "Not like this, Sunny. My God, I'm sorry. It's so wrong. So goddamn wrong."

"Colt—"

He moved away from her, sitting up, then rising and half stumbling off into the darkness for several minutes. Shaking, Sunny sat up herself, still feeling the fire in her blood, licking the taste of his sweet kiss on her lips, the smell of him lingering in the air, on her clothes. Her insides throbbed with aching, newly awakened desires.

"Colt?" Had she made a fool of herself? Did he think less of her now? Her breast burned from his touch, and an even hotter fire swelled deep in private places, places only Colt Travis had been allowed to touch. Did he think her brazen, perhaps as easy as the whores he visited? Why had she let him do that? Neither of them had said anything about love or commitment. They were as wrong for each other as fire and water. Blaine was the one who should have been allowed such privileges, and yet with Colt it had been so easy.

In the moonlight she could see him moving around near his horse. He brought the animal closer, and she could see that it was fully saddled. He leaned down and picked up his saddlebags.

"Colt, what are you doing?"

"Leaving—right now—before I do something we'd both regret."

"Colt, please don't go. I—I'm sorry if it was something I did or said."

"You're sorry!" He turned to face her, a fire still in his eyes. "Sunny, I had no right doing what I just did. No damn right! *I'm* the one who's sorry! The state I'm in right now, I probably shouldn't have come here. You're beautiful and sweet and understanding, and for a man in my emotional condition, that's dangerous. God knows there couldn't be a much worse match than the two of us, or a worse time in our lives to be getting all mixed up like this."

He leaned down and picked up the blanket, shaking out the sand and folding it. He threw it over Dancer's rump and rolled it up to tie it.

"I know what you're saying, Colt, but please don't let this end our friendship. I shouldn't have come down here. I shouldn't have let you—"

"It was my responsibility to know what was right and wrong to do, Sunny. And it's Blaine O'Brien who should be down here with you, not the likes of me. My God, we're totally wrong for each other. Besides that, I don't know what the hell I want right now. I'm just reaching out, trying to find answers, trying to stop thinking about LeeAnn. It isn't fair to use someone as sweet and innocent as you for something like that." He tied the blanket with hard, jerking movements, then turned to face her.

"Let's face facts, Sunny. We've always had an attraction for each other that goes beyond friendship, and it's dangerous, for both of us." He pointed to the bluffs above. "Up there. *That's* where you belong. That's your world. Like the man said earlier tonight, Sunny, together you and Blaine could buy all of Chicago. He understands your world, shares your dream of a railroad. He loves that life and he *belongs* in your world. I not only don't belong in it, I don't even *want* it! You have a railroad to build, an empire to run, and even if you wanted to, you could never walk away from any of it. It's in your *blood*. It's what you live for. You don't belong down here on the beach with a lonely drifter who right now would enjoy the feel of *any* woman in his arms, whether she was proper or a—" He closed his eyes and let out a sigh of disgust. "Damn!" He turned away. "Sunny, right now is not the time for me to be around somebody as pure and untouchable as you."

"I'm not untouchable. You know that now." Her eyes misted and she struggled with a mixture of glorious ecstasy and deep shame.

"Don't say that. You *are*, in all ways, not just . . . just physically." He turned and kicked sand over the fire to put it out. "I was way out of line."

"Colt, don't leave this way. We *are* still friends, aren't we? I don't want to lose that friendship. I want you to write me, please. Just write me here in Chicago, and wherever I am they'll see that I get the letters. I'll worry about you so. You've got to write and let me know you're all right."

He knew by her voice that she was close to crying. God, he hated himself! He put his head back and sighed deeply, wondering if she knew what agony it had been for him to move away from her, knowing that he could have had his way with her if he had kept feeding her need. He wanted her so badly that he was in pain, but common sense told him it was completely wrong, the timing, the place, most of all the woman.

"I'll see about it." He turned and stepped closer. "Sunny, I don't know if it's possible for us to be just friends. We both know that anything more than friendship is impossible. We would end up hating each other, and I would never want that to happen." He touched her face lightly. "We both have to get on with our lives and cope with our problems as best we can, but we can't *use* each other to solve those problems. We wrote those letters at a time when both of us needed the diversion and the companionship. We were both lonely, both wanting something to take us away from reality. But the reality is still there, and the reality is you're Sunny Landers, one of the richest women in the country, a woman who belongs with a man of equal wealth and power, a woman who is entering into one of the biggest and probably most historic events this country will ever know. You have a railroad to build, Sunny, so go build it. You don't need any more complications in your life right now."

Tears slipped down her cheeks, and she grasped his wrist. "I need you, Colt."

"No. You just *think* you need me. You're a Landers, Sunny. You'll be just fine, and so will I, after a time. They say time heals a lot of things. Maybe after the war I'll know more about what I want to do with my life, and you'll be married to a proper man by then. Just go up there where you belong, making deals with senators, entertaining foreign dignitaries, getting people to invest in your railroad. Go on with your life as though I don't exist, Sunny, because in a way I don't. I'm just someone who helped you get through a bad time, and that's what you did for me. We don't dare let it grow into anything more than that."

She let go of his wrist and choked in a sob, turning away and wiping her eyes. "You aren't going to write, are you? You aren't ever going to write or see me again, and I'll never know what happened to you."

"It's probably better that way, Sunny. At least I know someone really cares. I appreciate that more than you can know. I honestly intended to let the friendship and the letters continue, but it just isn't right. We both know that now. We know it could lead to more, and that to let that happen would be the biggest mistake of our lives. You know I'm right, don't you?"

Her shoulders shook with sobs. "I suppose. But it doesn't change anything. I'll go back and do what I have to do, but I won't ever, ever forget you or stop caring, no matter if I never hear from you again." She turned to face him. "I might even marry and all, but it won't change what's in my heart, Colt. If things were different—"

He put his fingers to her lips. "Don't say it, Sunny. It's

like that day I held you after the buffalo stampede. Some things are better left untouched, some words better left unspoken." He leaned down and gently kissed her forehead, then turned away to mount up. "Seems like we're always saying good-bye, doesn't it? I'll try to stay out of your life after this so we never have to say good-bye again."

"I don't mind, because each good-bye means I've seen you again," she answered, shivering with tears. "Good-bye, Colt."

"Bye, Sunny. Give your brother hell. Give *all* of them hell. Be strong, like your pa was. Do whatever you have to do to get your railroad built. When I come back from the war I want to hear that the Union Pacific is well under way. I'll be coming back out west to see for myself."

How wonderful he still looked on a horse, how handsome in the moonlight, tall and dangerous and wonderful. She walked over to him, reaching up and putting her hand over his. "I'll pray for you."

God, you're beautiful, he thought. How he hated himself for ruining everything by letting himself get carried away. "And I'll pray for you. I don't think you realize how strong you are, Sunny. And you're going to get stronger and more sure as time goes on. Your father chose well." Their eyes held a moment longer. He took his hat from where it hung over his saddle horn and raised it in the air. "Here's to the Union Pacific! Good luck, Sunny." He put the hat on his head and turned Dancer, riding off down the beach.

"Good-bye, Colt," Sunny whispered. She watched him until she could no longer make out his shadowy form, then touched her lips again, convinced that for the rest of her life, even if she never saw him again, she would not forget that fiery kiss or the feel of his warm lips at her breast, his hands exploring her most secret places. Colt Travis had wanted her, and she realized that if he had not stopped himself when he did . . .

She put a hand to her stomach, feeling the ache deep inside, sure no other man, not even Blaine, could make her feel like this again. She went to her knees, gazing out at the softly rolling waves that made little rushing noises when they washed up on the beach. "I love you, Colt Travis," she whispered, the tears coming again. "I'll always, always love you."

Chapter 16

Spring 1864

Colt knelt in the underbrush and pulled a wormy biscuit from the leather bag tied over his shoulder. He stared at it a moment, then angrily tossed it aside, deciding he would rather try to survive on edible plant life and bark than to have to pick the bugs out of one more rock-hard biscuit. If he could get back to his regiment, he could resupply himself, but in this tangled mess that was crawling with Confederates, he couldn't walk just anywhere he pleased.

General Grant called this place the Wilderness. Colt decided *wilderness* was not fitting enough. *Hell* was more like it. He would take the wide open spaces of the West any day to this tangled, buggy, thorny jungle. He had

had his fill of thick woods, and vines that gave a man the itch. The big hardwood trees of Virginia were beautiful, but he hated places where a man couldn't see more than ten feet in front of him for all the undergrowth; and when someone behind the next bush could be the enemy, it just made matters that much worse.

He groped through his supplies, ignoring his growling stomach and longing for a cigarette. He found his tobacco pouch, but there was barely enough tobacco in it to roll one cigarette. He put it back, deciding to save it for later, wondering when he would get the chance for another smoke once this last one was gone. Tobacco was hard to come by now, and his guess was that the camp supply was already gone. He could go for a long time without food. He had done it before once when he was stranded in a snowstorm in the mountains. But he wasn't sure how long he could go without a smoke.

He leaned against a tree trunk, contemplating his next move. He had worked as a scout for the Union Army for nearly two years now. Sunny had been right when she tried to explain how ugly this war was, and even she didn't realize the half of it. He thought he had seen it all when he first got into this mess, but nothing he had seen to that point compared to the bloody savagery of this war.

He had early on learned not to become too friendly with any man, because in the next instant that man could be dead or horribly wounded. Once he had been ordered to aid the company medic, an experience he would never forget. He could still hear the screams of one soldier he had to lean over and hold down while a doctor sawed off his leg above the knee, with nothing more than a little whiskey to dull the pain. He could still see that man's face, see the horror in his eyes; he could remember how badly his ear rang afterward from the man's screams.

He wondered if most of these men knew why they were fighting. It seemed things had gotten to the point where there was no cause anymore. It was simply a matter of winning, of not being the last man down. It was Yankees against Rebels, each side determined to show the other they could not be beat. He wondered what was happening in Washington, who was making the decisions that sent men against each other in bloody, pointless slaughter, who would decide that it was finally time to end all of this, and how many would be dead by then?

He checked his carbine, slowly standing up and looking around. For the first time in all his years of scouting and traveling, he was totally lost. He had come to scout ahead for Rebels, but these confusing wild woods had become a nightmare. He never knew if the next man he saw would be wearing gray or blue. Something bad was brewing, he could feel it in his bones. He had not been able to get back to his regiment, and all morning he had heard voices from every direction, occasional gunshots. He brushed at dried blood on the front of his own uniform, Rebel blood. Only two hours earlier he had surprised two Confederate soldiers, shooting one on sight and going hand-to-hand with the other. It had been easy for him, for he had fought many an Indian that way, and an Indian was much more vicious and skilled than any of these men. He had easily landed a knife into the man, then quietly lowered him to the ground. It was then he realized that man had not been a man at all. He couldn't have been more than seventeen, just another soldier fighting for what he thought was a just cause.

At that moment the war suddenly seemed ridiculous, a horrible waste of young men. In the beginning he had almost hoped he would be one of the casualties, but deeper instincts had caused him to fight back and protect himself. He supposed he simply was not the suicidal type, no matter how much he sometimes thought he would welcome death. Time was slowly healing his own wounds, and now he longed for this to be over so he could go home—home to the gentle prairie, home to the vast Plains in spite of all the danger there, home to the cool, magnificent mountains.

He couldn't help wondering what was happening with the Union Pacific, and with Sunny. He knew he would never forget the taste of her, the sweetness of her lips. He wished he could forget that night on the beach. He knew only moments after touching her that he had been a fool to allow his loneliness to overcome his better judgment. All he had done was stir up feelings better left alone.

Had he awakened the woman in her enough to cause her to turn to Blaine? Even though he knew Blaine was the best man for a woman like Sunny, the thought of the man taking enjoyment in that body, Blaine laying claim to Sunny Landers . . . it ate at his gut sometimes, but he supposed he would have to live with that.

A gunshot exploded nearby, and at the same instant Colt felt a fierce jolt. He saw the ground coming up to meet him, and his first thought was how strange it was that he felt no pain in spite of the fact that he was certain a bullet had just slammed across the left side of his neck, just under his ear. He wondered why he couldn't feel anything, why he wasn't even afraid. All he could think of was what an idiot he had been to allow himself to become so lost in thought that he had let himself be caught off guard. This was the result of his careless daydreaming.

Now it seemed that gunfire was exploding from every direction. Men were giving out Rebel yells, and were crashing through the underbrush surrounding him, yet he couldn't move, couldn't tell if they wore gray or blue. He felt a warm trickle at his shoulder, and he knew it was his own blood. He wondered if he was belatedly going to get his wish to die, and he thought how odd that it should happen now, when he had begun to want to live again.

He closed his eyes, realizing he must be stunned. In a few minutes he would be able to move, to think more clearly. He imagined himself riding free on the Plains, Dancer's mane flying in the wind. Would the man back in Chicago who had promised to keep Dancer still have him, or had he sold his beloved horse by now? Two years was a long time to wait for a man to come back and get his horse.

Gradually, the gunfire faded, and he thought the fighting must be over. He had no idea that the battle was actually growing more intense all around him, that the conflict between Grant's and Lee's men went on for the next several hours in the tangled maze of vines and trees and bushes, or that by nightfall hot sparks from the heavy barrage of gunfire had caused the underbrush to catch fire, trapping wounded but still-living soldiers. In the darkness their screams of horror could be heard as hundreds were burned alive. Colt heard none of it as he lay unconscious.

Sunny took rapid notes as Thomas Durant's right-hand man explained the situation at hand. She was aware that Blaine was watching her, and she wondered what he was thinking. She had not seen him in two years, since he left for Oregon shortly after the night of her party. They had had an intense argument before he left, over the fact that she had met with Colt Travis alone on the beach. Her meeting with Colt had left her shaken, unsure of how she felt about Blaine. She had never told Blaine about the kiss, or the intimacy she had shared with Colt. It was her special secret, a beautiful memory. Still, Blaine had been so angry. She had tried to explain that Colt was gone and would never be back, but Blaine simply would not believe her. Maybe now he would, as she had not heard a word from Colt since that one beautiful night.

Something had changed inside her after Colt left, his kiss still burning her lips, the fire in his touch leaving her shaken. She almost hated him for what he had done, awakening such exotic passion in her soul, bringing her such joy and yet such sorrow. She had lost two men that night. Perhaps in both cases it was her own fault, but the ordeal had left her harder, even more determined to guard her emotions, to turn to her business world and ignore her own needs. Need only led to dependency, and dependency to heartache. She was Sunny Landers, and she was expected to run an empire. Her position was the reason she could never love someone like Colt. She understood that more fully now. She had considered what it might be like to give up all that she had, and she knew she couldn't. It would be an insult to her father's memory and would go against all that she had learned and been trained for. She had something to prove now, to her father, to Vince, to Blaine, most of all to herself. She would spend her passions on Landers Enterprises and on the Union Pacific. She would make damn sure people stood up and took notice, that no one took her for granted because she was a woman.

That was the crux of it. Men like Blaine and Vince and so many others considered only her womanly side, tried to play on her emotions. She would show all of them that she could be as strong and formidable as the next man. Everyone kept dictating the role she must play in life, even Colt, and so she would play that role to the hilt.

Blaine spoke up, telling the others how lucrative the lumbering business was going to be when the railroad was completed. Sunny watched him. He was thirty-two now, and the trip west had apparently been good for him. He looked more handsome. He was tanned darker from the western sun, and he had put on a little weight in all the right places. As she listened to him speak, she realized he was after all the kind of man she should consider as a mate. She didn't particularly "need" Blaine, and that was good. She knew of several couples in her own circle whose marriages had been more for convenience and proper social standing than for love and passion. Maybe that was the way marriage was supposed to be.

At any rate, she doubted if Blaine was interested in her anymore. Since he first left, she focused her passions and energies on matters at hand. Over the last two years she worked tirelessly for the railroad, traveling back and forth between Omaha and Chicago, Chicago and New York, New York and Washington. She had grown stronger, had stood her ground against Vince until he seldom bothered rising up against her. She had a home and offices in Omaha, was received among the richest of the rich with honor and respect. When she spoke, important people listened. Perhaps most women of her age were already married and having children, but she had no time for such things. They were closer than ever to beginning construction on the U.P., and that was all that mattered now. She had dated a few male acquaintances, but only on a strictly social basis, nothing serious or intimate.

"So, gentlemen," Durant's man was saying. He turned to Sunny. "And gentleladies," he added with a grin, "we can only profit handsomely from the Doctor's plan. The Pennsylvania Fiscal Agency will come under control of the Union Pacific Railroad Company and will be called Credit Mobilier of America, a construction company for our own railroad. When Credit Mobilier contracts with the U.P., we will make sure our costs are padded high enough to use up all government grants. As I have already explained, we are working on getting the railroad act revised to increase the land grants and the amount of money the government will pay per mile. If that amount of money is more than is really needed, Credit Mobilier will make sure its construction costs make up the difference. Excess government money, my dear friends, will go into our pockets and make up for the money we have all personally put out for the railroad."

Grins and nods of satisfaction went around the table, a secret meeting of some of the country's wealthiest, discussing their latest scheme to begin making grand profits from their transcontinental railroad even before it was finished. Sunny had only the slightest qualm about the plan to build that railroad using their own construction company. She had fought too long and hard for the railroad to care whether or not the U.P. milked the government a little. Plenty of congressmen had milked her and the others at this table.

It was payback time, and in her world, ruthlessness and bribery and secret pacts were the name of the game. Besides that, an enormous profit would only prove to Vince that she and their father had been right all along to stick their necks out for this project. She had made sure over the last two years that there was no room in her life for anything but the U.P. and her growing interests in Omaha. Her almost constant traveling had kept her busy to the point of collapse, and after the miserable way she had handled her personal feelings, that was just what she wanted—little time for a personal social life, only for parties and meetings and fund-raising events—take a train to Chicago, sit in on a board meeting; take another train on to New York, still a dangerous venture in these times of war. She had made the trip so many times she knew the landscape by heart. In two days it would be on to Washington for some more palm-greasing.

It was imperative that a revised railroad act be passed, one that would allow Congress to release more funds up front so that serious construction could begin. Under the old act, a certain amount of construction had to be completed before the government would release any money, but it simply could not be done, and time was wasting. They had a huge project ahead of them, and the U.P. was still barely out of Omaha.

She watched Blaine scribble some figures, giving everyone an example of how much profit could be made through Credit Mobilier in the price of rails alone. Yes, she supposed, everyone else was right after all about Blaine. Even Vince had been right that someone like Blaine was a perfect match for her. Here was a man who understood this world, a man who discussed millions as though it were mere pennies, a man who could be totally ruthless in his dealings when it meant lining his own pockets. In many ways he was a lot like her own father. Men like that could love and be loved in spite of the tactics they used in boardrooms and secret meetings like this one. Maybe she had been wrong to hurt Blaine the way she had.

"Miss Landers?" Sunny blinked and looked at Tom Canary, a close associate of Dr. Durant.

Blaine noticed she had been almost startled. Canary had asked her a question and she had not even heard. What was she thinking about? She had been watching him off and on all through the meeting. Was she having regrets about their last parting? Had she heard from that damn half-breed?

"I'm sorry," Sunny was saying, blushing a little. "I was going over my notes and didn't hear you." God, how she hated the patronizing smile Canary gave her. *Typical woman,* he was probably thinking. She chastised herself for allowing her thoughts to wander.

"I was just asking if you followed up with the Doctor's suggestion as to how we can get more people to buy stock in the U.P."

Another move that was close to a swindle. What did it matter if it meant getting enough private funding to release government contributions? The government had required a certain amount of stock in the Union Pacific be sold before they would start dishing out money themselves. Because so many investors hesitated to put their money into a still-questionable project, Durant had come up with a way around the dilemma. For every purchase of stock, a ten percent down payment was required. Durant had simply told his prospective investors that if they would buy the stock in their name, he would pay the ten percent out of his own pocket and they could pay him back when the railroad began making a profit. It was a wonderful scheme, and Sunny and several others had done the same. It meant that they, and especially Durant, would own the bulk of U.P. stock, more than the government allowed them to own, but the government would not know. U.P. accounting showed the stock was owned by others.

"Yes," Sunny answered. "It's surprising how many new 'investors' I found when I offered to make their down payment for them."

There came a round of laughter at the statement, after which strategy for getting a new bill passed was discussed. Sunny could feel Blaine's eyes on her. She realized that in some ways she had missed him, missed their conversations about the railroad, the shipping industry, the stock market; missed going to the theater, going as a couple to functions in Washington, political conventions, and the like. They truly did have a lot in common, but now it seemed even Blaine was in her past.

The meeting finally broke up, and Blaine watched the men hover around Sunny, wondered how much she had been courted since he left. He damned himself for wanting her again the minute he set eyes on her. *Just look at them,* he thought. *Who wouldn't want to marry Sunny Landers and take her and her money to his bed?*

Sunny answered questions, laughed at the proper times, flirted with them as she had even as a little girl to gain their confidence and support. She had apparently learned to use her great powers as a female to get just about anything she wanted, and he wondered if he could make her want him again.

Blaine moved closer, and the others disbursed, most of them aware that this was the first meeting between these two old lovers since Blaine's return from Oregon. Sunny was almost surprised he was singling her out at all. "Hello, Sunny," he said, a hint of doubt and wariness still in his eyes. He studied her own blue eyes closely. How he wished those eyes would light up at seeing him again the way they had for Colt Travis the night of her party. Still, there was a certain warmth there.

"Hello, Blaine. You're looking well."

"I, uh, I'd like to talk. Will you come to dinner with me?"

She looked away. "I don't know."

He touched her arm. "At least let me tell you about my trip west, about Oregon. I imagine you'd like to hear all about it, seeing as how you carried on about the West yourself a couple of years back."

She looked at him again. Yes, he still wanted her, and she was a fool to keep turning away from him. "I would like to hear about it. It's almost dinnertime now. We can leave right from here if you like."

He brightened a little more. "Great." His eyes moved over her hungrily. "You're more beautiful than ever. I didn't think that was possible." He took a deep breath and let out a long sigh. "You know what I'm wondering, Sunny."

She held his eyes. "No. I have never heard from Colt and I don't expect to. I told you two years ago that he wanted nothing from me, Blaine. It should be obvious to you now that he came to see me only out of friendship. I wish you could have understood that. You had no right saying some of the things you said, especially when Colt was not there to defend himself."

Blaine touched her arm. "All right. For two years I've been wanting to apologize, Sunny. Let's go talk about this over a quiet table and a little wine, shall we?"

He took her shawl from her chair and draped it over her shoulders, wondering what she would think if she knew about the woman he had kept in Oregon. She was the virgin daughter of a Japanese prostitute who had been saving the girl for as much money as she could get for her. The girl had been trained to accept the eventual sale, and she had welcomed the wealthy, handsome Blaine O'Brien as her first and exclusive customer. He had paid dearly for the fifteen-year-old virgin so he wouldn't have to worry about disease, and the first night he took her he had imagined Sunny gasping with the pain and the glory of it.

Miko would be well paid to stay at his home in Oregon and wait for his return. It was a place Sunny would likely never go, so even after marriage he would have another warm body in his bed at night when he had to make trips to the West Coast.

Someday it *would* be Sunny in his bed. Now that he had set eyes on her again, he was determined to revitalize their relationship and pick up where they had left off. The fact remained that marrying Sunny Landers would bring him even more prestige and fame than he already had. Whether he loved her or not mattered little. Love was a ridiculous emotion. Desire, choosing just the right woman to present on his arm, marrying someone with a fortune that equaled his own—that was all that mattered. A man had to hold to his image, and marrying Sunny meant a grand wedding in New York City with lots of press coverage; it meant having children who could not help but be handsome and beautiful and intelligent; it meant that he had captured the most wanted but elusive single female in the United States, and probably the richest. Eventually, he intended to run for office, build his notoriety and reputation right up to the White House. A woman like Sunny for a wife could take a man a long way in life. She was worth going after again, worth waiting for. No other woman compared to Sunny—in looks, in wealth, in society's eyes.

He was not going to give up this time. Sunny Landers would belong to him no matter what he had to do to make that happen. Thank God that damn half-breed bastard was finally out of the picture. He realized now that he must have been crazy to think that someone like Sunny could ever have had any romantic notions about the man.

The smell of smoke aroused Colt, making him cough and roll to his knees. Now the pain hit him, a gripping vise at the side of his neck and left shoulder, a screaming headache. He looked around in a state of confusion. The night sky was black, but all around him the thick woods were ablaze, casting a bright orange glow on his surroundings, the flames licking toward him. He struggled to remember what had happened, where he was. He heard men screaming somewhere beyond the flames.

There was no time for reason or wonder. Instinct told him to run in spite of his pain, in spite of the weakness in his legs. It was either run or be burned alive. He turned and crawled through the underbrush, getting to his feet and heading for any area where there were no flames.

The heat was overwhelming, the smoke blinding. He stumbled over something, went down hard. He looked down, and by the light of the fire he saw staring eyes and an open mouth full of dried blood. He did not stop to see what color uniform the dead body wore. He ran again, putting his right arm over his face against the awful heat, unable to raise his left arm for the pain. He saw more dead bodies, and his injuries made his mind wander back to another fire, other smoke, a burning cabin. The dead bodies belonged to LeeAnn and his baby son. He screamed for LeeAnn, turning in a circle when the pathway ahead of him also burst into flames.

To his right he saw one small flameless area, and for a moment he was sure he saw LeeAnn standing there, beckoning him. "This way." The words were whispered, yet he could hear them clearly. He stumbled toward the only exit, and suddenly the woman before him had blond hair and blue eyes and a wonderful smile. He felt a rush of cooler air, and the woman's figure vanished.

He realized he had somehow found his way out of the inferno, but in his confusion he had left his rifle behind. He ran, and suddenly he was in thick smoke again. He fell down coughing, then began crawling, the only way to keep from breathing the smoke.

Again the air cleared, and he got to his feet and moved blindly through trees and underbrush, tripping on branches and vines, feeling crazy with a need to get out of the thick forest that was fast becoming a blazing inferno. How he hated this place! Maybe if he ran hard and fast enough, he could make his way out to the blessed open prairie, where he could ride free and forget this hell. He kept running, leaving the fire farther behind him. He reached a clearing, and across it he thought he saw softly glowing oil lamps. Maybe it was his own regiment!

The blinding pain in his head made it difficult to tell for certain, for he saw everything in a haze. He headed for the lights, sloshing through some swampy ground, falling once. The left side of his neck ached so badly, he could barely hold his head straight. Somewhere far behind him he could still hear men screaming for help. He headed toward the camp ahead, finally reaching it, only to realize he had walked right into enemy territory. Men in gray looked at him. A couple of them smiled.

"Well, well," one man muttered. "Look who stumbled in for a visit."

Colt went for his pistol, but something hit him hard from behind. He grunted and fell forward, feeling gravel scrape his face. He felt someone turn him onto his back and kick him. Hands began feeling around his body.

"Looks like he ain't got any dangerous wounds." Someone turned his head to the right, bringing on the excruciating pain at his neck. "Just superficial. Looks like we've got ourselves another prisoner, boys. Drag him over there with the others. First chance we get we'll get him on a wagon to Andersonville."

"He looks different," someone said, "like maybe he's Indian."

"I don't give a damn if he's Chinese or Apache. He's wearin' a Yankee uniform. That's all that matters. Once he's spent some time in prison, he'll wish he never put that uniform on. Get him out of here."

Colt felt himself being dragged, wondered if that was his scream he heard when the pain shot through his neck again. Someone kicked him in the groin. "Shut up, Yankee bastard!" He felt himself being tossed against something. It was not until that something moved that he realized it was a body. He heard someone groan, and the now-familiar odor of old dried blood stung his nostrils. He wondered if it was someone else's or his own.

Sunny sat and listened to Blaine talk about Oregon. It sounded beautiful, made her long to again go beyond Omaha to the plains and prairies and mountains. Such thoughts made her think again of Colt, but she pushed them away, deciding she would be wise to concentrate on Blaine. She had told him Colt was in her past, and she had to let it be that way.

"So, you love it too," she said aloud.

"Magnificent country! But the trip out is so dangerous. If not for being with some good men and an excellent guide, I don't suppose I ever would have made it through Indian country and through the mountains. I understand more than ever the need for the railroad, Sunny, just like you told me once. I have to admit I was in this at first strictly for the investment, but it's become more than that, just like with you." He took her hand. "I want to see you again, Sunny. Let's start over."

She sighed, staring at the candle that lit their secluded table softly. Blaine had asked for a table in the most private area of the posh restaurant, away from staring eyes. "I don't know, Blaine. I'm still far from ready for anything serious, what with construction barely under way, and all the traveling I have to do. I'll be in Omaha part of the time, and I have more things to do in Chicago to get things in shape so I can be gone for long periods of time."

"I know that. But we can share all this excitement together. Hell, I've got a lot of traveling of my own to do. Half the time I'll be here in New York tending to my own businesses. I just want to try again."

She met his eyes. "Part of our problem before was that you were eager to marry, Blaine, and I wasn't ready. I'm still not ready."

"I won't pressure you. We'll just let things happen as they may. Besides, once the construction gets started, you might change your mind. We can have a great life together, Sunny."

She wondered again if the words *I love you* ever entered his mind.

"I'm going to France to see my mother and sister, but I'll be back by late summer. I'll come out to Omaha and we'll see what happens. Will you wait for me?"

She pulled her hand away and picked up her wine. "You know I will. Seeing other men in any serious respect is the last thing on my mind right now."

Blaine wondered if there was any warmth to her at all. "Her name might be Sunny," he had heard one man tell another earlier in the day. "But she's more like cold winter—all business and no fooling around." He was convinced that somewhere deep inside this beautiful woman burned a passion as hot as the fires of hell. He just had to find a way to stir the coals.

Sunny drank a little wine, and suddenly she thought she heard someone call her name. An intense, inexplicable wave of deep sorrow moved through her, and she set down her wine and looked around the room.

"What is it?" Blaine asked her.

She shivered, pulling her shawl back around her shoulders. "I don't know. I feel like something is wrong." What was this ridiculous feeling? Had someone called to her? She looked around the room again, then back at Blaine. "I want to go back to my hotel, Blaine, and wire Chicago, make sure everything is all right."

"Of course everything is all right. What's wrong with you?"

"I told you, I don't know. Please take me back."

He shrugged. "If that's what you want. I'll go pay for our meal." He got up and left, and again Sunny scanned the room. What was this feeling? If she discovered everything was all right with Stuart and Vi in Chicago, then what could it be?

Colt? She rose, angry with herself for thinking it. She told herself this had to stop. Colt was gone and had no intention of ever allowing a relationship. For all she knew, he could even be dead.

Blaine returned, and she grasped his arm. "I've changed my mind. There is a play on Broadway I'd like to see. It isn't too late for the last show. Will you take me?"

He grinned. "With great pleasure."

They left the restaurant together, and other patrons stared and whispered. This was a place where only the very wealthy came to dine, and most knew Sunny and Blaine by sight.

"So, the beautiful couple is together again," one woman told another with a kind of sneer. "Maybe *this* time they'll marry."

"They say Sunny Landers is as cold as ice," her companion replied.

"Quit the gossip, Helen," the second woman's husband chided.

The woman sniffed. "You men are the ones who tell us these things, so who is *really* doing the gossiping?"

They all laughed lightly.

"All right, then," the husband replied. "I have a juicy tidbit I never told you." The women were quickly all ears, and the man grinned at their eagerness. "Word is," he told them, "the reason those two split up a couple of years ago was over some worthless drifter she knew— part Indian, no less. Something about him being a scout for Sunny and her father a few years back. They kept in touch and he came to see her. It made Blaine O'Brien furious and he left her."

"A Indian scout!" the first woman gasped.

"Good Lord," the second put in. "What would a woman of Sunny Landers's position want with a man like that!"

The man shrugged. "Who knows what her secret passions are? Apparently, it's done with and she's back with O'Brien. But can you imagine her walking into a place like this with some long-haired, dark-skinned, buckskin-clad oaf on her arm?"

They all snickered.

"Apparently, the prim and proper Miss Sunny Landers is not *always* so prim and proper," the first woman said snidely, relishing the chance to slam the wealthy Sunny Landers, who monopolized the society column every time she came to New York. It wasn't fair that any woman so young should be that rich and look that beautiful, let alone be the one to land the most eligible bachelor in New York City.

"Well, maybe it runs in her blood," the husband replied.

"Runs in her blood?" his wife asked. "What does *that* mean?"

The man hesitated. "Nothing in particular," he lied. "I just meant that Bo Landers used people as he saw fit. Maybe his daughter does the same. She probably decided on Blaine because of his wealth. Hell, together their fortune would be staggering."

He was relieved to see that his answer had satisfied the women. He had almost slipped, and he was not about to be the one to spread the story. He didn't even know for sure if the old rumor about Sunny Landers's mother was true, and considering Sunny's wealth and power, he sure as hell didn't want to be the one to start new fires of such damaging gossip. Female or not, Sunny could destroy any man she chose to destroy. Her father had done it years ago to those who had objected to his marriage to the lovely young Lucille Madison. He had no doubt the daughter was capable of being just as ruthless as the father.

Chapter 17

May 2, 1865

Colt watched from the window of the train that had brought him to Chicago. The engineer had slowed the engine to a stop in honor of the train passing them on the tracks to their right, also headed into Union Station but very slowly.

Men removed their hats, and women cried. The passing steam engine was decorated with United States flags, and each following passenger car was draped with black mourning cloth.

"That's it," someone behind him said quietly. "That's the funeral train."

The car in which Colt was riding was packed with people who had come from other areas of Indiana and

Illinois to view their assassinated President's body, which Colt had heard people say would be displayed at the Cook County courthouse in Chicago.

The President's death was the only topic of conversation Colt had heard since the news first hit over two weeks ago while he was in Columbus, Ohio, where he had been sent to recuperate for several days before going on to Chicago to be mustered out of the army. The whole city of Columbus had been in near chaos, people swarming the streets, holding newspapers with bold headlines about Lincoln's shooting at Ford's Theater in Washington. That chaos seemed to have spread to each city where Colt's train stopped.

Although the car in which Colt rode was stuffed to standing room only, the crowd was nearly silent. One woman wept openly, and a man sitting ahead of Colt took out a handkerchief and wiped his eyes. Colt thought how he would have dearly loved to have been the one to shoot John Wilkes Booth. What an ironic way for all this hell to end.

He was well aware of how people on the train had stared at him all the way here. He figured he must be as close to looking like a walking skeleton as a man could look. He wondered how long it would take for the nightmares to end, the awful dreams that made him wake up in a deep sweat. His hellish dreams of LeeAnn and Ethan had been replaced by haunting visions of life in Andersonville Prison—the ugly pain of his slow-healing wound, the lack of food and medical care. The polluted water they all were forced to drink, which came from the pitiful stream that ran through the dismal prison, gave everyone cramps and diarrhea, which were only compounded by the daily rations of three tablespoons of beans, a little salt, and cutting, unsifted corn meal that made a man feel like he had swallowed razors. For months he had seen nothing but gaunt, dying, dehydrated bodies, and he had become one of them. The only difference between him and most others was that he had survived.

Sometimes he thought the stench of blood and garbage and human waste and death would never leave him, as though the smell had penetrated his very skin. He had seen so much suffering and death that he felt numb, and he feared he had lost all human compassion. At one point the prisoners at Andersonville were dying at the rate of one hundred a day, buried in shallow mass graves like so much dead cattle. In the year he had spent in the hot, mosquito- and fly-infested hellhole, nearly thirteen thousand men died. But the camp was still overcrowded, thousands of men packed into twenty-seven acres. Many had tried to escape, none had succeeded. There was no place to hide in or beyond the compound, which was positioned in a wide-open, unshaded flat piece of land somewhere in Georgia. He had never been quite sure of its exact location, hardly aware of which direction he headed when he and several hundred others were told one day that the war was all but over and they were being released to return to federal troops.

Colt and the others had walked in sadly worn boots along a designated road, many of the men collapsing and dying along the way, some crawling. With what strength he had, Colt had managed to support one man he had befriended, getting him almost "home" to a Union camp, only to have the man become suddenly heavier as he slumped over in death. Colt did not have the strength to carry him. He left him in the road and kept going. He could still remember the gasps and stares of the men who greeted him, remembered his own shock when he looked at himself in a mirror for the first time.

He had been given clean clothes that didn't fit him very well, a few decent meals, and some kind of medicine that was supposed to be a revitalizing tonic. But he knew now that the only tonic he needed was to get back out to the open Plains and sandhills of Nebraska, to lie back in the western sun and let it bathe him. He would go on to the mountains, go to the highest damn peak he could reach and stand there, looking out over the country he loved, watching the eagles, feeling the cool wind, drinking from sparkling clean mountain streams.

He prayed Dancer was still being cared for and he

could get the horse back. He would collect the money he had left in a Chicago bank, as well as money the Union Army owed him, and he would leave the war and cities and people behind him. After Andersonville, the thought of being totally alone sounded wonderful.

The funeral train passed by, and his own train chugged slowly into the station. Colt waited as the rest of the passengers got off, then made his way slowly to disembark, grasping the rails tightly to keep from falling down the steps. At twenty-eight, he felt more like eighty. People swarmed everywhere, a few turning to gawk at him, most rushing farther ahead and practically falling over one another. He heard a few wails of grief, and he realized everyone had been running to view the funeral train.

Although it was daylight, it was rather dark inside the cavernous station, and hundreds of lamps were lit so people could see better. It was one of the busiest places Colt had ever seen, and again the feeling of suffocation began to press in on him. Talk and even shouting echoed in the huge railway center, more engines rumbled by, some entering, some leaving, steam hissing from the great belching bellies of the locomotives. An ornate gold-trimmed hearse clattered by, and Colt watched as a man shouted for people to get out of the way.

"From the looks of you, Mister, I'd say you've been in one of those godforsaken prison camps," someone nearby said. Colt turned to see a middle-aged, friendly looking man standing near him. He gave Colt a warm smile and took his arm. "I'm Jonathan Brinks, a hospital volunteer. My job is to watch for you fellows and help you to the nearest hospital, where you do some healing before getting back into civilian life."

Colt welcomed the help. He reached into the pocket of the lightweight Union jacket that had been issued to him and took out a piece of paper. "I'm damn glad to see you," he told Brinks. "I wasn't sure how to reach the hospital. Here are the papers from officers in Columbus with orders that I'm to get medical care here. I'm Colt Travis."

The man opened the paper to read the orders. "Well,

from that southern accent, I'm surprised you served the
Union."

"I just thought it was the right thing to do. Now I'm
not so sure the war itself was right. But it's over now."

"Well, you just come with me. I'll get you out of this
crowded mess."

The man led Colt in the opposite direction from the
funeral train, keeping hold of his arm for support. Colt
guessed the man to be about fifty. He was short and
plump, with graying hair and a great kindness in his
brown eyes. Colt was grateful for the thoughtful people
who volunteered their time to help the soldiers who had
no one to meet them when they came home. "Looks
like a lot of people are here just to see the President's
train," he commented.

"Yes, it's a sad, sad time for us all, Mr. Travis. I imagine just about everybody in Chicago will be going to the
courthouse over the next day or two to view President
Lincoln's body before it's taken to Springfield for burial,
but not even something that important can put a halt to
our hospital work. My job is to get you some help."

The station was so packed that a few people bumped
into them as they made their way outside. Colt glanced
in fascination at another monstrous, black steam engine,
noticing B&L painted on its boiler. So, here was another
part of Sunny's world, he thought. He had done a lot of
traveling by train the last few days, and he couldn't help
wondering how much of each person's ticket went into
the pockets of people like Sunny and others who owned
and invested in the railroad. He wondered what it must
be like to actually own a railroad, to sit in boardrooms
and make decisions that affected the way so many people traveled. He still preferred a nice, quiet horse, but
he couldn't help being a little awed by the eight-wheeled
monstrosities that pulled the trains, and he shivered to
think what people like White Buffalo would say when
these big engines rumbled across the plains and prairies.

Brinks led him to a waiting buggy, and Colt grimaced
with the effort it took to climb up into the seat. He
waited for Brinks to untie the horses, remembering Stuart telling him years before that more trains came into

and out of Chicago than any other city in the country. He could well believe it from all the activity. He watched a freight train arrive, a passenger train leave. Some engines read ILLINOIS CENTRAL, others CHICAGO & ROCK ISLAND; he saw yet another that read B&L.

"Washington wants to give the nation time to mourn and a chance to pay their respects," Brinks was saying. "The funeral train has been through several major cities on its way to Springfield, with funeral processions and viewing at each stop." The man climbed up beside Colt and picked up the reins, guiding the carriage slowly through crowds of people. "I read in the newspaper a few days ago that some people were actually injured in the rush to view the body at Independence Hall in Philadelphia. The whole nation is in grief and turmoil. The war may be over, Mr. Travis, but I am afraid that the hatred and bitterness will be with a lot of people for a long time to come."

Colt thought of his own personal hellish memories. "Yes. I imagine it will." He thought about the young boy he had killed back in the Wilderness, wondering if his body had been burned up in the brushfires that awful night he had managed to escape. In his present physical and emotional condition, the memory made him want to weep. Whose son was he? Had his family found out what happened to him? How many soldiers on both sides would simply never return, their families never knowing how or when they had died, what had happened to their bodies?

He took in the sights as Brinks headed for the hospital. He was amazed at how much Chicago had grown in the three years since he left. Was Sunny here, or was she in Omaha? Surely she was grieved over Lincoln's death, since she and her father had known the man and had worked so hard to get him elected his first term. Being here again brought back memories, memories of stolen kisses one night on a beach, the taste and feel of sweet, beautiful, forbidden Sunny. That seemed like such a long time ago now. He was a different person then. They both were. Sunny was probably up to her neck in railroad matters now, maybe engaged to Blaine, or even married. It didn't matter anymore. She had her life, and he had his; and in his present condition the last thing he cared about was trying to find her. He would never want her to see him like this, and it would be useless to see her anyway, even if he were healthy. When he left her that night on the beach it was with full knowledge that it was best never to see her again.

"Maybe you can help me find my way around after I get a little more of my strength back," he told Brinks. "I left my horse and some personal possessions with a Jake Winters before I left. He was volunteering to take care of such things for men who wanted to join the war for the Union cause. I hope he still has them."

"Well, I imagine we can find Mr. Winters through the center for volunteers. I'll check it out for you. I'll also see about your army pay."

"I appreciate the help. I have some money in a bank here too—First Federal, I think it's called. I'd like to get it out of there, get things together within a few days and head back west. That's where I grew up. I was a scout for several years, led wagon trains to Oregon, that kind of thing."

"My! How exciting!" Brinks glanced at him, squinting curiously. "You're Indian, aren't you?"

Colt figured he looked more Indian than ever, since he hadn't bothered to get his hair cut for quite some time. It hung past his shoulders. "Yes, sir, part Cherokee. My father was white. That's where I got my eyes—and my size." He looked down at his bony thighs. "My height, I guess I should say. Can't say much about my size right now. I used to be pretty big."

"Well, we'll fatten you up and give you more tonics. Within the year you'll be back to normal. Just don't go riding off into the sunset too soon. You need time to heal."

"I'll heal better when I get back out to the country I love, Mr. Brinks. That's all I want. Once I feel that western sun on my back, set my eyes on the Nebraska

Plains, see the Rockies on the horizon—then I'll start
to heal."

"Well, most every man wants to be wherever he
calls home, that's for sure. Me, I was born and raised
right here in Chicago. I've always wondered about
the West though. Looks like things are going to start
to grow and develop out there, especially if they build
that transcontinental railroad. The Union Pacific already has headquarters set up out in Omaha, I hear,
had their ground-breaking back in sixty-three, but
they're still having trouble getting construction
started. I imagine now that the war is over, things will
really get under way. Congress can give more attention to rebuilding the country." The man halted the
buggy in front of a large brick structure. "Fact is,
once you decide to head back west, you can get a real
head start by taking the Union Pacific. It connects
clear to Omaha now."

Omaha. Colt thought how many memories that city
held for him. He wondered if Billie was still there. He
imagined that Omaha, too, was growing rapidly. Everything was growing and changing. Time and cir-
cumstance stood still for no one. LeeAnn and little
Ethan were long buried, his short but happy married
life over. Slim was gone, his parents. He had been
through a hellish war and ungodly agony in a southern prison. Now here he was back in Chicago, where
he had held the beautiful, wealthy Sunny Landers in
his arms three years earlier. He had to grin at the
kind of reaction he would get if he told that to Jonathan Brinks. The man would think he had lost his
mind.

That was all in his past now. And when a man's
past was so full of painful memories, there was nothing to do but leave it all behind him and try his best
to start over. He followed Brinks into the hospital.

Sunny sat in the balcony of the courthouse, an area
reserved for privileged Chicago citizens. She stared at
the flag-draped coffin below, watching the endless

line of people who walked by to pay their respects, their low voices and occasional weeping echoing into the chambers above. This was the second day the President's body had lain resting here. They would take it away soon, put it back on the funeral train and take it to its final resting place in Springfield.

She had been there since the body first arrived, sleeping only a few hours last night in a hotel. Grieving for President Lincoln brought back painful memories of grieving over her own father. Bo Landers and the President had been good friends, and she could not help thinking back to how hard her father had worked to get Lincoln elected. He had literally died for that cause, and now, after serving the nation so well and so wisely, after suffering the hellish decisions a president must have to make during an agonizing civil war, Lincoln, too, was dead.

It didn't seem fair, but then, most things in life didn't seem fair. Slim never should have died, nor Miss Putnam. Her own mother shouldn't have died before she got to know her. Bo Landers should still be alive. There never should have been that horrible, ugly war. So many things happened in life that just shouldn't have. Why was it always the good people who died before their time?

Her tears were not just for the President and memories of her father, but for the nation as a whole. How would they ever rebuild and get back to the business of being a united country? She had read about the horrible destruction of whole cities in the South, some destroyed by Sherman, some destroyed by the southerners themselves who wanted to make sure that when Union soldiers arrived, there would be nothing to capture or steal. Atlanta, burned to the ground—Richmond, burned to the ground—so many other cities as well as elegant plantation homes lying in blackened ruins.

A way of life for the South was over. Slaves had been freed, but no one knew what to do with them. They were left to wander and fend for themselves, a poor, lost people who had no idea where to go. Some were already filtering into Chicago, others, she had heard, were heading west to find land of their own.

A lot of people would be heading west now, not just Negroes, but southerners who had lost everything and could not afford to rebuild—some who would lose their land because banks would foreclose on them—taxes would be applied that they would not be able to pay.

How could this happen? Everything was so wrong. The President's assassination had left her and many others in a kind of shock, especially when it came on the heels of a war that had touched so many lives. This latest tragedy had brought back memories she would rather not dwell on—memories of a man who had gone off to war after awakening her passions one moonlit night on the shores of Lake Michigan. She had never heard from Colt, and when she read the daily lists of so many wounded and dead, she had little hope that he was still alive. She had already made up her mind she must forget him, and now his memory was stirred in her soul all over again. If only she knew for certain what had happened to him, she could perhaps rest a little easier. She could only pray that if he was still alive, he was not hurting, or missing a limb; that he would at least send her one letter, just to tell her he was all right.

"Sunny, you should leave here and get some rest." Blaine came to sit down beside her again, after he'd left her to talk to some nearby dignitaries. "We have that train ride to Springfield and the funeral; and then the long trip to Omaha. This has all been too much for you."

"I'll be all right once I get back out to Omaha. When does the train leave for Springfield?"

"In three hours. I had Mae get all your things together and Page drove your trunks down to Union Station."

Sunny took a deep breath and wiped her eyes with a silk handkerchief. "I'm so glad we happened to be in Chicago when the body came through."

Blaine put an arm around her shoulders. "I just

wish I didn't have to leave you at Springfield and go back to New York. I hate these separations."

Sunny rose. "All the more reason we can't make any serious plans yet," she told him. She met his eyes. "I'm so sorry, Blaine." Just a couple of weeks before he had again asked her to marry him, and then the news came about President Lincoln, sending her spiraling back down into a world of confusion and grief. Again she had put off making a decision. How much longer was he going to wait? When would she know it was the right time, and why didn't she have enough passion for him to be more eager to be his wife?

"I know what this has done to you, Sunny," he answered. "After New York I'll stop to see you in Omaha and then I'll be going back to Oregon for a few months. Maybe this time when I get back, you'll finally be ready. Construction of the U.P. should be well under way by then. Maybe you and I could get married and go to France, meet my mother and sister, get away from *all* of this for a while. That's what you need, Sunny. You just need to get completely away, relax and be a woman—just a woman."

"I can't think about any of that now. All this has brought back so much—especially my promise to Father. I need to be *here,* Blaine. I want to follow every step of construction, be present when the rails meet."

"That could take another three or four years. I know this isn't the time or place to talk about it, Sunny, but I simply won't wait that long! I'll be back in another year, and I want to be able to place the biggest diamond on your finger money can buy, and then set a date. Surely we can do that much."

She took his hands, studying his dark eyes. "Maybe by then we can. You'll have a lot more straightened out as far as your new logging company, and I'll be more settled in Omaha. Now that I know I can count on Cyril Brown to do a good job of handling Landers Enterprises, I don't have as much here to worry about."

"Except Vince trying to stick his nose into things.

He must be furious that you appointed Cyril to the job."

"Cyril knows how to deal with Vince. He was Father's right-hand man for a lot of years and knows as much about the company as I do. And he doesn't give me any argument over using funds for the U.P. Even Vince seems to be coming around a little. He's been sitting in on meetings involving the railroad. He hasn't said a word, but I think he's beginning to realize what a lucrative investment I've made after all. I'll win him over yet."

Blaine sighed deeply. "You're not going to give up on him, are you? Do you realize how much of your life has been spent trying to prove things to your brother, Sunny? Not just to your brother, but to practically everyone you know."

She folded her arms and stepped over to the balcony railing, looking down at the coffin again. "I don't think you understand how hard it is being a woman in my position, Blaine. Certain people, especially Vince and Eve, have hurt me deeply. I see how men watch me, wait for me to make a mistake. Even you were that way in the beginning."

"Sunny, that's all in the past."

"Not completely. There are still a few men who won't meet with me directly. It's like, like there is something more wrong than my just being a woman. The way some of Father's old friends look at me—it's different from when I was a little girl. They accept my knowledge of the business, but there is still something about me they *don't* accept."

"They're just a bunch of old coots who think Bo Landers was the only one who could handle things. You're proving them wrong. To hell with them."

She sighed, turning to face him again. "It doesn't matter for the moment. Lying down there is one man who *did* listen, who received me with the same respect he would receive a foreign dignitary or one of his congressmen. He believed in the railroad, took time to give attention to it in spite of the ugly war around him. He was a good man, Blaine, one of the wisest I've ever known. Father saw that inner strength in him, knew this was the man who not only was capable of being broadminded about this nation's progress, but who could carry on his shoulders the turmoil that was about to beset us. I'm just glad Father didn't live to see this."

Blaine put his hands on her shoulders, feeling sorry for her, but in despair of ever getting her to the altar. He was beginning to wonder if she was incapable of physical passion. He knew people gossiped about their relationship, wondering when they would ever marry, and it annoyed him. He was beginning to consider it a slam to his own manhood, and it made him more determined to know the final victory.

Still, he had told himself he could not and would not wait forever. He already had his eye on the young daughter of a wealthy New York industrialist. She was only sixteen and not ready to be seeing someone his age, but she was a beauty and came from a family of good standing and great wealth. She was not as lovely as Sunny, or as rich or well known, but she was good enough material to mold into the beautiful wife of a congressman and future president. When he got back from Oregon he would be ready to get more involved in politics, and a married man was always thought better of by the public than a single one. Sunny was the only woman he wanted, but if she again refused to at least become engaged, he had already decided to begin courting Bess Hammond.

Much as he hated to think about it, he couldn't believe it was just the railroad and business and the war and all the other outside factors that were keeping Sunny from making a decision. He couldn't help the feeling that the woman was waiting for something . . . maybe for someone. She never mentioned Colt Travis's name anymore, but he guessed she was wondering if he had survived the war. How he hated the thought that she might think of him at all!

"Let's get out of here and get you something to eat before the train leaves," he told her. "My coach is waiting outside." He gently pulled her away from the railing. "You've been here long enough, Sunny. Let's go."

She reluctantly obeyed, letting him lead her down the stairs and outside, where they were literally attacked by reporters asking about Sunny's friendship with President Lincoln, her relationship with Blaine. Blaine shielded her in his arms and got her into the coach, pulling down the shades to shut out the faces while his driver snapped the horses into motion, nearly running over some of the onlookers.

"Bastards," Blaine fumed.

Sunny leaned back in the seat and closed her eyes as the buggy left. Minutes later, it clattered past a nearby hospital on its way to Union Station. Inside that hospital, Colt Travis lay resting.

Colt could see the fire creeping up on him, feel its heat. He rushed toward the only pathway out of the inferno, only to trip over something. He looked down to see a dead baby. He screamed and ran, then suddenly awoke with a gasp to find himself sitting up in bed, sweating and shaking.

"Here now, what is this?" a woman's voice asked. "You poor thing. Bad dreams about the war?" She set an oil lamp down near his bed. "Let me bathe you and cool you off. Do you want anything?"

Colt heard the sound of water as she dipped a cloth into a wash bowl and wrung it out. "A cigarette. I need a smoke," he answered, breathing in near gasps.

"I'll see what I can do. Here. Just breathe deeply and try to put the dream out of your mind. This happens often in here, men like you with horrible memories."

He felt a cool rag at his face, and he closed his eyes and breathed deeply as she moved the rag to his neck.

"Dear God," she suddenly whispered. "Colt?"

He opened his eyes to a familiar face, but he could not quite place her. "Do I know you?" he asked.

"It *is* you! I'm Violet Landers, Stuart's wife! I met you that night at Sunny's dinner party. Why, that must have been at least three years ago!"

Colt thought for a moment, then took the rag from her and rubbed the back of his neck. "Jesus, go away," he told her.

She touched his arm. "Why? Because of the way you look? For God's sake, Colt, we have a hundred men in here who look like this. It's only a matter of time before you're back to your old form."

"Please go."

She took the rag from his hand. "Don't be silly. Thank God you're alive and have all your limbs. Sunny will be so happy to know—"

"Don't tell Sunny!" he said in a louder voice. "Don't you *dare* tell Sunny I'm here!" He stood up on rubbery legs and grasped the bedrail, almost going down. Vi grasped his other arm.

"All right, Colt, I won't tell her. Just calm down and get back into bed, please. I'll go see about finding some tobacco."

He leaned over the bed, half falling into it. "Jesus Christ," he muttered.

Vi hurried away, returning moments later to find him sitting on the edge of the bed. "Here," she told him. "We keep some prerolled smokes on hand since so many men ask for them." She handed him a cigarette, then brought the lamp over and turned up the wick so he could light it. When she saw him in the brighter light, her heart ached at the embarrassment and agony in his eyes. She turned the lamp back down and set it aside again, then sat beside him on the bed. "Tell me where you've been, Colt. Belle Isle? Andersonville?"

He took a deep drag on the cigarette, closing his eyes and breathing deeply for a moment. "Andersonville," he finally answered, his voice quieter now. "If I died and went to hell tomorrow, it couldn't be any worse."

"I'm so sorry. We've all wondered what happened. You never wrote Sunny. She worried more than any of us, although she didn't speak of it. I saw it in her eyes."

He took the cigarette from his mouth and stared at it a moment. "Just don't tell her I'm here. I'd never want her to see me like this. Fact is, I don't want her to see me at all. It's best that way, for both of us."

Vi touched his back, wanting to cry at its boniness. "I think I understand. She's gone to Springfield for the President's funeral anyway, and from there she'll be going on to Omaha again."

"Let her go. If you send her any kind of message that I'm here, she'll come back first. Wait till I'm gone. Then you can tell her I'm alive and all right." He looked at her. "Why aren't you in Omaha? I thought you and Stuart were both going."

"Eventually. Stuart is out there now having a home built for us. I thought it my duty to continue my work here until the war was over. The children and I will be going out soon."

He put the cigarette back to his lips, resting his elbows on his knees. "How is Sunny?"

"She's fine—very distraught over the death of the President. It brought back painful memories for her. But she'll be all right as soon as she gets back to Omaha and her work with the railroad. That's all she seems to care about."

Colt nodded. "Figures." He paused, smoking quietly a moment. "What about that Blaine O'Brien? They engaged or married yet?"

Vi rose, going to the wash pan and rewetting the cloth. She wrung it out and came back over to him. "I've never quite been able to figure out how Sunny feels about Blaine. I don't think she knows herself. The day after you showed up at the party, they had some kind of falling out. Blaine left and didn't contact her for two years." She sat down beside him and started to wash his back, but he straightened, turning to face her.

"What the hell happened?"

Vi hesitated, watching his eyes. "Why don't *you* tell *me*, Colt? Sunny wouldn't. I know only that she met you on the beach, and after that she changed, grew somehow harder and more determined. She had an argument with Blaine and he left. I think he was terribly upset that she had met alone with you. What happened, Colt?"

He turned away again. "Nothing really. We just realized that trying to be only friends wouldn't work, that's all. And since it's ridiculous to think we could be more than that, we decided it was better not to stay in touch anymore. That's why I don't want her to see me now. She'd come rushing over here full of pity, and I'd look into those damn blue eyes of hers, and we'd be in the same miserable predicament all over again. She's better off with somebody like Blaine, although I don't particularly like the man myself."

"That's because you're nothing like him." Vi began washing his back again. "You both made the right decision, but then again, I care very much for Sunny, and I don't think she's very happy. Actually, I've never seen her quite as happy as she was that night at the party after you showed up, or quite so miserable as when you left." She laid the rag over the back of his neck. "That better? You woke up in a terrible sweat."

"Thanks. As far as the dreams, I get them all the time. Sometimes they get mixed up—the Indian attack on my family mixed in with memories of the war, watching the medics, the horrors of Andersonville. A few stiff drinks before I go to sleep might do the trick."

She touched his arm. "Don't do it, Colt. I've seen men turn into drunkards over the war, fall into complete ruin. You're too good a man for that."

He snickered. "You hardly know me."

"Oh, but I do know you through things Sunny used to tell me, things she let me read in her diary."

He grinned and took another puff on the cigarette. "She still keeping that journal?"

Vi smiled. "Yes. She has a fine talent for writing."

Colt sighed deeply, staring at the floor. "Yeah. She

has a *lot* of talents. She's one intelligent, sophisti-
cated, educated woman, and beautiful to boot. She
must have about a thousand men after her hand."

"Oh, there have been many, but she saw only a few
socially after you and Blaine left. There was never
anything serious. Now Blaine is back, and they're together again. I guess they patched things up. Blaine
would like to get married, but Sunny still insists she
can't give attention to that part of her life right now.
She's too wrapped up in the Union Pacific—traveling,
raising funds, trying to keep a reasonable hand in
Landers Enterprises and keep Vince from moving in
where he doesn't belong."

Colt put what was left of the cigarette between his
lips again. "So, Blaine is back." He rose, feeling
stronger now. He took the rag from his neck and
pressed it to his forehead, then ran it back through
his hair. "There must be *something* special between
them if she didn't take much interest in anyone else
the whole time they were apart."

"Maybe. Then again, maybe it wasn't Blaine she
was pining for."

He turned to face her, and he couldn't help a grin.
The woman had a lot of insight. "Maybe not. But I
imagine she's over it now."

Vi moved her eyes over him, noticing the scar at
his right side. "Is that from when the Pawnee
wounded you?"

He put a hand to his side. "This one and the one
over my eye." He realized then that he was standing
there barechested and wearing only his longjohns,
but somehow it didn't matter. If Vi had been working
much at this hospital, she had seen a lot more than
this. "I've got a scar on my right thigh from a Crow
knife, this one on my left arm is from camp robbers
who shot at me when I was camped alone in the
Rockies. That was before I met my wife. I got a couple of broken ribs when I rode for the Pony Express
and outlaws shot my horse from under me." He put a
hand to his neck. "Here's my newest—a Confederate
bullet."

She smiled softly. "Apparently, you're a hard man to put down."

"Yeah, well, Andersonville just about finished me off better than any bullet could have done." He grinned bashfully and sat back down.

Vi touched the scar under his left ear. "Poor Colt. So many scars, inside and out."

He met her eyes. "Is she happy with Blaine?"

So, it's back to Sunny, is it, she thought. "She seems to be, most of the time."

He looked away. "I suppose it's best. Somebody like him would understand her pretty good."

Vi smiled sadly. "He understands her *world,* Colt. I'm not so sure he understands the woman behind that beautiful face. I have a feeling there's a part of her that *you* understand more than anyone."

He shook his head. "Maybe. But some things just can't be. Even if everyone welcomed me into her world, which God knows would never happen in the first place, *I* wouldn't want any part of it. It would be just as wrong for me as it would be for her. Do you know what I'm saying?"

"I think I do."

He let out a light, clipped laugh. "The night I walked into that dinner party—" He ran a hand through his hair. "God, I was never so uncomfortable in my whole life. I couldn't live like that. Can you just imagine Sunny showing up at congressional parties with somebody like me on her arm?" His quick laugh had a note of bitterness to it. "Let alone how *I'd* feel trying to enjoy myself at things like that. No, it's done now, and it's best left undisturbed. She's got Blaine, and that's good. Something tells me he's a bastard in most ways, and I know from a certain little argument we had that he can be damn ruthless. But I think he cares for her. I don't think he'd be cruel to her or anything like that. So it's best."

Vi rose, touching his hair. "I suppose it is. What will you do when you leave here, Colt?"

He shrugged. "Head west, that's for sure. I think I'll leave tomorrow or the next day. Mr. Brinks is seeing about getting my horse and belongings back. I'll heal better when I get back out where I belong. I'll be all right. Once I'm strong enough, I'll get a job." He looked up at her. "You going to tell Sunny you saw me?"

"I think I should, don't you? She has a right to know you're all right, Colt."

"I suppose. Just keep your promise to wait till I'm gone." He studied the plain face, a face that seemed to grow more beautiful as they talked. "You're a nice lady, Vi. I don't imagine many women of your station would bother working here as volunteers, with the smell of blood and the dirty work involved. Why do you do it?"

She folded her arms. "I'm not sure myself. At first it was just an effort on my part to feel that I was doing something to help the cause, and I was the Landers token, so to speak. But then it became a very personal thing for me. I've had men cling to my hand and call me by their wife's name, or call me Mother in their delirium. My heart goes out to them. I just thank God it's over with now, and I especially thank Him that *you* survived."

He smiled sadly. "Thanks for the smoke. Tell Stuart hello for me."

"I will. Do you have any messages for Sunny?"

He shook his head. "No. Just that I'm alive. Don't say anything about, you know, some of the things I said tonight. Tell her I wish her and Blaine the best. She'll know what I mean."

Vi was beginning to have her doubts that Sunny and Colt's decision to never see each other again was such a good idea. She wondered if either one of them realized that they were in love. Was such a match so impossible? Perhaps it was. She had firmly believed it until now, but she decided it was not her place to meddle. "All right." She sighed in doubtful resignation. "I won't be back here until the day after tomorrow. I imagine you'll be gone by then." She touched his hair. "Sunny said once that you were like the wind, always drifting, hard to catch and hard to hold.

I guess she was right. You take care of yourself, Colt. I wish you only health and happiness."

He took her hand and squeezed it, surprised at how easy it was to talk to this woman he hardly knew. She couldn't be more than a couple of years older than he was, but it didn't seem to matter. "Thanks. And thanks for not saying anything to Sunny until I'm gone."

"Are you all right now? I have to go to another ward."

"I'm all right. Thanks again for the smoke, and for the talk." She started to leave, but Colt kept hold of her hand. "Do me a favor."

"What's that?"

"Kind of watch out for Sunny. She never had many women friends. I know by the way she talked about you a couple of times that she thinks a lot of you. She needs your friendship."

And perhaps she needs yours too, she thought. "I love Sunny like a sister, sometimes more like my own daughter, in spite of the fact that I'm not so very much older than she. Beneath that very businesslike, calculating, manipulating exterior lies a very sweet girl who sometimes gets terribly lonely, and who never had a mother to teach her how to be a woman. All she had was a bellowing father who could teach her only a man's ways, and I feel sorry for her having to take on so much at such a young age."

Colt lay back down. "Well, she's handled it pretty damn good."

"Yes, I suppose she has." Vi walked over and picked up the oil lamp. "Good-bye, Colt. God bless and be with you."

"Thanks. Same here."

Their eyes held a moment longer, and she turned and left. Colt stared into the darkness, old feelings aroused anew. He decided he would leave tomorrow, whether he was physically ready or not. He had a feeling Vi Landers just might not be able to keep her word about not telling Sunny about him before he left the hospital. It was time to get out of Chicago.

Part

Three

Chapter 18

Spring 1866

A sweet-smelling breeze caressed Colt's face and free-flowing hair as he ascended the gentle slope. He had to keep tugging at Dancer's reins to make the horse obey him, for the prairie was thick with fresh spring grass that was nearly as high as Dancer's belly.

"I swear if I let you, you'd eat yourself to death," Colt chided. "It's a damn good thing I keep you exercised or you'd bloat up and roll down these hills instead of walk down them."

Dancer shuddered and shook his mane. Colt grinned, stopping at the top of the rise and finally letting the animal nibble. He leaned over and patted the horse's neck, then sat up straighter and began rolling a cigarette, watching the construction crew below.

He had imagined that building a railroad would be quite an undertaking, but he still had not quite expected to see so many men involved that they could comprise a small town. He figured there were two or three hundred men down below, spread out from the end of track clear back to a second supply train and beyond to those who guarded a herd of beef to the north, which he figured was kept to feed the many hungry mouths at the end of a long day's work. The entire work camp covered close to a mile, maybe more.

From this distance he could only faintly hear shouted orders, but it appeared the men were working with precision, the actual track layers going at it like little machines. He could see men pounding in spikes, their mauls hitting silently at first, the sound coming to his ears a second or two later.

"What do you think, boy?" He sealed the paper and stuck the cigarette into his mouth. "Should I go on down there and see about work?" Dancer whinnied lightly and kept eating, moving ahead a little. Colt lit the cigarette and struggled with indecision. "Lord knows I've got to do *something* with my life." He looked around at the vastness that stretched in every direction. If he had to earn himself a living, he couldn't think of a much better job than scouting for the railroad, if they would have him. There weren't a lot of choices left for a man who enjoyed being out on the open prairie and plains, living under the stars.

Just as he had figured, coming back to this country had done more for him than any medicine he could have taken. He had needed time to be alone, had not been to one good-size town since leaving Chicago. He had at first contemplated stopping at Omaha to find Billie, but he had ruled that out. He just wanted to be alone, to let the quiet of the prairie and the mountains soothe his torn soul, erase the ugly memories that brought on the hated dreams. Yes, he was still lonely, but loneliness wasn't cured by being around a lot of people. A man could be lonely anywhere; and for him there were times when the loneliness was eased by not seeing anyone at all.

He let the reins go slack so that Dancer could continue to enjoy the treats of the prairie grass, and he rose up in the saddle a little to stretch his legs. He felt stronger, back to his old self, maybe even a little heavier than before the war. When he first came from Chicago, he often rode without shirt or hat, feeling a kind of healing from the sun that both warmed him and brought a rich color back to his skin. He stuffed himself with antelope and quail and rabbit and whatever wild game he could bag, as well as potatoes, carrots, bacon, beans, and other supplies he picked up at forts along the way. For a while food had become almost an obsession with him, and he had to grin now at teasing Dancer. He realized that for a while he hadn't been much different from his horse when it came to eating. He had spent the winter holed up in the Rockies, with little more to do than eat and sleep, taking down deer or moose when needed, just letting himself lie around and rest like a bear in hibernation. Sometimes he lifted rocks to help build his strength, or played cards with himself, or even studied a book of Shakespeare he had carried with him for years. It had never been easy reading, but parts were certainly exciting; and the challenge of sometimes having to study certain passages over and over to grasp their meaning kept his mind stimulated.

He felt healed now, in mind and spirit as well as physically. There were times when he wanted to shout with the joy of realizing he had survived personal and physical hell and now was back in the land he loved. Sometimes he would kick Dancer into a run, letting go of the reins and spreading his arms, riding hard, the wind in his face. He would yell and whoop like the wildest of Indians. He figured if anybody would see him at those times, they would think he was a crazy man. Maybe he was—crazy with a new eagerness to live, free of death and war and prison.

The only thing left that he was needing more and more was to lie with a woman, and he contemplated going back to Omaha and finding Billie before taking work. But going there meant risking the temptation to see Sunny Landers again, and that was something better left alone.

Sunny was truly in his past now. So were a lot of other things. He was twenty-nine years old and Slim's death, LeeAnn's and Ethan's deaths, the ugly war—all were behind him. There would always be a nagging, painful void in his life, times when thoughts of his baby son would bring the heavy pain to his chest; but he understood and accepted that now. The fact remained he was still alive and still young enough to love again and have another family someday. It was time to get back to living, to put aside what could not be and leave himself open to new possibilities.

Down below, one of the two huge locomotives that pulled the construction supply train blew its whistle, and a few men who had been sitting about moved to take the place of other workers, the men apparently working in shifts. *So,* he thought, *she really is building her railroad.* He had his own doubts in the beginning, but there it was, the Union Pacific, pushing its way west across the Nebraska prairie, edging toward the sandhills, right through the very country Colt had led Sunny and her father nine years ago. Life sure was strange, the way people moved into and out of each other's lives, the way things kept changing. He thought how Sunny must be busier than ever now, excited and happy at seeing her father's dream finally becoming a reality, proving to Vince that it could be done.

He already had a good idea of the enormity of the project, both in manpower and equipment, and in cost. Nearly three hundred miles to the west, graders were building a bed for the track layers. Colt had noticed the sod-covered dugouts that provided temporary housing for the graders, and when he rode in to talk to them, they had told him to come to the construction site to ask about work. He had not thought the project would be so strung out. The graders had explained that even farther west were the surveyors, who along with the graders were in the most danger, since they worked in smaller crews and were more at risk from Indian attack.

The Cheyenne had been on a wicked rampage against

the railroad, something Colt could fully understand. Once the railroad was completed, the West would fill up even faster with white settlers, let alone the fact that the big locomotives frightened away buffalo and other wild game. The graders had explained that sometimes sparks from the smokestack set fire to the prairie. But the Cheyenne had more reason to be at war, not just with the railroad but with all whites. On his way west last summer he had learned at Fort Laramie about a massacre of innocent Southern Cheyenne by Colorado Volunteers at a place called Sand Creek. Ever since then the Indians had been hot for revenge and had attacked and pillaged the town of Julesburg, in Colorado. They had raided and slaughtered whites on a bloody trail to the north, destroying telegraph lines, killing cattle, and burning towns and farms. The graders had told him gold had been discovered in the Black Hills, and now prospectors were flooding into land promised to the Sioux and Northern Cheyenne under the Laramie Treaty. That could mean only more trouble.

Colt wondered what had happened to White Buffalo and his family, wondered if the man ever thought about him. He couldn't help feeling some sympathy for the Indian plight. The same thing that had happened to his own people was now happening to the Sioux and Cheyenne and other Plains tribes. He knew what the future held for them, already realized that no matter how hard they fought, there could be only one outcome. According to the graders, more soldiers were already on their way west to protect the railroad, and hundreds more soldiers were being sent into the Black Hills and to Powder River country, where a Sioux leader called Red Cloud was wreaking so much havoc that some forts were being abandoned.

Sometimes he felt he should be with his Indian brothers, but he knew what they were trying to do was futile, and he had long ago chosen the path he would take in life. He had his special time to feel that side of his life when he spent the winter with White Buffalo, had experienced the savageness that lay just under his skin when he attacked the Pawnee. That, too, was behind him now.

He picked up the reins, taking a last puff on his cigarette and pressing the stub against his metal canteen to make sure it was out before throwing it into the grass. "Let's go, boy."

He headed down the slope toward the construction crew. Men swarmed everywhere, working almost like soldiers at precision drill, running with rails, spiking them into place. Colt tried to imagine what it would cost to pay so many men, let alone the cost of food and supplies, equipment, steel rails, freighting costs to get material to the site and such. It was easy to understand how much money such a project would take, but as he watched, it was also becoming easier to believe this could be done. He kicked Dancer into a gentle lope, riding toward a man who was shouting orders. He and several others turned to look at the approaching stranger.

"Hello," Colt called out. "Where's the boss?"

The man pointed toward the train that sat close to the construction site. "Last car before the wood box," he shouted.

Colt tipped his hat and rode alongside the train, looking up at gigantic boxcars that he guessed to be at least eighty feet long, each with three tiers of windows, almost like a three-story building but not quite as high. A few men stood on the platforms of the cars, some of them just staring at him, others nodding a hello. "Who do I see about a job?" he asked one of them.

The man looked him over. "You ever work as a scout?"

"Plenty of times. Is there a need for scouts?"

The man grinned, showing yellow teeth. "I expect so, seeing as how we just lost one to the Indians a couple of days ago. It's your neck, Mister. Go see General Casement. He's the construction engineer." He pointed to a passenger car next to the woodbox that carried fuel for the double locomotives. The big steam engines were used to push the train rather than pull it so that the last flatbed cars that carried tools and supplies could be closest to the work crew. Colt noticed the train was slowly moving, inching along the tracks as fast as rails could be laid.

Steam shot in one long gasp from the side of one of the engines, and Dancer whinnied and balked. "Easy, boy," Colt told him. "You'll have to get used to those damn things." He rode past the car the worker had indicated, deciding to first get a look at the engines, fascinating, massive power machines that almost seemed alive. He dismounted, keeping hold of Dancer's reins as he walked around the two locomotives, studying the amazing network of pipes and drive shafts, nuts and bolts and rods and gears that comprised the "iron horse," as one grader had told him the Indians called these things. They truly were an awesome sight, and in spite of his doubts that the presence of the railroad was good for the land, he could not help being caught up in the excitement, his curiosity stimulated by trying to figure the mechanics of the thing. When he had ridden trains back from prison and on to Chicago, he had been too sick to pay attention.

He nodded to an engineer.

"Looking for work?" the man asked.

"Yes, sir."

"Well, if you want to work for the railroad, it doesn't hurt to know a little bit about how these things operate. Want a look?"

"Don't mind if I do."

"Just tie your horse to the second car there. We don't move along fast enough that he couldn't keep up."

Colt tied Dancer and climbed into the cab, studying the maze of gadgets and gauges and levers. "Wood goes in here," a second engineer explained, opening a door to reveal the furnacelike belly of the engine. "The hotter the fire, the more steam she makes and the faster she goes. Hardest part out here is getting wood and water. The U.P. sends a train out every few days with new supplies. Eventually, there will be water towers and supply stations built all along the way, roundhouses where engines can be serviced and oiled and polished up, take on more wood and so forth. Some project, isn't it? Thousands of men and millions of dollars will be used before we're through, with way stations and new towns springing up all across this land. This is what you call progress, son, an example of how a few people's dreams become reality. Of course, it doesn't hurt when those people have big money of their own and friends in the right places."

The man laughed, and Colt could not help thinking of Sunny. "I expect so," he answered. "Tell me, is General Casement in his private car?"

"Sure is." The man looked him over. "Now, you look like some kind of scout. You're risking your skin if that's the kind of work you want. Indian trouble is going to get worse they say."

"I'm used to that kind of danger." Colt tipped his hat. "Thanks for the little lesson." He climbed down and headed for the car where Casement was supposed to be. The forward engine gave out a grunt and a puff and moved again.

Colt shook his head, wondering at how things change. He remembered the first time he had set eyes on a train, back before tracks reached Omaha, remembered laughing at Stuart Landers when the man told him his father wanted to build a railroad west. He climbed up on the platform of what looked like a passenger car, although when he went inside it had only a few seats. Several had been removed to make room for two desks, some file cabinets, and a cot.

A very small-built man looked up at him. "Yes?"

"I'm looking for General Casement."

The man rose, and Colt forced himself not to grin or look surprised at how short he was. He guessed the man couldn't be more than five feet and a couple of inches.

"I'm General Casement." The words were spoken crisply, and there was an authoritative air about him in spite of his stature. He barked an order to another man inside his quarters and the second man jumped to obedience, quickly leaving to procure the coffee Casement had asked for.

"My name is Colt Travis, and I'm looking for work," Colt told the general. "I've done a lot of scouting, heard you're in need of somebody like me."

"That's a fact. What's your experience?"

Colt removed his hat. "Before the war I led wagon trains west, since I was fourteen years old. I've been to Oregon and California, know the land, know the Indians. I can speak Cheyenne and Sioux and a couple of other tongues, and I'm not afraid to work alone out on the Plains. In fact, I prefer it that way. I rode for the Pony Express for a few months."

Casement looked him over. "We just lost a good scout. I hope you know what you're up against. If it's been awhile since you associated with any Indians, you'll find things have changed. By the way, you look Indian yourself."

"Part Cherokee, sir, but I was raised by a white father."

"Hmmm. Well, as I was saying, you might discover that parlaying with the Indians isn't as simple as it might once have been for you. They are no longer in a very sociable mood, and they view this railroad as an intrusion on their land, something that is scaring away the game, that sort of thing."

"I'm aware of the Indian situation. I know how they think. I really am good at what I do, General Casement, and I need the work."

The man studied him more, taking a seat. "With that southern drawl of yours, you must be a Confederate."

"No, sir. I fought for the Union. Spent about a year at Andersonville before the war ended."

"Andersonville!" A new respect moved into the man's eyes. "You're lucky to be alive, Mr. Travis."

"Yes, sir, I am."

"Well, we have all sorts of men on that crew out there —northern *and* southern, which makes it damn hard to keep order and keep them out of fights, but I do it. I don't tolerate laziness, fighting, or drinking, Mr. Travis. And for a job like yours I usually require references."

Colt thought about Sunny. A man couldn't get a better reference for a job like this one than from the woman who owned part of the whole project. She'd tell the man to hire him in a second, he guessed, but he didn't want to get the job that way. Casement would probably wire her, and then she'd know where he was. Much as he told himself there was nothing wrong with seeing her again, he preferred not to, not even sure himself why it mattered. He would just rather she didn't know he was doing this. With the hundreds of men who worked for the U.P., someone like Sunny probably didn't know the names of any of them other than the upper echelon who owned and managed the railroad. Only men like Casement were concerned with the names of the common workers, so it was unlikely Sunny would ever know what he was doing.

"Well, sir, I used to have some letters on me from people on wagon trains I took to Oregon and such, people who recommended me for this kind of work; but with the war and all, somehow I've lost them. I guess you'll just have to take my word."

"Well, I'm a pretty good judge of men, and you have an honesty about those white man's eyes of yours. You certainly look like a hardy, robust man who can take care of himself."

"I've done my share of fighting, sir, against Indians and in the war. I've got the scars to prove it."

Casement scrutinized the scar over his right eye. "Yes, I can see that." The man rose again. "What I need is a man who will ride the perimeter of the camp, Travis —keep an eye open for Indian attack. Believe me, we get them often. The Cheyenne are on a real rampage. I need a man who can spot trouble well before it reaches us, a man with a good horse who can ride fast and get back here to warn us so we can be ready. We keep a good supply of carbines for the men. When trouble comes, they drop their tools and pick up rifles. Things can get pretty wild out here sometimes."

"I'm your man, sir. Just give me the chance to prove it."

"All right. The pay is two dollars a day. Follow me. I'll explain how the camp operates."

Casement led him outside, and Colt felt like a giant as he walked behind the man. He figured that whatever Casement lacked in stature, he must have made up for in ability, or the Union Pacific would not have hired him. It was obvious only a man of extreme authority and determination could keep this project running smoothly. His secretary returned with the coffee, and Casement took it from him, sipping on it as they walked. Colt noticed that men seemed to jump at the little general's command or work a little harder when they knew he was watching them.

Casement stopped in front of one of the three huge boxcars that were part of what he told Colt was the work train. "Never stops rolling," he told Colt. "Keeps advancing as fast as the rails are laid. These bunker cars are where the men sleep, eighty-five feet long they are— regular rolling hotels. There's a triple deck of bunks inside, hammocks slung underneath some of them. The three cars can house up to four hundred men if some of them pitch tents on the tops of the cars. The car between mine and the housing cars is the dining car. We can feed only a hundred and twenty-five men at a time, so you have to eat in shifts. You'd be welcome to the sleeping quarters and the food when you're in camp, but of course if you're doing your job right, you won't be around most of the time. One end of the car where my quarters are is a kitchen and storeroom. And, of course, most of our meat comes from the cattle you see grazing to the north of the tracks."

The man had to nearly shout to be heard because of the noise of the camp.

"You just missed seeing the big timers of the U.P.," the general continued as both men walked past several horse-drawn wagons piled high with railroad ties. "Dr. Durant and his bunch were out here just a few days ago, threw a big party right out on the prairie to celebrate the U.P.'s arrival at the one hundredth meridian, nearly two hundred fifty miles out of Omaha. It was quite a bash—a couple of congressmen, celebrities of all sorts, and Miss Sunny Landers and her fiancé were also along. The men were falling all over each other to get a look at Miss Landers, but, of course, none of this motley crew was allowed anywhere near Durant and his bunch in their fancy frocks and top hats."

"I've, uh, I've heard of Miss Landers," Colt answered,

wondering why it bothered him more than it should have when the man mentioned Sunny's fiancé. "So, she's engaged, is she?"

"Yes, to that Blaine O'Brien fellow. Everyone says it's about time. They've been seeing each other for years, but Miss Landers has been so involved with the U.P. and Mr. O'Brien with his new logging industry and his own businesses in New York that they've just never been able to set a date. I think the wedding will take place sometime next year."

Colt struggled against the ridiculous feeling of hurt and disappointment. Sunny was doing exactly what she should. He forced himself to pay attention to Casement as the man explained more to him about the railroad camp.

"These men are not an easy bunch to keep organized and under control," the general was saying, "but by God they know they'd better stick to it or they're gone. We've got a mixture here of Civil War veterans like yourself, as well as German and Irish immigrants, Mormons, southerners who have lost their homes, drifters, prospectors, even a few Negroes—freed slaves needing work. They're a hardworking bunch when kept in line, but I don't like the damn tent towns full of gamblers and whores that follow them. There's one just a couple of miles to the east, and I imagine they'll be moving on farther west soon to keep up with us. They're good at bilking these men out of their hard-earned money, but I suppose if a man is foolish enough to let such riffraff take him for everything he has, there isn't much I can do about it. At the same time, they all know that if the whiskey and women keep any man from doing a proper day's work, he's through with the U.P."

The camp was filled with the shouts and curses of men, the banging of mauls, the occasional hiss of steam and sound of the whistle from the work train's locomotive. Men swarmed everywhere, some hauling ties from the wagons, others pounding spikes. A team of men hurried past Colt to pull a steel rail from a horse-drawn cart, the very last vehicle between the work train and the crew. Two men took hold of the end of a rail and pulled, the rest of the gang grabbing hold as the rail slid free of the cart. They ran with the rail to its required spot, a foreman gave a command, and the rail was dropped in place, after which the spike crew hurried forward and secured it.

Colt was astounded at the speed with which the rail was placed. He noticed Casement had his pocket watch out and was observing the whole process. "Thirty seconds," he said. "Very good." He looked up at Colt and smiled proudly. "With two rail gangs we can drop four rails a minute," he bragged. "Those rails weigh five hundred pounds each, but if things are organized, they can be handled like sticks of wood." He watched two more rails put in place. "When Dr. Durant contracted with me for this job, I promised him speed and efficiency, and that is what he will get. The man has a lot of money invested in this, as does Miss Landers and a lot of others, including the government. The sooner the railroad is completed, the sooner it can begin earning money for itself. Besides that, we're in a little race with the Central Pacific, Crocker and Strobridge and that bunch. We don't intend to come in second on how many miles of track we can lay in a day. The competition is part of the reason these men are willing to work so hard. They don't want to be outdone by Strobridge and his little Chinese men."

"Chinese? I've seen a few in California. The Central Pacific is using them?"

Casement laughed. "That's what I'm told. I guess for their size they work pretty good, but these men don't have any use for those little yellow people. They sure don't want to be outdone by them, so they just work all that much harder."

Colt noticed that the rail cart was nearly empty, and that the bed of the cart had rollers in it, making it easier to slide the rails out. Another cart was on its way, bringing a load of rails from the flatcar of the work train that held the bigger supply. As soon as the first car was empty, men literally dumped it off the track to make room for the next cart, which was pulled along at a fast gallop so that the rhythm of the work was not interrupted. Behind it was another horse and cart full of rails, waiting for its turn.

"Those carts are very light," Casement told him as they watched several more men right the empty cart, unhitch it, and run with horse and cart back to the flat-car full of rails, reposition the horse and cart and begin reloading it. A second train was parked to the east of the work train; and it contained even more rails. Men worked at that end just unloading rails and bringing them to the flat car at end of track for loading onto the carts. "That first train will head back for Omaha soon to pick up more rails," Casement told him. "It's a never-ending process, Mr. Travis—bring out the supplies, load them onto the work train, bring them to the end of the track on the carts and back again. When well orches-trated, the entire procedure reminds me of a kind of dance, don't you think? In fact, these men have a nick-name—gandy dancers, some kind of Irish term. Each man has a specific duty. The work train and the supply train behind it provide everything needed to keep us supplied, fed, and housed, as well as everything needed to lay tracks with speed and efficiency. We even have a blacksmith shop. I tell you, this whole thing is a grand machination of men, contractors, subcontractors, engi-neers, foremen, surveyors, graders, rust eaters—uh, that's what we call the men who handle the rails—spike men—an absolutely beautiful movement of muscle and iron. We have a lot to prove to the disbelievers, Mr. Travis, and we're doing it."

It was obvious the general was proud of his own ex-pertise at keeping everything in order, and Colt couldn't help being impressed. "I can certainly see that," he an-swered. There was movement everywhere, a general feeling of anxious determination to get the job done. His own excitement was due in part to knowing what an achievement this must be for Sunny, to come out here and see the progress being made, a railroad edging its way across a continent, just like her father dreamed could happen.

"We've had a hell of a time getting proper timber for the ties," Casement was telling him. "There's nothing out here but damn cottonwood, and even that can be found only along the river. It's nearly useless as far as durability, but we burnettize it, impregnate it with a solution of zinc chloride. That helps strengthen it. At any rate, with the difficulty in getting good cedar and oak ties shipped in from Minnesota, we have to make do with mostly these cottonwood ties. What we do is mix them on a ratio of four of the cottonwood ties to one strong, durable one. Eventually, the cottonwood ties will have to be replaced, but there will be time for that once the railroad is finished. Right now speed is essential." The man looked up at him, sticking his thumbs into the armholes of his vest. "Well, you're welcome to go over to the storage car and get whatever supplies you'll need, food and ammunition and such."

"I'm pretty well stocked for now."

"Good, then you might as well get started, Mr. Travis. There's no time like the present. Oh, and any wild game you can kill—antelope, even buffalo, is a welcome change—helps us preserve the beef."

Colt nodded, wondering, with all the noise and ruckus, how the man could think there would be much wild game anywhere close. He could understand why the Cheyenne hated this, but he was wise enough to understand there was no stopping it. He remembered White Buffalo's last words—that he should leave while they were still friends. If he was going to work for the Union Pacific, he would most certainly be considered an enemy. It made him sad to think of it, but he needed the work.

"Put me on the payroll," he told Casement. "And thanks."

The two men shook hands. "Report back here every couple of days just so we know you're all right. If you're in trouble or you know Indians are heading for us, give off three shots in quick succession. If we need you back here, you'll hear one long whistle from the engine, followed by two short blasts. That means you're to get back here just as fast as your horse can bring you. Try not to go more than a couple of miles beyond camp."

Colt nodded. "Yes, sir. And thanks again." He

headed back to Dancer and untied the horse, sensing the animal was very glad to get away from the frightening locomotive. "Let's get to work," he told the animal.

He headed southwest, leaving the noisy camp behind him and wondering what Sunny would think if she knew that he was now on her payroll.

Chapter 19

"Oh, Stuart, we've come so far! It just makes my heart skip a beat to see all of this!"

Although her small-brimmed, flat straw bonnet was well-pinned into her hair, Sunny clung to the hat with one hand while she clung with the other to the iron support bar of the train platform, on which she stood watching the scenery as her train rumbled along the freshly laid tracks of the Union Pacific, skimming across prairie land at the amazing speed of thirty miles an hour.

"Whoever thought nine years ago that this would come to be?" Stuart answered, his thinning hair blowing about in wisps as he watched from the other side of the platform. They shouted to each other to be heard above the rushing wind and clattering train.

"Not many," Sunny answered. "Has it really been nine years, Stuart?"

The man came over to stand beside her. "Seems impossible, doesn't it?"

Sunny kept her eyes on the passing landscape, watching a few buffalo far in the distance. They were in a run, heading away from the noise of the train. It was impossible to come out to this land without thinking of Colt, in spite of being resigned to the fact that she would surely never see him again. *Where is he?* she thought. *Why did he tell Vi to wait until he was gone before she could tell me she had seen him?* She couldn't help her concern for how he might be, after hearing about his condition when Vi had seen him. Poor Colt, imprisoned at Andersonville!

She told herself her past with him was all water over the dam now. She had matured, had faced the truth—Colt Travis was determined never to darken her doorway again—or brighten it, whatever the case may be. He knew what was best for both of them, and so did she. She had finally accepted a ring from Blaine, poor, patient, devoted Blaine. After three engagement parties, one in New York, another in Chicago, and yet another in Omaha, they had come out west four months earlier with Thomas Durant and celebrated reaching the one hundredth meridian. Now Blaine was back in New York, making the necessary preparations to run for governor of that state. It would take a lot of work, and he understood that Sunny would not take herself away from the railroad for that long. She had stayed in Omaha.

Blaine seemed satisfied just being able to say he was engaged to her and that they would marry in another year. That was enough of a boost to his reputation to help him win votes. It was time to plan further campaign strategies, even though elections would not come for nearly two years yet, and that meant staying in New York for now. "These things take a lot of time and planning," he had told her before leaving. "Now that the railroad is well under way, I can devote my attention to the elections."

Sunny knew that he expected her to be at his side for campaigning after their marriage next year. She had decided she owed him that much, even though it would be close to three years before the railroad was finished. He had promised that after the voting in '68, she could come back west for the final construction, be present for the joining of the rails, which was expected to take place sometime in '69. She hated the thought of leaving, but she couldn't very well marry the man and then stay behind for the first few months of their marriage. He would want her with him, not just for publicity's sake, but so that they could finally enjoy the consummation of their long relationship.

The thought of it made her shiver with a mixture of anticipation and apprehension. Blaine still had not stirred in her the desires she had once felt with Colt. They had shared enough kisses, enough touching for her to know Blaine would be kind, and she supposed that after their wedding night she would discover that being with a man was as pleasurable as Vi had told her it could be. Maybe with Blaine the passion would come after consummation, and she supposed there was nothing wrong with that.

She was glad Vi and the children were in Omaha now, so that she could talk often with the woman. She felt closer to her since Vi had been the one to help Colt. Although Vi and Stuart were well set and lived in a new home of their own, Vi still insisted on volunteering to help others. She assisted a doctor in Omaha now and was working on a funding drive to build a hospital for the fast-growing city. She thought how different Omaha was today from the dusty little settlement it had been when she first came west.

"We're well past the hundredth meridian site, Stuart," she called to her brother. "I can't believe how much track has been laid these last four months."

"You really don't have to come back out here, Sunny. Nothing has changed except for the new miles of track that have been laid."

"I *do* have to come, Stuart. It's like, I don't know, like I have to keep seeing for myself that this is really happening. When I do this, I feel like I'm bringing Father with me."

Stuart thought how beautiful she was, how much she

looked like her mother. He was glad Vince had never told her the truth about the woman. What was the sense of it, especially now that she had done so well and was engaged to a reputable, successful man like Blaine? Vince had grudgingly accepted the fact that Sunny had made the right decision to invest in the U.P. after all, and had even expressed an interest in investing himself. Sunny's engagement to Blaine seemed to have softened her belligerent brother to some degree, at least to the extent that he was actually planning a visit soon to see the progress for himself. Sunny wanted to be happy about it, but Vince had disappointed her enough times that she remained wary of his intentions.

"We should be reaching end of track soon," he told her aloud.

Sunny leaned forward a little to try to see ahead of the train. The rushing wind ruffled the deep blue plume that decorated her bonnet, which was also trimmed with deep blue ribbon that matched the tight-fitting paletot she wore over a white muslin blouse, a ruby and diamond broach at her throat. One thing was certain, his sister was all poise and beauty, and she dressed fit for a queen. Her skirt and the short train behind it were the same deep blue of the paletot, and the netting she wore to enclose the chignon into which her long, thick hair had been rolled at the base of her neck was the same deep blue, and was decorated with tiny beads. Her morocco leather boots were bleached white, with fancy stitching on the toes in the same blue as the rest of her day wear.

"I still don't like you coming out here like this," he told her. "You know the troubles there have been with the Indians."

Sunny waved him off and moved around him to the door of her specially built private car. "General Sherman has been sent out to take care of the Indian problems," she told him as she went inside.

Stuart followed her. "General Sherman can't be everyplace at once."

"No, but several of his men are camping right alongside the work crews. I've seen to that. There is nothing to worry about, Stuart." She removed the paletot, as the cool morning was turning warmer. She ordered Mae to go and see the cook about bringing some tea and biscuits for her and Stuart. "You should eat a little something yourself, Mae," she told the woman.

"Yes, ma'am. Thank you." Mae hurried away, thrilled as always to be brought along on these adventures. Her first train ride had been their first trip to Omaha, and the grand way in which Sunny Landers traveled made her feel like a queen herself. The social quarters of Sunny's private car were resplendent in Victorian elegance, designed by the master builder for the railroad, George Pullman, to whom she was sure Sunny must have paid a fortune. The richly upholstered car was furnished with stuffed chairs and sofas, and was carpeted. Rich, velvet draperies hung at the extra-large windows, and hand-carved, inlaid paneling led upward to a curved, gold-etched ceiling. Sunny's private sleeping quarters were just as luxurious, and a special room had been built into the car for Mae, which made her feel even more important.

The kitchen and dining car was just ahead of Sunny's private car, and there again, Sunny Landers spared nothing. She enjoyed only the best of wines, dined on ham and boiled tongue, steaks, corn on the cob, fresh fruit, corn bread, teal, all sorts of elegant foods, always kept on hand for any dignitaries who might travel with her. But this time she had come out alone, except for Stuart. Mae wondered sometimes how Sunny kept her lovely shape with so much fancy food, but then the woman was at the same time always busy and active, and she seldom ate big portions of anything. Mae ordered the food, and a cook prepared a silver tea tray. Mae carried it back to Sunny's car, struggling to keep her footing against the sway of the train. She poured a cup of tea for both Sunny and Stuart before leaving.

"Thank you for coming, Stuart," Sunny was saying. "It's nice to be able to share all of this with at least one of my brothers. Father would be proud of you."

Stuart snickered with a tone of bitterness, waiting for Mae to leave before answering. "God knows it took a lot to make that man stand up and take notice. I was never able to do it while he was alive."

Sunny set her cup in its saucer, holding the saucer in one hand and leaning back in her velvet chair. "You and Vince both always hated the attention he gave me, didn't you?"

Stuart just shrugged. "That's all in the past."

"Maybe. I still feel it sometimes, Stuart. I hope you understand that I never did one thing to ask for all that extra attention, and I never once tried to turn Father against either of you. I never manipulated Father in order to be given so much in that will. In fact, I didn't even want all of that to end up in my lap."

Stuart stared at the designs in the flowered carpeting. "I know, Sunny."

She sighed, closing her eyes for a moment. "It scared me to death. I would have gladly handed most of it over, if not for the trust Father had put in me to carry out his dream. I knew that neither you nor Vince at the time would have done that. If not for what I've done, there would be no Landers involvement in the Union Pacific. Now I think that you at least see that it was the right thing to do. With so much stock in Credit Mobilier, using our own construction company to build the railroad, we'll make a fortune."

Stuart thought how much the remark reminded him of his father. At times Sunny was capable of the same scheming and under-the-table dealings as Bo Landers, and why not? The man had taught her well. He himself had grown up with the opinion that bribery and deceit were simply part of running a business—whatever helped keep the family empire strong and wealthy was all right. He knew that deep inside, his sister didn't really like resorting to payoffs and bilking the government, but that she was not about to let anything stop her from building this railroad, or from making a fortune at doing it; for what was most important was proving to people like Vince that she could be as ruthless as the next man, as smart and cunning, and as successful. She had vowed not to let her railroad investments ruin Landers Enterprises, and she had done her job well.

"I have no more hard feelings, Sunny." He wished he could tell her that all along the bitterness had never really had anything to do with her as an individual. It was the way she had come to be in the family that had hurt, the way her mother had been put on such a pedestal; the way Bo Landers had accepted such a woman into the Landers empire and allowed her to hold such a cherished place, as though he had loved her more than he had loved Vince and Stuart's mother—Lucille Madison, of all women!

The locomotive gave off two long whistles, signaling that they were approaching the line camp. Sunny quickly rose, ignoring her biscuits. She pulled her jacket back on, buttoning it down the front so that it neatly fit her small waist. "We're here!" she said excitedly, her eyes always lighting up like a schoolgirl's when she visited the construction sites. She walked to Mae's quarters and told the girl to have the cook prepare wine goblets and a tray of liquid refreshments for General Casement. "I imagine the general will be dining with us at noon," she added. "I want lots of fruit, perhaps some boiled chicken." She came back to Stuart and took his arm. "Let's go back out on the platform."

"I still say I don't like this. You know that just two days ago the camp was attacked by Cheyenne. According to Casement's wire, if not for his scout's early warning, they would have lost a lot more men than they did."

"Well, then, the general must have hired a good scout, so we should be safe. Besides, if the Cheyenne attacked only a couple of days ago, I doubt they'll try again so soon."

"Who knows what those savages will do? Don't forget the scout before this one was murdered, and the one before that."

"And this one has managed to stay alive for four whole months," Sunny answered. "He must be smarter than the others. Don't be such a poop, Stuart. The threat of Indian attack only adds to the excitement, don't you think? Besides, we have six sharpshooters guarding this car alone. Now let's get out on the platform. I don't want to miss anything."

Stuart shook his head, grinning to himself. There was nothing cowardly about Sunny Landers. He remembered how brave she had been on that first trip west, and the times when she had bravely stood up to Vince. He realized she actually liked the danger of this land as much as she liked its beauty. Someone had once taught her to love it. He wondered how often she still thought about that man.

"That was a fine lunch, Miss Landers," General Casement said respectfully.

"Well, you certainly *deserve* the finest for the job you're doing, General," she answered. Sunny had long ago learned that praise was the wisest way to get a man to do his best. "You could give lessons to Strobridge and his bunch," she added. "I never thought such a mixed group of undisciplined men could be turned into such a well-organized group."

"Well, when Dr. Durant hired me, I promised him the C.P. would not outdo us. We're right on schedule. The Indian attack a couple of days ago slowed us only a little. There weren't so many of them, and we had plenty of warning. Still, the Indian problem is tremendous. And of course there are accidents, and the weather out here can be vicious."

"Statistics show we're losing an average of one man for every mile of track," Sunny replied. "I wish we could improve that. It upsets me tremendously."

"We're working on making the men more safety-conscious, but as far as the weather and Indians and prairie fires and the like, those are things we can't control, other than to have good scouts. I'm sorry there are only a few soldiers in camp today. The bulk of them went riding after those renegades who attacked us. There just don't seem to be enough soldiers to go around, with all this trouble."

"I know. Doctor Durant and I both have been pestering President Johnson to make sure enough troops are supplied for your protection. I think the President finally realizes the gravity of the situation. He and so many others just don't realize how big this land is, how isolated these men are."

Casement, Sunny, and Stuart had finished lunch and were walking past the Landers train and the first supply train, on down to the work train. Men standing on platforms stared, some of them removing their hats when Sunny looked at them. Stuart called out a "good afternoon" to them, going up and shaking some of their hands. Shouted orders became louder and more numerous and the men moved a little faster, knowing they were now being watched. Men ran for a rail, ripped it off the rail cart, ran back to the waiting ties, dropped it, and stepped back to let the spike men secure the rail in place.

"We're laying a good two miles of track a day," Casement told Sunny. "Been right on schedule since you were here in the spring." The man walked ahead of them to talk to a foreman, and Sunny shook her head.

"Do you see now why convincing Vince to buy out Don Harrison's steel mill was a smart move?" she asked Stuart. "Most of those rails were made at our own mill, shipped to St. Louis by rail and over to Omaha by steamship. Nearly every rail that gets laid means more money going back to Landers Enterprises, so even *in*directly we make money from the U.P., especially when we can pad the prices twice—first for the steel mill and again when Credit Mobilier bills the government. Because of me, my profits from shares in Credit Mobilier go back into Landers Enterprises."

Stuart laughed lightly, taking her arm as she stepped over horse dung. "You've turned into a hell of a businesswoman, dear sister. I'll never forget the look on Vince's face when you explained it all to the board. There wasn't a damn thing he could say against it. You really showed him up that day."

Sunny smiled, stopping to watch the workers again. Casement had to shout at some of them to "quit staring at the lady and show her what you're made of!" Sunny shook her head, breathing deeply with satisfaction. "It's a double joy, Stuart. Not only have I proven to Vince this can be done without damaging the company, but here it is—a transcontinental railroad—the very thing people used to laugh at my, I mean, *our* father over. Now those who failed to get involved are crying in their beer. Somehow, though, the profits and all aren't so important as proving this could be done, and knowing the benefit it's going to be some day to travelers—to the whole nation. There are wonderful new markets in California—their farm produce, wonderful spices and silks from the Orient, lumber. Blaine was smart to get in on the ground floor of the logging potential in California and Oregon."

"Blaine is a man who always stays one step ahead. You've chosen well, Sunny. Even Vince likes Blaine."

"In some ways they're two of a kind. And you know Vince. He's just happy I'm marrying someone who doesn't need my money."

Stuart chuckled. "Yes, I guess that's what he's most happy about. He—" He stopped mid-sentence when he heard three shots fired in quick succession. "What the hell?" He squinted to watch a rider approaching from the northwest. They had walked slightly beyond end of track, and the horizon was open to them. "That man is riding awfully hard. Maybe it's one of Casement's scouts. I wonder if there's some kind of trouble."

The man began waving a blanket and calling out in shrill war whoops. "My God, he's an Indian," Sunny said, her eyes widening.

"Miss Landers," Casement shouted, running up to Sunny and Stuart. "Get back in your car, quickly! That's our scout's signal that trouble is coming! Hurry!"

Sunny lifted her skirts, and the three of them started running back toward Sunny's train. "Your scout is an Indian?" Stuart asked, the words panted.

"Only half—Cherokee. You two get in your car and stay low!" Casement left them and began shouting more orders to the workers, who had instantly dropped their tools and were scrambling into the sleeper cars to grab their rifles. It seemed to Sunny that it was taking forever to run along the first two long trains. By the time they reached their own train, they could already hear more war whoops and some gunfire. She and Stuart scrambled onto the platform, and Sunny stopped to watch the oncoming Indians, a great number of them.

"Sunny, get inside!" Stuart shouted.

"Wait! They aren't that close yet!" She watched the scout, who was riding hard toward camp, his horse's mane and his own long dark hair flying in the wind. On his heels was a swarm of Indians, and she could hardly believe the scout had managed to dodge their bullets and arrows, let alone the fact that some of the railroad men were already shooting back. The poor scout was caught in the crossfire!

Part Cherokee, she thought. Could it be? It didn't seem possible, but then she had once told Colt he ought to try working for the railroad when he got back from the war. If it *was* Colt, why hadn't he come to her first? Why didn't she know he was working for her own company?

"Damn it, Sunny, get in here!" Stuart came out and grabbed her arm, forcing her inside, just as one of the men who had been hired to guard her own train jumped up onto the platform, rifle in hand. Stuart closed and locked the door, and Sunny rushed to a window to watch. The scout came closer, but in all the gunfire and mêlée, it was hard to tell if it might be Colt. His hair was much longer than she had ever seen Colt wear his, and his build was magnificent, not at all the way she imagined he might look, after the way Vi had described him. Of course by now he would be heavier again, but she had always thought of Colt with the more slender build of his younger years. He had been slightly more filled out that night he came to see her in Chicago, but the man she was watching now had more muscular arms and shoulders. Because the day had grown much warmer, he wore no shirt, just leggings and moccasins, a gunbelt slung around his shoulder and a rifle in one hand. His riding was superb, as he leaned into his horse to avoid flying bullets. His horse was sure-footed, darting first one way, then another.

He seemed to notice the extra train then. He headed toward it, apparently realizing some important U.P. official must be present and would need extra protection.

"Sunny, get away from the window," Stuart told her. He was crouched on the floor.

"Not yet. Oh, Stuart, you should watch! It's so exciting! And the scout! Stuart, I think it might be Colt!"

"What!"

"Come and look!" She no sooner said the words than the window ahead of her shattered. Sunny screamed and finally ducked down.

"Damn it, I told you! That could have been right where you were sitting!"

Mae let out a wild scream and came running from her private quarters. "We're going to die!" she sobbed. "The Indians will take us, Miss Landers! You know what they do to white women!"

"Be still, Mae! There are hundreds of men on this work crew, and they all have rifles. There are even soldiers out there. We'll be fine."

Sunny quickly removed her hat and inched her head up to look out the window again, just in time to see the scout charging up to her car. He jumped from his horse before the animal even came to a halt, and he raised his rifle and began firing. The attacking Indians now seemed to be zeroing in on her train, and her eyes widened as they came closer. One of them was carrying a flaming torch. The scout shot at him, and the Indian's horse stumbled and went down. The Indian tumbled through the prairie grass, setting some of it on fire, then got up and kept coming, apparently determined to set Sunny's railroad car on fire. She saw that the scout was having trouble with a jammed rifle, and in the next instant the attacking Indian threw the flaming torch at one of Sunny's windows. Sunny squinted, waiting for a shatter, but the torch bounced off and fell to the ground.

The scout whirled with his rifle and landed the butt of it against the back of the warrior's skull. By then another warrior was on him. Sunny gasped when the second warrior took a swing at the scout with a tomahawk, just nicking the scout's left shoulder. As the warrior's horse flew by, the scout reached up and grabbed the man's arm, yanking him off the horse and slamming him to the ground. Sunny's eyes widened then when the scout whipped out a huge knife and rammed it into the warrior's chest.

She sank away from the window then, holding her stomach. Mae crawled over to her and the two women held each other, while outside gunfire and war whoops raged on. Bullets shattered all but one of Sunny's windows on one side. She and Stuart and Mae remained huddled against the steel-lined walls of the sturdy rail car.

Sunny still could not be sure if it was Colt she had been watching. Whoever it was, he certainly knew how to fight like the very Indians who had attacked him. She hoped that whoever it was, he would be all right, for he had defended her particular train car valiantly. It seemed like forever before the sound of yipping, whooping Indians began to fade, and the gunfire began to dwindle. Sunny turned to take another look outside, to see several railroad men frantically pounding at a grass fire with shovels. A few bodies lay strewn about, both Indians and railroad men, and she felt a tightness in her chest at the loss. These men were literally risking their lives to build this railroad. She vowed then and there that they would be remembered with honor.

A figure emerged from the private rooms of the car, startling everyone when he stepped into the main quarters. "Is everybody all right in here?"

All three of them looked up, and Mae let out a horrified scream. "They got inside!"

Sunny's eyes widened, and she told Mae to be still as she slowly rose.

"Sunny?" Colt stared at her in surprise.

"My God! Colt, is it you?" Stuart had said the words as he also rose. "Jesus, man, you're bleeding! Sit down and we'll get something for that!"

Mae just stared in amazement that Stuart and apparently Sunny knew this wild-looking Indian who had just invaded their railroad car. Stuart barked at her to get some whiskey and bandages. She ran past Colt as though afraid he might reach out and grab her.

The shock of seeing Colt so unexpectedly left Sunny

speechless. His hair was much longer, his build much more manly and powerful, but it was Colt. There were those gentle hazel eyes, and they were looking her over as though she was the most precious thing he had ever seen. His physique seemed to fill the interior of her parlor car. He stood there covered with dust and blood, parts of him glistening with sweat, which only accented the hard muscles of his bare arms and chest.

The two of them could do no more than stare at each other, stunned. Stuart had followed Mae to try to find the right supplies. "What the hell are *you* doing out here?" Colt finally asked.

"I—I come out often." Why was her heart pounding so? What was it this man always managed to do to her in spite of their long periods of separation? She had not expected to ever see him again, had finally gotten him out of her blood, and now here he was again!

The shock and slight anger in his own eyes began to fade, and a hint of a smile crossed his mouth. "I knew somebody important had to be in this fancy car. I never thought it would be you." He looked down at his left shoulder and grabbed it with his right hand. "I'd better leave before I get blood and dirt all over your expensive carpeting."

"Don't be ridiculous," she said, rushing forward. "You sit right down." She urged him onto a velvet and oak window seat, and for the next few minutes confusion surrounded them. Stuart and Mae returned with bandages, Mae standing back and staring as Sunny and Stuart cleaned the wound and wrapped it, while General Casement came pounding at the door to ask if everyone inside was all right. Stuart let the man in, scolding Mae for leaving the door at the other end of the car unlocked.

"It's a good thing Colt and the others managed to keep those Indians at bay. They could have gotten inside the car, thanks to you."

"Don't pick on Mae," Sunny told her brother, wondering if Colt could tell how flustered she was as she wrapped his wound. Did he hear her heart beating, notice the color she knew had come to her cheeks? How many times had he thought about the passionate kiss they had shared, or remembered the feel and taste of her? "This is all new and frightening to her." She studied Colt's muscular arm as she bandaged it. It felt strangely exciting to realize this beautiful, wild-looking man was the only one who had ever touched her intimately.

Mae sat down and cried quietly while Casement questioned Stuart and Sunny, exclaiming over the fact that they both knew Colt Travis. "Why in God's name didn't you tell me you knew Miss Landers?" he asked Colt.

Colt glanced at Sunny. "I didn't want to get the job because of that," he answered. "Besides, it's been over four years since I last saw Miss Landers. We're just casual acquaintances."

Sunny looked down and tied off Colt's bandages, secretly grateful for the way he tried to keep things casual and respectful. Stuart explained to Casement how they knew Colt. Casement began apologizing for the damage to the car, as well as praising Colt for giving a warning in time for the men to get to their guns.

"The Cheyenne are getting more violent all the time," Colt answered the man. "You'd better get more soldiers out here right away, General. That's the biggest war party they've sent against us yet, and the closest they've come to burning down the trains and everything around them. And I think you'd better hire two or three more scouts."

"I'll get more soldiers out here," Sunny declared, straightening. "There will be no more delay! General Sherman is supposed to be taking care of the Indian problem, and we don't even know where he is at the moment!" She looked at Stuart. "You go tell the telegrapher to shimmy up the nearest pole and send a message off to Omaha. I want more protection out here, by *tomorrow!* There is no excuse for this! I want my men protected!"

Stuart nodded and left. Casement glanced at Colt. "I'll need you to ride out and make sure those Cheyenne aren't planning to come back today."

"I'll take care of it, sir."

"Take a minute to gather yourself. I have to go and assess the damage." The man left, and Sunny turned to a sniffling Mae.

"Stop crying, Mae. We're all right. This man is Colt Travis. You never got to meet him when he came to see me in Chicago."

Mae stared and rose slowly. She thought Colt both handsome and frightening, and she found it difficult to believe Sunny could be good friends with such a savage-looking man, although there was a stirring masculinity about him that made a woman's heart rush a little faster. "I'm glad to meet you, Mr. Travis," she told him. She looked at Sunny. "I'll go back to my quarters, ma'am."

She hurried off, and Sunny turned to Colt. "Mae is my personal maid. I take her everywhere with me." She knelt in front of him. "For heaven's sake, Colt, why didn't you tell me what you were doing? You must know I've wondered and worried about what happened to you after Vi told me how sick you were. And Andersonville! What kind of horrors you must have suffered there!" She looked him over, still shaken by his presence. "And look at you now! It's the land, isn't it?" She met his eyes again. "You came back out here to heal."

He nodded, his eyes moving over her in a way that made her feel too warm. "Last spring I decided it was time to put the past behind me and get back on my feet again. I needed work, remembered your comment about the railroad. As far as letting you know—" He shrugged. "I just figured it was better I didn't. I didn't think I'd actually run into you, and I knew somebody in your position wouldn't know the individual names of the men who worked for you."

"You don't have to put it that way. You work for the Union Pacific. I am just one of several owners. Dr. Durant is the biggest shareholder."

He grinned facetiously, glancing around at the Victorian elegance of the parlor car. "I'd say you're a pretty important factor in this whole thing." He shook his head and rose. "This is some private car. I've never seen anything like this—a far cry from those big old boxes the men sleep in, I'll say that."

"Would you like some kind of drink? A little wine perhaps? I can get you anything you want."

He moved his eyes back to hers, and they bore a strangely sad look. *No, you can't,* they told her. "One shot of whiskey might do it."

She touched his arm. "You sit back down, and I'll have Mae go and get it." She hurried away for a moment, through the private quarters.

Colt had seen those quarters on his way in, a small enclosure with a canopied bed and a dresser. The bed was all ruffles and silk and had been left unmade. Now that he knew who slept in it, old disturbing desires began to nudge at him. This was exactly what he did *not* want to happen. His plan had been to never set eyes on Sunny Landers again. Now here she was, in that beautiful blue outfit that made her eyes look even bluer. Her hair was all wound up into some kind of coif at the back of her neck and covered with blue netting, but he remembered how it looked brushed out long and golden around her shoulders.

Sunny returned a moment later with a whiskey bottle and a shot glass. She sat down beside him on the window seat and poured a shot, handing it over. Colt took it and gladly drank it in one quick gulp, deciding he needed it for more reasons than an Indian attack.

"I'm glad to see you again, Colt, to know how well you are." Their eyes met, and she blushed and looked down. "Colt—"

"Don't say it, Sunny." Did she know what she did to him, sitting this close, looking like that, smelling like that? He suddenly wished he had not put off taking care of his long-neglected need for a woman. The first thing he was going to do when things calmed down was go visit the whores at the camp town. Why hadn't that bothered him all that much until now? Damn her! "How about one more shot?" he asked.

She raised her eyes, and Colt noticed the misty look to them. She took the shot glass and filled it again, the huge diamond glittering on her left hand. He took the glass and drank down the whiskey, then took hold of her wrist with his other hand to look more closely at the ring. "Quite a rock," he told her. "But then, Blaine O'Brien can afford the best, I guess."

Sunny caught a hint of sarcasm in the words. She wondered if he realized the affect his touch still had on her. "I thought it was about time I gave the man an answer," she told him. "He's waited a long time."

Colt watched her eyes. *I'd wait forever too,* he thought. *But then, there would be no sense in that, would there? We already decided that.* All his resolve that he had finally gotten over ridiculous thoughts about this woman left him the moment he set eyes on her again. "I hope to hell the man knows how lucky he is," he told her. "And I hope you'll both be very happy. I really mean that." He rose. "You heard Casement. I've got to get back out there." *I've got to get away from you,* he thought.

"Colt, I hate to see you leave so soon. Come back later and have supper with us."

He looked down at her, and for several long seconds neither said a word. "You know I can't, Sunny," he finally answered quietly. "I do appreciate you fixing up the wound and your concern for what happened to me after I left Chicago. Now you know I'm all right."

Did he realize how wonderful he looked to her, standing there with all that power, his dark skin glistening, his long hair gracing those broad shoulders? He was more Indian than she had ever seen him. "I can't help the concern, Colt." She stepped a little closer, her eyes pleading. "If there's anything you need, anything at all, anytime—even after I'm married, you come to me, or to Stuart and Vi, do you hear? Promise me. I want you to be happy, Colt."

"I already am, just being out here doing what I'm doing."

She smiled sadly. "I suppose you are."

His eyes moved over her appreciatively. "By the way, you get more beautiful every time I see you. There must be a lot of men who envy Blaine O'Brien." He sighed. "Say hello to Vi for me. Tell her thanks for the nice talk we had back in Chicago."

"I will."

For a fleeting moment he thought of how exciting it would be to walk up to her and sweep her off her feet and carry her into that private room where the bed was still unmade. He wondered how much resistance he would get. Did she still want him that way, still think about that night on the beach, in spite of the ring on her hand? He quickly turned and left, furious with himself for the thought.

"Good-bye, Colt," she called from the platform.

He waved, walking out to his horse, which was grazing calmly not far away. In one quick leap he was on the animal's back. He rode off, and did not look back.

Chapter 20

A cold October rain and an almost perpetual headache since returning from the line camp kept Sunny from her normal workday. She sat at the window of the main-floor parlor of her Omaha home, a much more modest structure than her Chicago mansion, since she considered it only temporary, but a home she actually enjoyed more because she had had it built herself. It was warmer than the mansion, still three stories, but on far simpler a scale. The house was frame, with a circular balconied entry portico, large windows, and dormers in the top floor with swan's-neck pediments. Mae and the other servants lived on the top floor, all bedrooms and a parlor were on the second floor, the kitchen, elegant dining room, a library, living room, another parlor, and a marble-floored entranceway on the main floor. Every room was filled with plants and caged birds, and Sunny considered the house cheery and warm, much more fitting to her own personality than the Chicago mansion; more soothing to come home to after a long, busy day.

She had been happy here, loved it in Omaha, had struggled with her dread of having to move to New York with Blaine. She had made up her mind she could do it and be happy, since she would be a wife and probably soon after a mother. Now she was not so sure . . . now that she had seen Colt again. She wished she could hate him for always showing up in her life at the worst times, but then, when would be a right time? Now that she knew he was out there on the plains and in constant danger, how could she leave Omaha?

She watched a carriage come up the brick drive, recognized it as Stuart's. She watched Vi disembark and run through the rain to the portico. She heard the knock and she waited for one of the servants to answer. She turned away from the window then and leaned back in a rocker, waiting, suspecting the reason Vi had come to see her. She heard the servant ask for Vi's cape and gloves and hat, and a moment later Vi entered the parlor.

"What a nasty day! Even the bottom of my dress is wet." Vi looked down and shook at her dress slightly, then patted the sides of her hair.

"Hello, Vi."

The woman took a deep breath and walked closer. "I came to see if there is anything I can do for you, Sunny. Stuart says you haven't been in to the office since you got back from visiting the line camp." She squinted slightly, looking her over as she sat down in a silk love seat across from Sunny. "I must say, you don't look well at all. What's wrong, Sunny? Can I help?"

Sunny smiled sadly. "I wish you could." She rubbed her eyes. "Just a constant headache, that's all."

Vi leaned forward, folding her arms and resting them on her knees. "Maybe a good long talk would cure it."

"Maybe."

Vi hesitated a moment, hoping Sunny would offer to start, but she sat silent. Was she afraid to admit the truth? Vi suspected exactly what was wrong, and she decided to broach the subject head-on. "Sunny," she said, "Stuart told me about Colt scouting for the railroad." She watched Sunny's cheeks begin to flush. "He told me the whole exciting story of the Indian attack and all. I must say, his description of Colt certainly doesn't fit the way he looked when I saw him in the hospital in Chicago. I'm so glad to hear he's gotten so healthy again."

Sunny watched her eyes, knew good and well exactly what the woman was trying to do. Finally, she laughed almost sarcastically. "Healthy?" she answered. "Oh, Vi, he looked magnificent." She moved her eyes to gaze at a crackling fire in the nearby hearth. "That's what this land out here does for him. I've never seen him look more handsome, in spite of his scars, or more Indian. He's let his hair grow longer. The only thing that betrays his white side are those hazel eyes." She looked back at Vi. "I *do* need to talk, Vi. I'm in a terrible mess on the inside; and you, dear friend, already know it."

Vi smiled consolingly. "You've always loved him, haven't you?"

Sunny's eyes teared, and she closed them and leaned back again. "Yes," she answered in a near whisper. "That's the hell of it. God forgive me, but I want him, Vi, in a way I've never wanted Blaine." She swallowed, and a tear slipped down her cheek. "If I lived to be three hundred, it could never work, but I want him anyway." She took a long, deep breath. "God, it feels good to tell somebody." More tears came then, and she put her face in her hands and wept. "That night on the beach—if he hadn't been strong enough to stop, God only knows what I would have let him do. He touches me, and I have no control over myself." She jerked in a sob and straightened slightly to take a handkerchief from a pocket on her dress. She wiped her eyes. "I can go for years without seeing him, yet the moment I do, it's like . . . like he casts some kind of spell on me. And he doesn't try to do it. He fights it just as hard as I do."

Vi let her cry for a few minutes, feeling like crying herself.

"I don't know what to do, Vi. I just don't know what to do." Sunny met Vi's kind dark eyes. "How can I marry Blaine when I feel this way? And yet how could I explain it to him? And if I don't marry him, maybe I'll just grow into an old spinster." More tears came. "God knows Colt would never dream of marrying someone like me. He could never put up with this life, and I can't give it up, Vi."

Vi shook her head. "You don't have any idea what Colt would really want, because neither of you has allowed yourselves to say what you really feel."

Sunny blew her nose and breathed deeply to calm herself. She got up from the rocker and went to stand in front of the fire. "It's like I love two men, Vi." She sniffed and wiped her eyes again. "I love Blaine for being so patient, for the way he fits into my world, for his importance and his knowledge of business; but I don't—" She put her head back and closed her eyes. "I don't *want* him, not like I want Colt. I love Colt for all that's wild in him, his physical power, his bravery and skill. He's like a wonderful escape from everything that burdens me. He represents, I don't know, a kind of freedom, I guess, the simple life." She shook her head and turned to look at Vi. "But even if we wanted to try to be together, I can't stand the thought of the hell the people from my world would make for him. There isn't anyone, except maybe for you and Stuart, who would believe he didn't want my money. Can you just imagine how someone like Vince would treat him, and most of my friends and business associates? He's a proud man, Vi. He wouldn't be able to take it for long."

"He's also a very strong man, Sunny, inside and out. I'd wager he could take quite a bit if it meant being able to be with the woman he loves. And you remember how he handled Vince the night of your party. Colt might not be familiar with the kind of life you lead, Sunny, but he's no dummy. He's a smart man, a man who can learn quickly. My guess is he could handle himself with as much command and power in a boardroom as he can out on the prairie fighting Indians. He just doesn't know it yet." She smiled wryly. "Someone would have to teach him." She rose and walked closer. "But then maybe he wouldn't even have to *be* in a boardroom. Where love is concerned, sometimes people can reach all kinds of compromises in order to be together."

Sunny frowned. "Vi, do you realize what you're saying? It's impossible!"

"You don't know that for certain, Sunny. That's just what everyone else has been telling you. I believed it myself until I spoke with Colt at the hospital. I saw the look in his eyes when he talked about you. That man loves you, Sunny. He probably has loved you since you were fifteen years old. I'm sure he loved his wife very much and never would have gone any farther with his feelings for you if she and his son hadn't been killed. But the fact is they're gone, and he's alone, and I suspect he's just as unhappy as you are."

Sunny turned away. "It's all so ridiculous. And what about poor Blaine? He's waited so long to marry me. I don't know if I have *reason* to cancel our engagement. It might be the biggest mistake of my life. If I give back my ring, Vi, it will be over for good."

Vi touched her shoulder. "All you have to do is ask yourself—if you had to pick one of them and decide you would never see him again, which one would you choose?"

Sunny faced her. "You know which one."

Vi nodded. "Ask yourself one more thing. What if you *do* marry Blaine, feeling the way you do about Colt? In your heart, Sunny, in your soul, your dreams, who would you imagine was really sharing your bed?"

Sunny felt her cheeks getting hot, and she walked past Vi back to her rocker. "Don't say it, Vi."

"I *have* to say it. There are all kinds of adultery, Sunny. And adultery is one thing I don't think you're capable of living with, even if it *does* mean living the life of a spinster. You can be ruthless and scheming when it comes to business, but not when it comes to your heart and how you treat the people you love. It isn't in you."

Sunny sat down wearily, feeling physically and emotionally drained. "So, what should I do?"

Vi came over and knelt in front of her. "I think you

have to be fair, Sunny, to yourself, to Colt, *and* to Blaine. Blaine is going to be gone for several more months. You don't have to tell him a thing right away, not until you talk to Colt."

"I can't do that." Sunny closed her eyes, shivering with the thought of it. "What if it turned out like, like that last night I saw him at Fort Laramie? I made a fool of myself that night, and again when I met him on the beach. When I get around him I feel like the same silly lovestruck girl—the one he turned away because he was smart enough to know how impossible it was. He'd turn me away again, and I'd look like a fool again."

"You don't know *what* he'd do, Sunny. Isn't it better to risk getting a no than to never know at all? You certainly can't go on like this. You're killing yourself. And leaving it this way can mean you'll never be happy with Blaine, and that isn't fair to him, is it?"

Sunny shook her head, covering her eyes again.

"There is one more thing you need to consider, Sunny, and that's the two men themselves—their qualities, what they can give you in the way of love and support, what they want from you in return. I hate to put it this way, but as long as we're talking this out, do you really think Blaine loves you for *you?*"

"Yes, yes, he loves me."

"How often does he *tell* you he loves you?"

Sunny looked at her, blinking back more tears. "Not often, but he tells me sometimes."

"When it's convenient, I imagine." Vi rose. "Sunny, you of all people understand men like Blaine. You've run in their circle all your life. Men like that do what's best for their career and their fortune, and love has no place in their lives, not if it gets in the way of their power and prestige. Sometimes I don't think you understand just how important you are in the eyes of the general public. You're a famous woman, Sunny—beautiful, rich, eligible, acquainted with the wealthy and powerful. Do you think Blaine hasn't considered those things in choosing you for his wife? He's preparing to run for governor of New York. A man like that has to have the right woman on his arm. Do you honestly think you'd be breaking his heart if you decided not to marry him? I personally think he'd go find some other pretty little thing who came from a wealthy background, maybe the daughter of another industrialist or a congressman or anyone else who has power and influence."

"He loves me, Vi. I'm sure he loves me." Sunny leaned back in the rocker.

"And would he still love and marry you if you lost your fortune?"

"I don't know—"

"Yes, you do, Sunny. He'd drop you in a second! But not Colt Travis. He couldn't care less if you came to him in rags and carrying a tin cup! And that's the difference between them, a very important difference. You aren't made to marry for convenience, Sunny. You're too soft-hearted, too giving when it comes to your personal life. Even if you chose not to pursue your feelings for Colt, I don't think Blaine O'Brien is the right man for you. There *are* a few men of his stature who really would marry you for love, Sunny. I'm sorry, but I just don't happen to think Blaine is one of them."

Sunny sighed deeply, looking at the diamond Blaine had given her, remembering the look in Colt's eyes when he had noticed it. She shivered at the memory of how it had felt to be so close to him. She could still remember the smell of man and leather. How could a man's scent be that enticing when he had been fighting and sweating, when he was nothing but his raw self, wearing no fancy men's cologne like Blaine wore?

"I don't know, Vi. I have to think about this very deeply before I allow myself to see Colt again." She met the woman's eyes. "I can't believe you're telling me these things."

Vi walked back to the hearth. "I should have said them a long time ago, at least about Blaine. I tried, in my own way." She looked over at Sunny. "For years I've watched you do what everyone else thought was best for you, Sunny—inadvertently, you have even gone along with what Vince wanted. I have no doubt he's told you the kind of man you should marry. For the first part of your life Bo Landers told you how to act, speak, dress—

he brought you up in a man's world, and you've never quite known how to be a woman." She looked back at the fire. "I don't think Blaine is the man to teach you about that part of yourself."

The meaning of the words sent a near-painful wave of desire surging through Sunny's blood.

"Sometimes when it comes to matters of the heart," Vi continued, "risks are worth taking. I'm sure society didn't think Stuart should have married me, but he did anyway. Of course the difference between us isn't anything like you and Colt, but I certainly wasn't the glamorous, fabulously wealthy woman everyone *thought* a Landers should marry."

Sunny smiled through tears. "You're the best thing that ever happened to Stuart. And what would *I* do if you weren't around to talk to?"

Vi came closer again. "*I'm* not the one you should be talking to now. You have to tell Colt or go crazy, Sunny. You know that."

Sunny looked at her lap and swallowed. "It scares me. If something did come of it, can't you just see the cruel headlines slamming Colt? I don't know if I can do that to him, Vi. Maybe it would be selfish of me to tell him. Deep inside he's a kind, sweet man who's been hurt enough."

"You've been secretly hurting yourself, Sunny, for years."

Sunny shook her head. "That doesn't matter." She slowly rose. "Thanks for coming over, Vi. Would you like some tea?"

"Yes, on a day like today that sounds wonderful."

Sunny walked over and pulled the cord that rang the kitchen help.

"What are you going to do, Sunny?"

"I don't know yet. I do feel better talking about it though. You were right about that." She pushed a piece of hair away from her face. "I'll give it a little more time. Maybe if I get back to my work I can forget about it for a while. Maybe in the meantime Colt will leave the railroad and go on to something else, find another woman. For now I think I'll just concentrate on the railroad, as I've been doing."

"Just like that?" Vi smiled sadly. "You're a fool if you think you can forget him, Sunny."

A maid came into the parlor in response to being called. "Bring us some tea, Lilly," Sunny said. The girl nodded and darted away. Sunny looked at Vi. "How do you think Stuart would feel if I, if Colt and I—"

"Stuart thinks the world of Colt. As far as something serious between the two of you, that might be another story; but I can handle Stuart. Besides, he would just want you to be happy."

"Do you really think so? Before you came along he seemed to hate me almost as much as Vince does."

"I don't think Vince hates you as a person, Sunny. You're just in the way of his grand scheme, that's all. He's coming around a little."

"Yes, he seems to be." Sunny walked to the window again, picturing Colt riding out on the Plains in the cold rain. She hoped the coming winter would keep the Indians calm for a while so he would be safe until she decided what she should do about these painful, utterly forbidden wants that had plagued her since seeing him again. "Do you think he's thinking of me like I'm thinking of him?"

Vi watched her lovingly, feeling sorry for this young woman who had never had a normal childhood, who always had to be so strong when inside she was so soft. "Yes, Sunny. I think he thinks about you all the time."

Sunny watched one particular raindrop meander down the window. "I'll wait out the winter," she said quietly. "Maybe I'll feel different come spring."

Colt hunkered against the blizzard winds as he guided Dancer toward the lights in the distance. He had no doubt the lights came from the infamous "hell on wheels" camp town that followed the construction crews. He had tried to avoid the constantly migrating town and its whores and cheating gamblers, but in this blinding storm, and with night coming on, he knew he would never make it back to the construction site for shelter. With deep snows burying tracks, he would not be able to follow the rails back to Casement and the men. He had no choice now but to hit the camp town and find a place out of the wind, both for him and Dancer.

Dancer waded laboriously through snow as high as his belly, and getting higher all the time. This was one of the worst winters Colt could remember, and he figured he had seen some of the worst. He had no doubt that construction would be halted altogether for a few days, and in this kind of weather, there was little, if any, threat from Indians.

He felt solidly frozen by the time he reached the lights. He shouted at a man coming out of one of the tents, asking where he could put up his horse, and the man simply pointed to the street of makeshift tents and shanties. Colt could not see what lay beyond, so he headed Dancer in that direction until he saw what looked like a horse shed made of sod and a sign that read LIVERY STABLE. He dismounted and opened the door, which blew out of his hand.

"Hurry it up," someone shouted. "I'm tryin' to keep it warm in here!"

Colt smacked Dancer and herded him inside, then shut the door. "You got room for one more?" he asked.

"I reckon. Dollar a night."

Colt stomped his feet and removed his hat and a woolen scarf.

"You're an Indian!" the man grumbled.

Colt took a good look at the owner of the voice, seeing before him a small, bearded man who squinted back at him suspiciously. "I'm a scout for the U.P. I got caught in this blizzard and need some shelter." He untied his saddlebags and slung them over his shoulder, then took some coins from a leather bag tied to his belt. "Here's your dollar. Where does a man get a stiff drink and maybe a bath around here?"

The man looked him over more. "A ways back up the street—Billie's Place, it's called. You better watch yourself. Somebody looks like you can get himself in trouble."

"I can handle myself. Who's Billie?"

"Whore—Billie White—out of Omaha." Colt's eyes widened with surprise, but the livery owner didn't notice. He was checking over the horse. "I reckon if you need a woman, one of them she brought with her will accommodate an Indian if you've got the money."

Colt gave him a look of disgust. "Thanks," he said with a hint of anger. "Take good care of that horse. He means a lot to me." He turned and left, putting his hat and scarf back on and bending his head low against the wind. He struggled through the snow, going up close to each tent and cabin to peek inside and see if he had reached the right place yet. He finally reached a tent that was bigger than the others. Someone inside was actually playing a plunky tune on a piano. The wind howled so badly that he had not heard the music until he reached the entrance flap, and he wondered how in hell these people had gotten something as heavy as a piano clear out here. He supposed that where there was a will, or in this case a buck to be made, there was a way to do just about anything.

He pulled back the opening and stepped inside, and the piano music stopped for a moment as a motley bunch of strayed railroad workers looked up at him from four makeshift card tables. A black potbelly stove sat in the center of the tent, its pipe sticking through the top, a hot fire inside keeping the tent reasonably warm, although most everyone still wore jackets.

For a brief moment the only sound was the wind outside and the flapping of the tent's walls as people stared at Colt. He figured there were ten or eleven men inside, including a man serving drinks. A board placed over two barrels served as a bar. "Come on in," the bartender said.

Now that Colt had been fully scrutinized, everyone returned to their drinking and cards, and the piano player returned to his keyboard.

"Colt?"

Colt turned to the woman who had spoken his name,

and he broke into a grin. "Billie! The livery owner told me you were here."

Billie White brightened, jumping off a man's lap and walking up to hug him. Colt let his arms go around her, and it felt good. "Colt, you big, crazy Indian you!" Billie turned to the others. "Everybody, this is Colt Travis, an old friend."

"An old *customer,* you mean," one man teased. Most laughed good-naturedly.

Colt recognized the man and a couple of others from the work camp. How and when they had made it here were not his concern, except that to be here was to risk being fired. Casement hated these places, where whores and gamblers and whiskey peddlers took hardworking railroad men for everything they earned. He wouldn't be here himself if not for the storm.

"Colt, where have you been? My God, how long ago did you leave—sixty-two, wasn't it?"

"Over four years ago. I've been through a war since then—spent some time at Andersonville."

"Oh, Colt, you poor thing!" Billie stepped back, looking him over, her eyes filling with lust. "Well, you certainly don't look any the worse for wear now." She smiled seductively. "Want a drink?"

"Sure." Colt followed her over to the temporary bar, which took only five steps. He set down his saddlebags, and Billie ordered a whiskey. She turned and looked up at him, opening her woolen cape to expose a low-cut red dress that flaunted her bosom.

"Need anything else?"

Colt took a long, hard look. "I, uh, I don't think you know what you'd be in for. It's a long story, but I haven't been with a woman since I left you back in Omaha."

She smiled eagerly. "Well, well." She unbuttoned his wolfskin coat and ran a hand over his chest. "Somebody needs to reacquaint you with the more pleasant things in life."

He wished he could have explained to Sunny why he had left so quickly that day he saw her after the Indian raid. It was bad enough wanting her the way he did, but after this long abstinence, someone he had no right touching in the first place was far too dangerous for him to be around. *Damn her!* he thought. And damn himself for taking a job that left open the possibility of seeing her again. Part of him knew it was just what he had wanted, but another part of him told him he was completely crazy for constantly risking the pain it always caused him to see her. He was always hoping she would get uglier, or get the hell married—*some*thing, *any*thing! Why did she have to still have those beautiful blue eyes, and that look she always gave him that made him want to eat her up.

He pulled Billie to him and planted a long, hard kiss on her mouth. "I expect you're just the one to show me all over again," he told her.

She laughed, turning her wrist to grasp his hand and place it against her bosom, while she licked at his lips. "I never forgot you, Colt. It was just like I said it would be —I never found anybody else like you. Your name should be Stallion, not Colt."

He tightened his hold and kissed her again. Some of the men made lewd remarks, while others whistled.

"Give it to her good, Injun," somebody yelled.

The men all laughed, and Billie pulled away and handed Colt a shot of whiskey, which he downed immediately, mostly to warm his blood, partly to help ease the pain that thoughts of Sunny had given him since he'd seen her again.

"This place gets pretty wild in the warm months," Billie said, ordering Colt another whiskey. "The girls and I can hardly keep up with business. I've made a fortune following the railroad camps. Men who've been without awhile will pay anything for a woman." She handed him the second shot glass. "How about you?"

He leaned closer. "I figured after what you told me last time we were together, that you'd do it for free, considering what *you* get out of it."

She threw her head back and laughed again, and Colt downed the second drink. "By God, I just *might* do it for nothing," she told him.

"Hey, Travis," one of the men at a table shouted.

"What was it like being in the Icelander's private car back last fall? She the cold fish everybody says she is?"

Colt turned from Billie, scowling. "What?"

"The Icelander—you know, that there Sunny Landers —Queen of the Railroad, Miss High-and-Mighty-Big-Money. What's she really like? I seen you go inside her car the day them Indians raided us." He wiggled his eyebrows. "You were in there kind of a long time."

Chuckles and whistles moved throughout the tent, while outside the wind howled louder than ever. Colt stepped away from Billie and a little closer to the man who had made the remark, aware that his anger was as much from his own frustration at being so easily shaken by the sound of Sunny's name as it was from the remark itself. "Miss Landers's brother fixed up a wound I got," hc answered. "That's all."

The man, a well-built Irish spike man, laughed in a kind of growl. "Sure. I don't expect she'd get too friendly with the lower help. They say that one's cold as ice. That's why we call her the Icelander. Ice—Landers. Get it?" The man returned to dealing cards. "Only men with money and fancy suits can melt that one," he told the others. "They say she goes down only for rich men and congressmen—anybody who helps her financially or with the railroad."

The others laughed, but Colt was not smiling. He leaned over the table, looking big and menacing, and the other three men scooted away. "That's what they say, is it? You know that for a fact, Mister?"

The Irishman sobered, glaring right back at him. "Only fact I know is that there's no other way for a female to make it into that kind of money and power. We all know they can't think for themselves." The man smiled nervously. "Don't tell me you're sticking up for that rich bitch! Hell, she could buy and sell you a million times over, and she'd do it, too, if it meant money in her pockets! Or maybe she's the type who gets a thrill out of seducing her common help."

Colt grabbed the man by the jacket and jerked him out of his chair with such a force that the man's body hit the card table and spilled it to the dirt floor. "You don't know a damn thing about Sunny Landers," Colt raged. "She happens to be one of the nicest ladies there ever was—and you've got no right going around spouting lies about somebody you don't know anything about!" He brought a foot up into the man's groin, and the others inside the tent gasped; one of the other two prostitutes in the tent let out a startled scream. The Irishman doubled over, and Colt brought a knee up into his face, breaking his nose. He shoved him then, landing him into yet another card table. The men at the table sprang out of their seats, and the table and the Irishman went down together. Blood poured from the Irishman's nose, and he curled up against the pain in his scrotum.

Colt whirled, glaring at the others. "Anybody else want to insult Miss Landers?"

They all backed away, shaking their heads, some glancing at the pistol and knife he wore on his wide belt.

"Casement ain't gonna like hearing about this," one man said tentatively.

"I don't give a damn! I came here only for shelter, not for trouble; and I don't doubt the general would be more upset at the remarks made about Miss Landers than he would at me for shutting that man up! She's a highly respected woman, and indirectly all of us work for her, so keep your ignorant ideas about what the woman is like to yourselves!" Colt walked up and grabbed Billie's arm. "Do you have someplace private where we can go?"

She grinned, looking around rather haughtily at the others. "Follow me," she told him. "I have a feeling you'd better get out of here anyway." She sauntered outside, and Colt took a last threatening look around before picking up his saddlebags and following her. They both hurried into a small sod house next to the tent, and Billie quickly added some wood to a dying fire in the cast-iron stove that stood in a corner next to the bed. Besides the bed, the only furnishings were a table and a dresser. There were no windows.

Colt bolted the door and Billie turned, throwing off her cape. She reached under her skirts and pulled down leggings and drawers, kicking them aside. "What the hell was that all about?" she asked, coming closer.

She reached around his neck and Colt grabbed her at the waist, hoisting her up. She wrapped her legs around him, and he reached under her skirts, running big hands along her thighs and to her bared bottom. "It's a long story," he answered.

"Another one?" She pouted. "Sounds like you have a lot of storytelling to do, lover."

"Not just yet."

She threw her head back, and he carried her to the bed, kissing her breasts as he sat her on the edge of the bed. He pulled her dress away from her shoulders and off her breasts, and the chilly air made her nipples stand taut. Colt took one into his mouth, relishing the feel of it on his tongue, and this time it was not LeeAnn he imagined letting him do this to her. He stayed on his knees, unlacing his buckskin leggings and unbuttoning his longjohns. He pushed Billie's dress to her waist, and she gasped when he rammed himself into her almost savagely. She remained sitting on the edge of the bed, grasping his powerful shoulders, her head thrown back and her breasts exposed. Colt moved his mouth to her other breast, groaning and pushing at her until his release came all too quickly.

He began trembling then, resting his head at her breasts. "I told you it had been a long time. For a while, when I first got out of Andersonville, I wasn't even sure I could be a man again; then I put it off for so long I was almost afraid to try it."

She ran her hands through his thick hair. "Nobody would ever doubt your manhood, Colt Travis, and I've seen it all."

She laughed, and Colt covered her mouth, laying her back and climbing onto the bed with her. "Let's get undressed and do this right," he told her. "I intend to keep you here all night, and you won't need the fire in that stove to keep you hot."

She laughed more as they tumbled together and undressed each other. They crawled under the covers, and Colt moved on top of her, ready again to enjoy the pleasures of woman. She put a hand to his lips when he started to kiss her. "You've got it bad, don't you?"

"What do you mean?"

"Sunny Landers."

Colt stiffened slightly, meeting her eyes.

"I saw her name on that letter you were reading, back in Omaha. Why was she writing to you, Colt? How in hell is it you know a woman like that?"

He rolled away from her, stretching out on his back. Billie moved to rest on one elbow, reaching out to stroke his hair. "A man doesn't stick up for a woman that way unless he's in love with her, and if you are, I feel awful sorry for you if you think there's any future—"

"I *don't* think it. Leave it alone, Billie. I didn't come here to talk about Sunny Landers."

She studied him a moment, tracing her finger along the scar over his eye. "You seem to always come around when you're trying to forget a woman." She laid her head on his shoulder. "But then, that's part of what I'm here for. It really is good to see you, Colt. I'm glad you got through that awful war all right. I always worried and wondered about you."

His short laugh was bitter. "Don't waste your time." He sat up. "I need a smoke."

Billie pouted, sorry she had brought up Sunny Landers's name. She had seen the woman once in Omaha, and the thought of Colt with a woman like that was close to absurd, but she wisely guessed it was best not to point out that fact to Colt right then. He already knew it, and that was what was eating him. She wished she knew all the details, but Colt was a man who told a person what he wanted them to know only when he was ready to tell it. She had already made him a little angry, and she feared that to push him would make matters worse.

He rolled and lit a cigarette. "You breathe a word of anything to do with me and Sunny, and I'll be damn angry," he said, taking a drag on the cigarette.

"Discretion is part of my profession." She touched his back. "I'm sorry I said anything at all. You aren't going to sit there mad all night, are you? If you are, I'll just have to go find some other customer."

He laid back down, pulling the covers over himself and smoking quietly for a moment, listening to the winter winds outside, thinking how the howling matched the way he felt on the inside. "Don't worry. I'm not mad, and I'm not through with you yet." He put his arm out, and she snuggled against him. "Have you ever felt like you were wandering in a black tunnel, Billie? Every once in awhile you see a glimmer of light, a little bit of hope that you'll find your way out and find there's a purpose to your life—and then when you walk toward that light it gets snuffed out?"

She kissed his chest. "I know what you're saying."

"Yeah, I suppose you do." He took another drag on the cigarette. "She's going to marry a man she only thinks she loves, Billie, a man who I know damn well is just using her to enhance his own image, and it makes me crazy thinking about it. I know in my gut that he doesn't love her. He loves only what she represents— wealth, status, power. If she lost everything overnight, he'd be gone the next day, but there isn't a damn thing I can do about it. I sure as hell can't offer her anything to compare to what he can offer her. All I've got is love, and in her world that doesn't amount to a hill of beans. Even if we could be together, I'd probably end up killing half the people she deals with, including her asshole brother, and I'd be hanged. Worst part is, I think she could love me too, but like me, she knows that love alone wouldn't be enough to get us through the hell we'd know if we tried to do anything about our feelings."

"You don't know that for sure, Colt. Maybe you should tell her how you feel."

He chuckled, turning on his side to put out his cigarette. "Sure." He turned to face her. "She'll be married next summer, and that will be the end of it."

Outside the wind swept snow into deep drifts in a winter that would prove to be one of the worst in recent history, a winter that kept Sunny trapped in Omaha. No one dared venture beyond the safety of the city, and even in town there was danger because of short supplies. Snows were so deep that no trains were running between Omaha and Chicago.

Sunny wondered if the wicked weather was God's way of telling her she must not consider going back to the construction site to look for Colt. She had put it off, finding all kinds of arguments against it. Now the snow was so deep that she couldn't go anyway. There was nothing left but to wait until spring, just like she originally thought she should do. Maybe by then she could resolve her dilemma and learn once and for all to face the truth, whatever that truth was. She had until June to decide. That was when Blaine would come to Omaha to accompany her back to Chicago to make plans for one of the biggest, most publicized weddings that city had known in years. Even Vince and Eve were excited about it.

She turned to her journal, opening it to the yellowing pages where she had made some of her first entries. *Our guide is Mr. Colt Travis,* she read again. *I am sure that we will become good friends before this trip is over.*

She immediately scolded herself, closing the journal and taking up pen and paper. She owed Blaine a letter.

Chapter 21

May 1867

Colt heard the signal, one long whistle, followed by two short ones. Someone wanted him back at the construction site. Because the Indian problem was expected to worsen this summer, Casement had hired three more scouts, and had devised a distinctive signal for each to let him know when he was needed back at the base camp.

There it came again, the whistle's mournful wail capable of drifting across the Nebraska Plains for miles. However, today Colt was only a mile distant. He turned Dancer and headed to the end of the track, figuring that at a hard gallop Dancer could be back in a couple of minutes. He charged through tall spring grass, and the train was soon in sight. As he drew closer he realized a third train had arrived at the construction site. How long it had been there he couldn't be sure, since he had been several miles away earlier that morning. He stayed at a hard gallop until he recognized the fancy car that was part of the visiting train. The windows had all been repaired, as had siding that had been damaged by bullets, but it was the same car all right—Sunny Landers's car.

He yanked on Dancer's reins to slow the horse and felt the old mixture of apprehension and excitement. Why had he been called to camp? Sunny had not come back since the day of the Indian raid, nor had he heard from her all winter. He had supposed that by now she would be in Chicago planning her wedding.

He drew in a deep breath, hoping maybe only Stuart had come out; but as he urged Dancer into a gentler trot and approached the car, he saw Sunny herself come around the end of it, leading a shiny black mare and wearing a simple riding skirt and a plain blouse and riding cape, her hair pulled back into a thick braid. She looked no different from ten years previous, when they used to ride together on the journey west.

He couldn't help being glad he had bathed in the Platt River that morning and had shaved, then wondered why it mattered. What the hell was she doing here anyway, looking ready to ride and all? He had had all winter to stop thinking about her, and now here she was again. Did she enjoy torturing him, or was she really so innocent of his feelings that she didn't realize what she still did to him?

General Casement was standing beside her, but Colt didn't see Stuart anywhere. Had Sunny come alone? With two other trains between hers and the crewmen, few of the workers were in any kind of hearing distance; most kept too busy to pay any attention to his approach. With the time that had been lost over the winter, Casement was working the men at an even more rigorous pace in the renewed race to beat the Central Pacific's progress.

He watched Sunny's eyes as he drew Dancer to a halt near her and Casement. What was it that he saw there?

He couldn't quite read it, but her face was slightly flushed. She nodded to him, and he tipped his hat. "Miss Landers," he said respectfully, a wary look in his eye.

"Travis!" Casement frowned. "I was beginning to worry about you. You've been out for days."

"Just being extra careful. I rode a little farther north than normal. What's the problem?"

Casement finally grinned. "No problem. You have a very important job today, one that I am sure will be much more pleasurable than your regular duties. It seems Miss Landers has decided that before she goes back to Chicago, she wants a last look at the country she loves best. She'll be gone for quite a few months after this. She'd like to go riding, get a last look, so to speak."

Colt felt Sunny's eyes on him. "What's that got to do with me?"

"Well, she wants you to be the one to take her."

Colt scowled, looking back at Sunny, but she was turned toward her horse.

"I tried to talk her out of this—considering the danger and all," Casement continued. "But she seems to think that if she's with you, she'll be safe. She would rather ride completely alone, but that's out of the question. She doesn't want a whole army of strange men coming along, so that ruled out a soldier accompaniment and the other scouts. I guess it's just you. Just hang back and let her ride—keep an eye out."

Colt looked at Sunny again, and this time she met his gaze. It seemed she was trying to tell him something in that look, but he couldn't quite believe her eyes meant what he thought. What in hell was she after? Why was she doing this to him? "You probably should take more than just one man, Miss Landers," he told her.

She shook her head. "No. Just you."

There was a strange determination in the words. Apparently, she wanted to be alone with him, maybe needed to talk about something. But what? And why couldn't they talk right there? "It's too damn dangerous. We expect more Indian trouble than ever this summer."

"You know your job. It's my own risk. If something happens, it's my fault, not yours."

Why did he detect a double meaning to the words? All common sense told him to refuse, even if it meant losing his job. He looked at Casement. "I don't like the risk. She's too important."

"Well, I don't like it either, but when Miss Landers makes a request, we try to be obliging. You mind your manners now, and be extra alert. I would ride north if I were you. The Cheyenne most likely camped farther south for the winter. If they're coming, that's the direction they'll come from. Those in the North are probably on a spring hunt. I expect it will be another month before any real trouble comes." The man turned to Sunny and nodded. "You do what Colt tells you, Miss Landers. If he thinks it's wise to come back, then come back. He knows his business, and I know you'll be safe with him, since the two of you already know each other."

Sunny looked up at Colt. "I have every confidence in Mr. Travis."

She turned and mounted up, and Colt thought she looked as tempting straddled on a horse as ever. He felt his anger rising.

"Thank you, General," Sunny told Casement. "Don't you worry. I've got a rifle of my own along, the latest in the new Winchester repeaters; and I know how to use it. My brother made me learn after that Indian attack the last time we were out here." She glanced at Colt with a daring look in her blue eyes. "Maybe Mr. Travis and I can have a shooting match. It might be fun." She kicked her horse into a fast run, and Colt turned to Casement.

"Just remember, I objected to this. I don't want to be hung out to dry if something happens."

"You won't be. You heard the woman. Now, get going and stay alert." Casement turned to walk back to the crew, and Colt reluctantly rode out after Sunny, noticing she was slowing down deliberately so he could catch up. He reached her and grabbed her horse's bridle to stop the animal altogether. "What the hell is this, Sunny?"

Sunny wondered if he realized how hard her heart was pounding. Never had she done anything so daring, and never had she been so unsure that she *would* be able to tell him what she wanted to tell him, or be able to make the right decisions. Part of her wished she would have discovered he had left the railroad for parts unknown. It would have made this so much easier. She struggled to find her courage, wondering if she seemed to him like the foolish girl who had said good-bye to him at Fort Laramie.

"I just wanted to see you once more," she told him, looking away again. "You left too quickly for me to talk to you the last time I saw you, and it would have looked odd if I had just invited you into my private car. This was the only way I could think of to get you alone and talk to you."

He let go of the bridle. "About what? There's nothing left to discuss anymore."

She met his eyes again. "Yes, there is. You know it as well as I. Please, please don't laugh at me, Colt, and don't be angry. God knows I've never been more frightened in my life."

He studied the eyes that had haunted him for years, wishing he knew what she was after. Part of him wanted to drag her back to safety by her hair and another part of him gloried in this chance to be alone with her again. "It's a damn good thing that new regiment of soldiers that's supposed to be coming isn't here yet. Enough men have seen us ride off together as it is. Don't you know how this looks?"

She raised her chin slightly. "I don't *care* how it looks. After today I'll go home and never see any of them again until the railroad is finished, and by then I'll be—" She looked away. "Married." She swallowed nervously. "Please, Colt. I really do want to take this last ride," she said pleadingly. "Ever since I came out here, I haven't had the chance to enjoy this country the way I'd like. No one knows what I'm doing, not even Stuart, certainly not Blaine." She reached down and patted her horse's neck. "It's just something I need to do."

She faced him again. "I just want to ride and ride, to forget about boardrooms and decisions and wedding plans and even the U.P." She closed her eyes and breathed deeply of the fresh spring air. "For one day, just one day, I want to be completely free and do something *I* want to do. I was hoping that you of all people would understand." The pleading look he could never resist came back into her eyes. "Just be my friend today, Colt, like you always used to be. Be the man who wrote me those letters and who once taught me all about his land, taught me to love it. I want to laugh and be happy, and I want to share that freedom with someone who understands the need for it."

All anger and resistance left him, as well as the common sense that told him this was as dangerous as it could be—not because of possible Indian trouble, but because of his own heart. She still had that sweet charm that made it difficult for anyone to tell her no. He leaned back and smacked her horse's rump, and Sunny let out a little scream when the mare whinnied and took off at a hard gallop. Sunny leaned into the animal as though glorying in the ride, and Colt hung back a moment, watching her. There was a strange loneliness about her today, as though she were reaching out for something but not sure she wanted to grasp what might come to her. Was this some kind of final farewell to her freedom, to the land . . . and to him?

He goaded Dancer into a dead run, racing to catch up with her.

Whatever this day might hold for him, Colt had decided to quit worrying about it, and he knew Sunny felt the same. She seemed to want only to feel happy and free and unencumbered by the strains of her normal daily life and the enormity of the decisions she often had to make. She rode hard and wild, and before long Colt was caught up in her apparent quest to simply "be." At times it was hard to keep up with her, and he found himself laughing at the way she galloped her horse up and down the Nebraska sandhills, sometimes throwing back her head and yelling like an Indian, laughing, feeling the sun on her face. It reminded him of how he had felt after returning from the war.

What kind of battle had Sunny been fighting to bring her to this? It was almost as though she had just been released from prison herself. As the day warmed, she unhooked her riding cape and wrapped it into the gear on her horse. She took off at another run, opening her arms, screaming to him how much she loved the bigness of the land. "I wish it would swallow me," she called.

Colt kept chasing after her, wondering if she realized how watching her, having to keep coming after her, stirred desires in him that he had fought for so many years. He told himself it was his problem, not hers, that he was going to have to fight the pain. Was she afraid to marry Blaine? His heart ached at the thought that she was not going to be happy with the man.

It was well after one o'clock before she finally slowed her horse to a walk and asked him if he wanted some lunch. "Whatever you're ready for," he told her. "I do know you'd better rest that horse."

She was all smiles. "Yes, I suppose." She looked at him, her eyes running over him in a way that nearly destroyed his control. Why in hell did she keep looking at him that way? It was almost as though she were deliberately testing him. She stopped her horse completely and let it nibble at the sweet spring grasses. She turned and reached into one of her saddlebags, and Colt realized she had unbuttoned her blouse a little, he supposed because of the heat. He could see a good share of one breast, and he looked away.

"Here," she told him. He looked back to see her handing over a piece of beef jerky. "This is all I want for now. Enough for you?"

Again he felt a double meaning to the words. He took the jerky and nodded. She was smiling that smile that made his own mouth water to taste her lips again. Did she think he had forgotten about that delicious night on the beach? He bit into the jerky and rode slightly ahead of her. "Got kind of warm."

"Yes, but a beautiful day, isn't it? Oh, Colt, I've wanted to do this for such a long time. I just never had the chance. You don't have any idea how I used to sit in my room in Chicago and daydream about this, you and me riding wild and free—riding and riding and being a part of the land. It's always been that way for you, and I envy you for it. For me, something like this is such a glorious treat. When I finally moved to Omaha, I thought I could do this more often, but I brought my way of life right along with me, and nothing changed. And when I thought you were gone for good, it didn't matter anymore." She trotted her horse up next to him and bit off a piece of jerky.

"Sunny, I wish I knew—"

"Don't say it. Just enjoy the day, Colt." She chewed the meat and swallowed, unhooking the straps of her canteen and opening it to take a drink.

Colt stared ahead, afraid to look at her. He chewed on some more meat, then grasped his ammunition belt and ducked his head to take it from over his shoulder. He hung it around the pommel of his saddle, then stuck the remaining jerky in his mouth and reached down to grasp his buckskin shirt, pulling it off over his head.

Sunny allowed herself a glance. Would she have the courage to tell him what she needed to tell him? Was it better left unsaid? Wild fantasies about him returned at the sight of his powerful masculinity when his shirt came off, and she was touched by the scar left from the Pawnee arrow wound. She thought about how he had suffered, the horrors he had seen.

"It's getting almost too hot," he told her. "You sure you don't want to go back?"

"No. Not yet."

"Just be careful you don't let the sun burn that pretty face."

She laughed lightly, lifting the canteen and drinking some more water. She offered it to him, and Colt met her eyes. He swore if he didn't know her better, she was giving him a look of invitation, but he was not about to take that road. It could lead to nowhere but disaster for both of them. What in God's name was this all about? The woman was to be married soon! What the hell was he doing out here in no-man's land, riding with the richest woman in the country, a woman who dined with presidents and owned half of Chicago and dished out millions like pennies, a woman who was part owner of the very company for which he worked? This was the most absurd situation he had ever encountered! He took a swallow of water and handed back the canteen, then reached behind him to get out tobacco and a cigarette paper.

"That's the scar from when you were wounded by the Pawnee, isn't it?" she asked, her eyes resting at his right side.

Colt rolled himself a cigarette. "It is. I've finally managed to put all that behind me."

She began undoing her braid. "Where do you go from here, Colt?"

He lit his cigarette and took a deep drag. "I don't know. I guess I'll wait and see where life leads me. I've pretty much always done it that way." He removed his hat and hung it, too, around the saddle horn by its string. He ran a hand through his long dark hair, then turned to tie his shirt into his gear, the cigarette still in his mouth. "How about you? Why are you doing this, Sunny? You should be back in Chicago, making plans for a grand wedding, not out here riding like a wild woman who's scared to death of her future."

Sunny looked away, wondering if he knew what seeing him bare-chested did to her—his dark skin glistening in the sun, that cigarette between those full lips, those gentle hazel eyes. He was raw power, so sure, so handsome, so forbidden. "Who said I was scared?"

"Nobody. It's just written all over your face, that's all. Does it have something to do with marrying Blaine? You think you're going to find some kind of answer out here?"

She shook out her own hair, enjoying the feel of letting the long blond tresses fall free. "I don't know. I've never been sure about Blaine, and yet I should be." She sighed deeply. "I should be the happiest woman in the world right now. I have everything . . . everything." Her voice trailed off.

"That depends on what *everything* means. Look at what you have compared to me, and I pretty much feel *I* have everything, yet you could buy and sell me a million times over."

She stared off at the higher bluffs on the horizon. "No, Colt. No one buys and sells someone like you. You're your own man. You aren't impressed by money, and you don't judge people by it. That's why I feel so good when I'm with you, in spite of how hard it is for us to be just friends. With you I don't have to put on any airs, pretend I'm something I'm not."

"Do you pretend around Blaine?"

"Sometimes." She met his eyes. "I'm sorry. I know this is hard for you, and that I promised to let you go on with your life and me with mine. I know it's best we have absolutely nothing to do with each other, but when I think of never seeing you again, or even being able to write you, or—" She looked at him pleadingly, her eyes tearing. "Once I marry Blaine, it really will have to end. That's why I had to come out here, Colt. It isn't fair to you, and it makes no sense at all; but I felt almost led out here against my better judgment." She reached back and took a deep breath. "Now I don't regret it at all. This has been the most wonderful day I can remember since when Father and I came out here and he let me ride with you. It's strange, isn't it, how people move in and out of each other's lives—how some things change so much but other things stay the same, like the land. When I come out here it's as though the last ten years never happened."

Colt smoked quietly for a moment. "But they *did* happen, Sunny. I lost my best friend, a wife, and a son; you lost your pa and became one of the most powerful women in this country. I've been through a war and a hell worse than death in that prison camp while you became part owner of a transcontinental railroad and built another grand home and offices in Omaha—became engaged to a man whose wealth probably matches or tops your own. My life has been one of tragedy and pain and dirt and a sort of going on from one pointless thing to another. Yours is filled with balls and boardrooms and diamonds and soon a wedding that will make the papers in other countries. Things *do* change, people grow apart, especially those who have no business being involved in each other's lives."

She fought the tears, realizing what he was telling her. He could not be a part of her life. It was like that night at Fort Laramie, a gentle good-bye, a painful lesson in what was right and wrong. But she also remembered Vi's words about following her heart, about how love could conquer great obstacles. Did Colt believe that? She sniffed and wiped her tears, refusing to look at him.

"Dammit, Sunny, don't cry. I told you that ten years ago." He took another long drag on the cigarette, suddenly feeling awkward. He had spoiled her happy day. *Damn her!* he thought. How many times had he said that to himself? God, he loved her, and that was the hell of it. Should he tell her? How could it possibly help anything? It would only make everything worse.

She straightened in her saddle, retying her canteen. "I'll always treasure our friendship, Colt. One thing no one can take from me is my memories, or my dreams." She held her chin higher and faced him. "I'll race you," she told him.

"What?"

She gave him a daring look, a new boldness in her eyes. "I said I'll race you. If you catch me and manage to pull me off my horse, you've won!" She charged away, and Colt sat there a minute, wondering what she was up to. What was this sudden change in conversation? She was like a crazy woman today, and she had turned his feelings a thousand different ways.

He watched her, the way her bottom fit her saddle, the way her hair blew in the wind. Her daring look stirred his pride, and the race was on. He kicked Dancer into a hard run, manly desires stirring in him at the challenge of catching her. He held the reins with one hand and smashed out his cigarette against his saddle horn with the other, tossing the stub aside and leaning into the ride. "Get up there, Dancer," he shouted to the horse.

Dancer's mane flew up into Colt's face as he galloped up and down more sandhills. He noticed Sunny veer to the west rather than north, and he turned Dancer, tak-

ing a cut between two more sandhills and emerging near
Sunny as she came around the end of one hill. She
screamed and laughed when she saw him, and now he
knew he could catch her.

He came closer, the determination to reach her now a
burning need. It went against all reason, was totally foreign to all sense of maturity. They were like children for
the moment, and yet not children at all. The emotions it
stirred in him to think of catching her were dangerous,
yet he could not stop himself. He came ever closer, and
now he was on her!

Sunny screamed when she felt his strong arm come
around her. Suddenly, she was free of her horse and
sitting sideways on Dancer, a powerful arm holding her.
She covered her face and laughed as Colt slowed his
horse. "Now you are my captive," he teased.

She threw her head back and faced him, and both of
them sobered. For a moment they sat there breathing
heavily from the ride, watching each other.

"We had better go catch your horse," he finally told
her.

"We'll find it later," she answered. She moved her
hands to touch his powerful arms, ran her fingers over
his bare shoulders. "Tell me, Colt. What does an Indian
do with his captive?"

For a moment everything went silent for him. Nothing
existed but the utterly beautiful woman in his arms, her
tempting mouth, her open blouse, her blue eyes, her
golden hair. He moved a hand to rest against the flat of
her belly. "He takes her to his tipi and makes her his
slave," he answered, his voice gruff with passion.

She touched his face. "That's what I want you to do
with me, Colt. Make me your slave—today, tonight, tomorrow."

He shook his head. "Sunny—"

She touched his lips. "Don't say it, Colt." Her eyes
glistened with tears. "I don't know what's right and
wrong anymore, and today I don't care. I just want you.
I've always wanted you." A tear slipped down her cheek.
"It can't be anybody else, Colt, not the first time. I—"

His kiss cut off her words, a deep, hot kiss that removed any remaining inhibitions. She could barely get her breath for the thrill of it, the ecstasy of his hand moving to her breast, the ache of womanly desires that surged in her when his tongue moved between her lips. Dancer moved slightly, and she clung to Colt. He left her lips for a moment, keeping one arm around her as he slid off the horse and pulled her after him.

From then on they were each so possessed with passion and need that nothing else existed for them. He pulled her into the grass, and they both felt consumed by need and long-repressed desires. His kisses were hard and deep, leaving her no time to reason or to object, and hardly able to get her breath. She suspected that even if she wanted to stop him, she surely could not now. And why would she want to? This was what she had wanted for so long, what she had dreamed about for years; but it was so much more exciting and glorious than she had imagined.

Her breath came in gasps, and she could not stop her tears of joy as she lay there in the grass, his warm, delicious kisses smothering her until his lips left her mouth to move over her throat, down to the whites of her breasts. She closed her eyes, her heart pounding wildly as he pulled her blouse from the skirt and unbuttoned it, pushing it aside. He untied the front of her camisole and pushed it open, and she cried out when she felt the warmth of his mouth at her nipple, gently tasting her, each gentle sucking pull causing pleasurable painful surges deep in her belly.

She grasped his hair, pushing herself toward him, wanting to feed him, please him, be Colt Travis's woman. Every movement now was hard and deliberate and desperate, both of them breathing hard, fire tearing through them. There could be no slow movements, not this first time.

She felt dwarfed by his physique and power, a woman that this wild, beautiful man had to touch and taste and fill. His hand was running up her leg and under her skirt. He moved his lips back to her throat, and she could feel him trembling with the want of her. He pushed his hand up under her bloomers, and she gasped

his name when he touched the soft skin of her bottom.
She wondered if she might die from the ecstasy of it, for
it was hard to breathe, and her heart beat so hard that
her chest hurt. He took his hand away, and she closed
her eyes, shivering with awakened needs as he rolled her
to her side and began unbuttoning her riding skirt.

Somewhere deep inside Colt admitted this was the
biggest mistake he would ever make in his life, but there
was no going back now. Here she lay, Sunny Landers,
her hair undone, her full, firm breasts offered up to him,
her eyes closed in ecstasy, her whole body on fire for
him. She wanted him, and he was not going to put up
with the pain of wanting her any longer. Whether they
could join their lives was a question he couldn't answer,
but it was one that mattered little now. She wanted him
to be her first man, and by God he was not going to let it
be anybody else.

He rose to his knees and yanked, pulling off her riding skirt and bloomers both in one swift motion, tossing
them aside. He met her eyes, seeing the want still there,
seeing no hesitation. He moved his eyes downward
then, drinking in her naked splendor, leaning over her
and touching the flat belly, the blond hairs that hid her
virgin offering.

"God, Sunny," he whispered, leaning down to kiss her
belly.

"Colt," she whimpered. She repeated his name then
with each breath she took as he moved down to kiss at
private places only Colt Travis had touched. He kissed
her thighs, lingering for a moment at the scar left from
when he had cauterized her wound. He moved back to
secret places, and she opened herself to him in all her
soft, pink, untouched beauty.

Colt felt her grasp his hair, heard her scream his
name when his tongue found that magical place that
brought a woman unbearable pleasure. He allowed himself a moment of exquisite satisfaction, tasting her
sweetness, reveling in the knowledge she was totally
willing. He grasped her hips and sucked her pink fullness until he could feel her throbbing. With each breath
she cried out his name, and she pulled at his hair so

hard that it hurt. He moved back up her belly, lingering at her breasts again, moving on top of her, finding her mouth in a fiery kiss, giving her a taste of her own juices.

Sunny returned the kiss like a wanton woman, totally lost in the man who had just claimed her most private parts as though he owned her. She felt gloriously wicked and alive, in love and on fire. Colt moved an arm under her shoulders and rolled onto his own back, pulling her on top of him so that her hair hung down around her face and brushed his own. They hesitated just a moment, watching each other's eyes, seeing the need and the want and the passion there. He grasped her shoulders and pushed up slightly so that her breasts hung free, and she smiled, throwing her head back in the ecstasy of knowing Colt Travis was gazing at her nakedness. He gently caressed one nipple, rubbing it with his thumb.

She drew in her breath in a deep, shuddering sigh. "I didn't know it could be this wonderful," she told him in a whisper.

"Do you know how long I've wanted you?" he asked, his voice raspy.

Sunny met his eyes again, and she smiled. "I've wanted you longer."

"I don't think so." He moved his hands to pull her blouse farther off her shoulders, and she slipped her arms from the sleeves. Another piece of clothing was tossed into the grass. She sat on top of him, wearing only the camisole which hung open, her boots, and knee-high stockings. She leaned down to let him taste her breasts again, and then he grasped her hair and met her mouth, driving his tongue deep inside as he rolled her over on her back. His kisses became wilder and hotter, and she reveled in the way he made her lose control, the thrilling sensations he brought her. How strange that she could stand up to men of great wealth and social power, but this man who had nothing at all in the way of wealth took away all stubborn pride, all sense of reason, all inhibitions. This was one man she could not resist, who made her weak. She was glad, so glad she had decided to confess her desperate plea to be possessed by him.

"I love you, Colt. I love you so much," she murmured between kisses.

Somehow he had moved between her legs, or had she just opened them naturally and willingly? He grasped her face in his big, strong hands, resting on top of her for a moment, his powerful shoulders lifting him over her.

"God help me, I love you too," he told her, his jaw flexing as though he were struggling against the feeling. "I don't know what's going to happen after today, Sunny, but damn you, I do love you, and I want to be inside you. . . ." She closed her eyes and gasped his name. "I want to make love to you, Sunny, over and over," he groaned, "until neither of us can find the breath or the energy to move."

He kissed her eyes, licked her mouth while he reached down to unbuckle his gun belt. He tossed it aside and began unlacing his leggings and unbuttoning his longjohns.

"Say it again, Colt," she begged, her eyes closed. "Tell me what you'll do to me. I want to hear it, feel it—"

"I want you, Sunny. I need to feel myself inside of you. Give yourself to me."

The words made her feel wild and free. He met her mouth savagely then, shoving his tongue deep. She returned the kiss, her arms reaching around his neck and her tongue meeting his. She wondered at the wildness he brought out in her. She realized it had been there all the time, waiting to erupt at just the right moment. She arched against him, feeling as though she could not get close enough, touch deep enough, be wicked enough.

"Yes, Colt," she gasped. "Make love to me until I die. It has to be you, just you!" She screamed then, unable to say another word for the pain that hit her hard and fast. He surged inside of her, and for a brief moment she wanted to push him away and beg him to stop, but she understood that Colt would never cause her pain unless he could bring her indescribable pleasure too.

He reminded her of a grand stallion taking his mare.

The pain was cutting and deep, yet before he finished she began to experience through the pain another sensation, a deep need to take him inside herself, to please him greatly and take her own pleasure in return. She knew now the glory of it, the beauty of offering herself to a man she loved. She wondered briefly if she could have stood the pain if it had been Blaine. Surely loving and wanting the man the way she loved and wanted Colt made this first time more bearable.

Moments later she felt him shudder and then relax. For a moment neither of them said a word. "My God," Colt finally muttered, brushing her hair with his lips. "What have we done, Sunny?"

"It's all right," she answered.

"Sunny, it's not all right—"

"Don't say it! Don't say it," she begged. She leaned back and kissed him, and it was only then she realized he had tears on his cheeks. She brushed them away with her fingers. "Not yet, Colt. I don't want to talk yet. I don't care what Casement thinks. I told him I might want to camp out under the stars all night. I said it because I knew if this happened, I couldn't bear to leave you and go back to that train right away. Let's just be together, today, tonight, tomorrow."

He drew in a deep breath, resting on one elbow and moving his other hand to massage her belly. "I must have hurt you."

She smiled through tears. "Only at first. I don't care, Colt. I wanted it this way. No matter what happens, I'll always love you, and you'll have been my first man." Her tears came harder then. "Hold me, Colt. Just hold me."

He pulled her into his arms. Overhead a hawk circled, riding the winds and casting its shadow over the scene below—a black mare grazing nearly a half mile away, a painted Appaloosa a quarter of a mile in a different direction. A gun belt and various articles of clothing lay strewn along a pathway of crushed spring grass that in turn led to the nearly naked bodies of a man and a woman who lay holding each other, quietly weeping.

Chapter 22

"We'll camp here tonight." Colt led Dancer through a grove of cottonwood trees to the Platte. "We can wash in the river, and we're less likely to be seen down in here in case someone should come along."

Sunny watched him, loving the way he moved, the way he sat a horse, the look of his powerful forearms. After their first coupling, they had both fully undressed and had run and laughed in naked glory under the prairie sun. They had made love again in the soft grass, and after that second sweet union they had decided to find a place to camp. Finding all their clothes and running down the horses had been a wonderful game. They laughed at how a shirt lay here, a pair of pants there, here a stocking, there a gun belt. The two horses had been grazing so far apart that they had to whistle and call and walk a total of nearly a mile to get hold of them.

It was the happiest time Sunny could remember. Finally, she could voice the love she'd felt for so long, and now she knew Colt felt the same way for years. For now neither of them wanted to think about what might lie ahead. They enjoyed the moment, enjoyed the wonderful gift of being able to show their love. Sunny's body hurt with the sweet pain of being loved by the beautiful man who rode ahead of her, leading her horse. It gave her shivers to realize her handsome, sure, brave but gentle Colt had seen her naked, had tasted her breasts, had explored and claimed her most intimate parts, had plunged his glorious self deep in her belly and branded her his own. She had wanted him so fiercely that she let him take her with the utmost abandon. It seemed as natural as breathing, no hesitation, no embarrassment, no worry over whether it was wrong. Nothing could have felt more right. Ever since she was a girl of fifteen, she'd known this day was coming. It simply had to be. In spite of all her millions, this man of little wealth owned her now, heart and soul.

They reached the river, and Colt tied and unloaded the horses. Sunny helped him gather wood as the sky began to darken, and they spread out a blanket and built a fire. Colt dug into his supplies and took out some soap and towels, turning to watch her add a little wood to the fire. He was thinking how she looked like an ordinary woman, more beautiful than most, but plainer now, her hair tangled and undone, no makeup, her blouse only half tucked into her skirt. She wore no jewelry . . . except for that diamond ring. He felt a stab of pain at the sight of it still on her hand.

"I can't believe you're roughing it this way," he teased. "You look like a common settler woman."

She smiled that smile he loved. "I'm tougher than you think. I thought I proved that to you ten years ago. You're a hard one to convince, Colt Travis." She held his eyes challengingly as she began removing her blouse. "I'm ready for that river bath."

He came closer, putting the towels and soap on the blanket. "That river is pretty cold this time of year."

She unlaced her camisole and opened it along with

her blouse. "Not cold enough to take away the heat you bring out in me," she answered, reaching up around his neck.

Colt grinned, meeting her mouth in another hungry kiss, wondering at this insatiable appetite he had for her. He had not felt this good with a woman since Lee-Ann, and much as he had loved her, he had to admit that this feeling he had for Sunny was more intense, more demanding. He had never loved this way.

Sunny kissed his chest, enjoying the taste of him even though he had been sweating from their hard riding and their previous lovemaking. He had a stirring, manly scent about him. She looked down and began unlacing his pants, and she could see him swelling again with the want of her. She daringly knelt to pull off his buckskins, and she touched him gently.

Colt drew in his breath at the feel of her fingers. She kissed him, rubbed her cheek against him. "You're so beautiful, Colt," she said softly. "I've wanted you for such a long time." She kissed his flat, muscled belly, inching her way back up and kissing his neck. "I want to be better than any woman you've ever been with. Do I please you, Colt?"

He grasped her tangled hair, kissing the top of her head. "How could someone as beautiful and loving and willing as you not please a man?"

She looked up at him, and he found her mouth, keeping her face between his hands. She ran her hands over his powerful arms, reached around his neck. She reminded him of a little girl who couldn't get enough candy. When he left her mouth she kissed his neck again, her breathing heavy. "Do it all to me again, Colt," she whispered. "What happened when you kissed me down there? I never imagined—"

He ran his hands under her blouse and camisole, caressing her bare back and crushing her breasts against his chest. "It's just a way to make it feel all that much better for a woman."

"Do it to me again. I felt like I belonged totally to you. I want to feel like that again."

He kissed her hair, her eyes. He removed her blouse

and camisole, dropping them to the ground, then knelt to pull off her skirt. He helped her step out of her boots and stockings and underclothes, and Sunny marveled at how easy it was to let him see her naked. He kissed her belly, then reached over and grabbed the soap, surprising her when he scooped her up in his strong arms. "First my captive and I will bathe," he said, running with her to the river.

Sunny screamed and laughed when Colt threw her into the cold water. He laughed with her, quickly grabbing her and dunking her under the water for a kiss before coming up for air. They splashed each other as they floated toward a rock, where he propped her up and began lathering her.

Sunny threw her head back and closed her eyes, enjoying the feel of letting him bathe her, letting him wash every part of her. He pulled her from the rock and dunked her again, and she laughed and took the soap from him. "It's my turn," she told him.

They moved closer to the edge of the river, where it was shallower, and Colt stood in water that came only to his knees. He watched her as she soaped him, her hair slicked back from her face. It reminded him of that night when he had supper with her and her father out in this very same country, when she had bathed and then come to the table. That was the night Bo Landers had warned him to stay away from his daughter. The memory brought back the fear that he did not want to face yet—that he should have done just that.

Sunny washed him gently, exploring, watching how that most intriguing part of him swelled when she slid her hand over it with the slippery soap. "Don't stop," he told her, his voice gruff with ecstasy. Moments later his life spilled on her, and she was awed by this curious but wonderful thing between man and woman, this glorious way God had created for man and woman to consummate their love. Suddenly, she wanted babies—babies for Colt, a son to replace the one he had lost.

They went back into the river to wash and rinse off yet again. Colt threw the soap up onshore, and they swam for a while, playing like carefree children. He car-

ried her out of the water and laid her on the blanket,
handing her a towel. It was nearly dark now, and he
added a little more wood to the fire before picking up
another towel and drying himself off. He looked down
at her lying there watching him, a towel pulled over her.
He grinned, leaning over her and pulling the towel
away. "I'll warm you up the way you asked me to," he
told her, meeting her mouth. He explored deeply with
his tongue while he moved a big hand over her breasts,
her belly, down to that part of her that belonged to him
now.

She whimpered and returned his kisses wildly when
he moved a finger deep inside of her suggestively. Sunny
knew she would still feel pain, but this was Colt, her
precious Colt, and he loved her. He had a way of easing
the pain, a way of touching her that made her want him
in spite of it. She wondered at her own boldness, the
way he had of making her ignore all modesty, lose all
inhibitions. His lips moved down to again claim and explore her intimately. She gripped the blanket in her fists
as his warm lips and gentle tongue again pulled at that
secret part of her. She had not known her own body
until now, was not aware of the magical, wonderful feelings a woman could experience. Could a man claim his
woman more fully than this?

She felt the wonderful release pulse through her
again, and quickly Colt moved back over her, pushed
himself deep inside her. Her body needed him, and she
had no control over that need, not when it was Colt who
was touching her, Colt who was bringing to life all the
buried passions.

Colt grasped her under the hips, glorying in her
depths, rising up on his knees and lifting her to himself.
He thought how in spite of her boldness, she was truly
offering herself to him in sweet innocence, allowing him
to teach her the joy of being a woman, trusting in his
love. She was discovering something new and wonderful, and he loved her so. At last now there was something he could give her, a kind of freedom she had never
known.

Their eyes met, and Sunny arched up to him in wild

passion, thinking how he looked the conquering warrior. Yes, she truly was his captive now, and his touch was like a drug that made her lose all reserve. His hair hung over his bronze shoulders, and his muscles were hard from grasping her, his eyes on fire with his own ecstasy. She gloried in the fact that the pain was nearly gone now. He moved in ways that made her feel insane with the want of him, not just in deep thrusts, but in magical circles that brought such a thrill that she could hardly get her breath.

It was strange to think that this powerful man could break her in half if he chose to, yet he could be so gentle. He bore scars from fierce fighting; she had seen him kill men without a flinch. Yet here he was, mating with her. To her he was simply sweet, loving, gentle Colt, who was not just her friend but her lover.

His life spilled into her, and he slowly relaxed. He reached over and took hold of another blanket, lay down beside her then and covered them. They were still for several minutes, saying nothing. She settled against his shoulder, and Colt petted her hair. "You hungry?" he finally asked.

"A little."

He kissed her hair. "We have to talk, Sunny."

She rubbed his chest, and he noticed the diamond again. She closed her eyes. "I know. Let's wash and eat first. We have all night to talk."

He took her hand and kissed her palm, then turned the hand to look first at the ring, then into her eyes.

"Take it off," she told him.

He frowned. "Sunny—"

"Take it off. I'm not marrying Blaine."

He felt an odd heaviness of impending disaster as he removed the ring. She took it from him and rose, walking over to put it in her saddlebags. Colt watched her, thinking how firm and beautiful her bottom was. How could a man get enough of a woman like Sunny? How could he not love someone so sweet? He felt a fierce jealousy at the thought that Blaine might have married her and been first to take her, and he was glad it hadn't happened that way. He knew what she was doing was not easy for her, nor would it be easy for her to tell Blaine she was not marrying him.

Still, even with Blaine gone, could they really be together? He reminded himself who she was. That beautiful naked woman walking back to him was Sunny Landers, queen of the Union Pacific, the richest single woman in Chicago, maybe in the country. What the hell was he doing lying here with her along the Platte River, claiming her for his own?

"Let's go wash again," she told him. He saw the tears in her eyes. "Then we'll eat."

He got up and followed her to the river.

Colt rolled himself a cigarette and took a stick from the fire to light it. He threw back the stick and took a deep drag, feeling pleasantly full from the fresh bread and turkey meat Sunny had brought with her. He picked up a tin cup filled with coffee and watched her repack some of the food and their plates. She had slipped on a simple cotton sleeping gown, and on her it looked elegant. Colt decided she was the type of woman who could look good in a potato sack.

He sat wearing only his longjohns. It was one of the warmest nights so far this spring, made more pleasant by the fact that this time of year there were still no mosquitoes. Sunny leaned over the fire and poured herself some coffee, and he thought how pretty she looked in the firelight, while Sunny in turn was thinking how wonderfully handsome and dangerous and seductive he looked, his bronze skin glowing by the soft light of the flames. She sat down beside him and sighed deeply. "I've wanted this moment to come ever since I said good-bye to you at Fort Laramie," she told him. "So many times in my dreams, I—" She looked at him. "Did you dream about being with me sometimes?"

He met her gaze, the cigarette still in his mouth. "What do you think?"

She smiled softly. "I think you wanted me that night at Fort Laramie."

He gave her a teasing grin. "You were just a kid."

"I was old enough, especially in the eyes of someone like you who has lived among Indians and such. I've always heard Indian women marry quite young."

"Some do." The air hung silent for a moment. "You saying *we're* going to marry?"

She sipped some of her coffee. "It's not for me to say."

He smoked quietly for a moment. "Sunny, it isn't a matter of whether or not I want to marry you. You know damn well I'd love you to be my wife, to be a mother to my children. But you also know the problems we face, the reasons we both fought this for so long. I could never be a Blaine O'Brien or anything like your father or—"

"I would never want that. What I love about you is that you are what you are, no pretense, no concern for outspending the next man, no fancy notions. Surely we can find some kind of compromise, Colt."

He leaned back on one elbow. "Well, we sure as hell know we can't go through life trying to stay away from each other." He took the cigarette from his mouth and blew out smoke in a deep sigh. "All right, let's weigh the facts here. I could never go back to Omaha with you and start wearing fancy suits and going to board meetings and such—and if I left all that business part of it to you, what would I do there? I'd go crazy trying to make myself useful. And I sure as hell wouldn't want to just sit around living the high life, making Vince and everybody else believe I married you so I could lie around and live off your money, which we both know is exactly what they're going to think.

"Now, you," he continued, "in turn, can't come out here and live like just any common settler woman. For one thing, you have a railroad to finish. I know how much that means to you, Sunny, no matter how much you might love me. You also have a fiancé who'll be coming back here anytime now expecting to take you to Chicago to marry him. Maybe I *should* go back with you for the time being, just for moral support. I don't like the prospect of you facing Blaine alone, or Vince, for that matter."

She stared at the fire. "I'm not worried about Vince. I've been handling him alone for years now. He'll rant and rave, but there's really nothing he can do. I *am* a little worried about Blaine. After all these years, he'll be terribly angry."

Colt sat up a little straighter. "Would he hurt you?"

She met his eyes. "No." She smiled at the look in his eyes. "You'd kill for me, wouldn't you?"

He took another drag on the cigarette. "I already have in the past. Have you forgotten those buffalo hunters? You don't think I did that just as part of my job in protecting you, do you? It was the thought of what they had in mind to do to you. I wasn't about to let them touch something as beautiful and innocent as you, especially when I wanted you for myself."

She sighed and leaned closer. "I wish you would have told me then. I loved you so much, Colt."

He tossed the cigarette into the fire. "I figured such a relationship was impossible." He turned to meet her eyes. "Maybe it still is."

She felt the pain in her throat at the remark. He lay back and she stretched out beside him. "We'll find a way, Colt. I can't stand the thought of leaving you, but I suppose for the time being I'll have to. I'm going to go back to Omaha and tell Blaine when he comes that I can't marry him, that I just don't love him the way I should. I would take you with me, but I want to spare you as much as I can. Just breaking up with Blaine will bring terrible gossip. I don't want you involved right away."

"Sunny, I'm a man. I can take it. I don't want you going back alone."

"It has to be that way. I won't have people insulting you. We have to take this one step at a time. After a while we'll find ways to be together, slowly let people know what's happening—that we're in love and we're going to marry. If I break up with Blaine and we tell everyone at the same time about us, the cruel gossip will be that much worse."

She touched his face, studying his eyes. "There must be a way to make it work, Colt. I want to have your children. I want you always in my life, and we can't just carry on an affair forever. We have to make it legal so we can be free always to do this whenever we please." She stroked his hair back from his face, studying the scar over his eye. "We have to take a step at a time. The headlines will scream with the story, I can assure you, and we have to be prepared—*you* have to be prepared. I'm used to the attention, but you aren't." Her eyes teared. "I don't want all gossip and remarks and cruelty of others to change you, make you hate me in the end. That's what I fear most."

He took hold of her wrist and kissed her hand. "I could never hate you. But I understand why we have to do this slowly. You just remember that I'm here for you, and all I need is one telegram telling me to come to Omaha and I'll be there, gossip or not. In the meantime, maybe we'll find a solution to how in hell we're going to manage to live together. The only damn thing we have in common is that we love each other."

She kissed him. "It's going to have to be enough, Colt. That love will have to get us through some very bad times. I'm so sorry, because it's mostly my fault. I could just give everything over to Vince and Stuart—"

"No!" He sat up. "I don't want a damn thing to do with any of your money, Sunny, but I'd never ask you to give all that up. It would be like me just giving up everything I love out here, denying my heritage, putting on a silk suit and going to operas and pretending to be something I'm not. What you have is a part of you. You shouldn't have to lose part of yourself just so we can be together. I think we're both smart enough to find a way to make this work without losing ourselves, losing the very things we love most about each other."

He looked down at her, lying back down to rest on one elbow again. "It isn't the wealth and the power that I love, Sunny. It's your strength, your determination, the way you took all that on and wouldn't let Vince browbeat you out of it, wouldn't break your promises to your father. Now here you are building that railroad you and your father always dreamed about. I'd never take that away from you, just like you'd never make me sit in boardrooms instead of riding free here, where I belong. We can love each other and still be ourselves. And we can instill in our children the best of both of us."

She could not stop the tears, and he pulled her into his arms. "You make it sound like we really can do it, Colt."

"Of course we can. I know how strong you are, and I know how determined you can be when it's necessary. I'm just as stubborn." He moved on top of her. "We're going to make this work, Sunny. I'm not giving up, not now. I'll do whatever it takes to keep you right here in my arms, and neither one of us is going to give up everything that we are to make that happen." He kissed her eyes. "One thing that's different about me from any of those men in your life now—if you came to me tomorrow and said you weren't worth a dime, it wouldn't make a damn bit of difference."

A tear slipped out of her eye. "I know," she whispered. *But that isn't how it is, Colt,* she thought. She touched his face, thinking how little he understood of how he would be treated back in her world. The night of the dinner party was only one tiny example. Some had gossiped cruelly then, even when she and Colt were only old friends. They had looked upon him as a curiosity, asked ridiculous questions about his heritage. What would it be like if she told the world she was marrying the scout Colt Travis? She was probably wrong to have come out here and done this to him. Now that she realized how much she truly did love him, she couldn't bear the thought of him taking any kind of ridicule. He was such a proud man, and so untouched by greed and corruption and all the things she put up with almost daily.

She leaned up and kissed his shoulder. "You're right about the railroad. That's one thing I feel responsible to stay with, Colt. Once it's finished, I'll have so much more time to devote to a marriage and children. But that doesn't mean we have to wait until then to be husband and wife. I can hardly stand the thought of having to leave you for a few days."

He ran a hand along her slender leg, pushing up her

gown and stroking her hip. "And *only* a few days. Don't make me have to wait too long."

"Blaine will be in Omaha any day now. As soon as I've told him and gotten Stuart and Vi used to the idea —as soon as all the hullabaloo is over as far as the newspapers and all—I'll come back and we can decide how we're going to handle the rest of our lives together."

He sighed, moving between her legs. "You *sure* you don't want me to come with you?"

She traced her fingers over his lips, thinking how she would want to die if people were cruel to him. "Yes. Just be very, very careful while I'm gone, will you? I would hate to lose you now, after finally finding you. I'm your woman now, Colt, and you're my man, no matter how different we are. It's right. I know it in my heart."

He met her mouth in a sweet kiss, pressing himself against her belly. She wrapped her legs around him, and he reached down and unbuttoned his longjohns. He rubbed himself lightly against her, teasing with both his penis and his tongue until she begged him to finish it. Again he moved inside her in a sweet, slow rhythm. He rubbed his cheek against the fullness of her breasts beneath the soft flannel gown, taking comfort in resting against them. He met her mouth, moving his hands under her hips and pushing deep, softly rubbing against that secret place that made her breathing deepen, made her arch toward him until he gloried in the feel of her pulsating climax that pulled sweetly at him and made him groan with the want of her. She was tight and wild and exotic, and he owned every part of her, had tasted and explored and loved her in ways he knew she never would consent to with any other man. Here was one area in which he had more power than any of the men she faced in any boardroom or in Congress.

He shuddered with his release, then lay on top of her a moment before relaxing beside her.

Sunny snuggled against him. "We'll be happy, won't we, Colt?" she asked, sounding sleepy.

"Sure we will," he answered, kissing her hair. She closed her eyes, and he watched her awhile, her face looking small and almost childlike in the light of the fire, with no makeup, her thick hair a tumble. In moments like this she was so vulnerable and almost dependent, nothing like the kind of woman he imagined she had to be when she faced business and political enemies.

No more, he thought. *She won't face them alone anymore.* He might not be a full part of that world, but he would be there for her to turn to, cling to, draw strength from. And he would be her escape. She needed to get away from all that sometimes. That's why he was better for her if he didn't change too much. She didn't need a Blaine O'Brien. She needed a Colt Travis to keep her sane and strong and safe . . . and loved.

"You what?" Colt rolled up another blanket. Most everything else was packed into their gear.

"I told potential investors I would pay the required ten percent on their stock if they would sign and say they bought the stock. When the U.P. begins making a profit, they'll get their share and they can pay me the ten percent. In the meantime, I actually own much of the stock myself. Dr. Durant sold many shares that way."

Colt put on his hat. "Why doesn't that sound legal to me?"

"Probably because it isn't. But we had to get things going, Colt. Congress was stalling, demanding that a certain number of stocks be sold first, making us prove we had plenty of investors. So what if it's just names on paper? The money is still there."

He shook his head. "I couldn't do business that way."

Sunny checked the cinch under her horse's belly. "Oh, Colt, it's done all the time in my circle. We're even using our own construction company to supply the railroad. The government pays so much a mile, and we base our costs on cost of supplies, and so forth. We pad the prices for our own construction company, the government adjusts its share accordingly, and we make back some of our own invested money before the U.P. even starts taking on passengers and freight." She straightened and faced him. "It's called survival. Just like out here, Colt. The strongest, wiliest, most seasoned scouts like yourself live. The others die. In my world there are other ways to be strong and wily."

He stared at her a moment, wondering at how different she seemed when she talked this way. This was not the sweet, innocent, vulnerable woman who slept in his arms last night and to whom he had made love twice more this morning before they finally bathed again, ate, and dressed. This was the Sunny he didn't understand, the one who did not fit into his world, or he into hers. "If I was involved in all that, I'd have to be honest about everything. That's the only way I could run a business."

"Honest!" She laughed lightly. "Talk to our own congressmen about being honest. If I hadn't had to do so much bribing to get the railroad act passed in the first place, I wouldn't have to be thinking of ways to get my money back out of them. It's a common business practice, Colt. You scratch their backs, they scratch yours."

He kicked around at the fire to be sure it was out. "And you *stab* their backs, they stab *yours,*" he added.

Sunny mounted up, watching him a moment. "Sometimes. Colt, are you angry with me?"

He met her eyes, breathing in a deep sigh. "No. I just don't like your kind of enemy. Mine come at me with real weapons and a look to kill. Yours smile and shake your hand, and to fight them you have to be just like them. That's not the Sunny I know and love."

She smiled softly. "This Sunny is nothing like the one who will return to Omaha. The wrong decision, or sometimes just being too honest, can cost you millions in the business world, Colt."

He mounted his own horse, turning the animal to face her. "Isn't there a saying that honesty is the best policy?"

"You would soon learn that doesn't often apply where I come from."

Their eyes held, both of them feeling the burden of their differences. He rode closer, studying the proud way she sat, her blouse now neatly tucked again, her hair twisted up and pinned at the back of her head. She had to look proper when she returned to the train, and he wanted it that way too. He remembered the remark the man in Billie's saloon had made about her, and he wanted none of that kind of talk. When they made this public, it would be in the right place at the right time, in a way that would create the least gossip. Each of them was worried about the pain the other might suffer at the hands of the public because of their relationship.

"Well, Miss Landers, when you become my wife, I am going to have to show you that things can get done without all that bribing and scheming. Maybe your father thought that was the only way to do it, but I happen to disagree. I might not understand all the ins and outs of your little empire, but I understand human nature, and I understand right and wrong."

She shook her head, smiling sadly. "You make it sound so simple, Colt."

"It *can* be simple." He leaned over and kissed her cheek. "Just remember what we said, about our love getting us through this."

Her eyes teared. "I'm scared, Colt."

He took her hand. "You want to know something? So am I. But all I have to do is look into those blue eyes of yours and I know I can take just about anything to be with you." He squeezed her hand. "And all *you* have to do is trust me, lean on me, and not worry about how I'll be treated. I've been through a lot in my thirty years, Sunny. I can take it."

She clung to his hand, tears sliding out of her eyes now. "I don't want to leave this place. I've never known such happiness as I have had the last two days. I'm scared I'll never be this happy again."

Thunder rolled in the distance, and to Sunny it seemed ominous. "We don't have much choice now," he told her. "Storm's coming."

Yes, she thought. *I feel it too.*

He gave her a reassuring smile. "I love you, Sunny. That's not going to change. And remember, if you need me, you send me a wire. I might get fired, but I'll come running."

She managed a light laugh through her tears. "Who's going to fire you? I'm your boss, remember?"

He winked, trying to overlook his own sadness at leaving the place where he had found such happiness. "I guess you're right." He leaned over more and met her mouth, moving a hand to lightly caress one breast as the kiss lingered. He left her mouth and kissed her tears. "We'd better go before we end up spreading the blanket again. If we do, we'll get caught in the rain."

She reached out for him, grasping him around the neck, and he pulled her onto Dancer. "Hold me a little longer," she whispered. "Let me ride with you until we get in sight of the train." She sat sideways and rested her head against his shoulder. Colt took the reins to her horse and headed up the bank away from the river, through cottonwood trees and out to the sandhills, heading southeast.

They rode for over an hour without seeing a soul, neither of them talking, wanting only to enjoy the feel of their bodies touching, the strength they found in each other's arms. Sunny breathed deeply of his scent, wanting to remember. Colt in turn enjoyed the smell of her hair, and he was sure he would not forget the sweet taste of intimate places that belonged only to him. She had offered herself so willingly, with so much trust and love. Whatever lay in their future, they would always have this to remember, and nothing could change the fact that he had been her first man, first in her heart and first to invade her virgin depths.

They were in love, and it felt good to finally admit it, finally consummate that love, no matter what the odds against it. Bucking those odds could not be nearly as difficult or painful as it had been to try to stay away from each other. It simply could not be done. The attraction, the love, the need were all too powerful.

The storm moved closer, black clouds billowing on the western horizon and coming fast. Thunder again rolled through the heavens, and shortly afterward Colt heard the signal—one long blast and two short ones. It was followed by another signal, and he recognized it was for Quinn Dix, another scout. "You'll have to get on

your own horse, Sunny. There's some kind of trouble.
That's my signal—and one for another scout. For all we
know, we're in danger. We've got to ride hard."

He gave her a quick kiss and pulled her horse up next
to his own. She reluctantly left him and moved onto the
black mare. "You're the one who wanted a good ride,"
he told her. "Let's get in one more on the way back.
Maybe we can beat out that storm." He kicked Dancer
into a gallop, and Sunny followed, her heart pounding,
not with fear of trouble, but with dread. The glory and
ecstasy of the last two days were ending too quickly
now. The thunder on the plains seemed to echo her fear
of what was to come.

Chapter 23

The black clouds rolled in hard and fast on a high wind that brought the storm quickly as Sunny and Colt approached the construction camp. At least thirty army tents were stretched out in a neat line near the trains, their canvas billowing with the wind, flags flapping. Soldiers' horses grazed farther to the east, a few uniformed men keeping watch over them, having a difficult time keeping them from bolting because of the coming storm. More soldiers milled about the camp, some heading for their tents as a few large drops of rain began to pelt them.

"I wonder what's up," Colt shouted through the high wind. Stinging dirt lashed at their skin, and they both had to duck against it. "Those soldiers must have arrived yesterday."

"We sent for them," Sunny yelled back. "It doesn't mean there's trouble."

"They wouldn't signal in all the scouts if there wasn't."

Lightning slashed through the rumbling dark clouds, followed by a crack of thunder that made Sunny's horse whinny and balk. She urged the horse forward, feeling as though the coming storm only signified the storm that lay ahead for her. She had lied to Colt about wanting to go back to Omaha alone. She wanted nothing more than for him to come with her. It seemed that every time she said good-bye to him, it was always months or years before she saw him again. Still, she knew the ugly publicity that lay ahead once she broke her engagement to Blaine, and she did not want him involved in it. At least now she knew just how much she loved him, and that he loved her. She had no doubt in her heart that he would wait for her.

If only they could make love once more, just once more before she had to leave him. She still felt on fire with the want of him, burning inside at the memory of his naked skin touching her own, of letting him see and touch and worship every part of her, of taking Colt Travis in all his glorious manhood inside her own body and giving him pleasure. It all seemed too wonderful to be true, and sometimes she felt like pinching herself to make sure she was not dreaming. Now when she read her old journal entries, she could smile instead of weep, rejoice instead of fantasize.

As they drew closer, it became obvious that daydreaming would have to stop for the moment. Yet another train had arrived, and two men in top hats stood on the platform of Sunny's car, waiting expectantly. They clung to their hats so they would not blow off in the wind. Sunny recognized them as part of Durant's elite ten, a group of the Doctor's top people to which Blaine and Sunny belonged. General Casement was running toward Sunny and Colt with a couple of extra men, who grabbed the bridles of their horses.

"They'll take care of your mounts," Casement hollered. "Some of Durant's men are here, Miss Landers. We need to talk. Come inside your private car. The scouts are to come too!"

Colt grabbed her arm and they hurriedly climbed onto the platform and followed the two top-hatted men inside, where more men waited, a total of six. They all rose when Sunny entered, and those wearing hats removed them and bowed slightly. One of them, a tall, thin man with hard blue eyes and small, tight-set lips, looked Sunny over with a hint of contempt. Colt caught the look, knew what the man was thinking about her being out riding alone with a scout. He felt an instant defense of Sunny, but for the moment he hung back as Sunny greeted the men.

"I'm glad you were close enough to get back right away, Miss Landers," Casement told her.

"Yes. Your presence is needed," the thin man told her, glancing from her to Colt. Colt met the man's eyes boldly. When the man looked away again, Colt scanned the looks on the faces of the others, some of whom were also looking from him to Sunny with smirks on their faces. A few just stared, intrigued by his size and looks.

"What is happening? Why are all of you here?" Sunny asked, still a little breathless from the ride as she shook a few hands. She called out to Mae to go and see about bringing some tea and coffee, as well as a bottle of whiskey.

"The soldiers arrived late yesterday," Casement told her, "and just in time, I might add."

Colt moved to stand beside the scout Quinn, who had also been summoned. He could see by the man's eyes that Quinn, too, was wondering about Sunny riding alone with him. There was more a look of curious humor in his eyes than malice, and Colt gave him a scowl. It irritated him that all these men were here when they got back. He knew Sunny had planned on just the normal work crew, not this group of men who were so close to Blaine and who would be full of curiosity and ready with judgment. Colt had to admire her sudden poise and air of authority as she took the only seat left in the elegant parlor car, which seemed suddenly too small now that it was filled with so many people.

"We have an Indian problem," Casement was explaining. "One of our graders arrived last night on horseback. He was gravely wounded, said three other men are dead. We wired Omaha, and these gentlemen came out in representation of Dr. Durant. They said I should signal in the scouts so we can discuss what to do."

Mae brought in the drinks, and Sunny quickly became the gracious hostess, offering coffee, tea, and whiskey to the men. Mae poured whatever each man asked for. The men continued to glance at Sunny in curious wonder, and Colt figured it was not just from the fact that she had been out riding alone, but that probably none of them had ever seen Sunny looking quite so plain, wearing only a blouse and a riding skirt, her cheeks flushed from a hard ride—or was it from something else? He wanted her again already, wondering if he could bear to go more than a day without holding her beautiful body next to his own, without invading her again, enjoying her bold abandon, savoring every part of her. He liked her this way, no makeup, no frills, just plain, beautiful, wholesome Sunny.

"According to the surveyor, we have quite a problem," the thin man said again, apparently considering himself the spokesman for the others. He took a sip of whiskey. "We have a decision to make, Sunny, and Dr. Durant said it has to be made among us six and you. Blaine couldn't make it out just yet." He glanced at Colt on the last sentence, his blue eyes like ice. "He'll be in Omaha in another three days, but we don't have three days to wait."

Outside, the storm hit, the thunder making Sunny jump. She glanced at Colt, aching to go to him and let him hold her. How nice it would be if they could be alone, lie in her private bed and hold each other while the storm raged outside. She remembered another prairie storm, when she was in the covered wagon.

"Why the rush, Mr. Canary," she answered. She looked at Mae. "You can leave us now, Mae. Thank you."

Mae nodded and hurried off, glad to leave the presence of so much wealth and power but full of questions for Sunny about spending the last two days with Colt Travis.

"We took a train out last night," Canary answered. "Got here only about a half hour ago. It seems the surveyors laid out a route directly through some Cheyenne Indian burial ground over the winter while the Indians weren't around. Now the Cheyenne have discovered what's been done, and they're furious. They attacked the graders and are camped at the burial ground now, refusing to let us come through."

"Then go around," Colt said. "You'll save a lot of lives and trouble."

Canary shot him a look that told him he had not been asked to speak. Colt did not flinch. He glared back at the man, thinking how his name fit him—thin as a little bird. The smell of arrogance was so thick in the now-cramped car that Colt was on full defense.

"That is just the problem," Canary answered. He looked back at Sunny, as though to remind Colt he had been talking to her, not to him. "We came out here to discuss the matter, because to go around this gravesite, or whatever it is, would mean many extra miles of track. Its location is on the best soil, right in the middle of some very rugged, hard-rock country that does not offer a good path anywhere near on either side. Because of the past winter, we're falling behind, Sunny. Normally, we don't mind a few extra miles of track—it's just more government money in our pockets. But this time Durant does not want the delay. We have a lot of lost time to make up for, and it's time to be as efficient as possible, both with money and material as well as speed."

"But going straight through as planned will mean a heated fight with the Indians," another man put in. He reached over and poured himself more coffee from a silver pot that sat on a round oak table in front of the men. The rich elegance of Sunny's private car again reminded Colt of the kind of money and power and social standing Sunny represented, a way of life that was ingrained in her very blood. At the same time he was reminded what this kind of living did to him. Already he felt choked, needed to get out of the close confines of the parlor car.

"In other words, we're choosing here between putting on a lot of extra miles, which means lost time and money, or going through the burial ground and losing a lot of lives," Sunny was saying.

"That's about the size of it," Canary told Sunny. "You know the kind of money we're talking about, and you also know how important it is to the Doctor to keep up with Strobridge."

Sunny sighed, putting a hand to her head. How she hated coming back to a car full of men who were after her to make another decision. This one was made more difficult by the fact that deciding to go through could endanger Colt's life.

"We brought in the scouts to get their opinion," Casement was saying.

Sunny looked at Colt, thinking how he stood out from everyone else, so big and rugged-looking. It was almost humorous trying to picture him in a silk suit and top hat. An odd fear gripped her. Now that they were back to reality, had they been wrong to think they could be together? Yet she could no longer imagine her life without him in it. She saw the love there in those hazel eyes, knew he was telling her not to be afraid, not to give it up. "You know the Cheyenne, Mr. Travis," she spoke up, addressing him formally to help stave off the unspoken gossip she knew filled the minds of her business cohorts. "You even lived with them for a while. What are we in for?"

"Yes, I suppose it takes an Indian to know an Indian," Canary said derisively. "Let's hear it, Mr., uh, Travis, was it? We'll hear what you and the other scout here have to say, and then you can be off. We have some important decisions to make."

Sunny watched Colt stiffen at the rude remark, spoken as though Colt were just some common servant who should get in his say quickly and get out. "I would be careful how you address our scouts, Mr. Canary," she said before Colt could answer. "They happen to be our most important men. Without them a lot more lives would have been lost by now. Mr. Travis has already been wounded once protecting the U.P. and me and my brother a few months back. He is also a veteran of the Civil War who spent time at Andersonville. You will address him with more respect."

Canary reddened a little, and Colt grinned inwardly at Sunny's bold retort. She was back to Sunny Landers, the businesswoman, and he loved that Sunny just as much as he loved the vulnerable, totally submissive woman who had been completely in his control the last two days, or had it been the other way around? She certainly knew how to manipulate men.

Canary nodded to him. "My apologies for sounding short with you, Mr. Travis, but we've no time to lose here. This is a very grave situation."

Colt looked over at Quinn and saw the concern on his own face. Quinn was a good man who knew his job well, although he didn't know quite as much about how to handle Indians as Colt did.

Quinn nodded to him. "I'll let you do the talkin'," the man said.

Colt turned to Canary. "You're right," he answered. "This *is* a grave situation. There are few things more important to the Indian than their sacred burial grounds. I don't know how many are out there, but it doesn't take a lot of Indians to create a whole lot of trouble. The Cheyenne are some of the fiercest fighters on the Plains, and believe me, they'll fight for this one. Personally, if you do decide to go through, I'll help however I can, but I won't set foot in the burial ground itself. I happen to believe that it's too sacred. My advice is to try to find a way to go around." He looked at Sunny. "The Indians have lost enough land and dignity. Don't do this to them."

Their eyes held for a moment, both of them struggling to hide their love and passion, wishing they could talk about this alone. Outside, a wild storm raged, and Sunny felt one raging in her soul. Rain pelted the windows of the plush railroad car, and thunder seemed to literally shake the ground. Sunny tore her eyes away then, looking at Canary. "There must be some way to go around."

"Not without a great deal of lost time," Casement answered for the man.

"I say we risk it," Canary told Sunny. "We have over sixty soldiers with us now, with more to arrive tomorrow. They can rout out the Indians in no time, and there will be enough men to leave a few here to help protect the construction crew in case the Indians decide to attack here too. Once the tracks are laid through the burial ground, we can leave soldiers camped in the area for a while to keep guard until we're sure the Cheyenne won't try to come back and destroy the tracks, or until so many of them die that there are not enough left to give us a fight."

"It isn't right," Colt said, his anger obviously rising. "For God's sake, what's a couple more weeks, a few more miles! A burial ground is so important to the Indian. You're building right through land that's been theirs for centuries, chasing away their game, bringing out more white settlers, now this! To tear up that burial ground is as sacrilegious to them as burning a Bible would be to you! Someday the U.P. is going to rake in millions. Don't sit there and tell me you can't afford to lay a few extra miles of track."

Canary's face grew to a deeper red, and the others sat dumbfounded at the way Colt dared to talk to him. Canary rose, facing him. "I said earlier I was sorry for the remark I made, but I take it back. How dare you in your position talk to me that way!"

"You asked for my opinion," Colt growled. "You *got* it!"

There came another clap of thunder, and the rain came down so hard that one could not see more than a few inches beyond the torrent just outside the window.

"I asked for your opinion about the danger of the situation, not about the U.P. and what it can and cannot afford to do. What the hell would you know about the business end of this thing anyway? I'll remind you of your place, Mr. Travis, and if you want to *keep* your job with the U.P., you had better be a little more supportive of the railroad that pays your salary every month!"

"That's enough, Mr. Canary," Sunny spoke up, also rising. "Colt Travis is one of our best scouts. Mr. Casement can tell you that. I value his opinion, and he is upset only because he understands the Indians so well."

Canary looked him over scathingly. "He ought to." He held his chin haughtily, his thin nose high in the air. "In this particular case, I have to wonder just whose side you're on, Mr. Travis."

"Listening to you, I'm beginning to wonder myself," Colt sneered.

"Now, now, we have a problem here, and this is not the way to solve it," Casement broke in. "I have a crew out there laying two miles of track a day. Before long we'll reach this burial ground, and I've got to know what to do."

"White Buffalo ain't gonna budge," Quinn added.

Colt turned. "White Buffalo! Is that who's out there making all the trouble?"

Quinn nodded. "He sent a messenger to the interpreter working with the graders after their attack—said to tell the Great White Father that White Buffalo would never allow the iron horse to go through their burial grounds."

Colt turned to Sunny. "White Buffalo is the man who saved my life when I was wounded by the Pawnee. I lived with him and his people for months. Maybe I can talk to him."

He saw the fear in her eyes. "It would be too dangerous now," she answered. "He would look at you as the enemy."

"He would value our friendship enough not to harm me. Just let me tell him the U.P. will go around the burial ground. You've got pull, Sunny. You can do it."

Lightning continued to rip the sky outside, and a loud clap of thunder made Sunny jump again. It took all the self-control Colt could muster not to grab her and hold her. He saw the terrible indecision in her eyes, and at that moment he also saw how their differences were going to always be pulling her in two different directions.

Sunny stood there, feeling helpless, while the rest of them watched, wondering at the familiar way in which Colt had called her Sunny instead of Miss Landers. Canary thought the whole situation very strange, Sunny Landers out riding alone with such a wild-looking man, half Indian, no less. He wondered if Blaine O'Brien knew.

"I don't have that much pull," she told Colt. "In something like this, it's a matter of a majority vote. If it was up to me—"

"You're getting too sentimental, Miss Landers," Canary said. "It isn't like you, not the woman I've seen at our board meetings. You know the U.P. comes first, and you know what Dr. Durant wants. I vote to go through." He looked at the other five men present, and they all nodded. "I might add that we wired your fiancé," Canary added, "and Blaine O'Brien also votes to go through, as did the other two men who could not be here."

Colt looked at the man, no longer able to bear the torture in Sunny's eyes. "It's easy to vote on something like that when you aren't out there to see for yourself what you're up against," Colt said angrily. "You aren't the ones risking your lives."

"No, we aren't," Canary answered. "That's what soldiers and you scouts are for."

Quinn stiffened, and Colt just glared at Canary. "Yes, we're all *expendable*, aren't we? A small sacrifice for the U.P.!"

"I didn't mean it that way—"

"I know what you meant," Colt growled. He looked at Sunny. "Quite a bunch you run with, Miss Landers."

"Colt—"

He turned away from her to face Casement. "Let me go talk to White Buffalo. Give me at least that much. Maybe we can work something out. Let me go see him alone first."

"No! It's too dangerous," Sunny said, unable to hide

her personal concern for him. Some of the others watched in shock when she touched Colt's arm.

"White Buffalo would never harm me," Colt assured her. He looked at Canary. "Just give me a couple of days, then send the soldiers forward, but stay a mile or so back from the site. Have the lieutenant wait for me before doing anything rash. Whatever White Buffalo has to say, we can wire back to Omaha and get a decision. For God's sake, the *least* you can do is let me talk to the man!"

"We'll lose time in this storm. The site is at least a two-day ride from here, I'm told, a hard ride at that. With this storm—"

"I'll leave right now. I've ridden in this kind of rain before."

"Colt, this is no ordinary rain," Sunny protested.

He didn't seem to hear. He turned to the lieutenant. "You can wait and leave when the storm lets up. Just be sure to hold back like I said. I'll see if I can reason with White Buffalo."

"He's gotten pretty mean and nasty, Colt," Quinn said. "Lost a lot of family at Sand Creek. I doubt he's the man you remember."

"I know what it does to a man to lose his family. I understand him perfectly."

Sunny's heart went out to Colt at the remark, and she vowed that she would never let him be hurt again. He would always have the support of her love.

"Come to the kitchen quarters with me," she told him. "I'll make sure you have plenty of supplies."

"Good luck, Colt," Casement told him. "You watch yourself out there."

Colt nodded to the man, then glanced at Canary. "Just give me a couple of days. You and the others might as well go on back to Omaha. There's nothing you can do here."

Canary nodded. "Try to smooth things over, Travis. We don't want to lose too many men, and whether you believe it or not, we can't afford any more lost time or labor."

Colt held his eyes a moment, thinking how pleasant it

would be to rub the man's pointed nose in horse dung. He made no reply. "Follow me," Sunny told him. She led him through the other end of the car, past her private quarters and to a little enclosed area just before the platform, where shoes and capes could be stored when first entering the car. She closed the door and looked up at him, both of them close in the tiny compartment.

"I didn't really mean it about taking you to the kitchen," she told him, reaching up around his neck. "I just had to get you alone once more, Colt."

He pulled her close but hesitated before their lips met. "It's always going to be this way, isn't it?"

"What way?"

"You and I arguing over what decision to make. I can't put money and a company before what's morally right, Sunny."

"Colt, I told you if it was up to me, I'd go around. But this is something I can't control. Surely you can see that. Don't be angry, not now, when we have to be away from each other."

He sighed, his eyes changing to the look of gentle love that made her want him so. "The only thing I see is that in spite of all this I could never stay away from you. I love you, Sunny. Get yourself to Omaha and back here so when this is over we can be together again. We can shout it to the world that we're in love."

She smiled, tears in her eyes. "I was afraid you were already changing your mind."

He grinned then, leaning down and meeting her mouth. "You know better," he told her between light kisses. "I just wish to hell I could take you back in there to that bed and make love once more before I leave." The kisses grew hotter, deeper. He moved a hand to her bottom and squeezed lightly, already aching to be one with her again.

She moved her lips to kiss his neck, breathing in the scent of him. "Oh, Colt, I'm scared for you. I don't want you to go."

He kissed her hair. "I've been taking care of myself for a lot of years. You know you don't need to worry about that." He drew back a little, putting a big hand to the side of her face. "Besides, White Buffalo and I were good friends. He won't be real happy that I'm working for the railroad, but he won't hurt me. Of course, if I have to fight him, that's another story."

She closed her eyes, turning her face and kissing his palm. "I don't want to be apart, Colt," she whispered, the tears coming again. "Every time you leave me I wonder if I'll ever see you again."

"You'll see me, all right. You go back to Omaha and do what you need to do, and I'll go do what I need to do. We'll meet again wherever the work camp is by then, and we'll pick up where we left off. We'll find a way, Sunny, just like I promised. I'm sorry I lost my temper in there. I'll try to learn to get along with people like that."

She laughed through her tears. "Canary has always been an ass. When Durant isn't around, he likes to play the big cheese just because he's his right-hand man. He doesn't like me because I'm a woman, but I've never let him badger or snowball me."

Colt smiled lovingly, rubbing a thumb over her cheek. "I could see that. You amaze me, the way you handle yourself in those situations."

She reached up and touched his lips. "I can handle any man—except you. You completely undo me, Colt Travis."

He licked her fingers, taking one between his lips suggestively and nibbling at it. "Good. I like it that way." He sobered, touching her hair lovingly. "I'm glad you came out here, Sunny. I hated you for it at first. I thought I was going to have to go through the pain of wanting you again but being unable to touch you." He leaned down and kissed her, a sweet, promising kiss this time. "I love you," he whispered. "Come back soon, Sunny."

"You know that I will."

"You'll have to be very strong."

"All I have to do is think about how much I love you and need to be with you. Hold me, Colt, hold me tight." They clung to each other a moment longer. "I don't think of you as just my lover," she told him. "You're my best friend. You've been my best friend for the longest time."

He kissed her hair. "We might as well get this over with," he told her. "Bye, Sunny."

Oh, how she hated those words! She had heard them before, more than she cared to remember. "Good-bye," she whispered. "God be with you."

He pulled away, and she saw tears in his eyes. He hurried through the outer door to the platform, and Sunny followed, standing there out of the rain while he ducked into the torrent and literally disappeared. She strained to see, finally making out his form not too far away. She saw him pull something from his supplies and realized it was some kind of rubber rain gear. He threw it around himself and mounted, and the ground splashed beneath Dancer's hooves as he rode off. It took only a few seconds for her to be unable to see him anymore because of the rain.

A sick feeling engulfed her, and she went back inside, going to sit down on her bed. She rolled to her side and curled up, wondering how she was going to bear the next days or possibly weeks before she saw him again.

"Sunny?"

Sunny recognized Mae's voice. "I don't feel well, Mae. Please go tell the others I'm sorry, but I won't be able to rejoin them for a while. Maybe they should go ahead to Omaha. I'll be leaving myself soon."

Mae stepped closer, reaching out hesitantly and touching her shoulder. She noticed Sunny was not wearing her engagement ring. She well knew how Sunny felt about Colt Travis, although it amazed her. Still, she couldn't blame her in some ways. He surely was a man's man. "I'm here if you need me, Miss Sunny," she told her.

Sunny remained turned away, but she reached up and took her hand and squeezed it lightly. "I know. There's really nothing you can do, Mae. Thank you."

Bye, Sunny.

The words rang in Sunny's ears until she felt like covering them. She never realized love could hurt this much. The last two days had been like a wonderful dream. To have to part so suddenly left her in shock. This was not how she had planned their parting. Now her Colt was out there riding through that awful storm, headed for so much danger. Still, she was headed for a danger of her own, having to tell Blaine she could not marry him. She and Colt would both have to be very strong now, trusting in the special, beautiful love they had found to carry them through the days when they could be together again. "God protect him," she whispered.

Chapter 24

The enclosed carriage came to a stop in front of Sunny's home, and Sunny waited for her driver, a young Mormon named Matthew, to come and open the door for her. Her heart beat a little faster with a note of dread at the news Matthew had given her, that Vince was waiting for her at the house. He had arrived that morning. Sunny wanted to be glad he had come, since he had finally expressed an interest in the railroad and their holdings in Omaha; but even when it was for something good, she could not feel comfortable around him.

She wished he had picked a better time. She had wanted to have the next couple of days to herself, to think about Blaine, the Indian trouble, the danger Colt was in. She needed time to prepare herself for reality, to build up her courage, and to come down off the cloud she had been on since finally finding the only true love of her life. She wanted to be alone and lie in a tub and think about how it had felt to have Colt make love to her. The last two days had been so special, and she actually hurt from the want of Colt's reassuring arms around her again, especially now that Vince was here.

She hoped Blaine would arrive soon so that she could get the painful breakup over with. She didn't like doing that to him, but how could she marry him now? Her heart and body and soul belonged to someone else, the only man she had ever really loved. Dissolving the engagement was the only right thing to do. For once she was going to be truly happy, be with the man she had loved for ten years.

She climbed out of the coach, leaving a sleeping Mae inside. The train ride back had taken ten hours, and it was dark outside. Sunny had not bothered to change since leaving that morning, and she still wore her riding skirt and blouse. She had left the construction site within the hour after Colt had ridden off, her own train following the one that carried back Canary and his men. They would all wait now for a message from Casement.

Sunny had considered staying, wanting to be closer if something happened to Colt; but she knew that what was most important to him for now was that she come back home and get her personal life in order so that she could go back to him when the Indian trouble was over. There was nothing she could do at the site, since all the trouble was many miles farther ahead at the Indian burial grounds. Canary had said Blaine would be here in a few days, and she preferred to break the news to him in Omaha than to have him come to the construction site.

Matthew unloaded some of her baggage and followed her into the house. It had rained all the way back, but the downpour had finally let up, and a sultry humidity hung in the now-still night air. By the light of outdoor lanterns that hung in the portico, Sunny caught sight of a few spring flowers that were beginning to bloom around the front steps. She smiled, thinking of the wild-flowers in the sweet prairie grass where Colt Travis had first claimed her. Her cheeks burned at the memory of the things she had let him do to her, and she felt suddenly hot. She was not ashamed or embarrassed. It had all been so natural. After all these years of loving him, she had wanted to give herself totally, to please him in whatever way he took that pleasure. She wanted every intimate part of her to be owned by her handsome, brave, precious Colt; and she knew he revered her body, knew he touched and tasted and made love to her out of true love and passion and devotion. A woman couldn't want for more, and if all he could afford to buy her was a plain gold band, then that was good enough for her. It would mean so much more to her than the expensive diamond Blaine had given her, which was still packed away. She would not wear it again.

"I'll go get the rest of your things, ma'am," Matthew told her, setting down the baggage he had brought in.

"Thank you, Matthew. I guess you'll have to try to rouse Mae. Tell her to come in and go to bed. I don't need her anymore tonight."

"Yes, ma'am."

Sunny ordered a housemaid to take her bags upstairs. "Your brother is in the parlor, ma'am," the maid told her.

"Thank you, Sarah." The woman took some of her bags and headed up the stairs, and Sunny stood in the entranceway a moment, breathing deeply for courage, never knowing how she was going to be greeted by Vince. It irritated her that he had chosen this particular time to show up, and she had hoped that he would at least have already gone to bed so that she didn't have to talk to him until morning.

She headed for the parlor, thinking that she should be tired herself after the long trip, but being with Colt, being so hopelessly in love, had given her a new energy. How could she ever sleep again? She wanted to be awake so that she could do nothing but think about her magnificent lover, her precious friend, her breath of fresh air, the man who made her feel alive and wonderful and loved—oh, so loved. No one had ever loved her like Colt did, except for her father; but even he had not understood her inner being like Colt did.

She entered the parlor to see Vince sitting near the hearth, smoking a pipe and reading the latest edition of the Omaha newspaper. A silver tray with coffee and biscuits sat on a table in front of him. He looked up when she entered, and she did not miss the rather scathing look in his eyes as she greeted him. "Hello, Vince."

"What the hell are you doing dressed like that?" he asked.

"For heaven's sake, what difference does it make? Can't you give me a normal greeting?" She tried to smile, walking closer and sitting down in a cabriole chair on the other side of the coffee table.

Vince shrugged. "I'm disappointed that you weren't here when I arrived this morning. I went over to visit with Stuart, got a look at the U.P. offices. Stuart filled me in on some of the operations and all, but he said he had no idea why you had gone out to end-of-track alone."

Sunny caught the accusatory note in the words. "I often visit the construction site. Stuart knows that. You both know how important the railroad is to me." She leaned over and poured herself some coffee. "It's good to see you," she lied. "Have you come just to see our operations here then, or is something wrong back in Chicago?"

"I came for several reasons. I have to admit, my curiosity got the best of me. I would like to see more of the setup here, have a look at the businesses you've invested in—maybe even go out to end-of-track with you and get a firsthand look at the construction site."

How could she tell him that the next time she went out, she wouldn't want him along? She would be going back to be with Colt.

"Well, I'm glad you're interested," she answered, sipping the coffee. "I'm afraid that for the moment it's too dangerous. I came back because of Indian trouble. Some of Dr. Durant's men had also gone out to the site. They came back, too, just ahead of me."

"Oh, so you weren't alone out there after all?"

She held the cup of coffee in her hands, watching his eyes. What was he after? "Yes, I was when I first went out a couple of days ago. Durant's men didn't show up until early this morning." She looked at a grandfather clock that stood in a corner of the room. It was a little after ten P.M.

"How bad is the Indian thing?" he asked, leaning back in his chair and puffing on the pipe.

"Pretty bad. They expect this summer to be worse than last summer." She sipped more of the coffee. "Right now our biggest problem is that the best route out in the Nebraska sandhills goes right through an Indian burial ground. Some Cheyenne leader called White Buffalo is raising Cain about it. He's already killed a couple of our graders. A Lieutenant Tracer has taken some soldiers out there, and the scouts are going to try to talk to the Cheyenne first, see if we can come to some kind of compromise, but we don't expect to get any concessions. I'm afraid a real battle lies ahead." A sick feeling moved into her stomach at the thought of Colt being in the middle of that battle. Maybe she should have insisted he come back with her after all, but then Vince would have been here. She would rather Colt faced the Indians.

"Do you have good scouts?" he asked. "They know their business?"

She watched those searching blue eyes that had always frightened her so when she was younger. This time he looked at her as he had years ago when he had made the remark about who she slept with. She could see it in that damn smug look of his. He knew about Colt! But how? "Excellent," she answered. "One of them is very experienced with the Cheyenne."

"Mmmm-hmmm." He puffed the pipe a moment longer. "Well, I came out here to tell you you've won. I'm interested in investing some of my personal money in U.P. stock. This thing with Harrison Steel has really paid off. You made a smart move there, Sunny. You're quite a businesswoman after all, and Landers Enterprises is doing better than ever."

She breathed a sigh of relief, but his face was still a

little flushed, as though he were angry about something. "Well," she said, setting the coffee cup aside and leaning back in her chair. "I guess I should say thank you, but then, after all the other things that have happened between us, it's a little difficult to thank you for anything. Is Eve with you?"

He snickered. "You kidding? She thinks of Omaha as nothing but a cow town. She won't step foot out here. She *is* looking forward to you and Blaine returning for the wedding though. That's another reason I came. I've never gotten to know Blaine too well, considering he's had to kind of take sides between you and me. But we have a lot in common, I think. I'd like to get to know him better, travel back to Chicago with you and him. Since we're going to be brothers-in-law, I guess we ought to get some kind of rapport going between us. I figured that would make you happy."

Sunny tingled all over with dread. How she wished he had at least waited until morning for this. Telling Vince she wasn't marrying Blaine would be harder than telling Blaine himself. She felt herself shaking a little. It was easy for her to stand up to Vince when it came to business, but this was different. She knew good and well how he would treat Colt if she went through with this, and it pained her to think of it, let alone the tirade he was going to throw over the whole dilemma.

She rose, walking over to close the parlor doors, then turned to face him. "I'm not marrying Blaine," she told him. "I've changed my mind."

She stepped a little closer, wishing she could read those eyes that she hated. He sat a little straighter, his big frame overpowering even when he was sitting. He was looking more and more like his father, his heavy thighs filling out the pants of his silk suit, his stomach beginning to bulge, his hair thinning a little now and showing a trace of white at the temples. The only thing different was that Vince did not look at her with dancing, loving blue eyes like Bo Landers had looked at her. Vince's eyes were like slices of ice, and their coldness moved through her blood, making her shiver.

He took the pipe from his mouth and set it in an

ashtray, then rubbed his hands together as though trying to control himself, his face getting even redder. "It's that blood-sucking, renegade half-breed, isn't it?" he snarled. He looked her over as though she were a whore. "I know all about it, Sunny! I came out here in a great mood, ready to give in and admit that everything you've done has been right, ready to wish you and Blaine my best! And what happens?" He rose, stepping closer and towering over her. "I find you gone, and when I wire the work camp, I'm told you aren't there—that you're out riding, *alone* with Colt Travis! What in God's name are you *doing,* Sunny! Now you come back saying you aren't marrying Blaine? I wired this morning and learned you had left *yesterday!* You stayed out there all night with that goddamn worthless *Indian!* Did he *fuck* you, Sunny? Were you his *whore?"*

Her eyes widened, and she felt almost faint at the way he had put it. Without taking a moment to think, she slapped him hard. He instantly grabbed her wrist, squeezing it so tightly that it hurt. She felt the tears coming then, but she fought not to cry openly, the tears more from her terrible anger at his opinion of Colt than what he had called her. "I *love* Colt," she answered boldly, her teeth gritted. One tear slipped down her cheek. "And Colt loves me! If I was worth five cents, he would *still* love me! But that's something you would never understand, because *your* first love has always been *money!"*

"And you honestly believe Colt Travis isn't thinking in dollar signs? For God's sake, Sunny, how can you be so smart about business and so goddamn stupid about *men!"* He gave her a light shove. "You're more like your mother than I thought!"

She shivered, blinking back tears and rubbing her wrist. Her mother! What did he mean? *Colt,* she groaned inwardly. *How I wish you were here after all.* She wiped a tear with a shaking hand. "I'm twenty-five years old, Vince! I have a right to marry whomever I please—and marry for love! All my life I've tried to live up to everyone else's expectations of me! And why should I even *care* what *you* think! You've always hated me! Why, Vince? What did you mean about my mother!"

He sighed deeply, rubbing his eyes. "Damn you, Sunny. I thought if you married Blaine, none of it would matter." He whirled. "Did you sleep with Colt Travis?"

"That's my business."

He waved her off, his teeth gritted. "I can tell just by the *look* of you," he snarled. "All this time you've behaved like such a lady, saved yourself for Blaine! I was a little worried the night that half-breed interrupted your dinner party, but thank God he left right away. I thought he was out of your life for good this time! When in hell did you hire him for the railroad?"

"I didn't even know he worked for the U.P. until last fall when I went out to the camp and he helped protect me and Stuart from an Indian raid!"

"*Stuart* knows about this?"

She closed her eyes and turned away. "No. He knows only that Colt is a U.P. scout. He doesn't know I went out there just to see him. This was the first time I saw him after the Indian raid last summer. It was my first time out after those horrible winter snows."

"And after all those months you rode out there and lifted your skirts for the man? God, Sunny, as common as he is, even *he* must think you're easy! The man is probably laughing right now over the fact that he fucked Sunny Landers, the richest woman in the country!"

"Stop it!" she screamed. She whirled. "You don't know anything about it! We've loved each other for ten years, Vince. Ten *years!* We've been friends all that time. It wasn't just a sudden thing. It was beautiful. Colt loves me, and I'm going to *marry* him! If you're so worried about the money, I'll have him sign an agreement that he can't touch any of it if something happens to me. He'll *gladly* sign it, because he doesn't *care* about that! Why can't you understand that? Why can't you let me be happy? Why do you have to make it sound so ugly when it was so beautiful and right?"

She couldn't help the tears. She covered her face and wept, sinking into a chair. She heard Vince pacing, felt him come to stand near her.

"You want to know why? I'll *tell* you why!" He grasped her wrists, wrenching her hands away from her face. "It's because I don't intend any more shame to come into this family! It's because you're the only one who can prove to the world that your mother was a good woman—by being an honorable woman yourself! It isn't you I hate, Sunny; it's what you *represent!* I truly do care about you, and that's why how you conduct yourself and whom you marry means everything when it comes to what *others* think of *you!*"

Her shoulders shook with her sobs, tears streaming down her face. "I don't understand," she said, shaking her head. "What in God's name are you talking about, Vince?"

For the first time in her life she saw a flash of true concern in his eyes. "I'm not the bad guy you think I am, Sunny. *I* have feelings and pride too, *family* pride! And because you're *part* of this family, I care about the decisions you make. Do you want to know why I was so angry when you inherited so much? It wasn't you personally, Sunny. It was the fact that you were *her* daughter! If your mother had been an honorable woman, I could have accepted Father putting her on such a pedestal! But she *wasn't* honorable, Sunny. She was a *prostitute,* one of the most beautiful, highest paid prostitutes in New York City—the kind who cater only to the *wealthy!*"

She wondered if she might faint. She could feel the blood draining from her face. She stared at him a moment, a thousand thoughts converging at once in her mind. "You're lying," she whispered.

He let go of her wrists, straightening and running a hand through his hair. "I wish to hell I were." He almost groaned. He walked over to the hearth. "Stuart and I resented her when Father brought her home—I guess because we were young enough that we hated anyone who Father thought could take our real mother's place. Your mother was . . . truly beautiful. There's no argument about that. She was young and always smiling. Father really did love her. But he *paid* for her, Sunny! She was the daughter of a prostitute he used to visit when he went to New York."

"My God." Sunny covered her face again.

Vince sighed deeply. "Now you know Father wasn't the saint you thought he was. Stuart and I found out when we got a little older. Father was always a little evasive about Lucille's background, so we hired an investigator behind his back, did some checking. When we found out the truth, we couldn't help hating her. Her mother had already sold her to men—actually groomed her for what she was to be. When Father bought her, she was still pretty 'fresh,' you might say. He fell head over heels for her, paid thousands for her, told her if she'd marry him and never see other men, she'd live the life of a queen. She kept her promise. The few friends of Father's who knew about it were warned to keep their mouths shut or suffer the consequences. They knew Father could ruin them in an instant, and that he'd do it. In fact he *did* underhandedly bankrupt a couple of them for spreading rumors about Lucille that Father quickly put down, saying they were false. Most people believed Lucille was the sweet, pure thing that Father passed her off to be, because she was the prettiest thing who had ever graced Chicago, and the sweetest. It would have been hard for *anyone* to believe what she had been. My God, you're just like her, beautiful and sweet. Now you've let yourself be just like her in another way—the way I feared most. Like mother, like *daughter!*"

Sunny cringed at the words. She shook her head. "It's not the same," she sobbed. "Colt and I love each other. Blaine has never touched me. Colt is the only man who ever has." She gasped in a sob and faced him, rising. "I'm *not* a whore, Vince! How in God's name can you say that about me! I'm not like her!"

"Aren't you? What did you let Colt Travis do to you? How *willing* were you? You aren't even *married* to the man! And you were wearing Blaine's engagement ring, for Christ's sake!"

She turned away, stumbling back to a chair, feeling ill. Was he right? What did she really know about men? Was Colt thinking of her that way? Was what she had done that ugly and sinful? It had seemed so beautiful, so right. He loved her, didn't he? Yet even if what they had done was right because of that love, what would he think of her if he knew about her mother? Would he ever trust her again? Would he look at her and see a whore? She could not bear for Colt Travis to look at her with eyes like that, to have him be ashamed of her. Suddenly, it wasn't that Colt was not good enough for her— it was *she* who was not good enough for *him*.

She sank back into a chair. "Did Father . . . really love me?"

Vince jammed his hands into his pockets, walking to a window to look out at the lights of Omaha. "He worshipped you. He would never have wanted you to know. We confronted him with it, and he threatened us with full disinheritance if we ever said anything about it, especially to you. After a while people never said a word about it. Your mother was dead, and you were sweet and beautiful and innocent, a child who won people over with just a smile. You looked just like Lucille, and you were the be-all and end-all to Father."

He turned to face her, but she kept her hands over her face. "Now maybe you understand the hard feelings between us and Father," he told her. "And you understand why it's so important, Sunny, that you do everything in your power to bring honor to this family and put an end once and for all to some of the ugly rumors that are still whispered. The few who know are waiting for you to make a wrong move, eagerly looking for a hint of your mother in your blood. Can you imagine what they'll think if you bring that half-breed home? It's bad enough, him being a worthless Indian. Add to that what some of them know about your mother, and they'll think you chose him because he's wild and wicked. They'll think that when it comes to men you'll sleep with *anything*. Why in hell do you think Stuart and I were so happy you finally got engaged to Blaine? You couldn't have picked better. He might even end up governor of New York. He's wealthy, educated, well-mannered, a man of the world. Marry Blaine, Sunny, and save your reputation. It will help salvage people's memory of your mother. After all, she did treat Father well and was true to him. You can make up for all the shame, Sunny. And I think you owe it to me and Stuart. We didn't intend to ever tell you, but when I found out where you'd gone, and then you told me you weren't marrying Blaine, I knew I had no choice. Stuart doesn't know what I'm doing. This is between you and me. I like you, Sunny. I always have. For God's sake, my blood runs in your veins. I want only what's best for you. If that means putting an end to this Colt Travis thing and you hating me again, then I'll do it. Give it up! I don't want any more shame in this family or any more hideous gossip. Can't you imagine the headlines in the society pages if you tell the world you're marrying a half-breed scout who's worth no more than a month's railroad pay? Give it up, or I'll make sure there *is* no Colt Travis!"

Sunny felt her blood going cold. She raised her eyes to look at him. "What do you mean?"

His jaw was set rigid, a determined look in his eyes. "I mean that I'll do whatever it takes to make sure you do the honorable thing. Colt Travis is out there facing a lot of danger. One stray bullet, and he's dead. I'm sure I can find someone among all those itinerant railroad workers who would take a few thousand dollars to knock off a man whom no one would miss. With all the trouble out there, it would be easy to blame it on the Indians."

She slowly rose, shaking. "You wouldn't!"

He held her eyes firmly. "You'd better believe I *would!* Some men will take money for anything, Sunny. You know that firsthand. Take my advice and marry Blaine. Give up this thing with Colt Travis. I won't say anything to Blaine. He'll never know. Hell, it won't be so bad. He's a handsome, obliging man. He certainly isn't the type to be cruel in bed. In no time at all you'll forget Colt Travis, especially once you have a couple of kids. As far as Travis, what's he going to do about it? *You're* the one with the money and the power. You can shut him up plenty fast if you need to. But then, I imagine he won't do anything anyway. He'll figure you used him for a fling and gave him a damn good time for a day or two. A man like him should marry some common farmer's daughter, or maybe an Indian woman. He's not made for the likes of you, and you know it. And face it, Sunny. Even if you did marry him, the people in your circle would cut him down so fast he wouldn't know what hit him. He'd never survive. He'd end up hating you and everything you stand for. Without even trying, you'd *destroy* him. Is that what you want?"

She turned away, grasping the arms of a chair to keep from falling. All her fantasies about her mother and father were shattered, along with her own pride. She sank back into the chair. "Get out," she told Vince, her voice low and firm. "I've never hated anyone as much as I hate you at this moment. Get out, and don't ever step foot in this house again."

He let out a deep sigh. "Sunny, in time you'll know I told you for your own good. You'll realize I care about you. I didn't want to do this. For God's sake, you must know that, or I would have said something a long time ago, or when I sued you over the will. There are a hundred different times I could have told you, but I didn't."

"And Stuart knows too, then."

"Yes."

"What about Vi, and Eve?"

"No. We've never told our wives."

Sunny rubbed her forehead. Now she understood some of the looks she would get at times from certain of her father's business associates. They had all been waiting, mouths watering, waiting for her to prove she was like her mother. So many things were clearer now.

Colt! How could she bring him into her life! She already knew it would have been hard for him, but she never realized it would be this bad. Vince would surely tell him about her mother. After what she had let him do to her, he would lose his respect for her, think she was just a harlot at heart. But she would never get the chance to even know that. If she continued to see Colt, Vince would have him killed. Just knowing he existed, even if she could not have him, was better than Colt Travis being dead. She had no doubt whatsoever that Vince would hold true to his threat. She could never live knowing she was responsible for Colt suffering pain and death.

Still, even alive he would be dead to her now. Her precious, beautiful, gentle, loving Colt. He could not hold her again, touch her again, be one with her again. She would never know the glory and ecstasy of belonging only to him. She would never again ride free and happy in the prairie sun with Colt at her side, the wind in her hair, joy in her heart.

"Just leave," she told Vince.

"What are you going to do?"

She looked up at him, a new coldness in her eyes, a hatred Vince never thought she was capable of showing. "You leave me little choice. I'll marry Blaine, but I won't do it for you." She rose again, facing him boldly. "I won't even do it to save Colt's life, although you know I don't want him to die. I'm doing it for my mother."

He frowned in surprise. "Your *mother!*"

She swallowed at the pain in her throat. "I knew Father better than you or Stuart or anyone else. I don't care what you say about her. Father loved her, and I believe she loved him, even if he *did* buy her! I know by the way Father talked about her, and by how fiercely he apparently tried to protect her! If he visited her mother on his trips to New York, it was because he was lonely after *your* mother died. He was just a man like any other. He fell in love with Lucille, and I imagine her mother, horrible person as she must have been, was the one who *made* him pay for her."

She rose, looking up at him with a tear-stained face. "I'll marry Blaine to put a stop once and for all to the rumors about my mother. I'll show the world what an honorable daughter she and Bo Landers had. I'll give up Colt, not because he means little to me, but because he means *everything* to me! He's the only man I'll ever truly love, Vince, and no matter what you say, I *know* he loves *me* more than Blaine could ever *hope* to love me. Colt Travis is more man than Blaine will ever be, and certainly more man than *you!* You're a man without a heart, Vince Landers, and apparently a man capable of cold-blooded murder! If you hire someone to kill Colt, his blood would be as much on your hands as the man who pulls the trigger!"

He closed his eyes and sighed. "Sunny, I didn't want it to be this way. I did everything I could to stop it. And I never, never wanted to have to tell you. Dammit, Sunny, I truly do admire you. I'm only trying to protect you. Can't you see that?"

She shook her head. "I don't want to hear your excuses, Vince. If you weren't so arrogant and hateful of people you think are beneath you, we might have been able to work this out."

"It's what *other* people would have thought, not me, Sunny. It isn't just me Colt Travis would have to face and prove himself to. You remember that night he showed up at your dinner? Remember how some of those people looked at him? Surely you knew what they were whispering. Now you know why I was so upset by the way you took his hand and dragged him around. God only knows what some of them were thinking."

She turned away. "Just please go away before I scream. I can't bear to look at you or hear your voice a moment longer. Get out of my house and find a hotel for the night." She heard a deep sigh, footsteps. The parlor door slid open and was closed again, and the room was silent, except for the light crackle of a small fire in the hearth. Sunny went to her knees, wondering how such joy and ecstasy could so quickly change to such horror and despair.

"Colt, Colt, Colt!" she wept, bending her head to the floor. How could she live without him now, yet how could she risk losing him to death, or risk him finding out about her mother? Was Vince right about what Colt would think of her? What did she know about men? The only kind of prostitutes a man like Colt might have experience with were the slutty whores of the railroad camp towns. She could never bear to have Colt look at her and see one of them. Neither could she bear to see his free nature and sensitive pride destroyed by her world; or to see him physically destroyed by someone Vince might hire to kill him.

Colt Travis had belonged to her for two magical, wondrous days, and now she must set him free again. She would have to find a way to let him know that her decision was *because* she loved him so. She would have to find a way to convince him she was doing the right thing. He would surely end up hating her, but she could bear his hate and anger more than she could bear the thought of Colt being the one to scorn her and turn her away because of her mother; and she could bear his hate more than the thought of visiting Colt Travis's grave.

She got to her feet, deciding she had to be very strong, stronger than she had ever been in her life, even when facing down Vince or taking on the duties of her inheritance. She should never have invited Colt into her world, should never have allowed their love to blossom, should never have gone out to see him and build his hopes. He was too good and fine a man, proud and sensitive, worth so much more than the men in her world who boasted millions in the bank but were so lacking in matters of the heart. If she put an end to their affair immediately, most of the fine man that he was could be salvaged, and he would not be involved in ugly rumors or in scathing newspaper stories.

She would have to end it quickly. She would wire Blaine to wait for her in Chicago, and she would go there in the morning. She would tell him she wanted the wedding date moved closer, get married before the Indian problem was over and before Colt had a chance to discover what was happening and try to come to her. He would think nothing of not hearing from her for a couple of weeks. By then she would be Mrs. Blaine O'Brien.

She shuddered, grasping at the hot pain in her stomach.

Chapter 25

Colt approached the waiting band of Indians. It had taken him two full days to ride out here, and as he came closer to the area of the burial ground he saw a large circle of tipis, recognizing it not as a normal settlement of families with the men perhaps on a buffalo hunt, but rather the kind of village quickly set up by the few women who accompany and care for warriors ready to do battle. As soon as he got close, a line of at least thirty Indians formed. He knew he had been spotted much sooner by scouts, realized they could have already killed him if they chose, which was why he had tied a white shirt on the end of his rifle and held it up as a truce flag before coming any nearer. He could only hope they would honor the sign of peace.

Much as he wanted to, he couldn't think about Sunny now. He had to stay alert, for in spite of once living

among these people, they were not the friendly, accom-
modating Cheyenne he had left six years before. He
noticed they had camped just to the east of the burial
ground, which he could see in the distance now, looking
ghostly and foreboding in a morning mist.

He urged Dancer cautiously closer, eyeing the apparent spokesman for the warriors, who rode out ahead of
the others. Colt guessed him to be about his same age,
and by the time he got within a few yards of the man, he
recognized the face. He halted Dancer. "White Buffalo," he called out in the Cheyenne tongue. He made
the sign for friendship. "If you don't recognize me, you
must remember the horse I am riding. It was a gift from
you."

White Buffalo stared at him a moment, then rode
closer, his dark eyes losing some of their malice. "Colt
Travis, my old friend."

Neither man smiled a full smile, each suspecting that
after this conversation the friendship would be over,
neither wanting it to have to be that way.

"Yes, I *am* still your friend, White Buffalo. I looked
for you once, but you are not easy to find. I have
thought about you often over the years."

White Buffalo nodded. "And I have thought of you.
Come and smoke with me. We will talk."

"I'm here on behalf of the railroad, White Buffalo."

The man nodded, a sad look in his eyes. "I thought
so." He turned his horse. "Come."

Colt followed him into camp, edgy at the looks on the
faces of the rest of the warriors, most of them young,
and eager for a fight. They reached a tipi with many
buffalo painted on it, and White Buffalo indicated Colt
should dismount and come inside. Colt obeyed, and a
young Indian boy took hold of his horse for him.

"He is my nephew," White Buffalo told him. "Small
Horse is fourteen, and my brother said he could come
with us for the fight. I am teaching him the warrior
ways. This dwelling belongs to my brother and his wife. I
live with them."

They went inside, and old, familiar memories returned for Colt. He thought how much more he liked

something like this than hotel rooms. The memory of Sunny's mansion in Chicago flashed through his mind, how he had felt so suffocated in that huge, high-ceilinged room with a table so long one could hardly see from one end to the other. Yet in this simple tipi he felt free and alive.

White Buffalo offered him a place to sit, and Colt obeyed, careful not to walk between the fire and another person, something that was not done. White Buffalo introduced him to his brother, Two Teeth, and his wife, Blue Bird Woman. "You did not know them when you lived with me and Sits Tall, because at that time they stayed with the Southern Cheyenne on the little bit of land the Great White Father gave us down near old Bent's Fort," White Buffalo said. "Since then your government has moved the Southern Cheyenne clear back to that hot and worthless place they call Indian Territory. Most of us will not go there. We stay to the north now, join the Sioux."

White Buffalo's anger and agony were evident in his voice and his eyes. Colt waited quietly while the man lit his prayer pipe, offering it to the sky, the earth, the four directions. He took a puff, then handed it over to Colt. "Do you still carry the pipe that I gave you in friendship?"

Colt nodded. "I've been through a lot since then, but I still have it. I even have those scalps." He took the pipe, offering it himself to the God of heaven and earth, and to the four directions. He sucked on it a moment, then handed it to Two Teeth, who did the same as the first two men. He handed it to White Buffalo, who smoked it again, then lowered the pipe, watching Colt carefully. "I still carry the watch, but it stopped ticking long ago. Do you think that means something?"

Their eyes held in mutual sorrow. "I hope it doesn't mean the end of our friendship," Colt told him.

White Buffalo smiled sadly. "Sits Tall was killed at Sand Creek, along with our baby son and my father, Many Beaver, as well as the old medicine man, Dancing Otter and many others that you knew when you lived among us. *Zetapetaz-hetan,* the squaw killer, Chivington, showed us that day how the white man treats even peaceful Indians. So we no longer try to be peaceful. We do what we must do."

Colt closed his eyes. "I'm sorry, White Buffalo. You know that I understand how it feels to lose a wife and child." He met White Buffalo's eyes again. "You told me once that time can heal many things."

"*Ai.* But now *I* better understand your hatred for the Pawnee. Now *my* hatred is also great, not for the Pawnee, but for the *ve-ho-e.* I do not think time will heal these wounds, because the white man keeps opening them again. It is not just because of Sand Creek that my hatred will not go away, but for everything else. They are taking it all away, Colt—the land, the buffalo, our freedom. We can no longer live as we once lived, and some of our people on the reservations die of nothing more than broken hearts. Now comes the railroad, the great iron horse with its belly on fire, its black smoke darkening the sky, its noise chasing away the game. We try to stop it, but we know we cannot." He looked at Colt pleadingly. "Now all we ask is that it does not go through our sacred burial ground. It would be so easy for the powerful people who build this thing to send it around, far from this place that is beloved to my people. Have you come here to tell me they will think about doing this?"

Colt felt almost sick at being so torn. He removed his hat and ran a hand through his hair. "I wish they would, White Buffalo, just as much as you do. But in their world their way of thinking tells them that to lay that many extra miles of track would be too costly and take too much extra time. There is only one of them who would agree to go around, but it is a matter of votes of all those in charge. The rest have voted to go through. I am here only to warn you that many soldiers are coming. You have a chance to leave now, White Buffalo, peacefully."

White Buffalo shook his head. "If I did not fight for this, fight to protect the spirits of the loved ones who have gone before us, I would not be worthy to live. So if I am killed in this fight, it will be a much more honorable death than if I walk away from here and die an old man who remembers he was a coward and did not stand up for his people and their sacred lands."

Colt nodded. "The last time we parted, we were friends. You said then that it was best that I go while there were still good feelings between us. I wish it were not you here defending this burial ground. It would make it easier for me to do what I have to do."

White Buffalo handed him the pipe again. "Let us share one more smoke together then. You are still my friend, Colt Travis, but if I see you on the battlefield, I will have to kill you, as you will have to try to do to me."

A strange ache moved through Colt's shoulders and chest. He puffed the pipe and handed it to Two Teeth, who only sat listening. "I think the railroad is wrong in this, White Buffalo," he told the man. "I am totally against it. I respect the sacredness of your burial ground. I am only telling you that there are powers at hand here that all the fighting and bloodshed in the world won't stop."

He thought of Sunny again, how some of the decisions she made could affect hundreds of people, sometimes thousands—a go-ahead on this, a price on that, a bribe here to change a law, one there to take over a company. He told himself to stop thinking of her that way, to stop comparing their lives. His Sunny was the sweet, vulnerable, giving woman whose body he had shared on the prairie under the sun and stars. They had decided they could make their love work, and he was not going to let anything get in the way.

"I'm just trying to spare you, White Buffalo, you and many others. Why don't you let me talk to the railroad people. I'm sure they'd be willing to let you move some of the graves—"

"No! Do not even suggest it! You know the bones of dead ones must never be disturbed, or their spirits will never rest again! If we fight hard enough, the Great White Father will take notice. Maybe *he* will tell the railroad people they cannot do this!"

Colt rubbed his eyes, wishing he could hit something in his frustration. "White Buffalo, the Great White Father *wants* this railroad, as much or more than the people building it! He's not going to do one thing to slow it up. He'll go along with anything they decide to do, and they have already decided to go through."

White Buffalo stiffened and slowly nodded. "Then you should not be here, my friend. You should be back there with the soldiers who are coming."

Colt's jaw flexed in a sudden urge to weep. "I'm going to have to try to stay out of this one, White Buffalo. I can't bring myself to fight you. You saved my life once, gave me reason to live again. I'm sorry about all of it, sorry we have to meet like this after all these years. Under other circumstances, I would stay, and we could have a good, long talk."

"Yes, my friend, I would have liked that." White Buffalo took the pipe from his brother and raised it. "It is done now. Go back to your white world, Colt Travis. I think perhaps we will not see each other again."

Colt's misty eyes betrayed his feelings. "In another time, another place, we could have shared so much," he told the warrior.

White Buffalo looked away from him. "Go," he said softly.

Colt hesitated a moment longer, then rose and exited the tipi, realizing each extra moment he stayed could mean his life. He climbed onto Dancer, suddenly feeling weary and burdened. Part of him belonged here, maybe not with the Cheyenne, but with the Indian spirit. If not for certain decisions his father had made, he would still be living in Indian Territory among the Cherokee. Now here he was working for the Union Pacific, in love with a beautiful, rich white woman, yet his skin and his spirit were so close to these very people who were struggling to cling to what was left of their once-vast domain. Did he really belong in Sunny Landers's life, or did he belong with the Cherokee? Maybe he belonged with neither.

He headed Dancer slowly through the village, not sure if he would be allowed to leave without an arrow in his back. He hated the thought of what was to come, felt sad that he could not have spent more time with White Buffalo.

He rode a little harder as he got farther away, and it struck him that in a way he was saying a final good-bye to the Indian in him. Maybe it was supposed to be this way, slowly leaving behind the old, learning to change a little, just enough to make things work with Sunny. For ten years life had been leading him toward her, teaching him how to let go of things and move on. He could not imagine life now without her in it, no matter what the cost, and it was difficult to think of anything except seeing her again.

Still, for now he didn't have much choice. Lieutenant Tracer and his men would arrive anytime now to rout out White Buffalo and his people. The thought brought a tight feeling to his gut. He didn't want any part of this if he could possibly stay out of it.

The train rumbled through the dark, heading for Chicago. Sunny thought how the mournful sound of its whistle sounded on the night winds, reflecting the black mourning in her heart. Every mile the train covered was another mile farther away from Colt, from the Nebraska plains, from the only real happiness she had known. She had contemplated writing Colt a letter of explanation, something that sounded logical, something that would let him know her decision had nothing to do with how much she loved him; but she was afraid that to write him too soon and let him know what she was doing would bring him running, and she didn't want that to happen. It was best he didn't know at all until it was done and there would be no changing it. Maybe then she would write the letter.

It seemed so cruel to do it this way, knowing he was waiting for her to come back. He would find out through the newspapers or gossip at the work camp. How would he react when he read about the wedding of Sunny Landers and Blaine O'Brien? Each time she thought of it, the horrible black pain engulfed her, and she felt as though someone had died. In a way someone *had* died—a part of herself—the Sunny Landers who belonged to the wild land, and to Colt Travis.

Perhaps she had been a fool after all to think that she could share her life with Colt. If only she had never allowed it all to happen. Before it had been a fantasy she thought could never be real; but the reality had turned out to be so much more glorious and fulfilling than the fantasy. Colt had awakened things in her she did not know existed, but now they must be put to sleep again. Vince had made it all ugly and wrong. Now another man would touch her, but she would never belong to him, never feel the wanton desire and delightful ecstasy she had shared with Colt.

It seemed that someone with her money and power should be so free, free to do as she wished, love whoever she wanted to love. But her wealth had become her prison. The truth about her mother and father was the key that locked the door, and Vincent stood guard. Colt was the one who was free, and he had nothing at all— nothing but his pride, his sureness, his goodness, his love of the land and the animals. He didn't need any more than that.

The door to her private car opened, and Blaine came inside. He had arrived the morning after Sunny's argument with Vince, wanting to surprise her by arriving sooner than expected. Sunny had hardly had time to recover from the ugly things Vince had told her, or time to contemplate how she would bear leaving Colt forever. Blaine had spent a day going over the Indian problem with Canary and the others, after which he and Sunny, Vince, Stuart, and Vi had left for Chicago.

Blaine was overjoyed that Sunny wanted to move the wedding date closer. He couldn't wait to get back to Chicago and get things in motion. He had attached his own private car to her train, and Vince had done the same. They were all going back together, Vince riding with Blaine while Stuart and Vi and their children used Vince's car. Others were left in charge of the Omaha offices, and Vi had taken leave from her work for the new hospital, so they all could go back together for the grand wedding.

"Hello, darling," Blaine said, beaming. He walked over to pour himself a drink from a bottle of brandy that had been left on a nearby table from a small party they had shared earlier. Sunny shivered at the happy look on his face. Her life had become a maze of lies and make-believe now. She never wanted Colt or Blaine to know about her mother, or anyone else who didn't already know. She would have to lie to Colt about why she was marrying Blaine, to keep him from all the cruel gossip, and to make sure he wasn't killed. She had to lie to Blaine about loving him, pretend that she was happy. She had even lied to Vi about why she had made her decision, telling the woman that Colt had changed and had a new love interest and had gently told her that the old feelings he once had for her were gone. She suspected Vi didn't believe a word of it.

No one knew about her conversation with Vince, and they never would. As long as she never had to look into Colt's eyes again, she knew she could keep it all to herself. Colt was the only one who might be able to force it out of her; but even if he did, she didn't like to think of the look that she'd see on his face when she told him what her mother had been. She would rather he hated her than for him to look at her that way.

And hate me he will, she thought. The thought brought the sick pain back to her stomach with such force that she grasped it with her hand.

"Sunny! Are you sick? I swear you haven't acted right ever since I arrived." Blaine swallowed the brandy and came over to kneel in front of her. "This should be the happiest time of your life, but you certainly haven't acted like it. You smile, but I see no joy in your eyes." He grasped her hands. "Don't tell me you're having second thoughts again." His eyes turned to pleading. "Don't make me wait any longer, Sunny. For months I've thought of nothing but coming back here to marry you. Things are going well in the campaign, and when we get to New York, you can redecorate that big castle of a home I rattle around in any way you want." He squeezed her hands. "God, it's going to be nice to have you there and have you put a woman's touch to it." He leaned up and kissed her cheek. "What's wrong, Sunny? Have you been ill?"

Oh, how she wished she could love him; but she knew that she never had. He would never bring out the passion in her that Colt had. "A little," she answered. There. Another lie. "I'm just worried about that Indian trouble out at the construction site. I don't feel right leaving before finding out what's going to happen." *What if Colt gets hurt and I'm not there for him!*

Blaine just grinned. "Sunny, you're just one of many. For heaven's sake, Canary and his men are there, and if there's any more trouble, Durant himself will go out. They all know we can't be concerned with all that right now. Besides, there are soldiers out there and plenty of men. The thing will get settled and by the time we're back from Europe, the U.P. will be well into Wyoming. Next year will be the elections, and the year after that we'll take a train all the way to Utah for the joining of the rails. That's where they expect to meet, if Strobridge and his boys can get moving. I guess they had a devil of a time up in those mountains last winter."

He rose, keeping hold of her hands and pulling her up with him. "Sunny, relax and enjoy! Women are going to read about you and wish they were as beautiful, wish they led the life of a princess like you do, that they could have as grand a wedding. And it will get better once we're married. Just wait until you see Europe, the castles, the great cathedrals. You'll love France. I can't wait for you to meet my mother and sister! And Africa—the elephants and giraffes and all sorts of wild things. So much of Africa reminds me of the West, only bigger and more beautiful." He pulled her into his arms. "You'll love it, Sunny. You'll have the time of your life!"

She rested against him, praying that somehow she could let him consummate their marriage and make him think she was enjoying it. Perhaps Africa was bigger and more beautiful than the American West, but she doubted it would lift her heart to see it. It would only remind her of Colt. She would see him there, riding free.

"You *do* love me, don't you, Blaine?" She looked up at him. "I need you to love me, to be kind, patient."

"Of *course* I love you. What kind of a question is that?" He smiled, bending down to meet her lips, parting them gently with his tongue. How she wanted the kiss to be sweet and wonderful and stimulating the way Colt's kisses were. But she felt nothing. She could only pretend. She told herself that once they were married, once she had made vows to him and allowed him his husbandly privileges, it would change, especially once they were in Europe. There she would be so far away from the Sunny she had left back on the prairie, the Sunny who had lost a stocking out there . . . had lost so much more than that. Out there she had become a woman. No matter what she did now, that could not be changed. She would forever belong to someone else, in spite of her vows. She was expected to play a certain role, and she would do it, not to protect herself anymore, but to protect the man she truly loved, and to protect what little honor was left to her parents' memory.

Blaine kissed her neck, deciding her hesitancy was just a fear of the unknown. He would make a woman of her soon enough, and their marriage would be splattered all over the front pages of the New York newspapers—great campaign publicity. He thought how it was too bad about little Elsie Brown, the young girl who did his laundering and mending. He had caught her looks, knew she had been totally enamored with him; and during his long months apart from Sunny he had had a delightful affair with her. He wondered if the girl actually thought he might marry her. How stupid of her to let herself get pregnant. He had shipped her off to a special home in New England for wayward girls, with strict orders that the baby be taken from her once it was born and put in an orphanage so she couldn't come running back with it claiming it was his. Besides, how did he know that it was? Girls of her class usually went down for just about any man who smiled at them and had two dollars in his pocket. She had been a pleasant release for his needs while he campaigned and waited for his marriage to Sunny. Now, at last, the famous Sunny Landers would belong to him! He didn't doubt he would win votes just as much because of her as for himself.

"I'd better get out of here before I'm tempted to carry you back to your private bedroom," he told her. He pressed her close and whirled her around before setting her on her feet just as Vi opened the door to come inside. The woman looked embarrassed and started to leave. "No, it's all right," Blaine told her. He looked at Sunny. "I was just leaving." He leaned down and kissed her again. "We'll be in Chicago by morning."

She managed a smile and nodded. "I'll see you in the morning, then."

He gave her a wink and left, and Vi closed the door, then turned to face Sunny, who turned away.

"What are you doing, Sunny? I tried to talk to you once when you first got back, but you fed me a line of garbage. I want the truth. What happened with you and Colt? I know you love him and he loves you, and I say there is no reason why you can't be together. Why are you going ahead with this marriage?"

"I told you. Colt has found someone else, and he said he didn't think it could work anyway. The more I thought about it, the more I was convinced he was right. We can't recapture what we felt years ago, Vi. We've both grown and changed. I belong with someone like Blaine. It's that simple."

"I don't think it is. I think I should write to Colt—"

"No!" Sunny whirled. "I've never been angry with you, Vi, but I will be if you dare to interfere in this! I'll be married and on my way to Europe soon, and I don't want you doing something that will bring Colt running, do you hear?"

"Bring him running? I thought you said you and he agreed this was the way it should be—that he had found someone else."

Sunny's eyes teared. "Help me do this, Vi. Please! If you never do another thing for me, leave this alone.

Believe me, it's for Colt's sake. It's for *everyone's* sake! Just leave it alone! I'm begging you." She shivered, and a tear ran down her cheek. "You've got to trust me on this, Vi. Please, please don't contact Colt. I'll write him myself, after the wedding."

Vi shook her head. "I don't know what's happened, but I *do* know that you and Colt didn't just shake hands and say good-bye out there. When I heard you had gone out alone, I had a pretty good idea why. Now you're marrying Blaine, and I don't see any happiness in your eyes. Does Vince have something to do with this? It seems awfully strange, him being in Omaha when you got back and all."

"It doesn't matter, Vi. I've made my decision. It's better that one or two people get hurt than a whole lot of people." *I can't let the ugly rumor get to your children about their grandfather,* she thought. *And I can't let Colt be murdered, not my precious Colt.* "Blaine and I have been friends for a long time. He'll be good to me. Please just be here for me when I get back and don't make all of this more difficult than it already is. That's what you'll be doing if you get involved."

Vi breathed deeply with pity. "I think you're wrong, but I suppose it's your decision, Sunny. You know I'm here when you need me."

Sunny reached out and embraced her, clinging tightly to the woman and again longing to have had a real mother when she was growing up. What kind of mother would Lucille Madison have been? All she had had to cling to until now was the thought that she was a beautiful, pure, loving woman who would have been a wonderful mother if she had not died. She had at least been proud of the memory. Now she did not even have that.

Colt watched the intense fighting from a distance, torn between duty to the railroad and the army to which he had once belonged, and loyalty to his own race. In other skirmishes with Indians he had had no problem defending himself and the railroad, but this time White Buffalo

was involved. This time it was more personal. The man
had saved his life.

Still, to remain uninvolved was not easy. Men were
being killed in that valley between rocky bluffs, the
haunting burial ground just beyond them. It seemed
strangely symbolic. Dust rolled, the sound of gunfire
filled the air, horses whinnied. Part of him wanted to go
and defend Sunny's railroad, fight alongside soldiers as
he had in the war. Another part of him wanted to turn
on those very soldiers and join White Buffalo in one last
effort at preserving something precious and sacred.

He had explained to the lieutenant that White Buffalo would accept nothing but a route around the burial
ground. Lieutenant Tracer had sent a message back by
wire to Omaha, and the reply had come. "The railroad
goes through. Do what you have to do."

It was all the lieutenant needed. He and his men had
attacked at dawn the second day after they arrived,
charging forward, more men circling around the village.
White Buffalo and his warriors were ready. They ex-
acted a surprising toll on the soldiers. Colt nearly
groaned at just staying back and doing nothing, and he
wished there could be two of him. The soldiers re-
treated and now were attacking again in a battle that
lasted for over an hour. Through the dust and mayhem
he noticed one soldier caught under a fallen horse.
Dancer whinnied and pranced, sensing his master's anx-
iety.

Colt could hold back no longer. He galloped Dancer
down the hill, and in minutes he charged directly into
the mêlée, riding up to the soldier who was pinned under his horse, a young man of perhaps seventeen. Colt
dismounted and hurried to the boy's side, pushing at the
dead horse with all his strength.

"Get me out! Get me out!" the young man screamed,
his chest bleeding.

Horses thundered past them, men shooting and yelp-
ing. Colt gritted his teeth and pushed again. "Try harder
to pull yourself," he shouted to the soldier. The young
man put his free leg against the horse's back and used it
to push himself away from the animal when Colt man-

aged to lift it just enough that he could get free. Colt fell panting and sweating against the dead horse for a moment. He turned to the young soldier. "I'll get you to safety," he shouted, looking around for Dancer.

Just then a warrior rode down on him, screaming, his face painted, a tomahawk raised. Colt rose up and grabbed him by the bone breastplate he wore, ripping him from his horse. At the same time he felt the tomahawk glance off him at the right side of his back. Both men went down, but Colt stayed down longer because of his wound. Before he could rise he felt another blow to the back of his right thigh. There was no time to think about the pain or wonder how bad the wound might be. It didn't matter now if he had to fight the very Indians he had once befriended. It mattered only that he save himself. He had to live—for Sunny.

He rolled onto his back, knew the heavily painted warrior would come at him again. He found his pistol and managed to get it out just as the Indian raised his arm to bury the tomahawk in his skull. It was only then they recognized each other. White Buffalo and Colt Travis felt suddenly frozen in time, all sound around them dying away.

"If it is to be, then let it be you," White Buffalo finally said. "I will have died honorably."

Colt managed to scoot backward, shaking his head. "Go on, White Buffalo! Leave me!" The man shook his head and let out a war cry, coming at him with the tomahawk. Colt had no choice but to shoot. A hole opened up in White Buffalo's chest, and blood oozed out over the breastplate. The man went to his knees, staring at Colt, then fell across Colt's legs.

With all the strength he could muster, Colt managed to pull free of him, just then realizing the young soldier he had saved was no place around. He tried to stand, but it was impossible, and only then did he see that the back of his right legging was soaked with blood. He felt himself growing weaker and light-headed as he turned to crawl closer to White Buffalo. He rolled the man onto his back, a sick feeling welling up from his stomach. "White Buffalo," he muttered. "My old friend." He lay across the man's bloody chest as though to protect him. It was then that he noticed White Buffalo was wearing a gold watch and chain around his neck. It was the last thing Colt remembered.

Chapter 26

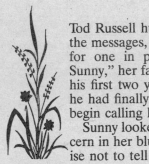

Tod Russell hurried into Sunny's office with the messages, knowing she had been waiting for one in particular. "I got word back, Sunny," her faithful secretary told her. After his first two years of employment with her, he had finally been able to bring himself to begin calling her Sunny again.

Sunny looked up from her desk, deep concern in her blue eyes. "You kept your promise not to tell Vince or Blaine?"

Tod thought the request odd, but his loyalty to Sunny Landers came first and everyone else second. "You know that I do whatever you ask."

Sunny thought about how he had changed since that first day she came to the office as his "boss" after her father died. He had been ready to quit. Now he was loyal and dependable, and most important, discreet. She had already received word about the heated battle over the burial ground, ten soldiers killed, several more wounded. The hated Cheyenne leader, White Buffalo was dead, killed by the scout Colt Travis. But there had been no word on Colt himself. "Is he all right?" she asked.

She could tell by the look on Tod's face that Colt was not all right at all. "I'm afraid the wire says he was badly hurt. They shipped him back to Omaha so he could get better care."

Sunny felt the life draining out of her. She closed her eyes and put her head in her hands. Colt! He needed her, and she couldn't be with him. "What's the other message?"

"It's, uh, it's from your fiancé. He says not to forget about the theater tonight. The mayor and his wife will be joining you. And your seamstress sent a messenger to tell you she's ready for another fitting for your wedding dress. She wants to know when you'll be by, and she says the sooner the better, now that the wedding is only ten days away."

"Yes, yes." Sunny rubbed her eyes. "I'll get back to her before the end of the day." She looked at Tod, and he was surprised to see tears in her eyes. He knew they were for Colt Travis—that savage-looking man he had met several years ago when he came to Sunny's office. What was this concern she had for the man? Tod's head swam with questions, but he knew he dared not ask. "I want to know more about Colt," she told him. "Wire back and find out just *how* badly hurt he is—if he's expected to live."

"Yes, ma'am." The man turned and left, and Sunny rose, feeling strangely old and weary. *Colt,* she thought. *My poor, sweet Colt. I should be there to hold you, to nurse you.* She had been back in Chicago for over a week now. Two days ago they had first received word about the Indian battle. Now she knew for certain what had happened to Colt, and she felt crazy with the need to be with him. She could perhaps go see him herself, could make up some excuse about needing to go back to Omaha to finish more railroad business before the wedding, but there was not enough time. Vince or Blaine might discover her real reason for going, and if she saw Colt again, touched him, how would she be able to bring herself home again? She would be right back in the awful predicament she was trying to avoid, putting Colt in danger.

Up until now she had always found the strength and courage to fight Vince. She could handle anything he tried to do to her; but when it came to threatening Colt's intense pride, let alone his very life, that was another story. She could not bear the thought of what Colt might think of her if he knew about her mother and grandmother. Was that why it had been so easy for her to let him ravish her body so freely? For her it had been nothing but a wonderful way to show her love for the only man she had ever wanted; but the truth might change everything, might make Colt look at her differently. She even saw herself differently, hardly able to look into her own eyes in the mirror.

Vince had taken the most beautiful, wonderful experience of her life and made it into something vulgar and sinful. Wasn't that how any man would look at it? For all she knew, Colt already thought less of her after he had had time to think about what they had done, how she had thrown herself at him while engaged to someone else. She already knew from the way some men had looked at her over the years how easily they could condemn a woman's behavior, how easily a woman could be labeled as bad and promiscuous. It was she who had gone to Colt, who had offered herself to him on a silver platter, so willingly, so brazenly.

She had surely been so wrong, and now she would have to live with her secret, live with a man she did not love; Colt would somehow have to get over the hurt. He would learn to love again, would find someone to treat him the way he deserved to be treated, give him children . . . help him forget. But the thought of him being with another woman made her stomach burn like fire.

Oh, how she wanted to go to him! But she realized she dared not see him or touch him again. It would only make him aware of what was happening, and she didn't want him to know until it was too late to do anything. She hurried to her door, in such agony that it was difficult to breathe. She opened it and looked out at Tod. "Find out more about Colt as soon as possible. And please send for Vi, will you? I need her to do something for me." Tod nodded, and she closed the door again. If she couldn't be with Colt, then she would send her love some other way, find some way to ease the emotional pain he would suffer when he discovered she had decided to marry Blaine. Colt liked Vi, and Vi was very good at comforting people.

She took deep breaths to keep from falling into a fit of sobbing. She walked back to the desk, feeling so filled with heartache that everything hurt. She rubbed her lower back as she eased herself back into her chair, then took out pen and paper. She would write Colt a letter—try to come up with an explanation that wouldn't destroy his love for her and his faith in that love, yet something that would convince him it was over. Vi would deliver it if she asked her to. Sunny could tell Stuart that she wanted Vi and Stuart to go and visit the wounded as a gesture of goodwill from the U.P. Stuart probably had some idea of how she felt about Colt, but he didn't know the extent of it, not like Vi did. Vi could visit Colt, give him some comfort. By the time he was recovered enough to try to do anything about her marriage to Blaine, if indeed he would want to, she would be Blaine's wife, and she and Blaine would be on their way to Europe.

Her hand shook as she put pen to paper, and she had to wait a moment, breathing deeply again for control. "God help me," she whispered. She was sure that in her whole life, before now and whatever lay in her future, this would be the hardest, most painful thing she would ever do.

Someone drew back the curtains, and Billie looked up from where she sat near Colt's bed. A rather plain-faced woman came closer, elegantly dressed, a woman of obvious wealth. Billie rose to face her, and the woman looked her over questioningly. "Can I help you?" Billie asked.

The woman moved closer, terrible sorrow filling her eyes when she looked down at Colt, his eyes closed, his face showing the pain he suffered. She looked back at Billie. "I'm Violet Landers. Who are you?"

Billie's eyes widened in surprise. Landers! "I'm Billie White. Colt and I are . . . kind of old friends." She smiled nervously, realizing this woman knew exactly what she was. "I heard he'd been hurt bad and they brought him back here," she explained. "I, uh, I work . . . here in Omaha . . . and other places." She looked away, bending over Colt and touching his hair. "Anyway, I know Colt doesn't have family or anything— nobody who really cares all that much about him. So I thought I'd come and sit with him, figured *some*body ought to." She looked back at Violet Landers and was surprised at the kindness in her eyes. "You're related to Sunny Landers, I guess?"

Vi took another chair near the bed. "Sunny is my husband's sister. She sent me here."

Billie scowled. "Why didn't she come herself? Colt keeps calling her name whenever he's conscious."

Vi closed her eyes and sighed, the words "dear God" exiting her lips. She seemed to be praying quietly for a moment before looking at Billie again. "How long have you known him?"

Billie self-consciously pushed a piece of her hair behind her ear, wishing she knew how to dress as elegantly as Vi Landers. She had made good money following the railroad crews, and her own dress had been expensive; yet now it seemed too gaudy. She pulled a shawl closer around herself to help hide the low-cut bodice. She realized the kind of wealth that was represented in the woman who sat across the bed from her, and she was surprised at the fact that Violet Landers spoke to her at all. "I don't know. About four years I guess. I met him in Omaha not long after his wife was killed. He was a pretty lonely man." She reddened a little. "I didn't see him again till last winter."

Vi frowned. "Colt wasn't in Omaha last winter. He was out scouting for the railroad."

Billie reddened even more. "He, uh, he got stranded in a bad snowstorm; had to come into the camp town to keep from freezing to death."

Vi looked down at her own gloved hands that clutched the purse on her lap. Everyone knew what the camp towns were like, the kind of people who ran them. "I see."

"No. I don't think you do," Billie spoke up defensively. "Look, lady, it's obvious what I do for a living, but sometimes I can be a good friend, too. I'll tell you something. I don't know how in hell Colt got hooked up with Miss Sunny Landers, but he's got it bad for her. I haven't seen him since last February, but I figure something must have happened between him and her, because he's been calling for her, and now you're here. Colt's a good man. I know one when I see one. If this Miss Landers thinks she can fool with his heart and treat him like he's nothing just because she's got money and he doesn't, I can tell you Colt's worth a *hundred* of her kind. I'm saying it straight out, even if she *is* your sister-in-law!"

Vi opened her purse, taking out an envelope. "It isn't like you think," she told Billie. She met her eyes again, and Billie felt a little sorry for what she had said. The woman looked ready to burst into tears. "You have no idea what life is like for Sunny. And I highly doubt anyone except me is aware of just how far she will go for someone she loves. She has been pulled in a hundred directions all her life, and the responsibilities she carries on her shoulders are awfully heavy for such a young woman. She's a good person, Billie. Her wealth has never affected her inner sweetness." She quickly took a handkerchief from her handbag and dabbed at a tear. "Sunny loves Colt, and I think they—" She hesitated. "It's up to Colt if he wants to tell you what happened between them. I only know something happened recently to convince Sunny it simply can't be. She won't tell me what it is, but I can tell you that she's sick over it. She's decided to go ahead and marry the man she's been engaged to all these months. She asked me to come here and give this letter to Colt." She handed it across the bed. "Can I trust you not to read it yourself, to save it and give it to him when he's well enough to read it?"

Billie reached out and took the letter. "I'm no snoop. A man wants to tell me something, fine. Otherwise I don't ask. And I don't go looking through his personal things."

No, Vi thought. *You only sleep with them.* She wanted to hate the woman, but at least she had cared enough to come and sit with Colt. If she weren't here, there would be no one. She understood men enough to know Colt certainly had a right to pay a visit to women like this one when he was a perfectly free man, before there had been anything between him and Sunny. She rose and leaned closer, touching his face. "Colt?" She frowned. "Dear God, he's so hot."

Colt's face contorted from pain, and he managed only a groan.

"He's running a fever—infection. That's what the doctors are worried about. He took two wounds from a tomahawk trying to save some soldier caught under his horse. There's one bad wound across his right shoulder in the back, but the worst one is on the back of his right thigh. I guess he lost an awful lot of blood. They say it takes a long time to build your blood back up again. The fever and loss of blood are why he keeps losing consciousness."

"Poor thing," Vi said softly. "And after all that suffering at Andersonville. He was just getting back to his old self." She studied the broad shoulders and powerful look to him. Yes, he was certainly a far cry from the man she had seen in Chicago after the war. Sunny was right about how this land was good for him. She could not help wondering if he and Sunny had made love, and she was sure she knew the answer. What had happened since then she could not imagine. Sunny seemed afraid of something. She had said it was Colt who wanted it to end, that he had found someone else. Billie was certainly not the kind of woman a man like Colt would choose to love and settle with. And if it was some other woman, where was she?

Sunny was lying. Colt had been calling for her, which meant there *was* no one else. She had been tempted to read Sunny's letter herself, but it was sealed, and she had a feeling that whatever it said, it was not the truth. She would never forget the look on Sunny's face when she asked her to bring the letter—the look more of someone headed for a hanging than a marriage.

"Sunny," Colt whispered then.

Vi took his hand. "I'm here, Colt," she lied, hoping the words would help him recover. She felt him squeeze her hand lightly before going limp again. She straightened, squeezing his hand in return before letting go of it and wiping her eyes again. She looked at Billie. "Maybe it would help if you answered as though you were Sunny when he calls for her," she told the woman. "Just until he's better. I would appreciate it, and I know Sunny would too."

"I don't know," Billie answered, leaning over and touching his arm. "I don't like fooling him like that. If she's never coming, he might as well know it. Maybe just for a couple of days, while he's too far gone to realize what's happening. I guess I can always tell him he dreamed it."

"Anything that will help him want to live is important."

Billie turned and slipped the letter into her own handbag. "Yes, I suppose."

Vi moved around the end of the bed, touching her shoulder. Billie turned and faced her. "Thank you for being here for him," Vi told her. "I'm glad you cared enough to come."

Billie shrugged. "Colt is easy to like. I mean, he's a hell of a man and all, but he's kind of sweet in ways. He always seemed so lonely. I always felt like he was wishing I was somebody else—first his wife, and then your sister-in-law. I'd sure like to see that fancy lady for myself." She turned away, putting on a cocky air. "I sure can't imagine how Colt got himself all tangled up with somebody like that. I remember they used to write to each other. It sure is strange, isn't it?"

Vi watched Colt sadly, feeling partly responsible for what had happened. She never should have encouraged Sunny to tell Colt how she felt about him. She was so sure it was the right thing to do. "Not so strange," she answered. "In some ways they're a lot alike, in spirit. They were good friends, understood each other in a special way. I think Sunny is making a big mistake, but I'm not the one who can change that. Only Colt can, and now here he lies helpless." She looked at Billie. "Is there anything you need while you're here? Are you staying in a hotel or something?"

Billie smoothed the skirt of her taffeta dress, feeling tacky and overdressed for the time of day. "No, thank you. I have a place to live when I'm in Omaha." She raised her chin, deciding this woman could think what she wanted. "It's over the Horseshoe Saloon, in case you ever want to write me and find out how Colt is doing."

"I see. Thank you for telling me. I just might get in touch with you at that."

Billie saw no ridicule or derision in Vi's eyes. To her astonishment, the woman stepped closer and hugged her, kissing her cheek.

"Thank you, Billie. And after he reads the letter, kind of stay with him awhile longer. He'll need a friend."

"Yes, ma'am, I will." Billie had to struggle to keep her mouth from dropping open. Women like Vi Landers were generally the kind who wouldn't even walk on the same side of the street with her, let alone touch her. She watched Vi move around to Colt again, bending close and kissing his cheek.

"God be with you," she said softly. "And with Sunny." She straightened, wiping at more tears. "Goodbye, Billie." She turned and left, skirts rustling.

Billie stared after her a moment, wondering if the entire episode had really taken place—a Landers coming here to see someone like Colt—hugging a prostitute and thanking her for being Colt's friend! She turned and picked up her purse, opening it and looking at the envelope again. Yes, it was real, and she feared that once Colt Travis read what was inside the envelope, he would be one hurt and angry man. But first he had to get better, and right now there was a chance he would die before he ever knew about Sunny and the letter.

"Sunny," he groaned again.

Billie leaned closer. "I'm right here, love," she said softly.

Sunny forced a happy look as she made her way down the aisle of the magnificent Lutheran cathedral, which was filled to capacity with some of the most important people in Chicago and Illinois as well as many from New York City and U.P. executives from Omaha. Organ music filled the church to its four-story-high dome, and lighting was softened by splendid stained glass windows.

Sunny knew her eyes should be on Blaine, but she stared only at the massive wooden cross that decorated the pulpit area, praying that she was doing the right thing, hoping God would forgive her if she was not. She had more reason to marry immediately now. She suspected she was pregnant with Colt's child. If she waited for Colt to be well, people would know she had conceived this child out of wedlock. They would be even more cruel to Colt, would brand his baby as a bastard; and still there was the awful fear that Vince would find a way to end Colt's life.

No one knew she had been sick all morning. No one knew she should have had her period a good ten days earlier. No one knew that she was secretly sure she was carrying Colt's child, a child they might once have shared with great joy, the child she had once dreamed of having to take the place of the little son Colt had lost. She had not meant it to happen this way, and she didn't want the horrible stigma put on her baby that was usually given to children conceived as hers had been. He was not a bastard. She knew who his father was, a kind, gentle, beautiful, brave man who would never know about the baby. She had no choice now but to allow Blaine his husbandly rights this very night so that she could claim the baby was his. It was important that Blaine believe it, for she wanted him to love the child and never resent it.

She dreaded the ocean trip that lay ahead, considering how ill she felt; but she couldn't object to that. She couldn't very well tell Blaine too soon that she was with child. She hoped she could hide her vomiting until they were on their way to Europe, so that she could pretend it was simply seasickness.

Stuart gave her away. She had not invited Vince to take any part in the ceremony itself, although for the sake of looks and gossip, she did have to invite him to the wedding. She thought how smug he must be feeling. He had won at last. She would rather he had won any other battle but this one, and sometimes she wondered if her illness was partly due to the hatred for her stepbrother that ate at her insides. She wanted to hate her father for what he had done, but she couldn't bring herself to that. Bo Landers had dearly loved her, tried to protect her, truly loved her mother, in spite of how she had become his wife. She could not help believing there had been some goodness in Lucille Madison. She *had* to believe it or go insane; and she had to protect the woman's memory.

Blaine was beside her now, beaming with joy and pride. She supposed she looked as beautiful as she ever had in her life, in a dress that was perfectly tailored to her still-slim waist, the train of the dress flowing out behind her for fifteen feet. Stuart's six-year-old daughter, he and Vi's third child, was flower girl; their eight-year-old son ring bearer. Their eleven-year-old daughter, Diana, Vince's fourteen- and ten-year-old daughters and his seventeen-year-old son all part of the wedding party. Much as she hated Vince, Sunny could not take that hatred out on his children, none of whom, amazingly, were anything like their witch of a mother and steam-roller father.

She was saying her vows now. She wondered where Mae was. She had not been able to scan the audience closely enough to find her. It was comforting to know that Mae, scatterbrained as she could sometimes be, knew this was not what Sunny really wanted. Mae and Vi both had tried so hard to cheer her up and tell her what a grand day this was for her, but Sunny knew by the looks in their eyes that they knew who really owned her heart. Vi had tried once more to talk her out of the marriage, but Vi didn't know the truth about Sunny's mother, and she didn't know that Sunny was carrying Colt's baby.

It was a truly beautiful wedding, and Sunny doubted anyone could look more handsome and debonair than Blaine O'Brien—except Colt. She would like to see him in a silk tuxedo. The thought of it made her smile. Blaine thought the smile was for him. She felt even sicker at the thought that she was doing Blaine an injustice, but then, Blaine didn't need or want her love. He wanted her beauty, her importance, her standing in society. She would help him win votes. He was not the sentimental, soft-hearted man Colt could be when it came to love, and as long as she knew that, it eased her own guilt. She would make up for not truly loving him by being the dutiful wife, playing her role as the ornamental wife he wanted. He was not a cruel man, just cold and calculating, picking his wife the way he might pick the proper investments. He had agreed that Sunny could stay in control of Landers Enterprises and of her shares in the U.P. and other railroad holdings. In case of death, a vast new wealth would fall into Sunny's hands, even after Blaine's mother and sister in Europe got their share. In case of her death, Blaine would inherit what she owned. Vince and Stuart didn't mind. They both liked Blaine, knew he would handle it well and probably let them run most everything. There were no stipulations for divorce. It was simply not something to be discussed, for neither of them would consider the shame of it.

Somehow she got through her vows, realizing that she was hardly aware of what she had said. Blaine was lifting her veil, kissing her. The church resounded with glorious organ music, and people oohed and aahed and clapped as Mr. and Mrs. Blaine Hadley O'Brien walked back down the aisle arm in arm, positioning themselves at the church entrance to greet their guests. Two more hours passed with handshakes, hugs, kisses, pictures, rice-throwing. Blaine and Sunny climbed into a white and gold coach pulled by four white horses, and off they went to a country club, where a reception would be held for only the most elite of Chicago and New York.

Blaine turned to Sunny. "Finally," he whispered, meeting her mouth in a savage kiss. Her mind floated to another time, to warm prairie sun and the smell of fresh spring grass and wildflowers, the feel of that grass against her back.

Stuart and Vi and the children sat down to Vince and Eve's elegant dining table. Ever since Sunny's wedding Vince had been a changed man, more friendly toward Stuart and Vi, more cooperative at the office, a smile on his face most of the time instead of a frown. Tonight he had even invited Stuart and his family to dinner at his magnificent home on the lake, not far from Sunny's mansion. Servants began bringing in a grand meal, and Vince held up a glass of wine.

"Well, here's to Sunny and Blaine. It's been six weeks now. They should be in France by now, sunning on the Riviera, or maybe in Africa. You know, all of us should take a break sometime and go to Europe ourselves, maybe after the railroad is finished."

"Not a bad idea," Stuart answered, lifting his own glass.

"Yes, especially now since Sunny has been there," Eve put in. "We can't let her get a leg up on us, now, can we?"

Vince laughed. "Now that she's married to Blaine, she'll *always* have a leg up on us, but the union certainly can't hurt Landers Enterprises. If things go badly for some reason, Sunny can just take from one pot and put it in another." He and Eve laughed lightly, but Vi did not care for the remark, and Stuart only smiled. Vi would never trust Vince, and she had never stopped wondering what his role had been in keeping Colt and Sunny apart. She had no doubt it was all his doing.

Everyone began digging into the food, talking business while the children discussed doings at the private school they attended. All of a sudden they all either stopped chewing or quickly swallowed their food when they heard shouting in the outer hall. "Where is he! Where's Vince Landers!"

Vi looked at Stuart, both of them realizing it sounded like Colt's voice.

"Sir, you can't go in there—"

"Don't tell me where I can and can't go!" Colt's big frame suddenly loomed into the dining room.

"What the hell—" Vince rose, his face turning a dark red. Eve gasped and put a hand to her mouth.

"Colt," Stuart exclaimed. "What in God's name are you doing here?"

Colt headed straight for Vince, and Vi noticed he was limping. Vince backed up when he saw the look on Colt's face, and he fell over his own chair, landing on his rear. Colt landed into him, grabbing him by the lapels and jerking him to his feet, making it look easy in spite of Vince's size. "I want the truth, you bastard!" Colt growled. He whirled the man around and slammed him facedown on the table, scattering food and plates. Vince's face landed in a bowl of mashed potatoes, and Eve screamed and backed away. Some of the children began crying.

"Colt, don't do this," Vi begged.

Colt shot her the look of an Indian on the warpath. He jerked Vince's face out of the potatoes but kept a firm grip around his neck. "I came here for the truth, and this sonofabitch is going to *tell* it! I want to know why Sunny married Blaine!"

"Go get the police," Eve screeched at the servants. "Hurry!"

Colt moved an arm under a choking Vince's chin, and he swiftly drew a knife, holding it at the side of the man's face. "You bring the police, your husband is a *dead* man!" he sneered, looking wild.

Eve stared wide-eyed at him, beginning to shake and cry. "Why are you doing this," she squeaked.

"Ask your husband. *He* knows!"

Vince's eyes were bulging, and servants stared. Stuart felt helpless, realizing only then that Vince had apparently been up to his old scheming ways again, and it had something to do with Colt and Sunny. What had he missed?

"Get . . . the kids . . . out of here," Vince told his wife, glad that his seventeen-year-old son was not present. The boy might try to defend him and get hurt.

"Go! Go!" Eve screamed at the children.

"The servants too," Colt growled. "I want just you four in this room, and I want some *answers!*"

The children ran, screaming and crying. Gaping servants scurried away, and Stuart hurried over to close the doors to the dining room. "Colt, what in God's name is this?" he asked. "You can't come into a man's house and threaten him this way!"

"Can't I?" He placed the knife at the top of Vince's forehead and nicked it just enough to draw blood. Eve gasped and withered into a chair. "The truth, Vince," he snarled. *"I take scalps! Remember?* I can have yours off in an instant!"

"No! No, stop!" Vince gasped, his face so red Vi thought he might have a stroke. "Please, let me go!"

"Colt, please don't do this," Vi begged again. "You know you'll never get away with it."

"You think I *care,* now that Sunny's married to someone else?"

"The letter—"

"That letter was a bunch of bullshit! Something happened, Vi, and I'm betting it has something to do with Vince Landers! What did you say to her when she got back, Landers? When I got well enough I did a little investigating—found out from Sunny's servants in Omaha that *you* were waiting for her the night she got back after seeing me! They heard yelling, heard Sunny crying! Everything changed after that, and I want to know why!"

Stuart looked at Vi. "What do you know about this? What is he talking about?"

Colt jerked Vince over to a bigger chair and slammed him into it. A butler banged on the outer doors, which

Stuart had locked. "Mr. Landers! Mr. Landers! Are you all right in there?"

"We're okay," Stuart called back. "Just stay out! And leave the police out of it!"

Vince sat in the chair panting, blood mixing with the potatoes on his face. He angrily wiped away some of the potatoes, then took a handkerchief from his pocket and pressed it to his forehead. "Good God," he muttered. "What kind of a madman are you!"

Colt stood over him, waving the knife. "I'm a savage *Indian,* remember?"

"Colt, this isn't you," Vi said, remaining calm. "Don't do it this way."

"This is the only way men like Vince understand!" he shouted. He walked around behind Vince's chair, grasping some of his hair in his hand. Vince looked ready to cry. "I *loved* her, Vi. You know that," Colt said then, pain in his eyes. "And she loved me." He moved his eyes to Stuart. "She came out alone to see me. We finally admitted our love for each other." His jaw flexed in anger. "In fact, we did more than just admit it, but the details are for me and Sunny to know about. All I know is that when she left me before I rode out to the Cheyenne, it was with a promise to break her engagement to Blaine and come back to me. We were going to find a way to work things out!"

"Dear God," Eve muttered, looking at him as though he were some kind of monster. "You can't be serious!"

"I don't want you to say a word," Colt warned her. "I've got no more use for snobby bitches than I do for lying bastards like your husband!" Eve put a hand to her throat. Colt jerked again at Vince's hair. "What did you say to Sunny when she got back?" he demanded.

"What difference does it make? She's married to Blaine now."

In one swift motion Colt whipped his knife through Vince's hair, cutting it off at the top to a stub and throwing a handful of the sandy and gray cuttings into the man's lap. Eve closed her eyes and wept. Colt reached down and grasped Vince under the chin. "The *truth,*" he warned.

Vince looked at Stuart. "Letting her be with this savage would have been a disaster, for her and the whole family," he choked out. "I . . . I told her I could easily find someone to put an end to you," he said then, directing his words to Colt. "A lot of men would take money for something like that. I told her if she pursued her sordid affair with you, I'd see you *dead!*"

"Vince!" Vi felt faint with anger. "Sunny *loved* Colt!"

"There's *more,* isn't there?" Colt asked. He moved around to stand in front of Vince, bending over the chair and laying the knife at his throat. With a quick flick he cut the string tie at the neck of Vince's silk shirt, and everyone gasped. "Sunny knows I can take care of myself," he told Vince. "She could have warned me. There's something else. What are you leaving out, Landers?"

Vince glanced at Stuart again, and Stuart's eyes widened with outrage. "Vince, you didn't *tell* her! We promised *never* to tell her!"

"How could I *not* tell her, after learning she'd been cavorting with this savage like a common *whore!*"

The room hung suddenly quiet. Vince trembled, watching Colt put his knife back in its sheath. Vince breathed a little easier until suddenly Colt jerked him out of the chair. "You filthy-minded *bastard!*" Colt sneered. He laid into the man with his fists, knocking Vince halfway down the long table and sending more food scattering and spilling. Eve screamed and wept more when Colt jerked the man back off the table, hit him again, sending him sprawling into two chairs.

"Colt, please stop!" Vi shouted.

"For God's sake, man, you'll kill him," Stuart put in.

"He *deserves* to die!" Colt raged. "How *dare* he call the woman I love, his own sister, a whore!"

"That's because her *mother* was one, and *her* mother before that!" Vince shouted. He managed to get to his knees, grasping at his stomach and spitting blood from his mouth. "Father . . . *bought* her . . . *paid* for her . . . the daughter of a high-class prostitute in New York City!"

Both Eve's and Vi's eyes widened in shock, and Colt

stumbled backward as though he'd been hit by something.

"You stupid bastard," Stuart shouted at his brother. "You *told* her, didn't you! My God, Vince, how could you *do* that! You know we promised Father! You *know* Sunny is nothing like that!"

"Vince! Tell me it's a lie," Eve groaned.

"It's the truth." The man tried to get up but managed only to turn and sit on the floor. He wiped the blood that dripped from his nose, and one eye was already swelling. "I didn't want any more shame . . . in this family! Not many knew, but those who did were just waiting for Sunny to show her true colors," he panted. He looked up at Colt, grimacing with pain and grasping his ribs again. "When I . . . found out she was rolling in the grass with this worthless . . . half-breed, I knew what people would say, how it would look, and I told her the truth about her mother!" He grabbed the seat of a chair and got to his knees, blood and potatoes now smearing the front of his shirt and jacket. "I told her even *Colt* wouldn't want her . . . if he knew! I told her if she wanted the family secret protected . . . if she wanted any respect left to her mother's and to Bo Landers's name, she'd better marry . . . a proper man and behave herself!"

Vi turned to Stuart, shivering with the shock of the news. "You *knew* this and never told me?"

Stuart glared at Vince. "We made a pact," he said through gritted teeth. "Father said he'd disinherit us if we ever broke Sunny's heart like that. When Sunny got older, she was so pretty and sweet and tried to be so good to us, we both decided to let it go. *I* let it go for *Sunny's* sake! *Vince* let it go only because he wanted to keep it covered up for the sake of gossip about the family, to save his *own* face!"

Colt turned away and grasped the back of a chair. "Do you really think something like that would have mattered to me?" he groaned.

"Hell no," Vince answered, still shaking. "But I knew . . . *Sunny* would think it mattered! I knew she'd . . . never want you to know. Between that . . . and my threat to have you killed . . . she knew what she had to do . . . and it was *right*, dammit! You know it never could have worked, Colt. It's as much for . . . your own good as hers!"

Colt closed his eyes, breathing deeply for self-control. Oh, how he wished he had Vince Landers out in a lawless land where he could do with him what he'd like. "Yeah," he said, his voice oddly quiet. "That's what she said in her letter—that it was best for both of us." He whirled, the chair in his hands. "I should *kill* you! You've destroyed Sunny's chance to ever be a truly happy woman. You're a selfish, arrogant *bastard*, Vince Landers. Nobody is *ever* going to love her like I did!" He turned with the chair, throwing it at a mirror over a huge stone fireplace. Eve screamed again when the mirror shattered into thousands of pieces, falling to the hearth along with the broken chair. Colt turned back to Vince, and Vince tried to scoot back again. Colt charged toward him, lifting him up and landing a booted foot into the man's groin. "You filthy-minded sonofabitch! You took something that was the most beautiful thing in the world to her and you made her ashamed of it!"

"Please, please don't kill him," Eve screamed.

"Colt, let him go!" Stuart begged. "His kids are right here in the house! So are my own!"

Colt just stood there a moment, as though deciding. Vince hung limp and groaning in his hands. "Don't even *think* about sending someone after me, Landers," he snarled, "because if I find out about it, you're a dead man for *sure*, even if I hang for it!"

He brought a knee up into the man's nose, and Vi grasped her stomach at a cracking sound. Colt threw the man across the table again, astonishing the others at how easily he tossed the man about. Vince weighed a good two hundred pounds or better. Colt looked at Vi, tears in his eyes. "He's not even *worth* killing, at least not *this* time! He'd just better never threaten me again!" He moved his eyes to Stuart. "Don't worry. I'll never give away your little secret. I'd never do that to Sunny! She's suffered enough!" He headed for the doors.

"Colt," Vi called out. "Where will you go?"

He stopped, his back to her. "I don't know. I sure as hell can't work for the U.P. anymore."

He charged through the doors, and several servants gasped and scattered. Eve stumbled over to Vince, who had rolled off the table and lay curled up on the floor, covered with blood and potatoes and a mixture of several other foods. He held his nose, which was bleeding profusely.

Stuart turned to Vi and shook his head, tears in his eyes. "I loved her, Vi. I never would have told her." He frowned. "You knew about her and Colt?"

"I knew she went out to the camp alone. I had an idea why." She wiped her tears. "I thought when she came back she'd tell everyone and they would be happy. I never could get her to tell me why she changed her mind."

Stuart closed his eyes and sank into a chair. "Sweet Jesus," he muttered. "I knew a long time ago she cared about Colt, but I never thought it was that serious. One of you should have come to me. I might have been able to straighten it out."

"She wouldn't let me, Stuart. She told me it was all Colt's doing, that he had told her it just wouldn't work, that he was interested in someone else."

He ran a hand through his hair. "Well, it's pretty obvious that wasn't true, isn't it?" He shook his head. "Poor Sunny. She's never been allowed to be happy."

"I'll go talk to the children—think up something to tell them." Vi hurried out of the room while Eve began ordering servants to clean up the mess. Vi hurried to the front doors first to try to catch Colt, wondering if there was anything she could say to ease the pain; but he was already gone.

"He took off on a horse, ma'am," one of the servants told her. "Went charging out of here like lightning. Who was he, ma'am?"

Vi turned back to the house. "It doesn't matter anymore. I highly doubt any of us will ever see him again." She walked wearily back inside, her heart aching for Colt, and for Sunny. She had no pity for Vince whatsoever, and for the first time in her life she thought how pleasant it might be to kill someone. Colt had shown amazing control, for surely he had wanted nothing more than to murder Vince Landers.

Part

Four

Chapter 27

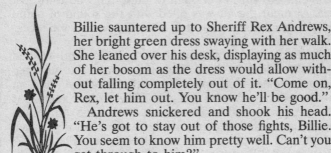

Billie sauntered up to Sheriff Rex Andrews, her bright green dress swaying with her walk. She leaned over his desk, displaying as much of her bosom as the dress would allow without falling completely out of it. "Come on, Rex, let him out. You know he'll be good."

Andrews snickered and shook his head. "He's got to stay out of those fights, Billie. You seem to know him pretty well. Can't you get through to him?"

She shrugged. "He's an angry man right now. He's really okay, Rex. Let him out and he'll ride out to sleep under the stars like he always does after he gets into a brawl." She reached out and touched his hair. Sheriff Andrews stood only five foot nine, but he was brawny and daring, a former guard for Wells Fargo who had settled in Cheyenne at the request of certain citizens who wanted their town to become more respectable.

"Come on, Rex. Please? You know he can't stand it in that jail. He goes crazy closed in like that. The poor guy lost his wife and son to Pawnee Indians, fought in the Civil War, spent time at Andersonville—give him a break. I'll give you a free night for it."

The sheriff scowled. "Billie, you know I'm married."

She reached between the cleavage of her bosom and pulled out a ten-dollar bill. "Will this cover the fine?"

Andrews rose with a deep sigh. "You win. He'd just better hightail it out of here for a couple of days, or next time he'll be in there for a good week."

Billie straightened, smiling. She liked it in Cheyenne, a booming town that was expecting the railroad to arrive by April. Omaha was getting too civilized for her kind, many prostitutes already run out of town. In Cheyenne she was free to do what she liked. She had opened her own saloon with profits from the camp town, and she was making more money than ever. The town over-flowed with single men, and some lonely married ones, men who worked for the railroad, bankers, lawyers, gamblers, freighters—men from all trades. There were women, too, but not enough to tame the wild town just yet. At night the air was filled with the sound of piano music, laughing prostitutes, shouting men, and occasional gunfire.

Andrews took the keys from a hook and walked through a door to the cells at the rear of the building. Moments later Colt appeared at the doorway, a cut on his lip and one over his left eye. Billie already knew that the man who had insulted Colt had come out much worse and was lying in a room at the doctor's house. "Colt, why do you always have to be such a bad boy," she pouted. "I can't always be leaving my customers to come over to bail you out."

He gave her a bashful smile. "Sorry. What do I owe you?"

She looked him over. "Oh, I'll get it out of you one way or another. I—"

Billie's words were cut off when gunfire crashed through a barred front window. Billie jolted forward, and Colt caught her as she went down, a bullet in her back.

"Billie!" Colt and Andrews both ducked down, and Andrews crawled to the door and bolted it.

"Send him out, Sheriff," someone outside yelled, "or we're comin' in after him!"

"It's those damn cattlemen that caused so much trouble earlier," Andrews told Colt. "I locked one of them up and the others said they'd be back for him, but I didn't expect something like this!" He crawled over to Billie. Colt had rolled her onto her back and was kneeling over her, feeling for a pulse. There was none.

"Sons of bitches," he groaned. He looked at Andrews. "Give me my gun. I'll help you."

Andrews quickly moved to where Colt's gun belt hung. He jumped up and grabbed it, and another shot came through a different window.

"Come on, Sheriff, let him go or you're a dead man!"

"They're all drunk," Andrews fumed. He looked down at Billie. "Bastards! Is she dead?"

Colt took his gun belt, nodding, tears in his eyes. "Somebody is going to pay for this! Billie's been a good friend to me the last few months, just a friend, nothing more." He tied the bottom of his holster around his thigh. He still felt a soreness and tingling in the back of the thigh, and he had lost a piece of muscle from the blow of White Buffalo's tomahawk, which caused him to walk with a slight limp. But he was strong as ever, and his shoulder wound had left no permanent damage. "How many of them do you think there are?"

"I'm not sure. Probably five or six."

"Close the shutters and turn out the oil lamps. I'll go out the back way. Once it's dark in here, you can get to a window without them seeing you."

"You heard us, Andrews! Send Mills out, or Cheyenne won't have no sheriff in the morning!"

Colt quickly crawled to the jail cells, where he stood up and ran out the back door. Andrews ran in a stoop back to the windows, reaching up with one hand to slam the wooden shutters closed. He stood up then and blew out the lamps, then made his way back to the windows. He opened the shutters on one and peeked out at seven men perched on horses outside the jail, guns leveled at the door. He wondered if Colt Travis would help him or just duck out on him.

"Come and get me," Sam Mills yelled from his jail cell. "There's only two of them!"

The men outside looked at each other, frowning. Two men? They all knew that Sheriff Andrews always worked alone. He had never been able to find anyone skilled or brave enough to take on the job of helping civilize the untamed town. Cheyenne was growing so fast with men who lived by their own law that the town council could not pay most men enough to take the risk. "Keep a lookout," one of them said to another.

"Hold it right there," came a voice from the shadows. "Everybody get down, or you can each wonder which one of you I'll shoot first."

They could not see the speaker. "We want Sam back, Mister," one of them spoke up. "No big deal. It's not worth dyin' over."

"That depends on whether it matters to me if I die. It doesn't. But I'll bet it matters to you."

The front door came open then, and Sheriff Andrews stepped out. "Get down off those horses, boys."

There was a moment of hesitation, and then one of them fired at Andrews. The man spun around when the bullet grazed his left arm, but he kept hold of his gun in his right hand. From the shadows came more gunfire, and three men went down in quick succession. Two rode off, and Andrews shot at them, wounding one. Colt fired from the alley, killing a fifth man. Two others managed to ride off unhurt.

"You all right?" Colt shouted to Andrews, moving out from the shadows.

Andrews was panting, holding his arm. "I will be."

A few people came out of saloons and gambling houses to have a look, but throughout most of the town the piano music went on, people so used to gunfire that they didn't bother to see what it was all about. Andrews looked up at Colt. "Thanks."

Colt holstered his gun. "You think the other two will come back?"

Andrews looked out in the street, where five bodies lay, one of them still alive and moaning. Their horses had scattered every which way. "Are you kidding? They'd be crazy." The man looked back at Colt. "You did good. You said earlier you used to scout for the U.P.?"

Colt nodded, opening the door and leading the man inside. "You'd better sit down. I'll relight the lamps and get the doc." He took a match from where he'd seen some in a box on Andrews's desk and lit one oil lamp, then the other. He walked around and looked down at Billie, the old familiar grief he had felt so often over the years returning. She had gotten him through some rough times, and he was still not over Sunny's marriage to Blaine. It had been Billie's idea to come to Cheyenne, but Colt's anger had caused him to get in a few fights and had landed him in jail more than once. He worked for a rancher outside of town, but he felt restless and unhappy, wondering if he would ever love again, ever care about anything again.

He knelt down and caressed Billie's face. "Poor Billie," he muttered. "This is my fault. If she hadn't come to bail me out, this wouldn't have happened." He closed his eyes and made a fist. "Damn! Everything I touch dies or leaves me."

"I know a good way to keep you busy and give you an outlet for all that anger, Travis," the sheriff told him.

Colt swallowed back an urge to weep. "How's that?" he asked, pain in his voice.

"Be my deputy. Nobody else around here has the guts to do it."

Colt shook his head. "Me? A lawman?" He turned to look at Andrews. "I don't know."

"What the hell? You got anything better to do? Pay's forty dollars a month. You said yourself you didn't give a damn what happened to you. A man who thinks like that is even braver, and I like the way you handle yourself." Andrews leaned back in his chair and shivered. "You'd better go get that doc right now. We'll talk about this later."

Colt nodded, taking a jacket from a nearby hat tree and laying it over Billie's face. "I'm sorry, Billie," he groaned, tears welling in his eyes. "I'll see you get a real nice burial." He rose, turning away from Andrews and sniffing. "I'll go get some help."

"Think about what I said, Travis," the sheriff answered. "You could start tonight. God knows I'll be out of commission for a while. I need the help."

Colt walked to the door. "I'll think about it."

"I'd want you to cut that hair and wear regular clothes instead of those buckskins. You too Indian to do that?"

Colt smiled sadly, thinking of White Buffalo, wondering if anyone had bothered to bury his body. God, how it hurt to know he'd been the one to kill the man who was once his good friend. "No," he answered. "I'm not too Indian." He looked back at Andrews, pain in his eyes. "Find me some kind of badge. I'll be back in a bit."

Andrews smiled. "Good. Now you can help me put other men in jail instead of it being you."

Colt nodded. "I suppose." He walked out and closed the door behind him.

"What's goin' on out there!" the cowpuncher Sam yelled from his cell.

"Shut up!" Andrews barked. "Four of your friends are dead and another one wounded. The other two rode off. The one still living is going to hang for the murder of Billie White!"

"You can't hang a man for killin' a damn whore! They ain't worth it!"

Andrews stared at Billie's cold, still body. "This one was," he said quietly.

Sunny lay in a bath of sweat, her face pale from loss of blood. The doctor had finally stopped her bleeding after she gave birth to an eight-pound son. Labor had lasted for hours, and Sunny barely had the strength to move when Vi came into the room, the baby in her arms. "Time for a feeding, if you have the strength, Sunny."

A nurse helped Sunny roll to her side and propped pillows behind her. She had come back to Chicago to have the baby, wanting to be near Vi when her time came; and Blaine had come just a few days before, taking time away from his renewed campaigning. It was an election year, and this coming summer he would be completely immersed in his effort to get into politics. He would expect his wife and child to be by his side, but right now Sunny liked the thought of being with her son.

She smiled when Vi lay the baby beside her. She helped her open her gown, and in moments the baby was suckling away at its nourishment. *My son,* Sunny thought. *You're as beautiful as your father.* His skin was still too red to tell if he would be brown or fair, but she already knew how he would look. He was perfect in every way, without a flaw on his skin. His shock of black hair was oiled and combed to the side. When he opened his eyes, they were not blue like Sunny's. They were hazel.

"How are you feeling, Sunny?" Vi asked.

She closed her eyes. "Like I died. Please stay here. I don't know how long I can just lie here and feed him."

Vi reached out and touched her hair. "I know. My second one was like this." She stroked her hair away from her face, thinking about the things she had learned about Sunny's mother. It had taken Vince some time to recover from Colt's beating, but Vi had not felt the least bit sorry for the man. She realized now the unhappiness with which Sunny must live, but now she at least had this baby. Vi had hoped the baby would change everything for her, but during the throes of birthing, Sunny had called out Colt's name. No one had heard but the doctor and nurse, and Vi had warned them to keep still about it.

Now, as she studied this baby, while she had bathed it, powdered it, looked into its eyes, she could not help wondering if the child might be Colt's; but she was afraid to ask. If she was wrong, Sunny would feel terribly insulted. She had never told Sunny what she knew about her mother or about the confrontation between Vince and Colt. She figured it was best now not to mention Colt's name anymore.

"Isn't he beautiful?" Sunny said weakly.

"He is perfect. How could you and Blaine *not* have a perfect baby?" Vi saw the clouds move into Sunny's blue eyes.

In the aftermath of birth Sunny felt vulnerable and sentimental, an odd depression engulfing her. Oh, how she wished she could tell Colt he had a son! How happy it would make him! But it would be cruel to tell him when she couldn't be with him, to let him know he had a son he could never hold or raise himself. "Vi," she whispered, her eyes tearing, "I have to tell someone. You're the only one I can trust."

"Tell me what, darling?"

Sunny looked past her. "Are the doctor and nurse gone?"

Vi frowned. "Yes."

Sunny looked at her with eyes of sorrow. "This is Colt's baby, not Blaine's." The tears came harder then.

Vi put her head in her hands. "Dear God, Sunny. Do you know what this child would mean to Colt?"

"I know." A tear dripped onto the baby's head, and Sunny quickly wiped it away. "Get me a handkerchief, will you?"

Vi rose wearily and walked to a chest of drawers. She found a hanky and brought it back to Sunny, sighing with sympathy as she sat down on the edge of the bed. She watched the baby grasp at Sunny's breast, noticing how dark his little hand looked against Sunny's white skin. "I suspected," she told Sunny. "You called out for Colt during labor."

"I did? Did Blaine hear?"

"I don't think so. I told the doctor and nurse to say nothing—said it was just the name of an old friend you must have thought of in your delirium."

Sunny closed her eyes again, more tears coming. Vi's heart ached for her and she touched her arm. "Sunny, don't do this. You'll lose your milk." She wiped at a few quiet tears of her own. "Honey, since you're the one who brought up Colt's name, you might as well know that he came looking for you after he recovered."

The baby stopped suckling, and Sunny gently pulled away, covering her breast but keeping the baby beside her. "When? What did he do?" She shivered, wiping at more tears. "Oh, how he must hate me!"

Vi took her hand. "I'm sure he doesn't hate you. He came to Vince's house while we were all having dinner, and he lit into Vince something awful. We all thought he was going to kill him. He made Vince tell the truth, figured this was all Vince's doing. Vince was a long time recovering."

Sunny's eyes widened with dread. "Then Vince told, in front of you and Eve?"

Vi frowned. "Sunny, you should have just shared it with Colt and let him decide what to do."

"I couldn't," Sunny sniffed. "I was afraid of how he'd look at me, what he'd think about the two days we spent together. And I had to protect my mother and father's memories. I couldn't let people gossip. And Vince threatened to kill Colt. I would rather live without him and know he's alive than to go to him and have him die."

"Colt can take care of himself. And the other, Sunny, how could you think that would matter to him?"

"Things like that always matter to a man. When I realized I was pregnant, I couldn't go running to Colt then either. If I had dropped everything and married Colt, you know what people would have said about my baby." She kissed the baby's hair. "I never want ugly things said about my child, or about Colt. Vince was right in saying that even if he didn't have him killed, the way we live would have destroyed Colt. It never could have worked."

"I think you're wrong, Sunny. But it's too late now to try to change any of it."

Sunny sniffed and blew her nose. "Where did Colt go? Is he still working for the railroad?"

"No. No one seems to know where he went."

Sunny pulled the baby closer. "Gone again, like the

wind. At least I have his son with me. I can bear anything now, Vi."

Unless the baby begins looking more and more like Colt, Vi thought. "Sunny, I am amazed at your strength and determination in the world of business; and yet you always place yourself second in your personal life. You've got to start being your true self, stop living the way everyone else expects you to live."

Sunny kissed her son's sweet-smelling hair. "It's like you said. It's too late now. I married Blaine, and I'll be true to him. Has he seen the baby yet?"

"Yes. He'll be in soon." Vi decided not to tell her how Blaine had frowned at first when he saw his son's black hair. He had quickly brightened, putting on a look of pure fatherly pride. Vi squeezed Sunny's hand. "You just remember that I'm always here when you need to talk, Sunny. You can always tell me the truth about anything. You know it will go no further."

"I know. Thank you for always being there, Vi. I'll be all right."

"Do you want me to take the baby?"

"No. I just want to hold him and look at him for as long as I can stay awake. Now I'll always have a little bit of Colt with me."

Vi rose, feeling sick at how wrong all this was. She left the room, looking for Blaine. "Where is Blaine?" she asked Stuart.

"Oh, he's left to wire New York—wants the birth to get splattered in the papers right away—good for publicity." Stuart made the remark with a hint of sarcasm.

Sunny heard him, even though he spoke quietly. *Yes,* she thought. *Anything for publicity.* Blaine had pulled her all over Europe in spite of her terrible morning sickness, showing her off, letting foreign papers take pictures, making sure many of them were sent home for articles in New York newspapers. Because of her sickness and her inner unhappiness, their sex life had been a disaster from the first night, when he accused her of being cold and unresponsive. He had been angry at first that she had gotten pregnant so soon and they had to cut short their European and African tour because she was so sick. It seemed that once she became his wife, he figured he had her where he wanted her and no longer needed to be kind and attentive.

She could still bear this marriage, be a good wife to him, if he didn't always make her feel like just a pretty ornament on his arm rather than making her feel like a loved and cherished wife. In all sincerity she had made up her mind to make him happy, but Blaine seemed to want only her bedroom favors, and to show her off to the general public, with little affection shown in their private moments. They could talk about stocks and bonds, the railroad and the progress of his logging industry; but then, Blaine could talk to anyone about those things. They were his favorite subjects. She had not realized how unfeeling he truly was until she met his mother and sister, two very cold and selfish women who cared about nothing but lying around on the Riviera and being taken care of by Blaine's money. Sometimes Sunny had to admire what a hardworking man he was, but his objective in life seemed only to get richer and be in the public eye. She realized that she had done a lot of things herself to increase her fortune, but it had been to prove something to everyone else, never for herself. Now that she had a son, she was determined to devote more time to her baby.

"My precious little son," she said softly. "If only your father could see you. How I would love to give him that happiness." The tears came again and she kissed the baby's tiny hand. Blaine came into the room then, all smiles.

"The announcement will be in all the newspapers," he bragged. "I imagine baby gifts will be flowing in from all over before long." He knelt beside the bed. "What do we call him?"

"Whatever you want, Blaine."

"Well, how about after your father—Beauregard—call him Bo."

She managed a smile, taking hope that the baby would bring a new closeness between her and Blaine. "Little Bo. All right. Beauregard Stuart, after my father and my brother."

Blaine grinned. "Hey, little Bo," he said, letting the infant grasp one of his fingers, "you, my son, are going to win an election for me, you and your beautiful mother." He looked at Sunny. "First my opponents said I was a poor candidate because I was single and didn't understand the difficulties of the average family. After I got married, they said I was too rich to identify with the common person's needs. Some of their damn headlines read that I've got looks and charm, but no heart—that I love money and I associate too closely with the most wealthy people of New York and will grant them favors. I suppose I will, but the general public doesn't need to know that. I'm working on some programs to benefit the poor, getting involved in a few things that will convince them that I'm on their side. When they see me out campaigning with you and little Bo, they'll see what a good family man I am. I'll talk about programs to help the average family. We'll win all kinds of votes."

Is that all little Bo is to you? she wondered. *Just a vote-getter?* She saw no tender, fatherly look in his eyes, only an excitement at the possibility of becoming governor.

"I've got some campaign work to do, love," he told her. "You certainly won't be needing me for the time being."

"Blaine, don't you want to spend some time with us? Don't you want to hold little Bo?"

He rose. "The kid is sleeping. I don't want to disturb him. You just hurry and get well so you and the baby can come with me when I hit the campaign trail in May."

"Blaine, please don't go. Can't you stay a few days so we can be a family for a while? No campaigning? No business? Just the three of us?"

"Now, Sunny, you of all people know some things can't wait. That's part of the reason I married you. You understand about the kind of life I lead." He leaned down and kissed her cheek. "You're just a little depressed from having a baby. The nurse says that happens sometimes." He patted her shoulder. "In no time at all you'll be up and about." He straightened and walked over to a mirror to smooth back his dark hair and check his appearance. "Maybe now that the baby

has come, you and I can get around to a decent sex life.
Little Bo came so soon that between you being sick in
the beginning and then getting so fat, we've never quite
gotten that part of our marriage in order, have we?" He
turned around and winked at her. "You take care of
yourself now. I'll be back later tonight."

He left then, and Sunny stared at the door. She
wanted so much to love him, and in some ways she did;
but he always left her feeling so empty. He seemed to
understand nothing at all about a woman's feelings and
needs, and she could already see he thought of little Bo
more as some kind of commodity rather than as his son.
And now, when she needed Blaine more than ever, he
was concerned with the political advantages of being a
new father. She had once worried about how she might
hurt him if she broke off the engagement. Now she realized he would have been angry only because he was
afraid it might hurt his political career. She could count
on one hand the number of times he had said he loved
her. Blaine O'Brien did not know the meaning of the
word.

Colt tilted back the chair inside the sheriff's office, putting his booted foot up on a table and picking up a tin
cup filled with coffee. "Not much longer till spring and
we can get rid of some of this damn snow," he commented to Rex Andrews. He sipped some of the coffee,
and Andrews got up from behind his desk and walked to
the potbelly stove that heated the jail, opening the door
and throwing in more wood. Both men wore jackets
against a bitter cold just outside the door that made it
difficult to keep things warm inside.

"Yeah," he answered. "Trouble with summer coming
is this town is going to be wilder than ever. The U.P. will
be here in a month or two. You're going to see more
cattle in this town than you've ever seen in your life.
They'll smell us clear back in Omaha."

Colt chuckled, picking up the morning newspaper.
"Just wait till they declare Wyoming officially a new Ter-

ritory. We'll have one hell of a time keeping order that day. Looks like it's going to be a busy year."

Andrews closed the stove door, then stayed near it to rub his hands together and absorb the heat. "I reckon." He turned to Colt. "But I expect you can handle it. You've been a big help, Colt. I wouldn't have made it this long without you. I'm glad I found a way to channel all that energy of yours—and that anger."

Colt set the paper aside a moment to roll himself a cigarette. "Yeah, well, I never said how long I'd do this. Too many people and too much civilization kind of wear on me after a while."

Andrews shrugged. "A man's got to settle sometime or other, Colt, find out what it is he wants to do and all. How old did you say you are? Thirty-one now?"

"Yup." Colt lit the cigarette.

"Well, I'd say it's time you took a wife—tried to have yourself another family to replace the one you lost. You can't roam aimlessly all your life."

"I suppose not. But when a man's already known the greatest love of his life, it's awfully hard to settle for second best."

Andrews sat back down at his desk. "Well, that wife of yours must have been some woman."

Colt didn't reply. How could he explain he hadn't been talking about LeeAnn, much as he cherished her memory. He took a deep drag on the cigarette and opened the newspaper, reading headlines about another Sioux rampage far to the north in Powder River country. Things were getting so bad that some forts had to be closed. He could not help secretly rooting for Red Cloud and his warriors, who were winning some decisive battles against miners flooding into Montana, where more gold had been discovered. But he knew how it would all ultimately end.

He scanned the rest of the front page, then saw the smaller headline. *Son Born to U.P. Magnate, Blaine O'Brien.* He removed the cigarette from his mouth and straightened in his chair, setting the cigarette in an ashtray on the table. *Mrs. Blaine O'Brien, formerly railroad and freighting heiress Sunny Landers, gave birth to an eight-pound two-ounce son, Beauregard Stuart, on February twenty-six of eighteen and sixty-eight. Mother and child are doing fine. The baby's father is currently on a speaking tour in his campaign for governor of the state of New York.* He read the article over again, feeling a strange tingle that he could not explain. He found himself counting back, remembered his liaison with Sunny had been near the end of May '67, almost nine months to the day. She had married Blaine over two weeks later.

He read the article again, reliving the torture that plagued him at the thought of Sunny lying in Blaine O'Brien's bed. He told himself he was crazy to think the baby could be his own. It must have been born a little early, but eight pounds was awfully big for an early baby.

He picked up his cigarette and tossed the paper into a wastebasket. There was no sense in thinking about Sunny anymore or considering the baby could be his. All such thoughts did was stir up this terrible hunger and jealousy, anger and frustration. Andrews was right. He should be thinking of his own future, having his own children. "I'm going to make the rounds, see if everybody made it through the night without anybody getting robbed or killed." He put the cigarette into his mouth again and took his heavier sheepskin jacket from a hook near the door.

"Oh, things get pretty quiet when it's this cold. It's this summer when you won't get any sleep."

Colt smiled, a great sadness filling him. He took out his revolver and checked it, then finished buttoning his coat and put on a hat. He walked out into a stinging wind. Bits of snow and sleet spit through the air, and he thought how the cold, gloomy weather reflected how he felt on the inside. He wished he had killed Vince Landers, but the man wasn't worth hanging for, and there was no changing the damage he had done.

Billie had been the only one left who knew how he felt, and now she was gone too. He missed her. How could he explain how he felt to someone like Rex Andrews, especially when it came to how much he had loved Sunny Landers? The man would think he had lost his mind.

He realized he was right back where he had started years ago, completely alone. Maybe that was just the way it was supposed to be for men like himself. He dropped the cigarette and stepped it out, pulling his hat down and ducking into the wind to cross the street.

Chapter 28

Blaine sat silent inside the coach as it splashed through fresh puddles from a recent rain. Sunny held little six-month-old Bo in her arms, feeling so weary she wondered how she found the energy to walk. "I'm so sorry, Blaine."

For a moment he remained silent. "How did it happen?" He finally spoke up. "I worked so hard for this, Sunny. To not even win the *primaries* . . . I don't understand it."

"Who knows how the minds of the general public think? Sometimes the common person just doesn't trust someone with as much wealth as we have. They think a man like you would serve only your own interests if you were elected."

"I don't need to hear it from my own wife."

She sighed in exasperation, leaning her head back

and closing her eyes. It had been a long night, waiting in the ballroom of a hotel owned by Blaine himself in the heart of Manhattan. He had ordered champagne and caviar, a bevy of fancy foods and celebration ornaments, but the big party he had planned never came to be. He had lost before even making it to the general elections in November. It was two A.M., and Sunny's legs ached from standing so much. Bo had been fussy all night from being in such noisy surroundings, and the general strain of the evening was catching up to Sunny, who had never truly had time to recover from Bo's birth. Blaine had her out campaigning by the time Bo was a month old.

"Blaine, I'm just trying to figure out—"

"Don't try, Sunny. It's partly your fault anyway."

She sat up a little straighter and looked at him. *"My* fault! What are you talking about? I worked so hard for you."

"You missed several stops because of the damn baby."

"The what?"

He made a groaning sound, putting his hand to his eyes. "Sunny, I never wanted a child this soon. I knew it would interfere with the campaigning. I thought afterward that it would be good for publicity, especially if you had the child along on public appearances; but he kept you from being at my side like you should have been."

"For God's sake, Blaine, he's your *son!* How can you talk about him like he's just a thing that's in your way!"

"Because he *is* in the way! You got pregnant with him right away, got fat right away—all before our marriage could even get off the ground! You were sick and we couldn't make love, you couldn't finish that trip. I missed my hunting expedition in Africa because of him. You couldn't campaign with me in your last months, and even a month after he was born you kept complaining about being too sick and too tired, and the damn baby cried all the time."

"He had colic! As far as my getting pregnant, that takes two, you know, and I don't recall you refusing to come to my bed."

"I might not have been so adamant about it if I had gotten some kind of decent response out of you. I kept wondering what was wrong with me, why I couldn't please you sexually. That's why I was always wanting you, hoping you'd loosen up and enjoy it. But you never have."

The carriage pulled up in front of their town house, and Blaine climbed out and marched up to the door without waiting for Sunny. Stunned by his remarks, Sunny climbed out on shaky legs, holding little Bo close, realizing more and more that he was all she had. Apparently, Blaine O'Brien had meant to use them both as tools to glory. Now that it had backfired, he would be colder and more distant than ever. Was this what she could expect for the rest of their married life?

She went inside after him, and Blaine had already shed his hat and light jacket. It was a hot, sultry August night, and for Sunny the air seemed heavier and more oppressive than it really was. She handed a sleeping Bo to a servant and told her to put the child to bed, then removed her straw hat and followed Blaine into the study, where he was lighting a thin cigar. She closed the study door. "Blaine, don't shut us out like this."

He turned, his dark eyes blazing. "He won after all, didn't he? He didn't have to beat me in a physical contest; the sonofabitch didn't have to beat me financially or socially, but he won all the same. He had my woman first, sired her *bastard,* and ultimately caused me to lose the elections!"

Sunny felt her cheeks going hot. "What are you talking about?"

He stepped a little closer. "I'm talking about Colt *Travis!*" he snapped.

Shivers ran through her. "I don't know what you mean—"

"The *hell* you don't! A few weeks ago I had occasion to talk to Tom Canary, Sunny! You know what he told me? The bastard made the snide remark that he didn't realize what a horsewoman you were. I asked him what he meant, and he told me that when he and other U.P. men had gone out to the work camp last year when they had all that Indian trouble, they had to call you in from God knows where—that you'd been out *riding* with Colt Travis! He said he thought I knew about it, and that was why he never mentioned it that first time I saw him in Omaha just before we left to come back to Chicago. That bastard never liked you anyway, Sunny—doesn't believe in women having any power. There's nothing he enjoys more than making you look bad, but then, he didn't really have to *try,* did he? *You* did that all by yourself!"

Sunny grasped the back of a chair, holding his eyes boldly. "So I went riding with Colt. So what? It's *you* I married, remember?"

"Save it, you *slut!*"

The word hit her like a physical blow. She thought about her mother and grandmother, took on all the guilt in that one statement. She literally gasped, turning away and grasping her stomach. Canary! He had always been an arrogant bastard, always voted opposite her at meetings, always made remarks about the U.P.'s "token woman." She could picture his face when he made the remark to Blaine.

"Tell me, Sunny. Just who *is* the father of that pretty, dark-skinned baby boy upstairs?" Blaine walked closer when he made the remark. "Is he the bastard I *think* he is?"

She whirled. "Don't talk about my baby that way! He's a sweet, innocent little boy who never needs to know the difference. I married *you,* and if you had shown one ounce of genuine love and compassion, one sign that you loved me for me and not for my name, I could *easily* have loved you the way I should, Blaine! I made vows to you that I intend to *keep.*"

The blow came from nowhere, sending her reeling. She fell to her right, crashing over a table and lamp, cutting her cheek on the glass bottom of the lamp when it broke. She felt herself being pulled to her feet, felt another blow. The suddenness and the power of her husband's fists so stunned her that she had no resistance at first. Blaine grabbed her by the hair after she went down the second time and yanked her to a sitting position, kneeling over her. "You lifted your skirts for Colt Travis like a common *whore,* didn't you!"

She could make no reply, barely able to see him through blurred vision. *It was beautiful and good,* she wanted to tell him. *Please don't say it that way! I loved him. Why can't anybody understand how much I loved Colt?*

"*Slut!* Why in hell did you go ahead and marry me, huh? Did you figure to get your jollies from your half-breed stud and then marry me for *prestige?* Is he the reason you're always talking about getting back out to Omaha and the railroad?"

"No," she managed to mutter. "You . . . don't understand, Blaine." Those words! Those horrible words! *Slut* and *whore.* "It wasn't like you . . . think," she muttered. "Please . . . don't make it . . . so ugly. You're my . . . husband, Blaine. I would never . . . never be untrue to my . . . wedding vows." She could feel blood running down the side of her neck from the cut on her cheek.

"I got all the answers I needed the minute I mentioned Colt Travis! I saw it in your eyes, bitch!" Again he yanked her to her feet. "If I had won that election like I should have, I wasn't going to say a thing! I was going to let it go, put on the image of happy husband and father for the public. But that's all changed now. I've *lost,* and I don't like losing at *anything,* Sunny!" He held her by the arms, and she stood there limp and in shock. "The worst part is you and that baby screwed it all up for me! And to know the kid isn't even mine makes it all that much more infuriating! I not only lost that election, but I lost because of that no good, worthless bastard *Indian!*"

"Blaine . . . please . . . let me talk. We can . . . work it out. We've been friends for so . . . long. You . . . loved me, and I . . . want to love you . . . be a good wife—"

"*Love* you? I never loved you, Sunny! I *picked* you because you were the perfect wife for a man of prestige and power, a woman who understood my world, who would look good in the governor's mansion—maybe even the White House! I *chose* you, Sunny, like a man chooses a prize horse! We were going to be the perfect couple, the talk of society, admired by everyone in the state of New York, maybe someday by the whole nation. But you went and ruined *all* of it!"

There came more blows, another ugly tirade of name-calling. Sunny had no idea where she was in the room, which furniture she was crashing into. She only knew she heard things breaking, heard his ugly words, felt blows to the face, to her ribs, her stomach, in total shock from the horror of discovering that the gentlemanly Blaine O'Brien could be capable of such violence. "He won," he kept saying. "Colt Travis outdid me after all! The sonofabitch can't give you as much as department store jewelry, but he won anyway!"

"Mr. O'Brien!" Sunny heard one of the servants calling from outside the doors. "What's wrong? What's—" Sunny heard the door slide open, heard a scream.

"Get the hell out of here," Blaine shouted. "Get out of here and keep your mouth shut!"

"But Mrs. O'Brien—"

"Get out!" The words were more of a roar.

Sunny heard the woman let out a wail. "My God! My God," she cried. Sunny could not move, and she thought how strange it was that at the moment she could not feel anything. She sensed she was on the floor, and she began crawling, something inside telling her she had to get away before Blaine killed her, wanting to live now only for the sake of poor little Bo. She had to protect Bo. Her movements were stopped when Blaine picked her up like a rag doll and threw her against a piano. Sunny heard the sound of the piano keys hitting their strings in odd notes as she again slid to the floor, her hand grasping the keyboard.

"Thanks to you I can't hold my head up in this town," Blaine stormed. "I've lost an election, and I don't like that, Sunny, not one bit! I won't say anything about what a slut my wife is, because I don't intend to live with that kind of shame and gossip! We'll put on a pretty front for others, but at home this marriage is *ended!* You, my little whore, are *stuck* with it! You're going to go the rest of your life without a man in your bed, because *I* won't be there, and if you take any other man, I'll beat you again! Understand? You're in my little prison, Sunny, and I'm *never* unlocking the doors!"

She could feel him leaning close then, heard his growled words. "If and when I *do* choose to come to your bed, it will be for sheer manly pleasure, not love. That's how it is with *whores,* you know! And it will be only to have children of our own so the marriage looks good, and so I have an heir to my fortune! But don't expect that little bastard upstairs to get one penny of what's mine! I'm cutting him out of my will! I'll let *you* explain to him when he's older!"

He kicked aside the piano bench against which Sunny was leaning, so that she tumbled all the way to the floor.

"We'll talk more when I get back," he growled, standing over her with authority. "You cost me a hunting trip to Africa, and I'm by God going to take it! If we're going to keep this marriage together, I have a lot to think about, and for a while I don't want to see your face or see that worthless baby upstairs! I'm getting the hell out of New York and away from the *both* of you!"

Sunny was vaguely aware of Blaine leaving the room. Moments later she heard the servant Trudy exclaiming over her, "Dear God! Oh, my God, what has he done to you, Mrs. O'Brien!" Sunny wished Mae were there. She had left her in Omaha. Blaine did not want any of her servants coming to New York with her. Mae would be such a comfort. Maybe Vi. If she could just talk, she'd tell Trudy to send for Vi.

"I'll get a doctor," Trudy was saying. Sunny heard a door slam. "Thank God he's left," Trudy said. "He can't hurt you anymore, ma'am. Oh, you poor thing." The woman yelled for help. Moments later Sunny heard the butler, Robert, also carrying on. She felt herself being lifted, and now the pain began to set in. It seemed to be everywhere, her head, her back, her ribs, her stomach, her insides. She tasted blood and Trudy went on about blood dripping on the carpet. "Get her to her bed," the woman told Robert. "I'll send for the doctor."

"What should we tell him, Trudy?"

"I don't know! Dear God, I never thought Mr. O'Brien was capable of something like this! I've always thought him an arrogant man and he certainly has never been overly kind to us, but this! Oh, such a beautiful, sweet woman she is! How could he do this!"

"Baby . . . my baby," Sunny mumbled.

"The boy is fine, sleeping soundly," Robert assured her, not realizing she meant the baby she thought she might be carrying by Blaine. She had been saving the surprise for after the elections, thinking to add to Blaine's celebration by telling him she was going to have another child. He had not given her the chance.

"I'll say she fell down the stairs," Trudy was saying. "Mr. O'Brien is much too important for the doctor to dare say it was anything else. I'll call Dr. Tims, Mr. O'Brien's personal physician. He'll be discreet about it."

"Yes, yes. Well, hurry and send someone for him. She's in a bad way."

Sunny rested her head on Robert's shoulder, and as consciousness began to leave her, she thought it was someone else holding her. "Colt," she whispered.

Since the Union Pacific had come through, the wild, fast-growing town of Cheyenne, Wyoming, was bursting at the seams with people from all walks of life. The summer of '68 saw thousands of cattle move through the town, brought in by surrounding ranchers and on drives from the south to be boarded onto trains that would take them to Chicago for slaughter. Numerous side tracks held additional locomotives and waiting cattle cars, and it had already been decided that more would be needed the next summer. The town citizens joked that if the dust or a stray bullet didn't choke or kill a person, the smell would do him in.

After a wild shootout with bank robbers the day before, Colt was given some time off to recover from a minor bullet wound that had grazed his left hip. He sat in his room at the Eat & Sleep boardinghouse, owned by an older couple by the name of Perry from the South who had lost everything they owned in the war and had come west to start over. It was Mrs. Perry who had brought the morning paper for him, along with a cup of coffee.

Colt picked up the paper and read the headline. *Infamous Cheyenne Leader, Roman Nose, Killed in Heated Battle. So,* he thought, *another good man down.* He had followed the Indian problems closely, wondering if he would ever get over his own guilt for killing White Buffalo. *The Cheyenne leader, Roman Nose, was killed recently during a siege against Major George A. Forsyth and approximately fifty experienced scouts, who were pinned down on an island along the Arikaree River in Kansas, from September 15 until September 25. The scouts were surrounded and held on the island by hundreds of attacking Cheyenne. Shielded only by their own hand-dug rifle pits, and many nearly starving to death, Forsyth's scouts hung on in a heroic effort against warring Cheyenne intent on a massacre. The scouts had been hired on order of General Phil Sheridan to help track those Indians who have been committing depredations against settlers throughout Kansas, Nebraska, and Colorado.*

On the morning of September 25 the 10th Cavalry arrived on the scene to find hungry, battered but cheering scouts still entrenched in what is now being called Beecher's Island, after a Lieutenant Frederick H. Beecher, who was killed in the fight. By the time the scouts were rescued, at least six had been killed and another fifteen wounded. Forsyth reported at least thirty Indians killed and close to a hundred wounded. For the last few days of the fight, Forsyth's men survived on boiled horse flesh.

It is hoped that the death of Roman Nose will take some of the fire out of the constantly warring Cheyenne. General Sheridan will continue to pursue the savages, and has promised General Sherman that there will be no peace for the Cheyenne for many months to come.

Colt folded the newspaper and sighed, reaching over to pick up a prerolled cigarette and lighting it. He winced with the stinging pain in his hip, a wound that was not major, but bad enough to make a man grimace when he moved around too much. He sat up on the edge of the bed, too restless to let the pain keep him on his back, but forced to gingerly lean to one side to avoid putting pressure on the sore spot.

He took a deep drag on the cigarette, thinking how he could have been there at Beecher's Island if he had answered the ad he had seen a few weeks earlier calling for experienced scouts. He had been tempted to take up his old profession and get back out on the Plains, but he had come to like Rex Andrews and knew the man depended on him to help with the demanding job of trying to keep some kind of order in Cheyenne.

He grasped the iron post at the foot of the bed and managed to stand up, then limped over to a window, watching the bustling, dusty street below. He had to admit that Andrews had had a good idea offering him a deputy's job. Although he usually hated so much noise and civilization, ever since Sunny had married Blaine O'Brien he had needed the excitement and danger, the busy schedule he kept and the outlet it gave him for all the pent-up anger. Being in Cheyenne left him little time to think about the hurt. To return to the open plains and be entirely alone again was now something he didn't think he could bear.

He smoked quietly, allowing himself a rare thought about Sunny. He had struggled against the memories, worked long hours so that sleep came quickly, all in an effort not to lie awake and think too much. It was times like this when it all came back so clearly for him—those blue eyes, that delicious smile, the feel of her body against his own, the ecstasy of claiming her.

He sighed angrily. That was the hell of it. *He* had claimed her first. Sunny belonged to him, and he knew damn well nobody else was going to love her as he had, although sometimes he almost hated her. As time went by he felt more and more angry that she had not come to him in the first place.

He turned away from the window, another painful shiver of remorse moving through him. God, how he had loved her, and much as he hated to admit it, he still did. The thought of her lying in Blaine O'Brien's bed stabbed at his gut like a knife. He would never forgive himself for riding off that day they had returned to camp and letting her go back to Omaha alone. He felt an explosive fury every time he imagined Vince lighting into her, insulting her, telling her the devastating news about her mother. The only thing that had kept him from killing Vince was the fact that his children were in the house. If he had gotten hold of the man alone, someplace where there was no law . . .

He couldn't bear sitting around like this. He smashed out the cigarette angrily and began dressing. He had to get out and keep busy in spite of his pain. Minutes later he left the room, leaving the newspaper on the floor for Mrs. Perry's housekeeper to pick up when she cleaned his room. He had not read it all, but he didn't care.

A few hours later the cleaning lady arrived, straightening his bed and emptying an ashtray. She picked up the paper, deciding to sit down for a moment and scan through it before throwing it away. One article in particular happened to catch her eye.

Railroad and Shipping Magnate Blaine O'Brien Drowned at Sea! the headline read on page three. *Blaine O'Brien, owner of the ocean freighting and passenger line bearing his name, died at sea in a raging storm on the Atlantic. O'Brien was also heavily invested in the Union Pacific branch of the nearly completed transcontinental railroad, as well as . . .* The woman skipped down through the long list of Blaine's holdings, as well as his social accomplishments. . . . *Lost his bid for governor of New York State in the August primaries . . . an avid big-game hunter . . . decided to journey again to Africa for a hunting vacation after a hard campaign . . .*

She scanned through more words, always eager to read about famous people. *Mrs. O'Brien, the former Sunny Landers, had not accompanied her husband on his voyage due to injuries from a bad fall sustained only one day before Mr. O'Brien left for Africa. The O'Briens have one son, Beauregard Stuart, who is six months old. . . . O'Brien's death leaves Sunny O'Brien heiress to an even greater fortune than that which she had already inherited from her father. It is estimated that her combined wealth surpasses even that of Cornelius Vanderbilt. . . . Memorial services were held September twenty-four, eighteen hundred and sixty-eight, at St. John's Lutheran Cathedral, New York City. Mrs. O'Brien remains in seclusion, refusing to speak to reporters.*

"Well, I'll be," the woman muttered, always enjoying reading about the misfortunes of rich people. She folded the newspaper and put it in with the rest of the collected trash.

February 1869

Sunny watched Bo crawl around beneath the huge Christmas tree in the downstairs parlor of her Omaha home. More and more the boy, a year old now, was looking like his father. He was strong and active and adventurous, and so beautiful. He was almost walking now, pulling himself up by grasping furniture, sometimes taking several steps with no help.

Whenever she looked at her son, she saw a reminder of how beautiful her love for Colt had been, not the ugly, whoring lust Blaine and Vince had both tried to make it seem. She wondered sometimes if she would ever get over the ugliness of that night when Blaine had beat her, not just the physical pain she had suffered for weeks afterward, but the emotional pain of his cruel words, and the deep abiding pain of having lost a baby. Maybe if she had told Blaine she was carrying his child . . . but then, life was full of maybes. The shock of learning about her mother, of loving Colt so intensely and then having to abandon that love, the emotional abuse she had suffered from Blaine, followed by the vicious beating and Blaine's untimely death, had all left her weary and near collapse. The only thing that kept her going and gave her a reason to go on in spite of her grief and guilt, was her son, her little bit of Colt Travis. In all that had happened, her little boy remained innocent of any wrongdoing. He was her only joy.

Sunny had come back to Omaha because it had become the only place she felt content and at peace. She decided that was because it was close to the land Colt loved, the land she and Colt together had loved. She had left others in charge and had come here to be alone, to think about what she should do, whether she should try to find Colt. Maybe it would hurt more to find him and discover he hated her and wanted nothing to do with her than to just let sleeping dogs lie and allow the poor man to go on with his life, leaving her out of it. Maybe he had found some other woman by now. Still, he had a son. It only seemed right that he should know about Bo. Even if he didn't love or want her anymore, he had a right to be aware of the existence of his own flesh and blood. She knew how important that would be to him.

She wondered how, with all her experience in the world of business and power, she could have made such a shambles of her personal life. Not only had she hurt Colt deeply, but she had destroyed the sweet love they had shared, and now she carried the guilt of feeling responsible for Blaine's death. If not for their fight that night over Colt, he might not have left. His cruelty could never be forgiven, and she would forever be haunted by his vicious abuse, yet the fact that he had left in anger and had ended up dying made her feel as though she were the cause. She still carried a faint scar on her cheek from that awful night, and to her it was like being branded a harlot.

Vi had told her over and over that it was Blaine's fault, not hers; but she could not shed her part of the responsibility, nor could she avoid the fact that all of it was more Vince's fault than anyone's. She was going to do her best to correct that today. She walked to a window to see if anyone had arrived yet for the special meeting she had called, and she saw a fancy coach approaching the curved, brick drive. "Good, Vince," she said softly, her eyes cold and hard. "You came."

Never had she been more determined, and in a sense she had never felt stronger. She thought how ironic it was that she was the richest woman in America, but the most unhappy, with no reason for living other than her little boy. What she was determined to do might bring her more trouble, but she had made a decision, and she was going to go through with it. What kind of problems would Colt give her over the boy? If he hated her and wanted no part of her life but wanted rights to Bo, how would it all be handled? Blaine had not yet changed anything in his will before leaving for Africa, which meant she and Bo had inherited a vast fortune. Little Bo, the son of a half-Indian scout who cared nothing for riches, stood to become one of the richest men in the country one day.

For now, though, the boy could do nothing to help his mother with the burdens she would face. Blaine's mother and sister had wanted no part of running any of the businesses. They were satisfied to simply live a life of leisure and travel, wiring Sunny for more money whenever they needed it. The bulk of the estate, which meant the bulk of the work and decisions, had fallen to Sunny, small shoulders that now carried a bigger burden than ever. Blaine had good men running his various enterprises, and Sunny was perfectly willing to leave things in their hands for the time being. She was not emotionally ready yet to take on her vast new holdings. She had left everything to the men already in charge, with a request for monthly reports to be sent to Omaha. In time, she supposed, she would make trips to New York to oversee her new interests there, perhaps sell some of the businesses; but she had not decided just what to do yet about the logging business Blaine had been building in Oregon.

Her new wealth was staggering, all too much to think about, overwhelming even for a Landers. The strange part was, she never wanted any of it, yet could not bring herself to shirk the responsibilities that had landed in her lap. She still found her greatest joy in the simplest things, like horseback riding, and now her little boy.

She watched Vince and Eve, Stuart and Vi climb out of Stuart's coach, and moments later she heard voices outside the parlor doors. She breathed deeply for the courage she would need, picked up Bo, and held him tightly as a servant led her two brothers and their wives into the room. She glared at Vince, seeing in his own eyes a trace of remorse but the ever-present belligerence. Eve marched in ahead of him, shoulders back, head erect.

"This had better be worth the trip, Sunny," she snipped. "We don't particularly care to be summoned all the way from Chicago on a whim. Vince is a busy man. With Stuart and Vi right here in Omaha, why couldn't you have settled whatever it is you need to settle with them and then written us?" She folded her arms. "Unless, of course, you wanted to personally rub it in about your newfound fortune. I must say—"

"Shut up, Eve," Sunny interrupted, her eyes still on Vince. "Sit down—all of you."

Eve sucked in her breath in fury at the personal affront. She started to speak again, but when Sunny met her eyes she stiffened at the cold hatred she saw there. She was already aware that Sunny had changed dramatically since Blaine's death. According to Vince, when she returned to Chicago for a few brief meetings before coming to Omaha, she had been a hard, bitter woman, nothing like the Sunny they used to know. Had her new wealth gone to her head? Was she just out to lord it over the rest of her family because of Vince's threats to Colt Travis? Surely the half-breed couldn't have meant *that* much to her, Eve thought. After all, look at how she had benefitted from marrying Blaine. Still, this was certainly not the old, forgiving Sunny. The look in her eyes made Eve back away and take a chair, as did the others.

Vince watched his sister warily. Sunny had not spoken to him since the night he told her about her mother other than at a couple of business meetings in Chicago. He was fully aware of the power she wielded now, power she could use to destroy him if she chose.

Sunny scanned all their faces, still holding Bo. "Vi already knows most of what I am going to tell you," she finally said.

Stuart thought how different she looked, still beautiful, but harder, her hair pulled straight back into a bun, a light scar on her cheek from her fall.

"I am tired of secrets in this family," she began. "I am going to clear up a few things today and put an end to *all* the secrets." She turned to Eve. "The things I have to say can't be put into a telegram or a letter or delivered verbally by someone else. They have to come from me, and you are going to sit there and listen."

Eve stiffened, her eyes little slits of haughty disgust, her thin lips pressed tightly together. Sunny turned her own hard blue eyes to Vince. "Vi told me that Colt paid you a little visit a while back," she said with a sneer. "As far as I am concerned, I wish Colt could have gotten away with *killing* you, and I am sure he would have if you had been out in the lawless land where he comes from." She leaned down to set Bo on the floor again. He shimmied over an Oriental rug to Vi, smiling and reaching up for her. Vince just glared angrily at Sunny.

"At any rate," Sunny went on, "the result of Colt's visit was that Vi and Eve discovered the truth about my mother, a truth that had been kept from me all my life and one that nearly destroyed me." She turned and began pacing, arms folded. "You all know that Vince used that truth to keep me from marrying Colt, the only man I have ever truly loved. He also threatened to have Colt killed. I suppose I should have trusted in Colt's love enough to realize he wouldn't have cared about my background, but at the time the news was so devastating, I couldn't think straight. When I look back on it now, I realize I should have told Vince that everything I have could be his if he would promise not to tell and would not make threats on Colt's life. I could have and *should* have gone to Colt and said to hell with my fortune. But sometimes we do foolish things when we are full of sorrow and torture, when someone we love is threatened, or when we fear we'll see something besides love in their eyes. Besides, giving everything over to Vince would have been a betrayal of father's trust in me. It would have been the ultimate victory for Vince." She stopped to concentrate a hateful glare at her brother. "And Colt would not have wanted that to happen." She stepped closer to Vince. "I married a man I didn't love because of you, and in some respects Blaine's death is also your fault. If not for that unhappy marriage—" She stopped and sighed. "Vi came to help me after my so-called fall. She knows it wasn't a fall at all. Blaine, the man who, according to you, Vince, was the proper man to marry, beat me within an inch of my life, blamed *me* for his losing the election. He used his fists on me brutally. He caused me to cut my face, and to lose a baby." She began to shiver, and she turned away.

"My God!" Stuart muttered.

"I suppose considering some of his other reasons, a man could be angry enough to do something like that," Sunny went on, "but there is never a reason for a man to beat a woman nearly to death. He could have divorced me, brought me all kinds of public shame—" Her voice began to break, and she stopped to regain her composure.

"Sunny, I'm sorry," Stuart spoke up. "If I had known what was really going on, how much you loved Colt—I thought you *wanted* to marry Blaine."

"Don't be sorry, Stuart. There is only one person in this room who is responsible. I called you and Vi here so that you would know about a decision I have made."

"Dammit, Sunny, I never thought Blaine was capable of that kind of cruelty," Vince told her, "or I—"

"Or you what?" Sunny stood staunchly before him, her hate-filled eyes now red with tears. "You wouldn't have changed a thing! Don't pretend your sympathy, Vince. I don't want to hear it!" She held her chin a little higher. "At any rate, the night of the beating Blaine also told me he had found out I had gone riding alone with Colt before our marriage. He accused Colt of being Bo's father." She held Vince's eyes. "And he was *right!*"

Eve's eyes widened, and she put a hand to her mouth.

"Jesus Christ," Vince muttered, looking away from her and taking a cigar from his pocket.

"I don't want to hear your judgment of me or your opinion of Colt," Sunny told him. "Nor do I want to hear your lamentations about how Colt Travis has won a part of my fortune after all through his son. Much as you refuse to believe it, Colt never wanted the money, Vince. He wanted only me, but I let you ruin the beautiful love we shared. I don't know if I can ever get it back, but I intend to try. Colt Travis has a son, and he deserves to know that. I am going to try to find Colt. He has lost so much in his lifetime. Knowing he has a son will mean a lot to him, and I owe it to him to tell him. And you, Vince, are not going to stop me or threaten Colt. I can destroy you in twenty-four hours. It doesn't matter if I have to destroy Landers Enterprises to do it, because I don't *need* Landers Enterprises anymore! I suggest you remember that. I would always see that Stuart and Vi are taken care of, and I might set up trust funds for your children, but if you threaten my son, or Colt, or any decision I make from now on, you and Eve will be living in the streets eating out of garbage barrels. Is that understood?" Vince's face glowed red, and Sunny enjoyed the look of defeat in his hated blue eyes. "Say it so I can hear it," she said, looking at Eve. "Both of you. Do you understand?"

Eve literally withered, looking at her lap. "I understand," she said quietly.

"Understood," Vince added. He lit his cigar, feeling the fury and frustration at being totally at his sister's mercy.

"Fine." Sunny scanned all their faces, feeling a little better at the look of approval on Vi's face. "From now on," she told them, "I am going to conduct my life the way I choose. If it brings gossip, then I will live with it. There is nothing anyone can do to me anymore. My mistake was in thinking I had to protect Colt from the same gossip, from those who would ridicule and insult him. He's more man than any I've ever known, and in spite of the violence he's known and participated in, even a man like Colt would never do to a woman what Blaine did to me. In that respect Colt is more the gentleman than Blaine ever was, and I realize now that I fully underestimated his strength, not just physical, but emotional. I should have given him the chance to prove he could find a way for us to be together, a way for us to survive in each other's worlds."

She walked over and took Bo from Vi's lap. "What's done is done. I don't care what you know, and I don't care what any of you think of me. The only tiny bit of happiness I have left is Bo, and probably the only remnant I can salvage of the love Colt and I shared is to at least let Colt share in the upbringing of his son. I can't think of a better father for a boy who will inherit a fortune and who will need someone who can keep his head the proper size. Colt can do that. He can teach him things all the universities and wealthy friends in the world could never teach him. I don't know if Colt can ever love or forgive me for hurting him like I did, but I think he'll want to know about Bo, and if letting him be a father to the boy means letting him into our lives, then that is what we will do. You, Vince and Eve, will welcome him and show the world that he has been accepted by the family—*if* I am lucky enough to even find him. Is *that* understood?"

Vince puffed angrily on his cigar. "You know what it will do to the family, Sunny, how it will look in the papers."

"I told you I don't give a damn. I am going to find Colt. It might take a while." Her voice softened slightly. "It's always difficult to capture the wind, but I'm going to try." She looked at Vince again. "What I have suffered, what Colt has suffered, is all ultimately because of you. It might as well have been your hands that beat me and broke my ribs and injured my kidneys and left this scar on my face."

She watched Vince's eyes widen at the words. "Oh, yes, my loving brother, Blaine did a fine job on me. I still have nightmares about it, still thank God he didn't decide to go upstairs and finish his anger on little Bo. But that is water over the dam. There was a time when I probably should have given up my share of our fortune to get you off my back. Colt and I even discussed that, believe it or not. But Colt told me that to give it all up would be to let you win. He said that together we could fight all outside forces, that neither of us would have to give up what we love just to be together. There was a time when giving up my fortune might have let me have the only true love of my life. Now it's my increased fortune that will defeat you, Vince. You can't touch me now. The only sad part is that it's probably too late for me. But it isn't too late for my son to grow up knowing the truth about his father." She looked at Stuart. "I want you to help me find Colt, Stuart. Check with the army forts farther west. Maybe he's scouting for them, what with all the Indian trouble. I want someone to check out Indian Territory. Colt is part Cherokee. Maybe he went back there. Check with the Texas Rangers. Have someone talk to some of the railroad workers. Someone has to have some idea where he is."

Vi decided not to mention Billie White. Out of her own curiosity she had looked for the woman herself, but the saloon where she used to work had been torn down and replaced by a church. She found only one person who had known Billie, but that person didn't know where she had gone.

Vi was glad Sunny was finally doing what she should have done two years before, but Sunny was right about one thing. Finding Colt Travis would be like chasing the wind. After all that had happened, holding him might be even harder.

Chapter 29

Late April 1869

 Sunny finished scanning the latest reports from New York, then signed a few letters, trying to get as much work done as possible before leaving for Utah. It was time to head west for the joining of the rails, expected to take place by mid-May, perhaps even sooner. She put down her pen and rose, walking to a window to watch the busy streets of Omaha, much more a thriving city than it was twelve years ago, when first she came here. The railroad was mostly responsible. She realized now that the railroad was responsible for many things that had taken place in her life. It was what had led her to meet Colt, and ultimately it had driven them apart.

From where she stood she could see the U.P.'s already-busy depot and the stockyards that lay beyond it. In spite of her bitterness over what she considered a kind of betrayal by the father she had loved so dearly, she knew that Bo Landers's dream had been very real, and so had his love for her. Vince had not been able to destroy that memory, and now that the railroad was nearing completion, she decided it was time to remember how important this had been to her father, remember the passion, the higher goals. She had promised on his deathbed that she would help finish the dream, and she had held true to that promise, but it had cost her so much.

She had never been able to bring herself to hate her father or to believe that he had not truly loved Lucille Madison. She certainly would never believe he had not loved his daughter with utter devotion and near worship. Now it seemed only fitting that she should be at the final ceremony for the Union Pacific, and she knew that on that day Bo Landers would be with her.

Someone else should also be there, but she had been unable to find Colt. The only thing she had salvaged from all these years she had loved him was their son, and now the dream of finishing the railroad took second place to her dream of finding Colt again.

She walked back to her desk to sign a few more letters. In just a couple of hours her train would be leaving, taking the entire family to Utah. Each member of the family would have their own private car, and Sunny would take Bo and Mae with her. Stuart and Vince were both bringing their wives and children. Sunny had decided to set aside her hatred for Vince for the time being, for the sake of his children, who were excited and eager to see the "Great American Desert" and be among the first to travel all the way to California by train.

Nineteen-year-old Vince, Jr., would not be with them. He was at Yale studying law. But sixteen-year-old Joyce, twelve-year-old Linda and eleven-year-old Mary were coming along. Stuart and Vi's daughter, Diana, now thirteen, as well as their ten-year-old son, Robert, and eight-year-old Sarah would make it a full family affair, and that was how Sunny intended things to be from now on. She would not have her son growing up in a family of hatred and back-biting. All the children had been told as delicately as possible who Bo's real father was, and as far as Sunny could tell, only Vince's eldest daughter, Joyce, who was beginning to closely resemble her mother in looks and personality, seemed to look down on her for it. The rest of the children were not particularly upset, although some were too young to truly comprehend what they had been told. Whether they liked it or not, Sunny was determined there would be no more secrets that could come out later in their lives and hurt them. And she was also determined that the family would become closer, even if it meant being civil to Vince. Bo was going to be raised in an atmosphere of love. In spite of his wealth, he was going to understand compassion and caring. Greed and malice would not be a part of his life, at least not while he was young. And even if Vince and Eve's participation was only out of fear of being financially destroyed, she figured that was better than Bo having to grow up with those two hating him and constantly attacking him as it had been for her all her own life.

The door to her Omaha office suddenly burst open, and Stuart came bounding in, his face showing his excitement. He carried a newspaper in his hand. "Sunny, look at this! All our work and expense trying to find Colt, and a damn newspaper article leads us right to him!"

Sunny felt the sudden, nearly painful tightness in her chest. She wanted so badly to find Bo's father; yet she desperately feared how he might react to her. To see him again and know he hated her would be a worse torture than anything she had endured so far. "What did you find?"

Stuart laid the Omaha newspaper in front of her. "Read that," he said, grinning excitedly and pointing to a headline.

Cheyenne Shootout Leaves Four Dead, Six Wounded
"A battle over water rights between two cattle ranch-

ers outside of Cheyenne, Wyoming, led to a major shootout inside the city limits four days ago," Sunny read aloud. "Men from both ranches got into a brawl at the Sundance Saloon after heavy drinking, and the fistfighting led to a gun battle outside in the street that was joined by a third party, that of Sheriff Rex Andrews and his deputy—" The name suddenly stuck in Sunny's throat.

"Colt Travis," Stuart finished for her. "Now, why am I not surprised that he's a deputy sheriff? Hell, he's done everything else." He took the paper from her. "Isn't this just the way you would expect to find him, shooting it out with a bunch of cattlemen in some wild western town?" He laughed lightly, but Sunny just sat in her chair, stunned.

"After nearly an hour of gunfire," Stuart continued for her, "the sheriff and his deputy, who was slightly wounded in the mélée—"

"Wounded?" Sunny looked up at him. "Colt was wounded?"

Stuart sat down on the edge of her desk. "It says only slightly. You know Colt. You could shoot his arm half off and he wouldn't think much of it. I'm sure he's okay, Sunny." He turned back to the article. "Let's see—the sheriff and his deputy . . . slightly wounded . . . arrested fourteen men, including those who had been wounded.

"A circuit judge is being called in to settle the water dispute and to determine who will pay for extensive damages to the Sundance Saloon. It is expected, as the West becomes more settled, that troubles over water rights will spread throughout Wyoming, Colorado, and Montana as well as other west and southwest territories where water is scarce.

"It is obvious from the shootout at Cheyenne that the West might be growing, but it is far from tamed. It is rumored that a novelist from New York City was present during the gunfight, and that he plans to write a book about it. More trouble is expected in Cheyenne from those men from both warring ranches who have not yet been jailed. Soldiers have been called in from Fort Laramie to help keep the peace."

Stuart laughed again, getting up and rolling the newspaper in his hand. "Doesn't that sound just like Colt? Right in the middle of things—a deputy sheriff. I wonder how he landed a job like that?"

"He probably welcomes the danger," Sunny answered. She rubbed her temples, her head suddenly aching from a surge of joy mixed with dread. It was hard for her to breathe, and her hands were shaking.

Stuart sobered, walking back to her desk. "Sunny, we know where to find him now. You should be happy."

She let out a halting, bitter laugh, putting her head back then to face him. "Oh, I am," she answered. "I just don't know what he'll do, Stuart, what he'll say. I want things to be like they were before, but I know they can't be. In a way I was almost hoping we *wouldn't* find him." Tears sprang into her eyes. "God, Stuart, he's going to hate me. I don't know if I can stand to see the look I know will be in those eyes when I see him."

Stuart came around the desk and put a hand on her shoulder. "Well, you won't know for certain unless you see him, will you? And you know damn well you can't *not* see him now that you know where he is. Come on, Sunny. You're the one who was so determined to do this. Just be strong about it like you are when you face Vince." He handed her a clean handkerchief from his jacket pocket.

"Facing Colt and facing Vince are not at all the same," she answered, wiping her eyes. "Colt can completely undo me with one look. My God, I love him so much, Stuart. I've loved him since I was fifteen years old. To see him again and have him hate me, to know he'll never hold me again, love me like he did before, it's going to be the worst thing I've ever faced."

"He has a son, Sunny. He can't hate the mother of his child."

She stared at the papers on her desk. "He can when he realizes that if not for Blaine's death, he might never have known."

"You did that to protect little Bo. He'll understand once he has time to think about it."

"I can only pray he will." Sunny rose, sighing deeply to control her tears. "I don't want him forewarned that we're coming," she said. "He won't know about Bo, and if he hears I'm coming, he just might bolt and run, figuring he's better off never seeing me again. He might not even know Blaine is dead. Either way, he's much too hard to find when he doesn't want to be found, so I'll just have to surprise him." She shivered. "I've faced a lot of powerful men, Stuart, but this one scares me more than anything I've faced till now. No decision I've ever made, even if it involved millions of dollars, has been as challenging as this one will be."

Stuart took her arm. "Come on. The train leaves in less than two hours. Get yourself home and finish packing. We have a trip to take, and little Bo is going to meet his father. It's all going to work out, Sunny. Sometimes I think I have more confidence in Colt than you have."

"Is that so?" She looked at the man and smiled affectionately. "You certainly have changed since marrying Vi. I'm glad I have one brother who cares about me."

He shrugged. "Vince cares too, Sunny. He just has a poor way of doing what he thinks is best for people, and he's a rotten judge of character. Besides, he doesn't have Vi for a wife."

They stopped near the doorway, and Sunny turned to him, more tears coming. "I need someone to hold me before I fall apart," she told him.

Stuart grinned a little bashfully. "Well, with the big salary you pay me, I guess I have to be good for *something,* don't I?" He put his arms around her, and Sunny couldn't help the bitter sobbing. She could not remember a time in her whole life when one of her brothers ever embraced her. She clung to him, and Stuart felt a tightness in his own throat.

"Hell, Sunny, I love you," he told her. "I'm sorry I never told you before." He kept a tight hold on her, praying Colt Travis was the compassionate, forgiving man he would need to be to handle what was to come.

He hated the thought of Sunny's heart being broken into any more pieces than it already was.

Colt tilted back the wooden chair outside the sheriff's office, putting a foot up on a railing. A group of cattle-men herded several hundred head past the end of the street, stirring up a cloud of dust that carried on the wind and made him turn away and rub his eyes. He had long ago gotten used to the smell of Cheyenne, with its dirt and a generous amount of horse and cow manure. He supposed the smell would get worse every summer, as more and more cattle were brought in to meet the trains heading east to the slaughterhouses in Chicago. Here it was only the first of May, and the real heat of summer was still ahead.

He lit a cigarette, nodding to a local farmer who drove a wagon past the office. He glanced at the cattle-men at the end of the street again. Since the judge had come and determined two men from the shootout should hang, and had set boundaries that allowed both warring ranchers involved to have access to a stream that ran between the two properties, things had not set-tled much. One rancher threatened to dam up his end of the stream, which was where the flow came from, and the judge warned that if he did such a thing, he would be arrested. A few more fistfights had broken out, but so far there had been no more gunfights.

Two young women walked past him on the boardwalk, one the daughter of a banker, the other the daughter of a blacksmith, both no more than eighteen years old. They stopped to say good morning to him, a look of invitation in their eyes. Colt grinned and greeted them, knowing full well their interest in him as a suitor. Both were pretty in their own way, but at thirty-two, they seemed too young to him now, and neither of them could compare to Sunny. He told himself he was a fool to always be comparing other women to one he could never have. He wanted very much to be able to love again, but he wasn't sure if he could. He watched the young ladies turn to each other and whisper and giggle as they walked away, watched the sway of their dresses, imagined how nice it would feel to have a decent woman love him and give him children again, like Lee-Ann, like Sunny might have done.

He knew from simple instinct that several available women in Cheyenne could be his for the asking, especially since that damn writer had been spreading it around that he was going to write a book about the shootout. He and Rex were being made out as heroes, but Colt's natural modesty and aversion to too much attention made the whole thing embarrassing for Colt. He kept trying to tell the pesty writer that he was just doing his job.

His side still ached from where a bullet had skimmed across a left rib during the shootout, nicking a piece of bone away, and he wondered how many more scars he would carry before going to his grave. Most of the soldiers were gone now, except for a small squad that remained to help keep an eye on things for a while. Colt felt bad about having killed one of the ranch hands himself, but when bullets were flying, a man had to do what he had to do. He could have predicted problems over water, seemed to remember mentioning that to Sunny once when they had talked about how the railroad would change the West.

Change it, it had. It had changed more than the land. It had changed a whole way of life for some people, especially the Indians. He thought how different everything was now from when he used to ride and scout with Slim. He was a different man himself from the twenty-year-old kid who took on the job of scouting for Bo Landers. Twelve years had passed.

He let out a whistling sigh of amazement, setting his chair back on all fours and rolling himself a cigarette. *Twelve years,* he thought. *I've loved her all that time.* What a fool he had been. Loving Sunny openly had led right smack into the disaster everyone had warned him it would. He lit the cigarette, finding it incredulous how much could happen to a man in twelve years, loving and losing a wife and son, living among the Cheyenne, fighting in that hideous war, spending time in a southern prison, going to work for the Union Pacific.

He could hear another train rolling in now, its whistle sounding throughout the city and to the mountains beyond. He took a deep drag on the cigarette, thinking how for two short days he had thought that maybe, just maybe, he had found the happiness for which he had searched for years, had finally won the love of his life, would be rid of all the loneliness and the one-nighters with whores who didn't really give a damn about him, except for Billie.

He smiled sadly, leaning back in the chair again and thinking what an unusual wife Sunny would have made if they had ever been able to marry. She would certainly not have been the conventional woman who would be waiting for him in a cozy little house every day, bread baked, clothes scrubbed. But then, what the hell? He could have lived with the businesswoman Sunny Landers, because the woman who came to his bed at night would have been completely different, as giving and loving and open as the best of them.

He angrily rose then, chiding himself for thinking about her. She had loved him with fiery passion, almost violently; but she had hurt him just as violently. Did she realize how shattered he had been, how empty his life had been since then, how hard it was for him to take an interest in another woman? There she was, lying in Blaine O'Brien's bed, and he was still visiting prostitutes, waking up with just as empty a feeling as when he fell into their beds the night before.

He leaned against a support post and watched the street with experienced eyes and ears, always ready for trouble. He had learned early on that a lawman couldn't be too careful. In spite of the growing civilization, most men figured it was all right to take the law into their own hands, something he still believed himself in some respects. He could think of one man he would have killed if he could have gotten him somewhere out in those hills beyond town. Killing Vince Landers slowly would have been a pleasure.

He swatted a fly, scowling at the fact that it existed at

all. He thought it was too early in the season for flies. There would be enough of the pesky things around once the real heat of summer set in at the stockyards on the other side of the railroad tracks. He watched the same two young women coming toward him again, packages in their hands. They stopped to ask how his wound was healing.

"I'm doing fine, thanks," he answered.

"Did you see the fancy train that pulled in at the depot a while ago?" the banker's daughter, Elaine Byron, asked him. "Three of the prettiest train cars I ever saw. Mrs. Herrod was at the depot, and she said they must belong to someone very rich."

Colt's smile faded some. "That so? Maybe I'll go take a look."

"Are you going to the dance Saturday, Mr. Travis?" the other said, quickly reddening with embarrassment that she had asked at all.

Colt folded his arms, towering over both of them. He allowed himself a closer look, both girls plain, but pretty just from their youth, young breasts untouched, innocent eagerness in their eyes. "I expect I'll try to make it."

"Then we'll both save a dance for you," Elaine answered.

Colt grinned. "I'd like that."

They smiled bashfully. "Have you really done all those things that writer is saying in the newspaper?" Elaine said, moving her eyes over him suggestively.

Colt had to grin at her youthful attempt at being seductive. "I haven't been reading those stories," he answered. "The man has pestered me to death. I hope he's been telling the truth."

"Oh, that you were once a mountain man, that you've lived with Indians and hunted buffalo, all sorts of exciting things," Elaine answered. "Are you really from Texas?"

"I was pretty young then. I've even lost most of my drawl, but people tell me it's still there sometimes. I can't ever tell myself. What do you think?"

"Oh, we can still tell," the blacksmith's daughter answered. Her mother called to her from across the street then, and the two young women gave Colt their best smiles before leaving him, giggling all the way across the street. Colt laughed lightly, shaking his head and putting his cigarette back to his lips to take another drag. He watched them cross the street, scanned others across the way.

It was then he noticed someone standing and watching him—a woman who even from this distance he could tell had a beautiful shape to her and was elegantly dressed. He felt as though the blood were draining out of him as she stepped off the boardwalk and started across the street, looking hesitant, almost as though she might not make it all the way on her own. He knew that body, that walk, that air of dignity and wealth, but he could hardly believe it could be who he thought it was.

A wagon clattered past, and she waited, then kept coming. She was dressed in black, the bodice of her dress tightly fitted to her slender waist and hips, then flaring out slightly just below the hips and flowing into a short gathered train at the back. The high neck of the dress was adorned with a necklace of purple gems set in gold, and a row of purple buttons down the front added the only color to the dress. Her gloves and boots were a matching purple, the black velvet hat on her head trimmed in purple ribbon and displaying small purple feathers.

She was all elegance and beauty, her blond hair pulled back at the sides and coiffed into a cascade of curls. She carried a little purple handbag, but when she came closer Colt noticed none of the accessories. He saw only the face, thinner, the blue eyes showing deep tragedy—and there was a thin scar on her left cheek. Where had that come from? Where had *she* come from?

She came closer, watching his eyes, the usual bright smile with which she used to greet him gone. There was only a look of deep remorse, and her lower lip quivered slightly when she stepped up onto the boardwalk to stand only a few feet from him, holding back as though a bit afraid. "Hello, Colt."

Colt took the cigarette from his lips and dropped it,

stomping it out. "Sunny," he managed to say when he finally found his voice. "What in God's name are you doing here?"

Sunny could not help admiring his powerful build, the way his denim pants fit him, the snakeskin boots, the gun slung low on his hip. He wore a blue shirt and a leather vest, a leather-strung turquoise stone at his neck, the first few buttons of his shirt undone. His hair was short now. She could see a few dark waves from under his wide-brimmed hat. *Still so handsome,* she thought. He would be thirty-two now, and here she was twenty-seven. Maybe for a man like him she didn't even compare anymore to the sweet young things with whom he had just been flirting. Maybe he was even interested in one of them. Maybe she was a stupid fool for coming here at all and butting into his life again.

"I . . . we have to talk," she told him, wondering if it was really her speaking. She felt removed from herself, felt as though she were floating in some kind of unreal world, could hardly sense the boardwalk beneath her feet. After all these weeks of searching, it seemed incredible she could walk across a street and find him so easily. She had looked for the sheriff's office, and here he was. Somehow she had thought it would be harder than this, and there had been times when she felt like he was some kind of distant dream who didn't exist anymore.

But he did exist, and he stood in front of her. To her devastation she saw his first look of surprise and the hint of lingering love quickly replaced by something else. Yes, there it was, the hurt, the hatred.

"Talk?" His eyes moved over her. "What the hell about? It's a little late for talking, isn't it?" He looked past her. "Where is your beloved husband?"

A few people were beginning to stare. Sunny closed her eyes and grasped a railing. "Please, Colt. Is there someplace where we can be alone?"

He let out a bitter snicker. "No, thanks. We've *been* alone before, remember? It was the biggest mistake we ever made. What the hell is this, Sunny? Do you actually *enjoy* doing this to me? You wait until I just begin to think I can go on with my life without you, and then you show up again! Jesus, Sunny, I'm a man with more than a little *pride,*" he nearly growled. "How did you find me anyway? I suppose a woman of your wealth can hunt down anyone she wants and bandy him about like one of your damn tennis balls. Where's Blaine? Did you decide *he* couldn't be a part of your life either?"

"Colt, stop it!" She put a shaking hand to her face, as though to cover her scar. "Blaine is dead. He drowned at sea last September." She clung to the railing, looking away from him.

"Dead!" Colt felt light headed from a myriad of emotions. A soldier came out from the jail and spoke to him for a moment, and Colt struggled to keep his composure until the man left. He stepped closer to Sunny then, wanting to throw her out into the street, yet wanting to hold her. Could a man love and hate the same woman with equal passion? "Don't tell me that just because Blaine is dead you think you can come running to me and pick up where we left off! What the hell kind of man do you take me for, Sunny?"

Her shoulders jerked in a sob, and Colt sensed she was nearly ready to pass out. "It isn't . . . like that. I have to . . . tell you something. Please, Colt, where . . . can we talk?"

"Jesus," he muttered. She felt him move away from her, heard him tell someone inside he would have to be gone for a while. He grasped her arm, and she felt the old fire move through her but sensed only coldness and anger on his part. He walked so fast that she had to hurry to keep up. He led her to Dancer, lifting her as though she weighed no more than a child. He plopped her on the horse and mounted up behind her, reaching around her to pick up the reins. He turned Dancer and headed out of town.

"I've been looking for you for nearly three months," Sunny said, for the first time in her life feeling awkward in his arms.

"I don't want to hear it," he answered. "Just wait until we get someplace where we can stop."

Sunny wondered if he knew how badly she was shaking—to see him again, looking so wonderful; to have his arms around her, arms that once held her so lovingly; to be so close. . . . If she turned her face, it would be only inches from his own. It was all as horribly painful as she feared it would be. He was so angry, so untouchable. In all the years she had known him, in all their other encounters, never once had he been like this, so cool and distant.

Colt headed Dancer toward a cottonwood tree near a stream, wondering in turn if she realized what it did to him to have her suddenly appear out of nowhere, to have to sit with her almost smack in his lap, to want to hold her and shove her off the horse both at the same time. Was this another torment, another short encounter that would leave him reeling? He halted Dancer and climbed down, wincing slightly from the lingering pain in his side. He reached up for her, and their eyes held as she let him lower her. He could feel her ribs, thought how terribly thin she was, noticed again the scar on her cheek.

"Are you all right now?" she asked when he set her on her feet. "I read you were wounded." She turned away. "That's how I found you—an article in the Omaha newspaper about some big shootout over water rights."

He turned and tied Dancer to a low tree branch. "My luck," he grumbled. "Yeah, I'm fine." He turned, but her back was to him. "I probably should say I'm sorry about Blaine, but I can't. I just wish he would have died a little sooner, like before you *married* him! You wanted to talk—so talk." He reached into an inside vest pocket and pulled out a cigarette paper. Sunny turned, watching him prepare a cigarette as she had seen him do in happier times.

"You shouldn't be sorry for Blaine even if you wanted to be. He's the reason for the scar on my cheek."

Colt stopped what he was doing and met her eyes. "How?"

She reddened a little, turned away again. "He beat me—not just a few slaps like some men might do, although even that much is unforgivable as far as I'm concerned. This was fists, my face, my stomach, my ribs. I was bedridden for weeks. I almost died from internal bleeding, and I . . . I lost a baby—a baby he knew nothing about."

Colt sealed the cigarette but didn't light it. He walked a few feet away from her, and for a moment there was nothing but the sound of a soft wind and birds singing. "Why?" He finally spoke up, their backs to each other.

"Tom Canary," she answered. "You probably remember him from that day we returned and met with U.P. men about the Indians. He told Blaine I had gone riding alone with you before Blaine and I married. He said . . . you had won after all . . . called me several names I don't care to repeat . . . made it out to be something dirty and sinful, just like—" Her voice choked. "Like . . . Vince did."

"Dammit, Sunny!" Colt turned and walked closer to her. "Why in hell didn't you *come* to me! Why didn't you trust me to help you? For God's sake, I've faced every danger there is! If you had told me Vince threatened my life, I could have been on the lookout. Jesus Christ, I've been taking care of myself in dangerous situations since I was fourteen years old!"

"It wasn't just that," she answered, turning to face him. "It was what he said he'd tell you about my mother and grandmother! Do you know how I felt when he told me that? Right after I spend two days with you, being intimate with you while engaged to someone else, my brother tells me what my *mother* was! Vince made me out to be hardly better than a harlot! He said you'd think of me the same way if you knew! He said others knew about my mother, that others were just waiting for me to show myself to be like her and the gossip about her would start all over again if I brought you into the family. He said you probably already thought of me that way, that you were probably laughing about how you got under Sunny Landers skirts!"

Colt turned in a circle, raising his hands in frustration.

"Is that all the trust you had in me? After all the years we were friends and longed to be lovers, a few words out of Vince's mouth and you're afraid to come to me with the *truth?* I *loved* you, Sunny!" He came closer, towering over her. "Love means accepting *everything* about a person, good *and* bad! And what your mother was doesn't make you bad! You let Vince make you think that way, and you didn't put enough trust in my love to come to me!"

He was so close, shouting the words, needing to get them out. Sunny cringed, putting an arm over her face, memories of Blaine's tirade becoming vivid. She tripped over a tree root as she backed away and fell. Colt reached down to help her up and she cringed, screaming for him not to hit her. Only then did it become clear to Colt that her beating had left lasting effects on her, and although he didn't know anymore how he felt about her himself, the thought of Blaine beating her made him feel crazy with frustration. How could any man hit someone like Sunny, hit *any* woman, for that matter. A man had to be one hell of a bastard to do something like that.

He leaned over her, and she jumped when he touched her shoulder. "Is that what you think, that I'd *hit* you? *Me?* For God's sake, Sunny, I've done a lot of things in my life, but hitting a woman has never been one of them. I thought you knew me so well."

She remained sitting, breaking into sobbing. "Oh, God, Colt, you don't know what it was like . . . finding out about my mother . . . marrying Blaine . . . all of it. I didn't know enough about men . . . how they thought about women that way . . . to be certain you would still . . . love me . . . if you knew. I made such a mess of everything. I loved you so. I still love you. I've . . . never loved anybody else. Just don't hate me. That's all . . . I ask. You don't have to love me. Just don't despise me, and don't hurt me."

He tossed aside the still-unlit cigarette and grasped her wrists, pulling her hands away from her face and looking again at the scar—a scar on his beautiful Sunny. She sat shivering and weeping and looking much too thin. "My God, what have Vince and Blaine done to you? What have *I* done to you? I never should have let you go back alone that day."

"It wasn't . . . your fault. It's never been your fault," she sobbed.

He kept hold of her arms. "Come on. Get up, Sunny. This isn't the Sunny I knew. Don't do this."

He helped her to her feet. "The Sunny you knew . . . died the day she got married." She wept.

Colt put an arm around her and led her to a spot of soft grass, making her sit down under the cottonwood tree. He sat beside her, taking off his hat and running a hand through his hair. "Just calm down and I promise not to yell anymore," he told her. He leaned back against the tree, his heart still torn between love and hate. "And for God's sake, I can't believe you think I would hurt you physically. It takes a hell of a coward to do something like that." He sighed with disgust. "Why don't you tell me why you're here," he said. "You had to know how insulting and cruel it would be to come running to me because your husband is dead."

She took a handkerchief from her handbag and blew her nose. "Yes, I know," she answered. "There is nothing I can do, Colt, about how you might feel about me now. I would never expect you to . . . come running back. I know I hurt you. But you have to know I never *meant* to hurt you. I was afraid . . . for your life, for what others would say about you, how ugly they might try to make our relationship look even if Vince didn't have you killed. It was . . . the news about my mother that destroyed my trust, Colt. I was in shock. All my life I had been told what a sweet, beautiful young woman she was, how much Father . . . loved her. I knew you were probably familiar with common prostitutes . . . from the way you lived before you loved me. I was afraid you would . . . picture me like them . . . look at me with shame and disappointment. I would rather have you hate me."

He shook his head in wonder at how convincing Vince must have been, how mercilessly he must have come down on her. He got up again, feeling restless and frustrated, wishing he could think straight. He put his hat back on and searched for the unused cigarette. Sunny noticed his slight limp with an aching heart.

"You still haven't been clear about why you're here now." He found the cigarette and picked it up, blowing grass off it and lighting it while he waited for an answer. He took a deep drag, turning to look at her when she still did not answer. He saw something close to terror in her eyes.

He frowned, keeping the cigarette between his lips. "What is it, Sunny?" God, she looked pitiful. He didn't want to have any feelings for her, but how could he not? This was Sunny, the sweet, vulnerable, willing woman he had loved so passionately for so long. All he could see was the bubbly, beautiful fifteen-year-old girl he had met twelve years before. He took the cigarette from his lips. "Sunny, this is me, *Colt*. We used to be able to tell each other everything, remember? Whatever it is, I'm not a woman beater, and I promise not to hate you. I honestly don't know what I feel anymore, other than a gut-wrenching hurt that has never gone away. But I don't hate you, all right? Just tell me why you're here." He frowned at the way she visibly trembled. She got to her feet, managing to stand and face him squarely, her eyes wide with apprehension, her hand still at her stomach.

"Colt, you . . . you have a son. I mean, *we* have a son. My son . . . he's not Blaine's. He's yours."

He stared at her a moment, pure shock in his eyes. He tossed the cigarette and stepped closer, searching her eyes. The air seemed suddenly too still. Even the birds were silent, or was it that neither of them could hear? Sunny wondered if a more beautiful man existed on earth, wondered how she was going to allow him into Bo's life and have to see him and talk to him without being able to touch him and be in his arms again.

"You're serious!" he said in a near whisper.

"Very." She felt her cheeks growing hotter. "I should have had my time of month—" She looked away. "Before the wedding. It . . . never happened. I married Blaine so soon that I was never totally positive, but I was afraid that if I waited to find out . . . with you wounded and the possibility of you dying . . . I didn't want my baby to be called a bastard. That's part of the reason I married Blaine as fast as possible, so he would think it was his. When he was born, such a beautiful, dark little boy with such black hair and those hazel eyes . . . I have no doubt, Colt. If you saw him, you would know."

He turned and walked away. Sunny knew how he must be struggling with his emotions. "I decided to try to find you, Colt. You had a right to know. I was hoping that somehow . . . in spite of what has happened between us . . . that you would agree to see the boy . . . be a father to him. I don't want any more lies, Colt. Everyone else knows—even Vince. With what I have inherited through Blaine, my riches far surpass Vince's. He knows I can destroy him financially with a nod of the head and that I will if he dares to interfere with anything you decide to do about our son. Vince is no longer a threat to us. I want so much for little Bo—that's his name, after my father—I want him to grow up knowing you, knowing a true freedom of the soul. He stands to one day inherit a massive fortune, Colt. He needs a man guiding him who can teach him how to handle that kind of wealth without letting it make him greedy and arrogant."

She stepped closer, taking hope that she had found something on which they could share common ground. "I can teach him the business end of it, but you can teach him the really important things, like loving the land, respecting it, not always putting his own interests first. There is an honesty and integrity about you I want him to learn. Colt, you can give him things that all the money in the world can't buy for him. In my whole life I never knew anyone like you. That was why I loved you so, why being with you was like leaving hell and going to heaven. For twelve years just the thought of you has been my strength. You were everything I wished I could be, everything I want my son to be. If Blaine hadn't died, I think I would have ended up divorcing him, in spite of the scandal, to keep him from raising little Bo. I knew after the beating he would have been cruel to the boy. I would still have tried to find you—not for myself, but for my son. I want you to be a father to him, no matter what kind of sacrifices I have to make to my life-style to do it. I'll do whatever you ask, give you whatever you ask. Just please don't ask me to give him up completely. Don't take my baby away from me. He's all I have left."

The words stunned him. Here she was, a woman who could destroy him at the flick of a finger, and *she* was afraid he'd take her son away from her! He supposed he could if he wanted. He could just take him and ride away with him, figure out a way to never be found. It was a thought. But much as he wanted to hurt her in return for all his own hurt, he knew he couldn't do that to her. The irony of the whole thing was astounding. Bo Landers had warned him once to stay away from Sunny. Vince had threatened to kill him. Blaine had said he would destroy him if he pursued his feelings for Sunny. Now his own son was heir to both the Landers *and* the O'Brien fortunes. It was almost laughable, but he felt no humor at the moment, only a deep joy inside that wanted to well up and engulf him.

He shook his head, his eyes tearing. He had a son! "*My* son is going to run your little empire someday?" He turned to face Sunny, and her heart went out to him at the look in his eyes. "*I* have a *son?*"

God, how it hurt to see a man like Colt close to tears. "Yes. I came out here with the whole family. We had planned the trip to be among the first to travel to California by train—were on our way to Utah to be present for the joining of the rails. Just before we left, Stuart found the article about you, so we stopped here on our way so that you could meet little Bo and have some time to think about what you want to do about him. I had already been searching everywhere for you."

She stepped a little closer, taking hope in the look of joy and love in his eyes. "He's so beautiful, Colt, just like . . . like you. He has a free spirit, is full of adventure."

Her face brightened, and Colt began to see a little of

the old Sunny in the way her eyes finally lit up. "I swear he'll never live to five, he's so daring. He's full of fire and love and courage. He's such an easy child to love." Her smile faded slightly. "Blaine figured it out. That was the other reason for the beating." She looked away. "He said he would disinherit both of us, but he failed to do it before he left for Africa. He left the very next day, saying my pregnancy had spoiled his first trip. We were supposed to go there on our honeymoon, but I was too sick. I lay near death from his own hands, and he left for Africa, apparently not caring if I lived or died. My injuries were passed off in the newspapers as caused by a fall."

She put a hand to her forehead, a raging headache suddenly setting in. "I never saw Blaine again. I know I betrayed him, but he betrayed me by marrying me strictly for appearance's sake. When he lost the elections he blamed me and Bo and said he had never loved me in the first place—said I would forever live in his own form of prison. I was ready to try to love him, but he simply didn't understand how to love." She looked up at Colt, wishing she knew for certain how he felt. "Do you want to see your son?"

He quickly moved away from her, wiping at his eyes with his fingers. "I need some time alone. Take Dancer back. I'll walk. Just leave Dancer in front of the jail. Which train car is yours?"

"Mine is the last one before the caboose. We aren't in any big hurry. It will be a couple weeks yet before the joining of the rails."

He faced her, his eyes looking bloodshot. "Is Vince along?"

He watched her stiffen. "Only because his children wanted to come. I'm trying to bring some harmony into the family, for Bo's sake. I will always hate Vince, but I won't let it show in front of the children. We are going to be one family from now on, even if I have to bribe Vince to do his share." She saw the hatred move into his eyes.

"I'll come see the boy. You just tell Vince Landers to

stay out of my way. I can't guarantee I won't kill him if we get into it again."

"He won't give you any trouble. When will you come?"

He turned away again. "I don't know. I have a lot to think about."

She walked over to Dancer, untying him. "Take your time, Colt. The important thing is Bo. We have to put him above our own hurt and anger."

"Yeah," he said quietly. "I guess this throws us right back together again, doesn't it? What a hell of a mess."

"I'm sorry, Colt, for always disrupting your life. But I'm not sorry for Bo. He's the light of my life. And I'm not sorry for having loved you, or for the fact that I still love you and always will. My feelings for you have never changed. If not for Bo, I would have ended my life, maybe even before Blaine's beating, but certainly after it. The only thing that kept me wanting to live was to be there for Bo, my little piece of Colt Travis, the only man I've truly loved with all my heart and soul and body. No matter how much you might hate me or look down on me, my feelings for you will never change. If I could go back and do things over, I would, but I can't, and that's the hell of it. I allowed Vince to destroy our love, and there are not enough words to—" Her voice began to choke. "To express how sorry I am that I hurt you, that I couldn't . . . be with you after you were wounded, that you had to wake up to find out . . . I had married someone else. All my millions will never bring me the happiness I knew those two days we spent together, Colt . . . or the joy our son brings me. All I want now is for him to know his father. If I can have that much, I can live with the rest."

Colt put a hand to his head. "Just go, Sunny. Leave me alone." He heard the sound of weeping, heard Dancer whinny lightly and then trot away. He went down on one knee and bent his head. "God help me know what to do," he groaned. "A son. I have a son."

Chapter 30

Mae answered the knock at the door, opening it to see two guards outside. "Deputy Colt Travis is here to see Mrs. O'Brien," one of them said. "Is it all right?"

"Oh, yes! Miss Sunny is expecting him."

The guard frowned curiously and stepped aside, nodding for Colt to enter. Mae stood aside, staring at Colt, who removed his hat. "Mae, isn't it?" he asked.

She blushed, glad for Sunny's sake that he had come. She knew how Sunny felt about this man, knew he was Bo's father. "Yes, sir. Come right in."

"That's some welcome committee Sunny's got," he said, sounding a little irritated.

"A necessary inconvenience, Miss Sunny says. When you're as rich as she is, and you're traveling with a child who could be held for ransom, you have to take precautions."

Again Sunny's staggering fortune seemed almost overwhelming to Colt. "Yes, I suppose," he answered. "It's pretty bad when even a deputy sheriff has to have permission to come visiting." *Especially when it's to see his own son,* he thought. Mae closed the door, and Colt glanced around, wondering if there was a chair in the parlor car that wasn't too good for him to sit on.

"Miss Sunny will be right out. She's changing the baby. Have you eaten, Mr. Travis?"

"I'm fine. I, uh, could use a drink though. You have any of that good whiskey Sunny usually keeps around?"

"I'll go and get some. Please sit down wherever you like." Mae hurried to the forward section of the car, which Colt guessed contained a small kitchen. This car was bigger than the last one of Sunny's he had been in, and even fancier, the walls and ceiling made completely of oak, carvings of trees and flowers in the ceiling that were highlighted by gold etching. The curtains at the windows were a pale yellow, and the same color dominated the designs in the upholstery of the Victorian furnishing and in the flowered carpeting. A gilt-framed painting of mountains hung on one wall, another painting of a Union Pacific locomotive on another, a picture that closely resembled the huge painting Colt had seen in Sunny's Chicago office, but smaller. He tried to remember how long ago he had been there. Was it '61 or '62? It seemed incredible they had moved in and out of each other's lives over so many years.

He still wore his denim pants and knee-high boots, but had changed his shirt to a simple white one with a black string tie. He wore a new black felt hat, had bathed and shaved but decided not to dress up any more than usual. He had decided not to be anything but himself for this first meeting with his son. He had left his six-gun at the sheriff's office, deciding not to wear it around the baby. He had told Rex Andrews he would explain later why he couldn't be on duty tonight, although he wondered how in hell he was going to tell the man he had sired a son by Sunny Landers O'Brien, just about the richest woman in the country. It would probably take Rex, who had become a good friend, a week to stop laughing before he realized Colt was not joking.

He heard a baby giggle, and his heart nearly skipped a beat. He removed his hat and sat down on a silk love seat, thinking how he hated fancy furniture. A moment later Sunny came out, holding a handsome baby boy in her arms. "Hello, Colt," she said softly. "Mae said you were here."

She could see he had eyes only for the baby, and she smiled sadly. "This is little Beauregard Stuart O'Brien. If you want, I can have his last name changed to Travis. It can be legally done."

Colt slowly rose, his eyes glued to the boy. Bo was wearing short pants and knee-high stockings with high-button shoes and a little dress shirt with a striped jacket. His nearly black hair was oiled and combed to the side. He stared at Colt with wide hazel eyes set against very brown skin, and he suddenly smiled, reaching out for Colt as though he sensed exactly who he was.

"You see what I mean about having no fear of strangers?" Sunny said, handing him over.

Colt reached out hesitantly, and the boy came right to him, putting chubby arms around his neck. "My God," Colt said softly, burying his face in the child's neck.

Tears formed in Sunny's eyes at the sight. She had done so many wrong things, but now she could give Colt a little bit of joy through this child. She knew how he had suffered over the loss of his baby son to the Pawnee, something that had left a lasting emptiness in his soul, as it would any man. "Would you like me to leave you alone with him?" she asked.

Colt could not reply at first. He simply shook his head, sitting down with the boy and quickly wiping his eyes. He set Bo out on his knee and looked him over, studying his perfect complexion, thinking how he resembled many Indian babies he had seen, grinning at the boy's dimples and the way he giggled when Colt bounced him lightly on his knee. He touched his hair, his face, his arms, held his chubby hands. Yes, this was his son all right. All anyone had to do was look at him to know that. He took a deep breath and cleared his throat before speaking. "What the hell kind of a way is this to dress a kid?" he asked. "He looks like he's ready to go to the office with you."

Sunny grinned. "I suppose you would rather he wore little buckskins?"

"Sounds more fitting to me, considering his looks."

Sunny was relieved to see him finally grinning. Mae came in with a silver tea tray that carried a teapot and cup, with a few slices of cheese and bread, as well as Colt's whiskey. "Thank you, Mae. Maybe you should go and stay with Stuart and Vi so we can be alone," Sunny suggested. "I'll call for you when I need you."

"Yes, ma'am," Mae answered, secretly hoping she didn't hear another thing from Sunny for the rest of the night. She quietly left, grinning to herself. She had grown to love Sunny, felt fury at the thought of Blaine O'Brien beating her like he had. *I'll bet Colt Travis would never beat a woman,* she thought as she went out.

"He's beautiful," Colt was telling Sunny as she poured him a shot of whiskey. "I can see he has a lot of your personality too. I imagine you're a good mother. You have the heart for it."

A warmth moved through Sunny at the words, along with the pain of knowing how she had hurt him. "Thank you," she said quietly.

Colt looked at her, noticing she was not wearing the fancy black velvet dress she had worn earlier. She was dressed in a plain blue cotton dress and wore no jewelry except small pearl earrings. She wore little makeup, and her hair was brushed out in long, thick tresses. To him she was prettiest this way, although whatever she wore, there was always an air of elegance to her composure. His eyes moved over her in a way that gave Sunny a new feeling of warmth, new hope. She saw no hate there. "You look nice tonight," he told her. "I always liked you better in simple clothes."

Her face felt suddenly hot. "Thank you again." She handed him the whiskey, and their fingers touched when he took it. She quickly looked away and poured herself some tea while Colt downed the whiskey and set the shot glass back on the tray. He stood then, picking up

Bo and holding him high so that the baby laughed, then he nuzzled the baby's neck again.

"God, Sunny, you don't know how many times I wondered what my Ethan would have been like at this age, dreamed about how it would be teaching him how to do things as he got older, taking him hunting, teaching him to ride. I want to do all those things with Bo."

"You can do whatever you want. I told you that was how it would be. Wherever you are, I can bring him out to you for a week every month, or a summer. If you like, you can live in Omaha and see him as often as you like. I think I'd prefer raising him there rather than Chicago or New York. In Omaha he'll be closer to the land you love. I'll have to make monthly trips to New York. You can spend all the time you want with him the times I'm gone. I would never give you a problem about how much you want to see him."

He met her eyes, and she thought he looked at her rather strangely. She wished his once-gentle eyes were not so unreadable now. She thought she saw some of the old love there, but then, maybe that was just wishful thinking.

"I, uh, I haven't decided yet how to handle that part of it," he told her. "I *would* like him to carry my name though. And I'd like to be in on any major decisions that involve him, including anything to do with when he inherits certain things, when he takes responsibilities, where he goes to college, things like that. And I don't want Vince to have anything to do with his upbringing."

"Fine." Sunny drank some tea and ate a piece of cheese while Colt continued to play with the baby, wrestling with him, letting Bo think he was stronger, tickling the infant, glorying in the sound of his giggling. They played so hard that when Colt finally got up and took a chair, holding the boy on his lap, Bo lay his head against his father's chest and was quickly asleep. Sunny sat quietly and said nothing, letting Colt hold his son and stroke his hair gently.

"It's like he knows," he finally said.

"I think maybe he does," Sunny answered. "Here, I'll take off his shoes and we can put him down. I'll just let him fall asleep in his clothes." She knelt in front of Colt and unbuttoned the baby's shoes and pulled them off, as well as his long stockings. "Bring him back here."

Colt rose, hugging the boy close and following her into a narrow hallway along one side of the car.

"That door at the end of the hall goes to our private kitchen," Sunny told him. "The other door on the side here is Mae's room and this is my room. I keep Bo's crib in here." She opened a door and went inside a small but luxurious room that contained a four-poster with lace curtains all around the canopy and a blue satin bedspread. Everything in the room was blue, with a dash of yellow. Sunny lifted a blanket from the crib and Colt laid the boy on his belly. Sunny covered him. "It always surprises me how cold it gets out here in this arid land at night," she said quietly, "no matter how warm the days are."

"No trees to hold the warmth and no humidity," Colt answered.

"I always remembered that from that first trip west," she said, turning to leave. Colt caught her shoulders.

"Sunny—"

"Please, let's get out of here, Colt."

"Why?"

She looked up at him, fire ripping through her at being so close to him in this room of all places. "You know why," she whispered.

"Because you think I don't love you? I might be damn mad, Sunny, but I never stopped loving you." His voice was tender, the words spoken softly to keep from disturbing Bo. "I spent most of the day by that creek, Sunny, thinking about all this. I don't want to be a part-time father. I want to be with my son all the time, and I want to be with *you* all the time. We both made a serious mistake letting other things come between us the last time, and I wanted so much to hate you. But part of this is my fault, too, and when I saw you standing there, holding my son—"

She turned her face away, tried to pull away from him, but Colt held her fast. "You said you still loved me, Sunny. I was ready to do it like you said, have visitation rights and all, but I want us to be a real family. I lost one family. I don't want to lose another."

"You're saying that because of Bo. It isn't me you want—"

"It *is* you I want! I didn't want to admit it, but I can't leave it this way, Sunny."

"Don't use me, Colt," she whispered. "I don't want you to think of me like my mother."

He held her arms tightly and lightly shook her. "*Stop* it, Sunny!" He said in an angry whisper. "I don't ever want to hear you talk about yourself that way again! You're Sunny Landers, a beautiful, good woman in your own right."

She raised her eyes to meet his own, thinking how wonderful he looked by the light of a dim lantern she kept in the room so Bo wouldn't wake up to darkness. She wondered how a man could get more handsome as he got older, wondered how, after twelve years, she could still feel the way she did that night she left him at Fort Laramie, so full of love and fire.

Colt traced a finger over the scar on her cheek. "I would never, never hurt you like this," he told her. "I love you, Sunny, much as those words have gotten me into a hell of a lot of trouble in the past. I feel like I'm taking a hell of a risk, but I'm not letting you get away this time."

She studied his eyes, so afraid to believe. "You wouldn't lie to me, would you, Colt? You wouldn't deliberately fool me just to hurt me? I know how much I hurt you."

He felt her trembling. "You know me better than that. All I want is for us to be a family, the way it should be. When I think how fast the last twelve years went by —twelve *wasted* years—" He shook his head. "Life's too short, Sunny, to spend it worrying about how to hurt each other more."

She clung to his shirt. "After all we've been through, it scares me to think about trying again."

He smiled softly. "You think *I'm* not scared? I'd rather face those cattlemen again, maybe even go back to war. I'm probably headed for a new kind of war, but I can handle the enemy, Sunny. That's where you have to trust me."

She reached up and touched the scar over his eye, put there by the Pawnee so many years before. He had fought them in revenge for his wife and son's deaths. "Yes," she answered. "I believe you *can* handle any enemy you face, even the kind in silk suits and top hats." Her eyes teared. "Do you have any idea how much I love you? I'm so sorry for all of it, all the years I fought my feelings for you."

"I was just as guilty there."

He was so close. How could their lips not touch? How could the passion not still be there when they did? His kiss was deep and lingering, from a man hungry for the only woman who could truly satisfy him. He backed her to the bed, searching her mouth as he gently laid her back. His kisses grew hotter, his whole body more urgent.

Sunny whispered his name, and magically she felt her dress and shoes come off. What was this spell he cast on her? She kissed his throat, his chest, untying his tie, unbuttoning his shirt and pulling it off his shoulders. He sat up and took it all the way off, and their eyes held in another brief moment of hesitation before he bent down to kiss her breasts lightly, fuller now from having nursed a baby.

"Colt," she whispered. "It's too soon, too sudden."

"No," he replied, untying her camisole and pushing it open. "It's been much too long for both of us." He tasted her taut nipples, shivering with the thought of bedding her again, the only woman who could satisfy him, the woman he had made love to so many times over the years in his dreams.

He moved down, and she lay trembling as he pulled off her drawers and stockings, kissed her thighs, kissed that most intimate part of her that had belonged to him first, his lips trailing back over her belly and breasts. He smothered her with more hot kisses, his tongue searching her mouth while his fingers found their mark. He felt her own fire burning his already-hot skin, felt her sweet moistness on his fingertips, felt that magical spot that was swollen from desire. It was so satisfying to touch her there again, to feel her breasts against his naked chest, to hear her whisper his name in ecstasy.

Sunny wondered if she might die from the joy of the moment, to think he still loved her, in spite of how she had hurt him. Her beautiful Colt was touching her again in that exotic way only he knew to touch a woman. His fingers worked in a circle of fire until she felt the throbbing release deep in her belly.

He rose to quickly remove the rest of his clothes, and Sunny kissed his chest and back as he did so, wanting to touch him and taste him and make sure this was real. "Tell me this isn't wrong, Colt," she asked, tears in her eyes. He turned, his eyes moving over her nakedness, eyes that had always so easily undone her.

"It isn't wrong. Making love was the most right thing we ever did, Sunny, and it's right now." He crawled on top of her, grasping her by the waist and scooting her farther up on the bed. "I didn't plan any of this. I don't know what happens to me when I get near you, Sunny Landers O'Brien, but you make me crazy."

She closed her eyes and drew in her breath as he moved between her legs. He kissed her eyes, her nose, the scar on her cheek.

"That bastard," he whispered. "Let me take it all away, Sunny." His lips moved over her throat, hot skin touching. He met her eyes, and she saw the look of pride and ownership there. "Do you know what it was like for me, knowing you were with him?" he groaned. "Tell me you never wanted him," he whispered, licking and tasting at her mouth again.

Her tears flowed freely. "I never wanted him," she answered, "not like you. I don't even want to talk about it."

"Shh." He kissed the scar again. "We won't then. You've never belonged to anyone but me, and that baby over there is proof of that. We have a son, and we belong together. We've belonged together for twelve years, but we were both too stubborn and too stupid to let ourselves believe it."

She gasped when he suddenly entered her, pushing

deep and hard. He grasped her hair, part of him hating her for letting Blaine O'Brien do this to her, another part of him loving her for the reasons she let it happen. He would make up for the awful beating, would remind her a man could be gentle, remind her who her first man had been, who her only man would be from then on.

Sunny groaned with shivering ecstasy to know he was in her arms again, reclaiming her, reawakening all the passion she thought she would never feel again. It was more glorious than the first time, so much more meaningful. This was the father of her child, her only true love, the man she had loved for so long.

Too quickly his life spilled into her. He rested his cheek against her own, whispering close to her ear. "Just lie still. I want to stay inside you." He kissed her neck, and it was then she felt his own tears against her skin.

"Colt, my precious Colt, I love you so," she wept. "It feels so good to say it again."

"We'll stay here all night," he whispered, kissing her again, running his tongue deep while he searched her depths, reclaiming her for himself. He left her mouth and kissed her eyes, those blue eyes that made him crazy. "I'll never get enough of you, ever again," he groaned. "I want to make love all night, Sunny, touch you, taste you, love you hard and deep, explore every part of you, make up for all the lost time."

She arched up to him as again he began moving rhythmically. Her every breath came in gasps of passion, his name whimpered with every thrust. He was back in her arms, back in her life. She would let him ravish her tonight, let him take back every inch of her, every part of her. She had always belonged to this man alone, and nothing had ever changed that. She vowed that from then on nothing was going to keep her from having him. Nothing was going to keep Bo from his father. This time was forever.

Her train had been pulled to a side track, and outside another train rumbled by them on the main track, its whistle crying into the night, its wheels thundering rhythmically. Sunny thought how fitting it was that it passed while she lay in the arms of the young scout who had first guided her father west to show him the best route for a transcontinental railroad. In a few days the dream would be a reality, but it was no longer her first and most important dream. That one was right there in her arms, and he would share her bed and her body for the rest of the night, and for the rest of her life.

There was only one church in Cheyenne, and it was Methodist. By two o'clock it was packed to overflowing with citizens of Cheyenne who had picked up on the rapidly spread rumor that their deputy sheriff was going to marry the wealthy widow, Sunny Landers O'Brien. Many had come simply because they knew and liked Colt, others out of sheer curiosity. Stories flew about how two such drastically different people had ended up together, and people gossiped that the fancy Mrs. O'Brien must have been taken by Colt Travis's rugged handsomeness, saying that eastern women couldn't resist western men. Others whispered about the fortune Colt was marrying into. Did he love the woman, or was he taking advantage of her fascination in him in order to get his hands on her wealth?

Those who knew Colt personally, including Rex Andrews and his family, were certain that for a man like Colt it could only be love. Andrews could still hardly believe Sunny O'Brien's son was Colt's own child. The sheriff stood at the front of the church as Colt's best man, still trying to comprehend the fantastic tale Colt had told him. Vi stood to his right as matron of honor for what would be a simple wedding, one that had been hastily planned. Neither Sunny nor Colt was going to let one more day go by without finally being husband and wife.

Vi was glad for Sunny, loved Colt for his amazing capacity to forgive. She glanced at Vince and Eve, who sat in a front pew of the little church, both of them looking angry and disgusted. Vi was sure they thought themselves too good to be sitting in the crude little chapel in the town of Cheyenne, where last night they had heard laughter and piano music coming from its many saloons. But Vince knew better than to raise a fuss. Sunny had ordered him to attend with his children and to act as though he were enjoying every minute of it.

Mae sat with Vi's children, holding little Bo, who was dressed in a little suit and behaving himself amazingly well for a child who was usually packed with energy. Vi scanned the gawking crowd, smiling at how people literally hung over the railing of the small balcony above. People were crammed along the walls and some even waited in the church foyer, more standing outside the open doors and beyond.

An old woman began plunking out the wedding march on a piano, and people began whispering and pointing again when Colt stepped through a door at the front of the church, followed by the minister, Reverend Harold Shores. Even Vi stared this time, taking her eyes from Colt only long enough to glance at Vince, who she could tell was himself surprised and impressed. Never had anyone present seen Colt Travis look the way he looked today. Vi wondered how he had managed to find such a fine-looking suit in a place like Cheyenne, but then, she had learned that out in these western towns people were amazingly ingenious at getting modern goods from the East. Now that the railroad had come through, suppliers could bring in the latest gadgets and the newest fashions.

She raised her chin and smiled smugly at Eve, thrilled that Colt had shown he could be a man of taste and elegance himself when the occasion called for it. He wore a gray tailcoat, short-waisted in the front, with black satin lapels. The matching gray pants were the newer, tighter-fitting style, and he wore a white shirt with a gray and black brocade vest and a black tie. If she didn't know better, she would have thought he had stepped out of a fine men's shop in Chicago, or was another U.P. executive on his way to a dinner party.

Colt moved his eyes to look at Vince, whom he had not seen or talked to since the family's arrival at Cheyenne yesterday. The look he gave Vince caused the man to redden slightly and quickly look away. Vince Landers would not soon forget the beating Colt had given him after Sunny married Blaine. He had a slightly crooked nose now as a lasting reminder. He knew he had no choice but to accept this marriage, much as it stuck in his craw.

The whispers grew louder when Sunny and Stuart came out from a small room off the foyer. The old woman at the piano, borrowed from a saloon, played even louder, and people gawked with envy, all kinds of imaginings running through their heads about this strange match about to be made.

Sunny and Stuart headed down the aisle, and as soon as Sunny saw Colt, her legs felt weak. She grasped Stuart's arm tighter. "Look at him, Stuart," she whispered, tears forming in her eyes. She thought she had seen Colt looking his best at other times, but today he was showing her he could hold up to the best-dressed men from her world. She preferred him in buckskins or denims, but she knew why he had done this today. Colt Travis was not a man to be judged or ridiculed. He obviously had taste, and she wondered when he had gotten the suit and how much it had set him back. She almost laughed out loud at the thought that she was worried how much he might have spent. After today, what was hers was his. There would be no prenuptial agreements, certainly no talk of who would get what in case of a divorce. If she died, Colt and Bo would get all of it, and Vince could just live with that. She had every confidence that Colt was intelligent enough to step into control of anything she had, and strong and bold enough to face down anyone who tried to ridicule him or get in his way.

She was sensitive to his pride. He would want to contribute in some way, and she would find a way for him to be his own man within her world. He would not work for her, but *with* her; but she knew that he would always remain the rugged, honest man he was. He would not want to get too deeply involved. He would concentrate first on being a good father, taking Bo out for horseback rides, teaching him to hunt, teaching him the basics of survival. Colt Travis would never be a Blaine O'Brien or a Vince Landers, no matter how fancy the suit he wore; and she already knew that the fancy suits were something he would seldom be seen in. Today was special. Today he was showing her he was willing to take an active role in her world, just as she was determined to learn to let go and take more time to feel the freedom of his.

They could not take their eyes off each other. Colt had never thought her more beautiful, even though she wore a simple, pale yellow dress, surprising everyone in the congregation with her refusal to dress like the near queen that she was. Colt could see that Sunny, in turn, was showing him she was not always one to dress like a royal princess; that she could be just plain Sunny, the way he liked her best. Her hair was pulled back at the sides and brushed out long down her back, simple spring wildflowers pinned into it. Her dress had just a slight fullness to the skirt, a wide yellow sash accenting her slender waist, the perfectly fitted bodice trimmed with white lace at the high neck and at the cuffs of her long sleeves. She wore tiny diamond earrings, and on her right hand she wore Blaine's diamonds out of respect for her first marriage. Her left hand was bare. Colt would place a plain gold band on her ring finger, and to her it would be worth millions.

Twelve years she had waited for this moment. Twelve years ago she had left Colt Travis standing by a campfire at Fort Laramie, loving him then, but never dreaming he would one day be her husband, share her bed, father her child. All her girlhood fantasies were coming true in this one moment, in this tiny church in a rugged western town, far from Chicago and New York, far from board meetings and theaters and politics; and she knew that if her little empire should fold, it wouldn't matter. She could live without all the extras, as long as she had Colt Travis at her side.

Stuart moved away and Colt took his place beside her. Sunny handed her bouquet of simple wildflowers to Vi, who was crying. Colt put an arm around Sunny then, taking her right hand in his own and holding it tightly, sensing that if he didn't hang on to her at that moment, she might not have the strength to remain standing. He could feel her trembling, and she squeezed his hand tightly. What they had shared last night would take nothing away from how beautiful tonight would be. It was only the beginning of many nights together. Each was sure they would never be able to make love often enough for the rest of their lives to make up for the time they had lost.

He looked down into her stunning but tear-filled blue eyes as he spoke his vows, grinning teasingly and winking when he got to "for richer or for poorer." It came Sunny's turn, and a few women who didn't even know her, including a few prostitutes who did know Colt, began quietly crying when Sunny could barely get out the words for her own tears. Her love for Colt Travis was obvious.

With shaking fingers Sunny slipped a gold band on Colt's hand, making another pledge. Colt did the same, both rings purchased by them together at a local jeweler, simple bands that represented more love than most expensive diamonds. The minister pronounced them husband and wife.

Sunny looked up at Colt, and he leaned down to kiss her. She put her arms around his neck and the kiss deepened. Colt slipped his own arms around her slender waist and lifted her, whirling her around, and the crowd in the church, made up of a few business people and respectable citizens, but peppered with a much bigger crowd of rowdy cattlemen, town drunks, prostitutes, saloon owners, and the like, burst into a din of shouts and cheers, a few men throwing their hats in the air. The minister's eyes widened when the woman at the piano, who he didn't realize was an ex-prostitute who played nights at the Red Spur saloon, began pounding out a rowdy song of celebration.

A bawdy female restaurant owner ran up to the pulpit and yelled that a royal feast had hastily been set up at Elmer Handy's new barn just outside of town, and a few men in town who were capable of playing instruments were prepared to come up with some music for dancing. An unrestrained crowd of cheering well-wishers gathered around Colt and Sunny and herded them out of the church.

Vince watched the rowdy group make their way out, while a few of Sunny's guards followed and the rest stayed with Mae and little Bo.

"God help us," Vince muttered as a few straggling reporters hurried out after the others, scribbling on their tablets. "I can just see the headlines in New York."

Stuart grinned. "Ought to be real interesting," he answered his brother. "Come on, Vince, let's go to the celebration. Sounds like fun to me. Let loose for once."

Vince glared at him. "Go ahead and make a fool of yourself! I'm going back to the train. I won't give that sonofabitch the satisfaction of attending a celebration of what he considers his victory over this family!"

Vi took Bo from Mae. "The only victory here, Vince, is that love has won out above all else," she told him. "Now you know that a love like Sunny and Colt share can't be defeated, and it can't be bought off at *any* price! Sunny is happy now, for the first time in her life, and it has nothing to do with how much money she has. If she lost it all tomorrow, she would still be the richest woman in the world. I hope someday you can understand that's all that has ever mattered to her, *and* to Colt."

Vi and Stuart and Mae and the children walked out after the others, followed by more guards. Vince and Eve glared after them, wondering how they were going to explain this to their friends back in Chicago. Already wires were being telegraphed to the bigger cities back east.

MILLIONAIRESS SUNNY LANDERS O'BRIEN, WIDOW OF SHIPPING TYCOON BLAINE O'BRIEN, WEDS DEPUTY SHERIFF COLT TRAVIS OF CHEYENNE, WYOMING, IN SIMPLE CEREMONY TODAY, MAY 5, 1869.

Chapter 31

The train whistle wailed through the night air, echoing against canyon walls as Sunny's train thundered through the rocky gorges of southwest Wyoming. Sunny lay in Colt's arms, relishing the unspeakable joy of having him beside her as her husband.

She kissed his chest, ran her hand over his firm muscles. "I think it was the most beautiful wedding there ever was," she said, pleasantly weary from heated lovemaking.

He massaged her back. "Well, people from your circle wouldn't agree, but I think you're right. Can't you picture some of those stuffed shirts from your bunch stomping their feet and whirling their skirts in a square dance?"

Sunny laughed lightly. "Oh, but you looked wonderful, Colt. How on earth did you find such a fancy suit in Cheyenne?"

"Oh, there are a *few* places that deal in the finer things out here. We aren't all *that* uncivilized, you know."

She turned her face up to kiss his lips. "I'm sorry you had to leave your job on such short notice. I'm sure Sheriff Andrews could use you in that wild town."

"Well, things are settling some." He rested a big hand on her belly. "I hated to do that to Rex myself. He's a good man and we got to be good friends." He moved his hand to the side of her face. "But I am not going to let you go away from me alone again, Mrs. Travis. You're stuck with me now."

She feined a sigh of dread. "Oh, poor me. I guess I'll just have to put up with you."

Colt grinned, moving on top of her. "I guess you will." He kissed her as hungrily as if it were the first time. She opened herself to him in renewed desire, and he entered her again, gently this time, moving in sweet, slow rhythm. They needed no foreplay, for both were still warm and on fire. This time was a soft joining by two people in their second night of rediscovering love after two years apart. Tonight they had tasted, explored, touched, had taken each other to the heights of ecstasy. Now they were finally beginning to realize this was real, to understand that they didn't have to make love with quite such fury, as though if they let go of each other, one or the other might disappear. Last night they had been renewed lovers, but still feared separation. Tonight they truly belonged to each other forever.

Sunny arched her head back, relishing the feel of his lips tracing over her throat, enjoying the sweet smell of him. She grasped his thick hair and pushed toward him, thinking how envied she would be by most women when they set eyes on her new husband. She knew that even the very rich ones, who might raise their eyebrows and gossip about her choice, would be wishing a man like Colt Travis were sharing their beds. The rugged qualities about him could not be hidden, even behind a suit, and his dark handsomeness, his build, and skills as a scout and lawman only lended to the male sexual aura about him. The scar over his eye seemed to enhance his good looks rather than detract from them, for it reminded her what a daring fighting man he was. Age had improved the somewhat lanky and bashful young man she had met twelve years before. He was all man now, honed hard by a life of danger and heartache. And because of him, she was fully a woman. Whatever lay ahead, Colt would be her strength, her protector, her beautiful lover.

He let out a soft moan as his release came, and she hoped that very soon his life would take hold so that she could give him another child. He kissed her lightly and pulled away from her, moving to his side of the bed to roll himself a cigarette. Sunny sighed deeply with sweet satisfaction, stretching and then getting up to go behind a curtained area to wash at a stand with a pitcher and bowl that was kept in her room.

Colt lit his cigarette and waited, smoking quietly, smiling when she came from behind the curtain wearing a baby-blue satin gown that clung to her every curve enticingly, her still-erect nipples making little points through the clingy material. "What's this?" Colt asked. "You're through with me for the night?"

She laughed lightly and crawled back onto the bed. "That's up to you." She stretched out on her back. "I just thought I'd clean up, and I wondered if you liked this gown."

He kept the cigarette between his lips and rose. "I like it well enough to yank it right off you." He walked behind the curtain to also wash himself, returning stark naked. He raised his arms out in a kind of shrug. "Sorry. I didn't have a fancy gown to put on."

Sunny smiled. "I like you just the way you are. You're—"

Before she could finish, they heard a loud rumbling sound, and almost at the same instant their car came to such a quick halt that Colt flew against the forward wall. Sunny screamed when she saw him fall, and she was herself plummeted against the headboard of the bed. Bo began to cry, and Sunny screamed Colt's name as she scrambled to check on the baby. Colt got up from the floor and leapt over the bed to check on them both, taking Bo from Sunny.

"You all right?"

"Yes, but Bo was thrown against the head of the crib!"

Colt held the crying baby close.

"My God, Colt, what happened? Are you all right?"

He laid Bo down on the bed, and Sunny began soothing the child herself.

"Just a bruised shoulder, I think," Colt answered, rubbing his left arm. Sunny saw the fear in his eyes as he bent down to look the baby over. "I just hope Bo isn't hurt. He seems to be okay." He turned his gaze to her then. "What about you? Jesus, your head is bleeding." He checked her scalp where blood had appeared.

"I'm all right, Colt. Please go find out what happened! I'm worried about Vince's and Stuart's children."

"Sunny!" Mae screamed from the next room.

"Stay with Bo," Colt told her, hurrying around the bed to pick up his longjohns and pull them on. He picked up his cigarette from where it had fallen to the floor and snuffed it out, then quickly pulled on his denim pants. He took a clean rag from near the washstand and handed it to Sunny. "Hold this to your head. I'll go see what's happened." He hurried out of the room, still shirtless, and Sunny heard him ordering Mae to go to Sunny's room and stay there.

Sunny froze when she felt an odd trembling beneath the train then, heard another rumble. Just as Mae came into the room there was a horrendous crashing sound. Mae screamed and crouched near Sunny, and Bo started crying again.

"Calm down, Mae!" Sunny ordered. "Screaming and carrying on will just frighten the baby more."

Sunny got up, tossing the rag aside and pulling on a flannel robe. "Go grab some blankets for yourself, Mae. We may have to leave the train. We're in the mountains, and it will be cold out there. Hurry!" Mae left to get some of her own blankets, and Sunny quickly wrapped Bo in the satin bedspread and grabbed another blanket, frightened for Colt. She ran with Bo into the parlor area of the car, then to the door and out onto the platform. "Colt!" she called. Her voice echoed strangely, and she sensed they were in some kind of canyon. She heard the sound of rushing waters far below. She dared to look down, and in bright moonlight she could see the train was on a wooden trestle, high above a canyon floor where a river surged, probably swollen from spring runoff.

She looked up then to see Lou Ballard, the train's brakeman, climbing down the narrow ladder of a boxcar that was positioned between Sunny's car and the caboose, from which Ballard had come. The boxcar had been attached to the train at Cheyenne to haul Colt's horse, Dancer. "What's happened!" Sunny asked him. "Are the guards all right?"

"I don't know yet what's going on, Mrs. Travis," Ballard answered. "The men in the caboose are all okay—a couple of injuries but none serious. You'd better have Colt check on his horse." He climbed over to her platform. "I'd like to go through and on up front to see what's going on."

"Of course, Lou. Colt already went up there. Please tell him if there is any danger that I want him to come back and not take any chances!" Sunny clung to Bo, shivering with fear for her son and her new husband. Lou hurried through her car and disappeared.

"Colt," Sunny whispered. She had loved and lost him so many times that the least hint of danger brought back the fear of losing him again. She looked up at a sky that was black and clear, stars and a nearly full moon shining brilliantly. For the moment things were eerily quiet, except for the roaring sound below.

Mae came running to Sunny's end of the car, carrying a blanket. Sunny ordered her to stay in one place and be very still. "We don't know what the distribution of weight might do," she told the woman. "Just wait until Colt and the brakeman get back." She looked down again when the sound of the torrential waters below was broken by a creaking, crunching sound, and Sunny could see a strange reddish glow, like hot coals. "My God," she whispered. Was the engine down there? She knew that the U.P. had built several of these trestles as temporary bridges over canyons until sturdier ones could be built—in some cases until a route could be carved out at the bottom or along the wall of a canyon. Had a spring melt turned the river into a raging torrent that had eroded the foundation of the trestle?

She heard a child's scream then, heard another child crying. Colt was herding Stuart and Vi and their three children through Sunny's car. Stuart was holding his arm and one of the girls had a bleeding leg. Lou was carrying a hysterical eight-year-old Sarah.

"We've got to get off this trestle," Colt ordered, herding everyone toward the far end of Sunny's car. "The damn thing collapsed and the engine is in the river at the bottom of the canyon, along with the woodbox."

"Dear God," Sunny exclaimed. "What about the engineers? What about Vince and his family? Theirs was the next car back!"

"It's still attached but it's hanging over the edge. I'm going to have to go back and see what I can do! Come on! Get up the ladder and head back to the caboose. You're all going to have to run back along this end of the trestle and get off the thing! Give Bo to me!"

There was no time to stop and question anything. The brakeman was already going up the ladder of the boxcar with Sarah in one arm. "Careful now," he warned the others. "Crawl across the top of the boxcar and climb down to the caboose. The guards back there will help you to safety. I'll have them bring some lanterns so you can see where you're going."

"Colt, I wish I could help you more, but I think my arm is broken," Stuart told him.

"Let me stay and do something," Vi asked. "Vince and his whole family are back there!"

"You stay with your children," Colt told her. "Come on now. The sooner all of you get to safety, the sooner a couple of the other men and I can help Vince."

Everyone scrambled up the ladder, and Sunny turned to Colt before taking her turn. "How bad is it, Colt?" She could see he was visibly shaken.

"Their car is about to go. It's at such an angle that they can't climb out to the other end. Everybody is hanging on to things. I'll try to get a couple of the other men to go back with me. Maybe if we tie ropes on ourselves we can get down to them."

"Colt, the whole thing could go at any time!"

"I know that, which means time is important, so get going!"

Sunny ordered a whimpering Mae up the ladder, then scrambled up herself, too frightened to realize how cold it was. Vi was still on top of the boxcar, forcing a terrified thirteen-year-old Diana to keep going. Sunny fought her own sickening fear, realizing that with one slip, any of them could fall hundreds of feet to the river below. They finally all managed to get to the caboose, hurrying through it then and on outside, where they made the perilous walk along the back end of the trestle. There was little human sound then, other than a few whimpers from the children. The river roared below, and wolves howled somewhere in the nearby rugged hills. It was dark and cold, and everyone concentrated on watching where they walked until finally they reached safe ground.

"Try to help Vi keep the children calm," Colt told Sunny. He gave Bo a kiss and handed him over to her.

"Mae and I brought a couple of extra blankets," Sunny told him.

"Good. Soon as I get back I'll try to find a place where we can hole up for the night against the cold. I'll grab some matches when I go back."

"Colt, you still don't have a shirt on!"

"I'll find something. You stay right here." He turned.

"Colt." She touched his arm, and their eyes held for a moment. "You're risking your life for Vince."

He leaned down and kissed her cheek. "It's Eve and the girls that matter. No man deserves to have to sit by helplessly and watch his wife and children die, not even Vince." He gave her a quick hug. "Don't worry. We haven't come this far to have anything happen to either one of us now. Just take care of Bo." He quickly left her, finding volunteers in the brakeman and two of the guards. The rest of the guards wanted to help, but Colt was afraid to return with any more weight than necessary.

"There's rope in the caboose," Ballard was telling Colt as all four men headed back. "I'll find you a jacket too."

"I'll get one once they're all out," Colt answered. "I can work better without any extra clothes."

They all headed back to the train, and soon all Sunny could see was the two lanterns the guards carried. Vi stepped up to her. "Come on, Sunny. Help me with the children."

"I just got him back, Vi. Something always took him away before." She shivered with tears. "If anything happened to him—"

"Nothing is going to happen. Let's get settled so we'll be ready when Vince's children get out. They're going to be so terrified."

"I wish I could see. It's so dark, Vi."

Reluctantly, Sunny walked back to the others, feeling sick at the thought that the railroad, of all things, could be responsible for killing Colt, after all the dangers he had survived in his life. The railroad—her grand dream. How hideously ironic! She sat down on a rock and held Bo close, bending her head and rocking the baby as she prayed silently.

Colt moved quickly through the caboose, telling one of the guards to grab some matches to use later to make a fire. He could only pray Dancer was not hurt. There was no time to check and see, but he could hear the horse whinnying with fright as he ran along the top of the boxcar. He knew the horse's constantly shifting weight was not going to help matters any, but there was nothing that could be done about it.

Lou Ballard and both guards followed him. They climbed down and moved back through Sunny's car, on through Stuart and Vi's car, which was just slightly askew, and out to the platform. The guard held up a lantern. "Jesus," he muttered. He could see by the position of this end of Vince's private car that it was dangerously tilted, most likely resting on a partially collapsed trestle that could thunder into the ravine below at any moment.

"Somebody! Help us!" They all heard the faint cry from Vince, the words sounding faraway.

"He must be clear at the other end of the car," Lou said. "What do you think we should do, Mr. Travis?"

Colt began tying one end of a rope around his waist. "There's no hope for the engineers or the fireman, but I think Vince and his family are all still alive. I'm going in there and try to lift them out. Two of you secure the other end of this rope around something that will give me some freedom to move. Hang on to the other end so I don't fall all the way. I'll bring them out one by one. Your third man can take each one to safety as I go back for the next one."

"That car could let go anytime," Lou reminded him. "If it does, we'll have to release this rope and let you go with it. You understand that, don't you?"

Colt nodded, checking the knot in the rope. "I understand."

"You've got a new wife and son. Let me go," Lou told him.

Colt eyed the aging brakeman, then glanced at the two guards. One was at least fifty, the other young and very slender. "I'm sorry, but I don't think anybody else here is strong enough. It's not going to be easy to keep hold of any of them, especially Vince. He's well over two hundred pounds. With your combined strength you can hang on to the rope, but individually I think I'm the only one who can do this."

"You be careful," Lou told him. "If it looks like it's going to go, climb out. You can do only so much, Mr. Travis."

"Let's get this over with, then." Colt left them, climbing onto the tilted platform of Vince's car. He reached out and took a lantern handed over by one of the guards and leaned down into Vince's car, holding it up for light. "Is everybody alive in here?"

"Who is it? Who's there?" Vince shouted from far below.

"It's me—Colt! I've come to help."

"Colt! Hurry!" Vince yelled back, sounding desperate. "Please, just get my wife and kids out! I don't know how much longer I can hang on!"

Colt leaned farther forward, holding the lantern out but unable to see Vince. He guessed the man was clear at the other end of the car, maybe all the way out on the platform on the opposite end.

"Please, get my daughters out," Eve begged.

Colt spotted her huddled against a bedroom wall with the youngest girl, Mary, who was eleven. For safety's sake, most of the furniture in the cars was bolted into place so that it would not fly around in case of a collision, a safety precaution Sunny had taken after a rash of accidents. Operators of the new railroad were still learning proper switching techniques. Colt was glad for the bolted furniture, or Vince's wife and children could have been badly injured. As it was, a chair lay against Eve, along with an array of dishes, a teapot, and knick-knacks that had spilled from tables.

"Stay as still as possible," he ordered them. He heard a whimpering sound near him and raised the lantern to see sixteen-year-old Joyce clinging to a lounge chair. He hung the lantern on a coat hook on the wall nearest him, so tilted that the lantern hung free from the hook rather than hanging too close to the wall. "Give me some slack!" he shouted to the men behind him. He turned and clung to the rope, putting his feet against the floor of the car like a mountain climber and inching down to Joyce. "Climb on my back," he told her. "Don't be afraid. There's no time for hesitation."

The girl obeyed, putting her arms around his neck from behind and wrapping her legs around his waist. Colt climbed to the top, his shoulder aching from his own tumble in the initial screeching halt of the train. He got Joyce to the top and helped her climb onto the platform of the next car, and one of the guards helped her run back to safety. Colt went back down, finding twelve-year-old Linda huddled under a sofa, clinging to its legs.

The girl was afraid to let go until her mother ordered her to do what Colt told her and save herself so Colt .could get back to the rest of them.

Again Colt climbed up, beginning to sweat in spite of the cold night air. Linda climbed to safety, and Colt went back down for Mary and Eve.

"What's happening!" Vince yelled from farther below.

"Just hang on," Colt shouted. "Joyce and Linda are out. I'm getting your wife and Mary now."

"Hurry!" Vince yelled, sounding terrified. "I can't hang on!"

"I can climb up the rope and hold on to furniture and things," young Mary told Colt. "You take my mother."

"You sure?"

The girl sniffed and wiped at her eyes. "I can do it if you're behind me."

"All right. You're a brave girl, Mary." Colt reached down and lifted her with one arm. She took hold of the rope and used his shoulders to push herself up. "Hang on!" Colt ordered. He reached down for Eve. "Grab the rope and we'll climb up together," he told her. The car shifted slightly, and mother and daughter screamed in terror. Eve grabbed Colt around the neck so tightly she was practically choking him. "Hang on, Mary!" Colt yelled to the child. "Scramble up! Scramble up!" He kept an arm around Eve's waist. "Come on."

Shaking with terror, Eve managed to let go of him enough to take hold of the rope. "Vince!" she screamed. "Vince, are you still with us?"

"I'm here!" he called back. "Just get yourselves out!"

Colt helped Eve climb to the top, and a guard reached out and grasped Mary, lifting her to the safer platform of the next car. Eve hesitated as she took hold of the platform railing of the collapsing car. She grasped Colt's arm tightly. "Please!" she begged, tears of grief and fear streaming down her face. "I know you hate him, but don't let him die! He's my husband!"

Colt thought how ironic her plea was, considering how she and Vince had never seemed to care how much Colt and Sunny had loved each other. "I'll do what I can, for the sake of your daughters, and because he's Sunny's brother."

"I'm sorry . . . how he treated you," the woman sobbed. "His life is in your hands. You wanted . . . to kill him once."

"I said I'd help him. Go on now, so I can get back to him."

To Colt's surprise, the woman hugged him around the neck. "Thank you for getting my daughters out." She left him, and Colt watched after her a moment, wondering why God had put him in this situation. He looked up at the stars. "You're asking a hell of a lot," he muttered with a scowl. He shouted to the men above then. "Give me plenty of slack this time!"

He moved back down through the car, letting his eyes adjust as he moved away from the lantern. He moved past the bedrooms, catching his feet on anything he could, on into the kitchen area, where he guessed Vince must have been when the accident happened. He strained to see, noticing the kitchen door was hanging open. "Vince!" he shouted.

"Here! Out here! Hurry!"

Colt moved on out to the platform, where by the light of the moon he could see Vince dangling off the end, hanging on to the railing of the platform steps.

"I can't get enough leverage . . . to get my knees back up on the steps," the man almost groaned.

Colt could see past him to the gaping canyon below. "Sweet Jesus," he muttered. He reached down. "Grab my arm and I'll try to pull you up enough to get your knees on the steps!"

Vince hung there a moment, and Colt realized the man was crying. "If I let go, it will be . . . the end of me," the man finally sobbed.

"Not if you take hold of my arm! I've got a rope tied around me."

"And if you let go . . . I'm a dead man. You *wanted* me dead once! It would be easy for you . . . to say you couldn't hang on. No one could prove otherwise!"

Colt gritted his teeth and scooted a little farther

down. "Grab on to me, dammit! I promised your wife I'd get you out of here!"

"My God, man, don't let go!"

"You'll just have to *trust* me, won't you? Hurry up before we both go down with this damn car!"

Vince made a choking sound, and suddenly Colt felt a hand grasp his upper arm. Colt took a powerful grip on Vince's own arm, having a harder time hanging on because Vince wore a shirt. Vince gripped his arm like a vise, and Colt grimaced with pain, pulling with all his might. "Come on! You can do it," he growled through clenched teeth.

Vince struggled to get a hold, his breath coming in grunts and gasps. He finally managed to get a knee on a step. "Pull! Pull!" he yelled.

Colt braced his feet against another railing and hung on until Vince got his other foot up and then fell against him on the platform, panting and weeping. "God, God, God," he moaned. "Thank God."

"We aren't out of this yet," Colt reminded him. "Come on. Do you have the strength to hang on to the rope? You'll have to do some climbing."

"I can do anything now," the man answered, his face against Colt's arm. "Just get me out of here."

"Grab on." Colt took his hand and put it on the rope. "We've got to climb all the way up to the next car. There isn't a second to lose."

Both men started up, Vince stopping every few seconds to get his breath. "I'm so tired . . . from hanging on so long," he panted. "I'm not used to . . . all this exertion."

"A man can do a lot of things when his life depends on it," Colt answered. He felt something cut into his sole and only then realized that he was barefoot.

"Yes, I suppose you would understand that," Vince answered. He sniffed. "You get me out of this, Colt, and I'll do what I can to help you learn what you need to learn about the business and all. You saved my wife and daughters, and that would be enough. To come back for me, of all people—"

"Don't worry about it. Let's get out of here."

Both men climbed more, the car shifting again. They scrambled even faster until finally Vince made his way out and into the next car. They could all feel more of the bridge giving way then, and Colt leapt to the next car. All five men ran through it to Sunny's car, feeling the trestle shifting beneath them. There came another blood-chilling, thundering crash just as they scrambled to the top of the boxcar and ran across it to the caboose. Colt could hear Sunny screaming his name, Eve screaming for Vince. He and the others ran through the caboose and along the trestle, led by one of the guards who carried the other lantern.

They reached safe ground, and Eve and Sunny started to run to their husbands, but Vi stopped them. "No! Leave them for a minute," she advised.

Sunny looked past her and realized the woman was right. This was a deeply personal moment for both men, and she was struck by a sight she never dreamed possible. One of the guards was holding up a lantern, and Vince was sitting on the ground, rocking and crying. Colt was knelt beside him, an arm around his shoulders.

Headlines about the daring rescue blazed in eastern newspapers. Not only had the wealthy Sunny Travis's new husband saved her brother and his family, but his skills of survival against the elements kept the entire entourage of the Landers family members, clothed only in nightwear or shirts and pants and no jackets, safe through a night that brought temperatures down to the teens. The stories told of how wolves had gathered threateningly, kept at bay by a campfire Colt had built, and by Colt running and shouting at them daringly through the night. Colt had found a small cavelike place, where the family huddled under a couple of blankets and branches torn by Colt from fir trees. Because of the danger of the whole train going down, no one had dared go back for more clothes or blankets. In spite of the threatening pack of wolves, Colt had gone out into the dark forest alone to get the branches. As the story spread, so did the embellishments of the circumstances surrounding the rescue, until a new respect for Sunny's second husband began to circulate among the elite circle in which Sunny moved.

Sunny's own train car and Stuart's had been salvaged when a U.P. supply train came along the next day. The whole family had awakened to morning light that showed a second, newer track built on concrete bedding across a shorter span of the canyon. Somehow her own engineer had gotten their train onto the wrong trestle, one that was not meant to be used permanently. Two engineers and a fireman had been killed, and Colt and the other men found and buried their bodies. The entire experience had been a trauma for everyone involved, but Sunny could not help being grateful for how it had drawn the family closer, especially for the changed relationship between Colt and Vince.

Dancer had been rescued and was not hurt, but Stuart was left with a broken arm, and they were all taken to Salt Lake City for treatment of cuts and abrasions. Colt's hands, arms, and chest were red with rope burns, and his left shoulder was badly bruised. He had also gotten a cut on his right foot. Sunny could not help the tears of relief that second night when she lay in Colt's arms and reminded herself again that they were all alive, thanks mostly to Colt. She had procured the services of another engine, and tomorrow they would go on to the site of the joining of the rails, Vince and his family sharing Vi and Stuart's parlor car. Things would be cramped, but no one seemed to care.

"Things have never felt more right," she said quietly, "in spite of the awful hell we've just been through. I guess we've had a wedding night we'll remember the rest of our lives."

They were back in Sunny's private car, and the train was pulled to a railroad siding for the night, everyone still too jittery to travel after dark.

Colt kissed her hair. "I've been thinking, Sunny. How about if we go find you a horse before we leave Salt Lake City in the morning? We can board it in the boxcar with Dancer. I thought it might be nice to ride back from Promontory, at least to Cheyenne. We could catch a train there to Omaha, or just keep riding if we want. The rest of the family can go on to California like they planned. I'd like to forget that part and just you and me and Bo have some time alone. We haven't been riding together since you came out to me two years ago."

She lay there quietly for a moment, thinking about the joy she had found those two beautiful days, the pain of having to give it all up and marry Blaine. "Yes," she answered softly. "I'd like that." She moved to look into his eyes. "Just you and me and Bo, riding free. I don't want to think about work and decisions and stocks and bonds and all those things for a while."

He frowned. "By the way, if I'm going to have a hand in all that, I say there should be no more bribing and underhanded stock deals and illegal bogus companies that double the money in our pockets at the government's expense."

"Oh, Colt, that's how business survives," she teased.

"Well, I say we try a new tactic—like honesty and integrity. You're the one who told me you admired those traits, wanted to teach them to Bo. You don't want him growing up knowing what a scheming trickster his mother is, do you?"

She laughed lightly. "All right. But you'll have a fine time persuading Vince to deal honestly and fairly with people. Here he is finally ready to teach you a few things, and you're going to hit him with things like integrity and above-the-table dealings? That should get the two of you off to a good start."

He tangled his hands in her hair. "Well, maybe *I'll* be the one to teach *him* a thing or two. Vince and I are going to get along just fine."

She grinned. "I'll have fun watching that one."

"You'll see." He kissed her eyes. "Right now I'm just glad to be alive, and so is he."

She sighed, studying him lovingly. "I think you've really won him over." She traced her fingers over his eyebrows. "You'll be taking me and Bo riding. I'd like to do something exciting for you too. I was thinking you would enjoy sailing on my yacht out on Lake Michigan. You should try it, Colt. I'll bet you'd love to learn how to sail, and I know you'd love it out on the lake. It kind of reminds me of the West—big and wide and endless. Father used to take me a lot when I was younger, but I haven't been sailing in years. Now I'm going to make more time, for *everything,* especially for my husband and son."

"Good," he said, kissing her lightly. "I don't know about me and that big lake. I've never been out on that much water. I'm more used to prairie grass under my feet—solid ground."

She grinned. "Well, we'll do a little of both." She found his lips and pressed against him, but Colt winced and pulled away a little. Sunny noticed the deep purple bruise on his upper right arm where Vince had grasped him so tightly. She kissed it. "Thank God," she whispered.

Colt stood beside Sunny as the speeches were made. She had been asked to speak herself, but this day was so emotional for her that she declined. Just being present for this historic moment, Colt standing beside her as her husband, was enough.

The golden spike was driven into place, and the message was telegraphed across the country with the simple word "Done." Unbeknownst to Sunny and the others, guns were fired into the air in many cities, bands played, people cheered and danced in the streets. The transcontinental railroad was completed, joined in the midst of the rugged Promontory Mountains, in the dry, barren area north of the Great Salt Lake.

Here at the actual site, Sunny could almost see Bo Landers standing on the U.P.'s huge locomotive *Engine 119,* as it steamed slowly ahead to touch cowcatchers with the Central Pacific's *Jupiter.* Men cheered, hats were thrown into the air, wine and whiskey were broken out. Sunny wept, thinking about all she had been through to come to this, and how right it was that Colt Travis should be there with her. Her joy of the moment had only been enhanced when before the ceremony several men congratulated Colt on his rescue of the Lan-

ders family, which, to Sunny's surprise, most people at
the site knew about. She had no idea how much the
news had spread and what a thrilling story the newspapers had made of it. Even Tom Canary had shaken
Colt's hand.

She wiped her eyes, looking up at Colt. "You were my
best friend through it all," she told him tearfully. Colt
embraced her, realizing how meaningful this moment
was for her, how she had fought for it, so much alone in
keeping the dream for her father. He looked past her to
see Vince approaching. Colt pulled away from Sunny,
and she turned when Vince said her name. To her surprise, the man embraced her.

"You did it, Sunny. I have to hand it to you," he told
her.

Sunny broke into bitter sobbing and hugged him
tighter. "This is more important," she managed to tell
him. Brother and sister stood embracing, and Vi stood
nearby, weeping at a sight she never thought possible.
Stuart, his broken arm in a sling, wiped quietly at his
eyes.

Colt left to get Dancer and a palomino mare he had
purchased in Salt Lake City for Sunny to ride. Both
horses were already packed with necessary supplies for
their ride back east, and he and Sunny had both already
dressed for their journey. In spite of the formal ceremony that had just taken place, Sunny had worn a simple brown suede riding habit, and Colt wore denims and
a calico shirt.

He strapped on his gun, wanting to be ready to protect his wife and son on their journey back through rugged country. Stuart had worried at first about their
traveling alone, but that was what they wanted. Colt
smiled with remembered embarrassment when he
thought of how Sunny had reminded Stuart it was Colt
Travis she would be with. "I'll have the best scout and
guide a person can hire right with me," she had boasted.

He secured the holster with ties around his thigh. No,
there would be no extra guards on this trip. For once
they would be totally alone in the land they loved, not as
tentative lovers who never knew how long they could be

together, but as husband and wife, the way it should have been years ago.

He took the horses from the train and brought them over to where Sunny was still talking to the rest of the family, now hugging Vi. There came a barrage of handshaking and good-byes, and Colt mounted up, reaching down and taking Bo from Sunny's arms. She mounted the palomino, and amid more cheers and gunfire from the surrounding crowd they rode off together, leaving the continued noisy celebrations behind them. They headed out into beautiful mountainous country.

"Tom Canary told me that Henry Villard is talking about another railroad farther north," Sunny told him.

"Who's Henry Villard?"

Sunny smiled. "A very rich business tycoon who doesn't know what else to do with all his money."

"Like somebody else I know?"

Sunny laughed. "They're calling it the Great Northern, and Canary is already thinking of investing."

"You trying to tell me something?"

"Sounds kind of exciting, don't you think? This railroad thing can get in a person's blood. What do you say, Mr. Travis? Should we invest?"

"Depends how involved you want to get. You planning on being out there at the construction sites?"

She shrugged. "You know that country better than I do. Is it really as pretty as they say up in the Dakotas and Montana?"

"Prettier than anything you can imagine."

They rode quietly for a moment, then looked at each other. "I imagine they could use someone to oversee the surveyors and scouts, someone with a lot of experience in that field," Sunny hinted. "If we owned enough shares, we would want to be very involved. It would certainly be exciting, wouldn't it?"

Colt grinned and shook his head. "What will we do with all the babies you're going to have?"

"Oh, where there's a will, and enough money, there is a way around any obstacle."

"You can't wait to go out and find something else spend your money on, can you?"

"It's just a thought. Right now it doesn't matter. Right now I'm having the most wonderful time of my life." She left him then, kicking the palomino into a hard run and riding ahead of him, yelling like an Indian.

Colt laughed, wondering how they both could have been such fools to deny themselves all these years. He swore he would by God make up for it. He would learn what he needed to learn, but he would make sure Sunny left that world of wealth and power often for simple pleasures like this. He urged Dancer into a harder run to catch up with her, letting out a war whoop. Little Bo screamed and giggled. His father's arm was around him, and he was not afraid.

Love is the emblem of eternity: it confounds all notion of time; effaces all memory of a beginning, all fear of an end.

—*Madame de Staël*, Corinne

I hope you have enjoyed my story. If you would like information about other books I have written and a personal bio, just send a self-addressed, stamped #10 envelope to me at 6013 North Coloma Road, Coloma, MI 49038-9309, and I will send you a newsletter and a bookmark. Thank you!

Rosanne Bittner

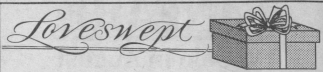